GREEN

Frontispiece: The Taj Mahal Emerald

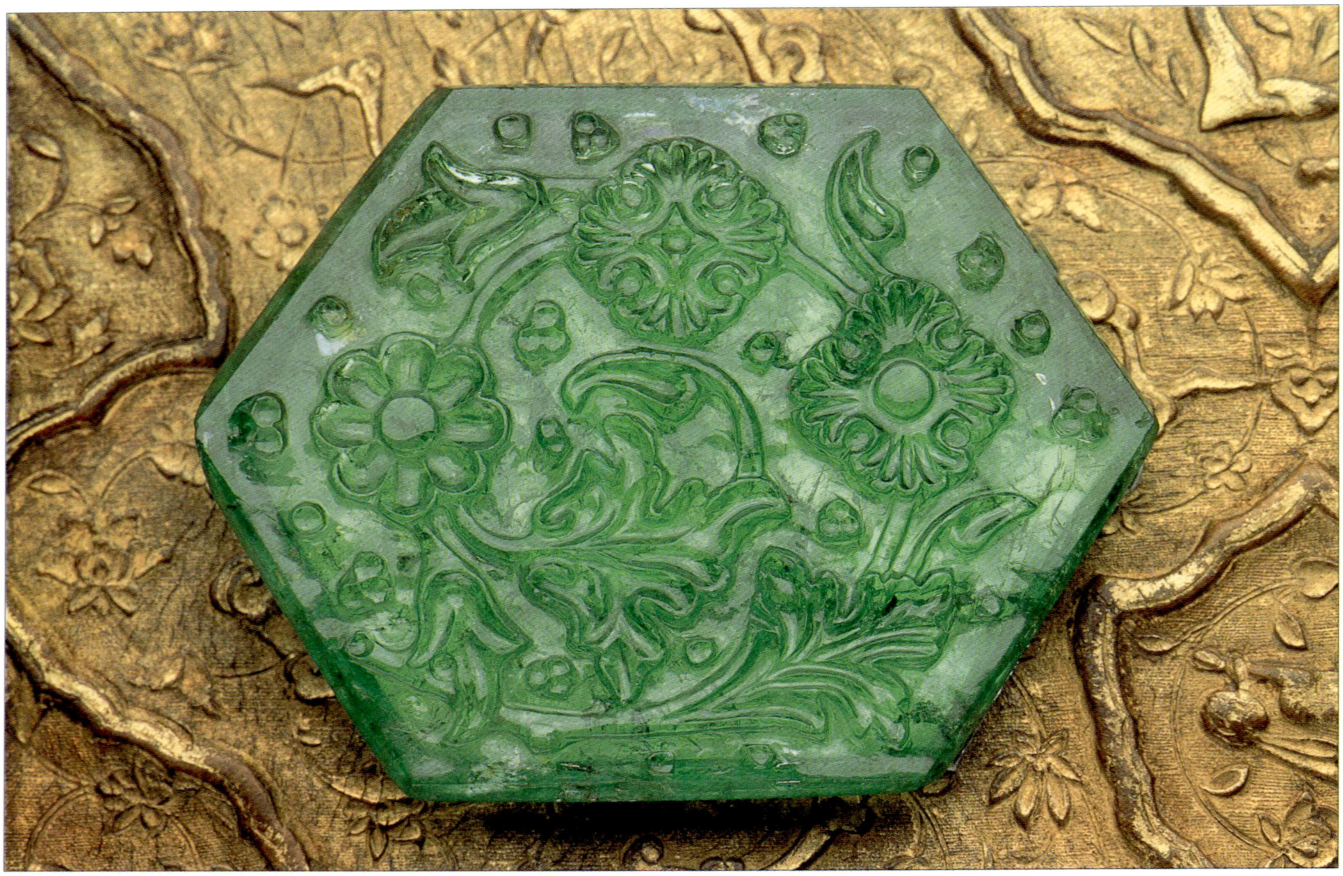

GREEN

A NOVEL

BENJAMIN ZUCKER

THE OVERLOOK PRESS
WOODSTOCK & NEW YORK

First published in paperback in the United States in 2002 by
The Overlook Press, Peter Mayer Publishers, Inc.
Woodstock & New York

WOODSTOCK:
One Overlook Drive
Woodstock, NY 12498
www.overlookpress.com
[for individual orders, bulk and special sales, contact our Woodstock office]

NEW YORK:
141 Wooster Street
New York, NY 10012

Copyright © 2002 by Benjamin Zucker

All Rights Reserved. No part of this publication may be reproduced or transmitted in any form or by any means, electronic or mechanical, including photocopy, recording, or any information storage and retrieval system now known or to be invented without permission in writing from the publisher, except by a reviewer who wishes to quote brief passages in connection with a review written for inclusion in a magazine, newspaper, or broadcast.

Library of Congress Cataloging-in-Publication Data

Zucker, Benjamin.
Green / Benjamin Zucker.
p. cm.
1. Jews—New York (State)—Fiction. 2. Greenwich Village—New York, N.Y.)—Fiction. 3. Diamond industry and trade—Fiction. 4. City and town life—Fiction. I. Title.
PS3576.U2259 G74   2001   813'.54—dc21   2001036568

Book design and type formatting by Bernard Schleifer

Manufactured in Hong Kong
1 3 5 7 9 8 6 4 2
ISBN 1-58567-174-6

Green is dedicated with all my heart to
(in order of their appearance in my life):

Charles Zucker: For the extraordinary man he was.

Joshua Abram Goren: For the marvelous man he is.

and to

Moses Zucker Goren and Abram Benjamin Zucker Goren:
For the wonderful men they are becoming.

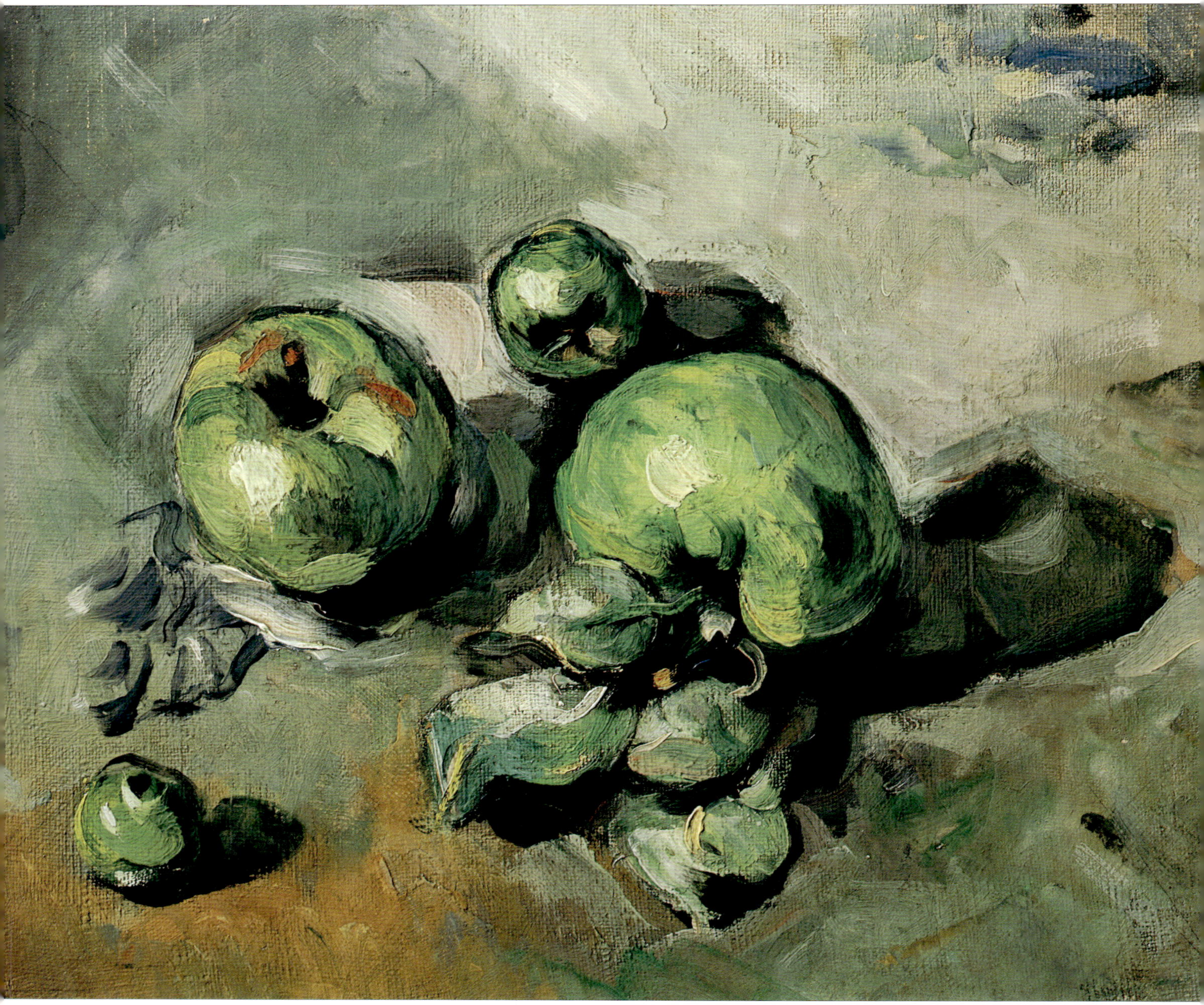

GUIDE TO THE READER

THIS NOVEL MAY BE READ AND UNDERSTOOD IN VARIOUS WAYS. I would suggest reading the central text of Chapter 1 first and then returning to the first page and reading the commentaries together with each page's central text. After reading Chapter 1 thusly, the reader should read the central text of Chapter 2 and then return to the beginning of the chapter to read the commentaries along with each page of Chapter 2. And then, by Joyce's slow "commodious vicus of recirculation," finish the remainder of the book, chapter by chapter.

The commentaries may be read starting from the upper left-hand corner of the page, clockwise around the page until one arrives—or, in Joycean, "rearrives"—at the upper left-hand corner. Each commentator takes a tag line from the central text and muses on it. The pictures offer further commentary on the text. And yet the central text and the commentary itself may also be seen as commentary on the pictures.

The order in which to read is ultimately your choice. To the extent that all of us accept commentary on our lives, welcome it or don't listen to it; to the extent that we feel the central text of our lives is of interest to others or not, still we persevere; to the extent that we feel our lives move forward chronologically, or that although Gatsby's green light "recedes before us . . . we beat on, boats against the current, borne back ceaselessly into the past"—so, too, can one read this novel forward or backward, circularly or in a linear vector.

Paul Cézanne, *Green Apples*.

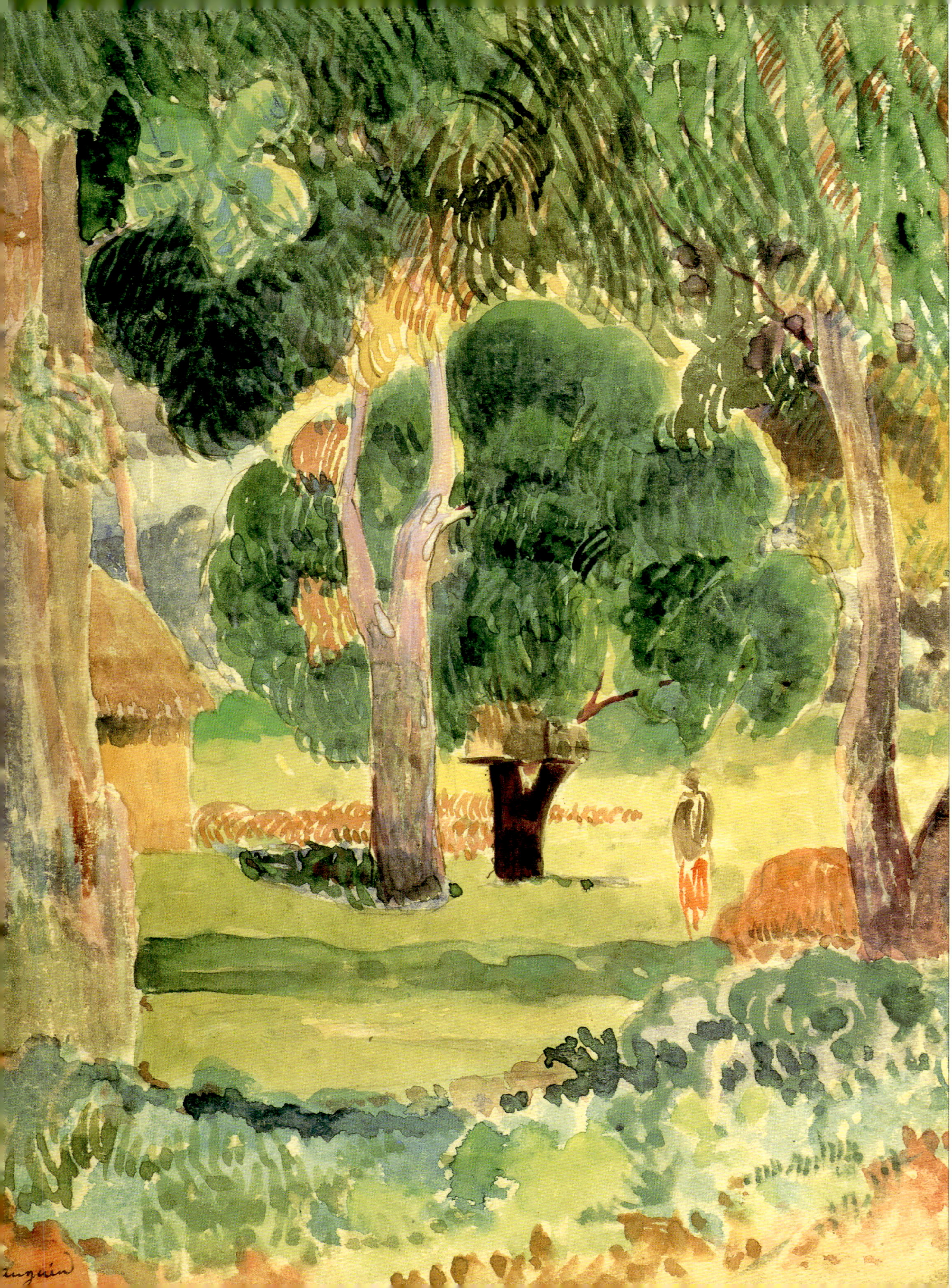

◆ Simha Padawer, Dosha's grandfather: Not four months—Amazing, the pair of them. My granddaughter and this man, Tal. Almost four months have passed and each doesn't know who created what.

When Judah Leib Eger became a Kotsker Hasid against the strong opposition of his father, Solomon ben Akiva Eger, he was asked what he learned from the Kotsker. "The first thing I learned—and the first thing one learns determines everything—was 'In the beginning God created.'" "For that you had to leave the path of your grandfather?" his father asked him incredulously. Judah Leib responded: "I learned that God created only the beginning. Everything else is up to human beings." But once the beginning was created, who can agree who created what. I would have expected more from my grandchild. Would that we all could have stayed in Slonim.

■ Paul Gauguin: A man in his early sixties although he could appear much younger—Appear to whom? And where? And when? When I was twenty-three and working at the Bank Bertin, I tried to look sixty by wearing clothes stitched in Peru at the time of my great uncle, Don Pio Tristan y Moscoso. But every Parisian could see I was either twenty-two or twenty-four. When ten years later, I still tried to look sixty so that I might pass as a friend of Pissarro in the rue des Fourneiux in Montparnasse, I fooled no one. Suddenly in Tahiti in front of Tehura, she thirteen or fourteen or whatever, and I forty-three in Paris, but sixty or one hundred and sixty to her. What did it matter? For she was offered in marriage to me.

At Taravao in Tahiti, I with Tehura on our endless honeymoon. Those Parisian eyes again on me and my ageless bride. Those Frenchwoman's eyes weighing me, counting me, appraising my years as late sixties, saying (not unpleasantly by the way, though not very kindly) "so I see you've brought a whore with you." and with her angry eyes, she undressed the young girl who was calm but who was now also aware of her own worth. The wilting bloom stared at the new blossom, socially acceptable virtue breathed impure breath over the pure, natural shamelessness of innocent trust. And it struck me painfully to see this dirty smoke-cloud in such a clear sky. I was ashamed of my race and my eyes turned away from the swamp which I then quickly forgot and I gazed instead at the golden creature whom I already loved I can still remember it vividly." The lushest green emerging from the blue of Paris.

■ Laurence Sterne: Ordered—*I wish I could have ordered an act of Parliament when the book of Tristram Shandy first appeared, that none but wise men should look into them. It is too much to write books and find heads to understand them.*

Paul Gauguin, *Noa Noa Album: Landscape*

CHAPTER I

"GREEN and blue are both wonderful, but this blue is more green than blue," Dosha said diplomatically, staring at the sand-painted walls of a large room on the ground floor of a Hudson and Perry Street apartment house. "And of course I should know because I painted it not four months ago for you, Tal."

"I am the one who gave the money to your "beau" young Fisher to fetch the paints. I ordered them, Dosha," said Tal, leaning toward her. He was dressed in a dark blue suit and a white shirt that glowed against the azure walls. "These walls are blue, not green," murmured Tal, resting his left hand on her right hand.

Dosha paused for a long time, stared at Tal, a man in his early sixties although he could appear much younger or much older. Dosha's center of the rainbow blue eyes rested on Tal while his eyes, greenish, shyly moved downward, gazing at her dark, red-flecked hair. Tal's eyes, searching for a focal point, fixed on the surface of the table.

Although he wasn't tired, his body slumped against the partly open drawer on his side of the Stickley library desk that Dosha had given him as a gift after his gift to her—"payment" for her having been allowed to complete the plastering and repainting of his downstairs Advice Shop cum studio on Hudson Street.

◆ Rickele Padawer, Dosha's grandmother: Green and blue are both wonderful—Everything is wonderful. The day is wonderful in America. Have a nice day. And of course it turns out to be. And the children are wonderful—until you don't know where they are—and people don't ask about them for fear you will ask them about their children. And of course the grandparents are wonderful, all together in a little bungalow home, far from their grandchildren who don't visit them because things are so wonderful with their grandparents so why disturb them.

But a yiddishe neshoma—a Jewish soul—still longs for its own flesh and blood. And when our two sons and one daughter had to leave us from Slonim, I told Simha they would send for us soon. As soon as they were settled in Chicago, America. And he said, there is a saying in Slonim: A father can support ten children, but ten children cannot sustain one father. And in America, I suspect that a father can support three children, but three children cannot sustain one father. My poor Dosha never sat at her grandfather's table. That is why she searches for some shred of wisdom in this man's house.

■ F. Scott Fitzgerald: Hair—Tal is staring at Dosha's hair. She must be in her early twenties and she'll stay that way. But he's not looking at her hair, her mouth, her body, with an old man's eyes. He is remembering his youthful vision—just as I, even I, after my crack-up still looked with my Zelda-seeking Montgomery remembering eyes and wrote: "*Her hair was soft as silk and faintly curling. Her hair was stiff fluff, her hair was a damp, thick shiny. It was not this kind or that kind, it was all hair.*" Same ending for Tal. Same ending for me. Where's her beau anyway?

■ Menachen Mendel Schneerson: Advice—"*As you are surely aware, the contemporary young generation, more than any other time in the past, is not afraid of a challenge, even if it should contain radical change and great hardship. It is rather those who are supposed to present this calling to them who fail to give our youngsters credit thinking that if it is offered in a diluted form, it will be more appealing and acceptable. Their fear of Tofasta miruba (too much at once) has gotten them down so much that all that they offer is "miut sheb'miut" very little—not realizing how self-defeating their approach is.*"

Tal may give good advice. Brilliant teaching. The only way he may today reach Dosha is through his advice shop. He may speak "good words" even quoting words of Torah, but they do not impress the listener and do not affect her in terms of "maise ekar." The deed is primary; otherwise they are "devarim Biteilem"—useless words. The blame must be put on the adviser since we have the rule that "words coming from the heart" penetrate the heart and are eventually effective." Tal is here for this moment. The young woman is here to hear. How they both hear will affect their hereafter. And not only theirs, but also many, many others.

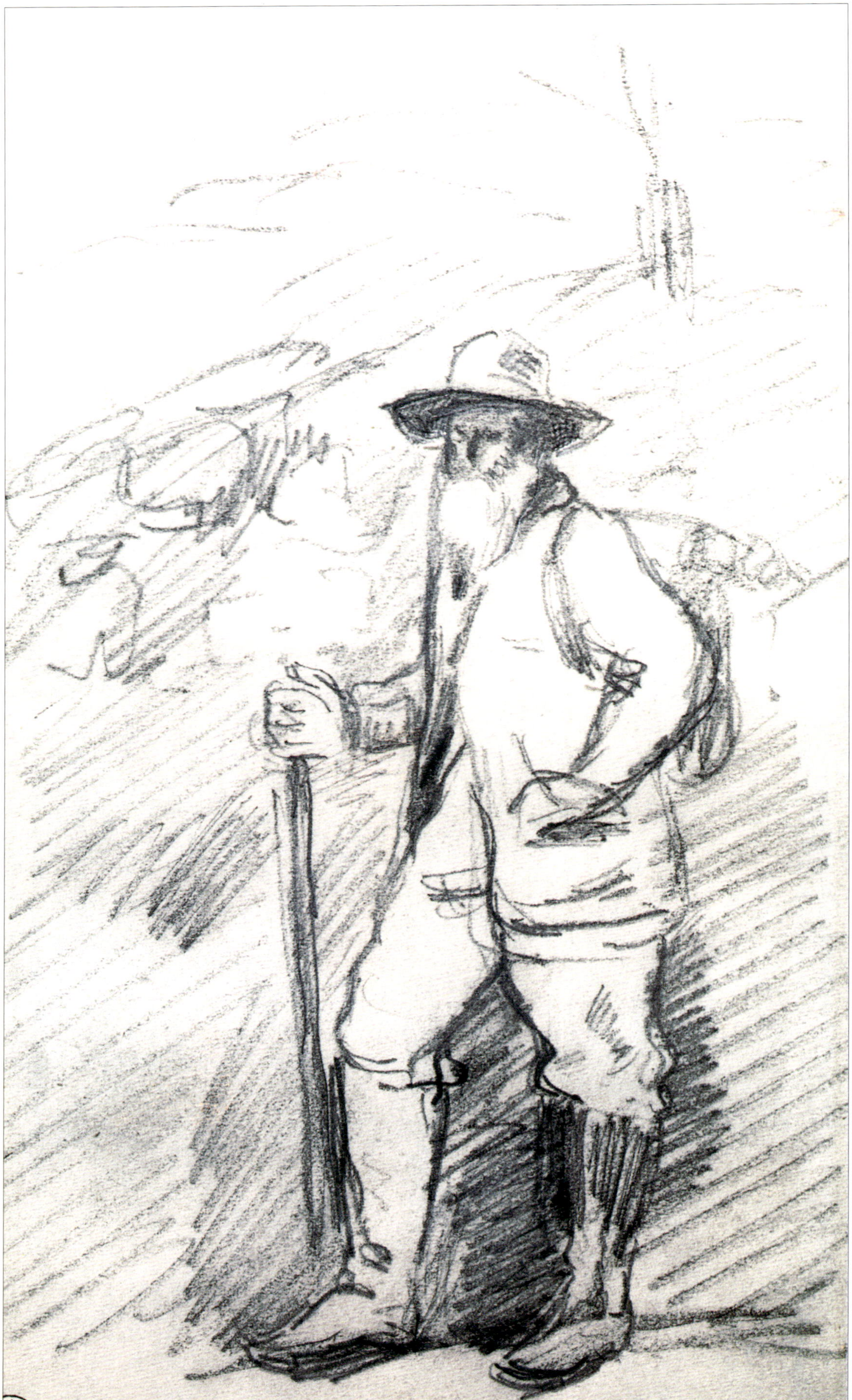

◆ EMILE VICTOR FISHER, FISHER'S FATHER: Did not say anything—My grandfather was a grocer. And not like Monsieur Saunter on rue le Petit Jacob whose groceries lit his Parisian nighttime windows more brilliantly than even Cartier's gem and jewel filled daytime vitrines. No, my grandfather Mendel was a simple grocer. An honorable one. Who said little in the daytime, all of which was spent in his store, dusting, cleaning, stacking, worrying about mice, fire and whom to extend credit to. He said very, very little at night.

To me the store was a palace. When I was a boy just turning nine in Poland, I can remember the weary look on my grandfather's face when he came home one hot spring night. "Do you know what today is Grandpa?" I rushed to him and threw myself into his arms. And when he didn't answer, I started to shout, "It's my…"

Grandfather sat me outside our house. The stars were already twinkling overhead. He said gently, "Of course I remember it's your birthday." I squealed with delight, running my hands through his pockets and even removing his hat, hoping something would fall out.

"Where is it Grandpa? Where's my birthday gift?" Even in the darkness I could make out the far away, sweet beyond sweet expression as he began:

"My birthday gift to you is the gift my father received from his father, a story. A story from my grandfather, a Breslover. And a gift you can tell your daughter or your son." I remember sitting on a rock in front of our house. And I remember thinking at first my grandfather forgot my birthday and then I remembered his opening words. "*Once there was a king. He had six sons and one daughter.*"

When I returned to Poland from Paris just before the War, my grandfather had already long died and I asked my heilige father, 'Tell me my grandfather's story once again. The one he told on my ninth birthday. I think I fell asleep.' My father looked at me and said, 'When you have children and your children have children, in the telling of the story to them they will remind you of the tale.'

My only chance is Raphael. G-d is my cure and his only medicine, his children's tale. Yet who will remember it and who will tell it to whom?

◆ Simha Padawer, Dosha's grandfather: Oddly he dressed with his winter formal suit—When I arrived in Slobodka before Stolin to study Mussar the Mashgiach pointed to Yakov Leiner, standing next to me and said "How long has Leiner been here?" And I answered, "I have just come Reb Yosef." And the Mashgiach pointed to the two Apfelbaum brothers, "And how long have they been here?" And I answered, "I just came here Reb. Yosef. How could I know?" And the Mashgiach placed Leiner, the two Apfelbaums and myself in front of him and I could see each of their formal winter suits, all in varying states of decay. The Apfelbaums' suits had started to fade, Leiner's completely tattered and mine was bright and fresh, my parent's gift to me. And I understood the Mashgiach. The hourglass of fashion. Tal's formal suit is threadbare, especially at the cuffs. He must have been in this village Yeshivah for at least ten years—more even than Leiner.

Tal didn't say anything. His mind seemed to be elsewhere. Odd he was, and oddly he dressed with his winter formal suit, a remarkably noble blue color—yet no tie—like an attorney without an office to go to, or a bank Vice President whose branch had been moved to another city.

"You paid for the paints, dear Tal." (Never call me Abraham, he had told Dosha after she moved to 551 Hudson Street and met him panting on the way upstairs to the top floor of the apartment house while she was descending.) "You paid, Tal," murmured Dosha, "but I mixed the paints and matched them against the swatch of color you gave me on that ragged piece of cardboard. You had me stencil four quotations in white brush work on each wall. Your neon advertisements, as you called them." Dosha looked up over Tal's head, turned to the left slightly, and read the words in white, pulsating against the wall's green-blue background.

If the doors of perception were cleansed, everything would appear as it is, infinite.

Returning to Tal's eyes again, Dosha added languidly, "These walls are more green than blue, dear Tal."

■ ELISABETH DE CLERMONT-TONNÈRRE speaks of Proust: Oddly he dressed with his winter formal suit—Of course I would come, Monsieur Marcel. Of course. Of course. As though his three invitations to me—lest perchance they had not found their way from our butler Alphonse who Marcel suspected of harboring resentment from that visit last July to our house, because Marcel would not surrender his fur coat to him. Marcel had thrice invited me, lest I refuse. The Petit Salon, the Ritz July 1, 1906. And of course the Princesse de Monaco, the Comtesse de Chevigné would come—no suddenly she won't come, no she will come but only after dinner. And Jacques-Emile Blache and Anna de Noailles. I could not bear Anna and, of course, she kept her fur coat on because Marcel, odd as he was with his winter formal suit, had kept his fur coat on. A pair of Eskimos they were, Anna de Noailles and Marcel.

■ PAUL CÉZANNE: His mind seemed to be elsewhere—Of course Tal is elsewhere. Of course Pissarro is elsewhere. And of course I was always elsewhere. And what if Pissarro were absolutely here? A man. An old man. A man with a stick. A man going off to paint. I wrote Pissarro how much I should like not always to talk of impossibilities and yet I always make plans that are most unlikely to come true. I imagine that the country where I am would suit you . "*The sun here is so tremendous that it seems to me as if the objects were silhouetted not only in black and white but in blue, red, brown and violet. I may be mistaken, but it seems to me to be the opposite of modeling.*"

Tal is not speaking to this young woman, but he is calling to her to join in elsewhere and she doesn't budge. Not a step. But in his artful power, he is carrying her through the blues. And greens. Across the water to place her on his blue mountainous bed. We're all alike: Pissarro, myself, and Tal. Posing as old. Ever young. In our green desires.

■ FRANZ KAFKA: Odd he was—Odd he was in the middle of summer, the Heilige Rebbe Issachar Dov of Belz who could see from Marienbad to Belz. "Easy," said my friend Jiri Langer. "Come with me and the Rebbe will teach you to see beyond Marienbad." And how odd it was that the Rebbe walked with Langer on his right and I on his left.

A "*silk caftan open at the front, a wide belt around his waist. And a tall fur hat, which was most striking of all. White stockings and, according to Langer, white trousers.*" And I shall make you a nation apart, sayeth the Lord. The aged Rebbe, skipping through the summer heat of Marienbad, fur-laden and winter formal with young Langer and my tubercular self, unable to keep pace.

■ WALLACE STEVENS: Odd he was and oddly he dressed with his winter formal suit—Tal: In short, a poet. I: The dean of surety-claims men in the whole country off to the Hartford Accident and Indemnity Company in a dark blue formal winter suit although autumn had barely announced its arrival, only to emerge "*sweatered and moccasined*" in my easy chair and all the time in or out of moccasin or blue formal moccasin, murmuring Mother's bedtime stories, lulling myself to an eternal sleep.

Paul Cézanne, *Camille Pissarro on his way to paint.*,

عمل گووردهن

● RICKELE PADAWER, DOSHA'S GRANDMOTHER: Change . . . change— On the edge of the chicken market in Mielec, you could see the magician opening and closing his hand. Sometimes one groschen and sometimes two. Sometimes a golden Hapsburg coin but sometimes nothing. If you could guess what was in his hand, you kept it. If you couldn't all it cost you was a kopek. And you could play over and over again. Even here all your friends advised you which hand to look. Over and over, Boynek the magician would change. And change again. And they would hit his closed fist with all the power they possessed. As though their force could change what, if anything, was inside Boynek's fist.

The Polish farmers came from the countryside with Boynek himself, always riding alongside. But in his own setting-sun-red wagon, the farmers who came with geese and ducks and chickens to sell in the town square, who came with not a groschen. They would all leave with Bonyek. He with half the coins in his reddened hands, cupped around his calico traveling bag and they with half for all their efforts. But he would reassure the farmers on the way back to their farms. Next month, your luck will change. This old man is as light on his feet as Boynek. What will she do next, my bubeleh? Move to a farm in the country?

■ THE LUBOVITCHER REBBE: For only one dollar, Dosha, I can give you advice—A Yiddishe Parnoseh (a Jewish living). From these fees Tal will earn a living? From this payment the young woman will feel she had consulted a specialist? A man who can change her life. But Tal can change her life. If only he would give her the dollar. For what she needs is a blessing. They are both holy: *"I shall make you a holy nation: A nation of priests."* And she too can change his life. If only he would ask her blessings and she would give him the dollar. That is why thousands of thousands—though I could not and would not number them—received one dollar from me standing in front of 770 Eastern Parkway. And did not they also bless me?

■ EMILY POST: Tal remained fixed in his position . . . nor removing his hand from hers.—*"A man of breeding does not slap strangers on the back nor so much as lay his finger tips on a lady. Nor does he punctuate his conversation by pushing on, nudging or patting people, nor take his conversation out of the drawing room!"*

Tal remained fixed in his position, neither answering Dosha nor removing his hand from hers. His eyes wandered over her head. At the top of the blue wall, Dosha had written, according to his inscriptive instructions, in white letters. "Not oyster white, G-d forbid," he had told her when she asked. "No, not off-white, that horrible Americanism. Pure white," he said. "And what does that mean?" Dosha had pressed him. "You know in your heart of hearts. Oh, you do," he had insisted.

*G-d Appears, and G-d is Light
To those poor Souls who dwell in Night;
But does a Human Form Display
To those who Dwell in Realms of Day.*

"And what does it mean?" Dosha had asked him. And he had told her, "It's an advertising slogan. It will bring people into my advice shop. They'll see my advertising above my client's head from across the street. That's the key point." Tal's mind wandered from Dosha's handwritten sign. It now fixed on Rachel, his mother, holding his tiny hand down the stairs in Antwerp as he descended, a boy not yet five, afraid when going down the stairs but eager and insistent to go up himself. Out of a fog he heard Dosha's voice, "Green . . . blue."

Tal's mind snapped back to the present and he exclaimed, "For only one dollar, Dosha, I can give you advice that will change your life and for two dollars I can give you advice that will change it back again."

■ KAREN BLIXEN ("ISAK DINESEN"): And for two dollars I can give you advice that will change it back again—And for three dollars can you do both? Both give her advice that will change her life and give her advice that will change her life back, yet with a memory, a clear memory of her life's blood—her new existence. And in any and all cases, all she wants is a story. Advice is merely the words of a character without the surrounding mystery. Tal more than a brother and less than a father to this young woman. My father *"who loved war for its own sake . . . with an artist's love. And could write of it 'Bayonets like diamonds have their beaux jours...It is young blood which enchants them both both.'"* My father, a suicide, and I a young woman. *"My dear dear and beloved friend, my wise and gentle brother. If you had been on earth still, I should have come to you and you would have taught me to love and approach thine but you are going away to higher worlds."*

And I wrote my mother from Africa, when my marriage and coffee farm were desperately sinking. *"If I can make something of myself again and can look at life calmly and clearly one day, then it is Father who has done it for me. It is his blood and his mind that will bring me through it. Often I get the feeling that he is beside me, helping me, many times by saying 'Don't give a damn about it.'"*

■ DARA SHIKOH: Change your life...and change it back again—If I could change my life. If I could change it back again. Not to the darbar where I placed my hand inside my father's. He, always silhouetted in profile against the sun. And not to the night when Aurangzeb swore fealty to me, before I left for Kandahar to fight our father's battles. But to go to Lake Dal with our sister Jahanara, hearing naked Sarmad speak of the illusion of change:

*"From saying One, one does not become a monotheist.
The mouth does not become sweet from saying sugar."*

Over and over, Sarmad whispered sugar to me. Over and over he said "One" in battle. But that did not change my end. Nor my father's.

■ SHAH JAHAN: Remained fixed in his position, neither answering nor removing his hand.— Aurangzeb remained fixed in his position. Where is your Dara. Your brother. I asked him over and over again. Collapsed at his feet. And I the Shadow of the Divine on Earth. Aurangzeb neither answering nor removing his hand from mine. But not a hand with a touch of warmth. Not a hand touched by the sun. A block of Kashmiri ice, Dara called him. Riding into battle. His head fixed on the Koran, spread before him whilst riding his bejeweled horse, riding more toward Mecca than toward the enemy.

Govardhan, *Akbar with Lion and Heifer.*

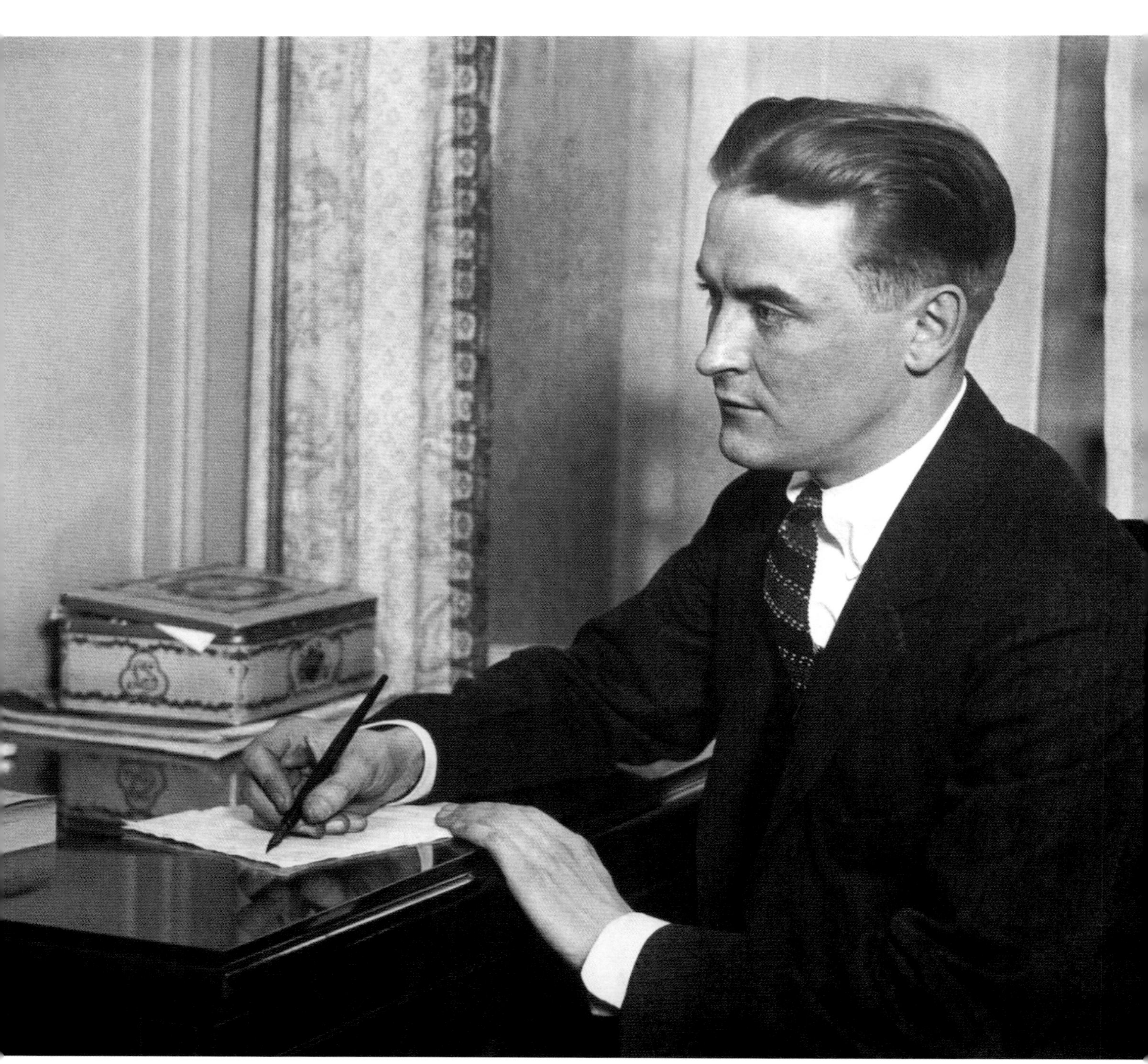

● SIMHA PADAWER, DOSHA'S GRANDFATHER: Unaware that she could see him—Once in the coldest day of the winter in Slonim, I was hurrying toward my daybreak class with the Rosh Yeshiva, Reb Abraham Weinberg. Across the town square, just to the right of the Bet Midrash (the hall of study), I saw Yakov Grunstein's sister Rickele standing in front of the stove in their house. I was lost in a dream thinking of her.

Suddenly I felt a slap on my back. "Simha," said Reb Abraham, for although he was already old, much past seventy, he knew every student's name and every student's face. He had examined me on the Tractate Ketubot two years before, and each time he saw me, he would stop and speak. "Simha, what are you doing?" And I was frozen. Reb Abraham looked with me at Yakov Grunstein's sister across the way. What could I say? But the Reb Abraham answered,

"To what may we compare the Torah, asked the Zohar Hakodesh. 'She may be compared to a beautiful and stately maiden, who is secluded in an isolated chamber of a palace and has a lover of whose existence she alone knows. For love of her, he passes by her gate increasingly, and turns his eyes in all directions to discover her. She is aware that he is forever hovering about the palace and what does she do? She opens a small door in her secret chamber, for a moment reveals her face to her lover, then quickly withdraws it. He alone, none else, notices it, and he is aware it is from love of him that she has revealed herself to him for that moment and his heart and soul and everything within him are drawn to her.'"

And Reb Abraham stopped speaking. But with his eyes, he asked me, does she know that Simha is looking at her? Somewhere within me, I understood that she could see me, only me. And Reb Abraham said, with his hands on my forehead, "Yes, what you are thinking is good. It will be good. It must be good. She will save you. Slonim will save you. And his voice cracked and he began to shake and to sob. "But you will not save Slonim."

Dosha looked out the window over Tal's shoulder at her boyfriend Fisher, a young man, who appeared even younger than his age. He was dressed in an Aran Island's wool sweater and corduroy pants, well worn at the cuffs. Fisher was standing stock still across Hudson Street, caught between staring and moving to his right or left. Frozen. He was unaware that Dosha could see him. Leaning on a fire hydrant to his left, Fisher was half concealed by an illegally parked car in a bus zone. He was all motion and no movement. But his eyes were transfixed on Tal's hand resting on Dosha's. And above Dosha's head, Fisher scanned the verse:

God Appears and God is Light
To those poor Souls who dwell in Night

"Poor Souls who dwell in Night." Must be poor Tal for sure, thought Fisher. "*But does a Human Form Display to those who Dwell in Realms of day?*" That must be Dosha.

Dosha, eyeing her boyfriend across the street, would not give him the satisfaction of removing her hand from Tal's.

The young man suddenly levered himself to the left, using his right hand as an imaginary fulcrum and spun on his heels counter-clockwise, disappearing westward down Perry Street.

■ J. P. MORGAN: All motion and no movement—"*Henry Ford put it simply. A man who is well needs no exercise and if he is ill, it will kill him.*" My breakfast consists of "*porridge, fruit, fried fish, eggs, bacon, tomato salad, rolls, butter and veal-tongue hash.*" I am all motion and no movement. Let Davison, Rainsford and others move for me. I told Rainsford that I trust people too easily and am rarely a good judge of them.

■ JAMES JOYCE: Aran Islands—1918. Regardless of the night before of wine of dreams of pain. Regardless of it all. I continued working. Chipping. Pasteing. My head closer than my pen to the page. But when Sykes proposed to launch Synge's *Riders to the Sea* in Paris, of course I agreed to help. At night, Nora lilting her Galway talk to me and by day preparing for the play, singing her Aran Island part as large as she would dare, as small as she would accept, I swam in her contralto waters.

■ GAUGUIN TO ÉMILE BERNARD: Light—"*You have discussed shadows with Laval and ask me whether I give a damn about them. As far as analysis of light is concerned, no. Look at the Japanese who are certainly excellent draftsmen and you will see life in the open air and sunshine without shadows. They use color only as a combination of tones, various harmonies, giving the impression of heat, etc...Besides, I consider Impressionism as a completely new movement, a deliberate attempt to move away from everything mechanical, such as photography, etc...That is why I would avoid as far as possible, everything that creates the illusion of something, and since shadow creates the illusion of sunshine, I am inclined to suppress it. If shadow constitutes a necessary part of your composition then that's an entirely different thing altogether. Thus, instead of a figure, you could just paint a person's shadow. That's an original point whose strangeness is quite deliberate.*"

■ F. SCOTT FITZGERALD: Boyfriend—There's her boyfriend, exactly as I pictured him: "*A thin, young man walking in a blue coat that was like pipe.*"

What's his story? It's the "*story of a man trying to live down his crazy past and encountering it everywhere.*" I'm not the old man in the room, I'm the thin young man. Ever the thin young man. So what if we're always trying to live down our crazy past? But Fisher's too young to have a past. Unless his past is me.

F. Scott Fitzgerald writing at his desk..

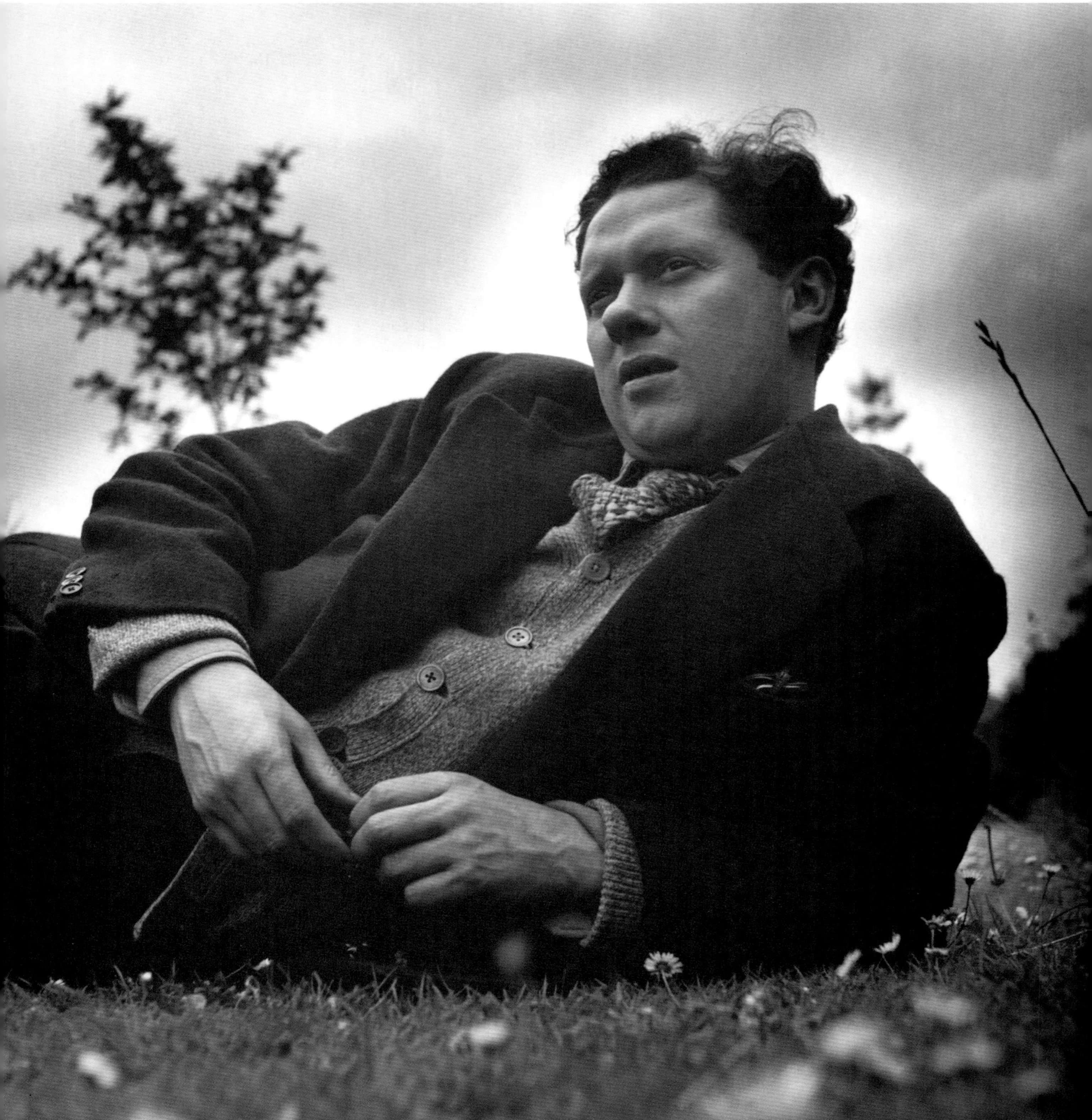

● RICKELE PADAWER, DOSHA'S GRANDMOTHER: You dear, sweet, ever-changing old man— In Meletz when I was a girl of seven, my father used to walk me to school, Beis Yakov. And when he was finished in the afternoon at the Sod Hatorah Yeshiva where he taught, he would come into Beis Yakov and bring me home. We would take the long way around the park by Rollak's lumber factory, through the fields just outside of town. Even in winter. Father would call these walks "work." "Oh do I have a lot of work ahead of me," he would say laughingly and I knew the walk home would be extra long. All the Jews would stand when they saw Father approach. *Rise before the beard of an old man—Kum lifney sevah.* I was the youngest of twelve. Later my daughter Deborah, a young woman in America, brought home Alexander. "This is my old man." I couldn't see the connection. And now Dosha, even younger, my granddaughter with this ever-changing old man—her Jonah—who, like Job himself, never was and never will be. And changing into what? One changes into old, G-d willing. Not from old into something else.

■ RUTHVEN TODD, FRIEND OF JOHN MALCOLM BRINNIN: Dear...old—Just like David Slivka said, quoting his grandfather: *Az melebt melearndt.* You live, you learn. I told poor Brinnin. It's taken fifteen years and Caitlin has given you the surprise of your life. John Malcolm, always eager for absolution at the hand of Caitlin. Caitlin found my copy of *Dylan Thomas in America* in her guest room. One morning, book in hand, she came to breakfast. Know what she said? *"Dear, funny old John, his book isn't nearly as bad as I thought."* Can you believe it? All these years, she'd never read it.

■ CAITLIN MCNAMARA THOMAS: Changing man hidden inside the . . . poet—Oh, he made it so simple. And Dylan's body not yet cool in death. I was to take out anything offensive, misapprehended, or otherwise troubling. So simple it was. Well then bring back my Lazarus to me, dear old John. I knew then I had to write: *"To give some dawning idea of the long growing years, with none of Brinnin's skill, but with a longer, and I hope, deeper understanding of the changing man hidden inside the poet."* But I knew it in 1954. And in 1955. And in 1956. And every year later, forever.

"If I waited a million years, I would never forget Dylan. He will not come blundering down the path again...and sing at the door impatiently and shout 'Cait, come down quick and let me in!' There will be nobody to bang at the door for he is in already...And Brinnin is responsible for me getting into such a mess and asking me to write an answer back and show another, different side of Dylan. All I am showing is that I can't write."

"For three dollars will you let go of my hand you dear sweet soul of a poet hidden in the body of an old man," said Dosha with all the gentleness she felt for Tal.

"I am not too old, you are too young," countered Tal, offended and troubled. Dosha thought of the first time she had seen him coming up the stairs, frozen between the third and fourth floor, hauling two bundles of books in dark blue canvas carry bags with three name tags carefully arranged on each bag with words: "Reward," "Please Return" and "Telephone Number."

Tal had stared at her as she descended the stairs until she arrived at the landing where he stood.

"Of course the old man had stopped," sneered Fisher when she told him that evening that she had met their next door neighbor. "He was trying to look up your skirt."

"Don't be vulgar, Dreamboat, I wasn't wearing a skirt. I had on the long calico dress you got me for our second anniversary last year on Nantucket." Dosha had dismissed Fisher's jealousy with a smile.

"Well then, he was dreaming of looking," said Fisher, trailing off. Dosha stared at Fisher. Extraordinary to be jealous of someone older than his father would have been, or a neighbor not yet met, already a rival.

■ DYLAN THOMAS: Carefully arranged—A letter from Thomas to John Malcolm Brinnin: *"I wired you again. You sent a cheque for 200 dollars. And so I had 400 dollars all together. 300 dollars I wired to Llewelyn's school. The other 100 I spent on a Vancouver ticket. So (again) HELP.*

On top of this Caitlin had carefully arranged for some laundry to be sent on from New York to San Francisco. This cost 40 dollars.

I can just manage to get to Vancouver. I'll leave Caitlin the fee from my San Francisco State College reading which is tonight and which will only be 50 dollars.

About other engagements: Is the date April 25 at the University of Chicago the same as that on April 24 at the Northwestern University, Chicago? Or can't I read?

It's summer here, not spring. Over 80 degrees. At Easter we go to Carmel & on to see Miller at Big Sur. We are both well. Please write very soon with any news, some love & a BIT OF MONEY. Caitlin sends her love. And as always, so do I. Yours, Dylan."

■ JOHN MALCOLM BRINNIN: offended...troubled—And without this letter. 1954. And without the others. How could I write of Dylan's life? And I needed Caitlin. "I made two requests of Caitlin. First, that she could excise anything from my book that might be offensive, incorrect, misapprehended, or otherwise troubling; second that she grant me permission to quote from or publish verbatim my letters from Dylan which alone could lend my account an essential degree of authenticity." Simple. Fair. They were letters to me after all. And she agreed with the proviso *"that the book be prefaced by a personal statement of her own."* And she wrote one. Simple. And never ceased from railing against me for years, and railing against *"the whole procession of diabolical bartenders, ravenous back handers and lascivious women for whose assaults upon Dylan's person and integrity, I was judged responsible."*

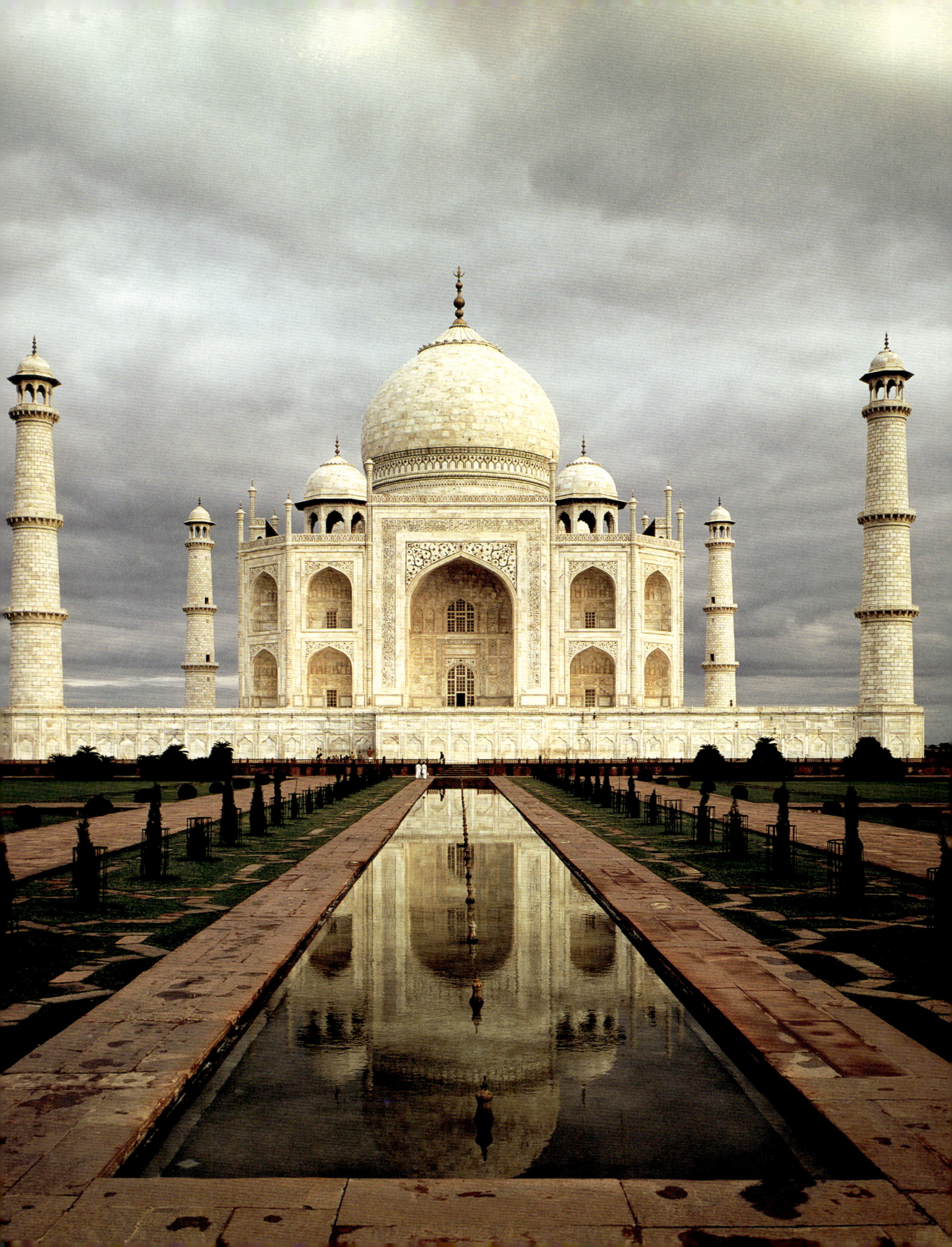

● SIMHA PADAWER, DOSHA'S GRANDFATHER: Face east—Oyfen Mul, opposite the eastern wall. "Padawer, sit here," Rickele's father told me. And I, a Yeshiva bocher (student), coming to visit my friend Yakov Grunstein. But his father insisted. "You sit here, facing the east." "Where is Yakov," I pleaded but searched everywhere for his sister. "They are both here, yinger man," said Rickele's father knowingly. "But why are you here, Padawer, and not there?" He said to me, pointing to the east. "What do you mean?" I stammered. "You know," he said. *My feet are in the west, but my heart, my heart is in the east.* Are you not Sephardi?"

"Oh," I said, suddenly understanding. "Yes, we are Padawers from Padua. Sephardim from Castile. My grandfather Isak would always tell me we went east as urged by Yehuda Halevi, but we also went a tiny bit north. "Young Padawer," came the quick reply. "My family will help you find your way, provided you don't object." I reddened all over and could not speak.

■ PAUL CÉZANNE: It's yourself you're seeing in him—Zola is always clear as a crystal with me. He, more a painter of me than I will ever be of him. Why can I not, even for a moment, accept my father? His life. His bank? Our bank, Heaven forbid.

It's yourself, Emile keeps chanting. It's yourself you're seeing in him. And I write to Emile: To Emile Zola. Aix 9 April 1858. "Since you left Aix, my dear fellow, dark sorrow has oppressed me; I am not lying, believe me. I no longer recognize myself, I am heavy, stupid and slow. By the way, Baille told me that in a fortnight he would have the pleasure of causing a sheet of paper to reach the hands of your most eminent Greatness in which he will express his sorrows and grief at being far away from you. Really I should love to see you and I think that I, we, shall see you, I and Baille (of course) during the holiday, and then we shall carry out, we shall complete those projects that we have planned, but in the meantime, I bemoan your absence."

Yes, Emile, we shall see you, and you shall see me, but I will be father, and you will be me. And who shall see all of us?

"Please," interrupted Fisher. "It's yourself, Fisher you're seeing yourself in him and it's yourself looking."

"All men are looking at you," said Fisher more to himself than to Dosha as she kissed him to interrupt his thoughts. While Fisher wasn't right about Tal, he wasn't completely wrong either.

Reluctantly Tal removed his hand from Dosha's, just as she had asked. "Listen Abraham, give me the two dollar advice and make it about Fisher. How can I get him to marry me?" Dosha pressed Tal.

"Go home tonight, dearest Dosha," Tal became animated. "Make love with him but not as you usually do. Cry. When he comes to you, sob uncontrollably. Sit down on your sofa and face East. Tell him you have just seen your father walking on the street and he wants to take you home to Chicago." With a flourish, Tal swept his hand to his right, pointing to yet another "advertisement" Dosha had written, again just a foot below the ceiling, again in "heavenly white" as Tal called it.

He who binds to himself a Joy
Does the winged life destroy
But he who kisses the Joy as it flies
Lives in Eternity's sunrise.

■ HE DOG: Face east—Eleanor Horman quoting He Dog: "*In spite of his ninety-two years and their infirmities, He Dog is possessed of remarkable memory. He is the living repository of Oglala tribal history and old time customs. Anyone digging very deeply into those subjects is likely to be referred to him. He Dog will remember about this.*" And that is why when He Dog spoke of Chief Crazy Horse saying, "Always face east," he hastened to explain, "My brother Chief Crazy Horse said always face east. Not because knowledge came from there, not because goodness came from there, not because blessing came from there, but because the stealers of the Black Hills will come from that direction. If you turn your back even for one moment to face west even for an instant, Pa Sapa (the Black Hills) will be lost forever.

■ SHAH JAHAN: Face east—Never face east. Face west, Dara. I built my mausoleum, my fabled marbled Mahal for Taj. 20,000 men. 20 years. A mountain of marble with my wife, Mumtaz. My cornerstone. And she facing Mecca. Soon I to lie in her line of sight. And she would face me and Mecca and I would face Mecca. The west. Never face east, Dara.

■ DARA SHIKOH: Face east—"Never," my father told me. "Never face east. And build a sign post towards the western paradise of Mecca. A sun dial for eternity."

And Sarmad's tales to me, Dara: "Once I was a Jew in a synagogue in Tabriz. A Sephardi arrived in temple and began to pray. We laughed and laughed until tears streamed down our faces, my father and my uncle and I. Why are you not facing towards Jerusalem, we pressed. The pure Sephardi said: 'My name is Ibn Abitur. And my ancestor, Yosef ben Yitzhak Ibn Abitur, was the greatest mind in Cordoba. He translated the entire Talmud into Arabic for the pleasure of the Caliph. And I face east for Jerusalem is in the east.' But you are now in Tabriz, we argued. 'Yes,' he wept. 'I am in Tabriz but I and my family have never left Cordoba.'" Sarmad told me this tale in the mountains of Kashmir en route to Lake Dal—a paradise on earth. An iron fort. The wind was blowing. I could not see Sarmad. Nor my brother Aurangzeb who accompanied us. But I could hear his voice: "And which is west? And which way is Mecca, Dara?" I suddenly understood that all directions lead towards paradise. I could not answer Sarmad. "And what do you say Aurangzeb, which way is Mecca, which way is"...And before he could finish the questions, my ever-holy brother spoke. "West is that way. Salvation is that way," his voice rose as he declaimed. "And how do you know?" I asked, with not a touch of astonishment. "Because that is the direction I face," answered my ever-holy brother. "And," he added quietly. "Your head will face there too, in the not too distant future." And then I knew it, as sure as my heart longed for Kashmir's sunsets, that in the fullness of time, my brother would behead me.

■ WILLIAM FAULKNER: Tell—Benjy's furious experience I found was so "*incomprehensible, even I could not have told what was going on then, so I had to write another chapter*."

"*That's how the book grew. It was not a deliberate tour de force at all, the book just grew that way...I was still trying to tell one story which moved me very much and each time I failed.*"

Tal's thrice told tale must and will be told yet again by another. And each hearer of these sounds, will he not tell it yet again, thrice?

The Taj Mahal, Agra, India.

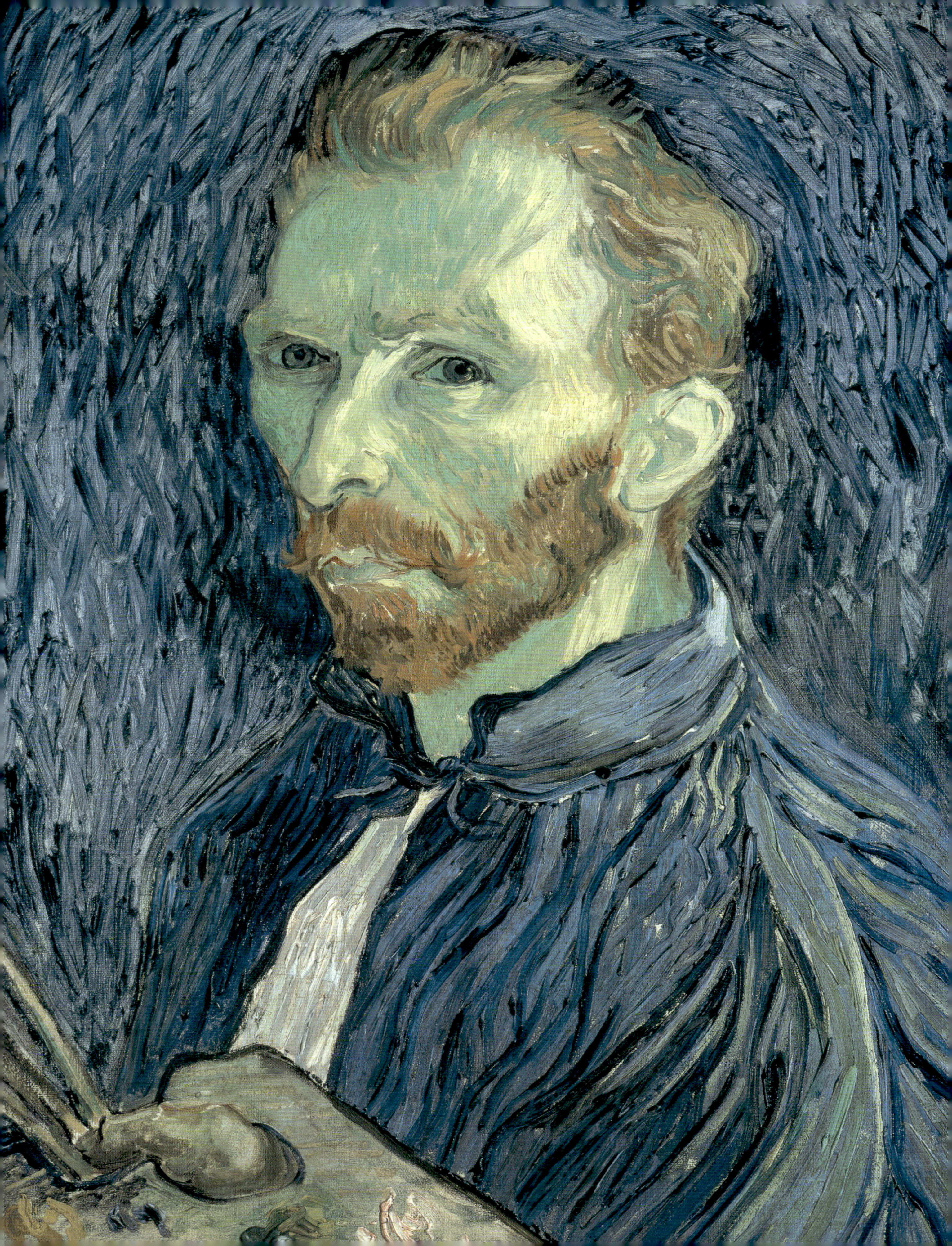

■ THEO VAN GOGH: I am not anyone's Rabbi—Vincent had written me: "*In our family, which is a Christian family in every sense, there always has been from generation to generation one who preached the gospel.*"

I could not preach and would not preach. But could I be a Rabbi to Vincent? I took him into my home. And shared my bread. And would have washed his feet. Or his soul. Anything, if only he would have consented to harken to me. Then, finally, he broke me in my house."

My home life is unbearable. Nobody wants to come and see me anymore because it always ends in quarrels, and besides, Vincent is untidy. His room always looks so unattractive. I wish he would go and live by himself."

Full of guilt, I entered Vincent's room. He was standing by his easel. Motionless. His two brushes. Green and blue, green for the eyes, blue for the blouse, forming a sign of the cross.

I don't know what came over me, but I knelt at his feet and implored him: "Vincent, be my Rabbi. And I will worship here in your cathedral every day." Vincent lifted me off my knees, dropping his two paint brushes to the floor. "*I prefer painting people's eyes to cathedrals. I am not anybody's Rabbi.*"

■ VINCENT VAN GOGH: Face—In a letter to his sister Wilhelmina in 1888: In this self-portrait "*I give a conception of mine, which is the result of a portrait I painted in the mirror...a pinkish-gray face with green eyes, ash colored hair, wrinkles on the forehead and around the mouth, stiff, wooden; a very red beard, neglected and mournful; but full lips, a blue peasant's blouse of coarse linen, and a palette with citron yellow, vermilion, malachite, cobalt blue. In short, all the colors on the palette, except the orange beard but only the whole colors.*"

It was the last portrait I painted in Paris. "It was the face of death." I knew it. Theo knew it. Even Jo knew it. And Wilhelmina, my dove, knew it, although she could not accept it.

■ PAYAG, court painter in Akbar, Jahanghir and Shah Jahan's reign: Tal...modestly lowered his eyes— He is frozen, Tal. Frozen. He is looking out at the young woman. And he is looking inward at himself. He is wounded. He is still. He is standing. As I am before my brother, Balchand. Before the emperors—all—Akbar, Jahanghir, Shah Jahan. A Hindu before them. And all my people, all frozen before Eternity's Sunrise. The everlasting Darshan.

But the Emperors too, are they not frozen before me and my brush. Never forget that, my brother Balchand always told me. And not just frozen before the one-haired brush of my brother, wonder of the age, and myself but before all the people of Hindustan. For we are all like drops of water frozen before the glistening overpowering light that blinds us all.

● RICHARD PADAWER, DOSHA'S FATHER: Father—Three months before my death, at the height of my troubles, Dosha called me. She had a dream that I wished to speak to her. And of course I did, I had all my life. And I said yes: I will come to see you this spring. And the time was given to me to fulfill my promise and she gave me a gift of a book. My life described. How does Tal know of Dosha's dream. He's neither a Rabbi nor psychiatrist. How can he speak to her as I never was able?

Tal slowly intoned the lines. As he read, "But he who kisses," he modestly lowered his eyes whispering, "lives in Eternity's sunrise."

"What does this quotation mean, Abraham?" Dosha asked. Tal remained silent. "Where does it come from?" Dosha persisted. "Is it from the Bible?"

"No, it's a side path," Tal winced. "Should I have you write: Mene Mene Tekel Upharsin? Thou art weighed in the balance and are found wanting? My advice business is bad enough without you totally wrecking it, Dosha."

"Are you completely crazy, Tal?" interrupted Dosha. "Why are you telling me I should lie to my Fisher?"

"Listen Dosha. If you see your father in your sleep, your therapist will tell you it is a wish fulfilled, your guru will tell you it's an omen and I, your Rabbi, will tell you that if you do this, Fisher will marry."

"You're not my Rabbi," laughed Dosha. "You are not anyone's Rabbi."

"I am not anyone's Rabbi but I could be your Rabbi if you'd let me."

● SIMHA PADAWER: You are not my Rabbi...I am not anyone's Rabbi but I could be your Rabbi—In Slonim, before the flames devoured our blessed fragment of Jerusalem in Lita, I stood before the Rosh Yeshiva, Reb Avraham Weinberg. He looked at me. Sixty years separated us, perhaps more. He put his hands on my head and he said simply: "Now that you've wed. Now that you've studied. Now that I have passed to you all that I can pass to you..." Through my brain could not accept the idea that the flow of his teaching me would end. But his hands held my head ever more tightly and he whispered again, "Now that I have passed all to you. You are a Rabbi in Israel." Through my tears I could see he was leaving me and I pleaded with him, sobbing, "I am not anyone's Rabbi, if you are not mine." And I wrapped my arms around him, trying to keep him on earth, but Reb Avraham, with a force I will remember forever, freed himself from me and said, "You are no longer my student. You are a Rabbi in Israel. It is time." It had to be. I knew it. Only my bride, my dewy dear from heaven, Rickele, gave me the strength to accept Reb. Avraham's *Smicha*—ordination. His hands but her arms.

■ RABBI NOSUN: A side path—Rabbi Nachman took me into his study. He stared directly at me as though he was watching his own face in the mirror. I was standing at his side, not touching him but feeling closer than I had ever felt. "You have been my brother," he whispered. "You have been my Hasid. Now you will be my pen. My teachings are not understood," he said to my image in the mirror. "My Hassidim do not change." "Why Nosun?" he thundered. Somewhere a voice came from my heart. *The children of Israel, a stiff-necked people.* I heard that Rabbi Nachman, when he was away in Medvedenka had told a story, a wondrous tale. "And why not to me I thought when I saw him the day he arrived back in Breslov. And did not Reb Nachman know what I was thinking? For immediately he said to me, "Yes, Nosun, children need stories, not only teachings. Tonight I will start. And you will listen to every word. You will be my pen. Do not change even a letter. And that night, when the moon was full, he began. And Gabriel and Raphael will be my witness, I was before Reb Nachman in Breslov but I was also with him in Medvedenka, saying to his followers: *My lessons and conversations with you are not having any effect in bringing you back to G-d, so I must now start telling stories.*" And he did, to them and to me:

Once there was a king. He had six sons and one daughter. The daughter was very precious to him. He was very fond of her and used to play with her. One day when they were together, he was annoyed at her, and the words flew from his lips, "May the evil one take you!"

That night she went to her room, and in the morning no one knew where she was. Her father, the King, was very distressed, and he sought her everywhere. On seeing that the king was in great sorrow, the king's chamberlain asked to be given a servant, a horse, and money for expenses, and he went to look for her. He searched for a very long time until he found her.

Vincent van Gogh, *Self-Portrait.*

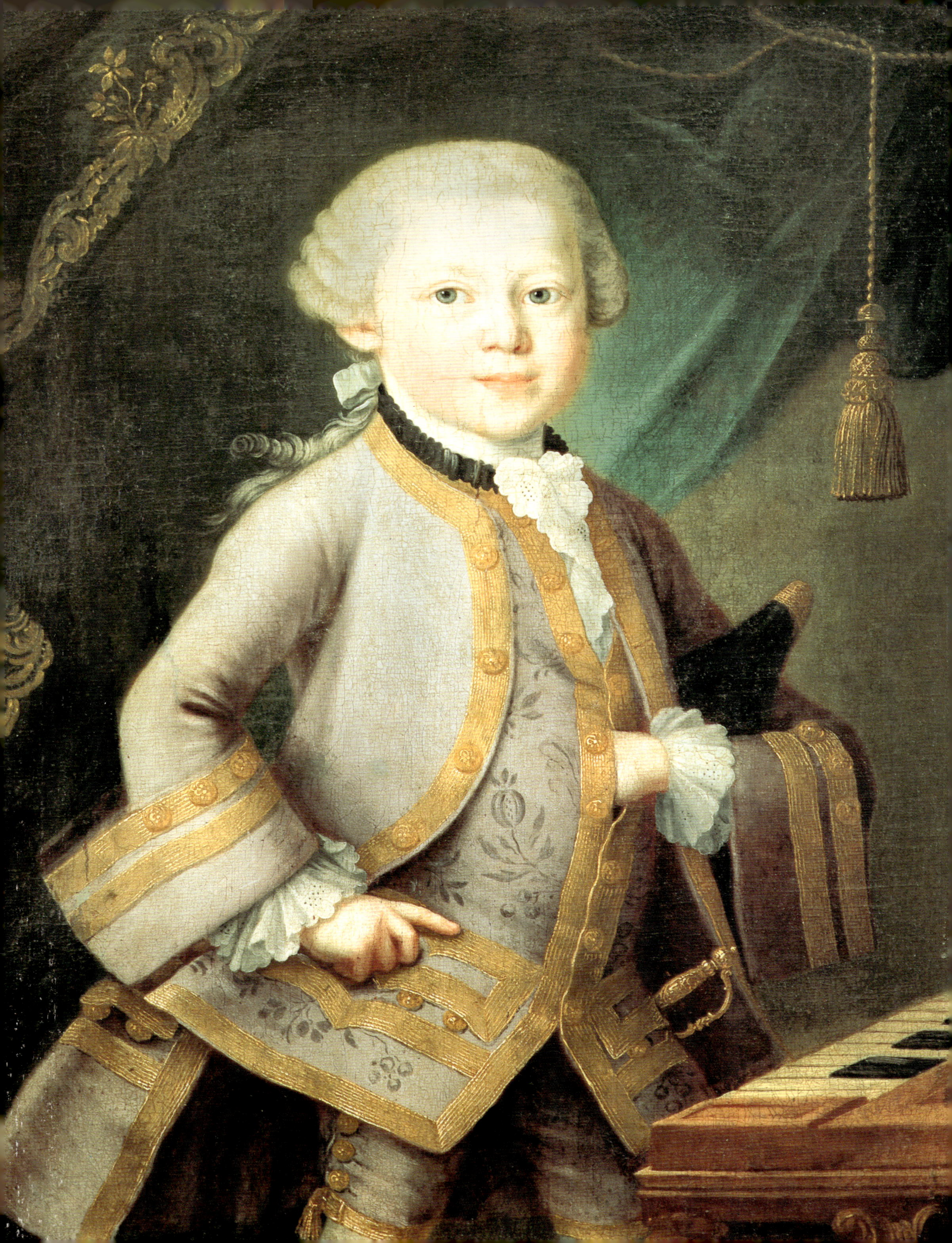

● MARGUERITE GUTWIRTH STOLZ, FISHER'S AUNT: And now your father—When I was seven, my older sister Sheindle and I were inseparable. My four brothers and my four sisters were close. Very close. But with Sheindle it was something else. Our mother was near blind and getting blinder each year. And my father each year, each month, each day, prayed for G-d to enter our home and cure the sick. But mother was as strict as she was courageous. We all had to be together each meal. We could eat food in the kitchen and in the dining room but not in any other room in the house. An hour after dinner, I was obliged to go up to the top floor of the house to Sheindle's and my room to prepare for bedtime. A half an hour later she would join me—a half of an eternity. One night I took two oranges from the kitchen and hid them in my pajama pockets after I came down to kiss my parents good night. On the stairs going up, Hessiah picked me up playfully and spun me head over heels. *"Malkele, Malkele du bist ah draidele* (Little Malkeh, little Malkeh, you are a little draidel top)." Suddenly, the oranges gaily cascaded down the stairs. My mother, not seeing, but hearing them, bounded up the stairs, shouting: "Do you not know the rules about not eating in your room and never, never taking food out from the ground floor to another room?" I burst into tears, but she persisted. "And now your father will speak to you." His eyes fixed on me and Mother who held his right arm tightly, urging him to speak. "Malkele, who is the second orange for?" And through my tears, I whispered "Sheindle." "Ah," said my father. "Because you thought of another, you can keep the oranges, one for you and one for her. But you are never to do it again."

"I'd let you but you would not accept the honor of the post in your dreams dear Tal," said Dosha.

"At least heed my advice. Cry. Throw yourself at Fisher's feet. Tell him of your cruel father, a gypsy who was born in the town of Ceneda just north of Venice. He and your mother separated when you were seven. How your father met your mother."

"Your father drank," intoned Tal. "When you came to New York, you were twenty-one and wanted to be a painter. Now your father wants you back."

"It's you who wants me, Tal. You. And my father is dead. And I won't resurrect him or create a Golem in his place to ask Fisher to ask me to marry," countered an astonished Dosha.

But Tal wasn't listening. "And then take off your locket, throw it out of the window, and scream 'I hate my father's violent and narrow visions and I will never return. I, Dosha, will never return. I swear by my name I will never...'"

■ ISAAC BASHEVIS SINGER: When you came to New York, you were twenty-one, and wanted to be a painter—When I was young, I came to Warsaw. To become. Before that I was a nobody. Or, more properly, I was my father's dream. Religion was the very air my father breathed... "Everything in our house was religion." *"But I wanted something else. To become my brother. And so I took as my writer's name Bashevis from Basheva, my mother. I made it masculine."* But it *vas nisht ahin nisht aher.* Neither here nor there. Half a man. What they would call in the Writer's club in Varsaw, a shlemiel, a shlmazl, a shlepper, but not a real man. And speaking of the Varsaw writer's club *"two things all the writers said about vone another. One that he couldn't write at all and two that he vas impotent. And after that, each man felt that he was the most virile of everyone and that he's the best writer and then he could write happily."* To become a writer. I have to become not my father. To become my brother, I had to leave myself. In becoming my brother, all the Varsaw writer's club told me I was only half a man.

■ I. J. SINGER, BASHEVIS' BROTHER: When you came to New York, you were twenty-one and wanted to be a painter—*"Our grandfather taught us simply. This vorld is the vorld of lies and the graveyard is the vorld of truth."*

And I told my brother: If this is so, one is alive only when one is not here. But beyond the curtain. And I, I.J. Singer, swear by Spinoza, that if I will reach twenty-one, I will reach life. I will become. Myself. A painter. A writer. A jester. An actor. Anything. In Warsaw. In London, in Paris, in New York. But not in Bilgoray. Not in Lublin. And you, if you wish, you can follow my path. For I have cut down the trees. And the path is clear. But in the cutting, believe me, I will pay with my life. I paid and Isaac enjoyed.

■ PAUL CÉZANNE: I hate my father's violent and narrow visions and I will never return—*"To Camille Pissarro. Aix 23 October 1866. My dear friend, here I am with my family with the most disgusting people in the world, those who compose my family stinking more than any. Let's say no more about it."*

Let's not speak of any of them. I hate my father's violent and narrow visions and I will never return to Paris, to Aix, to anywhere. My mother Honorine turning the pages of an Art Gazette for Paris, as soon as Father leaves the room—and walking me to my art classes, but rushing back home so she should be there when Papa arrives from the bank. They are all of a piece—even I, all of one color pressed together in one stinking tube of paint.

■ LEOPOLD MOZART, WOLFGANG'S FATHER: Honor—Amadeus *"is a miracle, who G-d has allowed to see the light in Salzburg...And if it ever to be my duty to convince the world of this miracle, it is so now when people are ridiculing whatever is called a miracle and denying all miracles...But because this miracle is too evident and consequently not to be denied, they want to suppress it. They refuse to let G-d have the honor."*

■ WOLFGANG AMADEUS MOZART: Breathlessly—All the world loves me. Who is this, that will not kiss me? I proclaimed breathlessly to Madame Pompadour—when she turned her face from me.

Oh I learned a peg from her and waited not for the Empress of Austria to buss me—I jumped onto her lap and declared for all world—Nannerel, my father, all the court, that *"I, Mozart, love you with all my heart"* and then the Empress kissed me. Kissed me. Kissed me. And I no more than a month past eight years of age.

Anonymous artist, Portrait of Wolfgang Amadeus Mozart as a child.

בתולה

*א נשאת ליום הרביעי ואלמנה ליום החמישי שפעמים בשבת בתי דינין יושבין בעיירות ביום השני וביום החמישי שאם היה לו טענת בתולים היה משכים לבית דין: **גמ'** אמר רב יוסף אמר רב יהודה אמר שמואל מפני מה אמרו בתולה נשאת ליום הרביעי לפי ששנינו *הגיע זמן ולא נישאו אוכלות משלו ואוכלות בתרומה יכול הגיע זמן באחד בשבת יהא מעלה לה מזונות לכך שנינו בתולה נשאת ליום הרביעי אמר רב יוסף *מריה דאברהם תלי תניא בדלא תניא הי תניא והי לא תניא הא תניא והא תניא אלא תלי תניא דמפרש טעמא בדתניא דלא מפרש טעמא אלא אי אתמר הכי אתמר אמר רב יהודה אמר שמואל מפני מה אמרו בתולה נשאת ליום הרביעי שאם היה לו טענת בתולין היה משכים לב"ד ותינשא באחד בשבת שאם היה לו טענת בתולים היה משכים לבית דין *ב שקדו חכמים על תקנת בנות ישראל שיהא טורח בסעודה שלשה ימים אחד בשבת ושני בשבת ושלישי בשבת וברביעי כונסה ועכשיו ששנינו שקדו אותה ששנינו הגיע זמן ולא נישאו אוכלות משלו ואוכלת בתרומה *הגיע זמן באחד בשבת מתוך שאינו יכול לכנוס אינו מעלה לה מזונות לפיכך *חלה הוא או שחלתה היא או שפירסה נדה אינו מעלה לה מזונות ואיכא דבעי ליה מיבעיא חלה הוא מהו התם טעמא מאי משום דאנים והכא נמי הא אנים או דילמא התם אנים בתקנתא דתקינו ליה רבנן הכא לא ואם תמצי לומר חלה הוא מעלה לה מזונות חלתה היא מהו מצי אמר לה אנא הא קאימנא או דילמא מצית אמרה ליה נסתחפה שדהו ואם תמצי לומר אמרה ליה נסתחפה שדהו פירסה נדה מהו בשעת וסתה לא תיבעי לך דלא

בתולה נשאת ליום הרביעי. תקנת חכמים הוא שתנשא ברביעי בשבת כדמפרש טעמא: שפעמים בשבת. אבתולה קאי: בשני ובחמישי. אחת מעשר תקנות שתקן עזרא בבבא קמא בפרק מרובה (דף פב.) ומפרש לכולה ולכך תקנו שתנשא ברביעי שאם היה לו טענת בתולין ישכים לבית דין בעוד כעסו עליו [ואם יש שהות בינתים יש לחוש שמא יתפייס ותתקרר דעתו ויקיימנה ושמא היא זינתה תחתיו ונאסרה עליו כדילפינן (סוטה כח.) מונסתרה והיא נטמאה] ומתוך שיבא לבית דין יתברר הדבר כשיצא הקול שמא יבואו עדים ובגמרא פריך ותינשא באחד בשבת: **גמ'** לפי ששנינו כו'. לקמן מקשי עלה: הגיע זמן ולא נישאו. לקמן בפרק אע"פ תנן נותנין לבתולה שנים עשר חודש משתבעה הבעל והזהיר על הנישואין לפרנס עצמה בתכשיטין: לפרנס קנדיר"ר בלע"ז ולאלמנה ל' יום: הגיע זמן. זה ולא נישאו לחופה לקמן מפרש שעכב הבעל: אוכלות משלו. שהבעל חייב במזונות אשתו מתקנת ב"ד כדלקמן בפרק נערה (דף נו:): ואוכלת בתרומה. אם כהן הוא והיא בת ישראל שהכהן מאכיל את אשתו תרומה כדיליף (לקמן דף נז:) מוכהן כי יקנה נפש: לכך שנינו בתולה נשאת כו'. להודיע שתקנת חכמים מעכבתו מלכנוס ואין עכבה זו שלו: מריה דאברהם כו'. תמה על דברי רבו ואמר מריה דאברהם מה זה היה לשמואל לומר כן ועוד שאלה רב יוסף ושכח תלמודו ותוהא על דבריו הראשונים: תלי תניא בדלא תניא. תולה טעם משנה שנויה במשנה שאינה שנויה: ומקשינן לרב יוסף הי תניא והי לא תניא: הא תניא והא תניא. זו שנויה וזו שנויה: אלא תלי תניא דמפרש טעמא בדתניא דלא מפרש טעמא. משנתינו טעמא מפורש בתוכה כדי שישכים לבית דין והגיע זמן אין שום טעם מפורש בה לומר מפני מה אם הגיע זמן באחד בשבת אינו מעלה לה מזונות: ותינשא באחד בשבת. כולה רב יוסף קאמר לה: ועכשיו ששנינו שקדו. ובשביל תקנה זו הוא מעוכב מליכנס בא' בשבת מעתה אותה ששנינו כו': לפיכך. רב יוסף מסיים לה משמיה דנפשיה ומסבריה ואמר לפיכך הואיל ולמדנו שהמעוכב מחמת אונס אינו חייב לזונה חלה הוא וכו': הא קאימנא. הנני מזומן: נסתחפה שדהו. לשון מטר סוחף (משלי כח) כשטפה שדך כלומר ומזלך גרם כי מהיום אני מוטלת עליך לזון:

בתולה. הא דלא קתני הבתולה כדתני האשה נקנית היבמה נקנית (קדושין דף ב:) משום דהתם אקרא קאי כי יקח איש אשה (דברים כב) האשה הכתובה וכן היבמה אבל הכא לא קאי אקרא והא דלא תנן בפ"ק דקדושין (דף יד:) העבד עברי אע"פ דכתי' בקרא (שמות כא) כי תקנה עבד עברי משום דא"כ ה"ל למתני העבד העברי שאינו דבוק ואין דרך הש"ס לדבר כן ומיהו גבי איש ואשה רגילים בכל מקום לשנות בהן אע"ג דלא קאי אקרא כמו האשה שהלכה (יבמות ד' קיד:) האשה שנתארמל' (לקמן ד' טו:) האיש מדיר את בנו בנזיר (נזיר ד' כח:): **נשאת.** הא דלא קתני נושאין את הבתולה כמו האיש מקדש (קדושין ד' מא.) לפי שעתה מקצר יותר ועוד דאי תנא הכי ה"א אפילו בעל כרחה כדמשני (שם דף ב:) גבי הא דפריך וליתני האיש קונה ועוד דהתם אקרא קאי כי יקח איש אשה: **ליום** הרביעי. ולא בליל חמישי כדאמר בפרק בתרא דנדה (דף סה.) *דליכא כתובה דלא רמי בה תיגר' כ"ש אם יעשה נשואין בליל ה' דאיכא למיחש שיטרד בנשואין וכתובה ולא יבעול: **שאם** היה לו טענת וכו'. ואם תאמר הא תינח אשת כהן או פחותה מבת שלש דליכא אלא חד ספיקא כדאמרי' בגמרא (דף ט.) אבל בשאר נשים דאיכא ספק ספקא אמאי תנשא ליום רביעי ואומר ר"ת דלא פלוג רבנן בתקנת' ומשום אשת כהן ופחותה מג' תקנו בכל הנשים שינשאו ביום ד' ובקונטרס פי' שמתוך כך יתברר הדבר ויבואו עדים שזינתה ברצון וקשה לפירושו דאמרי' בגמ' (שם:) אמר אביי אף אנן נמי תנינא דהאומר פתח פתוח מצאתי נאמן לאוסרה עליו בתולה נשאת כו' מאי לאו דטוען פתח פתוח והשת' היכי מייתי ראיה לפ"ה הא אע"ג דאינו נאמן מכל מקום ישכים לבית דין שמתוך כך יצא הקול ויבואו עדי' ויתברר הדבר וי"ל דלא מייתי אביי ראיה לר' אלעזר אלא שהוא בקי ומכיר אם הוא פתח פתוח דאם אינו בקי לא יצא הקול ולא יבא לידי בירור כי יאמרו שהוא טעה וסבר שמצא פתח פתוח ואינו כן ולא יחושו לדבריו וע"ל דגם לפ"ה לא היו מתקנים שתהא נישאת ליום ד' משום שמא יתברר ע"י עדים אבל כיון דבאשת כהן ובפחותה מבת שלש דנאמן לאוסרה עליו תקנו שתהא נישאת ברביעי גם בשאר נשים תקנו משום שמתוך כך יצא הקול ויתברר הדבר על ידי עדים והשתא מייתי אביי שפיר ממתניתין דבאשת כהן ובפחותה מבת שלש נאמן לאוסרה עליו תימה דהכא משמע דמשום חששא דזנות תקנו שתהא נישאת ברביעי ובפ"ב דגיטין (ד' יז. ושם) איכא מ"ד דתקנו זמן בגיטין משום פירי אבל משום שמא יחפה על בת אחותו לא חיישינן משום דזנות לא שכיח וי"ל דהתם קאמר זנות דאתי לידי מיתה דהיינו בהתראה ובעדי' דלא שכיח אי נמי הכא שלא תשב עמו באיסור כל ימיו חשו אפילו לזנות אע"ג דלא שכיח: **מפני** מה אמר בתולה נשאת ליום ד' לפי ששנינו כו'. אין שואל הטעם למה נשאת ברביעי דא"כ לא הוה משני מידי אלא הכי פירושו מפני מה אמרו כלומר מאי נפקא מינה שתיקנו שנשאת ברביעי ומשני נפק' מינה לענין מזונות ותרומה ורב יוסף קא מתמה מריה דאברהם דהא נפקות' מפרשה בהדי' שאם היה לו טענת בתולים והוא מניח נפקות' זו המפורשת ותופס נפקות' אחריתא: **אלא** אי אתמר הכי אתמר אמר רב יהודה אמר שמואל. ולא גרסינן רב יוסף דהא רב יוסף גופי' קאמר אלא אי אתמר: **מפני** מה אמרו כו'. בכימות' גרסינן לה ולא בא להקשות אלא ותינש' באחד בשבת: **ותנשא** באחד בשבת לא בעי לשנויי דנשאת ברביעי כדי שתבעל בחמישי משום ברכה שנאמרה בו לדגים כדאמרינן לקמן (דף ה.) ועוד ל"ל טעם דשקדו תיפוק ליה משום ברכה ואומר ר"י דטעם דברכה איננה אלא עצה טובה ולא מקרי עברייני' אבל משום שקדו מקרי עברייני' וכן משמע לקמן דאמר טעמא משום ברכה אבל משום איקרורי דעתא לא חיישינן ומאי נפקא מינה אלא ודאי משום ברכה לא מקרי עברייני':

מסורת הש"ס

כ"י כ"י

לקמן דף ע:

לקמן דף מח: ודף נז. ודף ע: נדרים עג:

[ב"ב דף קלד. שבת דף כג: עירובין עה:]

לקמן דף ג:

עין משפט נר מצוה

א
א מיי' פ"י מה' אישות הל' טו סמג עשין מח טוש"ע אה"ע סי' סד סעי' ג

ב
ב מיי' שם הל' יט וסמג שם טוש"ע אה"ע סי' כו סעי' ג

[הך דליכא כתובה וכו' ליתא בנדה אך בשבת קל. וכראה כוונ' התוס' במ"ש כדאמר בפ' בתרא דנדה סה ר"ל שאמרו שם שאלי כתובה דמגבי בה עפי ע' רש"י ועיין שם והא דכתב דליכא כתובה הוא טעות בפ"ע]

פשיט

מציא

- Tuviah Gutman Gutwirth, Fisher's grand-father, quoting his ancestor Ephraim Katz: Jerusalem—"*In the Jerusalem of the present anyone may enter, but in the Jerusalem of the World-to-come only the invited may enter*" (Talmud Bava Basra).

In Tal's room now only the invited may enter but in the world to come all may enter.

■ Paul Cézanne: "After you've told...—Over and over Hortense would shout at me. "After you're told Father, we can start to live. After you've told Father, we can have a child. After you've told Father, you can become a painter."

But was it true? I painted before I told Father—or before Mother told Father. And I certainly had a child before I told Father and as for the rest—first one must tell one's self: That's the key to it all.

■ Hortense Fiquet, Cézanne's mistress: After you've told father—"When can we start to live?" I shouted at Cézanne. When can we start to live? It's really quite simple. One needn't be rich. Or brilliant. Or a banker. Or a lawyer.

Simply a man. We can start to live after you're told Father. And not only my last name Mademoiselle Fiquet, but my first name Hortense. Better still, let me tell your father, myself."

At least this woman has spoken directly to Tal but until she tells him her true first name, how will he have the faintest idea of whom she is? I was even less a woman than Paul was a man.

■Abraham Abulafia (1240-1291): Jerusalem—Tal has Dosha write Jerusalem for he is in the lands of Edom. "*You are beautiful, my darling as Tirzah, comely as Jerusalem*." And he is afraid to have her write this passage from our beloved's beloved Song of Songs. The sixth chapter for do they not live on the sixth level of their building and the fourth verse, for is this not the fourth level of trust, *sod*, secret. And should Fisher see the inscription of Tirzah written in his beloved's hand—would he not set his feet toward Jerusalem before the next full-moon. For Tirzah is his desire. So Tal has her write in the language of Edom. But Jerusalem, is she not the heart's desire of all. And one holy word calls to another. Before many moonlit nights, both Dosha and Fisher will surely awake. But only truly in the True Jerusalem.

Talmud: Tractate Ketubot.

■ F. Scott Fitzgerald: Forever—And this Dosha. Who is she? Remarkable love of life she has. "*A beauty that has reached the point where it seems to contain in itself the secret of its own growth, as if it will go on increasing forever.*"

Tal is right. So right. Fisher will gather you in his arms and kiss your eyelids forever. And if he doesn't I'll return and play Miles Standish myself.

Dosha thought, at least I didn't tell Tal my first and second name, Dorothea Jerusha but just the diminutive, abbreviated almost at birth, certainly before school. "You gave me that locket, Tal."

"Don't worry," said Tal. "I'll be downstairs to retrieve it." Tal sat erect, a hunter with a deer in his cross hairs.

"And after you've told Fisher you're a gypsy's child, and after he realizes you're not Jewish, then he will gather you in his arms and kiss your eyelids moist with the tears that you have wept all night."

"And by morning, sail on those tears down the Hudson to Centre Street, paddling the boat of your body to the marriage hall."

Tal rose out of his chair and suddenly, more in a chant than in a reading voice, more as a prayer than a poem, more squinting than peering at the wall's surface directly behind him, he turned on his heels with feet together as he began reading the wall above the window facing Hudson Street:

*England! Awake, Awake, Awake
Jerusalem thy sister calls!
Why wilt thou sleep the sleep of death
And close her from thy ancient walls.*

■ Ned McLean: Locket...tears—My father always told me: "Ned, I don't need someone else to make me look foolish, I can do it quite well myself. Tom Walsh is not about to make a monkey out of me. I'll give you one hundred thousand dollars and he'll give your bride one hundred. Or I'll give you less if he gives her less. And I'll give you twice that if he gives your bride, Evalyn Walsh, twice that. Every house you buy, every trip you make, every locket you purchase should be equally funded. Or mind my words, there will be tears at the end of the day."

■ Evelyn Walsh McLean: Locket—We were on our honeymoon and in the swirl of it all, Father's gift of a hundred thousand dollars and Ned's father's gift of a hundred thousand dollars, still not spent.

"Perhaps a locket might do," said darling Ned.

"We have just the thing for you," said the salesman at Cartier. "*Then he hypnotized me by showing me an ornament that made bright spots before my eyes...a line of diamond fire in square links of platinum where it would touch my throat became a triple loop. And from the other circle was depended an entrancing pearl; it was the size of my little finger's end and weighed 32 1/2 grains. The pearl was but the supporting slave of another thing I craved at sight— an emerald. Some lapidary had shaped it with six sides so as to amplify or to find at least every trace of colour. It weighed 34 1/2 carats. This green jewel, in turn, was just the object supporting the Star of the East. This stone, a pear-shaped brilliant, was one of the most famous in the world—92 1/2 carats. All lapidaries know it. With fingers that fumbled from excitement, I put that gorgeous piece around my throat.*"

"Ned," I said in mock despair. "It's got me! I'll never get away from the spell of this."

"A shock might break the spell," said Ned. "Suppose you ask the price of this magnificence."

Sweet of Ned to find the world's most fabulous locket.

■ Pierre Cartier: You gave me that locket...moist with tears—They were young, Evalyn Walsh and Edward Beale McLean. Young and rich the way only Americans can be. Her father was Thomas Walsh who scratched the American earth in Colorado and found golden El Dorado wealth beyond counting. His father didn't have even to bend down but merely had the *Washington Post* newspaper dropped on people's doorstep each morning.

And at age twenty-five, on their honeymoon, they arrived at our Cartier doorstep, flushed with newlywed longings, certain their jeweled nights would continue forever—the Star of the East, a hexagonal emerald, mounted with the green of a moghul garden dangling from its pearl chandelier.

And of course the price had to be whispered. A jarring sum. For a locket. And this young Dosha, is she not the young American? And Tal, not me? All those lockets I fashioned. Moistened with the tears of history.

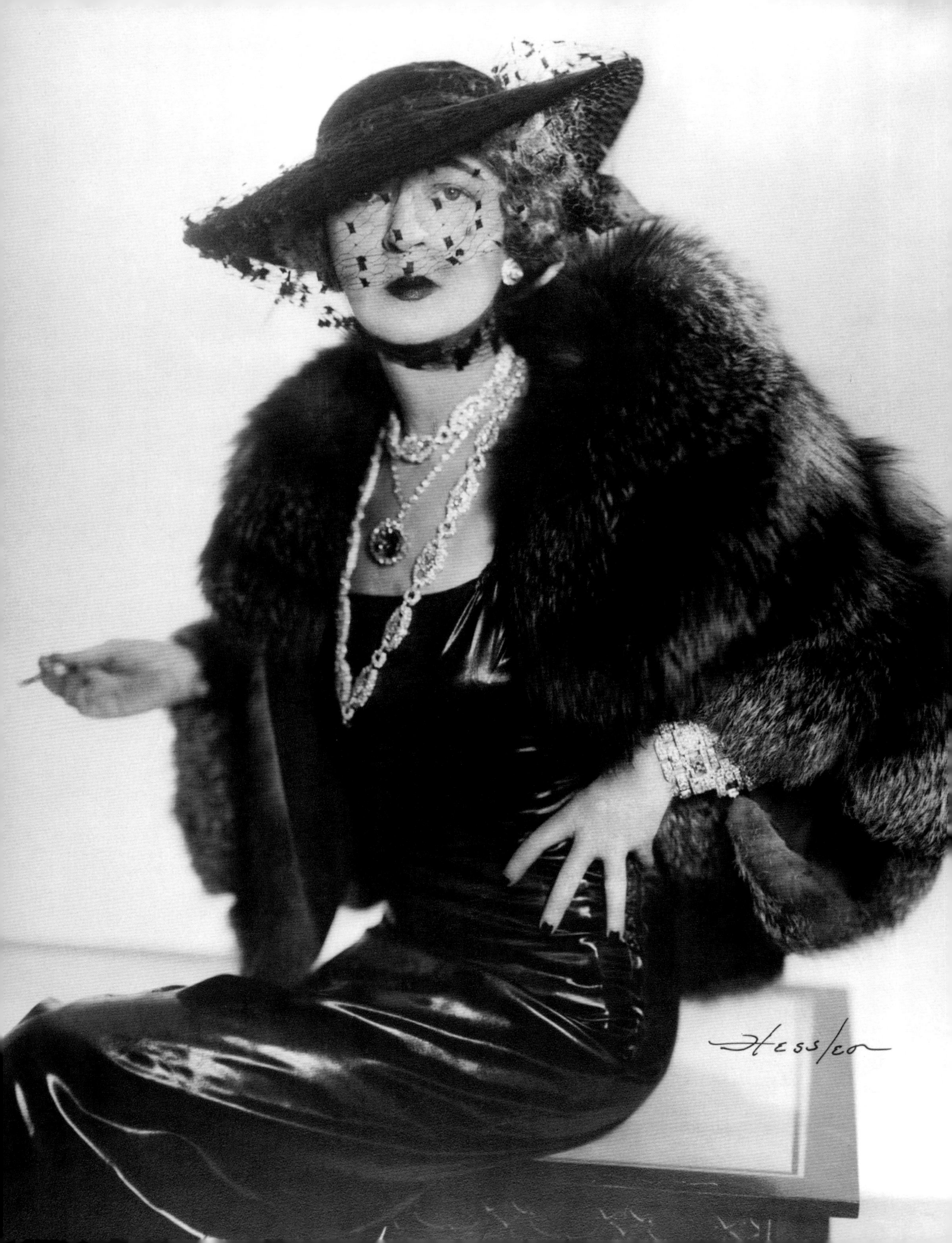
Hessler

■ EVALYN WALSH MCLEAN: Bluish green—Father had died just months before and I couldn't sleep, I couldn't eat. Dear, sweet Ned, very dear and very sweet at the time, said, "Let's go back to Paris." "And why Paris?" I asked. "Oh, we can visit your friend," he responded, referring to Pierre Cartier. "Oh, but I have the most marvelous of his treasures already," I said, but Ned persisted.

And what was to be lost? *My friend came to call on us not at the hotel Bristol in Paris. He carried tenderly a package tightly closed with wax seals. I suppose a Parisian jewel merchant who seeks trade among the ultra-rich has to be more or less a stage manager or an actor. Certainly, he must be one great salesman. Of course, Mr. Cartier was dressed as carefully as any woman going to her first big ball. His silk hat, which he swept outward with a flourish, had such a sheen that it almost made me believe it had been handed to him new as he crossed our threshold. His oyster colored spats, his knife-edged trousers, his morning coat, the pinkness of his fingernails, all these and other things about him made by him to be seen for me— for Madame McLean, one French compliment.*

"You told me," he said, "when you bought from me your wedding present, the Star of the East...that you had seen a jewel in the [Sultan's] harem [in Constantinople], a great blue stone that rested against the throat of the Sultan's favorite."

"I guess I did..." It was too early to argue and, after all, I had seen jewels on Turkish ladies that made my fingers itch."

And with a flourish, Monsieur Cartier handed me the stone. What a history of curses he recounted to me. And what a storm of protest from dear, sweet Ned.

What did I care for curses connected with the Blue Hope? My own father had just died. How could I suffer more, and in my case, one hundred and eighty thousand dollars was beyond me. And certainly, Ned was unwilling to stretch out his hand with green for blue.

■ EDWARD BEALE MCLEAN: Bluish green—
Astounding. That rogue Cartier. Not satisfied with robbing us blind on the price of the Star of the East. My father was furious when we each ran out of money. Oh, Thomas, Evalyn's captive father said "of course dear, I'll send you more money." And of course my father said curtly, "Come home immediately for the *Washington Post* board meeting." Then my father-in-law died. And Evalyn was not able to get up from her bed. I suggested, "Let's go back to Paris to get back on our honeymoon track."

Stunned I was when the old rogue suggested we celebrate her father's demise by purchasing a many times cursed diamond.

I could see us bankrupt immediately, one hundred eighty thousand dollars. Thank G-d I talked Evalyn out of it. But a woman always will out. And, of course, after we returned on the Rotterdam, the devilish Cartier sent the diamond "on approval for the weekend."

In the middle of the night, I awoke and there was Evalyn wide awake, murmuring, "that jewel is staring at me." And her solution. Simple. Follow Monsieur Cartier's suggestion: return the pearl and the heavenly green moghul emerald—the stone that she had told me would keep our love forever fresh— as credit against the purchase of the Hope Blue Diamond. As simple as that.

Her honeymoon was over. Her father had died. Green had turned to blue. And I was next to be jettisoned.

The word "Jerusalem" resounded inside of Dosha's head. Her right hand involuntarily twitched. Tal swiveled around once again. With tears in his eyes, he faced her.

"And in seven years if you're still married, you can burst out crying in the middle of the night and hit Fisher. As hard as you can, again with the same hand, and when he awakens, tell him you've lied. That your father came from Ceneda, north of Venice, but that Father was Jewish, very Jewish. More Jewish than anyone. Sephardic Jewish. And you, a Sephardic Princess. And if that won't keep him yours forever, I'll return your two dollars."

"Tal you're shrewder than you look and I love you, but I'd like a guarantee in writing. And these walls are still bluish green."

■ PIERRE CARTIER: Bluish green—I had just married Elma Rumsey and perhaps to impress her, perhaps to amuse myself, I showed her the sketch of the Star of the East with the pendant emerald and pear necklace I had sold Mrs. Edward McLean two years previously. She's coming next Thursday to the Bristol, dearest. I hope to sell her the Hope Diamond.

"For how much?" Elma inquired immediately, looking at the Hope which I held in my hand, the light bouncing off its adamantine surface, merging in the extraordinary beauty of her eyes. "One hundred fifty thousand," I said decisively.

"Pity," she said without reaching to touch the Hope—the way every woman who ever saw the Hope had done since we acquired it from Rosenau in 1909.

"Why pity, dearest?" I said, intrigued. "Do you want it?"

"Oh no, I want you, my pet, not any gem," she answered without any hint of a pause. "But you, Pierre, I'm not so sure you prefer me to some of your gems." I smiled and said, "So why pity?" "Pity, dear Pierre, because you stare over my shoulder at your brother's precious Moghul paintings behind me when I speak. And these great moghul princes, Shah Jahan and Jehanghir, what do they do? They stare down at their precious paradaisical green emeralds. Pity because you're so caught up in your world of trading that you've forgotten what you really want—the fabulous 34 carat hexagonal emerald that you told me was the greatest stone you've ever had." I felt myself go limp. And hoarsely said, "Elma, you're right but how do I do it?"

"Simple. Five steps. First, you ask one hundred eighty thousand dollars which even a McLean won't have. Second, you suggest an old-fashioned American trade and swap. She buys the Hope, you get the pearl and the emerald back. And third, we decide your outfit." And then she picked out my oyster colored spats, my pale trousers and my beautiful grey morning coat.

And fourth and fifth we turn the blue night into green so that never even for an instant do you trade me in for a Moghul bauble.

American socialite Evalyn Walsh Mclean wearing the 44.5 Hope Diamond.

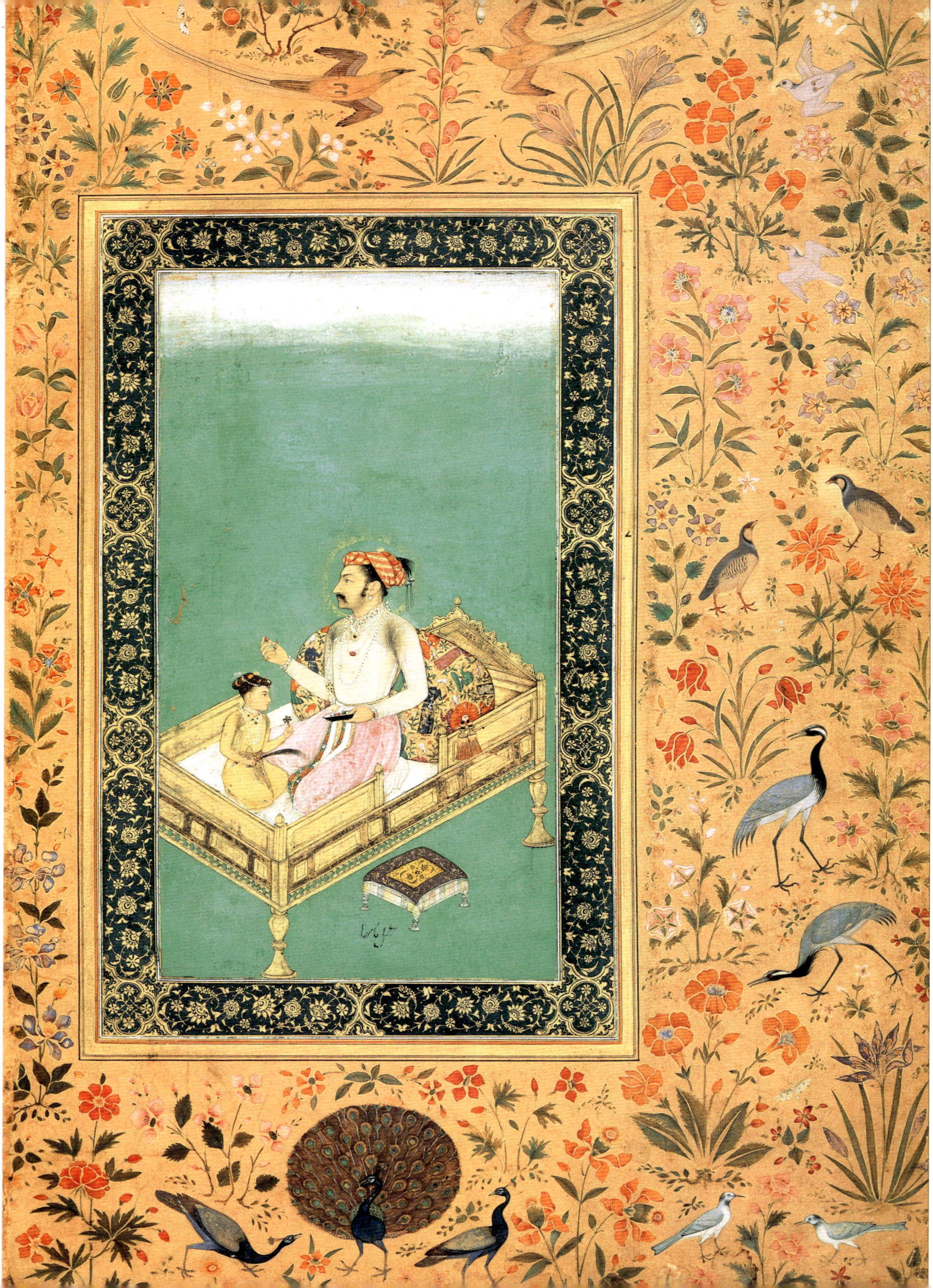

◆ Isaac Tal, Abraham Tal's father: Ein Eglaim—How like Abraham to give this young Fisher the same text he kept asking me about more than fifty years ago. "Where is Ein-Eglaim, Father?" he would ask me. And ask his brother Tuviah. And ask his mother, and I know he will ask this Fisher too. But Fisher will not know any more than he knows that his own father's name is Ezekiel. No, not to Fisher, his father's name will always be Emil. "Meir Mazel Vi Sechel" Pollak my partner in rough diamonds would tell me in the diamond Bourse—"more luck than brains"—Abraham is lucky in his choice of texts to teach Ezekiel's son, but Abraham should not take young Fisher as his Rabbi but rather as his student. Anyway, why should it end differently in New York than it started in Antwerp? Questions piled upon questions without the mortar of answers.

■ Payag, court painter of miniatures: Leaned down—I sat at my brother Balchand's left in the Kitab Khana and watched him work, from sunrise to sunset. I, mixing his colors, fetching him tea, boiling his rice. I, massaging his feet, washing his painting gown—though never did I see a spot of color on it. "Still you must wash," said Balchand "and everyday, for Akbar himself visits and by two things does his majesty judge his artist's perfection: whiteness of clothing and the color on the cheeks of the painted figures."

How skillfully my brother moved his hand and his brush—a butterfly resting, now on one corner of the painting now on the other.

One day he looked at me and said: "Payag, you've got a spot of color on your cloak, let me wash for you!" I protested, "But you are the painter not I."

He took my hand in his and guided it across the page. "There you've done it. The eyes of Babur." And two more strokes, his hand on mine, "And now the eyebrows." And removing my cloak, he was off. "When I return from the river, I expect you to have finished the outline of the page."

Before I could protest, he had scampered down the stairs and was halfway across the courtyard racing toward the banks of the river. I shouted at my brother: "How will I paint the landscape?" And my brother, my guide, my father and mother at once—for had he not shepherded me as a child from Sirohi across all of Rajistan after our parents died--turned and shouted, "Don't worry about the landscape, only the face of Babur is important." I shouted back, "What of the other faces, How will I draw them?" "They will draw themselves, but make sure the figures all lean down towards the divine light of Babur!" He did not return quickly from the river. It took an eternity. But return he did, an instant after I finished.

He bowed toward me and whispered, "Today your figures lean toward Babur, tomorrow all in the Kitab Khana will lean toward you—even you, Payag, do not see yourself as you will be."

Nanha, Prince Khurram (Shah Jahan) with his son, Dara Shikoh.

CHAPTER 2

Green-bordered, Fisher read the card even before he picked it up from the floor just inside his apartment. It was undoubtedly from his next door neighbor, Abraham Tal.

"And it shall come to pass that Fishers shall stand by these waters from Ein-Gedi, even unto Ein Eglaim. There shall be a place for the spreading of nets. Their fish shall be after their kind, as the fish of the great sea, exceeding many...

And by the river upon the bank thereof on this side and on that side shall grow every tree for food, whose leaf shall not whither, neither shall the fruit thereof fail; it shall bring forth new fruit every month, because the waters thereof issue out of the sanctuary; and the fruit thereof shall be for food, and the leaf thereof for healing."

Fisher leaned down, still in his underwear, and went lazily to his desk—a simple library table from Maine, Tal had told him, maybe more than one hundred years old. Slipping into an oak chair, he rested his back against the wooden slats and wearily put his feet on the table, knocking a huge pile of lined paper onto the floor.

■ Rabbi Sol Fisch: Ein Eglaim—"Perhaps the village of Ain el Feskah at the northwest end of the Dead Sea said Professor Lofthouse." Ein Feshkha or Ein Fashah, as the Arabs call it, was excavated in 1958. Water channels in buildings with large reservoirs for the breeding of fish were discovered at the site. Abraham and Fisher, Professor Sukenik and de Vaux, they are digging but in different directions.

◆ Rachel Abendana Tal, Abraham Tal's mother: Ein Eglaim and Ein Gedi—I remember Ein Gedi and I remember Ein Eglaim. Abraham had come home, not much after his Bar Mitzvah, chanting the names as he climbed the stairs. The words resounded; he had my father's voice. He hugged me as he entered the kitchen, I was cooking and chopping nuts for Isaac's salad, and he said, "Where is Eglaim?" "Ask your father tonight if..." I smiled as Abraham interrupted me; he was always ahead. "Oh, Father doesn't know." "Then ask," I responded. And Abraham interrupted me, "Tuviah doesn't know. And I suppose I should ask my teacher too which I did and he said, 'Abraham, where is Ein Gedi?' And what is the point of such an answer mother?"

Suddenly, with tears in his eyes, my Abraham, my treasure, pleaded with me. "Ask Isaac Sardo Abendana." I was stunned. My blessed father had passed into the next world two years before Abraham's Bar Mitzvah. I held Abraham's head between my hands and stared into his eyes. But I was speechless. After a long time Abraham whispered, "You can do anything, Mother." And as the angels Michael and Raphael are my witnesses, that night my father's face came to me in my sleep and I heard him whisper: "Only the Ari himself knows." I woke Abraham early the next morning and told him. What this meant to my son I do not know but of this I am certain: each question our children ask us, we as children can ask those who have come before us and each answer we receive can be heard long, long afterward. If only we can open our ears to truly listen.

■ Haim Vital in the name of Isaac Luria, the holy Ari: Ein Gedi and Ein Eglaim—My holy Master, the Lion of Safed, Isaac Luria would look at me and say each of us is one sentence of Torah. And your sentence, Haim, is from Ein-Gedi unto Ein Eglaim. Ein Gedi is first. The Yeshiva above. And the spring of waters nourishes every tree to yield fruit. And Ein Eglaim is where we are. And the waters of Ein Gedi reach us here. Rush through us. Pass through us. Nourish us. Cleanse us. Haim Vital, you are the pure water of life. My master would tell me, this sentence is your secret self. And where do the waters of Ein Gedi and Eglaim originate, my master? The Ari would not answer. But a year to the day after, he appeared before me and put his head to my ear and I heard the roaring of the words: Ein Sof.

■ Sarmad: Ein Gedi and Ein Eglaim—And what are these places asked the Emperor Shah Jahan.

They are green oases, ever green, green beyond dreams. Ein Gedi is the paradise of Judaism and Ein Eglaim the paradise of Islam. They flow one from the other. I told his Majesty that that was what I believed. And that is what I would teach Dara Shikoh, his most beloved son. My most beloved pupil. A shadow crossed his Majesty's face. He called for Aurangzeb to join Dara Shikoh and me. At once Aurangzeb came, sullenly, as always. My Emperor bade me to walk across the field and wait for him to speak to his seedlings: as he called young Dara. I was out of earshot but I could see the Shadow of G-d on Earth, Shah Jahan's lips move. My beard turned white that day. I could see my end.

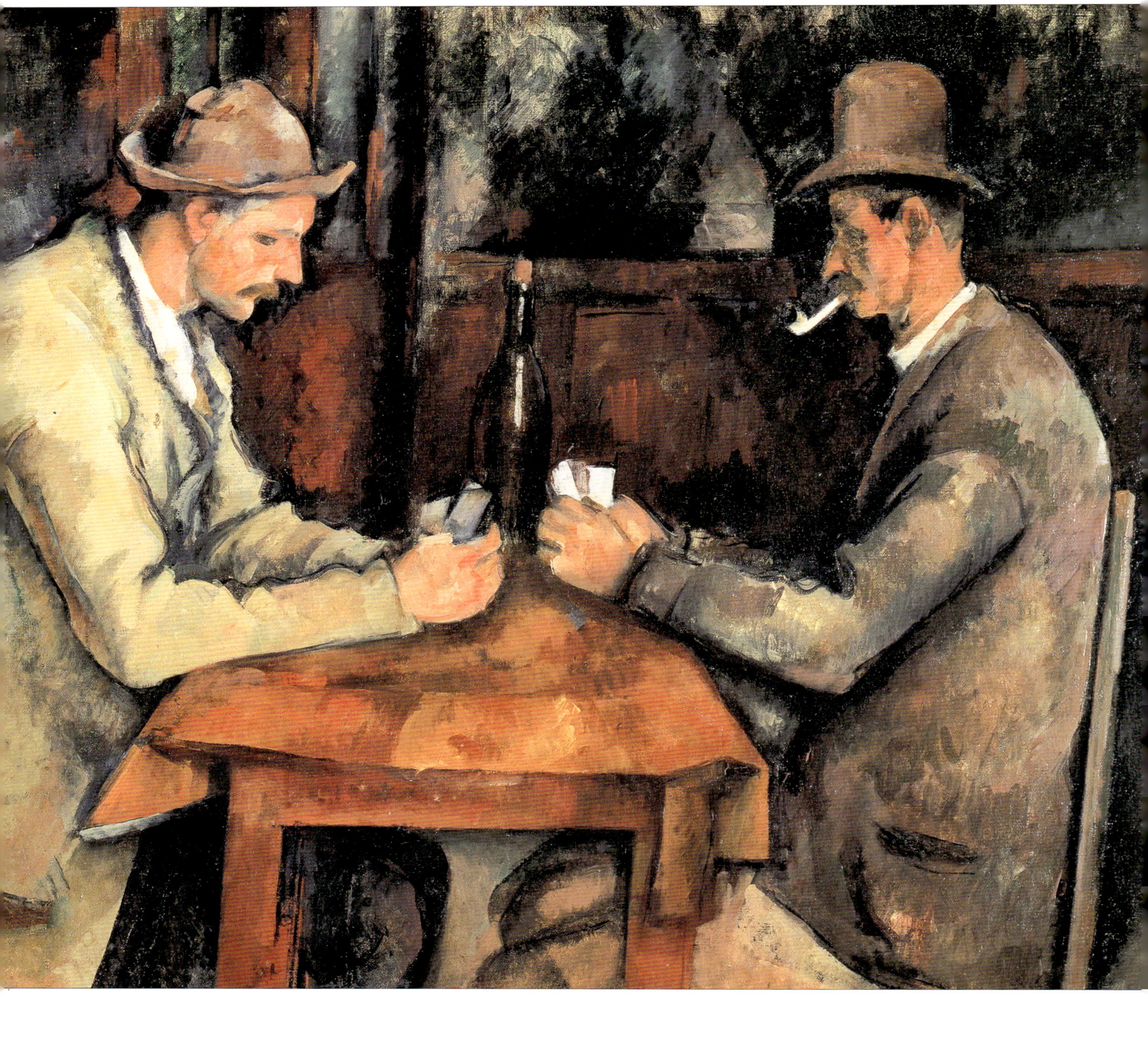

■ JACOB ABULAFIA: He looked out the window—Fisher looks out of the window but not at the passing traffic. He is still. I can see his lips moving. He is alone. He is praying. He is facing Jerusalem:

Outside the Land of Israel those who pray should direct their hearts toward the land of Israel, as it is said, 'and pray in the direction of their land' (2 Chronicles 6:38). In the land of Israel those who pray should direct their hearts toward Jerusalem, as it is said: 'and they pray to you in the direction of the city You have chosen' (2 Chronicles 6:34). *In Jerusalem, those who pray should direct their hearts toward the Holy Temple, as it is said: 'if he comes toward this house'* (2 Chronicles 6:32). *In the Holy Temple, those who pray should direct their hearts towards the Holy of Holies, as it is said: 'the supplications which your servant and your people offer this place'* (I Kings 8:30).

Those in the north, face the south. Those in the south, face north. Those in the east, face west and those in the west, face east. So that all Israel prays towards one place (Tosefta Berachot 3:16).

Fisher has begun his journey to Jerusalem. All journeys begin with prayer.

■ CÉZANNE: Fingering the card sideways, Fisher stared—And what is Fisher staring at? The Card? Hardly. In my study for *The Card Players* that I finished in October '91, I sketched in broad charcoal strokes five cards which had the bulk value of two cards. The cards had an ethereal edge, more floating ever upward. Only to be grasped by one of the card players—lest the cards disappear altogether.

In 1892 I finished the painting. The sketch had no reality as I explained over and over. *"Painting is classifying one's sensation of colour."* Only colour breathes life in the card player. When Zola, Lefèrre and I were young in Aix, each day after school we would play cards. Lefèrre would lose month after month, Zola would be even and I would triumph. "You're cheating!" screamed Lefèrre to me one day. "And you, Zola, are helping Cézanne." "Oh no," said Zola. "You do nothing but watch your cards. And I do nothing but watch you and Paul. And he simply watches me watching you and you looking at your cards." "So how is it that Cézanne always wins?" simpered Lefèrre.

"Monsieur Paul is also standing behind us watching himself," answered Zola with the look of a patron owning a mansion on rue Raspail in the center of Aix. Monsieur Paul is also standing behind us watching himself. Zola understood. That is why in '92, I didn't even bother to paint the cards. Young Fisher should stand behind himself. Maybe he will someday.

Fingering the card sideways, Fisher stared at the curious deep green border Tal had traced around the edge of the card and noticed that the lines didn't quite meet at the right angles.

He looked out the window at the passing Hudson Street traffic—"Five floors up and it's still so damn noisy here," he thought. Tal had once offered to change: "Of course I'll change castle rooms with you, my dear neighbor," Signor Tal told Fisher. "But one week without this light and you'll have to pay me my next years rent to induce me to switch again."

No fool, Tal, although an old fool, thought Fisher, as he flipped the card onto his desk.

Suddenly he saw the reverse of the card. "Fisher: You and I have an appointment together at my apartment. 3:00 this afternoon. All my blessings, Tal. A."

And the signature, bold with Tal, half-illegible with the final letter A trailing downward.

■ SIMHA BUNAM OF PSHISKE: Cards—Once when I was a lumber merchant, a partner of mine asked me to take his son on a business trip to Danzig. One night the son disappeared from an inn we were staying. I walked the streets until I heard piano music coming from a house. Through the window I saw a woman singing and watched as she finished her song. Suddenly I saw my charge, the lumber merchant's son, disappear into a side room. Entering quickly, I paid the woman a gulden to sing her most beautiful song. The lad returned to the singer and the piano player.

I convinced him to leave the house and we went back to our inn where we played cards through the night. In the morning, we recited psalms together and he accomplished a great returning. Years later I told a friend, *"That time in the brothel, I learned that the Divine Presence can descend anywhere and if in a certain place, there is only a single being who receives it, that being receives all of its blessing."* New York is Danzig. And Tal and Fisher are playing cards with each other.

■ RABBI NOSUN: Castle rooms—My head was swimming. "Do not change even a letter," Rabbi Nachman had warned me. I am a pen. But I wasn't writing. How could I listen, remember and write? Yet how could I refuse? As though to help me, Reb Nachman continued speaking each word as slowly as one would cut a diamond:

"He journeyed through deserts, fields and forests. Once when he was traveling in the desert, he saw a side path. He decided that, since he had been in the desert for such a long time and had not found her, he should try that path, and perhaps he would reach a town or village. He went for a long time, and in the end he saw a castle and many soldiers standing guard all around it.

"The castle was beautiful and finely laid out, with well-trained guards. He was afraid that the guards would not let him in. But he decided, "I shall take the risk." So he left the horse and went up to the castle. He was allowed to go in—no one hindered him—and he went from room to room. He came to a great hall and saw a king wearing his crown and many soldiers standing about. Many musicians were playing their instruments before the king, and it was all very beautiful and fine. And neither the king nor anyone else asked him anything. He saw good food, and went and ate. Then he went and lay down in the corner, to watch what was happening. He saw the king order that the queen be brought, and servants went to bring her. Then there was a great commotion and much joy, and the musicians played and sang when she was brought. A throne was brought for her, and she was seated next to the king. The chamberlain saw her and recognized her. It was the lost daughter of the king."

Paul Cézanne, *The Card Players*.

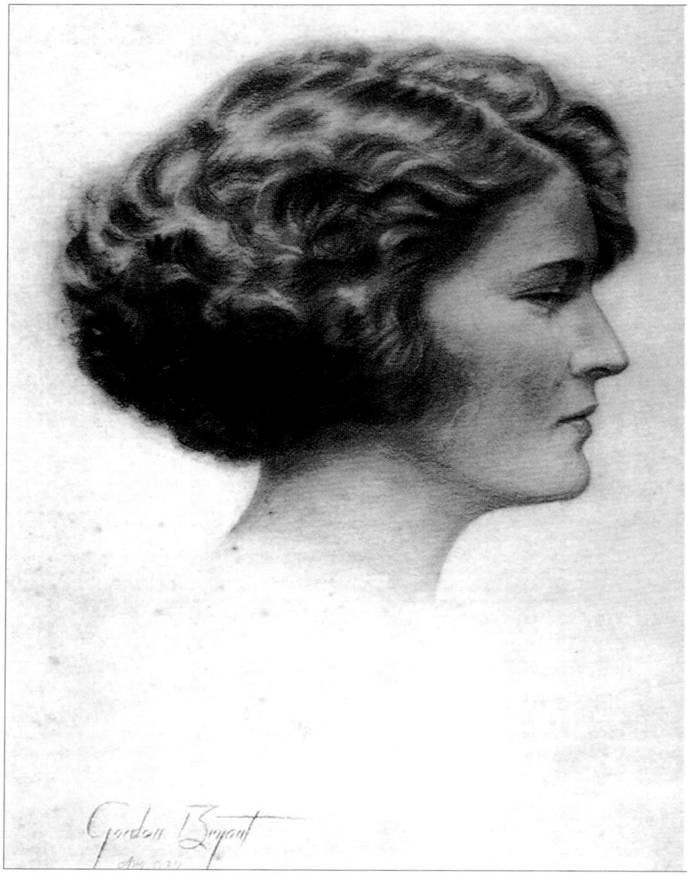
Gordon Bryant

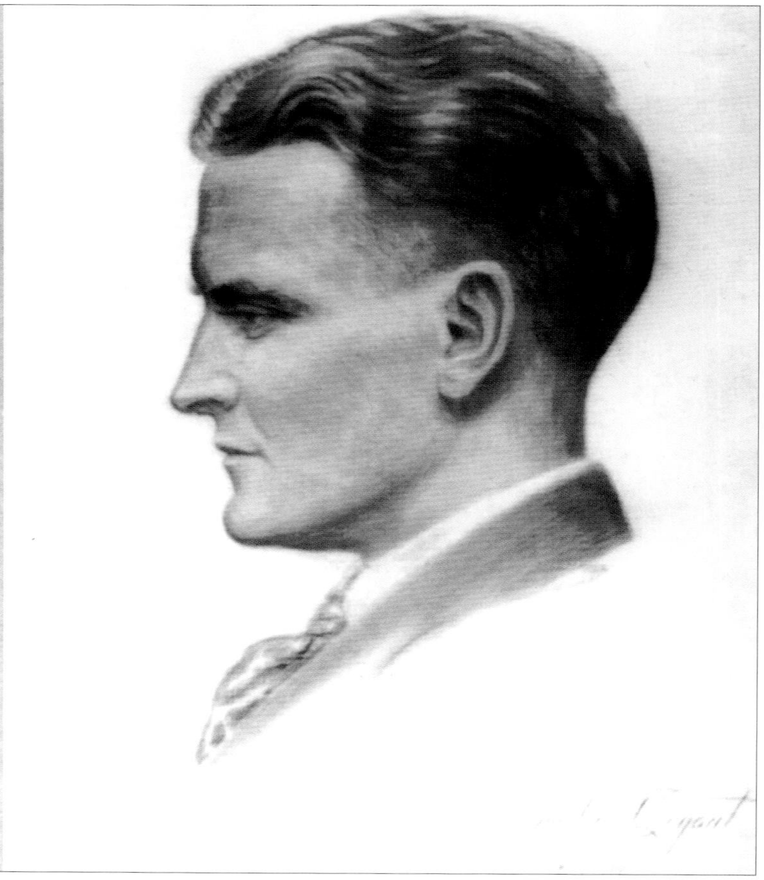

■ Yehezkel Schrage ben Yitzhak Bunam: December 22, 1940—I walked all the way from the hospital on rue Tsarovitch in the dark. No street lamps. Even stopped twice by gendarmes in front of rue Saint Sulpice, asking me why I was out on the streets at night and I told them truthfully my wife had just given birth and I couldn't sleep. And I couldn't stay in our apartment and I couldn't go to a cafe or bar. Everything was closed because of the blackout fear of the Germans bombing. I walked all night until six-thirty in the morning. Monsieur LeDruot opened normally at seven sharp, and there he was inviting me to the bar. A young American was standing, drinking a Pernod, weeping as he drank. "Soyez heureux," I said to the youngster—who must have been of university age—beard and black cravat. "My wife just gave birth to a son and I'll pay for your Pernod and anything else anyone wants."

This didn't seem to cheer him in any way. When I asked him why he was weeping, he mumbled in English—which I barely understood— an American writer, famous, had just died. I didn't catch the full name. Gatsby, I think. I looked at my Journale Nice Matin but there was no mention of it. When I tried to show the young man the paper, he simply said "le radio" and left Monsieur LeDruot's cafe abruptly. LeDruot shrugged at me and said, "Monsieur, Charles, Santé. Oubliez-le, c'est un jeune artiste americain—completement foux"—amazing, I had just told my dear wife, that's where we had to go immediately. Crazy that American staying in Nice. And weeping over a Mr. Gatsby.

■ The 13th Dalai Lama: December 22—"In my lifetime conditions will be as they are now, peaceful and quiet. But the future holds darkness and misery. I have warned you of these things."

"And the signs of my reincarnated self: clear as the mountains and subtle as dawn. The leg's skin ought to be striped like a tiger's; the eyes wide and the brows turned outward; the ears large, two fleshy excrescence should be found near the shoulder-blades, a token of the two extra arms of the chenrezig, the G-d whose earthly embodiment the Dalai Lama is supposed to be, and lastly, the palms should bear the pattern of a sea shell."

Fisher was stunned, half-annoyed, and completely baffled. A Tuesday. How did Tal know he'd be home, trying to write his Great American Novel? Putting it off so he could finish his assignment for Hamilton which was due yesterday.

And Hamilton was less than no help at all. Absolutely none. He had asked Hamilton last month to have lunch with him on December 22. "Are we celebrating Christmas early? Fisher of Men?" Hamilton had asked. "No, my birthday," answered Fisher.

They celebrated each year together. And each year Fisher had to remind Hamilton of the event. Always a lunch, always a bottle of champagne each and a long Hamilton toast delivered through two desserts and four espressos.

■ James Donoghue, a visitor who saw Fitzgerald's body in the Wordsworth room of Pierce Brothers Mortuary: December 22, 1940—I visited Scott's body more to pay respect to his work than to him. The hand that created Gatsby. That's what I wanted to see.

"Except for one bouquet of flowers and a few empty chairs, there was nothing to keep him company but his casket...I never saw a sadder scene than the end of the father of all sad, young men. Fitzgerald was laid out to look like a cross between a floor walker and a wax dummy... But in Technicolor...His hands were horribly wrinkled and thin, the only proof left after death that for all the props of youth, he actually had suffered and died an old man."

■ Sheilah Graham: December 22, 1940—Scott one day dead. December 22, 1940. He had a heart attack. Just inside the Pantages Theater. Barely getting back to Laurel Canyon Boulevard. December 21, 1940. Scott in my apartment, finishing a chocolate bar, making notes for an article for the Princeton Alumni Weekly: "An analytical long range view of the 1940 football team." And sweetly talking about the child he was going to give me. Calling me Sheilah, Sheilah—but not with the liquor-crazy disdain he sometimes had for the English and for Jews. I patted his hand. "Oh, but the child would be Jewish dearest and half British," he added smiling. "And aren't we a wee bit old," I added and he smiled with that glorious smile, that smile he would reserve for the moments when he would explain his creations. His Gatsby, I never read, rather, he read it to me. He smiled and said, "By divine right, I will our child into..."

Then he rose out of his chair, staggered toward me, collapsed, clutched at the mantle piece clock and fell backward, dead.

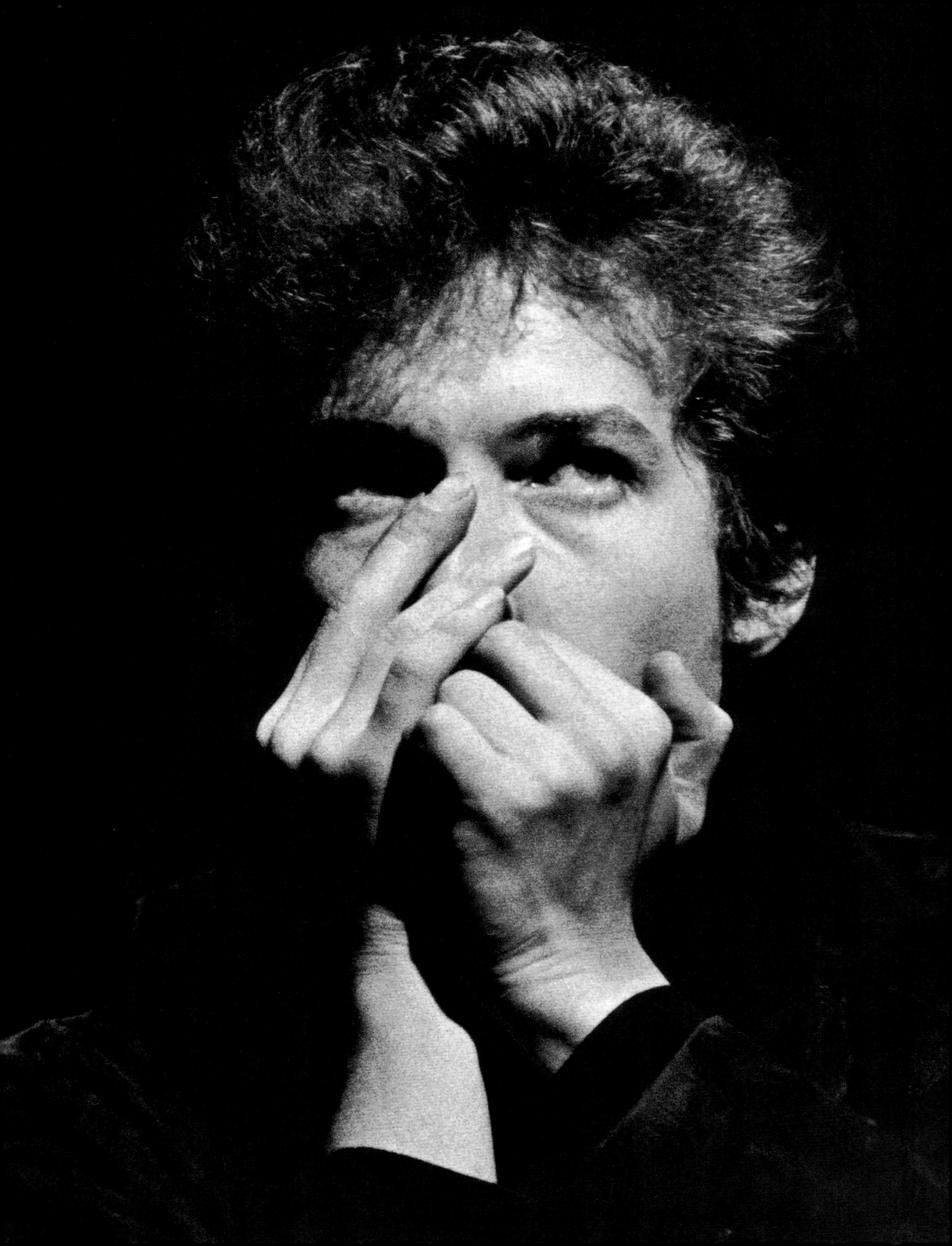

■ BALCHAND: Of course, I remember—"Of course I remember this lad," said his Majesty Abu'l-Fath Jalal Ad-Din Muhammad Akbar. "He is your brother. You carried him at the age of nine across the Aravalli mountains, saving him when he almost drowned in the river near your native place—Sirohi.

Akbar the Great was speaking but not looking at my little brother, Payag. He was looking at a page that Payag had drawn. He swept his eyes from face to face and smiled at the watermelons piled high in front of the watermelon seller. Suddenly his majesty's eyes rested on the right hand side of the page, and he lowered his head to better see the tiny script on the coins. "What is written here? Is it your name written in my language, brother of Balchand?"

Payag began to tremble—was our Majesty testing him? And before he said a word, so terrified was Payag, I put my hand on his shoulder and said gently, "What did I teach you to say when you don't know what to say, my brother?"

Payag, without raising his head, whispered, "Balchand, you tell me always, 'just speak the truth.'"

"And what is the truth, Payag? The Lord of all the world is asking you a question," Payag looked at the tiny script as though seeing his creation for the first time. It is not writing, it is simply brush strokes. I and my brother are not Muslims, my lord, we are your Hindu servants from Rajasthan, from across the Aravalli mountains we came.

Akbar burst into laughter and suddenly Price Salim, who had been standing silently in the doorway of the Kitab Khana moved towards his father Akbar and stood next to his Majesty.

"We are a pair," said Akbar, "This Hindu brush worker and myself, neither of us can read nor write our Persian script. We are one. Do not forget that, Salim. Do not forget that this Payag and your father Akbar, Salim, are two side of the same coin."

I knew that day that to the ends of our days, we could find refuge in the house of Akbar and Salim, as long as they lived.

"Of course I remember it's your birthday," Hamilton said to him across the desk they shared at Time Inc. "Of course, I remembered. The secret of life is my gift to you."

"What do you want most of all?" queried Hamilton. "What do you—not you and Dosha—want most of all? What do you—and not the next door neighbor or is he sharing your man-in-the-iron-mask prison cell with both of you—want most of all?"

And, of course, Fisher waited for Hamilton to complete his sentence—four years at Yale and almost four years afterward and he could barely get in a word. A would-be-Rembrant. Hamilton, perched languidly on his throne, was quite a talker. "Yes. What I want is..." Fisher stretched his hand out halfway across the Time Inc. desk, signaling Hamilton to finish.

"What you want is..." Hamilton dove into a pile of papers on his side of the desk and triumphantly fished out a white 6 inch by 8 inch sketch pad and lifted it up quickly, flashing it at Fisher face down on the mound of crumpled work papers.

■ MOSES HAYYIM LUZZATTO quotes Shir ha Shirim Rabbah: Throne—*Jerusalem in days to come will ascend higher and higher until she will have reached the throne of Glory."*

■ VAN GOGH: Would be Rembrandt—I would have given anything to be Rembrant. But nothing I had to give would make me a Rembrandt.

Why would I have given anything and everything to be Rembrandt? Because I finally could be me. Only through Rembrandt could I become me. And through him I d d.

These two men, Fisher and Hamilton. Are they not Anton and me? Young Mr. Anton Kersemaker and young Mr. Vincent van Gogh. In autumn 1885. The Rijksmuseum just opened in Amsterdam.

And as we reach *The Jewish Bride*, Anton walks on but I am overcome. At the end of the day, Anton returns. I am still in front of *The Jewish Bride*. *"Would you believe it—and I honestly mean what I say—I should be happy to give ten years of my life if I could go on sitting here in front of this picture for a fortnight with only a crust of bread for food?"*
That was Anton's gift to me, to go on a voyage with me. My ship was Rembrandt but my distant port of call was myself. And Fisher too and Hamilton too and even Anton. They—we—all travel to the same destination.

■ BOB DYLAN: What do you want?—
*"Your debutante just knows what
You need
But I know what you want.
Oh mama can this really be
The end
To be stuck inside of Mobile
With the Memphis Blues again."*

■ RABBI NACHMAN OF BRESLOV: Remember—*You must also take care not to talk in a bad way. Talking maliciously and derogatorily about other people is very damaging to one's memory. If you work on yourself and even force yourself to be happy, it is a help in developing a good memory.*

Bob Dylan.

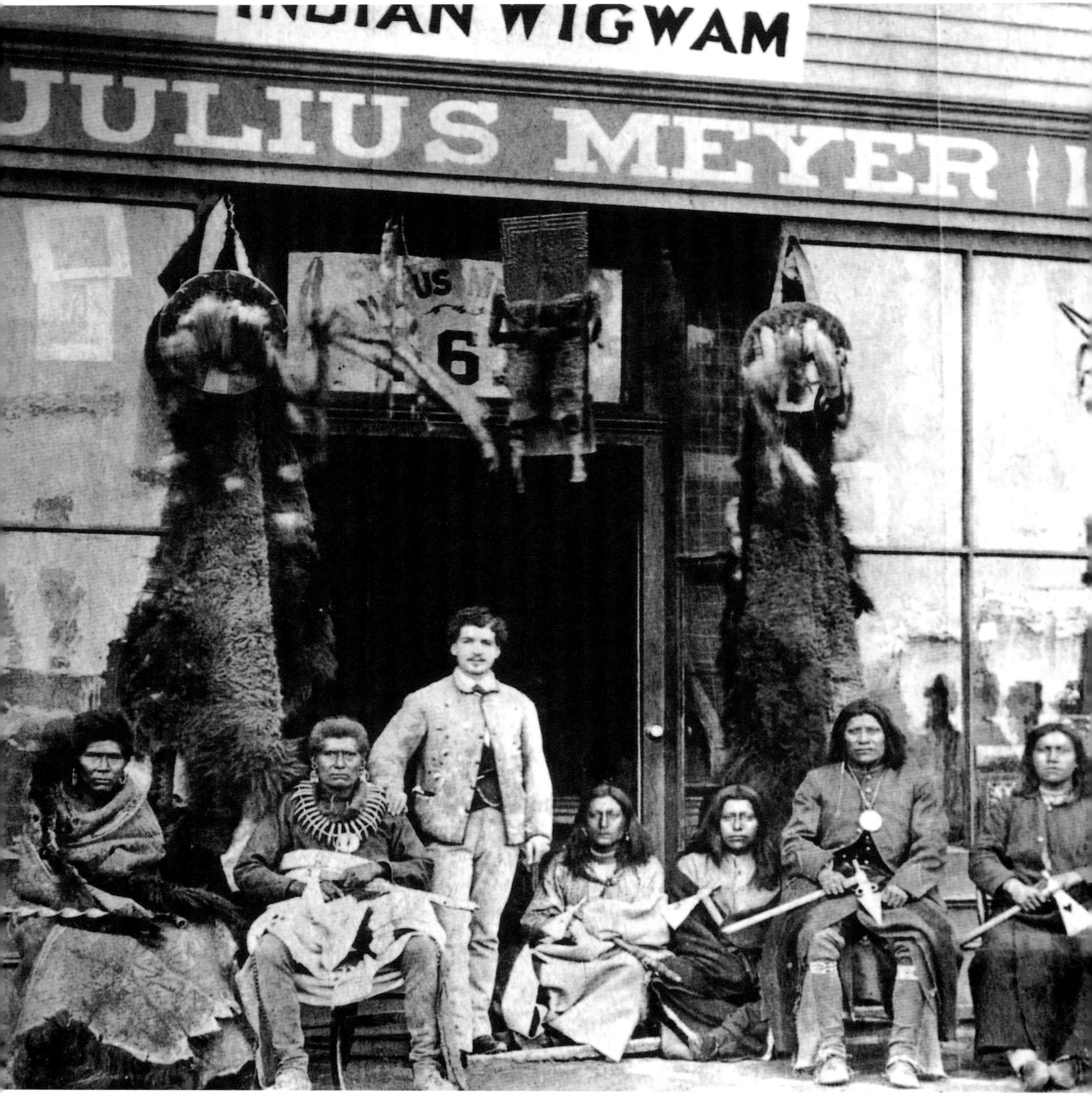
INDIAN WIGWAM
JULIUS MEYER
US
6

● RICKELE PADAWER, DOSHA'S GRANDMOTHER: Home—In Slobodka, I would ask my bridal groom, chusan boche, what time he would return home. And he would always delay answering. Back and forth his eyes would roam. He'd lower his head and minutes later murmur "by nine o'clock for sure. For sure." Then of course I would wait by the door at thirty minutes past eight and not longer than a minute later, my dear precious Simha would appear at the end of the street not winded from the long walk up Tamozhne Street but with a smile-radiant, floating toward me. Each and every night except Friday, when he finished learning at midday and went to the Mikveh three hours before sunset—always he would say nine and always it would be half past eight—a *daitcher* was not more prompt. And finally, after our beloved Hesche was born, I asked my Simha, "Why say nine when it's always earlier?" He smiled and said, "As Chofetz Haim once said, 'The way home is always short.'" I smiled and looked in his eyes, over our child Hesche's tiny body, gently repeating his answer to him, "And where is home, my Simha?"

He took Hesche from my arms and cradled his head and looked out our window, peering down Tamozhne Street, past the market, even past the river. When he turned around, I could see his tears, and Hesche too, crying, but both with no sound and everything held inside. He said: "You ask the best questions. From you I've learned everything." I never asked him again for the answer that I saw, I knew was beyond tears, beyond everything we could begin to imagine.

● JULIUS MEYER, DOSHA'S GRANDFATHER'S BROTHER: Home—Home. Home. Home. In the Omaha tongue, in the Winnebago and in the Brule, Swift Bear and Spotted Tail would use one word for home, in Pawnee. Sitting Bull and Red Cloud, would mutter another word in their Oglala Sioux fashion: Standing Bear would never pronounce the word in Ponca at all. Everywhere was home. And nowhere was home. And Max and Moritz and even mama and everyone in Blomberg, Germany, everyone all sitting alive and together and well in Adolph's living room. All of them living together in the Metropolitan Club that I put together in Omaha, still wouldn't have made a home.

"What you want is to be a…what the secret of life is…what your deepest, darkest, fondest, sweetest hope is…"

And again Hamilton flashed his cartoon artwork at Fisher. This time holding it up so that Fisher could make it out more clearly.

Three men playing Klaberjass Poker around a table, the fourth with his back to the viewer. Lots of square chips in front of each of them. One man with his head barely above the table and the Eiffel Tower in the window and the man on the right, eye-patched with thick glasses, leaning backward in his seat, recoiling from his hand. Clearly James Joyce. Just like the photograph by Berenice Abbott of Joyce in his home in Paris, Joyce astigmatic, his eyes barely visible behind his thick glasses, peering directly at the viewer. It was the photograph Hamilton had given Fisher at his twenty-third birthday as his twenty-fourth anniversary. "Nine months on the inside are like twelve on the outside," Hamilton quipped. "Next year it's a quarter of a century for you, my lad."

"I'll still be older than you," Hamilton had noted over the last espresso. "Always a bit ahead of you."

● MAX MEYER, DOSHA'S GRANDFATHER: Home—My brother Julius was one of a kind. I pleaded with him. Why live with Rosenblum, live with us. Live with our brother Adolph. Live with Moritz but no, even at fourteen, Julius' home was out on the prairie with the Brulé, with the Omaha. Anywhere but with us. I once asked him: Why not live in your own tepee and call it home? At least you'd be more comfortable than in that tiny rooming house that Adler overcharges you for. The thought of Julius asleep among all those trinkets, moccasins, bows and arrows, amused me. But Julius would have none of it. Home was someplace you didn't live in. Home was someplace you left.

■ STANDING BEAR, PONCA INDIAN CHIEF: Home—I saved Julius Meyer. I saved the white: Julius Meyer. As simple as the moon rests in its bed in the sky and appears fully clothed fourteen days later, I saved him.

But Meyer, whom the Pawnee called Box-Ka-Re-Hash-Ta-Ka, Curly-headed White Chief Who Speaks With One Tongue, and who called me chief and whom I called my white chief, would shake when he said the word, Home. He would whisper in my ear: his eyes aflame. "Never say the word, Standing Bear, Home. They will steal it from you. They will rob it. They will twist it. They will borrow it. They will never return it to you." I thought him mad, possessed, but one whose life you save, even a white, and especially a white, you become forever responsible for. "When will they steal it, this unpronounced word?" I asked my white chief. "It will take a hundred years. If you don't pronounce it. And it will take a hundred days if you do." I didn't believe him but I followed him across the waters and I ate with him in France and I feared his flaming eyes and I never pronounced the name and a hundred years later to the day, in 1966, our tribe's reservation, with 442 members and only 34 acres left to steal, was terminated. Now we are free. To own our home and pay taxes and pay for our medicine and pay for everything, including the right to stand on our land in front of our home and gaze at the moon. And without money, what were we to do? Of course, the white man had a ready answer. "Of course you are free to sell your home."

Julius Meyer's Indian Wigwam, Omaha, Nebraska.

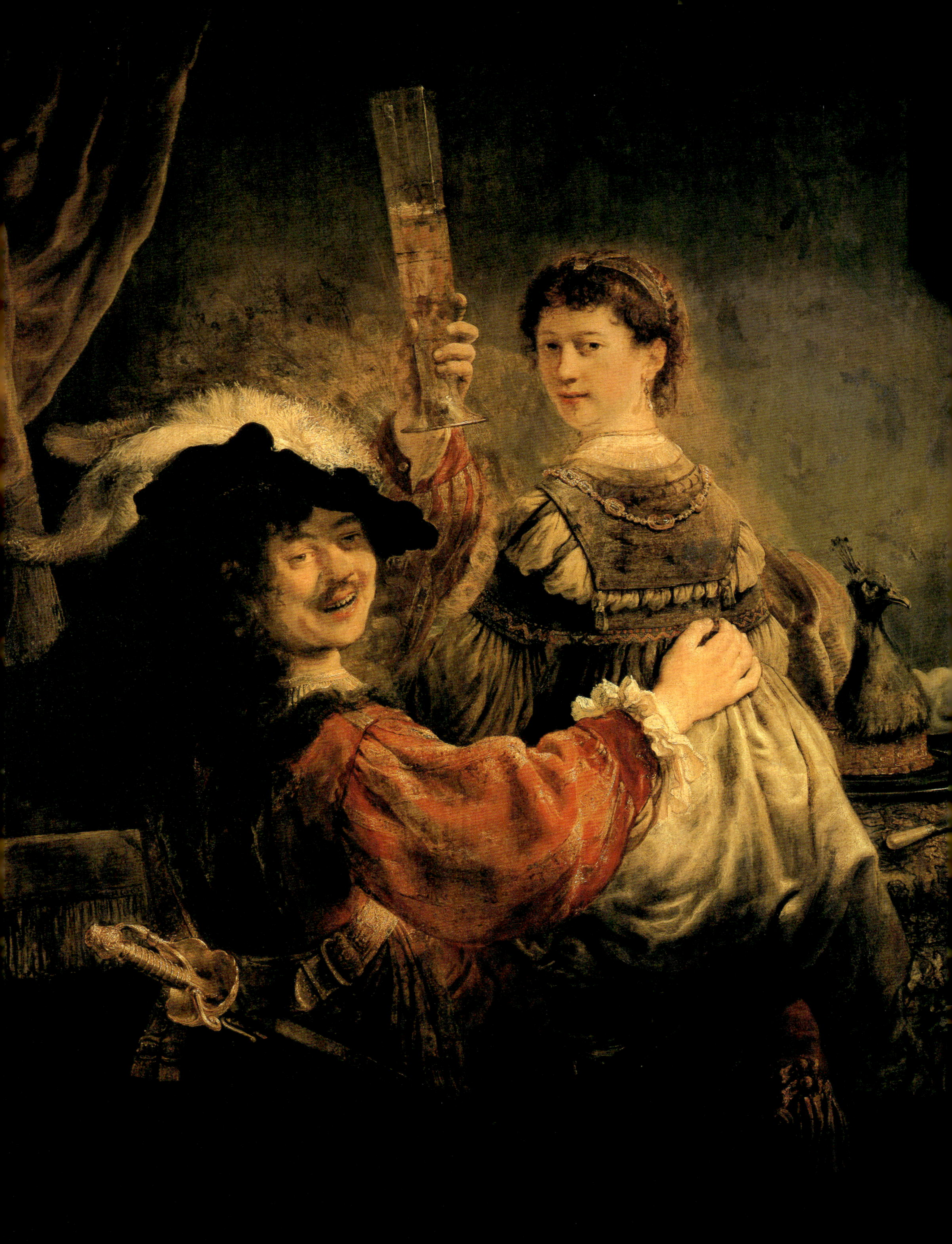

■ PLUTARCH: Suddenly Fisher could see—*"Often some trivial event, a word or joke, will serve better than great campaigns and battles as a revelation of character."*

This young man can see the small, small books. The words on their spines. Titles of works they had written. Because he read them all. Thought of them all. Committed them all to memory. They have become his own. The sudden has been slow process. Chewing each piece slowly. Without these efforts, without this knowledge, without this thought, suddenly would become never.

■ LOUIS CARTIER: What's your big question—It was ridiculous really. A younger brother always trying to act the older brother. Little Pierre, proudly strutting into my library and proclaiming "I've done wonders—saved the firm.

Les Riches Americaines have purchased the Star of the East, a pear shape that you said would take more than a decade to move." I suppose he expected me to applaud like a seal.

All I could do was look over his shoulder and see that 17th century glorious moghul miniature of Shah Jahan sitting on the peacock throne.

Half profile, all noble, halo around his head. A gem encrusted throne he had and all captured by a one-haired brush for more than three centuries. And Pierre talking in terms of a decade.

"Pierre, dear Pierre," I began softly, "When La Maison Cartier acquires a moghul gem, what's your big question? How much can we sell it for?

"We must think as Moghuls do. The big question for us should be, how can we find other yet greater treasures? Oh I know dear Pierre, what you will say. How will we pay for them? How can we afford even this past purchase? And on and on but I must tell you we will end up as second rate tradesmen in les Marchés puce if we're not careful."

"Yes Louis, that's exactly what we'll be if I am not careful," Pierre shouted and he stormed out of my study.

"Well, it's your secret life. What's your big question, Raphael? It's, how do I become a writer? How the devil would I, the all-seeing Rembrant, know? But like the good librarian that I am, I know where to find the answer. Invite Joyce, Fitzgerald and Kafka to a card game" Hamilton displayed the drawing proudly.

"It's Paris," said Fisher, noting La Tour Eiffel in the window.

"Ah," said Hamilton, "my pearls are not wasted upon you."

"But who is the fellow whose head is facing toward Joyce, Kafka and Fitzgerald?"

"Why, that's you. Go for it."

"But I don't look that way," said Fisher petulantly. "I don't have a bald spot on the back of my head."

"Oh but you will, you will, Gertrude Stein," said Hamilton.

Suddenly Fisher could see that the square chips in front of each figure were small books with tiny words on each spine—titles of works they had written.

■ DIMITRIJE BJELICA: Fisher could see—*"The Olympiad had ended. At the closing ceremony, Tal and Fischer were again in the spotlight. Bobby and I were sitting at the same table. He was very cheery and said, turning to me, 'Did you ever hear me sing in Bled? If I hadn't become a Grand Master, I probably would have become a singer'...*

When Tal came up to our table, Bobby said to him, 'Let me tell you your chess fortune'...He took Tal's palm and slowly began telling him his fortune. 'I see that you're a very gifted chess player'...Many Masters and Grand Masters had gathered at our table. Everyone was listening and watching. Cameramen began taking pictures. 'Your palm even shows you play sharply, in a combative style.' Tal, of course, was laughing. There was also a smile on the face of the American William Lombardy who was standing next to him. Meanwhile, the grinning Bobby was continuing. 'But I can also see that you will soon lose the title of World Champion to a young American Grand Master'...Needless to say, Bobby was referring to himself. But Tal promptly turned to Lombardy and shaking his hands said, 'Bravo Billy. So it's you who is destined to succeed me at my post!' Everyone roared with laughter. I don't know what had amused them more, Fischer's fortune telling or Tal's witty riposte."

■ MIKHAIL TAL: Suddenly Fisher could see that—Suddenly Fischer could see that. Yes, Bobby could see that. He could write that. In his article in *Chessworld* on the ten greatest masters in chess history, he said of me:

"Tal appears to have no respect for his opponents, and frightens almost every player he opposes."

Then I knew that he knew I could no longer frighten him. And that for the first time he could see the squares. Not like Botvinnik whom he did not even include on his list. And whom I always managed to frighten. To scare him I arrived late at the Fourteenth World Chess Olympiad in October 1960.

'Tal played well,' said Bobby after the game ended in a draw. *If I had lost, Bobby would have said I played brilliantly."* But the fear would be gone and Fischer could see.

31

Rembrandt van Rijn, *Rembrandt and, Saskia in the Parable of the Prodigal Son.*

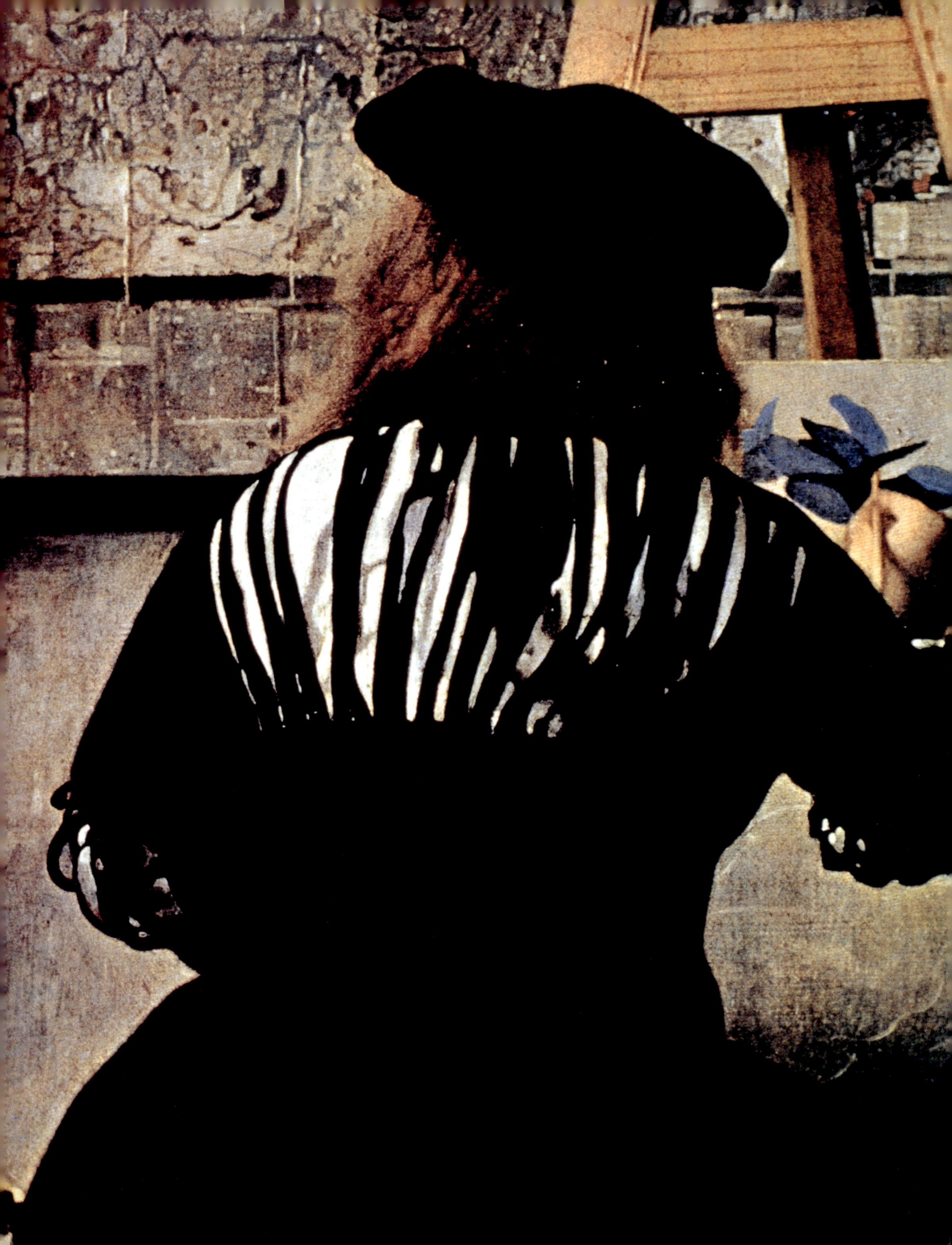

■ Rabbi Shimon, the first Hasid of Rabbi Nachman of Breslav: Then he closed his eyes—Reb. Nachman was once traveling with his Hasidim by carriage, and as it grew dark, they came to an inn where they spent the night. During the night, Reb Nachman began to cry out loudly in his sleep, waking up everyone in the inn, all of whom came running to see what had happened.

When he awoke, the first thing Reb Nachman did was to take out a book he had brought with him. Then he closed his eyes, opened the book and pointed to a passage. And there it was written: "Cutting down a tree before its time is like killing a soul."

Then Reb Nachman asked the inn keeper if the walls of that inn had been built out of saplings, cut down before their time. The innkeeper admitted this was true, but how did the Rabbi know?

And Reb Nachman said: "All night I dreamed I was surrounded by the bodies of those who had been murdered. I was very frightened. Now I know that it was the souls of the trees that cried out to me."

■ Emily Post: Hamilton shut up for a moment—"A few maxims for those who talk too much and easily—The faults of commission are far more serious than those of omission; regrets are seldom for what is left unsaid. The chatterer reveals every corner of his shallow mind: One who keeps silent can not have his depth plumbed. Above all, stop and think what you are saying! This is really the first, last and only rule. If you 'stop' you can't chatter or expound or flounder ceaselessly and if you think, you will find a topic and a manner of presenting your topic so that your neighbor will be interested rather than long suffering."

Such a pair, these two—Messieurs Fisher and Hamilton. I quite like their annual birthday celebrations. Heaven forbid, the lads cease to convene together. Diamonds in the rough, they both are, and not requiring more than a bit of polishing.

"Why is Kafka standing and why is he so frail?" Fisher asked, utterly charmed by Hamilton's drawing.

"Well, quite simple. It is 1928. June. Paris. Joyce and Fitzgerald have met. Kafka is invited. You'd be frail too if you'd walked all the way from Prague to Paris and were also dead for the last four years."

Fisher burst out laughing. "Hamilton, no pun intended, you're a real card."

"None taken, Fisher."

Without a moment's hesitation, Hamilton took out his set of brushes, a large bottle of white-out and set to work on the drawing with his eyes closed.

"What are you doing?" screeched Fisher. "If they catch you doodling, we'll lose our jobs."

"If I don't finish this before lunch time, we can't celebrate your birthday. We'll be thrown back one year, and you won't get any older. Maybe, Heaven forbid and the Saints take us, you'll get a year younger," said Hamilton in the direction of his drawing.

"Hamilton, shut up for a moment. Look at me. Seriously, how can this drawing truly be the secret of life for me?"

■ Vermeer: With his eyes closed—The only way to look at one's own work. To close my eyes in front of my canvas. And think to be able to see what I already painted and the space on the canvas. My brush in my hand, I looking at the canvas, my eyes closed. More important, that moment, than when I opened my eyes and looked at Morika, my Sephardi soul, more important than the moment my hand started to move down towards the canvas. More important than the moment of my hand steadied by my drawing stick, placed the dabs of paint on the canvas. For my hand had not a muscle in it. Involuntary. Guiced by my eyes, which closed could visualize the painting already on my canvas, my eyes closed so that I could not see Morika, and did I need my eyes to see my Morika who did not need her eyes to see me? Together with eyes closed, we see and feel the Holy Book, the Blessed One who had brought us together. Praise be the blessed book of the all seeing name.

■ Cézanne, Paris, 15 March 1865: Eyes closed—Eyes closed. And look, look until your eyelids feel so heavy they could roll your eyeballs out of your head. Camille Pissarro would circle about chanting "Eyes closed, Paul. And don't open them until you can visualize every stroke you are about to paint." Before Pissarro, in the Aix Drawing Academy, I was painstakingly taught to sketch, prepare, outline, plan before any painting was attempted.

And Camille simply told me: "Paul, you can sketch and plan and prepare with your eyes open and you will end up as a drawing in an Aix Gypsy caravan. Or you can let me teach you to become a painter. A great painter. Simply by closing your eyes." And Pissarro's broad, warm fingers would pass down on my eyelids, closing them with a Jew's gentleness—as though I didn't know how to close my own eyes, which I didn't. I would write letters to Pissarro over and over.

"Forgive me for not coming to see you...If sometimes you should wish to see me, I go every morning to Suiss and am at home in the evening. On Saturday, we are going to the barracks of the Champs-Élysées to bring our canvasses which will make the institute blush with rage and despair. I hope you will draw some fine landscapes. I shake you warmly by the hand." My hand. His hand. Closing my eyes—So I could see.

Johannes Vermeer, *The Art of Painting*, detail.

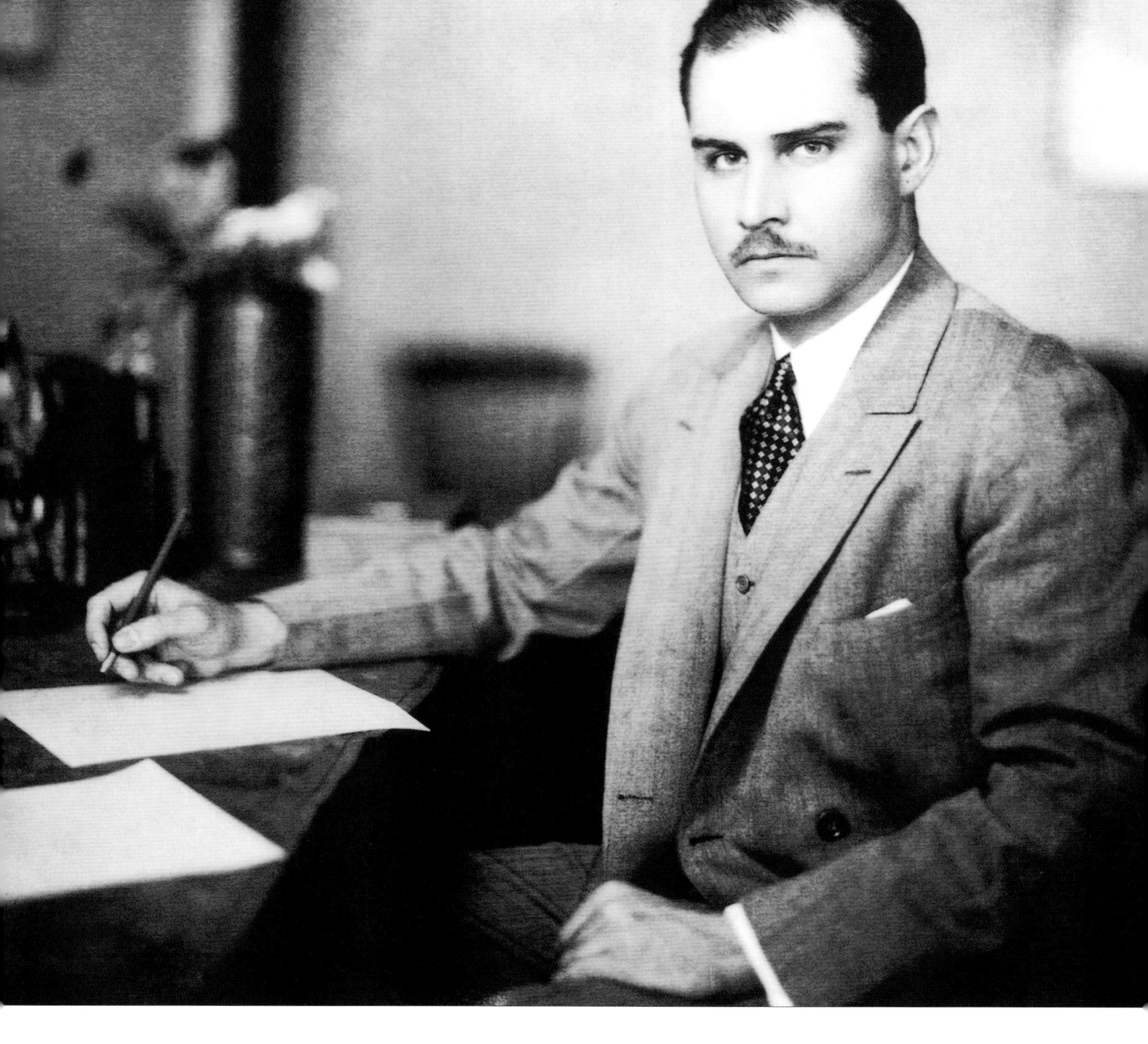

● TUVIAH GUTMAN GUTWIRTH, FISHER'S MOTHER'S FATHER: Drawing...perfect—Here they are, my grandson and his friend. And asking each other questions: Neither truly listening to each other but still asking questions. And does the question, if asked with a full heart, not bring the answer with it swift as an arrow? The Dubno Maggid in his home in Setil told a parable for each verse in the Torah. As soon as a question was asked of him, the Maggid immediately related a tale. And the Vilna Gaon, a tower of answers, asked him, "Reb Yaakov, tell me how it is that you always have a ready answer, a parable, a story, for each question brought to you, ever before..."

And the Maggid of Dubno interrupted the Vilna Gaon with a tale: "Once a Prince, interested in archery, wanted to perfect himself in that sport. Try as he would, practice as he did, the Prince could rarely hit a bull's eye. One day, while walking in the forest, the Prince saw on many trees arrows in the very center of each circle. Amazed, the Prince hid himself and waited to see the perfect marksman. Hours later, a man appeared, aimed an arrow at a tree, and calmly walked up to it and drew a perfect circle around the arrow."

"So it is with me," said the Dubna Maggid to the Vilna Gaon. "I prepare the story first. And I wait." And the Vilna Gaon himself became a disciple of the Master of parables, united by friendship for the rest of their lives.

Hamilton and Fisher. Friends for life, if only they will continue to question each other.

■ BRITON HADDEN: Let's go celebrate—There was Luce. Face lined with ink shadows, smudged with worry. Frozen in thought, peering up at the Harkness bells which were caroling, the crisp March air too warm for all his mufflers, and his Shanghai-made overcoat shabby even ten years before, sensible only for a Manchurian winter. Luce frozen in thought. I slipped up behind him and shouted in his ear, "Look out Harry, you'll drop the college."

Luce didn't move. But he did smile. "Let's celebrate," I offered. And I pulled on his overcoat, dragging him across Dwight for a drink at Mory's, he, and I, toddies for the both of us. At least in those days, he would celebrate.

"Well, you're cutting into my toast. Anyway, you're playing cards with Kafka, Joyce and Fitzgerald. But they don't have money. You know. Joyce, always broke, depending on Pound for shoes. Fitzgerald spending the year's earnings before it's sent from Scribner's. And Kafka, well the raging Czech inflation of the twenties. Anyway, in a spirit of camaraderie, you ask them their tricks of the trade. You pick up their chips, their chits, their chitter, chatter etc. etc.. Get it, Raphael?"

"Out of curiosity, why not have Aristotle one of the players?"

"Marvelous suggestion. One photograph of Aristotle please, so I can draw him. Seriously Raphael, let me do the artwork."

"What are you doing now? This drawing is perfect. Don't spoil my present."

"Aren't you the urban Pope to young Angel Michael. Aren't you the young Baron educating Dink Stover. When and where to stop. Fisher let's go celebrate."

They did. Marvelously.

Hamilton's drawing still resting on Fisher's non-writing table on Hudson Street. Inspiring, but still no inspiration. No novel. Only secret dreams.

■ MORIKA ABENDANA, Vermeer's painting model: What are you doing now?—"Close your eyes," he would tell me. Over and over. And at first I was afraid. Of course, I would hear him if he walked toward me across the studio. But the silence was eerie. As when my family hid on the roof of our house for more than a year in Cordoba before coming to Amsterdam. "Close your eyes so that I can better see you," Johannes would whisper. "It is not fair," I would tease him, "Why should you see me and I not see you." "Oh, but my eyes are closed too," he replied to me with a gentleness I had only heard when I was a girl living in the Plaza Réal, when my grandmother whispered to me tales of our people. "How can you paint me if your eyes are closed?" I parried. "How can I paint you if our eyes are open?" Johannes answered with a whisper across the room.

"What are you doing, Vermeer?" I asked with only half a voice, chilled with the heat of his gaze. And without answering, I knew his answer and without opening my eyes I could see into his closed eyes. And we both could touch and see what followed.

■ OWEN JOHNSON in *Stover at Yale*: Le Baron educating Stover—"You'll hear a good deal of talk inside the college, and out of it too, about the system. It has its faults but its the best system there is, and it makes Yale what it is today. It makes fellows go out and work, it gives them ambitions, stops loafing and going to seed..."

"I know nothing at all about it," said Stover, perplexed.

"The seniors have fifteen in each secret society, they give out their elections end of junior year, end of May. That's what we're working for."

"Already?" said Stover, involuntarily.

"There are fellows in your classes who've been working all summer so as to get ahead of the competition, for the Yale Daily News or the Lit, or to make the leader of the glee club—fellows, of course who know."

"But that's three years off."

"Yes, it's three years off," said LeBaron quietly.

אחד מי יודע

אחד מי יודע ׳ אחד אני יודע ׳ אחד אלהינו שבשמים ובארץ
שנים מי יודע ׳ שנים אני יודע ׳ שני לוחת הברית ׳ אחד אלהינו בֿ
שלשה מי יודע ׳ שלשה אני יודע ׳ שלשה אבות ׳ שני לחת הברית ׳ אֿ אֿ
ארבעה מי יודע ׳ ארבעה אני יודע ׳ ארבע אמהות ׳ שלשה אבות ׳ שלֿ אֿ אֿ
חמשה מי יודע ׳ חמשה אני יודע ׳ חמשי חומשי תורה ׳ ארבע אמהות ׳ וכו
ששה מי יודע ׳ ששה אני יודע ׳ ששה סדרי משנה ׳ חֿ חומשי התורה ארבע אֿ ׳ וכו
שבעה מי יודע ׳ שבעה אני יודע ׳ שבעה ימי שבתא ׳ ששה סדרי משנה ׳ וכו
שמונה מי יודע ׳ שמונה אני יודע ׳ שמנה ימי מילה ׳ שֿ יֿמי שבתא שֿ סדרי מֿ ׳ וכו
תשעה מי יודע ׳ תשעה אני יודע ׳ תֿ ירחי לידה ׳ שֿ יֿמי מילה שֿ יֿמי שֿ ׳ וכו
עשרה מי יודע ׳ עשרה אני יודע ׳ עֿ דבריא ׳ עֿ ירחי לידה שֿ ימי מילה ׳ וֿ
אחד עשר מי יודע ׳ אֿ אֿ אני יודע ׳ אֿ כוכביא ׳ עֿ דבריא תֿ ירחי לידה וכו
שנים עשר מי יודע ׳ שֿ עֿ אני יודע ׳ שֿ עֿ שבטיא אֿ עֿ כוכביא עֿ דבריא ׳ וכו
שלשה עשר מי יודע ׳ שֿ עֿ אני יודע ׳ שֿ עֿ מֿ ׳ שֿ עֿ שבטיא אֿ עֿ כוכביא
עֿ דבריא תֿ ירחי לידה ׳ שֿ ימי מילה ׳ שבעה ימי שבתא ששה סדרי משנה ׳ חֿ
חומשי התורה ׳ ארבע אמהות ׳ שלשה אבות ׳ שני לוחת הברית ׳ אֿ אלֿהינו
שבשמים ובארץ :

חד גדיא

חד גדיא ׳ דזבין אבא ׳ בתרי זוזי ׳ חד גדיא חד גדיא ׳
ואתא שונרא ׳ ואכלא לגדיא ׳ דזבין אבא בתרי זוזי ׳ חד גדיא חד גדיא ׳
ואתא כלבא ׳ ונשך לשונרא ׳ דאכלה לגדיא ׳ דזבין אבא בתרי זוזי ׳ חג חג
ואתא חוטרא ׳ והכה לכלבא ׳ דנשך לשונרא ׳ דאכלא לגדיא ׳ דזבין אבא בֿ
חד גֿ חֿ
ואתא נורא ׳ ושרף לחוטרא ׳ דהכה לכלבא ׳ דנשך לשונרא ׳ דאכלא לגדיא

דזבין אבא בתרי זוזי ׳ חד גדיא חד גדיא ׳ ואתא מיא וכבא לנורא דשרף
לחוטרא ׳ דהכא לכלבא דנשך לשונרא ׳ דאכלא לגדיא ׳ דזבין אבא
בתרי זוזי ׳ חד גֿ

ואתא תורא ׳ ושתא למיא ׳ דכבא לנורא ׳ דשרף לחוטרא
דהכא לכלבא ׳ דנשך לשונרא ׳ דאכלא לגדיא ׳ דזבין אבא בתר
זוזי ׳ חד גדיא חד גדיא

ואתא השוחט ׳ ושחט לתורא ׳ דשתא למיא ׳ דכבא לנורא ׳ דשרף
לחוטרא ׳ דהכה לכלבא ׳ דנשך לשונרא ׳ דאכלא לגדיא ׳ דזבין אבא
בתרי זוזי ׳ חד גדיא ׳ חד גדיא

ואתא מלאך המות ׳ ושחט לשוחט ׳ ושחט לתורא ׳ דשֿ
למיא ׳ דכבא לנורא ׳ דשרף לחוטרא ׳ דהכא לכלבא ׳ דנשך
לשונרא ׳ דאכלא לגדיא ׳ דזבין אבא ׳ בתרי זוזי ׳ חד גדיא
חד גדיא

ואתא הקדוש ברוך הוא ׳ ושחט למלאך המות ׳ דשחט
לשוחט ׳ דשחט לתורא ׳ דשתא למיא ׳ דכבא לנורא ׳ דשרף
לחוטרא ׳ דהכה לכלבא ׳ דנשך לשונרא ׳ דאכלא לגדיא ׳ דזֿ
אבא בתרי זוזי ׳ חד גדיא חד גדיא ׳

זה הספר אשכול הכפר ׳ כמעשה ידי להתפאר ׳ שבתי בכונה שעטנו
בזהב ותהלתו החסיד כמוהרר זלמן דיין מגורשן וויין ממשפחת אוייר בֿ

◆ TAL'S FATHER: Fathers—America. Streets paved with gold. Fathers writing messages in nail polish with notes on the backs of clocks. And of course who believes any of it. "He who rebukes not his son leads him into delinquency."

I pleaded with my wife Rachel, "If we do not speak plainly to Abraham what will become of him? Who will teach him, the street? The air? And she would say again and again. "A son inherits from his father looks, strength, wealth, brains and longevity."

"I will speak to him gently," my wife whispered. Why did I listen to Rachel? I should have spoken plainly and not have allowed her to speak in my name.

"We choose our own teachers, we choose our own fathers. Abraham, young Fisher, all of us."

And what of me? When I think "Fathers are often respected because of the merit of their sons." I tremble.

■ HENRY DAVID THOREAU: Clock...Mother...Father—*"I love a broad margin to my life. Sometimes in a summer morning, having taken my accustomed bath, I sat in my sunny doorway from sunrise till noon, rapt in a reverie amidst the pines and hickories and sumacs, in undisturbed solitude and stillness while the birds sang around or fluttered noiselessly through the house until by the sun falling in my west window, or the noise of some traveler's wagon on the distant highway, I was reminded of the lapse of time...For the most part I minded not how the hours went."*

This young lad's mother should have given him passenger fare straight away, away from the city. But not a clock. She has him where she wants him. Like mine. In an attic I lived. In my mother's boarding house. Not that I came down more than at mealtimes. Not that they were meals, rather some "indigestible compound, the pudding especially terrible." When they would ask me which of my mother's dishes I preferred, I would answer without appetite "the nearest." This lad's wish should be to move the farthest away. Still, the journey must be started by him, not by his mother.

■ F. SCOTT FITZGERALD: Know—*"I don't know why, but I think of all Harvard men as sissies, like I used to be, and all Yale men as wearing big blue sweaters and smoking pipes...I think of Princeton as being lazy and good looking and aristocratic—you know, like a spring day."*

How did Tal know he was back? Fisher wondered, noticing the card on his desk. Dosha had probably seen him looking at them across the street. But Tal's back had been turned and he Fisher, hadn't returned until Dosha had left that crackpot's Advice Salon, the "almost blue room" as she so delicately put it.

Fisher had just entered 551 from walking down Hudson, and anyway the old man was always sleeping in his upstairs blue den at noon.

Fisher moved into the living room where his pants hung over the Bukhara bolster on the floor. Slipping into his trousers with the measured pace of a young man intent on neither creating nor working, Fisher moved into the bathroom to look at the clock his father had insisted he maintain in his apartment.

"Dear Raphael: Your mother and I thought this might come in handy, Your Father," read the note which was written in nail polish on its facing.

"Ah," said Tal on seeing the clock. "The hand is the hand of Mother Fisher but the face is the face of Jacob."

■ T.S. ELIOT: Clock—*"I do not want the clock to stop in the dark."*

◆ RACHEL ABENDANA TAL, ABRAHAM TAL'S MOTHER: Father—Fisher's mother's hand, bringing his father's hand to his. Each generation. In all countries. Each father worrying aloud: "A father is responsible for his son's debt even if the endorsement is faulty."

■ TALMUD: Bava Batra, "Fathers are often respected because of the merit of their sons. A second chance for each father." But of course every father worries: Is it a blessing or a curse? How many lectures will exhaust the child before he will no longer hear his father? But a mother's hand upon her son's, whispering softly her husband's words, better yet, merely thinking them, those words are remembered and honored forever.

Honor thy father and thy mother, even as thou honorest G-d—for all three have been partners in thy creation.

Fisher's mother and, thank G-d I, bridges connecting fathers, children and the Eternal One.

■ MENACHEM MENDEL SCHNEERSON, the Lubavitcher Rebbe: Your mother...your father—In America, the mother will quote the father's words. But it is the mother talking

When I was young, a boy of ten. My father and mother bought me new shoes for Passover. My father noticed while we were all working, baking for Passover, how much I looked at my shoes. I couldn't take my eyes off them. My father called me and gave me a lecture on how low it was for a Jewish boy to have in his mind such low things like nice shoes. Such small things. He lectured me until I started to cry, until I vomited out everything I had eaten.

My mother came to my father and said, "What do you want from him?"

"I want him to be my son, not a piece of meat. He's supposed to be my son. "Don't worry," she said. "He'll be all right."

Direct. Direct. The father should speak to the son direct. And it should be in his words. Or with his lips. And of course, the mother should speak to the son. Direct. And with her words. But at least the mother writes in the father's name. And certainly this will be Fisher's blessing. That his time will be spent in a worthwhile way. An important way. Not a piece of meat, G-d forbid. Not only will Fisher be all right, his child will be all right also.

Seventeenth century Haggadah, Prague.

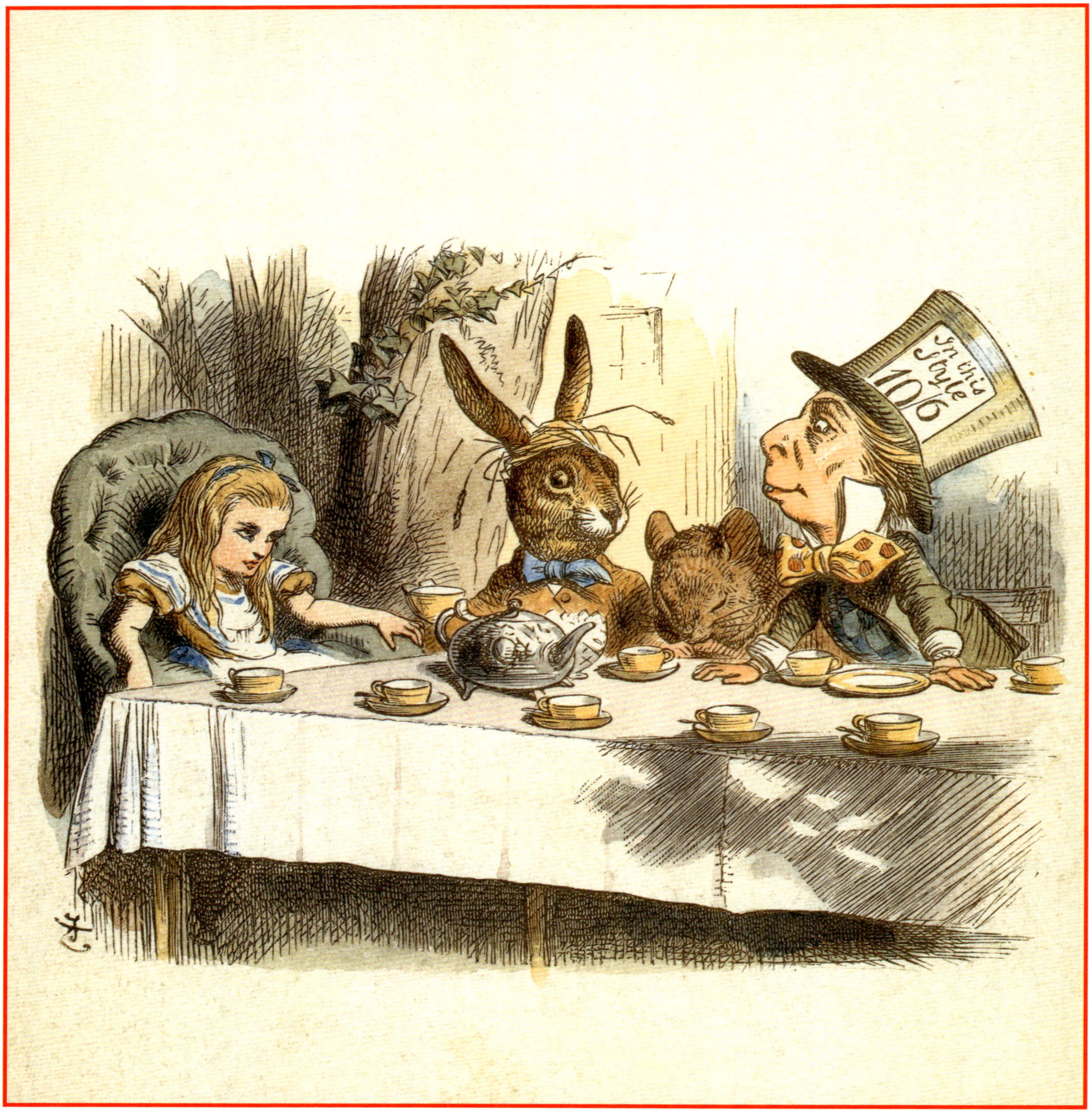
In this Style 10/6

■ JACOB ABULAFIA (1550-1622): Rabbi—Why do you keep the secrets you do, I don't understand. I asked my holy Rabbi Solomon Absaban and he did not answer. And I journeyed to Damascus and asked Moses Besodo "Why do you keep the secrets you do. I don't understand." And he did not answer. But when I asked Isaac Luria, may my life be fit to be a commentary on even one word of his teachings: He smiled and placed the holy Zohar before me. And opened it to a page [I, 186, A] and I read and I understood, all at once, and of course it was not secret.

"When the world was created, it was created from the single point of the world, and the center of all. And what is it? Zion, as it is written, 'A psalm of Asaph. G-d, G-d, the lord has spoken and called the earth, from the rising of the sun, to its setting'" (Psalm 50:1). From which place? From Zion as it is written, "Out of Zion, the perfection of beauty, has G-d shined forth" (Psalm 50:2). From the place that is the limit of the perfection of complete faith, as it should be. Zion is the strength and the point of the whole world, and from that place the whole world was made and completed, and from it the whole world is nourished. Come and see. "The lord thundered in the heavens," what need has it to say "and the most High gave forth this voice?" But here we have a mystery of faith. When I say that Zion is the perfection and beauty of the world, and the world is nourished by it, there are really two levels, namely Zion and Jerusalem. One is judgment and one is mercy. And both are one, judgment on one side, mercy on the other [Zohar I, 186 A]. Fisher's parents are on the Parisian fifth floor. The same as the New York sixth. Paris and New York. But all their secrets are one big secret: Zion and Jerusalem.

■ LAURENCE STERNE: The clock read 3:22—Why always 3:22? Because the author likes the number. It is his number, his *Hobby Horsical* number. And he is right on time with it. Just like my quotations. Citing the learning of the world. All from Rev. Mr. Clarke's collection. 700 volumes: *"dog cheap and many good."* And I spending a week setting my books up at Shandy Hall. And I plundering, learning from them. To record the birth of Tristram, forcibly ejecting him with obstetrical magic not invented. Who is to tell me, THE Author, about the year 1718. Or the day, the hour or the minute. *"I am this month one whole year older than I was this time twelve months ago and this Author, having got as you perceive almost into his second volume— 'And I am in my fourth volume, no farther than my first day's life tis demonstrable that...instead of advancing as a common writer in my work with what I have been doing at it. On the contrary, I am just thrown so many volumes back."*

And who is to say that it is not always 3:22. Is not the Author always right? Even his stopped *Hobby Horsical* clock is right twice a day.

Of course his mother had written the message and of course she'd chosen to attribute it to his father to give it the veneer of parental authority.

The clock read 3:22. "I've got at least an hour to go. Tal is always late," thought Fisher.

"What does he want with me? What he wants with Dosha is crystal clear on a foggy day. But why me?" Then suddenly, Fisher heard pounding on the door.

"It's me, Rabbi Tal," shouted Tal who Fisher sensed was on his knees bleating his message under the door jam as though he couldn't be heard otherwise.

"Tal I won't let you in now or anytime today," bellowed Fisher, rising to the sport. No self-respecting Rabbi would hold services at three in the afternoon."

"Listen Fisher, these are not services, these are lessons."

"Well then, no self-respecting Rabbi would hold lessons with his student without giving him time to prepare."

"I am not self-respecting, Fisher."

■ YOSEF BEN CHIYA: The message—Of course, his mother has written The message. Fisher, the son, knows well that his mother has written THE MESSAGE. And of course, he understands where it has come from. In the same way that my mother wrote the message for me. And when one's mother has such a message, the Holy One, blessed be He, guides her hand in the writing for she trembles and often the hand cannot pen the words. The greater the love, the shakier the hand, often beyond what a son even in his love and honoring of her, can read. And THE MESSAGE cannot be said or whispered, shouted or spoken, murmured or hinted at it must be written. For only the eyes of the son can accept it. And not the ear, ever.

■ SCHLOMO DOV GOITEIN: His mother—*"When Rav Joseph (who was blind) heard the steps of his mother, he said to his students: 'Let me stand up; I perceive the Presence of G-d approaching.'* In loving memory of my mother. Frida Goitein née Braunschweiger (1870-1920). My world shattered with my mother's death. I had asked Mother what will become of me? Shall I go to the Holy Land? I cannot leave you. Shall I stay? I cannot remain here in Europe. In Hungary, I will be trapped alive in a coffin. And I cannot push the pine lid that presses down on my face, Mother, tell me where shall I go? And Mother on her death bed, understanding all. Weakly but decisively bidding me to leave the room, her index finger shaking as though she had a pen in her hand. And she to her grave. I alone, frozen in my pine prison.

Three years later, I found a scrap of paper. *"Shlomo Dov: My angel, my answer: You will leave to the Holy Land. You will be reborn. You will leave from the Holy land to a distant land. And you will dream of a yet more distant land. And you will be my blessing to our people. And I shall always be your guardian Angel: Mother."* The next day I left for Haifa. And a lifetime of pouring over Arabic scripts of long dead Jews who became my friends, a world of humanity, Judaism and Islam brought back to life again. A world of possibility. Whom should I dedicate my work to? Of course, to Mother.

"After the death of Rav Yehudah, Rav Yosef and Rabbah were the candidates for the position of Rosh Yeshiva of Pumpedita. Each one said the other should receive the position." Imagine. Just imagine. My Princeton colleagues would say: Could such a thing happen today? I would hear a soft hint of my mother's voice: *Teaching revives the teacher. So the sages asked the opinion of the Rabbis of Eretz Yisroel who said that Rav Yosef had preference because of his comprehensive knowledge. Nevertheless, Rav Yosef refused to accept the position since the astrologers had told his mother that he would only be Rosh Yeshiva for two and a half years. and then he would die. Rabban thereupon accepted the position which he held for twenty-two years, whereupon R. Yosef became Rosh Yeshiva after Rabbah's death. He was the Rosh Yeshiva of Pumpedita for two and a half years from 320 C.E. to 323 C.E.* And I knew, I always knew that Rav Yosef had received the astrologer's words in writing from his mother and had my mother told me to leave Europe and leave her, for she was Europe and Europe was her, I would have been frozen. But a message from her, this I could decipher. Understand and devote my life to. And what was my life but understanding her message to me?

■ LEWIS CARROLL: Today—*"The rule is, jam tomorrow and jam yesterday.—but never jam today."*

John Tenniel, "The Mad Tea Party."

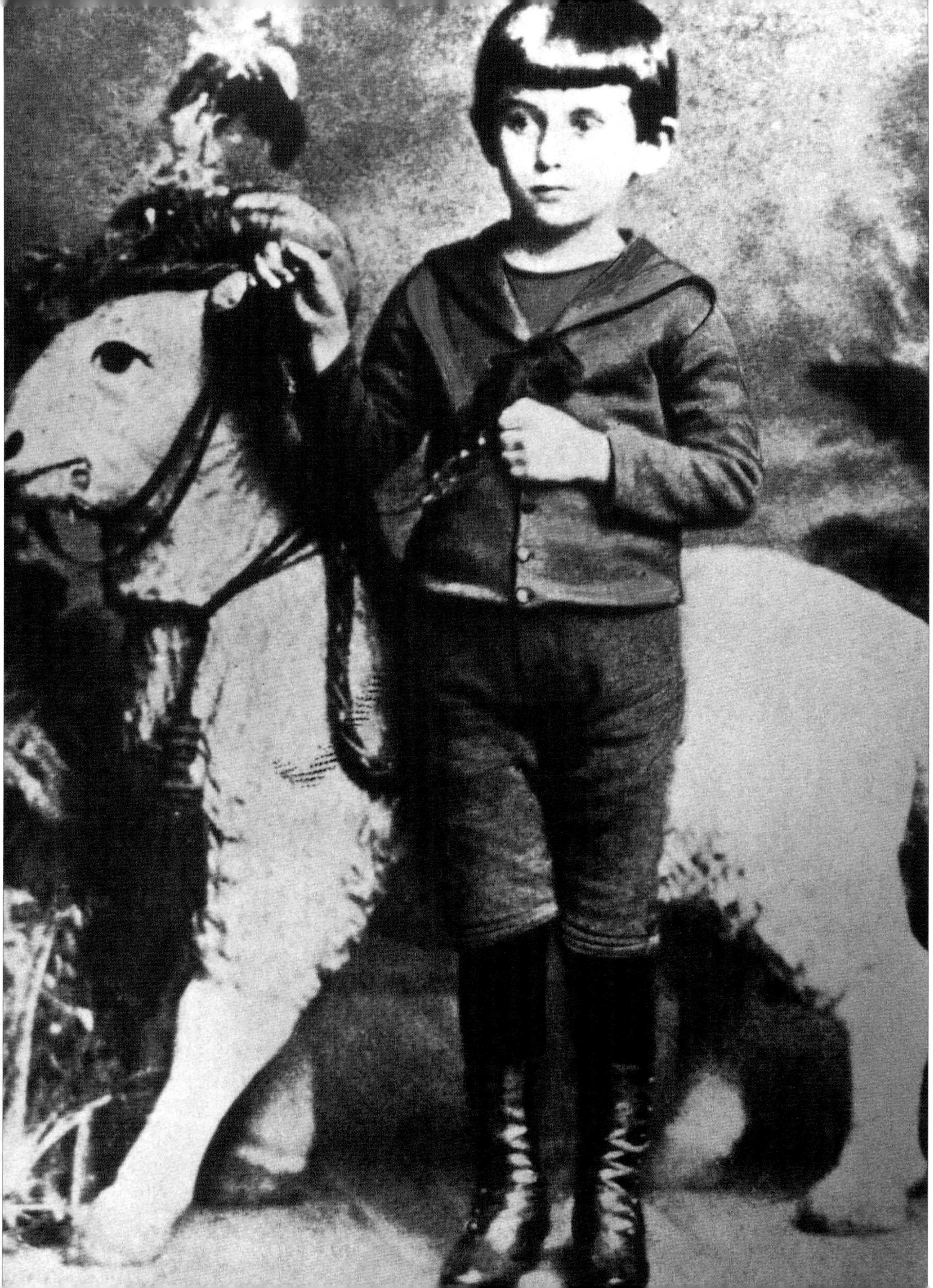

■ FRANZ KAFKA: It's your apartment or nothing—1916. November. A little blue structure, more an apartment than a house on the Alchimistengasse. Ottla had rented it but insisted I use it. "Franz, it's your apartment or nothing," she said to me. And I wrote to Felice:

"To sum up its advantages, the lovely way up to it, the quiet there. From my sole neighbor, I am separated by only a very thin wall, but the neighbor is quiet enough, and generally stays there until midnight. And then the benefit of the walk home: I have to make up my mind to stop. I then have the walk that cools my head. And the life there, it is something special to have one's own house, to shut in the face of the world the door not of your room, not of your apartment, but of your own house, to step out through the door of your lodgings straight into the snow of a quiet alley."

A gift from Ottla, and all because of two words: Ten Jews.

■ MILENA JESENSKA: It's your apartment or nothing—-It's your apartment or nothing Franz I insist. Not for Franz, but for myself I insist. Not for my father, for his hatred of Jews, for his hatred of mother and for his greatest hatred, for himself. Certainly not for Father, do I insist.

And certainly even less for Ernest, ever faithful in his unfaithfulness. No. For myself, I insist. Into Frank's apartment. Into Frank's life. Into Frank's body. Into Frank's head. To eat food out of him, to lick his palms. To be the tiniest of birds fluttering inside the rooms of his skull forever. He knew of my bird-like dreams, not that I told him or needed him to. "Milena," he wrote to me:

"On the balcony is a sparrow which expects me to throw some bread from the table onto the balcony instead of which I drop the bread beside me on the floor, in the middle of the room. It stands outside and from there in the semi-darkness, sees the food of its life, terribly tempting, its shaking itself, its more here than there, but here is the dark and beside the bread am I, the secret power. Nevertheless, it hops over the threshold, a few more hops. But farther, it doesn't dare to go and in sudden fright, it flies away. But with what energy does this wretched bird abound? After a while it's back again and inspects the situation. I scatter a little more to make it easier for it and if I hadn't intentionally-unintentionally (this is how the secret powers work) chased it with a sudden movement, it would have got the bread."

I am a little bird. A tiny, little bird. My father and my husband are swinging wildly at me. And Frank, almost. Welcoming me. Into. To his. Apartment. Or to his. Nothingness.

Franz Kafka as a young boy.

Fisher laughed and said, "You can't come in. I'll come to your apartment in ten minutes."

"No. I want us to study in your apartment, Fisher," rasped Tal through the peep hole, as though it were a microphone.

"Listen, who's the boss, the congregant or the Rabbi? Tal, it's your apartment or nothing. This is America, Tal."

"This is not America, Fisher, this is Greenwich Village. But all right, be at my place in seven minutes, we're wasting valuable study time and..."

Tal's voice droned on as he wearily wended his way to his apartment to prepare for Fisher.

"How can you live like this? There must be ten thousand books in this place," said Fisher almost to himself as he let himself in with his own key.

"I have no secrets from you my son. You will be my spiritual heir, Fisher." Tal had told him this when they first met.

"How about simply gifting me your vast estate, Tal, and let me develop my own spiritual palace?" Fisher had answered.

■ OTTLA KAFKA, Kafka's sister: It's your apartment or nothing. This is America— Franz," I said to my older brother, my only brother. My youngest sibling. "Franz it's your apartment or nothing. This is America. And you can come back each day to Mutti for lunch."

Franz's eyes grew large. As he surveyed the house's interior up and down the narrow stairs across the street, he scampered, waving playfully on the other side of Goldsmith Street. "Why are you doing this for me?" he whispered through the window, peering into the house from the outside. And I, like an innocent, gossiping with a next-door neighbor, simply put up two fingers in front of Franz's face. And then lifted both my hands with their ten fingers showing. And his glorious smile, shy and self-effacing, amazed that anyone in his family would notice him, acknowledge him, care for him, love him, lit the entire street with an alchemical glow.

How could he know of my afternoons with Josef David in the house? How could Franz know of what his blessing meant to me when I asked, dare I marry Josef— a gentile, a Czech, a conservative. And Franz had simply said, "You two," holding up and intertwining his two index fingers. "Ottla, it will be better than marrying ten Jews" and this he stated, holding up ten fingers shakily.

I was younger than all my family, screeching at Father, and Father's shopkeeper's skillful tongue screaming back, "Those same ten fingers will be the minyan at my grave site." Nothing I did, Zionism, my work in the shop, my dreams, my talking with Franz, nothing was enough for Father. And everything, everything I did for Franz was too much for Franz. How magical it was on Alchemy Street. Love for me by day. Amerika for Franz by moonlight.

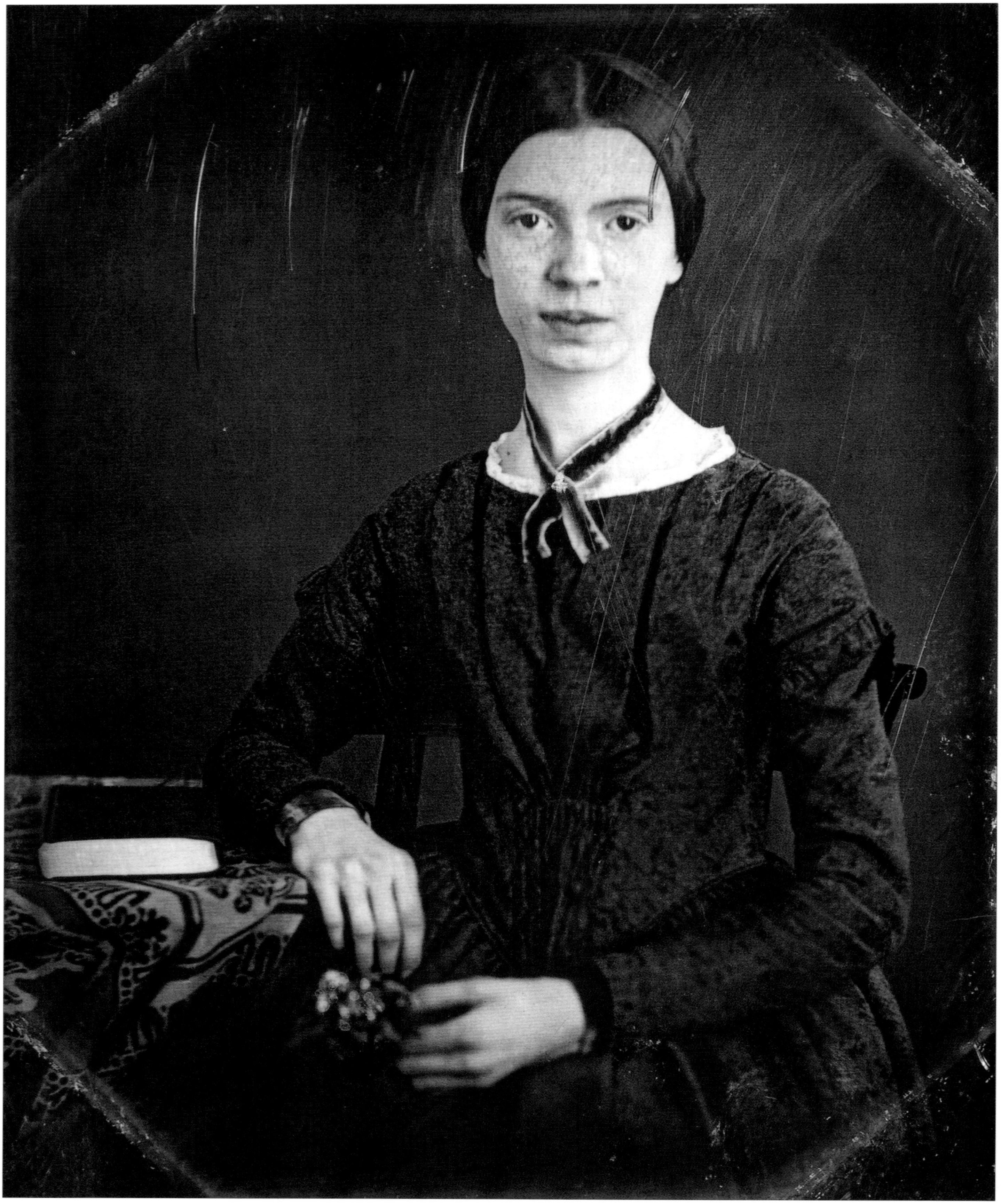

◆ SIMHA PADAWER, DOSHA'S GRANDFATHER: Of course Tal wants you to have his key. Darling Dosha—We learn from the Heilige (holy) Rashi. It is not only the words that matter, it is the line endings that matter. And it is not only the words that matter and the line endings but the spaces between the words and the lines, according to the Zohar Hakodesh, the Holy Zohar.

In Slonim, I learned from Rashi that *"Noah was a just, righteous man in his generation. These are the generations of Noah."* I learned that the good deeds a righteous person does are their true descendants. And this Tal: his good deeds touch Fisher. And touch Dosha. Most of all Dosha. Dosha knows. Read not, Rashi would say, his key, darling "Dosha" but read: his key: Darling Dosha. For Dosha, darling, is Tal's key to the world above. In the Zohar Hakodesh that I also studied in Slonim, there is no space between "Tal wants you to have his key: Darling Dosha." Tal can and does give Fisher his entire blessing (for his name itself means blessing): his Darling Dosha.

And she is his to give. Just as my children's children were across the seas in America. And I and the enemies in Slonim. Together Thank G-d with my Angel Rickele.

■ EMILY DICKINSON to editor Thomas Wentworth: There are 12,260 volumes here— *"For several years, my Lexicon was my only companion."* Two volumes. Webster's American Dictionary of the English Language. Published at Amherst in 1844 by J. S. and C. Adams. Either one reads a lot or one writes a little.

■ GERALD MURPHY: "That's not what he wants from you"—Sara whispered to me so as not to alert Scott, "My G-d, Gerald, it's so simple, really. 'He's a sort of a masher' That's what Scott wants from me. To take each part of me. And put me inside him. My fingers, my toes, my heart even. He dreams of running his tongue inside the crook of my arm, down the long side of my outside thigh—bathing me with his lips, and whispering, talking, singing, chanting, writing on my body like foolscap. That's what he wants to do."

"That's not what he wants from you, Sara," I protested, albeit faintly. "Or not what Scott could even pretend to dream of."

"Then why dear," Sara protested, "does he stare, day after day. At me, on the beach, in our house, why doesn't he move his eyes from where I am, even when I've left the room? Everyone knows it is so. Why does Scott stare at me. Always." What could I do but pretend to be asleep.

■ MOSES HAYYIM LUZZATTO: Great wonders of nature— *"Be open-eyed to the great wonders of nature, familiar though they be. But men are more wont to be astonished at the sun's eclipse than at its unfailing rise."*

"I've already given you the key. Simply write the history of the Taj Mahal emerald, one of the great wonders of nature, for my brother and myself and we will make your fortune," said Tal. Fisher winced. The gem and its story were extraordinary but how could they be a key to a livelihood, let alone a key to treasure? thought Fisher. "A key," Fisher mused on Tal's phrase. A word that Tal used with disquieting frequency.

"Of course Tal wants you to have his key, darling," Dosha had told Fisher. "He's a lonely old man and afraid he'll have a stroke. His dreadful brother never calls him and he wants us to be his attentive children."

"That's not what he wants from you, dear Dosha."

"Don't be disgusting, Fisher."

"Anyway," said Tal, interrupting Fisher's musing. "There are 12,260 volumes here."

Not including the socks, thought Fisher. "And in which Green Village do Dosha and I live happily ever after? And by the bye, where's Ezekiel, Tal?" Fisher, moved to Tal's table in the center of the room.

Tal pointed to the empty chair opposite his. Tea was steaming on a 1930s gas stove. "Ezekiel is sitting here. And may God give him strength. Read his note aloud."

◆ RICKELE PADAWER, DOSHA'S GRANDMOTHER: Tal wants you to have his key—On December 8, 1942, Captain Bobkov's sleigh with two Red Army Apparatchiks suddenly appeared among our group of 72 men and 63 women and children.

All that survived from Slonim's glory were ashes of humans scattered among the highest snows I ever remembered. Much higher than my mother's house in Troki so close to Vilna and yet so different. Lt. Vladimir Ivanovich wanted to be the first speaker. So anxious he was to denounce us, but Colonel Bobkov insisted on the first words: "Jews," he shouted over the roaring wind. "You could be great partisans but you sit here eating the fruits of the peasants' labor." At first we thought he was joking. What fruit? Moynek answered him immediately, "It is the general staff that prohibited Jewish partisans from fighting against the enemy." Vladimir Ivanovich shouted down Moynek, screaming, "You are informers. Your raids against the enemy have led to partisans being killed."

And on and on he raved. I clutched Simha's arm and whispered, "Argue with this Vanse." But my husband looked shriveled, lost, and simply shrugged wearily, muttering, "I don't have the key to understanding this Ivanovich's illogic." With every ounce of strength I had, I lifted Simha up and said, "To quote you Simha, The Holy one, Tal Minhashamayin, the dew from heaven wants you to have his key." And Simha once again was in his Slonim Yeshiva. He began slowly whispering yet he was strangely audible,

"Heroic Lt. Vladimir, you charge us Jews of attacking and provoking responses that endanger peasants and Partisans alike. Hero of the Soviet Union, Captain Bobkov argues that we Jews have done nothing. We Jews would not presume to decide between you two but rather ask your guest, the third of you who has come to give us guidance.'" The third Russian, with a newly sprouted beard, was wearing the dress of a Russian Cossack. Without introducing himself he began talking with authority. He had heard many things about the Jews here, he said. He knew some of the accusations against them were not true. He knew that many Jews were fighting heroically at the front. He knew that Jews were working night and day in the factories back home to produce vital supplies for the front. He believed that the Jews were capable and devoted Partisans who should be used in the life and death struggle. Whatever happened between them and the general Partisan staff should be relegated to the past. The Jews should now reorganize themselves and become active against the fight. And then Bobkov gave us guns and we moved into the Rafalovka forest.

That was the turning point. Simha's speech. I only dared ask him after the War, in America: "How did you trust that Cossack to save us?" And my Simha answered so sweetly, "I didn't see a Cossack, I saw the Prophet Eiljah."

Emily Dickinson.

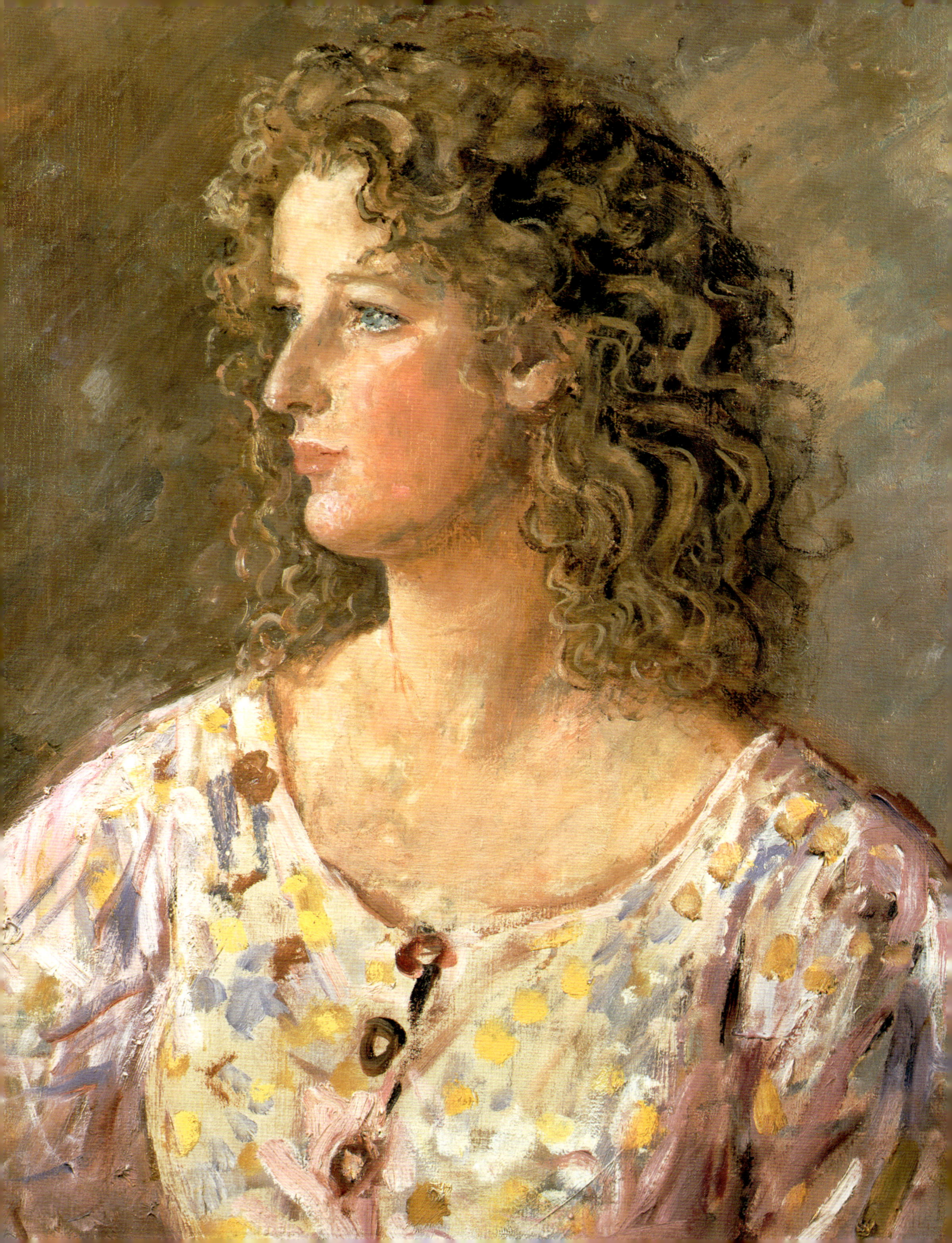

■ DYLAN THOMAS: Green—
*Now as I was young and easy under
   the apple boughs.
About the lilting house and happy as
   the grass was green,
The night above the dingle starry,
Time let me hail and climb
Golden in the heydays of his eyes,*

He came back, our down the road and across the street white fence neighbor, Vera's officer husband. Demobbed from heroics in the Peloponnesus with his sub machine-gun spraying our bungalow with bullets. "*To put the wind up we wee buggers.*" Teach us a lesson. All the way from Greece. He came to remind us of a thing or two.

And then I understood the war would never be over. I knew it as simply as the pen trembled in my hand. Sing to me. Aunt Annie calling me from the Gothic window. "Dylan, Dylan." And I beyond the house high hay on the hill, before the stream in the garden itself.

The ever green Eden of my youth. "*Time let me play and be.*"

And my hand moving automatically.

"*Time held me green and dying Though I sang in my chains like the sea.*"

And then under the bed with drink or no drink. Caitlin and I could survive a thousand years of bombardment and still the bullets would find us senseless in their predictability, undeniable in their ordinariness.

And who could sleep after that? With Cait under the bed at the least sound outside and one night the pen lifted my hand.

Now as I was young and easy…"

And the apple orchard near Laugharne started to sing in me to Cailtin. "*Shining. It was Adam and Maiden.*" And I whispered to her in the horn of her ear: We are young and easy. And we sang in orchards like the sea.

Fisher smiled at Tal and began:
"And it shall come to pass that fishers shall stand."
"Tal, could these fishers be me?"
"Of course, if you let it be."
"But why plural? I'm only one!"
"And what of Dosha?" smiled Tal like a patriarch.
"Again, Tal, with Dosha. I don't want to get married. And I don't want to marry Dosha. And I don't want to have children. And I don't care if there are new fishers."
"But," interrupted Tal, "you do want to have new fruit each month and you do dream of holiness. And you do wish your leaves to heal and you do long to ever be green."

■ BOBBY FISCHER: I don't care if there are new Fisher's—Sammy Reshevsky went crazy. 1961. Sixteen games set up. Only him. Only me: the winner to be crowned the king of American chess.

Four games in New York. Eight in Los Angeles. Four in New York. Reshevsky wins the first. I, the second. By the end of the eleventh, it's five and a half games each. Sammy tried his European spook tricks of freezing me with air conditioning but I wasn't born in Brooklyn for nothing. Judges back me. Why should I reschedule Saturday's game for the attack at dawn on Sunday just because Reshevsky is an Orthodox Jew. Sunday afternoon would be just fine. And it would have been fine for Sammy too but that old biddy Mrs. Gregor Piatigorsky who had funded the tournament refused to have the game scheduled for Sunday afternoon. Her precious Piatigorsky husband had a concert. And why should I show up early Sunday morning for the twelfth game. Or the thirteenth game?

Reshevsky lost his mind screaming: "I won when I was six in Lublin, in Cracow, in Warsaw. I defeated those Gutwirth boys in Antwerp in 1919, when I was nine years old. In 1920 I triumphed over 120 West Point cadets. Not bad for a youngster. Never a second player, only me. I beat Fischer. And I don't care if there are new Fischers. I'll beat them." Stupid to talk about new Fischers when he hadn't defeated me. It was only a question of time.

■ CAITLIN THOMAS: Green—"Dive under the bed darling!" I shouted to Dylan. The sound of machine-gun fire echoing in my ears. Like the *March of Time* films we would see on Thursday at the Royalton Cinema. His hand ever on my thigh.

But Dylan didn't move. Vera's captain: dark glasses with a hand grenade and machine gun aimed menacingly at Dylan.

Dylan raised his right hand and pointed at the tiny kitchen. "Wee Aeronwy is asleep in there Captain. Please release your weapons for inspection!"

Under the bed, I screamed. But Dylan persisted with his insistent *March of Time* narrator's voice. "Captain your colonel is ordering you. Your weapons, this instant." And "Colonel" Thomas saluting smartly. I myself cowering under the sofa bed, peering out at the crazed Captain returning Dylan's salute and meekly handing over his machine gun, already spent, and a loaded hand grenade to boot.

Hero he was. So cool, my Dylan, through the police examiner's questions, recreating it all for drinks on the house at the Black Lion, staggering home.

And still Aeron asleep through it all as only children can sleep. And then Dylan crawling on all fours under the sofa bed. Each night for months, years. And only when I would hide there with him. He whispering, intoning, chanting "*O as I was young and easy / in the mercy of his means. / Time held me green and dying / though I sang in my chains like the sea.*" Chattering, frozen, terrified. Only when asleep and snoring could I drag him to our pillowy sea comforter bed.

■ SAMUEL RESHEVSKY: And Fisher smiled at Tal and began— Fischer would smile at Tal and begin. Fourteen years old at Portoroz with blue jeans and a T-shirt. Smiling at Tal, the winner. A draw with Tal. Fischer smiling. In 1959 Zurich, smiling still at Tal and tied still at 10-3.

But then Bled, Zagreb and Belgrade. Fischer still smiling but losing four games to Tal. Stockholm smiles: and onto Curacao. 1962. Botvinnik laconically noting that "In his entire career, Tal has won every tournament he had to win." But Fisher still smiled. He knew Tal's end game. Only Tal could defeat Tal. And he did.

Augustus John, *Portrait of Caitlin Thomas.*

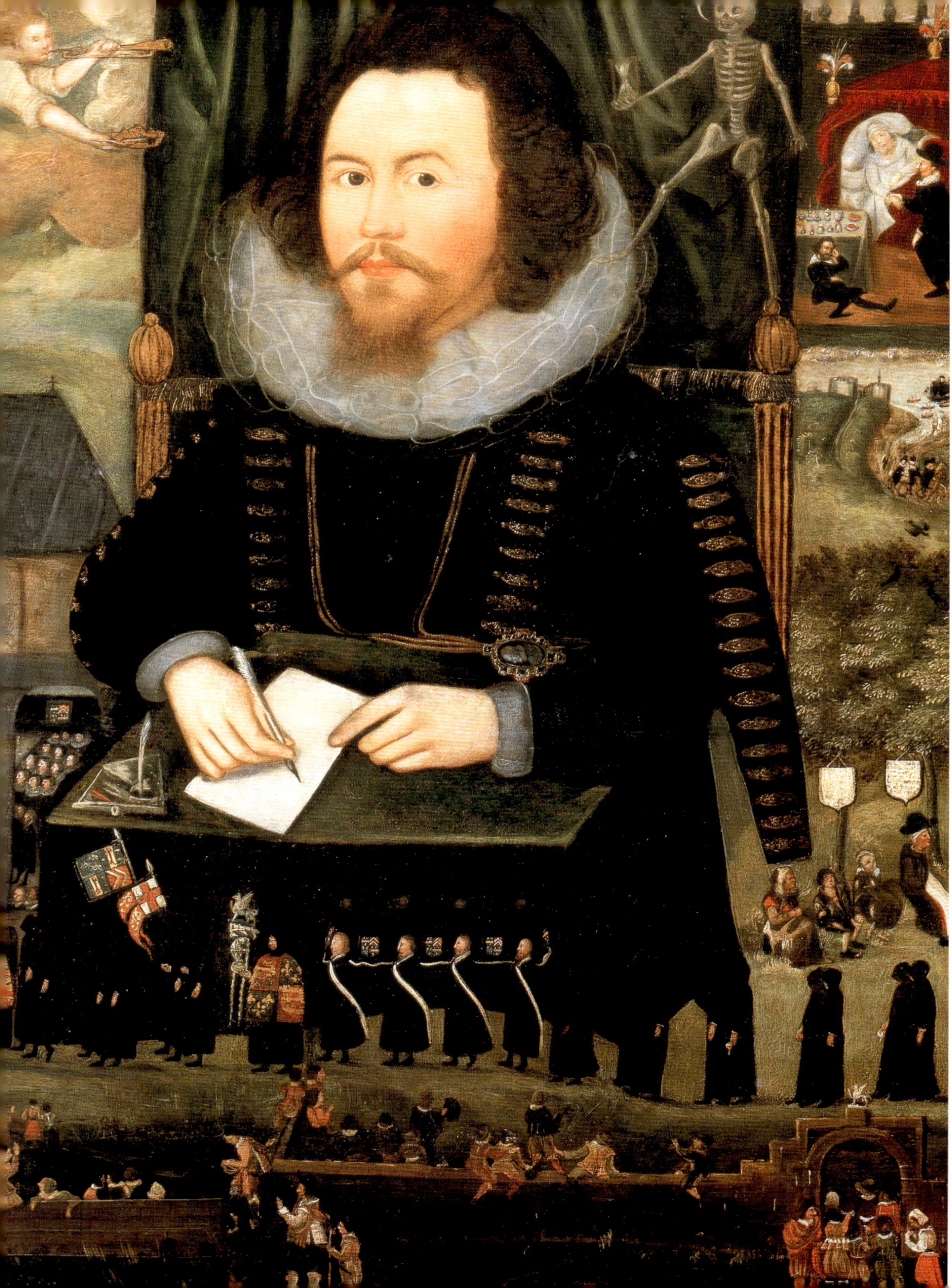

■ SIR EDWARD COKE (1552-1634), jurist: Time Inc.—How strange, this Time Incorporated. This corporation of Time. "*Corporations cannot commit treason, nor be outlawed, nor be excommunicated, for they have no souls.*"

And these two petitioners, these two young souls, pilgrims, almost, sweet William and young Raphael being interviewed by a corporation which by definition is beyond Time, above Time, below Time also— yet named Time. An oxymoron, a legal fiction, yet all too real.

■ J. B. PRIESTLEY: Time—Time is an appearance not a reality. "*All Time,*" said McTaggart to me when I was up at Cambridge, "*is series A and series B. And Time is an appearance, and as such real things appear to us to be in Time because we perceive them.*"

And I went to the National Portrait Gallery and looked at myself in Unton's eyes. A blank sheet of paper. The future ahead of me. A blessed birth. A sanctified end. I, rising above it all. Greater than the byways cunningly laid out as highways but rather traps, detours, a cul de sac, mirrors. But still, I above. Ever fame to crown me: an angelic woman with fiery hair, trumpeting fame sensuously in my ear.

"*While listening to McTaggart I could never find a flaw in his lucid and highly ingenious arguments but rarely believed anything he had told me once I was out of his presence.*" Touching this desire of Hamilton and Fisher to incorporate Time.

■ RABBI NOSUN: An entire year later—Reb Nachman's voice lowered as he spoke the next words. "The queen looked around and saw someone lying in *the corner…*" He continued, "*And she recognized him. She got up and went over to him, and then she touched him and asked, "Do you recognize me?"*

He answered, "Yes, I recognize you—you are the king's daughter who was lost." He asked her, "How do you come to be here?"

She answered, "Because of the words that flew from my father's lips, that the Evil One take me. This is the evil one's place."

He told her that her father was grief-stricken and had been looking for her for many years. Then he asked her, "How can I get you out of here?" She answered, "You cannot, unless you choose a place and remain there for a year, and for the entire year you yearn to get me out of here. Whenever you have a free moment, you must do nothing but yearn for me and hope to get me out of here. And on the last day of the year, you must fast and not sleep for twenty-four hours."

So he went away and did all that she said. At the end of the year, on the last day, he fasted and did not sleep all night. Then he got up and went to the king's daughter, to take her away. On the way he saw a tree on which fine apples were growing, and he was filled with longing and he ate one of them. As soon as he ate the apple, he fell down, and a deep sleep overcame him. He slept for a very long time. His servant shook him but could not rouse him.

CHAPTER 3

GREEN PILES OF photographs, growing on Fisher's Time Inc. desk—more properly his cubicle—almost totally obstructed Hamilton's view of Fisher. Moghul Emerald photographs, museum transparencies of Shah Jahan's portrait, haloed in green, miniatures drawn by Mansur of Kashmiri flowers, were all Hamilton saw.

"I know you're in here, Raphael," trumpeted William Hamilton. Twenty-eight years of age. Six years out of Yale, and four years past their initial interview at Time, Inc.

In Fisher's apartment—in his pre-D celibate days, as Hamilton called them—the two Yale graduates paced up and down, back and forth, through the rooms that faced Hudson street.

"If they see my grades," said Hamilton, "I'll never get the job on Mount Time."

"Why don't you apply first, Raphael, and then after you get the job, an entire year later you can recommend me and I'll come waltzing in through the back door."

■ NANNERL MOZART, MOZART'S SISTER: Time—Wolfgangerl until he "*was almost nine was terribly afraid of the trumpet when it was blown alone without other music. Merely to hold a trumpet in front of him was like aiming a loaded pistol at his heart.*" "*One time, Papa wanted to wean him out of this childish fear and once told me to blow [the trumpet] at him despite his reluctance, but my G-d! I should not have been persuaded to do it; Wolfgangerl scarcely heard the blaring sound when he grew pale and began to collapse, and if I had continued, he surely would have had a fit.*"

■ EDWARD FIRST BARON THURLOW (1731-1806): Time Inc.—"*Did you ever expect a corporation to have a conscience when it has no soul to be damned and no body to be kicked?*" Quite so, here. For Time, too, does it have a conscience? Or a soul? Or a body? But these lads are not going to Compostela nor to Lourdes nor to Jerusalem nor on Haj. They are seeking a job.

■ WILLIAM FAULKNER: Time Inc.—They should take themselves out right down by the waterfront on Gansevoort Street. As far from traffic as they can get. And load up pistols and shoot themselves. Or better yet, have one total night on the town. If they can't get to the French Quarter, then get blind drunk every night and get reborn each morning.

Time Inc. I came to New York City to get started. "*I had one hundred dollars. I had been painting, you know. So with sixty dollars of my stake spent for railroad fare, I went to New York.*"

My room was two dollars and fifty cents and I made eleven dollars a week as wages from Miss Elizabeth Prall's bookstore. All to wait on ladies over sixty. Good wages. Good books. And a birth. "*Time is dead as long as it is being clocked off by little wheels. Only when the clock stops does Time come to life.*" And these two, why are they digging their own graves, each for the other? Will the one really be an artist, the other a novelist inside a corporation clock?

■ THE VILNA GAON: Green piles of photographs growing on Fisher's Time…desk—And how can green piles of photographs-paper grow on Fisher's time. And on his desk.

For it is his time now. It is his duty to "thank, praise, laud, glorify, aggrandize, extol, bless, exalt and acclaim the One who performed all of these miracles for our ancestors and for us."

"And there is an ability of His servants to change the course of nature." Piles of papers can become green. They can grow under this young man's inspiration. The sweat of his brow while he studies over his desk, day and night, night and day, if he is "*thanking, praising, lauding, glorifying the One.*"

Anonymous artist, *The Life and Death of Sir Henry Unton*, detail.

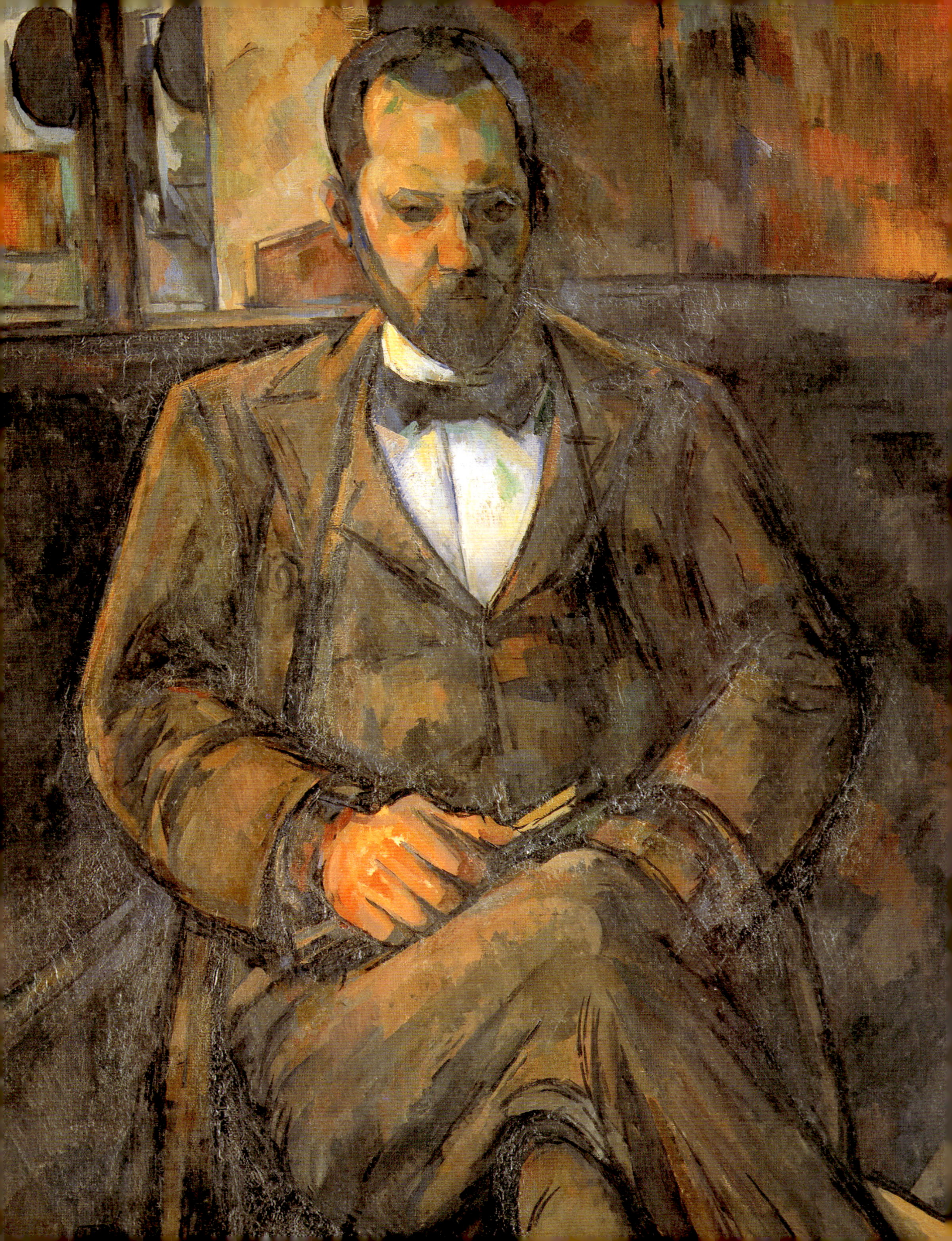

◆ SIMHA PADAWER, DOSHA'S GRANDFATHER: I'm right and you follow my decision— Can this man, Fisher, be the right one for my granddaughter Dosha? He doesn't claim he's right and that his study companion should follow him. He doesn't claim his study companion is right and he will follow him. He simply regards right as a game of chance.

And what would our ancestor the Heilige Rashi have said? *"To the right or to the left even if the judge tells you about what appears to you to be right that is left or about what appears to you to be left that is right, you have to obey him (the judge); how much the more is this so if actually the judge tells you about what is evidently right that it is right about what is left that it is left."* Everything is upside down here. Will Fisher end by worshiping a lucky coin?

■ AMBROSE VOLLARD: Right—*I saw Cézanne on each of his trips to Paris and his good will was such that one day I ventured to ask him to paint my portrait. He consented at once, and arranged a sitting at his studio in rue Hégésippe-Moreau for the following day.*

Upon arriving I saw a chair in the middle of the studio, arranged on a packing case which was in turn supported by four rickety legs. I surveyed this platform with misgiving. Cézanne divined my apprehension. "I prepared the model stand with my own hands. Oh, you want to run the least risk of falling Monsieur Vollard, if you just keep your balance. Anyway, you mustn't budge an inch when you pose."

Not to the right, not to the left. And what of your two portraits of Madame Cézanne? One in a red dress and one in a yellow armchair? In one, Madame leans to the right and in the other to the left. But Cézanne wouldn't hear of it.*"*

Seated at last and with such care I watched myself in order not to make a single false move; in fact I sat absolutely motionless; but my very immobility brought on in the end a drowsiness against which I successfully struggled a long time. At last, however, my head dropped over my shoulder. The balance was destroyed and the chair, the packing-case and I all crashed to the floor together! Cézanne pounced upon me. 'You wretch! You've spoiled the pose. Do I have to tell you again you must sit like an apple? Does an apple move?' From that day on, I adopted the plan of drinking a cup of black coffee before going for a sitting; as an added precaution, Cézanne would watch me attentively and if he thought he saw signs of fatigue or symptoms of sleep, he had a way of looking at me so significantly that I returned immediately to the pose like an angel—I mean like an apple, an apple never moves!"

Paul Cézanne, *Portrait of M. Ambroise Vollard, the art dealer.*

"Oh, I the mole," said Fisher. "And you the 'agent provocateur.' A leaf from Professor Westerfield's *Manual of Espionage*."

"Oh, no. You apply first, William: You fit their profile right down to the shoe size. You get in. You're the mole. And I'm the waltzer."

"Pour me some more Chianti," said Hamilton. "Let's think on it."

"There is no more Chianti," intoned Fisher.

"Let's go down to the White Horse then."

"All right but let's settle up here: Heads, you win Hamilton. And I go in to Time and apply with my glorious academic record, my Ten Eyk triumph and my Gallic charm. Tails, I'm right and you go in—the spirit of Napa Valley with a whiff of the wine country and a memory of the Highlands thrown in."

"And what if the coin falls and rests on its edge?" asked Hamilton with a surprising talmudic twist.

◆ RICKELE PADAWER: Right—When I would say to my dear Simha, "I am telling you simply and clearly, I am right, you should follow my judgment," Simha would smile and cup his hands over my ears and whisper. "You might think that if the sages tell you that the right is left or the left is right, you are to heed them. The text states, 'to the right and to the left.' When they tell you the right is right and the left is left." "So what is the decision, Reb Simha?" I smiled at him while I cupped his hands with mine. And though I couldn't hear his words, I could see him smiling, shaking his head in agreement. I was right! I like this Fisher. Not so certain what is right. He will be good for my Jerusha.

■ LEON DE MODENA: Right—What is Fisher to do if not to gamble? Toss a coin. Turn a card. Read coffee grounds. In 1625, I earned 72 ducats a year at the Ashkenazi Torah Study Society. At the Italian synagogue, an additional 22 ducats a year. An occasional wedding, a bris, or a charm 12 ducats more a year. And 50 ducats in a blessed year for writing. Over 150 ducats, perhaps. And our house ate up more than half.

Of course I gambled and would again today. And Fisher is quoting Nachmanides: *"The need to follow the ruling of the Sanhedrin, the high court, is very great since the Torah was given in writing. Now it is well known that no two people can agree on all matters that arise. Controversy is thus bound to increase, and the Torah will be subject to various interpretations. Scripture therefore laid down the law that we should obey the great Sanhedrin that sits before the Lord in the place which He shall choose whatever they instruct you in their interpretation of the Torah. Whether it was transmitted to them in unbroken succession by oral testimony or when it is based on their understanding of the sacred text.*

For the Torah was given on condition, they were vested with its interpretation even if they seemed to call the right left. How much more so should you give them the benefit of the doubt and accept their right as right, for the Spirit of God rests on the ministers to his sanctuary. He will never forsake them and always preserve them from error and stumbling."

Fisher's right. Hamilton should accept his judgment. But in Venice and in this Village that they live in one must gamble to earn one's bread, to pay one's rent, to sleep, and of course to earn the Divine Blessing to study.

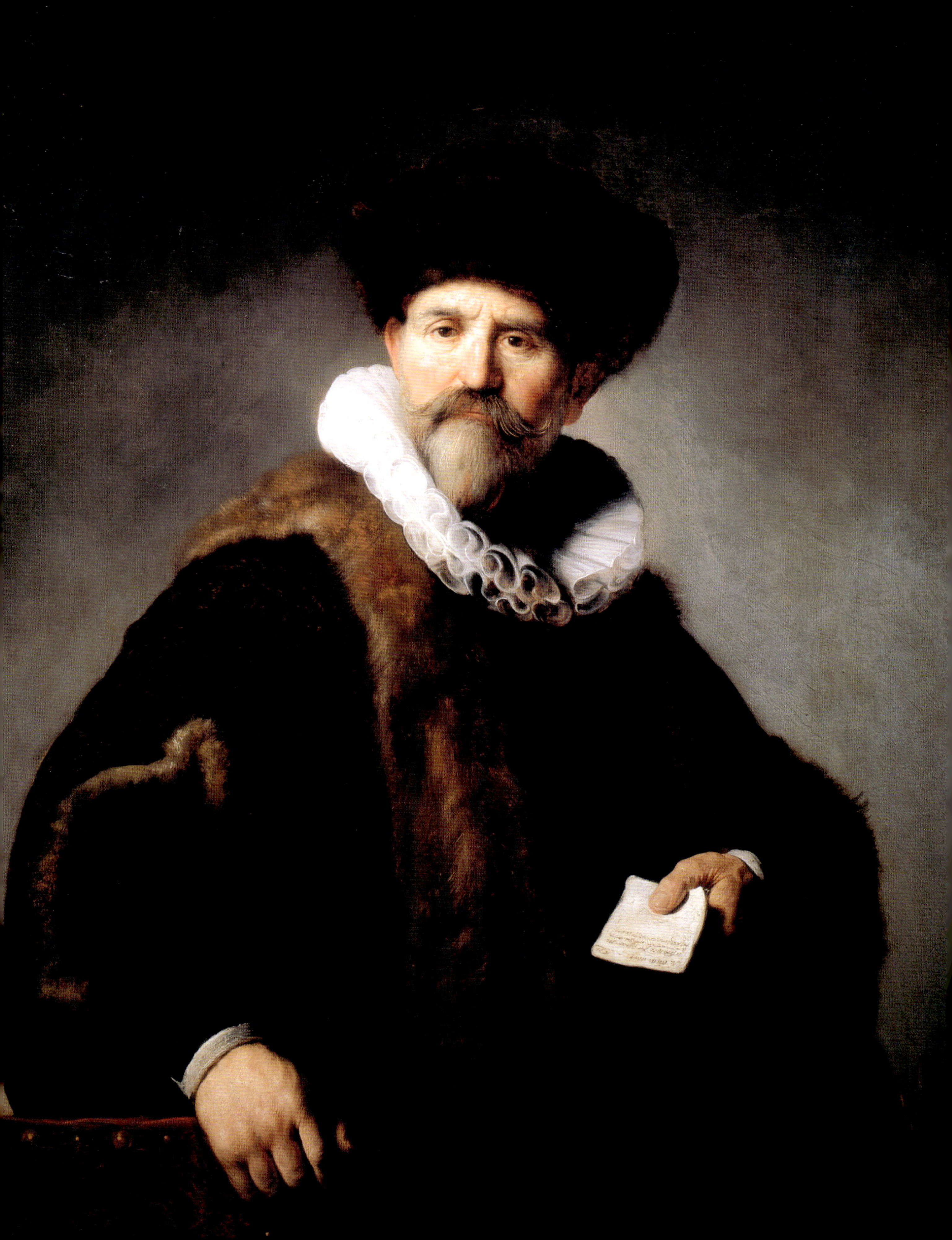

◆ RICKELE PADAWER, DOSHA'S GRANDMOTHER: We go together—In the forest near Byten, just outside of Slonim, in the winter of 1943, Simha and I would wake each morning. Together. I would have slept beyond dawn—cold as it was—but Simha would talk in his sleep. *"The world is a narrow bridge. The key is not to be afraid."* And as many times as he said it in his sleep, over and over, quoting his Rebbe, the Breslover, I knew he was terrified. He would tighten his grip around my arm and say "Rickele, Rickele, get up we must go together." He was terrified of being left alone. Of course, we would both go together. What did he think? That we would go to that place of fire and smoke where Lt. Yakov Fyodorovich told us the men and women were separated and then some women went to the right and some to the left and the men were further separated, some went to the right and some G-d-forbid to the left. So if you don't follow Lt. Chaim Podolski and me and we don't all of us go together as one partisan unit, we will certainly perish. Not a night went by that my arm was not numb from Simha's grip. And even after the War, for two years, even when we came to Brooklyn sponsored by our sons and visited by our granddaughter, Jerusha, he still could not let go of my arm or let me sleep after he awoke, until we met the Rebbe.

■ REMBRANDT: We go together—"What will it be like for me?" Saskia had asked when her cousin Uylenburgh had introduced me to her. "You gave me a luminescent gem of the Portrait of Nicolas Ruts and I give you a wondrous pearl of my cousin Saskia Uylenburgh." And Hendrik Uylenburgh pushed his cousin ever so gently a half a step toward me. Saskia's eyes were downcast. Both her parents had died seven years before and seven lean years were not lightened by that dimwit guardian brother-in-law of hers, Gerrit van Loo.

I could see her left hand support her head as she lowered her eyes, wondering what I would say. Would I abandon her as Rombardtus, her father, had, or Antje, her sister, to illness? "Clever you are and brazen too Uylenburgh, for you still owe me for my portrait of Nicolas Ruts. Hand over my commission which you received, spent and have not yet given me my half. Is this pearl yours to give, Uylenburgh?" I placed my hand gently under Saskia's chin and lifted her face. She neither rouged nor protested but just gazed at me.

"Don't be a swine, Rembrandt to speak of the Mennonite merchant Nicolas Ruts and a pearl of great price in one breath. Roll together through the streets of Amsterdam," Uylenburgh laughed as he shepherded us out of his house.

"This isn't exactly Leyden, Rembrandt," shouted Saskia's cousin as we walked together down the Breestraat. "People won't know you aren't married, yet." Saskia and I both heard Uylenburgh's last word "yet" as we headed for the Nieuwe Doelenstraat. All day and even past dinner we walked. I told Saskia of Marten Looten's portrait and how much I had been paid and of Nicola Ruts and what he said when her cousin gave him my portrait. "But what will it be like for me?" Saskia kept asking me until I could no longer hold back. I looked into her eyes and pledged with my soul. "We will go together," and added, with my heart, "forever." "And where are my witnesses to your pledge?" she persisted. I held Saskia in my arms and said, "The witnesses are the portraits of you that I shall draw. And etch and paint. They too will last forever."

Rembrandt van Rijn, *Portrait of Nicolas Ruts*.

"Well then," Fisher assured him, "We go together."

And who could believe it? Hamilton flipped. The coin rolled and rolled and rolled out of the living room into the kitchen only to drop between the floor boards to the floor below.

"Well, that settles it," said Hamilton. "Tomorrow we're off to Time, but for today, to the White Horse we go."

The next day, they met in the Time Inc. lobby.

"I'm Hadden and you're Luce," Hamilton had said to Fisher as they rode up the elevator to the personnel office for their interview.

"No," insisted Fisher. "I'm Hadden, you're Luce."

Together they had walked to the personnel office with an oak leaf rolled up job application scroll over their shoulders.

The secretary in Wyllys Terry III's office politely inquired, "Who is going in first, Mr. Fisher, or you, Mr. Hamilton?"

◆ SIMHA PADAWER, DOSHA'S GRANDFATHER: We go together—When my granddaughter Jerusha, whose American parents couldn't pronounce my mother's name and had only time for the diminutive Dosha, saw us after the War, she burst into tears. "Ghosts!" she shouted, pointing her finger at me and Rickele. Poor child, terrified of us. I suppose we were as thin as ghosts. And that no gudnik, that Stalinist mother of hers who made my son dance like the marionettes I saw in Vilna at a Purim Spiel, just smiled. "Oh my dear child, Bubbie and Zaidie will watch you and cook your dinner, your Father and I are going out," they would say to our Jerusha. And before a year had passed, my Rickele was making Jerusha little cookies and every day on the way home Jerusha would stop by us. One day she was different. "Zaidie, you must see the Rebbe I saw today after school. He will make you feel better." And our Jerushaleh insisted to her no gudnik mother and her stum-silent father that we should see the Lubovitcher.

And in we went together. My Jerusha spoke first. "Last month Mr. Rebbe, my school class came to visit you and you told us we could come back if we had a question. And here is my question. My Zaidie is very tired. And my Bubbie who brought him from Europe and gives me cookies every day cannot sleep at night. Can you make them better?"

The Rebbe stretched out his hand toward me and said, *"Fin Ven Kimt a Yid?* From where does a Jew come?" And without knowing why, I simply answered, *"Ich bin a pushette Litvak fin* Slonim. I am a simple *litvak* from Slonim." "Why have you all come together here," said the Rebbe looking at Jerusha who spoke no Yiddish. Before I could answer for my English was not so ayyayai, Rickele said "All through the War in Slonim, in Byten, in the forest of Belorusse, my Simha would say we go together. He would repeat this without end." And suddenly the Rebbe spoke in a whisper, not with a sigh, not with an accusation, but simply stating a fact:

"On the third day, Abraham lifted up his eyes, and saw the place afar off. And Abraham said unto his young men, 'Abide ye here with the ass and I and the lad will go yonder and we will worship and come back to you. And Abraham took the wood of the burnt offering and laid it upon Isaac his son; and he took in his hand the fire and the knife and they went both of them together.'"

I looked at the Rebbe's eyes, bluer than I had seen in any Yeshivah, bluer than any in any partisan group. And I said, "Speaking of the fire and the knife…" And the Rebbe with tears in his eyes said "By my life, I cannot answer but this I can tell you," pointing to our Jerusha and placing his hands upon her forehead in blessing,

"I will bless you and in multiplying I will multiply your seed as the stars of the heaven and as the sand which is upon the seashore."

Suddenly the Rebbe was silent and we all wept. After a long time the gabbai came in and gently ushered us out. Poor Jerusha held my head and said, "Zaidie, you'll be alright won't you?" And in truth for the first time since the War, I could sleep. But more important, the *interstika shira*, the key thing, was that Jerusha was blessed.

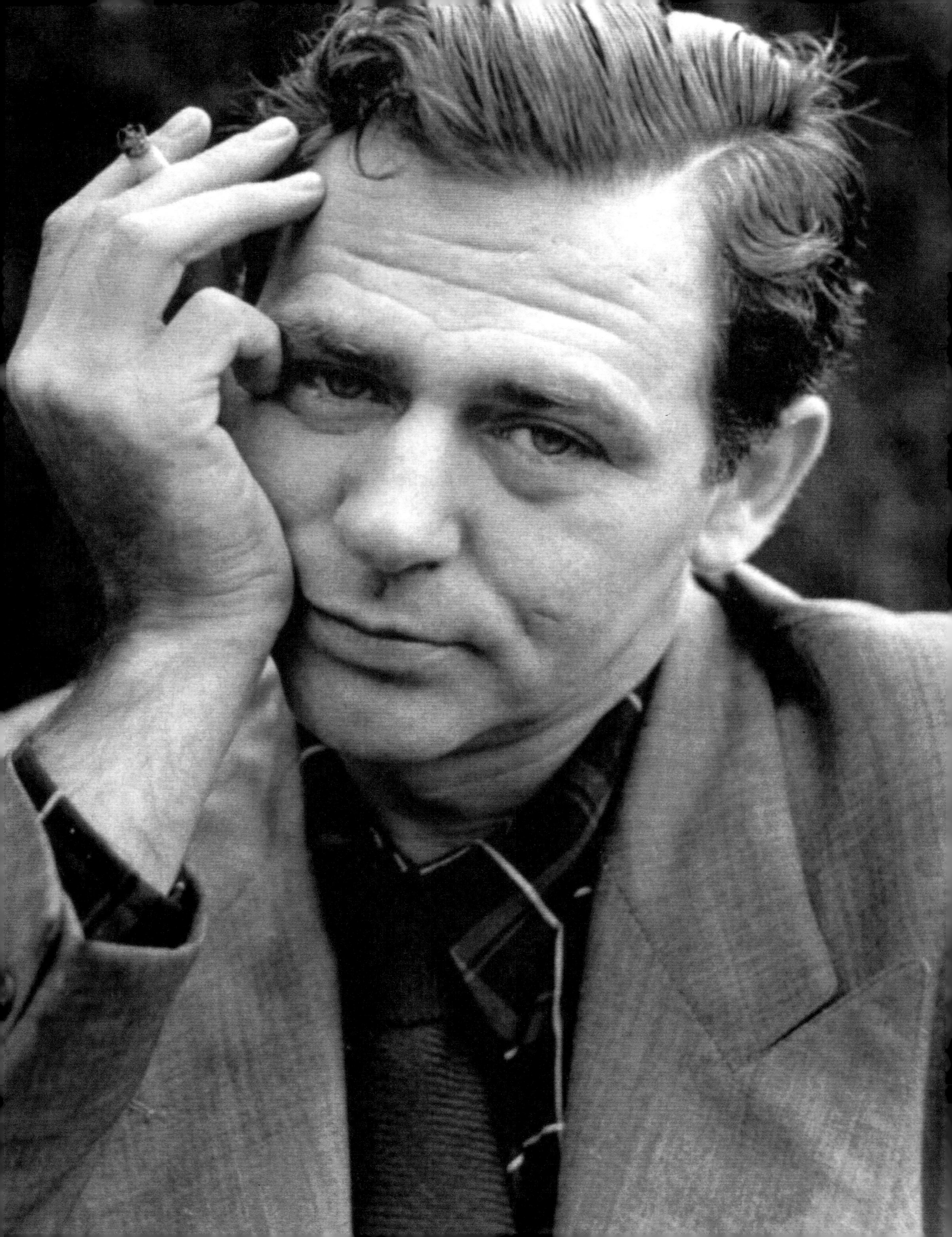

■ BRITON HADDEN: Mr. Luce hired Agee himself—Henry hadn't hired Agee himself. Ralph Ingersoll had, on a recommendation from Dwight MacDonald. But Agee had it. An elegance of style. Wit. People smiled when he entered a room. Laughed when he talked. There was music in his voice. Of course he would die young. Luce knew it. Just as he knew I would die early. Henry never aged because he was old already at Yale. Never brilliant like Agee. Luce read Agee's *Fortune* poems on orchids, Bordeaux wines and the ten most precious jewels in the world and insisted "Mr. Agee, your next assignment of free verse is the Price of Steel Rails. I will personally edit your article."

Jim could write on everything and he did. Twelve thousand words on the price of steel rails, the contour of land outside of Gary, Indiana, the complexion of young steel workers in Pontiac, Michigan and shades of greyness embedded in the fingernails of Bethlehem steel workers and foremen after a twelve hour shift.

"Remarkable , Mr. Agee," said Henry. "Extraordinary writing. Twelve thousand words, and only one hundred and twenty six usable ones for *Fortune* readers." "Are you firing me, Henry?" asked Agee standing in front of Henry's desk which Henry particularly detested considering Agee's height, six feet three I believe, a considerable edge over Mr. Luce, over half a foot.

"Sit down, Mr. Agee quite to the contrary. I have a proposition. Attend Harvard Business School and I'll triple your salary." "And treble assignments on steel, aluminum and copper. Thank you, Henry, but I'll stick to my element. Good night." Agee breezed out of the Founder's room, leaving Henry as he always was, since my death—quite alone.

■ ROBERT FITZGERALD: Luce hired Agee—Between them, you could draw a map of all America. And a measure of all men. Like Fisher and Hamilton, Agee and I toiling for Luce. Agee *"was visited on at least one occasion by a fantasy of shooting our employer. This was no less knowingly histrionic and hyperbolic than the other. Our employer, the Founder, was a poker-faced strong man with a dented nose, well-modeled lips, and distant grey-blue eyes under bushy brows; from his boyhood in China he retained something of a trace of facial mannerism that suggested the Oriental. His family name was New England and rather a seafaring name…*

The Founder had that sea coast somewhere in him, behind his mask, and he had a Yankee voice rather abrupt and twangy undeterred by an occasional stammer. A Bones man at Yale, a driving man and civilized as well. Quick and quizzical, interested and shrewd, he had a fast sure script on memoranda and as much ability as anyone in the place. He had nothing to fear from the likes of us. Jim imagined himself laying the barrel of the pistol at chest level on the Founder's desk and making a great bang. I imagine he imagined himself assuming the memorable look of the avenger whom John Ford photographed behind a blazing pistol from the Informer. It is conceivable that the Founder on occasion and after his own fashion, returned the compliment."

"That's not Mr. Fisher, that's Mr. Hamilton, ma'm. And we're going in together. We're our generation's Luce and Hadden."

"Mr. Luce? Are you a relative?" asked the astonished secretary. She abruptly got up and walked to Terry's office, closing the door behind her.

"Mr. Terry, these two odd Yale men who sent in their manuscripts yesterday are here. And one of them, the tall one, may be kin to Henry Luce," she whispered, bowing her head while pronouncing the ineffable name.

And of course Terry couldn't stop smiling throughout the interview with Fisher and Hamilton. "Naturally we'll take you both. Mr. Luce himself hired James Agee himself. And yes there is a place for novelists at Time Inc. Even today. Even in our Time." Terry chuckled, pausing to make sure they'd caught his witticism. "No, we don't pay those kinds of wages to beginners and you will be drawing separate checks…yes…no…yes…later perhaps."

■ JOHN HUSTON: Mr. Luce hired James Agee himself—Mr. Luce. Himself. Hired James Agee. Himself. That's how it should read. For Jim was more rare than one of a kind. Perhaps he didn't even exist. Only his creation of himself, the shadow of his hand, dancing before us, really happened. Rare was too common a word to describe him. Jim "*never attempted to win anyone to his way of thinking, far less to try to prove anyone's mistakes or in the wrong. He would take a contrary opinion regardless of how foolish it was and hold it up to the light and turn it this way and that, examining its facets as though it was a gem of great worth, and if it turned out to be a piece of cracked glass, why then he, Jim, must have misunderstood. The other fellow had meant something else, hadn't he…this perhaps. And sure enough Jim would come up with some variation of the opinion that would make it flawless as a specimen jewel. And the other fellow would be very proud of having meant precisely that, and they would go on from there."*

And Mr. Luce. Himself. He would fashion himself into a gem. Never the other fellow. All the difference in the world. And Jim and MacLeish, and Hersey and, and, and they were all lapidaries hired to shape, brute, polish, engrave, fashion, the Great One Himself.

■ DWIGHT MACDONALD: Agee—Agee worked for Time but more precisely for Henry Luce for fourteen years. Twice the biblical seven. For in the pharonic scheme of things it was seven years of plenty and seven years of famine. But for Time, the years were all of a piece, days of famine, night filled with the freedom of plenty.

"*In his last letter to Father Flye written a day or two before he died, Agee sketches out a fantasy about elephants, how they have been degraded by man from the most intelligent and the noblest of beasts to figures of fun. He felt he was dying and this was his last, most extraordinary insight. For wasn't this just what happened to him? Wasn't he also a large, powerful being who was put to base uses?*

There is something helpless about elephants precisely because of their combination of size and intelligence. It is a fact that they can be tamed and trained as few wild animals can. Henry Luce was a decent fellow when Jim and I worked for him at Fortune and I'm sure Luce was like me, charmed and impressed by Agee. But what a waste, what pathetic docility, what illusions…"

James Agee.

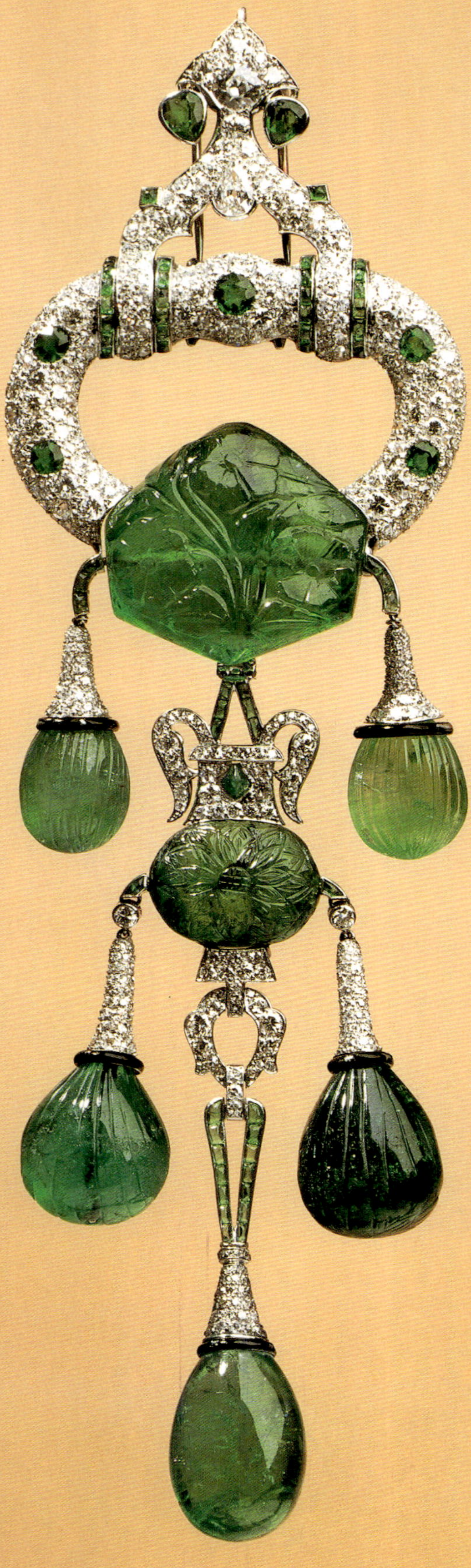

◆ SIMHA PADAWER: Wake up—Wake up, my mother would shake me in the middle of the night in Slonim. Even my heilige father couldn't awaken me. I could have slept for years. We would start studying in the Troki Yeshiva when it was dark even earlier than in Slonim. Wake up: Abraham *"It was early morning. Abraham rose in good time, had the asses saddled and left his tent, taking Isaac with him, but Sarah watched them from the window as they went down the valley until she could see them no more."* The book Yakov Beller, the apikoras, showed me. "And what of the mother, Sarah?" Yakov kept at me. "How could she have allowed her son, her only son to go?" And my mother could wake me, and no other. And where was she when…

■ SASKIA UYLENBURGH: Rembrandt—We go together. Together. Or we together. Rembrandt always said to me on our walks in Amsterdam. The first night, moonlit. I remember his hand quivering as we walked. I thought to myself, he has the palsy and my sly cousin Hendrik has passed another half-guilder where one was due. Always trading was Hendrik, I'll give you this if you give me that. "Come to my Breestraat house," he had told my Rembrandt to be, "And you will be the Lion of Amsterdam."

"But I am an independent master in Leyden," Rembrandt had replied to my ever-crafty cousin. "I will not be made member of the Guild of St. Lukes and what rent will I pay you, Uylenburgh?" "Do not call me Uylenburgh, call me Hendrik. Are we not family? Rembrandt, there will be no rent between us." "Uylenburgh," Rembrandt replied to my cousin. "We are not family, not by marriage." "Not yet. Not now. But soon, Rembrandt," my cousin had protested and like a magician at the Maastricht fair, Hendrik pulled me out of his sleeve and sent the two of us walking by moonlight. And Rembrandt talking all the time at the moon, his palsied hand shaking and I, his rent, suddenly could not contain myself. "Trying to wake up?" I stuttered. "Why is your hand shaking so? Do you have India palsy?"

He stopped and stared at me for what seemed an hour and pulled out a piece of charcoal and kneeled down on the ground furiously slashing at the cobblestone street. After not more than three minutes, he stepped back, his hand perfectly still, and with a flourish he beckoned me to examine.

On my hands and knees I bowed down to the ground before him and there I was, a likeness of me, more a reflection of myself in a pool of moonlight, a wilted rose in my white hand, even the rouge on my face, white to eye, and Rembrandt with his chalk held upright, dancing about me singing. "Oh we go together. Forever. Everywhere. Together. Forever." "Rembrandt," I rose trembling. "You'll wake the dead. Be still. We can wed but we will never be forever."

And he, gaily dancing in front of me, behind me, around me, waving his charcoal stick by moonlight at me, I leaping, trying to hold it but never quite touching it. "Oh, with my drawing we will be together forever." Rembrandt trumpeted gaily.

And there they were, four years later, still at Time, Inc..

By now Hamilton had agreed to be Luce, and Fisher happily accepted his position as Briton Hadden. The two earned identical sums of $405 a week minus $83 for Social Security and New York state and federal taxes.

"Wake up, Fisher," said Hamilton as he scooped up the photographs of Indian Moghuls. Shoveling through the sheaf of documents, he lectured. "Raphael, we've got to get the captions for these photos by next Monday. This is serious. John Walsh is taking our outline to editorial, and if they don't have the story boards all set upstairs, we're out of here. History. Newsreels."

"So what, Rembrandt." (Rembrandt was the name Hamilton preferred to be called in moments of crisis.) "Aren't you always telling me that you'd rather be a cartoonist who dreams of painting *The Nightwatch* than assistant to the Vice President of Special Projects?"

■ VAN GOGH: Wake up—"Wake up," Monsieur le Docteur Gachet would whisper to me. "Wake up. Wake up." Perhaps Gachet was afraid that I would fall asleep at my canvas while painting him. But he was the patient and I the doctor. Les Frères Goncourt were his bed sheets. If only Gachet had the strength to pull them over his eyes and get one good, long nights sleep.

I wrote to my dear Theo, *"The preface of their novel tells the story of what the de Goncourts went through and how at the end of their lives they were melancholy, yes, but felt sure of themselves, knowing that their work would remain. What fellows they were! If they were more of one mind than we are now, if we could agree completely, why shouldn't we do the same?"*

■ THEO VAN GOGH: Wake up—Wake up Vincent. And you painting Dr. Gachet to wake him up. And he sitting for you, his strength almost beyond him. You, sagging. I can feel Dr. Gachet sinking below the canvas, below your easel. And he doesn't have my Johanna or you, my angelic brother Vincent, to hold him up or watch over him in his sleep. The de Goncourts had each other. And we, dear Vincent, have each other. But the world is falling asleep, Vincent. Each of us and our reveille call only dimly heard, each by their lovers, in their dreams. Wake up, Vincent. And wake me up. And I'll awaken you. And you, Dr. Gachet. And we all together can wake up the world

■ LAURENCE STERNE: Wake up—Wake up Eliza, I pleaded. Walking about the James' house in Soho. Round and round the house I marched half the night. More. At the very start of the year of '67. And my Eliza fevered and withered by her wretched husband Draper. No pharaoh was more cruel—to separate us.

"Write your husband, Eliza, tell him the truth in your case. If he is the generous, humane man you describe him to be, he cannot but applaud your conduct. Wake up Eliza and accept me." "It is true I am ninety-five in constitution and you but twenty-five—rather too great a disparity, this—but what I want in youth, I will make up in wit and good humor. Not Swift so loved Stella, Scarron his Maintenon or Waller his Sacharissa, as I will love and sing thee, my wife elect!"

Cartier Brooch, c. 1920

55

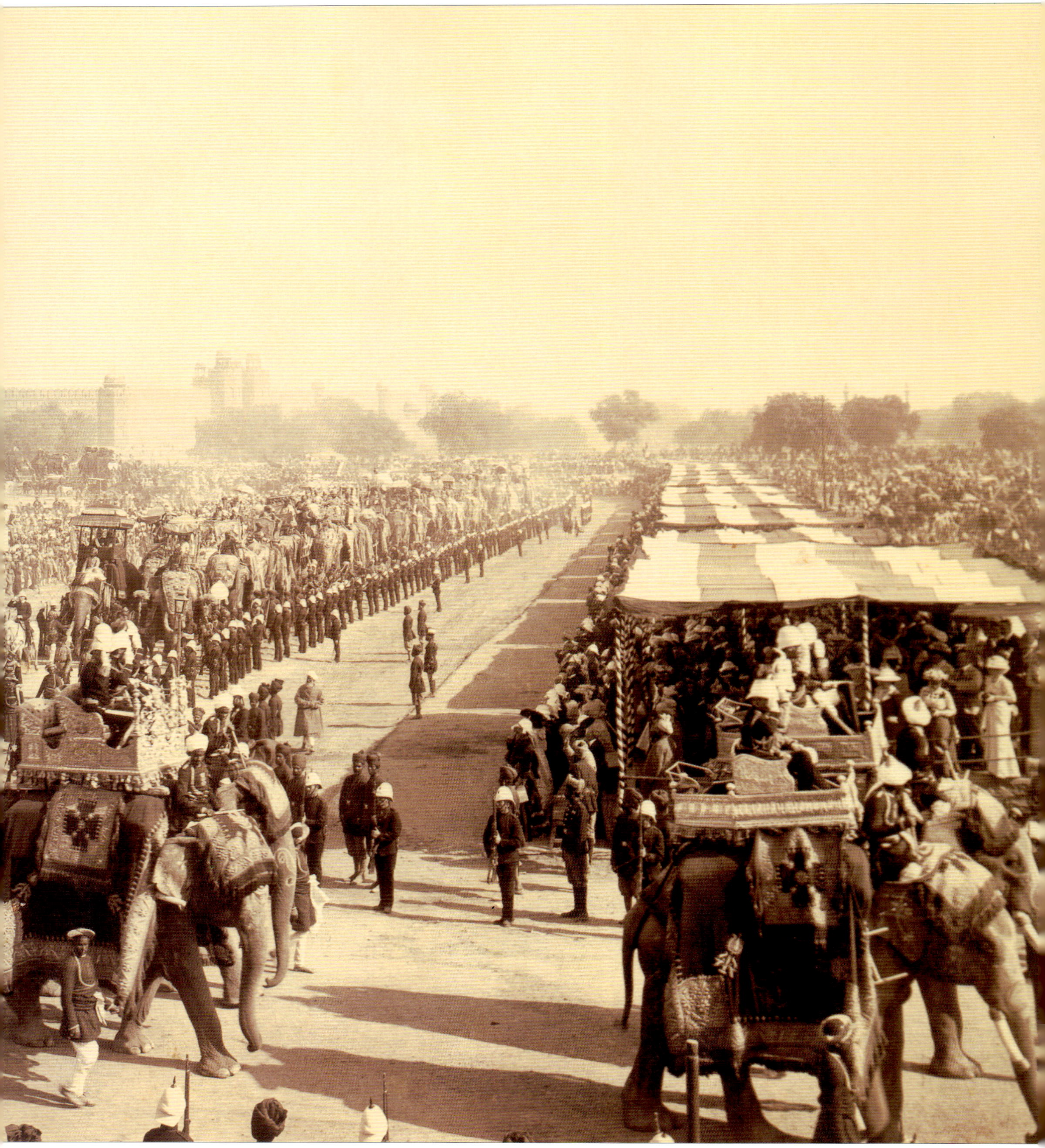

■ FRANZ KAFKA to Milena Jesenská: hallucinating—"*It occurs to me that I can't remember your face in any precise detail.*" Only how you finally walked away between the tables of the coffee house, your figure, your dress, these I can still see. But between your entrance walking slowly towards me in the Arco, I with Brod at his favorite table in front, on the right: "Franz from here we can see everything," "Any woman approaching, who to wave at. We can turn to our left and snub those who will snub us if we give them half a chance. We command the heights here, General Kafka." And how disappointed Brod was as you approached our table, eyes riveted on me. I can feel their flame. Let no man look upon my face and live, we are taught by my father's father and still I could feel the heat of your gaze on me and I couldn't breathe, much less speak. And you, approaching like an eagle, neither looking at Brod nor anyone else but mouthing words as you floated toward me. How disappointed Brod was that your words and your eyes were directed only at me.

"The Genius of Prague: The wonder of our age." I heard your words only in Brod's echo.

"Just what I tell Franz," said Brod gallantly. "He is the genius of Prague and he will be the wonder of our age, Mademoiselle Jesenska, if I'm not mistaken." And I am unwilling, and incapable of speaking, only to see Brod on his feet, stretching his hand over my head, hoping to touch you, hallucinating: you and I are letters pressed together in an envelope posted to China. Forever.

"How you are correct, Milena Jesenska. And am I correct, Max Brod I presume? But what does the Genius of Prague have to say?" And you, my Milena, mine forever, still not touching Brod's outstretched hand. What can I say? I can write everything. I can mouth nothing. "I hear the genius of Prague says two people must anoint a genius. A man must be anointed by his mother before the age of six and a woman by her father before the age of seven and both a man and a woman must be anointed by a friend in their twenties and only then they can be declared genius." Brod withdrew his hand and settled in his seat. And shrewdly eyed you, my almost, my Milena..

Without hesitating, without withdrawing your gaze from me, you said, "I would like to translate your work into my mother tongue, Czech, so that you can become the wonder of our age." Before I could utter a peep from my nest, Brod rose to his feet and said. "But of course, Milena. We will send you *The Stoker* by return express mail." He extended his hand only to have you walk away. "*Between the tables of the coffee house, your figure, your dress. These I can still see.*"

India Durbar of 1903.

"Actually, I'd rather be Rembrandt hallucinating he was the Moghul Shah Jahan: The Shadow of God on Earth."

Fisher smiled. "Listen, there are five reasons we're fine. The first is my neighbor's brother owns the Taj Mahal moghul emerald. Second, anything to do with the Taj Mahal is always timely."

"Spare the puns please," winced Hamilton.

"Thirdly, Walsh made the strategic mistake of writing a memo and sending it to T. Brooks who certainly has mentioned it to the Great Man."

"Punt the spare explications, Raphael," said Hamilton.

"Fourthly, they still believe you and the Great Man are somehow connected."

Hamilton absentmindedly looked at the cutout version of the Taj Mahal emerald, sketching the outline of the flower petals with his right hand.

■ MILENA JESENSKÁ to Franz Kafka: You and the Great Man are somehow connected—In the Arco as I came toward you and Brod, I could see the plane of your cheekbone and the light that rested, caressing your neck, moving down under the whiteness of your starched collar.

I could feel the whiteness of your chest and my fingers could feel your heart and I approached, swimming upstream, toward you, past all the spectators in the Arco. I could see Brod waving wildly at me, as though I might not be able to brave the currents between the tables set with islands of coffee pots and tea trays and I, swimming ever upstream with an undertow at my feet. And your glorious smile and the whiteness of your teeth, strange how they were covered with letters:

"*As Gregor Samsa awoke one morning from uneasy dreams, he found himself transformed in his bed into a gigantic insect.*" And as I swam toward you, I was drawn by the rope of your words which I held onto, despite the extraordinary thunderous sounds of all of the vile mockers sitting on the shores of the coffee house. Screaming at their tables, gesticulating at me, the undertow of my father's hands clutching at my feet, trying to sabotage my every stroke. And poor Mother, already floating by me like some jetsam and flotsam, a death mask grin on her face. I was only sixteen when she died. She, elegant crucifix, was too frail a boat to carry me on my voyage.

And you Franz, my Franz, my always Frank, in German or in Czech. My Genius. Brod was right. He was always right. Right from the start, Brod told me: "Milena, you and the great man are somehow connected. Franz is a genius. Brod anointed you." And you were six. And swimming toward you, Brod held his hand out to me. In friendship, I know, but men are men and always will be in Vienna and even in Prague and certainly in their dreams. It must have been my angelic mother's crucifix, whispering to me. Swimming toward Frank's smile.

And the text of your teeth brought us face to face. "*And it was like a confirmation of our new dreams and excellent intentions…*" And I awoke facing you, my Frank, my ship, my ocean, my real mother and unreal father. My second chance, my genius. And you didn't have to say anything. Do anything, be anything. Just SMILE with words flowing out of you. And I would be your bed and my head: Your embroidered pillow. My ears a rest for your tongue, my shoulder solace for eyes. Four days in Vienna with you alone would be two lifetimes for us.

عمل گوردهن

■ FRANZ KAFKA: Out of Greenwich Village and out of New York—Hamilton understands as Brod understood. Fisher does not understand as I did not understand. Out of Greenwich Village and out of New York. Out of paradise and into paradise.

"We are sinful not simply because we have eaten from the Tree of Knowledge, but also because we haven't eaten yet from the Tree of Life." Brod singing to me to follow him to the Paradise of Palestine and I leaden-footed in the coffee house aromas of the Paradisiacal Prague. Either wonderful, either more than enough. Once having eaten from the Tree of Knowledge, one must not hesitate to grasp the fruit of the Tree of Life. Young Hamilton will save himself, but Fisher will need more than his daily Brod, only Dosha will do. Just as Milena was my only hope for Eden.

■ YOCHANAN BEN ZAKAI: Paradise—"Two students who study night and day together, Paradise will be their portion," I said to Rabbi Jose, the priest. "In my dream I saw the two of us reclining upon Mount Sinai and a 'Bat Kol,' a heavenly voice, issued from Heaven concerning us "Ascend hither, ascend hither! Large banquet couches and beautiful coverlets are prepared for you. You, your disciples, and the disciples of your disciples are invited into the third lecture hall. As for the disciples of the sages who wrinkle their foreheads with study of Torah in this world, the Holy One, blessed be He, will reveal to them its mysteries in the world to come."

■ SHAH JAHAN: Paradise— And Dara, my son, sat between me and his teacher, Sarmad, at the edge of the garden pool at Shalimar. The sun drifted toward the horizon and neither Dara nor Sarmad said a word. I waited for either of them to speak for I was the Shadow of God on Earth, I was eternal.

The sun moved slowly across the sky allowing Dara to formulate his questions which Sarmad knew in advance, but while he was the teacher, he could not speak first for Dara was my seed and would soon rule Hindustan.

So we waited, Sarmad and his Emperor, for the last rays of the sun in the Heaven that is Kashmir to form the words in the mind of young Dara.

Without turning to the right or the left, while facing neither his teacher nor his father Dara, said: "Speak to me of Paradise."

This world is the seed bed for the other world, I remember hearing my grandfather Akbar say. Yet it was Sarmad's mouth that uttered these words. And Dara repeated what Sarmad had uttered. My words too, and the great Akbar's also, with the very same music as my blessed star, Akbar, had chanted to me when I was a boy half Dara's age.

"A disciple who does not know the Koran by heart is like lemon without scent," said Sarmad as much to Dara as to himself.

Then we all went silent again. And the sun set on all of Hindustan. And beyond to Mecca. And beyond this world to the next. And that day never came again.

Without looking up from the photo, he said, "No one believes that we are, or were, or ever will be Hadden or Luce. No one here has even heard of Hadden. Listen, Fisher, you need this job or you're out of Greenwich Village and out of New York."

"And the fifth reason," said Fisher, powering ahead to a Clarence Darrow-like summation, "is over the weekend I noticed next year's annual budget on Brewster's desk and we're a line item: The Green Moghul Mirror of Paradise—The Taj Mahal Emerald." And with that Fisher took the photograph out of Hamilton's hands and dropped it into the document pile on his desk, an extraordinary carved emerald—a roiling sea of green.

■ MILENA JESENSKÁ: Paradise—Frank longed for Paradise. He had found it, or it had found him, when I walked into the Café Arco. Of course, how could he accept Paradise? I twenty-three, he thirty-seven, but about to turn 969. The Methuselah of fear.

Paradise could not exist. Or it had existed and had been destroyed by a suspicious conflagration. Or still existed but was closed to all Mittel Europeans. Or would be discovered by our child, who could not be born without our sojourning in Paradise. My "poor brain is unable to think." I wrote him in the café across the street from the poste restante. Even when a letter he wrote me arrived in the morning I would still go to the post office in the afternoon hoping for yet another. Hopeless, helpless, under the spell of his words.

"It would be a lie for me to say that I miss you, it's the most complete, most painful magic, you are here as much as I and more intensely.: Wherever I am, you're there as much as I am, and indeed more so."

That's it Frank. We are here for each other. Letters between us flying over the skies Poste Restante Vienna to Prague. And back and forth. And I like a siren, calling to my Frank, come to Vienna, come to me, come to Paradise. And Franz instead hears the police siren of his father. Frank writes to me speaking of himself in the third person. The fourth person. Another person's voice.

"All right, and Milena calls you with a voice which penetrates your reason and your heart with equal intensity. Of course Milena doesn't know you, a few stories and letters have dazzled her; she is like the sea, strong as the sea with its vast volume of water and yet mistaken, tumbling down with all its strength when the dead and all distant moon desires it…Milena thinks only of the opening of the door. It will indeed open, but then? Then a long thin creature will stand there, with a friendly smile…He's unlikely to talk much, lacking the vitality…you see, Milena, I'm speaking frankly."

Frank, Frank, this is not you speaking. It is your father speaking. Come to me in Vienna. And we shall sing so loud together that our father's voices will not be heard. Our roaring Paradise. Come. Frank. Come. Soon.

Nanha, Prince Khurram (Shah Jahan) with his son, Dara Shikoh.

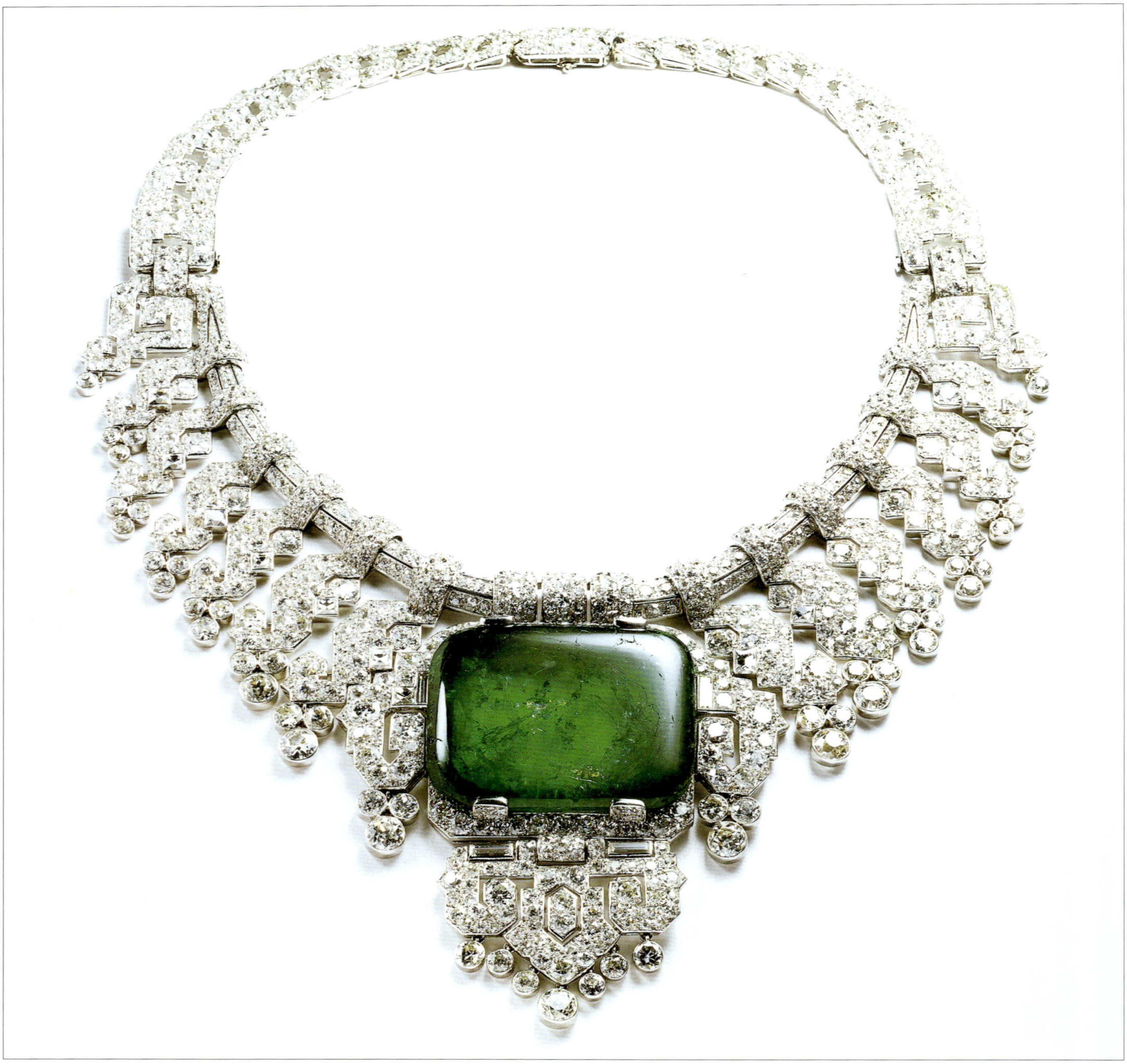

■ AN ASSYRIAN TABLET: Every man wants—*Our earth is degenerate in these latter days. Bribery and corruption are common. Children no longer obey their parents. Every man wants to write a book. And the end of the world is evidently approaching.*

■ BRITON HADDEN: Gog—Gog and Magog, how strange that Hamilton should taunt Fisher with the name Gog. The same name that Luce baited me with. Ezekiel 38, if my memory serves, and it always did and ever more shall: once learnt, not forgotten. And thus saith Ezekiel: "*Gog of the land of Magog, the chief prince of Meshech and Tubal.*"

Even stranger a name for Fisher than I, he a young Israelite and Gog coming from the north after the Temple is established at the end of days, with many peoples to, plunder Israel and carry away spoil. And the Lord, Himself, punishes Gog "*with pestilence and with blood and with overflowing rain.*"

"Not a terribly nice nickname, Henry. Why do you call me that?" "Because you call me Alexander," replied Luce. "But Henry, Alexander conquered the world and so will you in the fullness of time, at the end of days." But Henry stared at me and quoted from the classics:

"Why do you weep Alexander, his generals asked. They say that there are many world empires in the universe, and I have not even conquered one, answered Alexander." Young Fisher knows that Hamilton will not be Rembrandt, sufficient to the day if he be Hamilton. And yet of course Fisher will continue to bait Hamilton as Rembrandt. He cannot stop himself. Any more than I could avoid calling Luce Alexander or he and Hamilton calling us Gog.

CHAPTER 4

THE GREEN identity card, sine qua non of Fisher's right to travel to floor 14, was pinned to Fisher's rumpled shirt as he bounded past the downstairs guard to the staff elevator bank in the Time Life fortress. It was well past midnight and Fisher had only ten hours to finish the proposal.

"Finish or perish," Hamilton said as he ambled out of his cubicle next to Fisher the previous day.

"Which do you prefer, Rembrandt?" asked Fisher.

"Which do I prefer?" echolaliated Hamilton and continued. "That you not call me Rembrandt, dear Gog, and that we perish so that we may finish something worthwhile and not simply be paid to paint Luce's fantasy. And which do you prefer, Gog?'

"Likewise, that you not call me Gog and that we perish so that we can start something."

■ ABDALLAH IBN SALAM, Muslim cleric: Gog—It is a narrow, narrow gate. And it opens to a yet more narrow, narrow bridge across the valley of Hinnom from the Mount of Olives to the Temple Mount. And must we all not cross that Siraj, that narrow bridge? One by one, each bearing his sins as baggage across the narrow walkway, swaying in the violent winds of wars of Yajuj and Majuj— the Gog and Magog of my youthful teaching in Medina.

At the day of Resurrection, the very hour of daybreak, we all assemble on the white ground of Sahira, the base of the Mount of Olives. Loaded down with our misdeeds, our good deeds dancing in front of us, freely like angels proclaiming our arrival, hoping to influence our judgment for the good before we trudging, pushing ahead, arrive in Jerusalem for our judgment.

■ VAN GOGH: Green—"*I have tried to express the terrible passions of humanity by means of the red and green…The room is blood red and dark yellow with a green billiard table in the middle: there are four citron yellow lamps with a glow of orange and green…Everywhere there is clash and contrast.*"

We are all meant to help each other. Dr. Gachet is meant to help me. And I, Dr. Gachet: Hamilton, to help this young man Fisher and young Hamilton to be helped by young Fisher. And the maître de Café de la Gare, Joseph-Michel, where I rented an upstairs room was he not meant to help me as I paid my rent, en avance or at least Theo did—but we are at each other's throats. But for Fisher's card of green, laissez-passer, the guard would turn like a jackal on him. I can see the specks of blood red surrounding the pistol on the guard's hip. Are we not meant to be brothers, Théo and I? Are not Fisher and the young guard part of the same family and yet, the cathedral in which we all live is as hard to enter as it is to escape from.

■ RABBI AKIVA: Gog—The battles of Gog will last for twelve months. All the previous calamities of Israel will fade into insignificance. But the vision of Ezekiel will burn brightly in the mind of our people: For seven years the inhabitants of Israel will use the weapons of the enemy for fuel. G-d himself will battle Gog. The last of ten occasions of the Shekina's descent to the world will be in the time of Gog and Magog. The war of Gog and Magog will be the final war.

■ GERALD MURPHY: Asked—How like Fitzgerald is this young Fisher. Asked questions. Asking questions. Always to etrnity. And not only of me, of Sara. Always gathering grist for his novel.

Scott had decided to use Sara and me as characters in his novel.

"He questioned us constantly in a really intrusive and irritating way. He kept asking things like what our income really was, and how I had gotten into Skull and Bones and whether Sara and I had lived together before we were married. I just couldn't take seriously the idea that he was going to write about us—somehow I couldn't believe anything would come of questions like that. But I certainly recall his peering at me with a sort of thin-lipped, supercilious scrutiny, as though he were trying to decide what made me tick."

Lady Granard's necklace, Cartier, 1932..

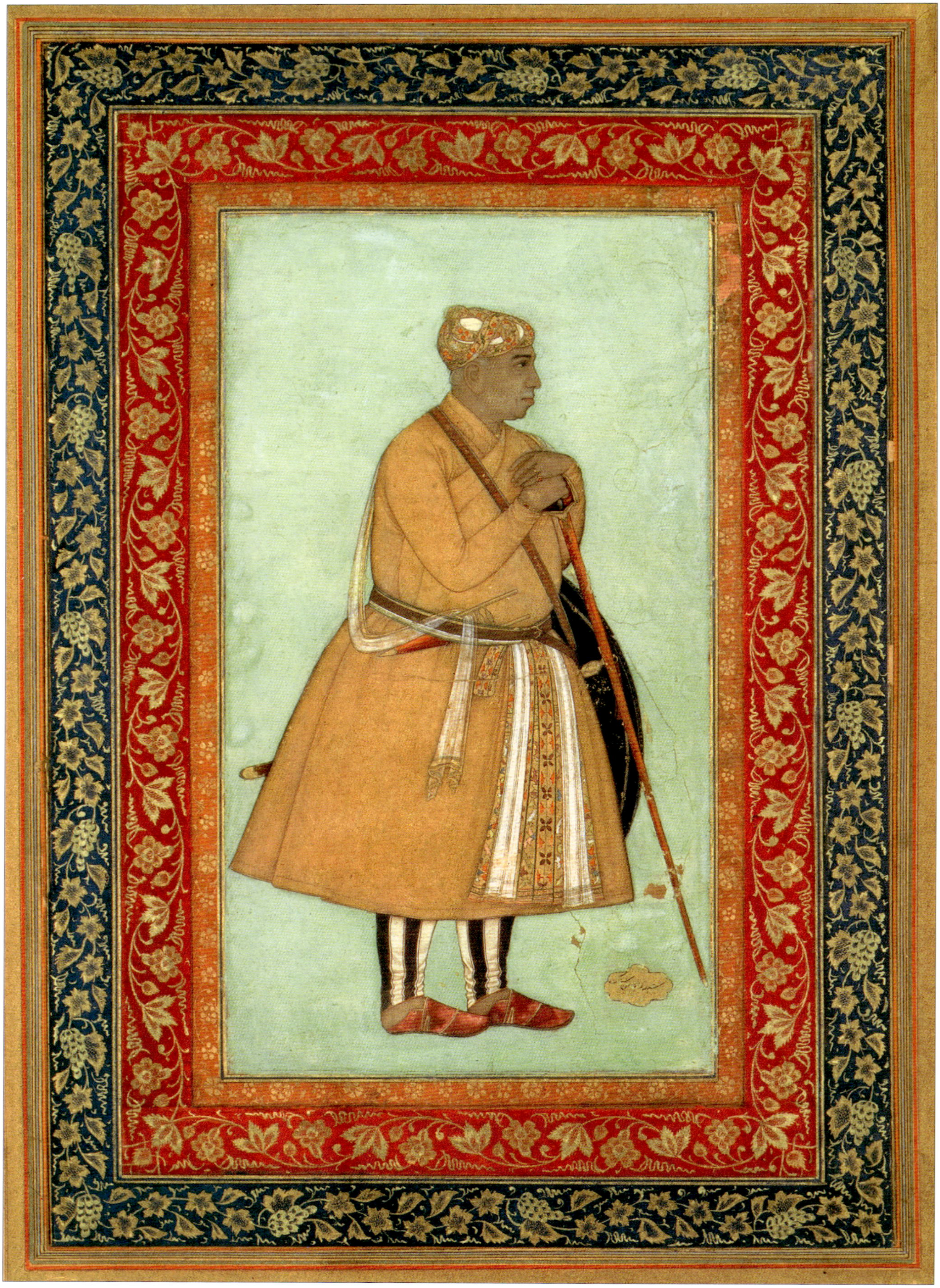

■ JAHANGHIR: Old—Payag painted the old warrior, Man Singh, in the last winter of Man Singh's life. By the time I held the painting in my hand, Man Singh had departed this world for wherever the Hindus travel to.

I looked down Payag's portrait: at the white hair, the weight of Man Singh resting upon his sword, the look of Man Singh that could see beyond mountain ranges. He was standing before my very eyes—not dead but more alive than ever.

I said, "Payag, you have shown the Rajput Man Singh as he is. How did he think? Was he ever afraid? He would tell you, for you are of his people."

Pagag, hesitated and then said: "Man Singh was afraid of nothing other than a Brahmin."

"And what is a Brahmin?" And Payag answered, "Here you must summon my brother Balchand, and we together will attempt to tell you, for one alone may not speak of the Holy to the young—even though he be Emperor."

This is what they said:

"There are four major castes in India. Each has its own particular customs and ways, and each has its own special day. First is the caste of the Brahmin, which means one who makes the unqualifiable deity known: their duties consist of six things: to acquire knowledge, to teach others, to worship fire, to guide the people to worship, to give something to the needy and to receive gifts…This caste has a specific day, which is the end of the month of Savan, the second month after the rainy season. They consider this day holy and on it their devotees go to the banks of rivers and reservoirs, recite incantations, and blow on ropes and threads. The next day, which is the beginning of the New Year, they tie the threads around the hands of rajas and elders as votives and consider them good omens. They call these threads rakhi, which means maintenance."

I said to Payag: "Now that Man Singh, the Rajput, is no longer alive, and you have explained to me what a Brahmin is, you will be my Brahmin. Come and put the *Rakhi* thread upon me."

Payag walked toward me and I bade my vizier to let him—though a Hindu—come as near to me as a son. Payag took the painting I held in my hand and placed it on both my hands which he clasped together to balance the painting evenly, holding my hands together, he said, "This is your *rakhi*. Just as Balchand and I placed our offering for your blessed father Emperor Akbar, before you, on his hands."

"So too we will place our painting as *Rakhi* on the next Emperor's hands if that be the divine kismet."

Payag's actions and words pleased me greatly and I added immediately: "and upon my grandson afterwards also."

But Payag lowered his head. I could see the color drain from his face. He did not so much as move his head in assent. Quite to the contrary, he did not move a single part of his body.

It is said by the Chisti Sufis that a true Brahmin has the gift of seeing the future. Can it be different with my Brahmin painter Payag, who sees the present so clearly.

Payag, Man Singh of Amber

It was quite perverse, the arrangement of Fisher's desk. A slim volume of Agee's *Let Us Now Praise Famous Men* rested just beneath Archibald MacLeish's *J.B.*, a first edition signed and bought in the Gotham bookstore, just four blocks away from the office during a sinfully long lunch hour, Hersey's *A Bell For Adano* and, of course, *The Wall*. It was a rogue's gallery of former Time writers along with *Stover At Yale*, the Hiram Bingham biography of dear old Elihu Yale, and a museum reproduction portrait of Shah Jahan, builder of the Taj Mahal, sitting on a peacock throne.

And finally, perched on top of all the books, was a photo of an Orthodox Rabbi lost in thought and looking at a page in the Talmud, taken anywhere in Europe and in any century.

■ HIRAM BINGHAM III: Arrangement—I would arrange the books differently were I young Fisher. Pride of Place to my own. Place it on top of the papers, all the other books. Like my Machu Picchu above the clouds, waiting to be discovered. For its bait to catch Luce. After all, Henry swims ever upstream. Ever the explorer. In the words of Kipling:

"One everlasting whisper, and night repeated, so: Something hidden. Go and find it. Go and look behind the ranges. Something lost behind the ranges. Lost and waiting for you. Go."

Yes, "Before the war it was exciting to go and find behind the ranges of the Andes the white temples of Machu Picchu and the palace of the last of the Incas. Recently it has been just as exciting to find behind the ranges of monumental archives in the India office in London, a journal kept by Elihu Yale…to find with my wife in the musty files of the little newspapers of the time of George I scores of notices of the forty days of auction sales of the incredible 'Collection of Elihu Yale, Esq, the late governor of Fort St. George."

Elihu is a far brighter blue lure for Henry. Perhaps young Fisher wanted only a Bones Man, MacLeish or Hersey to interest Luce. But *Stover at Yale*, how childish, neither fact nor fiction, neither fowl nor fish. Fisher still has time to reorder the pile and place my Elihu on top. Fisher's still young.

■ ARCHIBALD MACLEISH: On top—At least my words are on the top of the heap of books. Friends with them all in the twenties: Dos Passos, Hemingway and Gerald Murphy — skiing with our wives all together in the Austrian Alps. And onto the Riviera all together. And off again and on again to Paris, Hemingway's burly body and artless air and charming smile and sanctimonious guile. All friends wanting to be on the top of the heap.

And now to balance my thin book on top of that hulk Agee. O, Henry Luce himself is bound to arrive at any moment. It's his arrival after all but it's my setting, my art: My Job:

"The scene throughout is a corner inside an enormous circus tent where a side show of some kind has been set up…the feel is of a public place late at night, the audience is gone, no one about but maybe a stage hand somewhere cleaning up, fooling with lights."

Mr. Zuss vi Zucker, as we say sweet Mr. Fisher is already here:

"I heard upon his dry dung heap
That man cry out who cannot sleep
If G-d is G-d, he is not good
If G-d is good, he is not G-d;
Take the even, take the odd
I would not sleep here if I could
Except for the little green leaves in the wood
And the wind on the water."

Can He Himself, Mr. Luce, be far behind?

■ PAYAG: Old—Jahanghir bade me enter and sit down in front of him. He was kneeling–Moghul style–much as I had seen my brother Balchand paint his Majesty's grandfather Humayun the year before.

"You will paint the warrior Man Singh who brought me a present of Orissa and Bihar. How long will he live, this Rajput of Amber? I should like to have a remembrance of him—a portrait of him—not of someone else."

I nodded and said quickly, "It shall be done as you have said—and I began to step back from the shadow of G-d on Earth—as he was called—but I asked myself, Why me?

"For in that time Mansur was the Nadir al'Asr, the wonder of the age, and Abu'l Hasan, the wonder of the time.

They are not you, and you are not them. You will show Man Singh to me as he is, and you will tell me how he thinks. Go immediately to the Deccan. But alone, without your brother Balchand, for an old warrior will reveal his secrets to one but never to two."

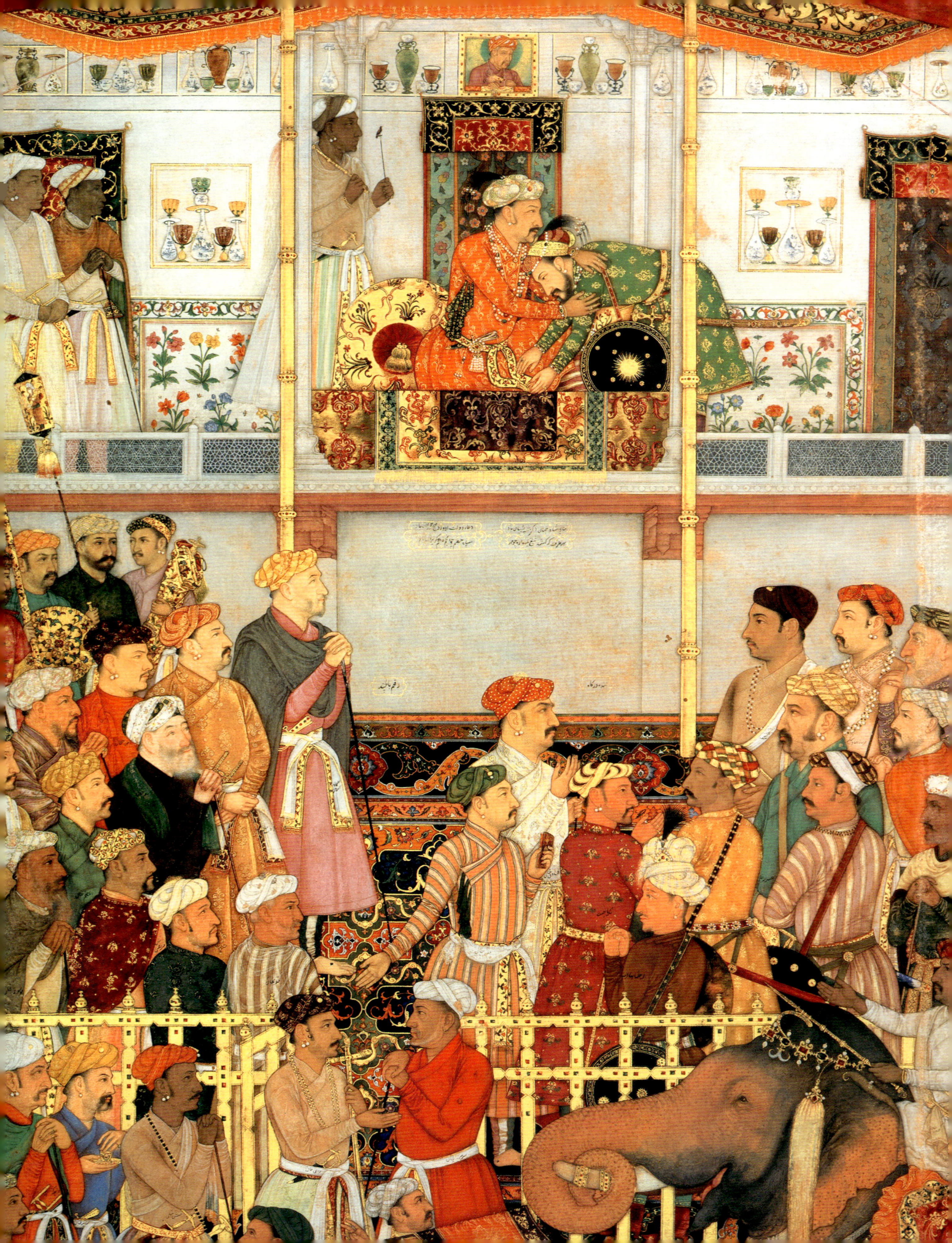

■ F. SCOTT FITZGERALD: Electric typewriter—Already making a mistake he is, young Fisher. Writing longhand is what he should be doing. And then have Hamilton type it up. Here is my list for him. Or for myself. Or for all of us. Best written in longhand. And then to Isabel Owens to type up. And then to keep on a shelf in a not so neat pile of papers, a soft coaster for my midnight glass of whiskey. Future fodder for the Princeton Graduate School library. My catalog for my life.

List of Troubles:

Heart Burn
Eczema
Piles
Flu
Night Sweats
Alcoholism
Infected nose
Insomnia
Ruined nerves
Chronic cough
Aching Teeth
Shortness of Breath
Falling Hair
Cramps in feet
Tingling feet
Constipation
Cirrhosis of the liver
Stomach ulcers
Depression and Melancholia

■ BALCHAND: Greatest Moghul of All Time— He summoned me in the middle of the night and asked me if I remembered when he had been summoned to his father's court when he was Prince Khurram after his glorious defeat of the Rana of Merwar.

I could see a half-smile on my Emperor's face and I wondered why I was summoned and not Murad or Ramdas, the other great painters of the court. But I held my tongue, as I always told Payag: Never add to the words of the Emperor and do not answer immediately for often the Emperor will answer for you. That is ever the safest, I would tell Payag over and over again.

Why the Emperors kept us was the greatest mystery to me—Akbar, Jahanghir and G-d's Shadow on Earth—the Ruler of all the World, Shah Jahan. But keep us they did. And for certain before I answered, Shah Jahan said, "Of course, you remember—you and your brother—to have seen the House of Merwar humbled.

"I want you to paint my portrait on that day of victory over the Rana of Merwar." And the Emperor stopped speaking.

After the longest silence I questioned: Do you want an enormous portrait of Shah Jahan: For we had to refer to the Shadow of his excellence in the third person.

"No, it must be a portrait of Prince Khurram on that day. As it was with Karan Singh. The son of Rana Amar Singh, as he was." So asked, so shall it be done. But my heart was broken—for on that day Hindustan had ceased to breathe.

Balchand, *Jahanghir receives Prince Khurram.*

Resting his electric typewriter lightly on *Let Us Now Praise Famous Men* and *J.B.*, Fisher checked his watch and started to type:

Raphael Fisher/William Hamilton:

PROJECT GREEN:
MOGHUL/ THE TAJ MAHAL/
THE TAJ MAHAL EMERALD

Chapters:

1. Elihu Yale Connection.
2. Green.
3. Paradise. Gardens.
4. Emeralds. Diamonds.
5. Moghuls. The Sun.
6. Greatest Moghul of All Time.
7. Taj Mahal Tomb: Love or Power.
8. Taj Mahal Emerald: Power or Love.
9. What Is Love? The Moon.
10. What is power?

■ SHAH JAHAN reading from the Tuzuk-I-Jahanghiri: Greatest Moghul— I summoned Payag's brother Balchand and spoke in the voice of my father Jahanghir. Place the Hindu rakhi offering on my hands: Paint for all in the world, from Hindustan to Mecca, the moment I was destined to become the greatest Moghul Emperor: I summoned Abdul Hamid Lahawri to read to Balchand from my father's diary. Balchand would illustrate the passage on the immortal face of time:

"*The next day the 11th of the month [19 Feb. 1615] Prince Khurram was to attain the felicity of being received [by me his father, Emperor Jahanghir]. Khurram entered the Hall of Public and Private audience with all splendor and magnificence surrounded by all the victorious soldiers who had been assigned to him on this campaign…he had the fortune to perform Körünüsh [formal 'kowtow'] prostrations, and salutes…I summoned my son forward, embraced him, and kissed his head and face, singling him out for particular affection and kindness. When he had finished the rites of service, he had his vow and alms displayed and said if it was ordered, Karan should be allowed to prostrate himself and perform körünüsh. I ordered Karan brought in. The Bakhshis [military officials] brought him in the usual ceremonials.*"

Balchand listened and went to the Kharkana to illustrate my father's vision before the eyes of all the world.

■ A.B. MARTIN: Green, Paradise, Taj Mahal— "*All in all, I have made several serious mistakes not buying wonderful things. But over the years I have noticed that other collectors have made even more serious mistakes in buying or not buying. There are times when I feel that in my collection, I have been brilliant to the top of my shoes, that my collection will be viewed when the Mona Lisa and the Winged Victory are forgotten, that I have the eye of a mole, that I might as well pound rice with paper lanterns. Once in a while come blue-bird days when I obtain something that is capolavoro, and then I dream that Guennol is another white dwarf; another Taj Mahal; I feel every crow in my collection is a bird of Paradise (all birds of Paradise are members of the crow family). Anyway, I know there are one or two objects in the collection to keep ever-bright the name of Guennol, at least till time is wound up and put in a bottle. These special objects, like the green feathers of the quetzal, will never fade even after all the spring times have come and gone.*"

■ COTTON MATHER: Elihu Yale Connection— For was it my hand that penned the letter to Elihu Yale in 1718?

"*Sir though you have your felicities in your family which I pray G-d continue and multiply, yet certainly if what is forming at New Haven might wear the name of Yale College, it would be better than a name of sons and daughters. And your munificence might easily obtain for you such a commemoration and perpetuation of your valuable name, which would indeed be much better than an Egyptian pyramid.*"

Was it my hand? And was it my hand several months later that penned a letter to Governor Saltonstall confessing "*that it was a great and inexcusable presumption in me to make myself so far the godfather of the beloved infant as to propose a name for it. But I assured myself that if a succession of solid and lasting benefits might be entailed upon it, your Honor and the Honorable trustees would pardon me, and the proposal would be complied withall.*"

And is it young Fisher's fingers that pen this note to the missionary's son, Mr. Luce? Or was it His Hand and is it His Finger?

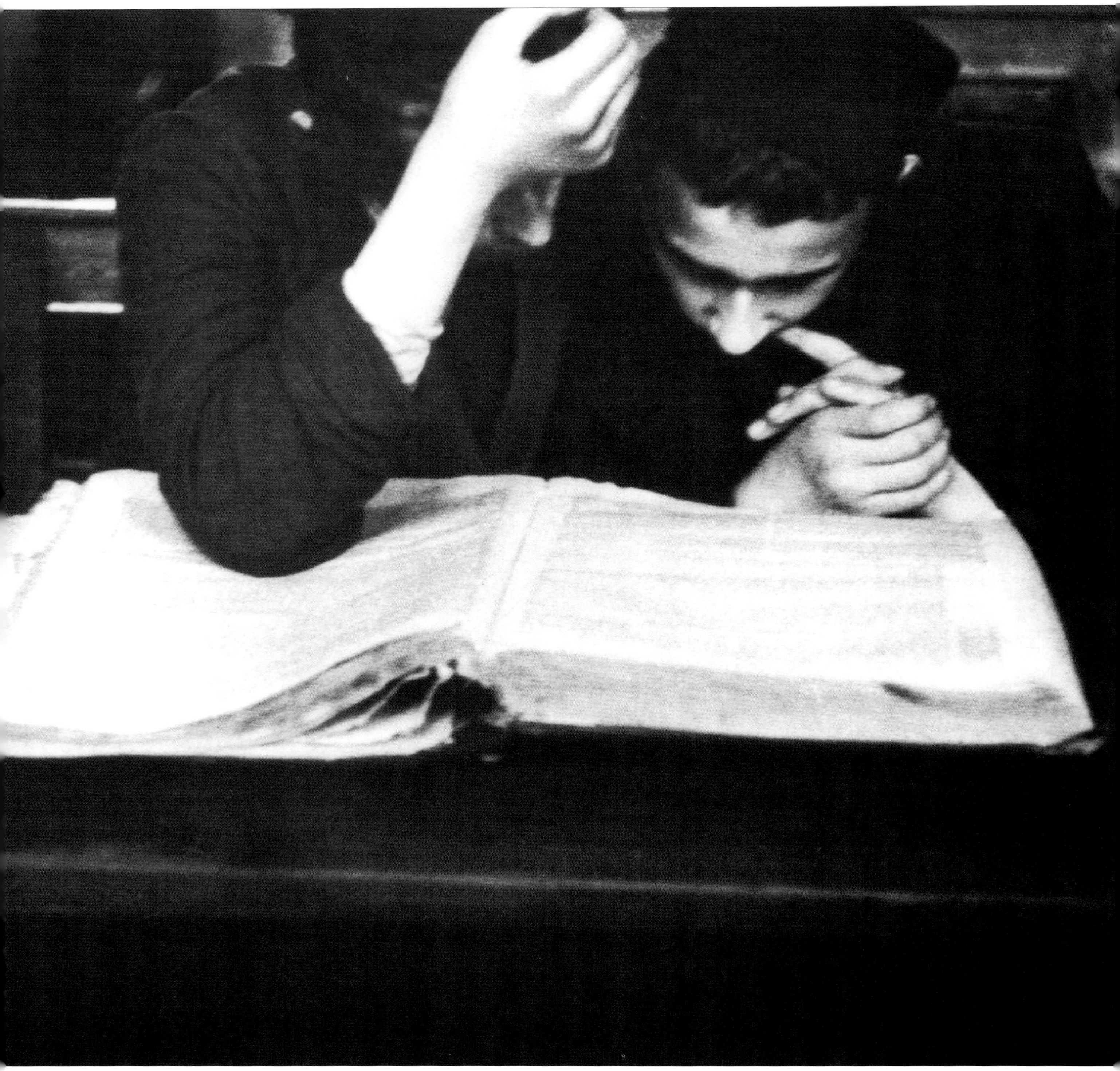

◆ RICKELE PADAWER, DOSHA'S GRANDMOTHER: As though playing solitaire with himself—Simha would return from the Yeshiva. Sometimes at eight o'clock, sometimes at seven. Sometimes at nine. And sometimes the food would long have gone cold. With one of the children already asleep and fed, no question, no problem. But when there were three and Jerusha's father had come into the world, I couldn't put his elder brother and sister to sleep and feed him and cook and wait. And one day I couldn't stand it and marched over to Sod Hatorah and peered through the window. There through the icicles, I could see Simha swaying back and forth, staring at his open Talmud, and then at the open Talmud of Wilamovsky next to him. Both tractates open to the same page. But Wilamovsky wasn't there with Simha.

I stood transfixed for an hour and Simha didn't turn to his left, my face as close to his as Wilamovsky was when they studied together all day and often all night. And Simha swaying slowly, back and forth, looking between the two identical pages.

When I returned to our house, he came perhaps fifteen minutes later. He took off his overcoat, brushed the snow off with his pale hands and sat down quietly at the table, still not speaking.

I asked him gently, "how did it go in the Yeshiva today?" "I studied alone," he said. "Why? I thought you studied with Wilamovsky." "Wilamovsky was sick. He wasn't there today. G-d willing, he'll come tomorrow." "I saw, Simha. I can't stand it when you don't return before dinner. With two children it was all right but with another I can't…I can't…." And I told him I had watched through the Yeshiva window.

"What did I look like?" Simha asked with the fascination of a *heder boychik*. "You looked as though you were playing solitaire." Simha held my hand in his and smiled with a smile that illuminated the room. "Yes, I was playing solitaire with Himself."

"And why was Wilamovsky's Talmud open?" I asked through my tears because although in fact I was hungry and the children were too, I was fascinated. "And were you and Wilamovsky playing solitaire with our children as well?" "Yes with Himself. And with Reuben and with his future daughter. And with Daniel Benjamin because Wilamovsky was sick. With his Talmud. With him. With his daughter Naomi and with her daughter, still unborn but to come, and with you my wife and always with Himself may His Name be blessed throughout the world and in all times through our children's children."

Fisher took out ten green folders and started to label them, taking the photographs and placing them into each folder as though playing solitaire.

The third folder, Paradise, was bulging. Pictures of gardens, Alhambra Oases in the desert, Samarkand and trees. Kashmir in summer. Rows of poppies. Meconopsis in the Royal Botanical Gardens of Edinburgh.

Two black and white photos—one a portrait of Elihu Yale in the Elizabethan Club in New Haven, the other of Yale and his son-in-law—constituted the only contents of Folder One.

■ REGINE SCHLEGEL: As though playing solitaire —I can remember visiting people my own age at the home of Mrs. Catrine Rordam (the widow of Dean Thomas Schat Rordam) in 1831 when Kierkegaard chanced to pay a visit.

Søren spoke constantly. Of what, I do not remember. How he gazed at me, talked to me, talked about me. He wrote: "*My G-d, why should this tendency awaken just now? Oh, how I feel that I am alone. Oh, damned be this proud satisfaction with standing alone. Thou O G-d, do not remove they hand!*"

Søren was playing solitaire and I was a pack of cards. When he wrote of me "*she was not religiously inclined,*" he was not right. I would have sat quietly, patiently by his side. Not moved an inch, inanimate as a deck of playing cards, yet full of life, like the hereafter.

■ BALCHAND: Portrait—Payag, my brother, always asking me, questioning me, badgering me, imploring me, threatening me, cajoling me, bidding me: "Paint yourself, Balchand, in a corner of a page. With your painting tablet under your arm. For the Emperor, for me, for all the future to see." I did. Could I refuse my brother?

■ SHAH JAHAN: Kashmir in summer. Rows of poppies—Mansur would walk me to the spot where he sat with my father, Jahanghir, and he would shake his hand at the valley's end. And say that is where we would sit, your father and I. I would say take me there and he would. Even at eighty, Mansur would hurry ahead of me, doubling back, changing directions. He knew every blade of grass, every flower.

And suddenly Mansur would stop and take out a brush and a slip of paper from his *jama* under his *padka*. He would point to a blue poppy standing alone. "That is your grandfather Akbar's. The one I painted for him. The one he gave to his son Jahanghir when you were a boy, Khurram."

Mansur always called me by my childhood name, the name my mother Jodh Bai and my aunt Ruqayyah Sultan Begum called me even after I became the Ruler of the world. Only Mother and Mansur were permitted to call me Khurram. When Mansur said my name, I remembered Akbar's words to my father Jahanghir, my advent has made the world joyous (*khurram*).

"Khurram, this is the poppy I painted," Mansur continued. And I looked at the blue, glistening drop of light shining more blue in his hand than any sapphire even glistened on my Peacock Throne. And I said to Mansur, "But the poppy you painted is long dead. And my father, too, has passed." Mansur did not hear, for his right hand, by the grace of Allah, had stopped shaking and he was painting the flower on the paper as quickly as the flower faded, plucked out of the Kashmir earth. And then and there I whispered to Mansur, "My flower of Kashmir will be an emerald forever green. It will be a reflection of my gift to the earth. It will be seen here forever white, a Taj of brightness, a qarina of paradise. And I and my house will be illuminated in both realms."

But Mansur did not hear my words for he was busily creating the Kashmir Paradise of my father's time. Creating and recreating each moment of his life.

■ CLINT MURCHISON: Playing solitaire with himself—Sid Richardson used to kid me, long and hard. "Clint," he'd drawl, "Why in the name of the land of Goshen, do you have all of these down home boys playing poker with you every night? And what in tarnation do you talk about to them all night long? Why not do business in the day time and sleep at night?" And I'd say, "Sid, in 1919 I busted into your poker game in Witchita Falls and we snuck past guards on the Texas border. And we damn near could smell the oil when we got past those lay-about guards on the fields that had just hit across Oklahoma." And then the next morning me n' Sid bought every darn lease we could for $50,000. Money I had and he didn't. And we cleared four times that very next day. Not a bad day's work. A thousand times more than we could have made playing poker that night. And a million times more than he could have made playing solitaire with himself.

Hell, Sid. I ain't gonna get me a business secretary. I'm just gonna have a passel of houses from the Sierra mountain range to west Texas. And one I'm going to fix up with eight beds "*so a group of us boys can talk oil all night.*"

Searching for the truth in the Talmud.

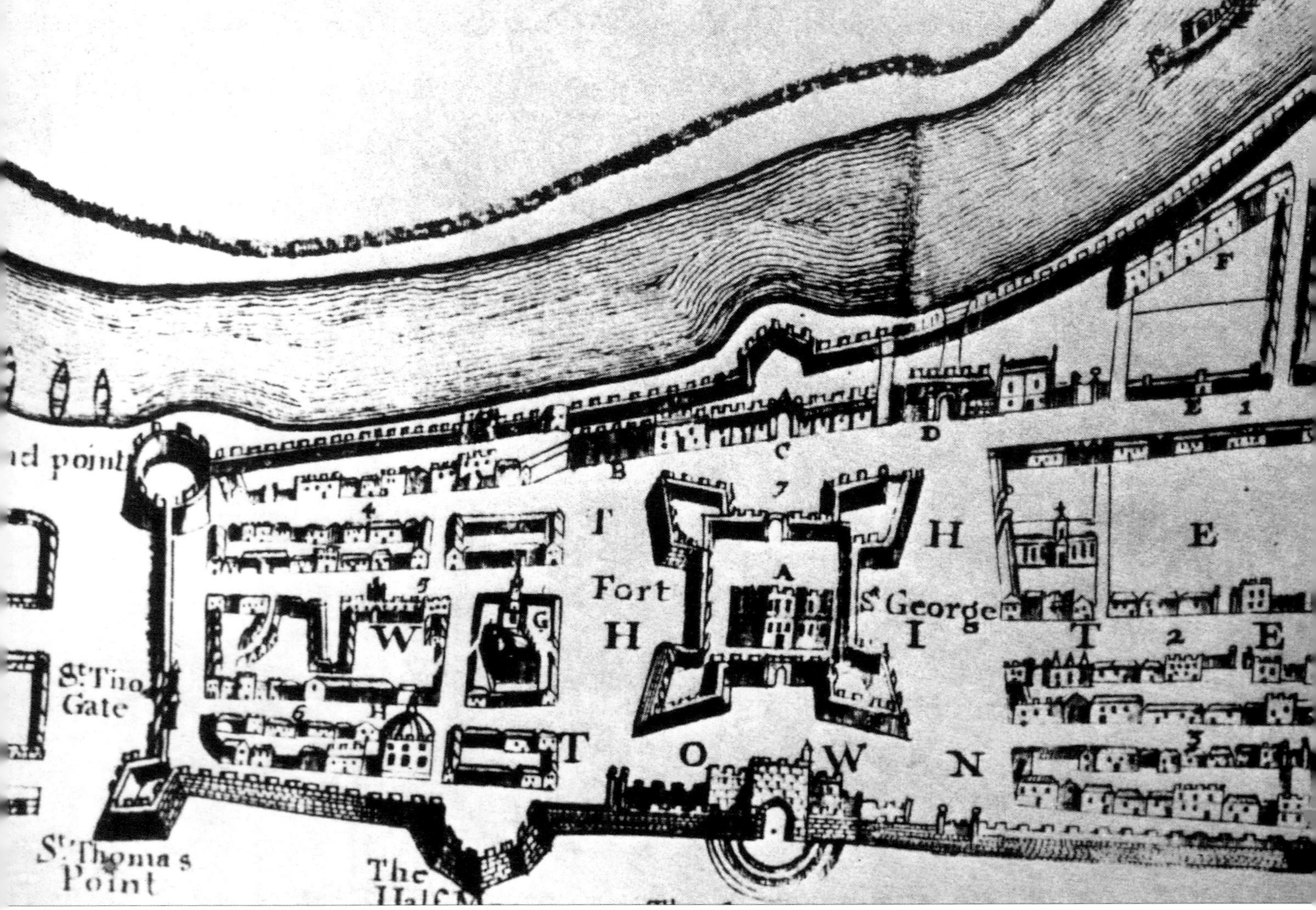

point
St. Tho Gate
St. Thomas Point
The
Fort
St. George
W
H
T
H
E
I
T
E
T
O
W
N
A
B
C
D
E
F
G
1
2
3
4
5
6
7

◆ TUVIAH GUTMAN GUTWIRTH, FISHER'S MOTHER'S FATHER: One—Number one. As though there could be an order. I was on my way to visit my father-in-law, my teacher, to ask him where I should send my son Baruch to Yeshiva. "Ask your father-in-law which is the number one Yeshiva today," I had been told before the Great War. And I in Antwerp, remembering the Belzer Yeshiva in Poland, a world away from my home in Western Europe. A world away from Riglitz, where I had grown up. Ask your father-in-law, said Morgenstein to me after the morning prayers.

As I walked toward Abish Rheinhold's house, I thought, My father-in-law always taught me: think about how you phrase the question and the answer will come when you cross my doorstep—when you see my face even before you ask the question.

I thought of the Yeshiva, of Belz, established by Sar Shalom. Tens of thousands studied there. Was this the number one Yeshiva? And then I thought of Shalom of Belz. One thousand days and nights he studied both revealed and Kabbalistic Torah. His Yeshiva, only one student, himself. For three years after his marriage, this was the number one Yeshiva.

And the holy Ari's teaching the very books Shalom of Belz studied from, were they not his Yeshiva and weren't they number one? Suddenly I had crossed the threshold of my father-in-law's house. I could hear Reb Rheinhold's footsteps and the words he had told me when he lay his hands upon me and gave me Smicha, The words of Pinchas of Koretz suddenly appeared before my eyes: *"Said the Koretzer, G-d and prayer are one. G-d and truth are one. G-d, Israel and Torah are one."*

Then I saw my father-in-law, and he smiled and said "Reb Tuviah, I don't know why you have come but I am as happy to see you, for you look happy to be here. With the Blessed Holy One, we are all one."

"Why make Elihu Yale Folder One?" Hamilton had asked.

"Maybe this will go all the way to the top and if HE, HEnry, HENRY LUCE, sees it, we can live off this for three years. All we need are HIS initials on the margins of our proposal," Fisher had replied.

It was already two in the morning. Fisher knew without looking at his clock. "All we need are his initials," Fisher kept mumbling to himself, as if in prayer. Over and over as he typed. Without looking at his watch which was turned over face down. His old Yale trick, only turn it over when you're ten minutes and one big idea away from finishing.

Fisher typed on, mouthing the words, "All we need are HIS initials. Or is it initial? Or is it?"

■ ALFRED BINGHAM, son of Hiram Bingham III the biographer of Yale: Yale…number one—*"When I first heard about G-d, I could make no clear distinction between G-d and my father. A higher power that both punished and loved that was clearly my father. He was immensely tall, not only compared to me but, at six feet four inches, compared to everybody else as well. He was to be feared but also to be admired and glorified.*

"Father was absent for months at a time in my childhood, exploring in Peru and the threat 'wait till Father comes home and hears about this' seems to have been common when I misbehaved. And then in 1924 on Elm Street at Yale. Had I become my father? G-d to the "little shoe-shine boys from New Haven's slums…each had a box for the tools of his trade with a footrest on top and if he snared a customer, he would get down on his knees and proceed with a flourish to clean and polish one shoe at a time…to have a little boy with unwashed hands and face go down on his knees before me so discomforted me that I seldom become a patron." But I had become number one. For Father had become number one. Hiram Bingham III; missionary's son from Hawaii, scholarship student to Yale, discoverer of Machu Picchu the Inca heavenly city, husband to Alfreda Mitchell, the Tiffany fortune heiress, newly elected Senator from Connecticut.

Almost G-ds, we were—myself, my father, the future biographer of Elihu Yale himself, and Yale's loyal sons and daughters.

■ ELIHU YALE: Number one—To be the first. Not primo inter pares. But to be the first. To be the first in Mother's eyes. And how to do that? I, in India and she across the waters in Wales. Or dead. Or both. For who in Wales was not dead? Not that we were alive in Madras. From the moment my feet touched the sands on the beach, walking towards the Fort, devilish hot, hotter than Purgatory. Why did I come to the port? To be the first. The first among the writers at the East India Company.

The first to be noticed by Mrs. Hynmers. Her husband was "the second" under Sir William Langhorn. And with their two children sitting five rows in front of me in a pew of St. Mary's, directly to the left of Sir William. Mrs. Hynmers' eyes searching for mine as she left the church, moving from mine to Sir William's. I understood immediately to be one in Madras, I had to become the second Mr. Hynmers. The Good Lord took Joseph Hynmers, took him though he had given 32 pounds, one third of his yearly salary, to build St. Mary, took him though he had two babes, took him to His bosom and Catherine took me to hers. I became a second, soon to become number one but only in Madras.

■ HIRAM BINGHAM, Yale biographer, discoverer of Machu Picchu: Elihu Yale—Oh how he wanted to be number one in Madras. In Queen's Square, London. On earth and ever after. His mountainous ambition pierced through the white paper documents I navigated through month after month and year after year in the India office in London.

His life: my Machu Picchu waiting to be rediscovered. Understood. Fathomed. Ordered. Perhaps, just perhaps to relive my own but not to record my own for my son would do that or some other son or daughter. But to be number one, that was the key. It was the only way to find an eternity of peace. To be unassailable.

Penniless, but not G-dless, understood. You needn't be a missionary's son to fathom it. No, to be number one. To have all look up to you. Your wife, your Mother (which is more difficult), your children, your friends, the readers of your obituary. Elihu Yale, going to India as a writer, a lad of twenty-one, penniless but not G-dless. Of course he knew that John Harvard sailed on the same boat as his father to America in 1637. And that his father, David, and John Harvard had landed in Boston on June 26, 1637. And that Harvard's name was known, now and forever because of his fortune. Elihu Yale dreamed of becoming number one. Do not we all?

Fort St. George (Madras) at the time of Elihu Yale.

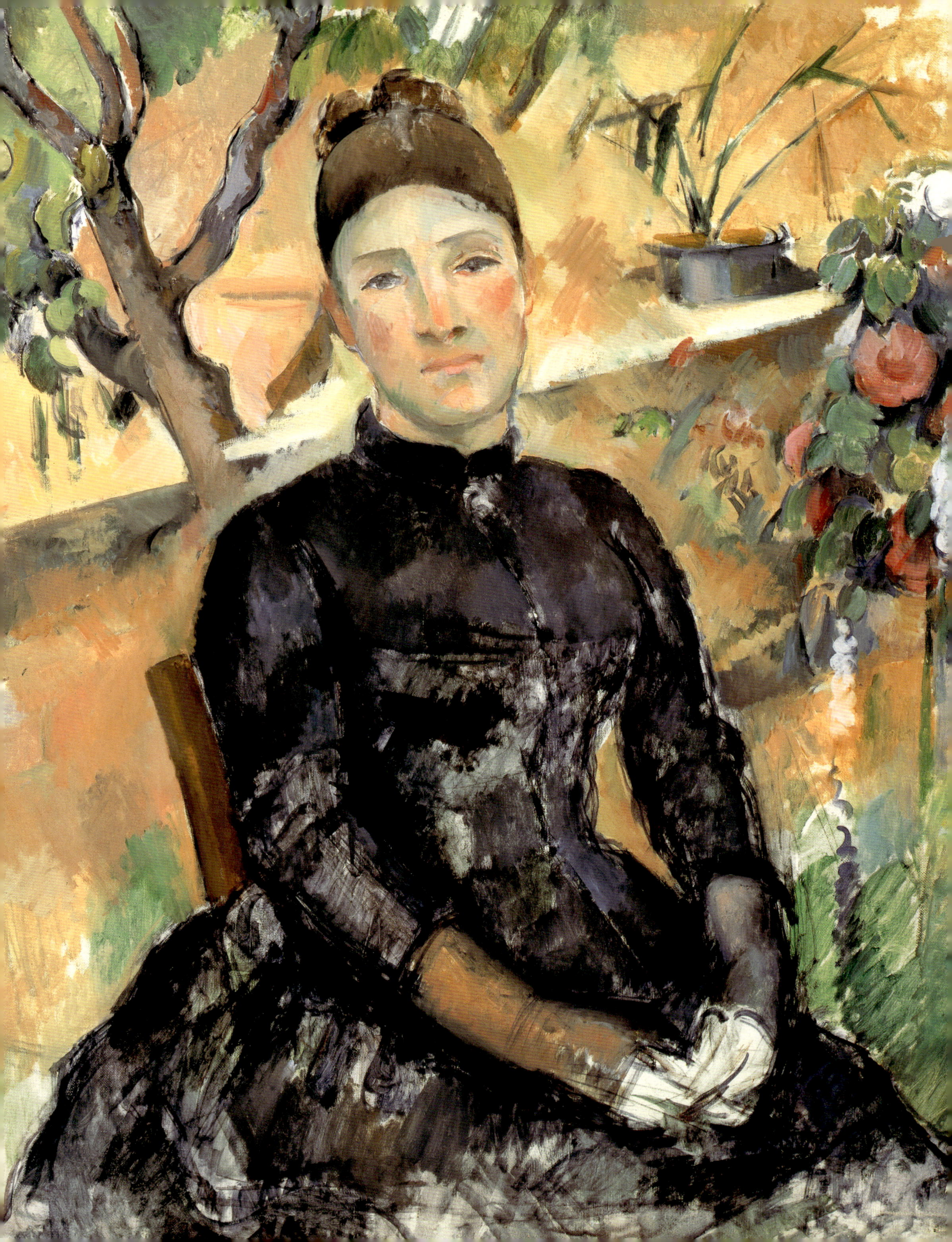

■ LAURENCE STERNE: What is love? Does it last?—Brave lad, to pose the question. Rude of the lad to change the subject. What is love anyway? "*For to say a man is fallen in love or that he is deeply in love or up to his ears in love and sometimes even over head and ears in it, carries an idiomatical kind of implication that love is a thing below man— that is recurring again to Plato's opinion, which, with all his divinityship, I hold damnable and heretical and so much for that. Let love therefore be what it will, my Uncle Toby fell into it.*"

This young Fisher doesn't know how deeply he is in love but seeks to measure another man's love, the love of an Indian trader, Elihu Yale, no less, or an Indian Potentate, Shah Jahan, no less: Blind elephants leading each other in circles of love.

■ MOZART'S MOTHER: Will love last?—"*We lead a most delightful life. Up early, late to bed and visitors all day long. We live like the children of princes until the hangman comes to haul us away.*"

■ JAMES AGEE: Staggered toward the men's room…green—I staggered toward the men's room…cut to the present: Fisher staggered towards the men's room. Of course, he's writing by night. All night. The deadline of his life coming up. Time's deadline. Charming, really if it weren't so predictable. Generation upon generation. He's changing his folders from Blue to Green. Perfect really. Even for a Yale man. Oh they made fine blue doppelgangers all of them.

Luce and Hadden; Luce and MacLeish; Luce and Hersey. All those old blues. And will it be HIMSELF, himself and the young lad, Fisher? G-d help them all and suffer them not to come into…Into the elevator I strode. I had been told that Luce HIMSELF did not relish the way I looked. Different. From eveyone. Not Old Blue enough. Lord knows why he expected me to crimson when I received his memo on the subject: "Watch it" into the elevator I strode.

Wearing a Times Square purchase: "*A little rolled brim hat. Strange people would wear them. A green feather was in it.*" I rode up and down the elevator. Time of My Life. Fisher's changing. Bless him. Blue to green.

Fisher yawned. He staggered toward the men's room, more lit by the moon washing across Sixth Avenue and 49th Street than by the dim Time-Life overhead late night lights.

Weaving back to his desk, Fisher looked at the folders, changing Folder Two to Blue and Green. And adding cryptically to Chapters 9 and 10:

What is love? What is its taste? Does it last? What is power? Does it last longer?

Must be past three, almost three fifteen. I'll lay my head down for my patented seven minute nap and wrap this baby up, thought Fisher. Even Hamilton was envious of how, in their senior year at Yale, Fisher could doze for seven minutes and then awaken in mid-sentence and finish a convoluted New Criticism paper for Prof. Wimsatt. Fisher pushed aside the photos on his desk and laid his head down wearily.

■ JUDAH HALEVI: Taste—
"*My heart is in the East
And I am at the edge of the West!*

*Then how can I taste what I eat,
How can I enjoy it.
How can I fulfill my vows and pledges
While Zion is in the domain of Edom,
And I am in the bonds of Arabia?*

*It would be easy for me
To leave behind all the good things of Spain;
It would be glorious
To see the dust of the ruined shrine.*"

◆ CHAYA BAS REB ABISH RHEINHOLD, FISHER'S GRANDMOTHER: Does it last— And I growing blind by the minute. By the week. By the month. And my husband, Reb Tuviah, closeted with my father, his teacher, Reb Abish. I can hear their voices in the library. I can hear the sobbing of my father *Gotse Helfen*. G-d will provide, G-d will help. I can see into the room, beyond the closed library door. Even though I cannot see the door anymore, I can see my husband, the father of our nine children, looking at my father's tears. I am trembling. Will Tuviah's love for me last? For I cannot see his face clearly anymore. And does an unseeable love exist? Is not love like a mirror? Reflecting back what one receives? Tuviah has come out of the library study, and my father has left to his house across the garden path.

Tuviah is holding my hand and quoting to himself, "*And Jacob served seven years for Rachel and they seemed to him but a few days for the love had to her.*" How many times did Tuviah take my hand and hold it and sing to me Jacob's song. Tuviah was my Jacob and, praise G-d, I could always see I was his everlasting Rachel.

■ CÉZANNE: What is love, does it last?— Hortense Fiquet, Mon petit chou chou, my little cabbage. A model in Paris. My love. My secret. Don't mention her name in any correspondence to Jas de Bouffan for my father will open my mail and father is not to know of Hortense.

Of course Marie, my sister, was the first to discover my "petite secrète" as she called Hortense when she didn't call her "dumpling."

Father found out soon enough. 'Your so-called love will never last," he thundered. Even after we married, Hortense and I, in April 1886, our son Paul already fourteen years old, still father thundered, "Your love will never last." He thundered on, straight to his deathbed in October '86. The pears I painted lasted a week, perhaps a day longer, but my love for Hortense lasted my life.

And Hortense's love for me? My sister Marie sent a telegram addressed to our son Paul, telling him to come quickly for I was dying, could not last more than two days, but Hortense hid the telegram from Paul. Why should she have to cancel a dress fitting? My love, our love, her love. Did it last? For how long? But my painting of our love, of her love for me, will last for…

Paul Cézanne, *Madame Cézanne*.

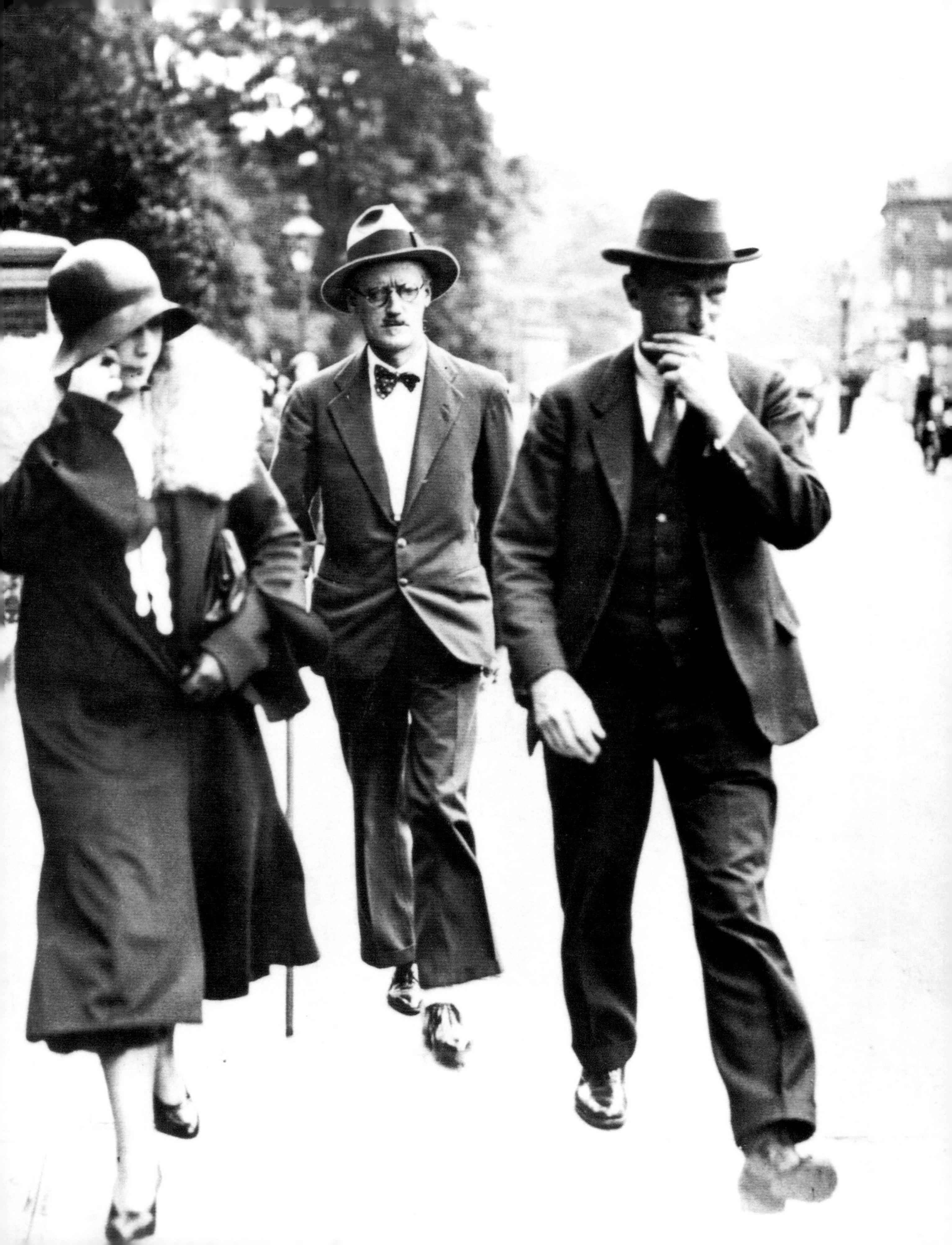

■ LEON DE MODENA: The Rialto Bridge—"*In the month of Heshvan 5369 (Sept. 1608), I moved into the Ghetto Nuova, on the ground floor of the house belonging to Zanvil of Udine. May G-d, his rock protect him and grant him long life. There I had many pupils throughout the winter. But I did what the angel messengers said to Sarah in answer to her denial.*" Isaac but you did laugh, tzehok, which I translated for my students as "sahak" playing games of chance. And so did I laugh and play games of chance "*until my behavior became so wild that I agreed to go and live away from Venice.*"

This young Fisher is me. Rooted in his youth and dreaming of flying towards the Rialto Bridge. My wife and I settling in Florence. Safe from the bandits who robbed me nightly of my teacher's wages. But the night air. We could sleep and not dream. Could we dream of anything other than the Rialto?

"*The air bothered my eyes and my wife's and we constantly longed for and yearned to return to Venice. Finally, after Passover (April 15, 1610) almost exactly one year to the day since my arrival in Florence, I departed and came back to Venice.*"

■ RABBI NOSUN: The whole story—My master had paused. As though he had lost the way. He closed his eyes and it seemed for an instant that he was asleep. But suddenly he continued loudly:

"*Then, when he awoke, he asked the servant, 'Where am I in the world?' The servant told him the whole story: 'You have been sleeping for many years. I kept myself alive by eating the fruit.'*

He was grief-stricken and went back to the king's daughter. She was in great sorrow and said, 'Because of one day, because you could not restrain yourself for one day and you ate the apple, you have lost everything. Had you come on that day, you would have taken me out of here. True, it is difficult not to eat, especially on the last day, when the evil impulse is so strong. Go, therefore, and choose yourself another place and remain there for a year. On the last day you may eat, but you must not slumber; and you must drink no wine, lest you fall asleep. The main thing is sleep.'

He went away and did what she said. On the last day, he returned to her. On the way he saw a flowing spring. It was red, and its smell was the smell of wine. He said to his servant, 'Look, there is a spring, and water should be flowing from it, but it is red, and its smell is the smell of wine.' And he went and tasted a little of the spring, and immediately he fell down and slept for seventy years."

Nora and James Joyce on their wedding day.

Visions of Harkness Towers with green moss rising on the brownish-red facade. A High Street bird flying towards the Rialto Bridge, crossing into the Art Gallery.

A hand tapped Fisher's shoulder, rocked him back and forth. Back and...

"Who are you, Fisher or Hamilton?" said the voice, which seemed to emanate from the thickest eyebrows Raphael had ever seen.

"Fisher or Hamilton?" the voice persisted. A man, perhaps sixty—perhaps seventy or perhaps eighty wore the darkest blue suit imaginable with a jet black tie. He had cold, unyielding eyes. His shirt's starched white collar was as hard as marble. In his right hand he held the photograph of Fisher's Rabbinic grandfather as a schoolmaster, pointing at a truant lower former.

"Who are you, Fisher or Hamilton? Tell me the whole story," he persisted in a stentorian form.

■ THE SEER OF LUBLIN: A hand tapping his shoulder—"*The holy Ari Rabbi Isaac Luria had two chief merits: he made plain and translucent the mysteries of the Zohar and he placed rejoicing foremost in the ways to serve G-d.*" And thus was the Ari awoken each night, with Elijah's hand tapping his shoulder, and Elijah's voice gently whispering, whispering Torah so softly in his ear that he did not awaken. And here Fisher is being asked, Who are you? Are you yourself or someone else? And so too are we all being asked each night by ourselves, often not softly, Who are we?

■ JAMES JOYCE: Rialto—"*We calls him the journey all Buggaloffs since he went Jerusalemfaring in Arissia Manor.*" "*He first got rid of a few mitsmillers and hurooshoos and levanted off…to keep some crow-plucking with some rival Rialtos anywheres between Pearidge and the littlehorn.*" Both journeying towards each other. Fisher swimming downstream. Hamilton on the Scottish high road. Tweedledee-dee and Tweedledee-dumb. Bloom more dedalus than alive. But Mother of Mary. Those deepset eyes will bring back Raphael all the way from Metatron's secretarial desk.

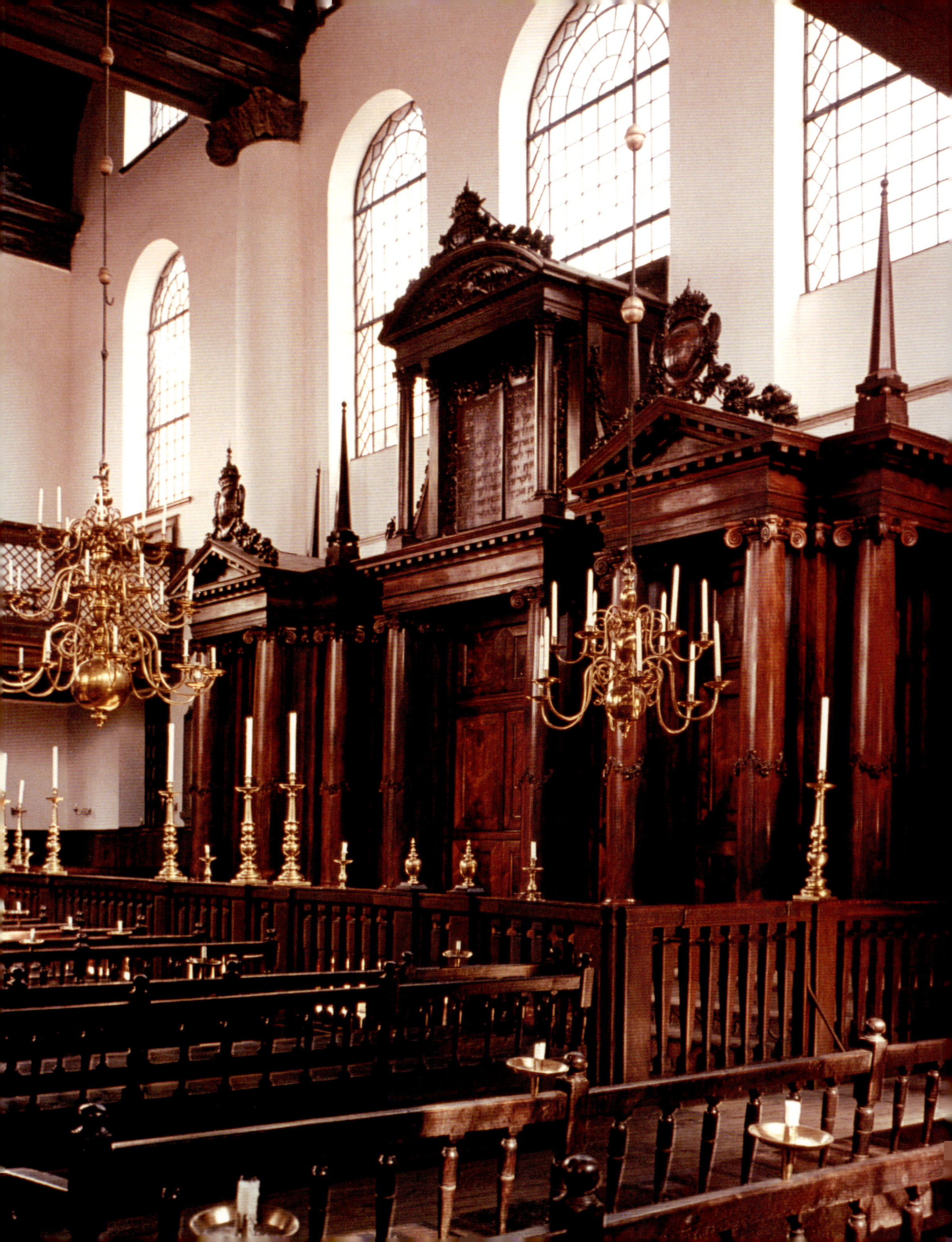

■ Rabbi Abba on the Zohar I: Raphael—"*Raphael is charged to heal the earth and through him...the earth furnishes an abode for man.*"

■ Clare Boothe Luce: Are you—"*Kindly fill out and return, I wrote to Henry. A Domestic Questionnaire with room for his answers.*

Question: Are you one to leave a party at eleven because you have to rise early and allow your mate to remain if she is enjoying herself?

Answer: Yes.

Question: Do you abhor twin beds?

Answer: Yes.

Question: Are you one to refrain from converting a wife or reforming her?

Answer: Yes.

Question: And will you insist she do the same?

Answer: No. I perceive I have spent a good part of my life reforming and/or educating others and I have a passion to feel how it feels.

Question: If your lady suddenly takes it into her head to elope with a belted earl or an Egyptologist, are you one to pursue her with a poker face and knock her gently on the head and nurse her tenderly until she comes to her senses?

Answer: Am not quite so dumb to answer this one. Let the lady take her own chance of being left by her G-ddamned earl.

Yes, Henry is asking the questions here. And yes this young man is answering. And yes Henry said yes to me. But if Henry doesn't like the answer or the question the young man poses, he'll leave before the young man finishes a declarative sentence."

■ Vilna Gaon: Could it be him—HIM. HE. This is Fisher's king. Will he too, even he, not die? "*We read on Passover: And we cried out unto Hashem the G-d of our fathers.*" As it is said, "*During those many days, the king of Egypt died, and the children of Israel sighed because of the labor and cried out, and their moaning rose up to G-d from their labor.*" "*As long as the king of Egypt was alive, the children of Israel were enslaved by him alone. Once he died, all of the Egyptians began to enslave them. First they sighed, a personal private response to their new situation. Then they cried out.*"

Fisher sighs now. Soon he will cry out.

"Put down that picture. It's a family heirloom," said Fisher, agitated. Could it be HIM, Fisher wondered.

"Then you're Fisher," said the patriarchal figure. "I've taken the liberty of looking at your draft suggestions and..."

"And who are you?" Fisher shot back, thinking he best be on the offensive.

The old man was unfazed. He carefully picked up the volume of *J.B.* and looked at the inscription of Archibald Macleish, scanning the fly leaf in a distant manner.

Archibald Macleish's inscription was written with curlicue Founding Father penmanship. The man's eyes peered at the bookseller's penciled notation: Rare. Why not rarissimo? Seller's puffery. But I suppose Archy was quite rare. As rare as a Patriarch.

■ Archibald MacLeish: Who are you?—I would ask Henry and he would never answer. "*After the great war, in 1919, I returned to Henry Seidel Canby's Yale class and there was Henry sitting next to Briton Hadden. And Stephen Vincent Benet on Henry's left: Hadden and Benet reading aloud from their poems. Hadden from memory and Benet from his already published book. Class after class. I looked at Henry and asked who are you? He neither answered nor replied in 1923 but wrote me a check for my part-time work at Time Inc. and because he knew I had one child and certainly would abandon neither child nor Muse.*

Nor in 1932 when he said to me 'Well, then you can work for Fortune as much of the time as you need to pay your bills and take the rest of the time off for poetry.'

Henry really thought that there was nothing he could not do so he often did it."

Perhaps he was a man who simply went around asking other people who they were, hoping to glimpse a clue of himself.

■ Briton Hadden: And who are you?—"And who are you?" I said to Henry Luce. He just stared at me open-mouthed with that look I had come to know in New Haven. Open-mouthed when I had approached him blindsided as he crossed High Street, passing just under the Rialto bridge entrance to the Art School. "And who are you," I persisted, walking directly along his left. It was a hot, stuffy New Haven June day in 1926 and Henry was to be rewarded with an honorary Master of Arts degree from Yale. But Henry did not look hot. Of course he looked stuffy but he always looked stuffy. He said cooly, "Briton, I can well appreciate you're hurt that Yale has not chosen to honor you with a Master of Art degree and has chosen me to…"

"And who are you?" I repeated, riveting my eyes on his eyes. I knew his tricks for he had learned them from me.

"I am not you, Briton. This is evident. Last week we spoke of our $8,541 profit for this year. We have agreed to each take $10,000 in salary. I am willing to recommend that…"

"But who are you Henry?" I persisted. And Henry grew silent. And I could see his father's face in front of him, thundering "I am the Lord thy G-d. I am who I am becoming."

"Yes, that's who you are, Henry, exactly who you are." I stormed off, never for an instant again to think of him as a friend and most certainly never to let him forget who I was—the founder and partner of Time Inc.

■ James Agee: Who are you?—Henry would mumble at me, standing over me, towering over me.

Nervously fingering a bottle of whiskey, I always kept an eye on the elevator. I always had a bottle pasted with a blue Tiffany engraved invitation with the initials H.R.L., ever ready for Henry's surprise visit.

"Who are you?" Henry would ask me, warily eyeing my Benzedrine tablets. And half-smiling at his Tiffany initials on the Jack Daniells bottle. With his stammer, Luce would repeat first, "How are you? How are you?" And then, "Who are you? Who are you?"

Then he'd leaf through my work, reading aloud his corrections more to himself than to me. And I would say, "Henry I'll be happy to tell you who I am if you'll just sit down and pour me a drink from your bottle." I'd push the bottle towards him. "Jim, let's go to a movie," he'd say.

Afterward his idea of socializing was Child's restaurant. He'd push the bottle toward me with the deftness of a card shark at three in the morning. Just like they do in those Hazard, Kentucky all night poker palaces. And I'd go to the movies with Henry, and have a midnight meal and walk all night down to the Village with him. But I'd never tell him who I was because, after all, he was always the dealer, wasn't he?

Hechal (Holy Ark), the Sephardi Synagogue of Amsterdam.

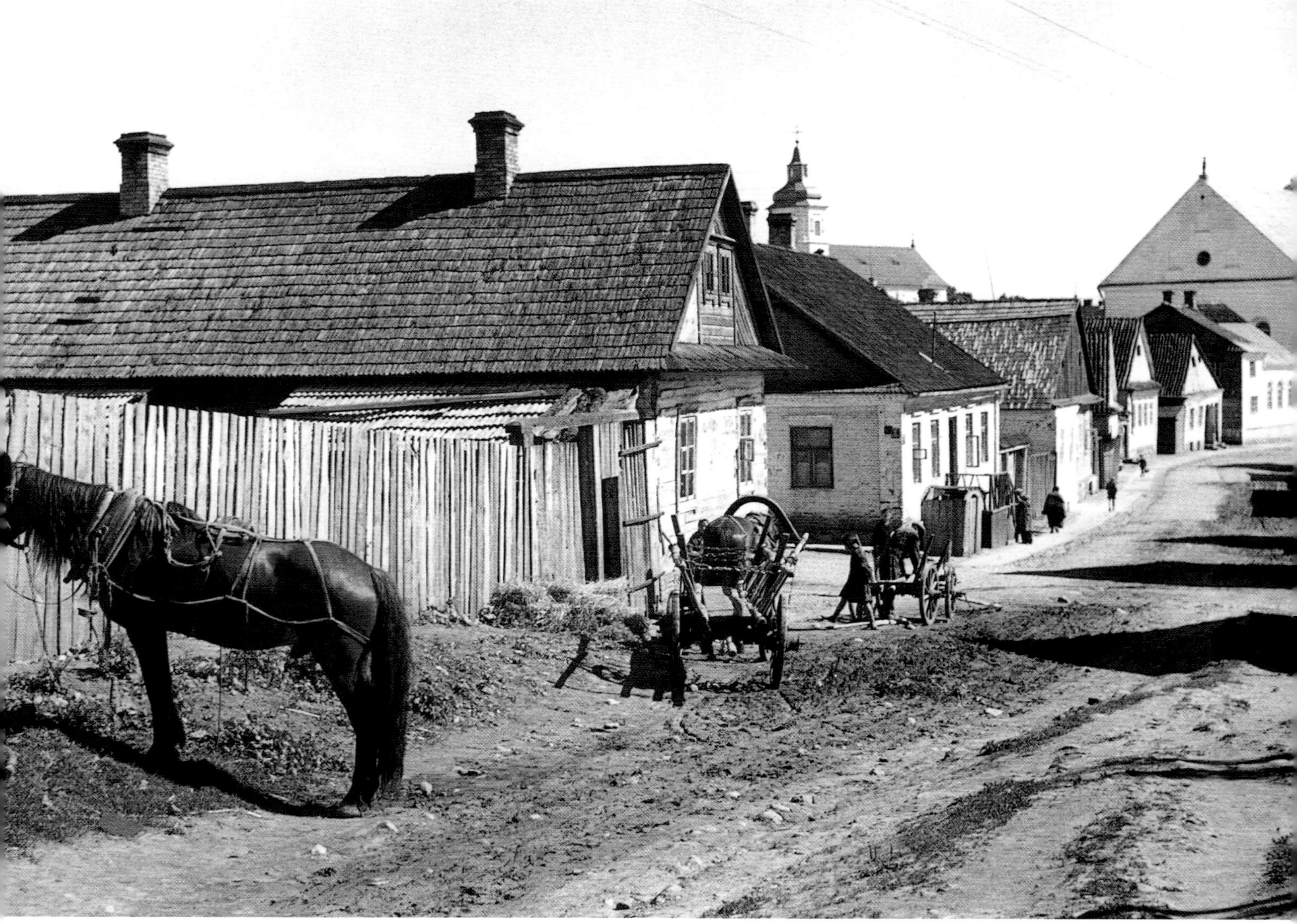

● TUVIAH GUTMAN GUTWIRTH, FISHER'S MATERNAL GRANDFATHER: He was my grandfather—He. Was. My grandfather. He is my grandfather, my grandson, Fisher is saying. I can remember it as if it were yesterday. When I was a boy of thirteen, ascending to the Torah in Riglitz outside the synagogue, my father stopped before we went in and spoke to me.

"Tuviah, my earthly treasure, when you go up to Heaven, what will be asked of you? The Heavenly One will ask you who are you and I give you my blessing that you are your grandfather, the Gaon Moreinu Rav Kalman the Kohen, judge of our scattered people in Cracow, huddled in Cracow, in Tarnov even in your village Riglitz." Father held onto my shoulder, unsure whether to go into the synagogue or not, to continue talking or be silent.

I felt the pull of people waiting inside the synagogue, but I also felt an incredible gentleness on my other shoulder.

"But Father I am your child and Yittel's child and is that not enough for me?" Father laughed and said, "And what am I but a Rav in Riglitz and what is Riglitz but a town where if all the Jews were to get married one day and if all the Jews here were to get called to the Torah for their Bar Mitzvah and G-d forbid, all of our town's Jews died on that same day, still I could not make a living."

"And what of my mother, Yittel?" Father froze, for Ittel was his whole world.

He said, "You are a blessing to me. With my grandfather's grandfather's blessing, I bless you. With the blessing of my grandfather Rav Zevi, the blessing of his grandfather Gaon Moreinu Raphael the Kohen of Bobov, receive all these blessings I bestow on you."

■ ARYEH YEHUDAH LEIB KATZ of Jerusalem (1658-1720), ancestor of Rav Tuviah Gutman Gutwirth, the grandfather of Fisher: my grandfather—My father, Ephraim ben Jacob, didn't speak much. Night after night my nephew Aaron and I would study his handwritten papers. *"It involved much trouble because of the confusing handwriting and the loss of many pages."*

My father Ephraim, the light of my exile, he didn't speak much of himself. But he did speak of his grandfather the Gaon Moreinu Ephraim the Kohen of Jerusalem, the head of the rabbinical court in Jerusalem may it be rebuilt and established in our day. My father did speak of his Jerusalem of the Exile, Vilna, and he wept. He hinted of my mother's father, my kabbalist grandfather, Reb Eliyahu Baal Shem of Chelm who created a golem and who saved Israel in a time of trouble, may his merit protect us and all of Israel.

At the end of my father's life, he was invited back to Jerusalem to be the Rabbinic head of all the Ashkenazim in Jerusalem, a post his grandfather, Ephraim Ha Cohen, had held. It was not to be the will of G-d and my saintly father passed away on 13 Sivan 5438, 1678. And I, could I be my father? And what gave me the strength to try? For I could not refuse to attempt to bring his writings to light. Only the memory of his work spoken and unspoken gave me the courage. I am my grandfather and my grandfather's father. When I had to leave the holy city of Jerusalem, when I returned to Prague a year later, could I forget my father's Jerusalem? And praised be to my grandfather Eliyahu the Baal Shem who said to me, "You will voyage to Jerusalem and you will voyage back. But when you return, you will go to Safed. You will end your earthly voyage in Safed and from there you will never be separated from the land of our forefathers. And Safed became my eternal Jerusalem."

Jewish Street, Slonim, Poland.

"Who am I?" said the man, slowly putting down the photograph with a gentleness that surprised Fisher.

"Who am I? A colleague of...of theirs," the man said, pointing at Agee's book.

"Excuse me for a moment," he continued. And just as Fisher rubbed his eyes in disbelief, the old man returned with a worn wooden chair trailing behind him with a grace that belied his age. He sat directly opposite Fisher.

"You mentioned family. You mentioned heirloom. Which is it Fisher, family or heirloom?"

"Both," said Fisher firmly.

"How family?"

"He was my grandfather." Fisher could feel the perspiration on the back of his neck. The inquisitor's eyes had not left his. He noticed the fingers of the man's left hand slowly moving, almost as though he were transcribing his words in some midnight star chamber.

● YITTEL, FISHER'S GREAT GRANDMOTHER AND THE WIFE OF YEKUSIEL ZALMAN THE KOHEN GUTWIRTH: Grandfather—My saintly father was the head of the Rabbinical court of the community of Riglitz. And my father invited us to live with him in Riglitz. To study with him in Riglitz. But Riglitz was tiny. Riglitz could fit in the suit pocket of Tarnov just as Tarnov could fit in the suit pocket of Cracow. My dear Zalman, my bridegroom for a month. He never mentioned any of his inclinations to move to his father, the dayan of Cracow, So I knew as sure as that G-d would provide for us, that Zalman's thoughts were never far from him. How could I know, as he never for a minute mentioned it to me.

And Praise be to G-d that in the middle of one night, in a dream wrapped in a dream, a month to the day after we were wed, G-d brought the answer to me. "Ask Zalman to speak of me," said the wife of Raphael Gutwirth the Kohen of Bobov. Ask Zalman to speak of me and ZuZan Git. It will be good."

Immediately, I awoke my husband and said, "I want to talk of Riglitz." Zalman held me and said gently, "Yittel can't it wait until morning." And I said with the same gentleness, "Speak to me of your grandfather's grandfather. And speak to me of his wife." It was dark outside our room. Very dark. But as the Lord is my protector, I could see Zalman's eyes.

His grandfather's grandfather's wife was the daughter of Rav Moreinu Rav Yakov of Bobov, a holy woman, a *Tzaddekis*. A woman whose name in Bobov alone was uttered as a blessing. "But why do you ask," whispered my husband. And in truth I didn't know what I was asking so I said nothing. Suddenly, Zalman was pacing around the room. "Oy guttenyu, G-d has sent you to me. Of course Raphael went to Bobov and left Cracow. And became the head of the Rabbinical court in Bobov. Of course I will leave Cracow and go together with you to Riglitz. What am I but my grandfather's grandfather and what are you but my entire house, my world, my entire blessing. As it is written in Bava Metziah, 'Whatever blessing dwells in the house comes from one's wife.'"

And never, ever, did Zalman mention Cracow after we moved our house in Riglitz.

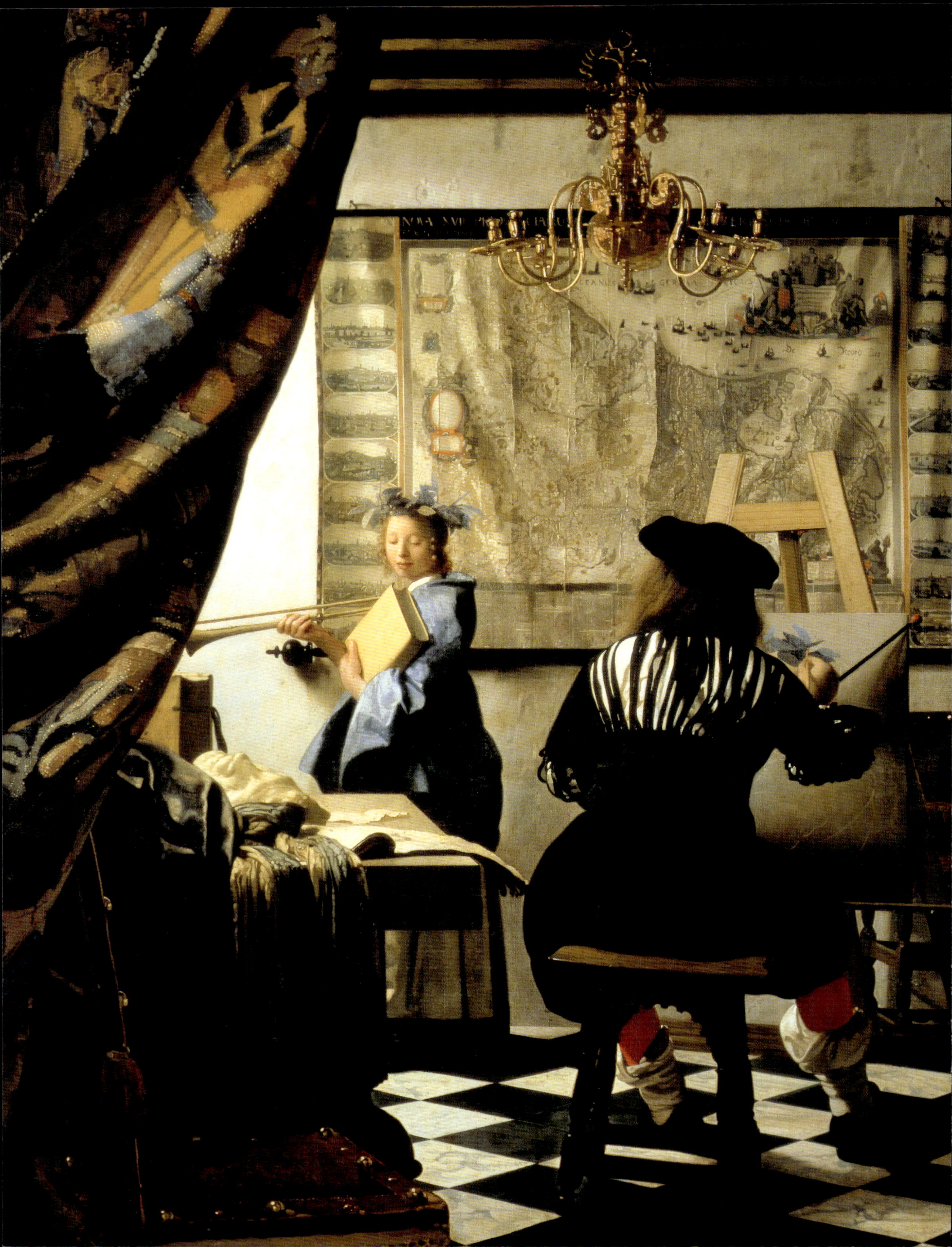

■ VERMEER: I've never seen the face—They will never see my face. Never. And she will never see my face. And I will never see Morika's eyes. I will paint her as Fama and make her famous. And I will paint her as Cleo and keep her lovely for all history.

But she calls to me softly. No one in the house can hear her. "Johannes. You are not painting me, you are painting yourself." I plead with her to be still. For my hand is trembling and even my Mahlstick cannot steady me. Am I painting? Or am I painting myself not painting? For I am really painting only Cleo's crown. And certainly not Cleo or Morika. And certainly, most certainly, she can see me though her eyes are closed.

She says to me, "Johannes, why will you not let me wear the pearl earring you gave me last month?" My Mahlstick is shaking so violently I fear my canvas will topple over, and I with it. And the curtain will fall and we will be together at last, my Morika and I. She whispers to me, "Johannes, I am tired. Tired of posing. Tired of holding this heavy book. Of holding your trumpet. Johannes, draw the curtain and light the lights and let me look upon your face, the face I've never seen."

■ KAY GLENN, in charge of Howard Hughes' personal staff: Just the highlights…I've never seen the face—If I had a dollar, just one dollar for every time anyone asked me in the 1960s about Hughes. "Oh, Kay, Hughes is the richest man in the world and you can see his face. What's it like? It must be fascinating. I know it's a super secret: tell me just the highlights. One day I just exploded. I'll tell you about yesterday. Friday, December 17. All about Howard.

12:10 Chair
1:20 Screening "Wrecking Room"
2:15 Bathroom
2:45 Chair
3:25 Chicken and dessert
5:20 Finished food.
5:25 Bathroom
5:45 Bed and asleep
7:50 Bathroom and shower
8:35 Chair
9:00 Screening "Arabesque"
10:15 Bathroom
10:40 Chair, 8 Codeine tablets 23 left
11:30 Chicken
1:00 Bathroom
1:20 Chair. "Arabesque" Reel 3
2:50 Bathroom
3:25 Chair
5:00 Bathroom. Call Gordon
5:50 Chair. Resume screening "Deadlier than Male"
6:40 Food. Chicken only.
7:35 Finished eating.
8:00 Bathroom.
8:20 Chair. Screening "Daring Game."
9:45 "Daring Game"
10:15 Chair. Resumed screening "Daring Game" reels 1 and 2.
11:10 Bathroom
11:45 Chair. Screening film "Tension at Table Rock."

So much for the highlights of the day in the life of the richest and most fascinating man in the Western world.

"And how is this an heirloom?" The man's eyebrows virtually superimposed themselves, hanging onto Fisher's eyes.

"Are you Mr. Luce?" Fisher stammered.

"Do you want me to be?" answered the gentleman, putting his right hand inside his buttoned vest to hide the fingers still moving.

"The photo is an heirloom because of what he means to me and what he meant to others," Fisher answered tentatively.

"If you are his heir, weave me a story on your loom," he commanded. "But make it less than an hour long. Just the highlights."

It must be Luce, thought Fisher. I've never seen the face but the word play is pure Hadden quoted by Luce.

"My grandfather is sitting in a moonlit room," said Fisher. It is not on an upper floor like we are here. And it, my grandfather's room, is never dark, just like here. Or cold and windy. My grandfather is not lonely.

● MENACHEM MENDEL OF RIMINOV to his in-law Zalman Hakohen Gutwirth, Fisher's ancestor, 1810: My grandfather is not lonely—When Reb Zalman, the Kohen, came from Myacznitza with his wife and his daughter before the wedding of my dear son Nosun Leib, he looked me straight in the eye as he crossed the threshold and said, "My wife has a simple question for you."

Before I could even welcome them and offer a chair, she began. "Reb Menahem Mendel, you have the power to bless. You prayed for the emperor Napoleon and he has become a king, a ruler throughout all the lands of our exile. Now Zalman and I are giving your son our most precious Rivka, the daughter of our old age. What blessing do you give us in return?" My gabbai stepped forward with Kvittel paper but I raised my hand immediately. I knew what a shamed Mechutunum in-law would mean.

"I give you and I give all your children's children this blessing: 'If ten Jews come together and converse regarding subjects of the Torah, they feel none of the hardships of the exile. But when they separate, each in his own corner, every individual among them begins to feel the rigor of the exile.' Even in the exile, until the great coming of the Messiah, your children and your children's children throughout all their wanderings will not feel utterly alone.'"

■ JAMES JOYCE TO HARRIET WEAVER, Joyce's publisher. 8 Feb. 1922: Weave me a story on your loom—And by a strange coincidence our name and Penelope, the weaver, the same. And therefore no coincidence. For you are the loom on which I will weave Ulysses. And I asked Weaver—like myself she could not bear being called by her first name by anyone except members of her family—"Did she have a little Irish blood" and she replied, "Joyce, I am afraid I am hopelessly English."

"And what will you write next?" Weaver asked me after she published *Ulysses*. "I think I will write a history of the world," I replied.

■ JACQUES CARTIER: How is this an heirloom—In 1911 when I went to the Durbar in Dehli to mix with all the Princes, Maharajas and Maharanis (if I could only meet them), Nawabs, Gaekwars, court treasurers, in short tout L'Inde. I went with Pierre's words ringing in my ears.

"Look my boy, look. And sketch each night. Whatever jewel you see, we may have something like it in La Maison Cartier." Pierre never said London or Paris or New York. And most certainly he never said, "What you may have" no it was always La Maison Cartier.

Of course I thought in terms of London. I was twenty-five. The London office was mine to run. In '09 I had gotten Louis and Pierre to agree (for once): London was to be in charge of all the trade in India.

Suddenly I had become frightened, what if Louis insisted on going to India—he was already thirty-six, un certain age, but he didn't. He simply said: "When you go, keep your eyes and ears open. Ask of each stone, of every diamond, every emerald, of each Maharajah, ask the same question as you gaze on a jewel: How is this an heirloom?

And for heaven's sake, don't follow Pierre's obsession, how can we sell something, anything, everything—

They can read your mind in India. Ask every Maharajah, Nawab, Nizam, each court treasurer, every gem cutter. How is this an heirloom? They all have bits and pieces of the most magnificent tale."

Johannes Vermeer, *The Art of Painting*.

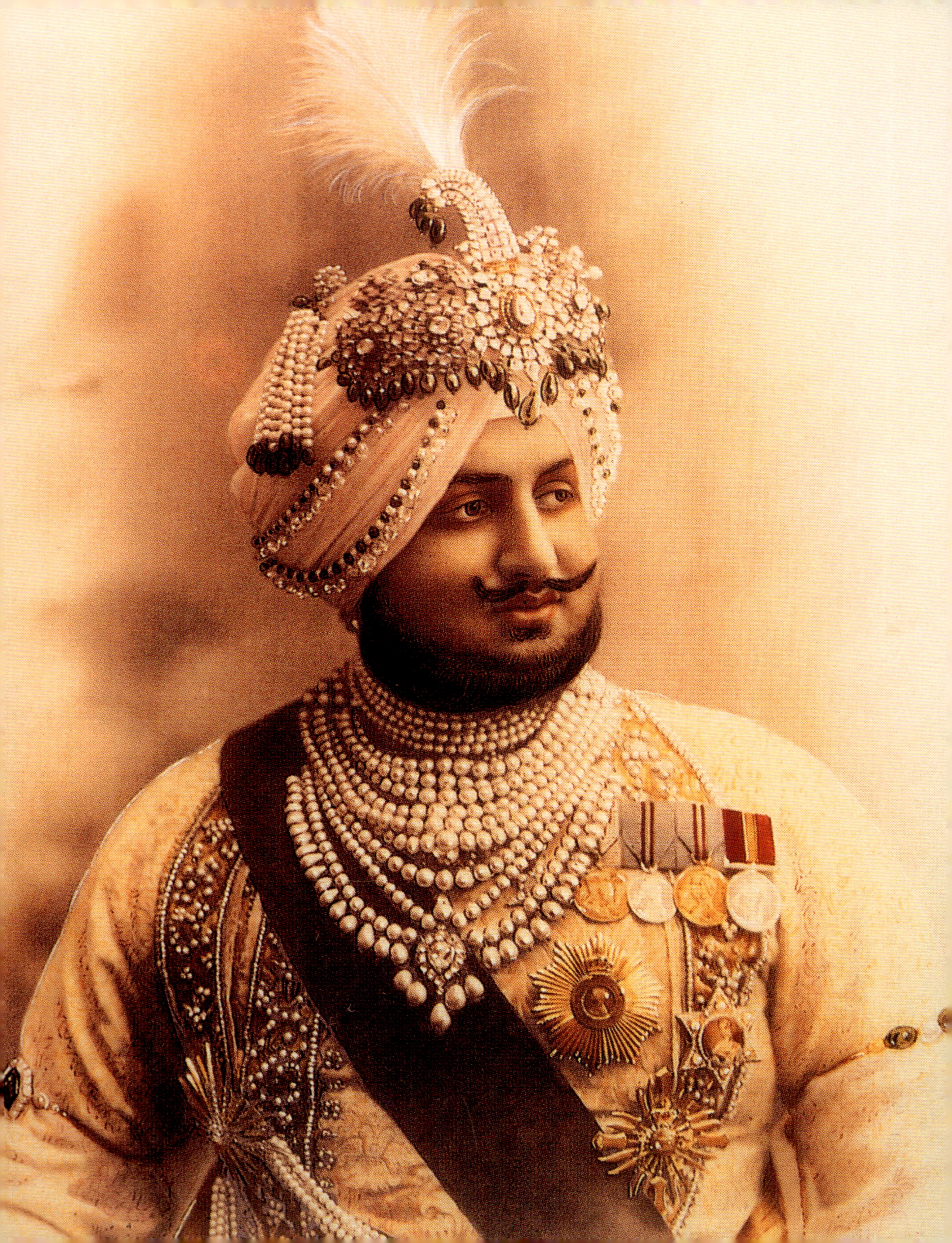

◆ KALMAN KATZ BEN ZALMAN GUTWIRTH, Fisher's grandfather's grandfather: Rabbi Judah of India was fond of narrating fairy tales—My blessed father Zalman told me when he came to page 74 of tractate Bava Batra that his father would whisper to my father: "Where is India?"

And to me who knew of blessed Jerusalem, the Jerusalem of my ancestor, the Shaar Ephraim and the Jerusalem of his grandfather Ephraim Katz, who knew of Safed where Aryeh Judah Leib ben Ephraim Hakohen, the Sha'ar Ephraim's son was buried. Jerusalem and Safed seemed beyond the ends of the world.

Or else why did the Messiah have to come to lead us there: destinations so distant only a heavenly guide could bring us there. But India, India was even farther away. Even farther from Cracow than heavenly Jerusalem. Perhaps India did not exist. It itself was a fairy tale land.

But the page of the Talmud states clearly: Rabbi Judah of India: And in the sea of the Talmud, whatever swims is true for all time, for Israel will forever fish there for wisdom.

I simply shrugged my shoulders and waited for my father to enlighten me just as I am sure my great great grandfather Judah Leib waited for his father Ephraim Katz to enlighten him.

Of one thing I was sure. From the way my father leaned forward to me and whispered to me this very same question "Where is India" This query had been passed from generation to generation. Who knows from how far back, a Yihhus Brief of questioning. Always remember that the Yihhus Brief of Ephraim Katz of Jerusalem, the Sha'ar Ephraim, show our family's lineage back to Aaron the High Priest.

Generations of Rabbis in Vilna, Jerusalem, Prague, Riglitz, Ofen, Buda, Bobov, asking of India.

"Look," said my father. Out the window. I could see the mountains. "Look beyond those mountains and imagine an ocean and beyond that ocean another ocean and there is India. We know of this far away ocean through our ocean of the Talmud. We fish here. We feed on stories. And if G-d forbid we lose our skill in fishing, we will surely perish.

But G-d has in his mercy, in his belovedness, in all countries and in all generations, in our family, opened our hearts to this page: The ocean of India is far far away but here it is before us."

And he began in a sweet voice to chant. Rabbi Judah of India was fond of narrating fairy tales. And my father's tongue lingered over the word India with a sweetness that has never left me.

His desk is covered with papers, just like mine. The papers are in Hebrew and Aramaic. They are old. Dream laden. Hidden. Cursive. Pages upon pages. And they form a frame for a solitary book which my grandfather has opened. It is many pages, long and narrow. The story, or the core, if you will, is on the inside and the explanation, or the commentary, on the outside of the book is called..."

"The Talmud!" cried the elderly man. "Do not take me for a fool. I am an heir too, and I have heirlooms as well."

"Excuse me. You're correct. It is the Talmud and it is opened to page 74 of the Tractate Bava Batra. My grandfather reads: "Rabbi Judah of India was fond of narrating fairy tales."

■ BABUR, 1483-1530: India—*"India (Hindustan) is a wonderful country. Compared with all other countries, it is a different world. Its mountains, rivers, jungles and deserts, its towns, its cultivated lands, its animals and plants, its people and their tongues, its rains and its winds, are all different."*

■ PROUST: India—*"When I was asked by a newspaperman what I would do if I had only a few hours left before the earth was destroyed, I calmly replied, 'I would throw myself at the feet of Madame X, go to the Louvre and take a llittle excursion to India."*

■ HIRAM BINGHAM III: India—For Elihu Yale: India was a six month journey from London, December 1671 to June 23, 1672. Brought into Madras, Fort St. George at peril of life. Taking Yale to the shore were *"boats—musoolas—8 feet deep and 7 feet broad and 20 feet long being sewed with ropes...the boat is not strengthened with knee timber as ours is. The boat is sewed together with rope yarn in the coco, and chalked with a sort of rosin taken out of the sea, so artificially that it yields to every ambitious surf. Otherwise we could not get ashore, the bar knocking in pieces all that are inflexible."*

And India knocking into pieces all that are inflexible. And Elihu Yale's India: a Welsh dream of riches, a vision of jewels, bartered over-schemed for, paid for, fretted over, hidden, promoted, brought back to London.

Like Marco Polo's China, only imaginable when one returns home. Once gone, one can never return. Even Elihu Yale could not permit himself to re-dream India once he left it.

Nor I, Machu Picchu.

■ JACQUES CARTIER: India—When I returned from the Durbar, I said "I will bring India to Paris. And I will give Paris to India."

Patiala jewels. The soul of India. The crown jewels of Sir Bhupindra Singh. When Louis my brother told me stories of the Patiala jewels, I didn't believe him. When Louis brought me a miniature of Shah Jahan on a peacock throne, I told him:

"Louis, this is India one hundred fifty years ago. Do not speak of what you have seen or what others have seen. Bring me the jewels."

Louis said, "I will bring India to you and to the people of Paris." And he did. Caskets of jewels. Old mine Indian emeralds of Colombian origin. Moghul-carved emeralds. Pearls from the gulf. A magnificent huge fiery star sapphire, more than 204 carats, and other ambassadors from the depths of the earth: cascades of rubies, bead necklaces, Golconda diamonds, some of them pale pink, uncut diamonds, one cut weighing 234 carats. Rings, buttons, belts. When they arrived in Paris to be remounted and remodeled á la façon Cartier, à la Parisienne, in platinum, Louis breathlessly called me to our office on rue de la Paix. "I told you I would bring India to Paris," he said grandly. I politely but firmly corrected him. "Our house, Cartier, has brought India to Paris. Now we must invite Tout le monde. Tout le monde. Only then did Pierre smile.

The Maharajah of Patiala.

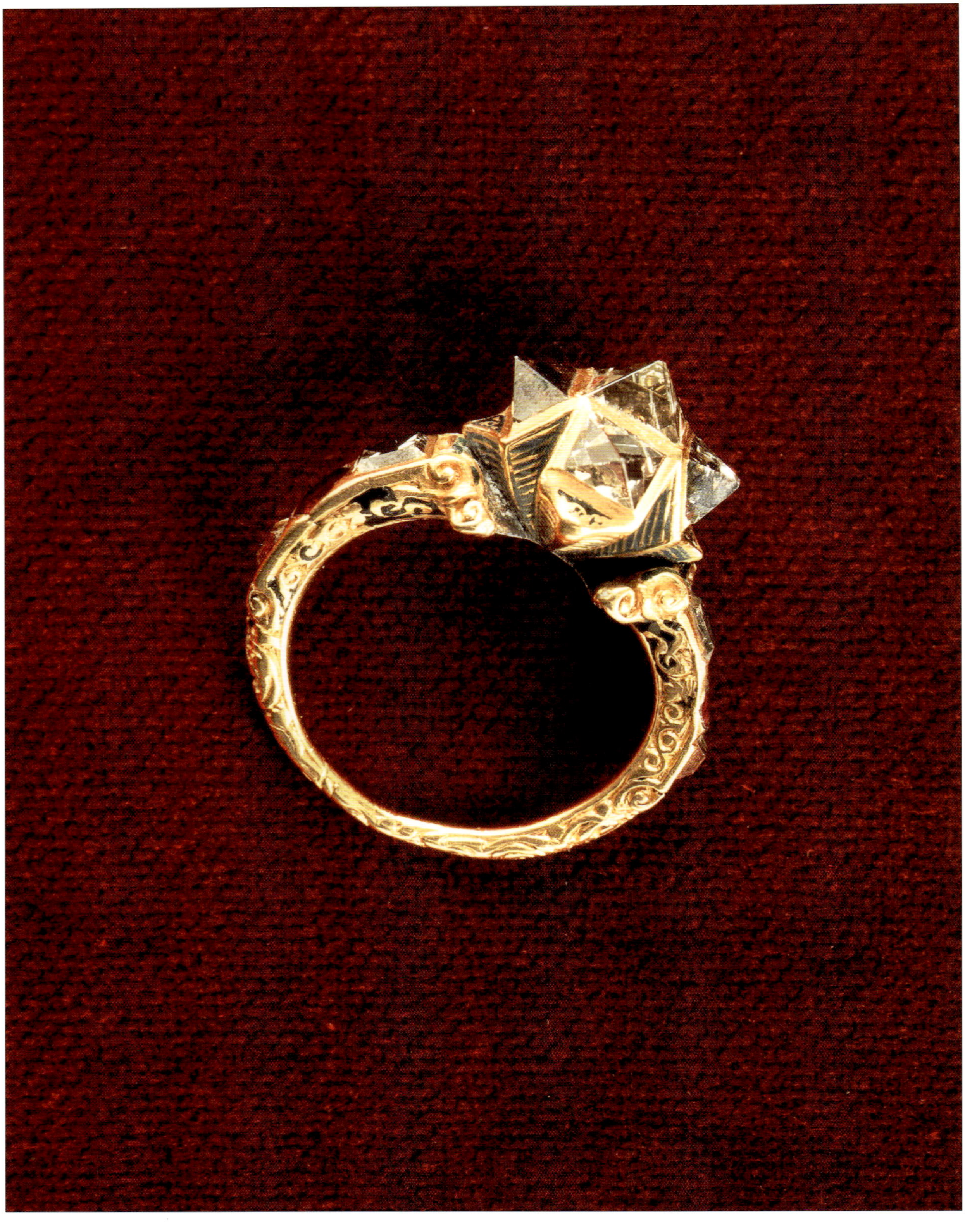

■ Henry Winters Luce, Henry Robinson Luce's father: Story—"I took Edward Hume for a walk when he was a freshman at Yale. We stood on a hill and looked toward the horizon. Hume was looking forward to becoming a physician. I could see far beyond his dream. 'Let this be a hill of vision to you. Let your view include the whole world. Where else except as a medical missionary could you possibly find so unlimited a place of opportunity and service?' And Hume went back to his Yale dormitory room and signed the student volunteer card. He went to China and rose to become head of Yale in China."

Hudson Taylor preached in those days: "A million a month in China are dying without G-d." A million souls destined for Purgatory. What did I, or Elizabeth, care that "eleven missionaries had been murdered in China in 1895." My wife, Elizabeth, told my son Henry these stories. Stories of his birth. My story. Her story. And we became Henry's story. Just as Fisher's story is his grandfather's story. Fisher is preaching to the converted. Thanks to G-d and to Elizabeth and me.

◆ Yehuda Leib Gutwirth Katz, Fisher's ancestor, (1658-1720): On one occasion he narrated the following story—My father Ephraim (1616-1678) was the light of my life and the light of all my generation. May his name be as great a blessing to all Israel as it has been to me. He would study from the Talmud each morning after Shachris. I can remember his eyes as he held my hand tightly and read from the Talmud. Rabbi Judah of India was fond of narrating fairy tales. On one occasion he narrated the following story.

"The first time I heard the story I was a boy of eight in a small room in the Yeshiva in Ofen that my father—the Sha'ar Ephraim—had founded.

I remember it like yesterday. Father asked when he finished the story, "What does this mean? Where is the gem today? Is it still lost? What is the miracle?" I was spellbound. I couldn't answer. Waters rushed before my eyes. So clear was the recounting of my father's tale, I could feel his hand in mine.

I looked at Father. "I don't understand even a word of this. The miracle is that Rabbi Judah only told this story once." And Father laughed and laughed. He called my heilige mother Nehama bas Eliyahu HaBaal Shem Tov and repeated what I said.

She laughed too. Suddenly my father grew serious and said to my mother, "Bless our child that he continue my teachings." And she said, "Bless him yourself, my dear Ephraim." My father looked beyond me and could see I think my future and without saying another word, my mother understood. And blessed me then and there and forever. Praise be to G-d who gave me the strength to voyage to Jerusalem and complete my father, Sha'ar Ephraim's, words.

"On one occasion, Rabbi Judah narrated the following story: 'Once upon a time I chanced to be traveling upon a ship in the Indian Ocean. We beheld a great fish, a whale, swimming about with a sparkling stone in its mouth. A strong swimmer leaped overboard in an attempt to secure the gem. The great fish was annoyed and tried to damage the ship.

"Then a huge creature of the sea fell upon the fish and killed it. All about us, the sea became red. A companion whale seized the gem, applied it to the wound of the fish and the whale revived. Again it tried to overturn the ship; again a monster fell upon the fish and slew it. This time, however, the monster secured the gem, and hurled it onto the ship.

"Foolishly, we applied the revivifying jewel on a salted fish. The fish came back to life again and jumped into the water, carrying the jewel with it."

Fisher paused. The old man nodded his head. His eyes asked Fisher to continue.

■ Elizabeth Middleton Root Luce, Henry Luce's mother: On one occasion he narrated the following story—"Don't hide your light under a bushel," H.W. would tell our son. And then my husband would tell our son of his birth in Tengchow. In a house without electricity. Windows that rattled with wind each winter. No matter how much we caulked and re-caulked them. No plumbing, No gas.

Over and over H.W. would narrate the story. And H.W. would insist that I be present to hear the tale, as though I had not been there in the East Shantung Mission, as though I had not borne Henry into the world without benefit of midwife. "All one can ask for is the help of the Holy One," H.W. said.

And even after Henry went to St. Alban's school north of London after he finished Hotchkiss, to cure his stuttering, the story of his birth was told over and over until it became a tale of wonder, a tale of family, an election by G-d, to spring forth from a Chinese manger into Life Everlasting.

■ Sir Thomas Pitt to Sir Stephen Evans, Ft. St. George November 6, 1701: Gem—"This accompanyes the modell of a stone I have lately seene; itt weighs...cartts 426...the price they ask for it is prodigious being two hundred thousand pags. Tho I believe less than one hundred thousand would buy it...Pro rata as stones goe I thinke 'tis inestimable. Since I saw it I have bin perusing of Tavernier where there is no gem soe large as this will bee when cutt...I write this singly to you, and no one else, and desire it may bee kept private...for itt being of soe great a value I believe there are few or none that can buy it.

Your most obliged humble servant, T. Pitt."

As to how I got this stone "I doe here declare and assert under my hand, in the presence of G-d almighty, as I hope for salvation, through the merritts and intercession of our savior Jesus Christ, that this is the truth and if it bee not let G-d deny it to mee and my children for ever."

Great gems make the strongest men mad. None can resist to follow a gem—even to perdition itself.

Seventeenth century octahedral diamond ring (side view).

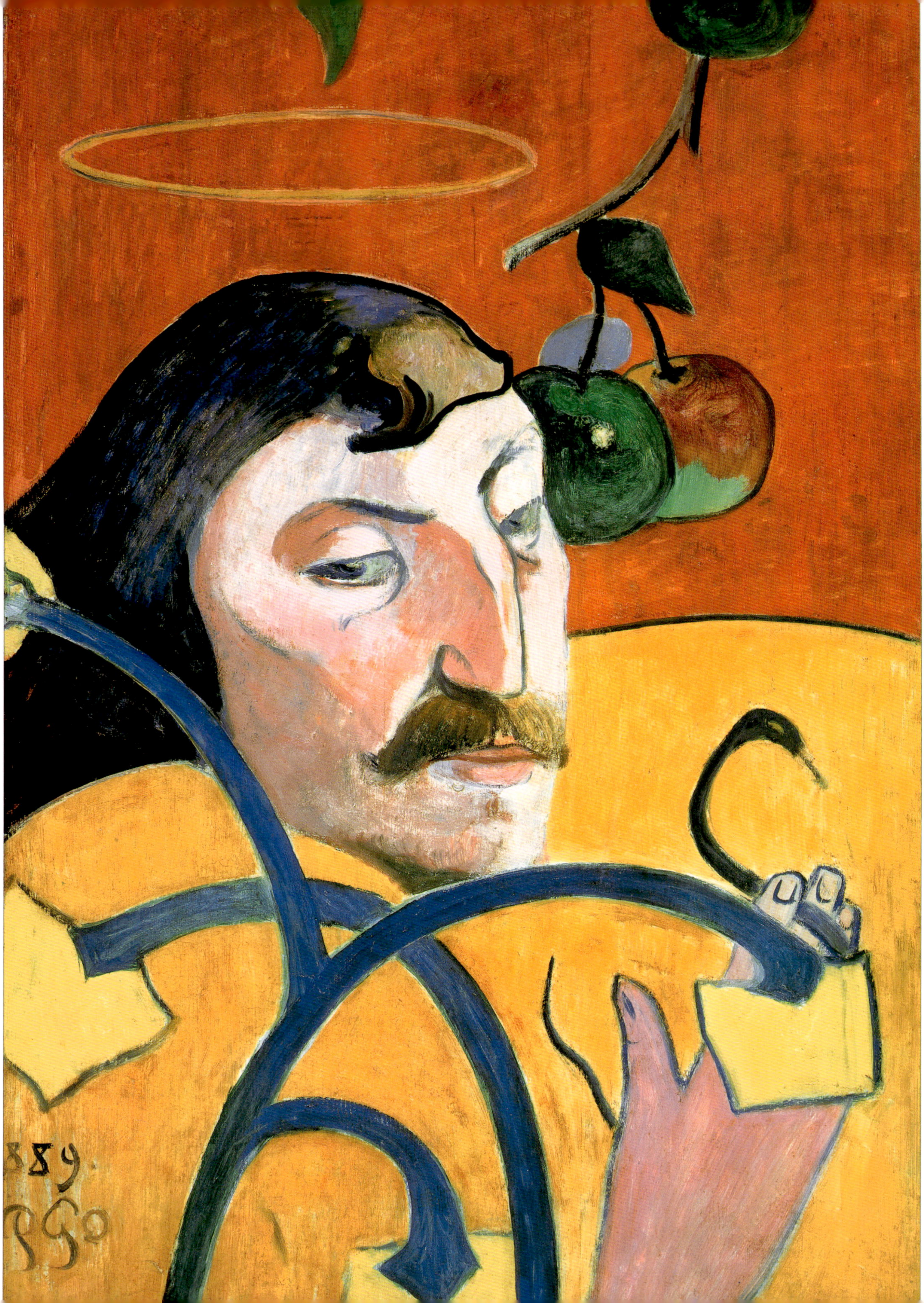

◆ TUVIAH GUTMAN GUTWIRTH, Fisher's grandfather: My grandfather is staring at that page—I am staring at the page, a page from the Babylonian Talmud. A copy of which I studied in Tarnov with Abish Rheinhold, my Rabbi. I married his daughter, Chaya, and the very same Talmud he used to teach was the very same Talmud he gave me as my wedding gift.

I stare at the page not looking for the sparkling gemstone in the mouth of the great fish whose brilliance illuminates the entire world. That gem is the Talmud itself, and in studying it, the gem is clearly before me. I am staring at the page of Talmud because it was printed in Vilna some twenty years before and sent to Cracow and purchased by my father-in-law and later gifted to me in Tarnov. Soon I will travel to Antwerp, and the pages of the Talmud will travel across the ocean after being buried with my library during the War and Fisher, my grandson, will stare at a page of my wedding Talmud, and he will stare and stare but will he understand that the true gem is study?

■ HERMAN MELVILLE: Staring at the page..., dreaming of voyaging—My mother is turning the pages of a book. I am ten and my father is reading my school report aloud to my mother. I am tiny in my chair at my desk, staring at the page of the book Mother has opened. Father is reading, more chanting than reading.

"Herman is making more progress than formerly, and without being a bright scholar, he maintains a respectable standing and would proceed further if he could be induced to study more. Being a most amiable and innocent child, I cannot find it in my heart to coerce him, especially as he seems to have chosen commerce as a favorite pursuit."

And what can I do but stare at the page. A fine merchant I'll make with one grandfather who threw British tea into the waters of the Boston Harbor, and the other grandfather, General Peter Gansevoort, with his vast fortune, who would brook no commerce with simple merchants. And my father ruined in Albany, not much capital to reestablish the family fortune. And my mother turning the pages before my eyes. I staring and seeing nothing, absolutely nothing on their blank surfaces. For I was dreaming of voyaging far from my narrow house, the gloom of my father, to the paradise of mother's Gansevoort youth. I would fill the pages with my own voyage and draw fish on the page of my life.

"I opened my eyes and the before sunlit room was now wrapped in outer darkness. Instantly I felt a shock running through all my frame; nothing was to be seen, and nothing was to be heard but a supernatural hand seemed placed in mine. My arm hung over the counterpane and the nameless, unimaginable, silent form or phantoms, to which the hand belonged, seemed closely seated by my bedside. For what seemed like ages piled upon ages, I lay there frozen with the most awful fears, not daring to drag away my hands, yet ever thinking that if I could but stir it one single inch, the horrid spell would be broken. I know not how this consciousness at last glided away from me…"

Paul Gauguin, *Self-Portrait*.

"My grandfather is staring at that page of Talmud, printed in Vilna some twenty years before. The Talmud was given to him by his father-in-law. The manuscript pages surrounding the text were annotations written by his father-in-law and manuscripts in his father-in-law's library. My grandfather, Gutman Gutwirth, was dreaming of traveling to Antwerp.

"In Antwerp he saw gems in the mouths of great fish and he was a strong swimmer. He went on voyages across the water, and eventually he told me of the gem that appears and reappears, a gem that is almost within our grasp but we possess it only to use it for purposes that belittle both the search and the vision."

"And where is the gem now, young Fisher?" asked the old man, on the edge of his chair.

■ GAUGUIN: Dreaming of voyaging—*"I am off to Panama to live there like a savage…I am off to Martinique. The matter is irrevocably decided: I am off to Madagascar. As for my self I have taken my decision. I shall be leaving shortly for Tahiti, a small island in the Pacific where one can live without money. I am laid flat today, conquered by destitution and above all by the illness of an entirely premature old age. I dream of voyaging to the Marquesas. And then to…And then to voyage to…and then to voyage…And then, and then…and."*

◆ ABISH RHEINHOLD, Fisher's grandfather's father-in-law: Gutman was dreaming of voyaging to Antwerp—Gutman was an *illui*. His gaze could take in an entire page with one glance. He could remember the page of Talmud underneath the page he was staring at. He asked me, "You are my Rabbi. Can I go to Antwerp? Your daughter wants us to go to Antwerp." The year was 1888. Diamonds had been discovered in South Africa. Already five students from my Yeshiva had voyaged to Antwerp to make a living. What was I to say to Gutman? He had my treasure, my daughter Chaya. He was also my treasure, my greatest student.

Did I not rise before him when he entered my room? For I knew that while I was his Rabbi, in the world to come, he would be the commentary on my work. How I would miss him. My daughter Chaya and I could not bring myself to answer.

Gutman pressed me with his eyes and I said, "We are all on a ship voyaging. We all can see the precious stone glistening in the water. Ask Reb Jehoshua, the Belzer Rebbe." "You are my Rabbi," Gutman persisted. "But I cannot bring myself to advise you, my son-in-law. I am nogeh ba Davar." "Then what will the Belzer tell me of my proposed voyage to Antwerp, away from Poland." "He will tell you, Gutman, that wherever you voyage you will be able to learn." "And what will he tell me of my children? And my children's children. Will they be able to learn?"

And what could I tell Gutman? My treasure. Both of us could see the great fish in the fiery waters of Poland. And should Belgium be so different? Or America? Or France? Or the land of Palestine that so many people speak of?

Gutman must have seen my tears for he embraced me and said, "I will go to Belz immediately. And ask the questions, but know one thing: Chaya and I would be so happy to take you with us if only you will come."

Gutman went to Belz. He returned the day after the following Shabbas. We voyaged to Antwerp together. But when I asked him what Jehoshua of Belz had said about his question: "Will his children's children be able to learn?" Gutman was silent. He knew it was not permitted to lie. He knew it was permitted not to tell all you knew of the truth. He said, "The Belzer told me, 'Bring as many fellow sailors as you can on the ship's voyage so that you do not lose sight of Rabbi Judah's gem when the sea grows dark.'"

85

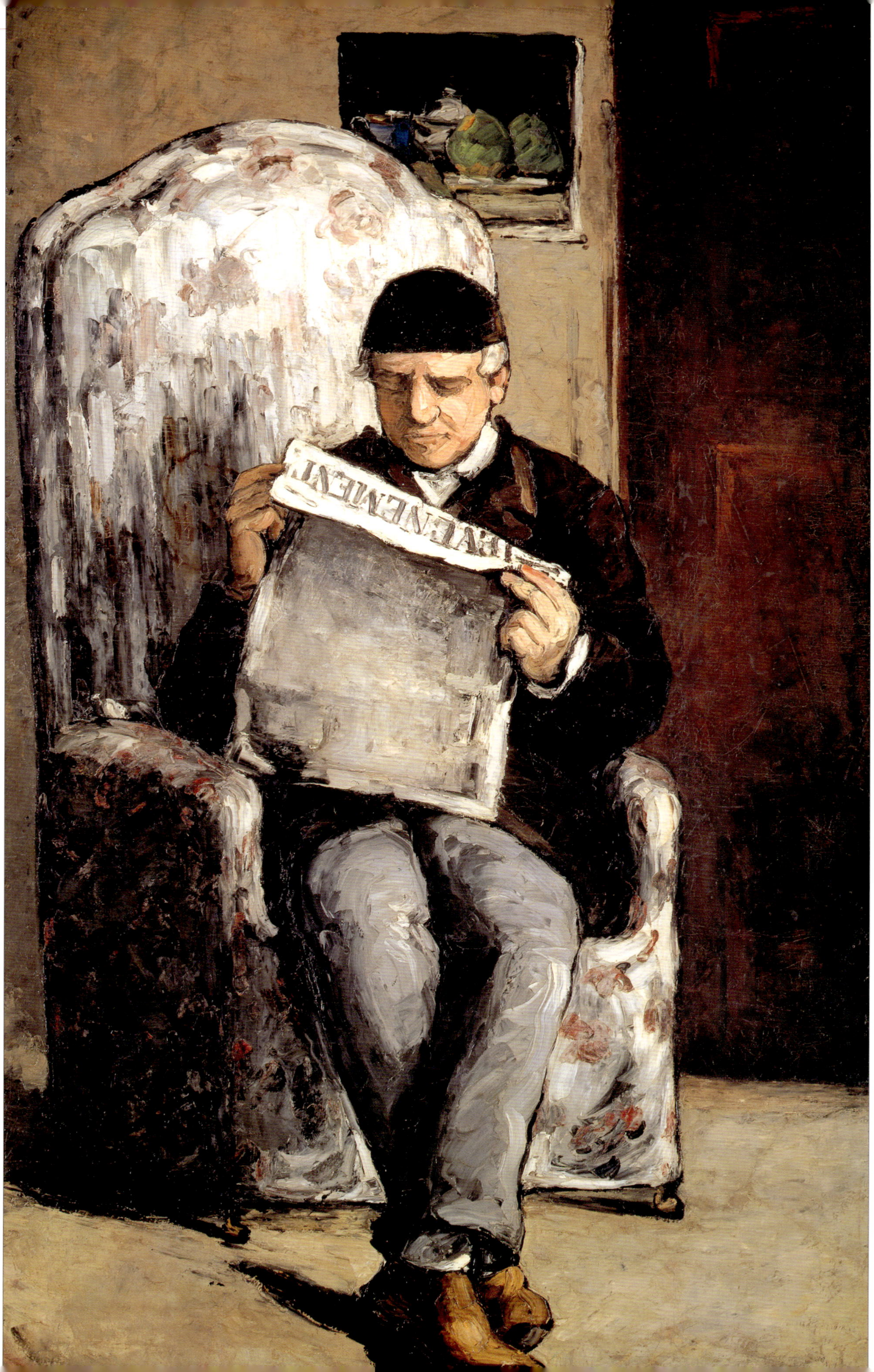

◆ EMIL FISHER, FISHER'S FATHER: Story—I would tell Raphael story after story about my father, about my grandfather in Paris, about my family in Poland, about crossing over to America from Paris during the War. Raphael would listen carefully, never interrupting me. I knew I repeated myself over and over, for after all, how many different stories does one know about one's parents?

How often can one describe the walk to our neighbor's barn in the depths of the Polish winter. I was five and Marek, my protector, a Polish farmer's son, was all of seven. I was walking toward their farm in the gloom of winter, off on my errand to bring fresh goat's milk to my aged tubercular aunt. Suddenly, in the dark, Marek punched me as hard as he could for no reason except that we were different. How often do different stories occur to us, so different that we can tell them to our children, so different that we must tell them to our children?

And how few of these stories, my gems, that I have told Raphael, will he tell his children? So few stories, like wine, rarely last more than a generation. Enthralling stories like fine wine even if buried, inspected, watched over, tended lovingly in the cellars of our mind run off into a cold forgetting earth.

■ LOUIS AUGUSTE CÉZANNE, CÉZANNE'S FATHER: Only a picture of—If you would only paint a picture of me instead of painting a two franc demoiselle in every six franc walk-up apartment in Montparnasse you ever lived in.

My G-d, to hear of your great friend Professor Zola commissioning a portrait of a fair-skinned woman, seduced, abducted and ravished by a man, surely no Frenchman, and twice her size from what I hear. How does he think of such subjects? And why do you hang on his every word?

Where is your bread buttered? I pay your rent. I pay for the brushes, for the models, for who knows what else? But I told your mother, Anne Elizabeth-Tonorine Aubert: as G-d is my witness. My manna shall not fall on you forever.

"I have only a picture of my grandfather reading the story of Rabbi Jehudah telling of the gem, 'may it be enough for you.'"

The man stood up and glancing at Fisher's story outline.

He put the project folder on the table decisively and rose to his full height. Then he reached into his pocket and wrote in a broad hand: December 22—Double young Fisher and Hamilton's salary for six months. If the project meets approval, contact Brooks. If not, fire Fisher and Hamilton."

And then with the tiniest of signatures, he signed his calling card. He left the card on Fisher's desk, and strode out.

Fisher peered down at the card and read the minuscule message and signature:

Luce, H.—for project Green.

■ ALMA MAILMAN, wife of James Agee: Time-Life—"*Shortly before I went to Mexico, I went to the Time-Life Building at night. Jim had a deadline to meet and it was very late. We quarreled, and I insisted I wanted to go, but he wanted me to stay. He threatened me. He said he was going to jump out of the window. It was on the twentieth floor. There was a glass ledge, and he went over and put one long leg over the glass ledge and looked back at me with this defiant look on his face. I just looked at him and left—walked down the hall to the elevator. As I got to the elevator I thought, oh my G-d, I've made him do it! and I ran back into the room. This was very late at night, and no one else was working, I ran into the room and the window was open and there was no Jim. The room was empty. I ran over to the window, frightened, really frightened, and I looked down. I don't know what I expected to find. I saw nothing, except what you see when you look out the twentieth floor from a window, and turned around and there was Jim behind the door, looking a little sheepish. I think I left about two weeks later.*"

■ CÉZANNE: A picture of my grandfather—"Paint a picture of my grandfather. Or, better yet, paint my portrait," Father would roar at me. And scream obscenities about Hortense, although he hadn't met her and hadn't heard of her, but he knew she had to exist. Of course, I would hide my paintings of Hortense more carefully than a Dordogne peasant hid his gold coins. "Why paint every putain who mounts your staircase, you could paint me," Father would shout.

"And why should I paint you, Father?" I would ask him in that neutral tone Father Pierre used when he would hear confession from Father first, and later me, in the Eglise St. Victor in Aix when I was a boy of nine.

"Why should I paint you, Father?" "Because I feed you, you sparrow. I shelter you. I am central to you. Without me..." and on and on he would sputter.

Rather than hear the catalog of threats, sadness, tricks and whimpering, I said: "As you are my patron, step into my studio tomorrow at noon." And paint Father I did. In all his glory, beautified by the Journal des Événements. Looking at me obliquely through the financial spectacles he always wore. Remote. Distant. Aloof. Dying.

"I am not that man," Father bellowed when he saw the work. Work that I had hidden from him through three months of sitting and invective.

And of course, I knew about him and Mother. Courting Mother in '36. I was born in '39, sister Marie in '41 and their blessed marriage in '44.

All the hidden passions. Hidden behind newspapers, buried in the garden, to be interred in the family plot. "If that is not you, dear Father," I said evenly, "you should become the painter and henceforth I shall sit in your chair in the bank."

Paul Cézanne, *The Artist's Father*.

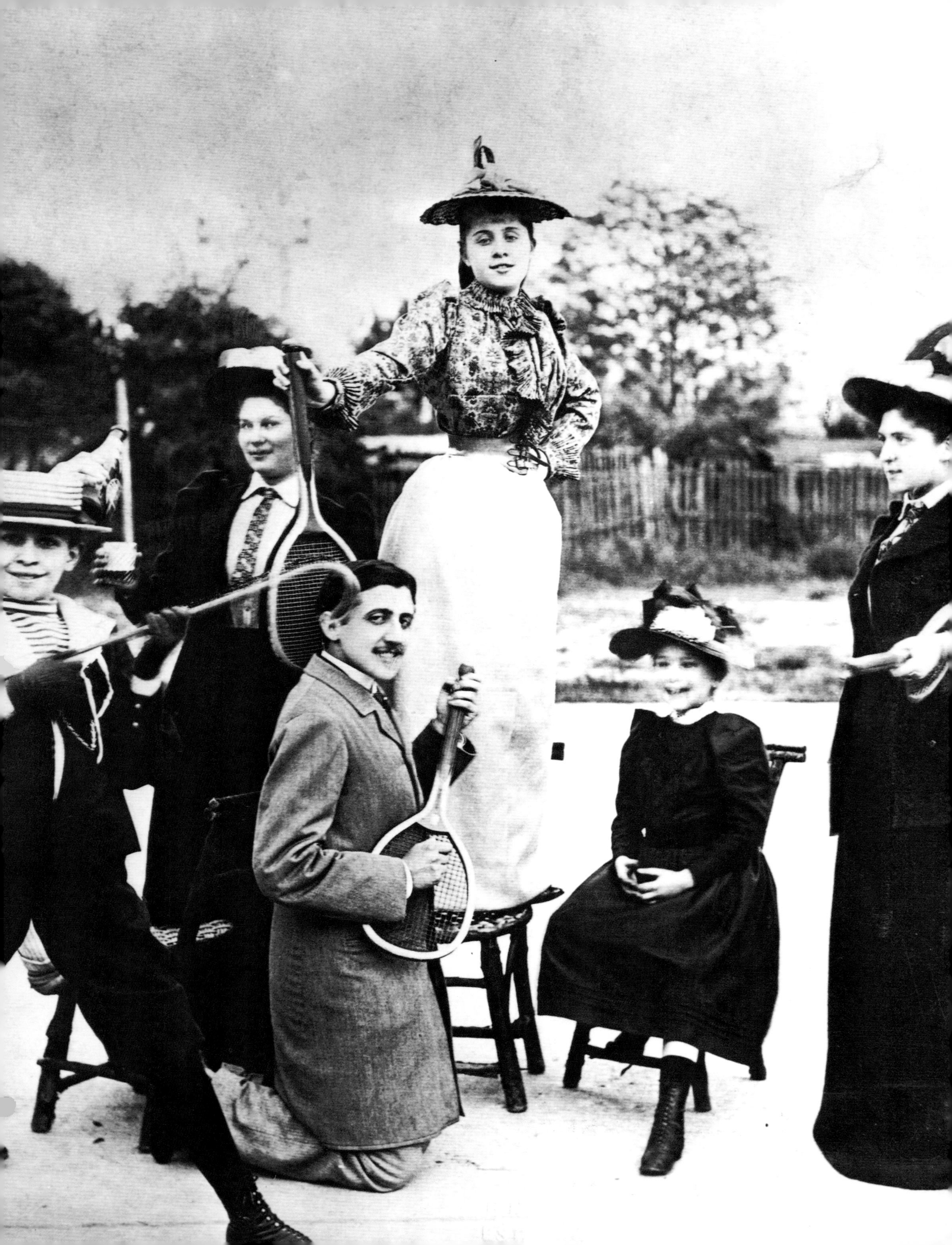

■ NEVIL MASKELYNE, Fifth Astronomer Royal: Greenwich Village…time— Of course young Fisher is on Greenwich time. I lived in the village of Greenwich from the time of 1765 until 1811. Years. And hours. And seconds.

Or I lived in the the village of Greenwich for forty-six issues of the Nautical Almanac, each copy fingered, gazed at, grasped at, poured over by sailors, shippers, Lloyds brokers throughout the world to reckon their longitude from Greenwich. My work, indispensable.

Or I lived in the idea of the village of Greenwich from 1765 to my death in 1811. Was I not in the center of the world? Not that Rome wasn't, or that Paris wasn't or that even London wasn't. All considered their meridian prime. But my calculations, page by page, figure by figure, checked, rechecked, calculated, recalculated again and again, ten times more brilliant than Harrison's chronometer and one thousand times more useful. Yes, my twelve pages of calculations for each month fixed Greenwich in the center of the world. And beyond my death too.

Even Fisher's mother doesn't know whereof she speaks, but she's spot on. She, her precious Fisher, his yet more precious Dosha, all for all time on my Greenwich time.

■ THEODOR HERZL: You'll never know when you'll have to…—And why couldn't Fisher's father finish the sentence? Flee. Travel. Voyage. Leave. Run. Escape.

On January 5, 1895, I could hear them in the Paris streets. Dreyfus convicted. "Death to the Jews!" Parisian mobs cried and that cry echoed in every one of my nights sleep afterward.

My friend Schiff in my room. I was reading my manifesto addressed to the Rothschild family out loud to him. My solution to the Jewish Question

Schiff had an idiotic look on his face as though he could not hear, as though he could not understand my German. I shouted at him in French. The Jewish state can speak what language it wishes. German, French. What do I care?

"Language will be no problem. Switzerland too is a federation of different nationalities. We recognize ourselves as a nation by our faith. Besides, in all llkelihood German will become the official language, out of necessity the Jew's German! Like the yellow star as a merit badge. But I have nothing against French or English."

And Schiff gaping at me. And what do you say of my plan to address the Rothschilds? I shouted, and Schiff mumbled, "Let me take your pulse, Dori."

CHAPTER 5

"Greenwich Village…time?" Fisher heard his mother say as he turned the lock and entered his parents' apartment on upper West End Avenue. His mother, Johanna Charlotte, was born and raised in the low countries, before "the War" as she put it. She pronounced Greenwich as the color plus half of the word "sandwich."

"What did you say, Mom?" asked Fisher, searching for his mother's voice in one of the eight rent controlled rooms his parents had occupied since arriving in America in 1941. "You'll never know," his father would chant, "when you'll have to run…" in an explanation of why they never purchased an apartment on the Upper East Side to live near his many sisters.

"What did you say?" asked Fisher, moving from the foyer into his old bedroom and then into the living room all the while knowing, of course, exactly where his mother was.

"I'm in the kitchen Raphael," she chirped from her slender frame. Fisher walked slowly—always the same hide and seek ritual, she never hiding and he ever seeking.

■ FRIEDRICH SCHIFF: You'll never know when you'll have to—"You never know when you'll have to run," shouted Herzl to me while he was explaining his book. A long letter to the Rothschilds. A call to the front. A love note to wake our people from the nightmare of our Dreyfussard history. But Dori was pacing, sweating, chanting, mumbling. He was unkempt, uncombed.

So different from the last time I had seen him. I asked to take his pulse. It was racing. I begged Herzl to burn his manuscript. He desperately needed a doctor.

■ WILLIAM EMPSON: Greenwich Village… time—Chapter III: *"The condition for the third type of ambiguity is that two apparently unconnected meanings are given simultaneously. Puns for Milton, Marvell, Johnson, Pope, Hood. Generalized form when there is reference to more than one universe of discourse."*

Fisher and his mother, Mother and I. Fisher in New York and I in England. Or Fisher and his mother in New York and I in Peking and mother in England. But we four are lines of one quatrain.

Our meter is ambiguity. Seven types of ambiguity. Seven times seven times seven Time.

For Fisher's mother is from Northern Europe judging by the sound of her, and the sight of her. And Fisher, learned as he is, hears the words "Greenwich Village" and time and winces at the word "time" as I wince even in Peking half a world away from Mother and half a century earlier at the word "mean."

Mother's words and Fisher's mother's words are a rich broth of ambiguity, filling our childhoods which last forever.

"The study of Hebrew by the way, and the existence of English Bibles with alternatives in the margins, may have influence on the capacity of English for ambiguity; Donne, Herbert, Johnson, and Cranshaw for instance, and the flowering of poetry at the end of the sixteenth century, corresponded with the first thorough permeation of the English language by the translated texts. This is of interest because Hebrew, having very unreliable tenses, extraordinary idioms, and a strong taste for puns, possesses all the poetical advantages of a thorough primitive disorder."

Hebrew runs through Fisher's mother's veins, fourteen generations of Rabbinical learning before her, to him with ambiguity galloping alongside.

Marcel Proust, playing on a tennis racket, with Jeanne Pouquet.

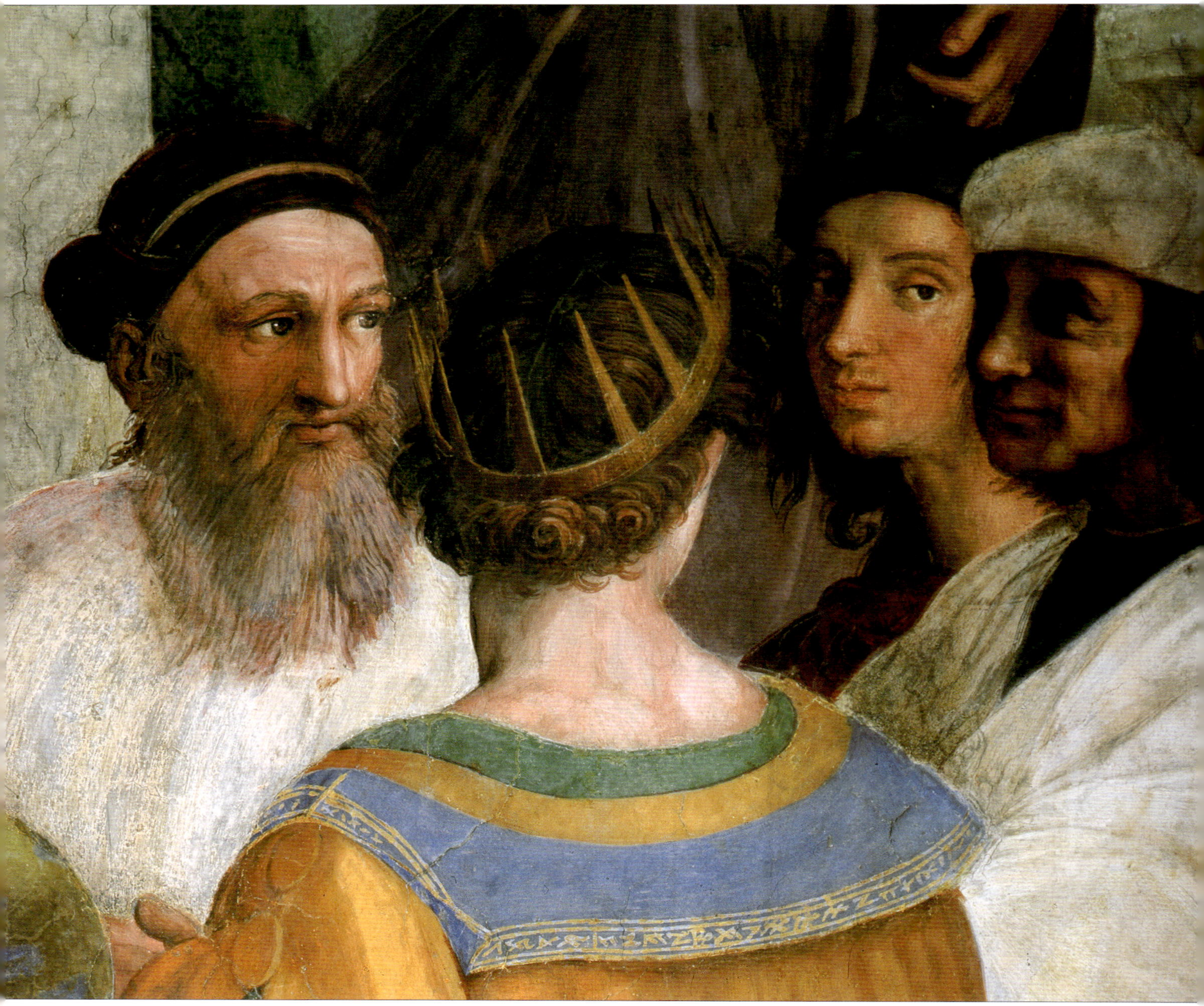

◆ EMIL FISHER, FISHER'S FATHER: Her obstreperous but bright second grade student—If I had a question for my father, when I was young in Paris, he would listen and then ask me to speak to my mother.

She would answer with confidence, each word chosen as though she had come into a classroom—not that I had been to school after the age of eight—not that I ever had a teacher in Poland, before Paris.

Once I said to my father, "Why do you always send me to Mother to answer questions that I pose to you?" My father laughed, the laugh that caused my seven sisters to name their sons after him; Bernards in France, Bertons and Bentleys in America but and always Bunam in Hebrew wherever they were born. Father picked up my hand, pointed it to the synagogue across the way and said, *"As our heilege Rebbe, Isaac Herzog, teaches us, the Talmud Niddah says: 'The Lord gave more wisdom to women than to men.'"*

And I smiled at Father and said, "Why Papa do you not send me to Rabbi Herzog himself?" Papa looked down at his shoes, unaware that I was teasing him, and after a time he spoke simply. "Because you wouldn't go to the Reb Herzog even if I sent you."

One day I decided to go directly to Mother, bypassing Father, and I asked her a question. She said to me, "I should give you advice? Don't you respect your father? Go to him. He will tell you what's best." My dear Lotty Johanna, my father was right and Herzog was right and the Talmud Niddah was right.

Not only do women have more understanding than men but also as Rabbi Herzog taught me and my father told me, the man to whom a miracle happens is not aware of it himself.

I always knew my wife was special, but did I know she was a miracle? Look how she speaks to our son, Raphael. Look how she sees the potential in him. She is his greatest teacher.

"That's not what you said," smiled Fisher as he pushed the white swinging door, the twenty times over painted wooden entrance to the kitchen. "This way you can't see the finger marks," she would tell him. Only to say three years later, "The kitchen looks terrible. When your father goes to Japan next month, I'm going to have the whole house done." Fisher entered the kitchen. His mother was not more than five feet tall with dark brown eyes that met his, half-laughing and half in philosophical mid-sentence, waiting to hear him speak more than thinking to speak first herself.

"Dear Raphael," she began again, patiently as though addressing an obstreperous but bright second-grade student.

Fisher kissed her on both cheeks the same way generations of their family kissed each other; it always ended with an obligatory two pats on her left shoulder.

■ EPHRAIM ZALMAN MARGOLIOTH 1760-1828: over to his mother—*"It is not the custom to visit one's friend in his house on Rosh Ha-Shanah as on other holidays, nor even to visit the Rabbi of the city on Rosh Hashanah. But one visits one's father and mother to receive their blessings, especially if he knows that they wish it."*

This young man walks briskly to his mother's house. He has no rabbi. His father is no longer with him. Every day for him is Rosh Ha-Shanah. But in going of his own free will, joyfully, to his mother's house, he will receive her blessing.

■ RABBI ISAAC HERZOG, 1888-1959: Waiting to hear him speak more than thinking to speak himself—I received Smihah from Jacob David Wilkowsky of Safed.

For me to study through the day and continue through the night was not unusual. But to receive Smihah and become a Rabbi and be called up to dispense advice, that was frightening to me. I asked Jacob David, "I think, please G-d, I could be a Dayan, a Judge, but how will I be able to dispense advice to people?"

"Ask your wife," replied Jacob David. "She will help you give advice." I blushed because I was not married yet. Reb Wilkowsky added a blessing from proverbs, *"House and wealth are inherited from fathers but a wise wife is from the Lord."* Thank G-d for Niddah's wife, the Lord gave more wisdom to women than to men.

I quoted my house, my wife Sarah, the daughter of Samuel Isaac Hillman, whenever I could. Her thoughts, my words. And she working in Ezras Nashim Hospital in Jerusalem, her deeds, my advice.

So the generations continue. A fine man Bunam Fisher and his son too and this Raphael all learning from Talmud Niddah. A mother in Israel waiting to hear her son speak more than thinking to speak herself. *"When Rabbi Yosef heard the footsteps of his mother, he said, Let me stand up for the Divine Presence is approaching."*

■ LAURENCE STERNE: Fisher kissed her on both cheeks—And lucky lad he is, an Angel Raphael himself, to be able kiss his mother on both cheeks.

My mother left me at ten. When I saw her next at twenty 'twas no more than for twenty minutes! Though she wanted to see me, appeared at my doorstep eager to share in my wife Elizabeth's fortune for the honey of the Lumley fortune drew her angelically across the seas from Ireland.

"The very hour I received notice of her landing at Liverpool, I took post to prevent her coming nearer me—stay'd three days with her—used all the arguments I could fairly to engage her to return to Ireland and end her days with her own relations."

Thrice blessed is Raphael: youth, Dosha, and an angelic mother. Thrice cursed was I.

Raphael, *The School of Athens*, detail of Raphael's self-portrait.

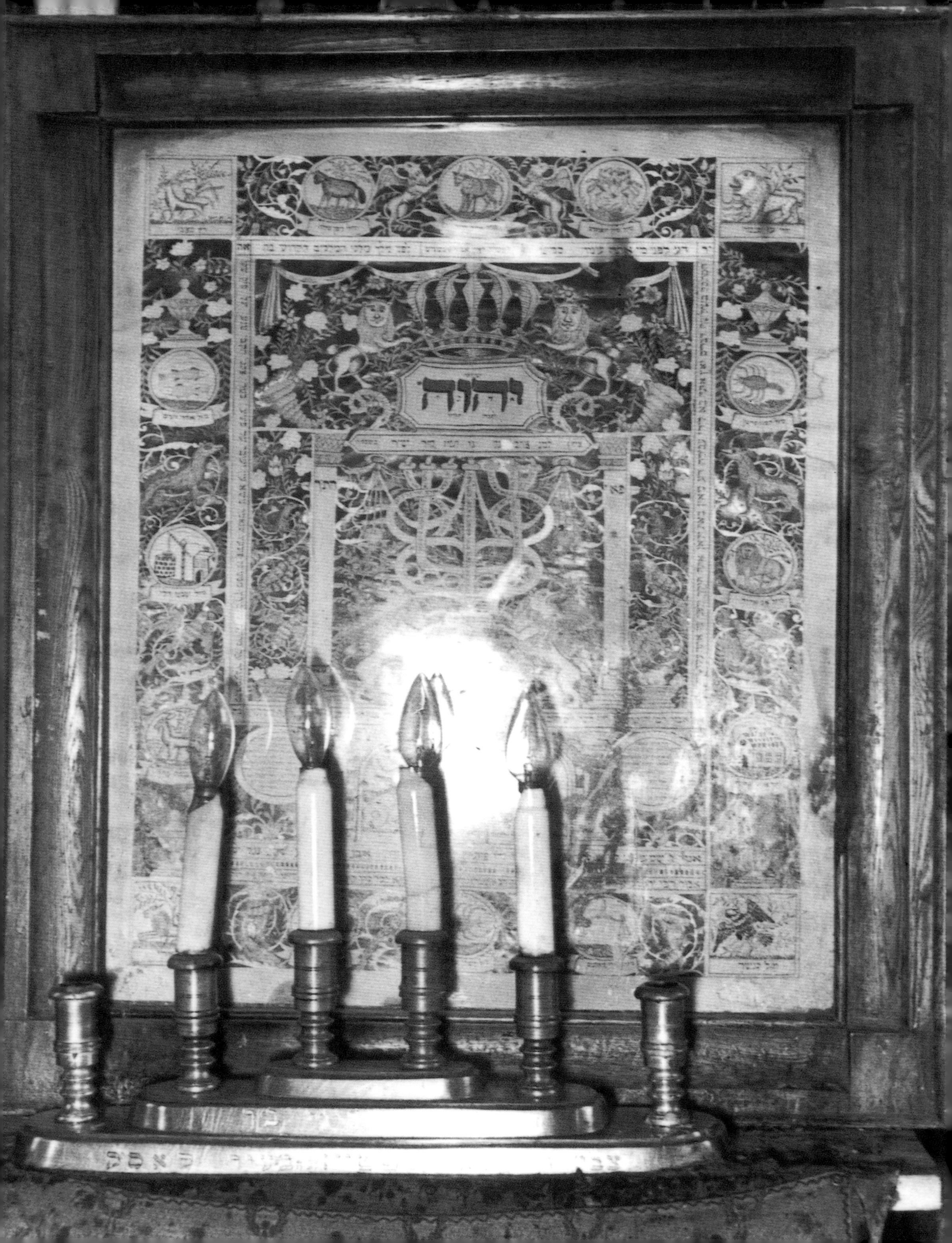
יהוה

◆ ARYEH JUDAH LEIB BEN EPHRAIM HA-KOHEN, Fisher's great great great great great grandfather (1658-1720): think—In Ofen (Buda), my father was a *posek*. And in Vienna and in Prague and in Istanbul and in Jerusalem too and when my father would sing, "And is not the whole world full of his glory," angels themselves would sing Amen.

In Ofen, my father would ask questions but his answers were rarer than rubies. In fact, in our study room on the top floor of our house where Hezekiah, the light of my youth, and my nephew Zevi Hirsch and I would sit each night, we would read by turn from Father's Shas and Hezekiah would re-read and my father would raise a question. I remember before the Plague in Ofen how Father motioned to Hezekiah not to answer. I remember Father whispering (It seems more a dream than a memory): "Hezekiah my son, you cannot answer."

Soon, so soon, Hezekiah was taken from us, leaving his poor son Aaron. And I within the next weeks, days, months, minutes, on the verge of dying. Father paced around my bed, asking the question over and over to the One True Judge. I couldn't believe my ears. It couldn't be that I was feverish. I was without words. I couldn't think. Even the question my father had lovingly put in my mouth could not come out. Suddenly, Father too passed into the world beyond the curtain.

◆ SHA'AR EPHRAIM, FISHER'S ANCESTOR, 1616-1678: Not that she commented unless a question constituted an answer—A question and an answer. A question. And my son Hezekiah in Ofen and my son Aryeh Judah Leib and my grandson Zevi Hirsch Ashkenazi and I.

Sitting in a room in Ofen I asking a question: a man should not say the grace after meals mentally but if he does so, has he performed his obligation? And they looking at my Shas intently.

And Zevi Hirsch not answering with his lips but with his eyes. I can see an answer. But he will not answer. For if he answers, he must first answer his father Jacob Sak and his father must answer back. But his father cannot answer to anyone. For Sabbetai Zevi, may his name disappear, had led my son-in-law Jacob down a path toward an abyss that none will climb out of.

But praise be G-d that Zevi Hirsch is here with me, with us, with Israel. Zevi listens, he looks, but he does not answer.

Hezekiah repeats my question, a man should not say grace, as though his repetition constitutes an answer and I can see that he will try to answer but suddenly Aryeh Judah Leib raises his hand to quiet his brother.

And staring at me, he whispers, "Father…you…speak…you commented…what is the…" And as I live, the voice of Elijah of Chelm comes into my mouth. "You cannot answer," I say, looking at Hezekiah. "And you cannot answer yet," I say looking at Zevi Hirsch. You are the answer because you are the question.

My words are more tears than sentences and I cannot sit erect in my chair. A bat Kol, for my dear father-in-law Elijah has been gone for so long. And can they hear me or understand me? They are all crowded near my face so close to me, I can hear them breathe but a world away.

Blessed be the true judge.

"What did you say about Greenwich Village Time, Mother?"

"Oh, that," she laughed, "I only asked, do you work in Greenwich Village or sleep at Time?"

Fisher laughed. "Just the latter, Mother dearest. But why do you ask and how did you know?"

For more than a decade she had noticed everything about him. Uncanny, not that she commented unless a question constituted an answer.

Well, what am I to think seeing you in your work clothes. Or as you put it, your blue corduroy pants, blue shirt and the Brooks Brothers blue tie with polka dots your father gave you, wound around your neck like you've been sleeping all night in a washing machine, she thought, not speaking, but he understood.

◆ ZEVI HIRSCH BEN JACOB SAK ASHKENAZI (1660-1718) the Haham Zevi, Fisher's ancestor, Ephraim ben Jacob's grandson: Not that she commented unless a question constituted an answer—We were as close to my grandfather Ephraim's face as when he would bless me going to synagogue before Rosh Hashanah in Ofen.

We were all three beings blessed, but not by Ephraim. Hezekiah was told that he could not answer. And I was told that I could not answer yet.

And the lamp of my youth—who saved me and guided my feet to the shores of wisdom—who never reproached me with his eyes for the sins of my father—may G-d judge him as a deer running hither and yonder in search of His light but blinded by an Istanbuli noonday sun. My thrice blessed uncle Aryeh Judah Leib, was he not given the sign he would be the question? Does not a question always constitute an answer. But it was not my grandfather speaking.

This Hezekiah did not understand. It was not Aryeh Judah Leib's father who was speaking—for he had not at that time gone to Safed—no, this he didn't understand.

I too did not understand. But I came to understand in Salonika with Elijah Covo, more Sephardi than Ashkenazi, more a voice from Heaven than a teacher on earth. My Uncle Hezekiah, I was told in my Yeshiva in Saloniki, has perished in the Plague. My uncle, my light, Aryeh Judah Leib was sick unto death but spared.

And my grandfather, hoping to return to Israel, perished in the awful Hungarian Plague too, after imploring the Merciful to choose him and not his sick son, Aryeh Judah Leib.

Elijah Covo, holding my head in his hands and whispering to me and now you and your uncle must be the blessed question—you will become a Haham in Israel, and your uncle will be both the Sheelah and Teshuvah, the question and answer, of your grandfather.

"Blessed be the true judge," said my grandfather, Elijah of Chelm, the creator of a Golem. Praise be to G-d that my life has been an Amen to these words.

◆ TUVIAH GUTMAN GUTWIRTH, FISHER'S MOTHER'S FATHER: Not that she commented unless a question constituted an answer—My blessed daughter. For is she not blessed to have a son who holds her dear? Was she not as a child so dear to me? A miracle: her questions falling on Fisher's ears as answers. On the deepest of deepest levels, commentary.

Are we not all answers to our parents if we are questions to our children?

Did not my forefather Aryeh Judah Leib take his father's Responsa on the Shulhan Arukh to Eretz Yisroel and the son of his late brother Hezekiah who died in the Plague in Ofen. They stitched together a volume of responsa: Sha'ar Ephraim's questions and answers. But only in Prague could Aryeh Judah Leib complete his father's work, and only in Safed could he complete his own—may his grave serve as a blessing—for us, generation after generation, question after question, answer after answer, commentary: The love of G-d, our commentary without end.

Altar of the Lask Synagogue, Lodz, Poland.

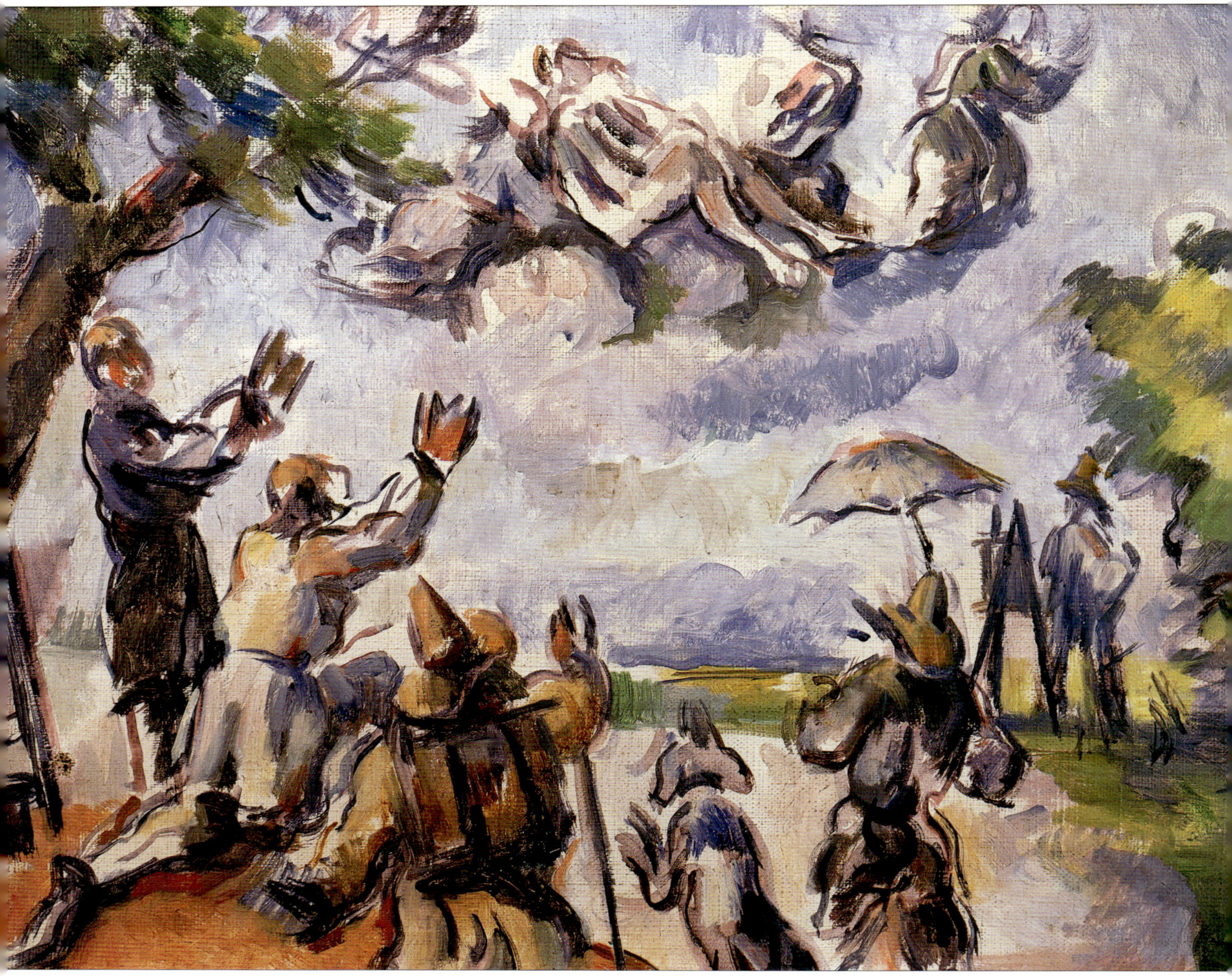

■ ARTHUR POWER ON JAMES JOYCE: Vermeer-like—Jim was a great artist. But he cared only for art that flowed from him. I would leave my office and have coffee with Jim not far from rue Monsieur le Prince. But never could I cajole him to look at Amedeo Modigliani's painting hanging not far away in the vitrine of Zboroski's gallery.

Modigliani is Italian. A Jew. The demi mondaine Paris Herald talks of him. Just a short walk, Jim. But Jim would have none of it. "Aren't you interested in seeing Modigliani's *Portrait of the Perfect Woman*?" She stretched, on every square inch of canvas, halfway down the Boulevard only at "spectacle" level to you?" I asked knowing that Joyce needed my help to cross the street so blind he was.

But Jim merely mumbled, "*Oh I write over every square inch of the foolscap available, my own body, till by its corrosive sublimation, one continuous present tense will slowly unfold.*' And besides Mr. Power, I already have the greatest painter of them all in my house, Vermeer."

How could I argue with him? While it seemed scarcely possible, all was possible with Jim.

■ PAUL CÉZANNE: Vermeer-like— In Aix in November '58, Joseph Gilbert would place a pen in my hand and squeeze my fingers mumbling: "Comme les anciens" like the Classicists. Pissarro would look at me and say, Can you not be like the morning light of Auvers? We both knew he meant—more like Monsieur Pissarro. I wrote Pissarro from L'Estaque 2 July 1876: "*I am forced to reply to the charm of your magic crayon with an iron point (that is with a metal pen)…the sun here is so tremendous that it seems to me as if the objects were silhouetted not only in black and white but in blue, red, brown, and violet. I may be mistaken, but this seems to me to be the opposite of modeling.*"

Van Gogh, shouting at me with a bread knife in hand, "If only we could all be more Vermeer-like." I said to Gilbert what I said to Pissarro, what I repeated to Van Gogh: "*One does not put one's self in place of the past, one only adds a new link.*" In the end, we are all ourselves, or we are nothing.

"Mother, how did you know what I was wearing when you're in the kitchen and I hadn't come in yet?"

His mother smiled at him and looked over his shoulder at the early morning light streaming in, Vermeer-like, through the kitchen window, illuminating the simple white enamel table with three chairs set alongside.

On the edge of the white enamel table was a small black chip. Fisher's eyes fixed on the chip. Suddenly he imagined seeing his late father sitting across the table, drinking coffee, *The New York Times* open to the Business section, or the front page; Fisher was allowed to read the sports section, the only interesting part of the paper.

■ MARCEL PROUST, May 1917: Vermeer-like—There is nothing Vermeer-like. For he is like everything. Thus nothing can be likened unto him. Or Him. In the last week of May at 9:15 in the morning, I sent Albaret to fetch Vaudoyer to take me to the Jeu de Paume to view my masterpiece, painted especially for me, "The View of Delft" by Vermeer.

Mine, all mine, for it can be everyone's. "*The gables of the house are like precious objects. The pink sand and the little characters and the roofs so meticulously painted you'd think they'd been lacquered. And of course the painting could only be viewed by daylight and I would not be able to rouse myself in the morning so I had stayed up all night eating boiled potatoes to give myself strength.*"

Vermeer's light, my oldest and truest companion, accompanied me to death. "*The good death, the one which gives us courage to walk into the evening.*"

■ HARRIET WEAVER, JOYCE'S PUBLISHER: Vermeer-like—Arthur Power wrote to me that Mr. Joyce had boasted to him of acquiring a Vermeer for the new flat Mr. and Mrs. James Joyce had rented off rue de Grenelle.

I had receieved the letter with grave doubt, for Mr. Joyce had indicated to me that the color scheme he and his wife had chosen in my honor were "my colors," blue and yellow. Certainly the colors of Vermeer. Could that be what Mr. Joyce's 125,000 franc bills were really for: a Vermeer?

I crossed the Channel in 1925 in the hottest June month since the Great War. Arthur Power had telephoned the Joyces, Segur 95-20.

Mr. Joyce had told me the house telephone and all was a tribute to me. The phone number, a cipher, Segur 95-20=1:15=S. 1915=September 15, 1915, my birthday and the day I promised to complete the final installment in "The Egoist" of *A Portrait of the Artist as a Young Man*. Started of course on 2 February 1914, Mr. Joyce's birthday. But did all this have to do with me or Mr. Joyce or Vermeer?

I shall meet you, Miss Weaver, at the foot of Square Robiac and together we will mount the stairs to visit the Joyces, et Vermeer en famille, added Mr. Power. I will wear my English silk tie of violet and red checks in your honor and my red silk handkerchief peeking from my pocket in Johannes' honor.

Imagine the look on Power's face when we went from room to room and blue and yellow they were, robin's egg Vermeer blue walls. Suddenly Mr. Power shouted, "Jim by Jaysus this is no Vermeer, this is a reproduction! I've brought Miss Weaver all this way from London to see this spurious article. It's not a Vermeer, it's Vermeer-like," Power continued to sputter. And calm Mr. Joyce, without skipping a beat, answered languidly, "Yes, Arthur. Vermeer-like. I like it very much, do you?" It was all quite comical. He was mad, Joyce, but not crazy.

Paul Cézanne, *Apotheosis of Delacroix*.

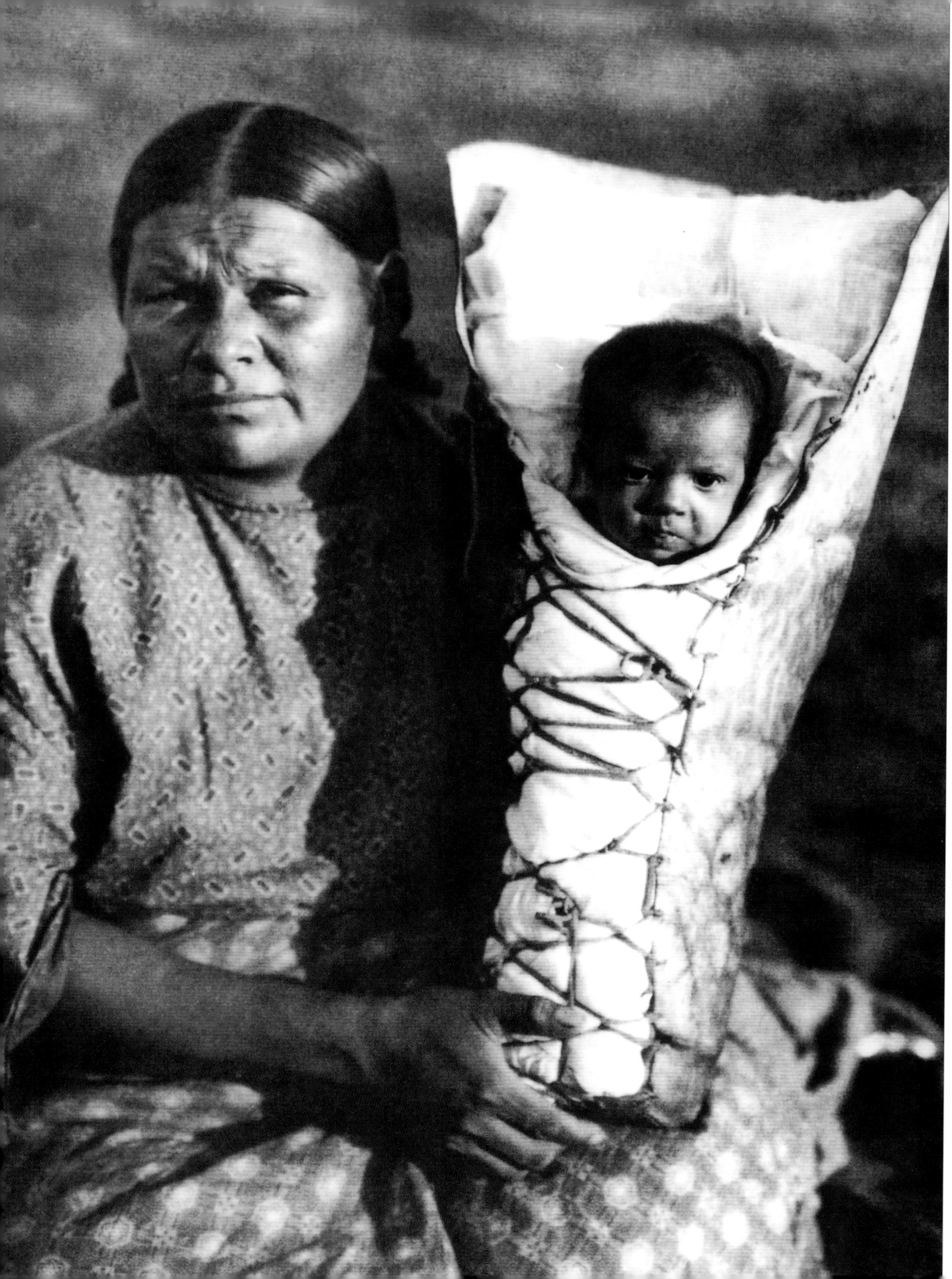

■ Rebecca Neugin, a three year old Cherokee girl on the Trail of Tears in 1838: Ten years old…with his father—What good fortune this young white man Fisher has, to be ten years old with his father.

"When the soldiers came to our house my father wanted to fight but my mother told him if he did, we would all be killed and we surrendered without a fight. They drove us out of our house to join other prisoners in a stockade. And after they took us away, my mother begged them to let her go back and get some bedding. So they let her go back and she brought what bedding and a few cooking utensils she could carry and had to leave behind all of our other household possessions."

■ Rabbi Nosun: She recognized him—Rabbi Nachman of Breslov was now speaking so slowly that each word seem to hang above my head. Tall as I was, and far as I could stretch, I could barely reach each phrase.

"While he was sleeping, many soldiers marched past, and their baggage trains went after them. The servant hid himself from the soldiers. Then a carriage went past, and the king's daughter was in it. She stepped down and sat next to the chamberlain. She recognized him and tried to rouse him, but he did not wake up. She then began to complain that after all the troubles and tribulations, after all the years that he had spent trying to get her away, "because of one day, on which you might have succeeded, you have lost everything." And she wept a great deal and said, "It's a great pity for you and me. I have been here for such a long time, and I cannot get away." Then she took a kerchief from her head, and she wrote on it with her tears and left it by his side, and she rose and seated herself in the carriage and drove away.

When he woke up, he asked the servant, "Where am I in the world?" The servant told him the whole story: how many soldiers had marched past, and then a carriage had gone by, and the king's daughter had stepped down and wept over him, and that she had said it was a great pity for both of them.

He looked about him and saw the kerchief lying nearby. He asked, "Where is this from?"

The servant answered, "She left it here and wrote on it with her tears."

So he took the kerchief and raised it to the sun, and he began to see letters, and he read her complaints and weeping, and that she was no longer in the same castle, and he should search for a golden mountain on which stood a castle of pearl, "and there you will find me."

A Comanche mother.

What good fortune he'd had, thought Fisher, ten years old, with the sports pages, his father forty-five, reading the adult news. Fisher's hot chocolate and sunny-side up eggs, white as the enameled table.

Now, more than ten years later, suddenly seeing his hot chocolate replaced by deep brown coffee, steaming in a cup, in front of his seat, by the china cabinet, Fisher laughed and said, "You were in the living room, you looked out the window and saw me. You went into the kitchen, you made coffee and you put it here for me."

Fisher uttered the last words with a Sherlock Holmes flourish, but as he sat down to drink his coffee, he thought of another question. Why had his mother been looking out the window at that particular moment? Of course she recognized him but why at that instant. He hadn't called her from Time to say he'd be dropping by. It was barely seven-thirty in the morning.

■ Andrew Jackson in his Farewell Address in 1837: father—I, as the Great White Father, have removed and caused to be removed all eastern Indians "beyond the reach of injury or oppression, and that the paternal care of the general government will hereafter watch over them and protect them."

For did I not always try to guide my Indian children from "savagism" to "civilization." Did I not adopt a Cree Indian orphan, Lin Coyer, and raise him as my own son at the Hermitage.

No one knows the mind of an Indian better than I. A thousand nights have I spent with them, in Peace and in War. And I will tell you simply: Removal will spell life for the Cherokee, for the Chocktaw and indeed for all Indians. To let the Indians remain in the East will spell death to them or am I not their father, and they are not my children.

■ Rebecca Neugin's father, a Cherokee who led the family in 1838 on the Long March from Georgia to Oklahoma: What good fortune—The Great White father, Andrew Jackson, told the Cherokee nation of the great good fortune awaiting us in the land in the west, Oklahoma.

Heat had killed so many of us in stockades, in hiding—and fever, plague, and starvation that we pleaded with General Scott to let us wait until the fall to move. These crumbs of kindness, much as a dying pet would be offered a final meal, were granted.

"In September 1838, we started to voyage westward across Tennessee and Kentucky, across Illinois and Missouri to Fort Gibson. Day by day we limped, crawled, struggled, and died…

I had a wagon pulled by two span of oxen to haul us in. Eight of my sons and daughters and three widow women and children rode along. My son Dick walked along with a long whip which he popped over the backs of oxen and drove them all the way. My wife and I walked all the way. Our people got so tired of eating salt pork on the journey that I would walk through the woods as we traveled, hunting for turkey and deer, which I brought into camp to feed us. Camp was usually made at some place where water was to be had, and when we stopped and prepared to cook our food, other emigrants who had been driven from their homes without opportunity to secure cooking utensils came to our camp to use our pots and kettles. There was much sickness among the emigrants, and a great many little children died of whooping cough."

And across the broad land in our shadows, the white men eat and sit and read. We are forgotten. Yet, they too are not in peace—indoors or in the great outside. They wander about, encircling each other, dreamlike but restless. All motion and no direction.

■ Spotted Tail, a Sioux chief: Father—"Why does not the Great Father put his red children on wheels so he can move them as he will?"

■ Wolfgang Amadeus Mozart: Father—"After G-d comes Papa."

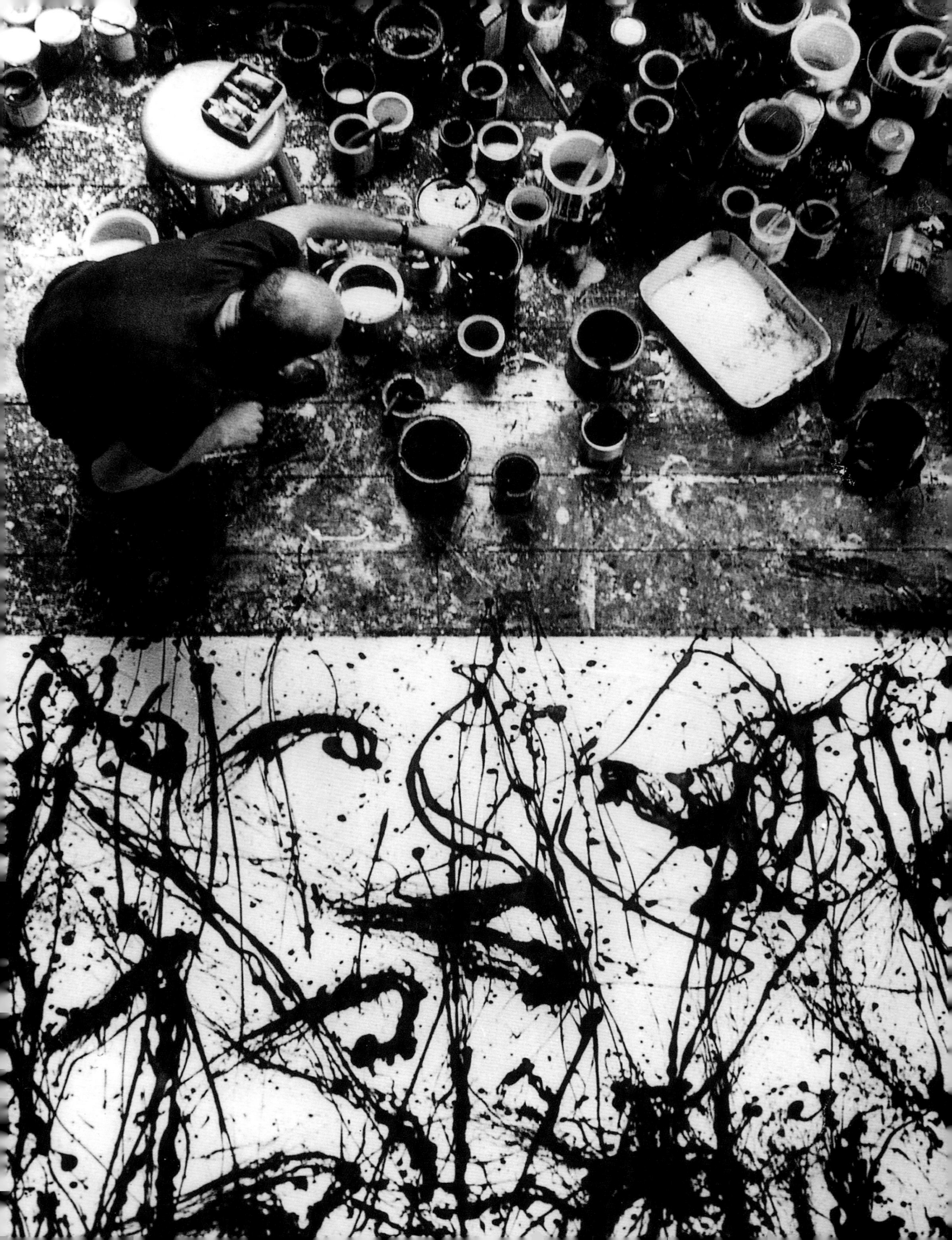

◆ TUVIAH GUTMAN GUTWIRTH, FISHER'S GRANDFATHER: "Did you expect me?" When I would enter the living room on the second floor of my house, my wife who could not see, but thank G-d saw everything, would turn her face toward me. I would often say to her, "Did you expect me?" And she would laughingly answer, "Always."

My grandson, even in America, the same question and the same answer. And that will be the answer given at the end of days when the Messiah comes—may it be in my grandchild's time— to his question, "Did you expect me?" And my grandchild will say, "Always."

"*And it shall come to pass in the end of days that the nations shall flow unto the Lord's house, and many peoples shall go and say Come you and let us go up to the mountain of the Lord (Jerusalem) and He shall be a guide between the nations…and they shall beat their swords into plowshares and their spears into pruning hooks; nation shall not lift up sword against nation neither shall they learn war anymore.*"

■ WALLACE STEVENS: Father superimposed…on mother's face—"*My 'imagination' I got from my mother and my 'practical' sense of reality from my father.*" Father who could write me in November 1897 during my first year at Harvard. "*You have discovered I suppose, that the sun is not a ball of fire sending light and heat like a stone but that radiation and reflection are the mystery and that the higher up we get, and the nearer to the sun the colder it gets and a few odd things like that but you are taught and directed in your studies in a way that you must acknowledge widens your range of vision and upsets your previous notions, teaches you to think, compels you to reason and provides you with positive facts by which you know a conclusion is correct. When this comes to you, you will first begin to absorb and philosophize and but for eccentricities in your genius you may be fitted for a Chair—do not be contented with a smattering of all things—be strong in something. Yours as ever, Garrett.*"

And Mother chanting to me, "*Eat your meat. You need strength and blood. String beans aren't enough.*" All the while, through the letters from Father, above her own lessons to me, the echo of her voice reading to me from Heaven's Bible. Music for my mind, poetry for my soul.

Father's words superimposed on Mother's face.

"*The quiet
The summer night is like perfection of thought.
The house was quiet because it had to be.
The quiet was part of the meaning, part of the mind.
The access of perfection to the page.*"

"Did you expect me?" he asked tentatively.

"Always," she answered with a mother's delight.

"Seriously, Mom." Fisher drained his cup. Whatever she put in the coffee wasn't cream. No matter how often he tried the mixture she used, it never tasted the same.

"Let me pour another cup. Such logic you use, you should be the boss of Time Incorporated."

"I met HIM last night, Mother, I can't believe it."

"You met or you dreamed you met HIM while you were sleeping in your clothing?"

Suddenly the image of the Patriarch Luce looking at the picture of his grandfather—his mother's father—superimposed itself on his mother's face.

■ JACKSON POLLOCK: I met him last night—Oh HE short for HENRY and HIM, long for every patriarch that ever lived but most especially those Presbyterian fathers. How we spooked the unsaved souls we've met. Just say nothing. Sit still and before you know it we've convinced even the People of the Book we have known them, we have met them, we can judge them.

Luce is all black and Fisher is a white canvas waiting to be dripped on. Luce can only appear at night for by daylight he doesn't exist. But true Presbyterian soul that he is, he neither sleeps nor slumbers. Still they are meant for each other, Him and Fisher. Just as I and Lee, one really. Try to peel Luce off the canvas of Fisher's life. Lee was on my brushes and no amount of whiskey or turpentine could remove her.

Lord knows how I tried, how I did try.

■ LEE KRASNER: I met him—"*When I met him I was terribly drawn to Jackson and I fell in love with him— physically, mentally, in every sense of the word. I had a conviction when I met Jackson that he had something important to say. When we began going together, my own work became irrelevant. He was the important thing.*"

Jackson heard me say that a thousand thousand times. He more afraid of the night than I. Even my childhood night times when my two sisters and I "*peering out the window at Mrs. Macvoy,*" mad Mrs. Macvoy. Emerging at night shouting at the moon, thinking she was talking to her long dead husband.

Only Mama could lead us back to sleep and my father he was different for all his mysticism, his close chats with the Holy One, Blessed be His name. Only Papa's mother could shlug kopores, swing a chicken, above his head to pardon his sins.

Jackson knew it, and my father knew it and I: *That thine is the kingdom and the glory*. But mine is the power. Always was. Always will be. So why is this nice young Jewish novelist boy talking about Henry Luce? To Henry's Presbyterian self, Himself, to Mama. And why isn't young Fisher bragging about spending his nights with Dosha herself because he can see where it all will lead. For Dosha is the power. Forever and ever. Plus ça change.

Jackson Pollock.

◆ RICKELE PADAWER, DOSHA'S GRANDMOTHER: Being in the present and being in the past—It is impossible to believe. In America after the war. After Slonim. After my entire family was lost. After our two boys and our daughter had gone to the *Guldeneh Medinah*, the golden country, in the 1920's. Chicago. Streets with gold, all you had to do was bend down and the gold was yours, wrote my brother to my husband, inviting us all to live with him in Chicago. "Don't you have to wait and see who has lost the gold?" innocently asked my Yeshiva trained husband. "Oh, it's so easy here. What's lost is small potatoes. No one cares about lost and found in America," Bubba Meysehs said to my husband by return mail. Bubbe Mayses and not Bava Metsiah. That's why I won't go to America.

But my brother Yankel now Jack Margolies—Real Estate—didn't take no or maybe for an answer. And Yankel was clever. Yankel sent three tickets for the children and two tickets for us, six months later. The children went. We stayed and stayed and stayed.

"I won't go if I don't have a livelihood as a teacher in a Yeshiva in Chicago," Simha insisted. "I am not Real Estate and Real Estate is not me." "Yankel can support us just as he supports our children," I pleaded. "I won't live off his charity!" Simha cried. And every week that went by, another letter from our children—Joseph, Malkeh and Reuven. Always the longest from Joseph and the shortest from Reuven. I was caught between two worlds. My children longed for their mother and Simha said, "I won't abandon my Yeshiva. My home. My past." And Yankel writing: "You and Rickele will come to Chicago when your past will be destroyed." Finally he did accept to come to Chicago—to teach at the Yeshiva that Yacob had arranged for us.

Two weeks after the tickets arrived, the War! The hiding. The partisans. Thank G-d we survived. But did we? For Simha was broken, just broken. How could our granddaughter Jerusha, the only one whom he could talk to in America, have known enough to have insisted Simha and I go to the Rebbe. She could not have been more than seven. She held my Simha's hand, putting it in the Rebbe's hand and saying, "Tell this man why you never laugh, Grandfather."

Simha looked at the Rebbe and answered, "I don't want to be in the present, I want to be in the past."

◆ SIMHA PADAWER: You are blessed my son—She hocked me and hocked me until I agreed to listen to Jerusha, until I agreed to go and see the Rebbe in Crown Heights. She would never let up, Rickele, once she got an idea. Just like when her no guddnik brother, a total luftmensh, the Wizard of the Windy City, he called himself, convinced her to send our children to America.

She never let up before the War and during to talk about America. She worshiped her brother. Of course, Rickele thought she saved the children's lives or America saved the children's lives or her luftmensh brother had. But what was a life in Chicago or New York? Did not Uri the Angel of Strehlitz say of the Yom Kippur that passed *"what I would not give to have those days return."* What I would not give to have one day, just one day, back in Volozhin in the Etz Chaim Yeshiva with Reb Naphtali Berlin. Of course, all the Yeshivot and all the batei medrashot and all my teachers and my students and their grave stones and all my past, gone and destroyed. Disappeared. And whom should I talk to?

The same taut skin, the same sense both his mother and grandfather gave of being in the present and being in the past at the same instant.

"Mother, do you remember when you asked Grandfather to bless me to be a good student when I was five years old?"

"And..." Fisher's mother interrupted. "And my father said, 'If Raphael will study he will be a good student,'" his mother continued with her eyes directly on his, exactly as they had been years before. Fisher stared down at his shoes.

"Did Grandfather bless me?" persisted Fisher.

"You are blessed," she said. "You are blessed, my son."

"Are you blessed, mother?"

And go to Brooklyn to speak to a Rebbe. Even the Rebbe. For what? For Jerusha was still a child. Of course Rickele knew how to convince me. With my own words.

"Yes, dear Simha. Jerusha is a child but did you not always tell me in Europe, at home, that after the destruction of the Temple, prophecy was given to fools and children?" What could I do but go to the Rebbe? What could I say but nothing? What could I think but that I didn't want to be in the present but in the past?

How the Rebbe knew what I thought only Hashem can understand. I am not sure why he said: "You are blessed, my son."

I want to believe. Believe me, I want to believe.

■ THE REBBE MENACHEM MENDEL SCHNEERSON: You are blessed—"And did he bless me. You are blessed," she said evenly. You are blessed my son. Are you blessed, Mother? They walked into my room. Three of them. The old man, with steady blue eyes, like only the misnagdim have—those who studied in Volozhin or in Mir.

With his wife who led him. And with their granddaughter. And he and his granddaughter alike, like two drops of dew. And who walked with whom? "And Abraham said to his young men: stay here with the donkey; the lad and I will go yonder and worship and we will come back to you." For did not Abraham know that he and his child would and will come back. Jerusha, the grandchild, has taken the grandfather's hand and put it in mine. In America, we are one generation farther from Sinai but we are one generation closer to redemption. The old man was weeping and his eyes asked for my blessing. He wanted to be in the past. I looked at the child and I saw the verse:

"By myself have I sworn, saith the Lord. In Blessing I will bless you, and in multiplying I will multiply your descendants as the stars of the heaven and as the sand which is on the seashore."

Because the old man wants to be in the past, he is with his grandchild in the present. She will be his Jerushah. His inheritance forever. She will be our Jerushah. And mine too. Jerusha is *"obliged to learn Torah, women's Torah study connects to the same essence of Torah."*

Jerusha must teach her daughter. In our day, women are the bridge to and from Sinai. And this old man, he did bless me. I could tell him, amid my tears. For do I not see our yeshivot day by day before my eyes. Do I not see the flames. Do I not weep? But do we not all see what we can be? And the binding of Isaac is not a sacrifice. Yes, I must say to the old man, "You are blessed. Blessed because of your Jerusha. Is not Israel blessed? Yes, because of our mother, Em be Yisroel. A mother in Israel. Our Jerusha."

Rembrandt van Rijn, *Abraham and Isaac.*

And this the form of mighty Hand sitting on Albions cliffs
Before the face of Albion, a mighty threatning Form.

His bosom wide & shoulders huge overspreading wondrous
Bear Three strong sinewy Necks & Three awful & terrible Heads
Three Brains in contradictory council brooding incessantly.
Neither daring to put in act its councils, fearing each other,
Therefore rejecting Ideas as nothing & holding all Wisdom
To consist. in the agreements & disagreents of Ideas.
Plotting to devour Albions Body of Humanity & Love.

Such Form the aggregate of the Twelve Sons of Albion took; & such
Their appearance when combind: but often by birth-pangs & loud groans
They divide to Twelve: the key-bones & the chest dividing in pain
Disclose a hideous orifice; thence issuing the Giant-brood
Arise as the smoke of the furnace, shaking the rocks from sea to sea.
And there they combine into Three Forms, named Bacon & Newton & Locke
In the Oak Groves of Albion which overspread all the Earth.

Imputing Sin & Righteousness to Individuals: Rahab
Sat deep within him hid: his Feminine Power unreveald
Brooding Abstract Philosophy. to destroy Imagination, the Divine-
-Humanity A Three-fold Wonder: feminine: most beautiful: Three-fold
Each within other. On her white marble & even Neck, her Heart
Inorb'd and bonified: with locks of shadowing modesty, shining
Over her beautiful Female features, soft flourishing in beauty
Beams mild, all love and all perfection, that when the lips
Recieve a kiss from Gods or Men, a threefold kiss returns
From the pressed loveliness: so her whole immortal form three-fold
Three-fold embrace returns: consuming lives of Gods & Men
In fires of beauty melting them as gold & silver in the furnace
Her Brain enlabyrinths the whole heaven of her bosom & loins
To put in act what her Heart wills; O who can withstand her power
Her name is Vala in Eternity: in Time her name is Rahab

The Starry Heavens all were fled from the mighty limbs of Albion

◆ **Tuviah Gutman Gutwirth, Fisher's grandfather**: Shalom, Tzu Zan Matzleach. Peace be with you. May you be successful—My grandfather, Kalman Gutwirth Katz, the heilige Dayan of Cracow, would take me to the door of his house. He always insisted to give charity with his own hand, *a varmer hand*, he called it and to see the person to whom he was giving.

When I was ten, I helped my grandfather walk back to his study, for in those days his health was always fleeing from him but G-d forbid not his clearness of mind.

I asked him, "Grandfather, Maimonides teaches us that a high level of giving is that neither the recipient nor the giver see each other. So why don't you give the money to another to give the poor person who comes to the door?"

And Grandfather, whose hand I can often feel on mine when I am tired, and when I feel I cannot go on studying, spoke softly. "You asked. You answer." I thought for a long time and said, "It must be that here something additional is required. The blessing is additional. Is that what the people come for?" And my grandfather asked, "And who are the people who receive a blessing?" Suddenly I could see that I was walking grandfather to the door and I too was being blessed: Torah, Huppah and Maaysim tovim. To study Torah, ascend to the marriage canopy and do good deeds. Grandfather could see my head shake back and forth as I reasoned out and when I had finished, he said, "Blessed art thou G-d who has created man."

■ Jahanghir in his diary in Tuzuk-I-Jahanghiri: Eternal—"*On Thursday the 9th [30 November 1617] a drinking party was convened. On this day, I gave my son Shah Jahan a flawless ruby weighing nine tanks and five surkhs [184 carats] worth 125,000 rupees set with two pearls. This was the ruby Her Majesty Maryam-Makani, His Majesty Arsh-Auhyani's [Akbar's mother,] gave me as a present at my birth. For years, it was in his [Akbar's] turban band and thereafter I too kept it in my turban band for good luck. Aside from its monetary value, since it has been a good luck charm for this eternal dynasty, it was given to my son [Shah Jahan].*"

"Yes, I am blessed, with the same eternal blessing as you. When your grandfather would be told, even at dinner-time in Antwerp, that there was a needy person who wanted charity at the door, he would tell one of his eight children to say he would be there in two minutes. He would go to his bedroom and get the charity money. Then go to the door and personally hand the money to the recipient. For my father it wasn't enough to give the money, he had to do it personally. And then, after he gave the money, he would smile at the poor man and his smile would contain a hint of sadness which showed that he understood how difficult it was to be poor.

"And then he would shake hands with the man and say '*Shalom, Tzu Zan Matzleach*. Peace be with you. May you be successful.' And then he would say from the depths of his heart, 'thank you,' while looking straight at the man. After the poor man had left, Father would often tell me: "Don't ever forget, even for a moment, that we—both you and I, and all our family could also one day be on the other side of the door. Asking. Hoping. Begging. Praying. For charity. For a door can open two ways. And in an instant.

■ Zohar: Blessing—"*From the day that Jerusalem was destroyed, blessings have been rare and curses frequent in the world*" (Zohar iii 74b).

■ William Blake: It wasn't enough to give, he had to do it personally—Milton. His eyes. My eyes. Were not my jewels gifts from him?

"*The cabinet is formed of gold*
And pearl and crystal shining bright
And within it opens into a world
And a little lovely moony night."

But seeing my master Milton's words upon a page, glowing though they might, even by moonlight, does not reveal their subtle mystery.

Nay, it wasn't enough to give, Milton had to do it personally. To come to me and speak in the perch of my ear. "*Time will run back and fetch the Age of Gold.*"

"*From infancy, I have had the faculty of vision. All men partake of this ability. But it is lost by not being cultivated…And I do write only when commanded to do so, only by my angels who come to me personally.*" And the moment I have written I see the words fly about the room in all directions.

■ Allen Ginsberg: He had to do it personally—Of course he had to do it personally. If he did not, he might as well hand out counterfeit money. Or pieces of shredded newspaper or burst balloons. But true gold. Money has to be given in person and then it can be given across the seas in ethereal realms, beyond one's breathing.

William Blake and his gifts to me, the setting sun in my cityscape apartment. I, on my back, hearing "a deep rich voice, my own reciting Blake's 'Ah, Sunflower'."

"*Ah, Sunflower! Weary of time*
Who counts the steps of the sun
Seeking after that sweet gold clime
When the traveler's journey is love."

Suddenly the voice has changed. It is the voice of Blake and it is speaking to me, across the room, across the oceans of time and space, lulling me in my crib, rocking me back and forth oh so gently, gifting me with a voice.

"*Where the youth pined away with desire*
And the pale virgin shrouded in the snow
Arise from the graves and aspire
Where my sunflower wishes to go!"

What could I do but climb on the fireplace and tap on the half open window pane of the two women neighbors living on my landing. "I've seen G-d," I exclaimed.

And what could they do but slam down their window. As did my analyst. As did Kerouac and my father. "*Madness the world would believe, visions it would not.*"

William Blake, Jerusalem.

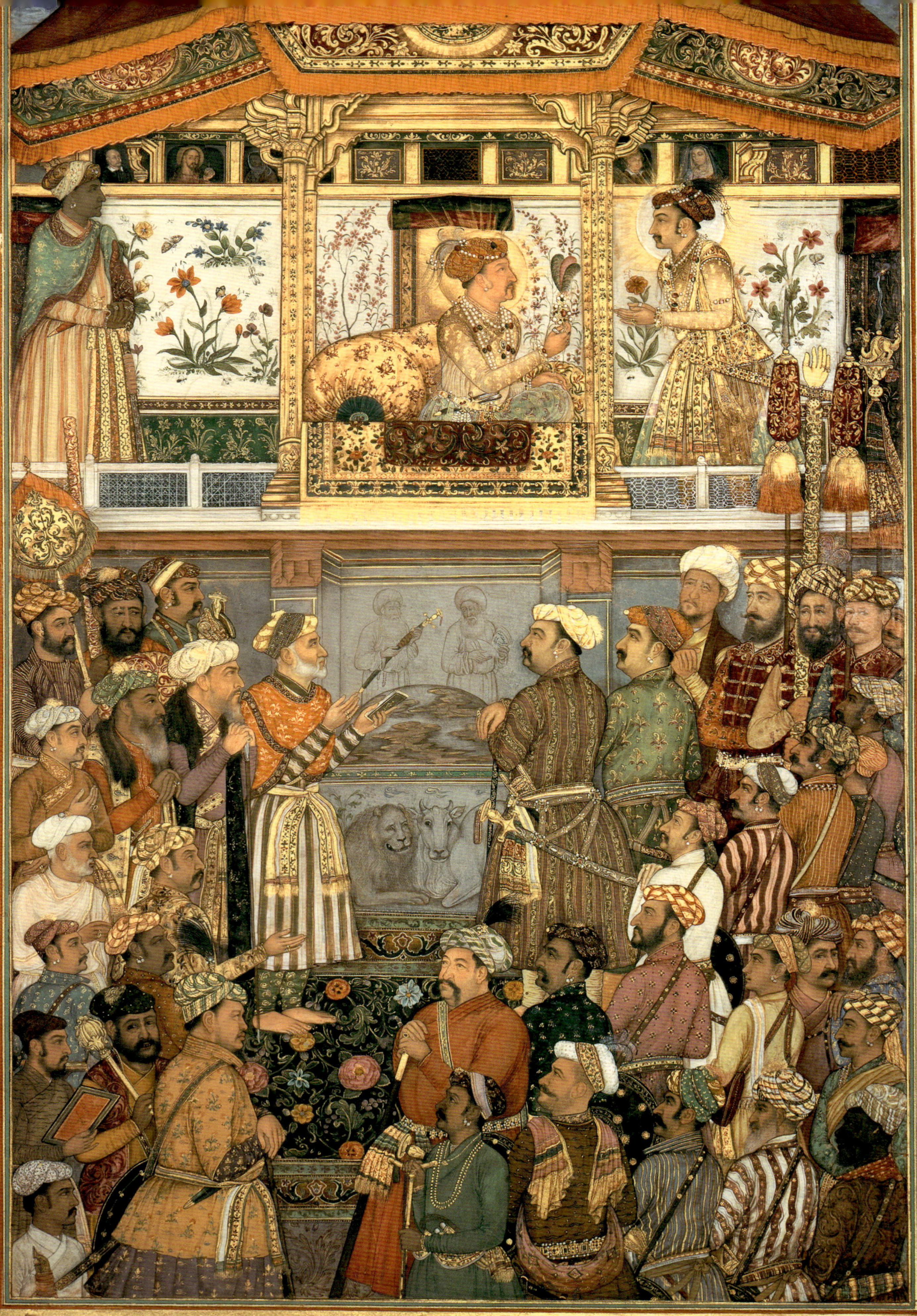

◆ Tuviah Gutman Gutwirth, Fisher's grandfather: Father would always tell me—My father would always tell me stories that his grandfather had told him in Cracow.

He would tell me stories when we studied, when we walked together on the street to Meisel's shul in Cracow, even when we traveled on the train to Belz.

Once on a platform waiting for a train to Warsaw, he turned to me as the passengers next to us were talking and laughing about someone who lived not far from us. Father led me down the platform a bit: "My father, Kalman Katz, told me on this very train platform that 'when one is in a public place, one should be careful not to use a person's last name if you're saying something bad about him.'"

Stories about everything. G-d, work, Israel, the world, the Sabbath that animals enjoy, the creation of the stars, long stories, stories as short as an aphorism, even a story without words.

When he was offered the post of Dayan of Riglitz, Father went to his father. "I am happy to go to Riglitz," Father said. "Although it is a town of only two synagogues and very few Jewish souls. I am afraid that my children will find it too small. And they will leave for much larger places, even to the West. Then their children, G-d forbid, will be raised among Jews far more removed from Sinai than we are."

More Sodom than Po-lin, our Poland.

My grandfather stared and froze and did not move or answer or make a sign. But my father persisted, for the question kept him awake, and his wife Yittal insisted she would not go without Kalman's answer for in truth it was her question for it was to her hometown Zalman and she were travelling.

Finally my great grandfather spoke.

"Reb Menahem Mendel of Kotz once traveled outside of Warsaw to see Mendel of Worke. You have mastered the art of silence. From where did you learn it?"

And neither did my grandfather speak. And neither did my blessed father speak when I spoke to him of my desire to go to Antwerp and of my worries for my children. When I could not tell my own children what to do, I told them what my father would always tell me.

"And then Father would take my hand, if I had been chosen to accompany him to greet the poor man at the door, and he would walk back into the dining room or wherever we were seated and Father's face would be shining.

Father would always tell me that he thanked people when he gave them charity because they were a blessing to him and he would also say a blessing for his children's children.

"Did he say for his children's children's children, Mother?"

Fisher's mother stared straight at him as light continued to stream through the window—a haze of blue and white. His mother's eyes had turned inward—thinking most probably of her father or perhaps of Antwerp, maybe of the War, of all that had vanished, but not everything, never everything. Her head slowly nodded back and forth. Was she going backward in time or forward, forward through his life to his children's yet unborn, he not married yet.

▪ Leonardo da Vinci: hand—Young Fisher's grandfather's father is a supreme teacher.

Fisher's mother's hand is in her father's hand, for all creation comes from the hand. *And with her thin hand, each vein a portrait, in his: Curiosita*— Fisher's grandfather is stimulating her curiosity, a quest for learning that will continue. At the door of their house *dimostrazione* a commitment to demonstrate knowledge of morality through *sensazione*, the refinement of the senses, the sight of the poor person, this means to enliven the experience.

Then the central paradox *sfumato*—going up in smoke—who is giving alms to whom? Who is receiving the blessing? *Arte e Scienza*, logic and imagination, mingle like a river, *Corporalita*, the daughter, cultivates grace, fitness and poise and the three, the poor man, the father and the daughter have *connessione* —the vision that all things are connected and being true, they will be transmitted unsoiled, unvarnished and handed down to the next generation.

▪ Chief Joseph (1840-1904): And then my father would take my hand—My father, Tuckakas, was called Old Chief Joseph by the white man. But he was never old. Henry Spalding, who converted my father, was always old.

"If I become a Christian," Father asked Spalding in Lapwai, "Will I become an old man? Because if I become old, the white man will turn me into a plaything, a slave."

"You will be called Joseph, freed from slavery and an adviser to the Great White Father."

Father gave his hand in friendship to Spalding. All this was before I was born. Father gave me a name from my people Hin-mah-too-yah-lat-kekt, Thunder Rolling in the Mountains. Father took my hand and pointed it to the rising sun. He said, "This land from where the sun rises, until the sun sets, is ours— all the Wallowa."

But when the White Man took our land, my father took my hand and lit a match and my hand burned his New Testament and his American flag and his membership to the church. We moved to hunt the buffalo in Montana, far from the White Man who then began to call Father Old Chief Joseph. Father laughed and said, "They can call me what they will, and they can and will call you Chief Joseph." But taking my hand in his he swore, "My son, you will always be Hin-mah-too-yah-laht-ket, the thunder that will roll forever down from the mountains."

▪ Payag: Thinking most probably of Father…maybe of all that had vanished, but not everything— Who were the moghuls? What were they? We Hindus could not even pronounce their name— mongols—and we called them moghuls.

In the middle of the night, Shah Jahan summoned me. Had he not summoned my brother, my fatherly teacher, my protector Balchand, also in the middle of the night? And just as with Balchand, Abul-Fazl reading aloud to me the portion of the Tuzuk-I Jahanghir that I was to illustrate. Over and over, Abul-Fazl read: "*On Thursday the ninth a drinking party was convened…this was the ruby…It has been a good luck charm for this eternal dynasty.*"

And Prince Khurram (how could I not see him as a boy—for I had been a court painter forty-five years before in his grandfather's court) said to me: "*Draw the picture of those days: bring them back before my eyes.*"

I said I will, your Majesty, but what were you thinking when your father gave you his nine tank ruby." "Thinking?" repeated Khurram. "Thinking? Most probably of Father. Maybe of the War…of all that had vanished, but not everything, never everything."

By the light of the sun that was just above the horizon, I could see the splendid ruby in the hand of my Emperor slowly moving back and forth, back and forth—from Akbar to Jahanghir to himself. All that had vanished, I could not see—but not everything, never everything.

Payag, *Jahngir presents Prince Khurram with a turban ornament.*

210.

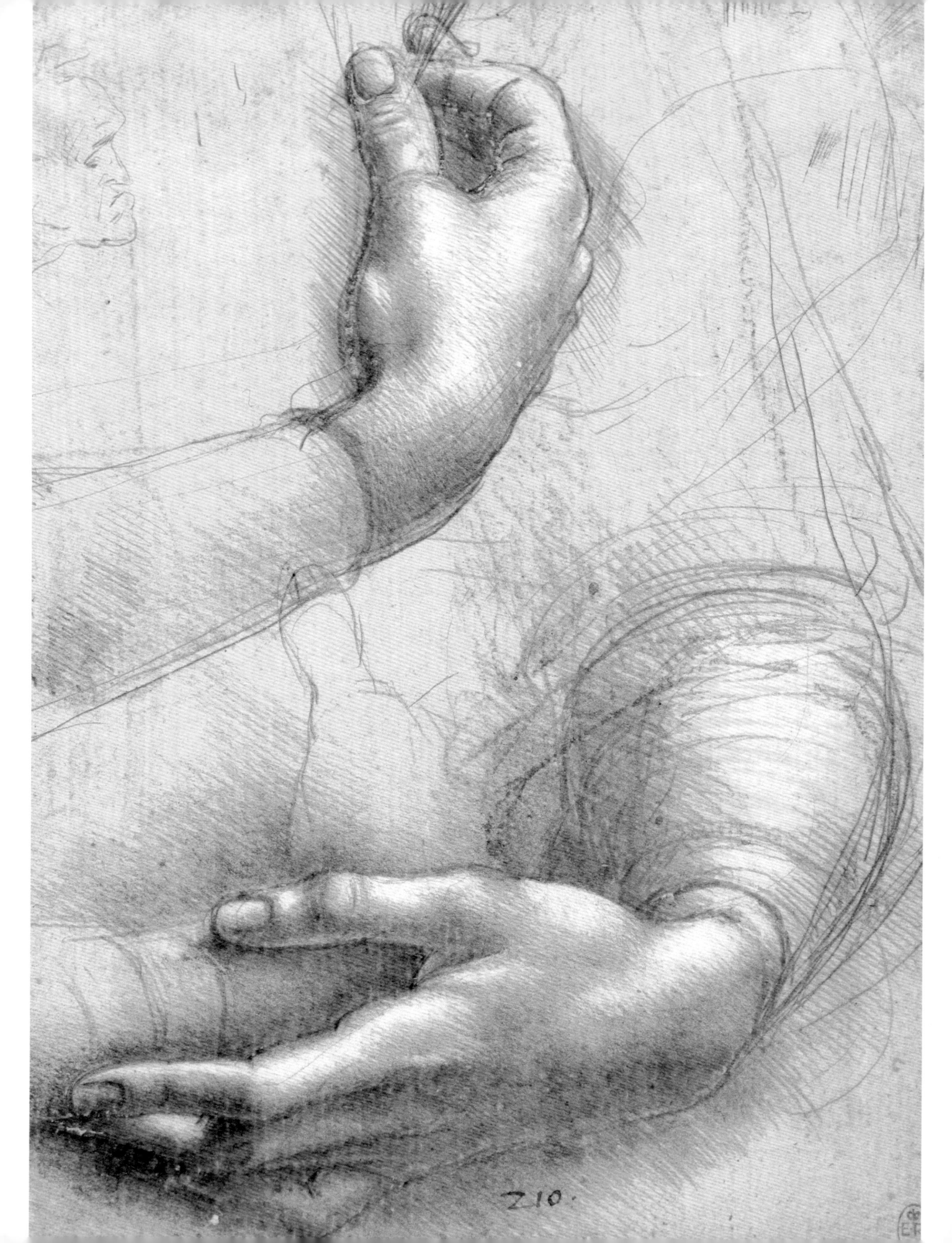

■ MONET: Fugitive—"*In the end the only merit that I have is to have painted directly from nature with the air of conveying my impressions in front of the most fugitive effects.*" Fisher worries that his garden flower will vanish. A fugitive. And she will reappear after a season. Or she will peep at him suddenly behind mist. Evade his eye but her perfume will send him all a quiver. Cache-cache. A million times. Even in one day.

And everyone is asking me, "Monsieur Claude, how old are you? Do you think you will be able to paint when you are one hundred?" But I know they meant ninety. And when I was sixty, they wondered could I paint at seventy. Of all the foolish questions ever asked, the most foolish, imprecise, meaningless and unanswerable surely must be, how old are you?

Did I not live for a thousand years each afternoon in Giverny? The colors changing every second. The sun rearranging itself before my palette, my hand racing to follow my eyes. If I did not paint with my heart, I would have collapsed long ago.

■ PAYAG: Name—"And what of you, Payag?" my brother Balchand said. He quoted my words back to me—when I had begged him to paint his own picture into his own painting. He was clever, Balchand. He studied the drawings of the West. The ones that the Italian traders and Jesuits brought back to Shah Jahan. The Emperor would give the drawings to him to study, to master.

"I am the ruler of the world—Shah Jahan—you, Payag must be the painter of the world."

And Balchand said: "Do not think your signature is enough. The Foreigners paint themselves. Even I, Balchand, a Hindu, in a Muslim river have drawn my self-portrait as you bade me to do. Payag, portray yourself in a corner of a painting, just as I did." So in a quadrant just above where Balchand had painted his own picture, I painted mine. Could I refuse my brother?

Leonardo da Vinci, *Study of a Woman's Hands.*

Ridiculous, he thought of Tal and the money. Eighteen hundred dollars. He had his own father and his own mother without Tal as a double set of parents and in-laws rolled into one. Dosha's name rolling around in his body.

Senseless to ask his mother what she thought. She would ask him back. And what blessing did he want from her or from Tal or Luce. He got up and kissed his mother good-bye on both cheeks. "Well, I'm off, Mother. Back to Greenwich."

With his mother, Johanna Charlotte, hearing only the first half of his last word.

■ PROUST: A fugitive—Monet cultivated a kaleidoscope of color in his garden, "*less the old florist garden than a colorist garden.*" The old florist shops with Hortensias, lasting a brace of days, a week perhaps—truly fugitive, but Giverny's canvas…

And Monet's canvases, a dream of a flower of a woman that will not fade, an eternal amaranth of light.

■ HIERONYMA DE PAIVA: A fugitive garden flower—What our Lord, Elihu Yale would call me. "You are my fugitive garden flower," Elihu would explain wearily as he entered the Garden House and sit me beside me turning the flat Hollandi diamonds, this way and that. While I looked at the diamond crystals, he would be shifting in his chair, pushing the stones backward and forward like a regiment marching up and down Middlegate Street.

■ HIRAM BINGHAM, biographer of Elihu Yale. Discoverer of Machu Picchu, Ridiculous… without a home…ask her to wed…senseless…overwhelmed…a sense of calm—Ridiculous in a sense. Yet so human. Marrying Alfreda with the endless Tiffany fortune. Then scaling the even greater lost treasures of Machu Picchu. And then and only then driven to write Elihu Yale's history. Both of us, Elihu and I, without a true home. Exiled. Far from Wales and Hawaii. From Mother.

Surrounded by moghul's wealth. Elihu: vigorous, young. The widow Hynmers with a fortune, of course he should ask her to wed…senseless to have it all. My professorship. Fame. Family. The senate. Elihu: the governor—lord of the subcontinent—Madras, then Fort George—senseless for me to be overwhelmed by Suzanne Carroll Hill—married she was, to a Congressman, and I married to Alfreda, to Tiffany, to my "standing." Elihu overwhelmed by Hieronyma de Paiva, a housemaid in his home, she widowed from Jacques de Paiva, died at the Indian mines. Elihu's three children running about the house. His wife, the widow Hynmers watching him, overwhelmed by a Portugese, a Jewess, the body of the East, the hot milky fragrance of earliest times.

Elihu and I, overwhelmed. And after eating the forbidden fruit banished from Eden, Could we ever in old age, in cool remembrance find a sense of calm?

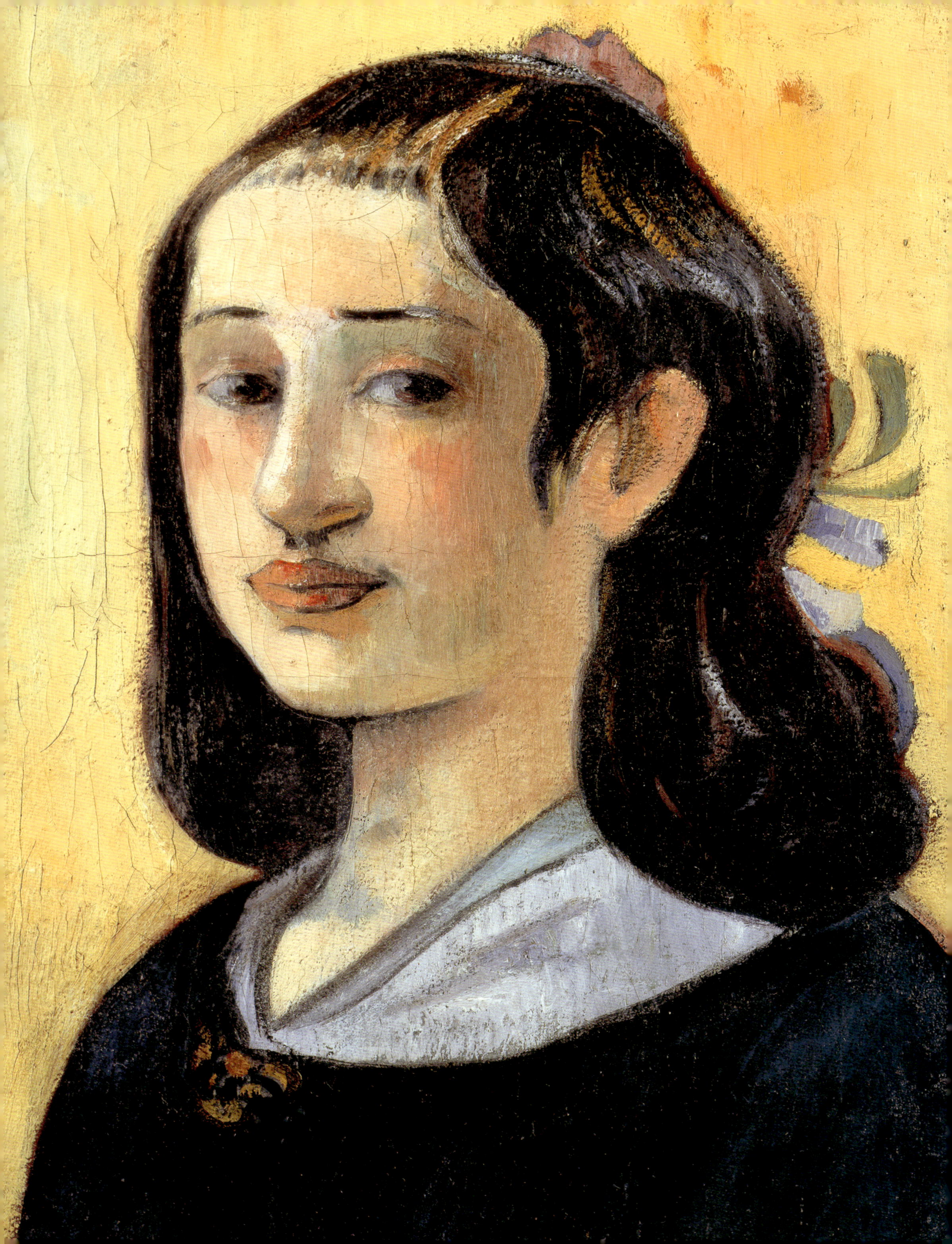

■ GAUGUIN: From Paris at thirty-six,—Fisher's father and I. Forever immigrants, forever refugees. Never Parisian, certainly not French with a place fixe each day at the corner restaurant, with a prix fixe meal and the comme-il-faux children.

My hunger as an immigrant to Paris twice as grand, for was I not a refugee to Peru at less than half twelve years of age? Eden it was in Lima, with my grandmother Flora's uncle, Don Pio de Tristan y Moscoso. To an old man's eyes, did not my mother Aline, his brother Mariano de Tristan y Moscoso's grandchild, look just alike? The very same intense eyes, the jut of her jaw, her long neck, the quivering of her nostrils when she felt trapped. Peasant stock and mixed Montezuma's blood.

A Peruvian Eden, I barely four years old hiding "*between two barrels of molasses sucking on sugar cane.*"

And my mother, distraught, searching for me, "*how graceful with a silk mantilla covering her face, revealing only one eye, that eye so gentle and imperious, so pure and mild.*"

And I being found, returned to my maternal home, "*slapped by my mother's hand, supple as rubber. It is true that a few minutes later, crying, she was hugging and caressing me.*"

And to leave Montezuma's sun. To return to Paris, fatherless, at age six. My mother was offered a 5,000 Piastres legacy by her now dead but ever-adoring uncle, aged 113 when he, Don Pio de Tristan y Moscoso, passed. Of course her Peruvian vulture relatives would not hear of it, blocked the will and sent their wily representative to France, offering my mother a fraction of what she deserved but more, far more than we needed. She, an aristocrat, uttered, "*All or nothing.*" It was to be nothing.

And when "*I came back one day with a few colored glass marbles, my mother, furious, asked me where I had gotten those marbles. I lowered my head and said that I had exchanged them for my rubber ball.*

'*What? You, my son, you engage in trade?*'"

Of course I knew that just as I was an immigrant to France so too would I be forever a refugee from Paris, never a tradesman, ever an artist.

CHAPTER 6

"Greener. That's what you'll be, a greener at Yale." Fisher's father had told the first time he came up to Yale to visit his son. Fisher: a prodigy, an immigrant's son, A French refugee, admitted to Yale.

And his father walking around the campus with him shaking, anxious to return to New York, uncomfortable. Perhaps the admissions officer might see him and decide his son wasn't the type for Yale.

One has no idea what it's like to come to America in the midst of war, a refugee from Paris at thirty-six, a refugee to France from Hungary at twelve, a refugee from Poland to Hungary at seven.

And before that, how many times had his own father or grandfather or mother's family fled? Didn't they originally come from Szechev? He wasn't sure.

"Raphael," his father had said, "when I arrived in New York and saw my brother, Nathan, who saved me and our whole family, I saw Nathan meeting me at the boat and I said to him simply, 'What do I look like? Nossun? The old Fisher of Fisher Feathers, Paris?'"

■ RABBI NACHMAN OF BRESLOV: Shaking—It is not Fisher's father who is shaking. It is his father being shaken by Der Alter Yidden, the grandparents of Fisher, the great grandparents who shake us all.

Fisher's father can sense why he is being shaken. He and his son are entering a strange kingdom. A story about a turkey. "*The king's son once went mad and decided that he was a turkey. As a turkey, the son had a need to sit naked under the table and gobble up crumbs of bread and bones. The doctors all despaired of helping him, and the king was greatly troubled. Then a wise man came and announced that he would take it upon himself to heal the prince. He stripped naked and sat under the table alongside the king's son, pecking with him at the crumbs and bones. The prince asked him: Who are you and what are you doing here? The wiseman replied, What are you doing here? I, said the king's son, am a turkey. And I, said the sage, am a turkey too.*

The two of them sat there together for some time, until they got used to each other. Then, at the wise man's signal, a shirt was thrown to them. Do you think, said the turkey-sage to the prince, that a turkey cannot wear a shirt? You can wear a shirt and still be a turkey! After a time he signaled again and they were given trousers. He said the same thing again. Do you think that with pants on you can't be a turkey? Thus they both put on pants and all the rest of their clothing. The wiseman signaled again and regular human food was thrown to them from the table and he said. You think if you eat good food, you're not a turkey? You can eat and still be a turkey! And so they ate. Then the sage said, Do you think that a turkey can only sit under the table? You can be a turkey and sit right at the table. Thus he went on with him until he had cured him completely."

And where is the wise sage who will heal Fisher? But Fisher can see his father shaking. And he will come eventually to understand, for we are all royal children.

■ SIR JOHN CHARDIN, Elihu Yale's partner: I came up to Yale to visit him— The first time I came up to Yale in London, after he returned from India, I cried, "*You are home at last Elihu and in blessed good health.*" And resplendent Yale was. After that first visit to Elihu on January 2, 1700, I wrote my brother Daniel who was still stationed in India. I went to see the nabob Yale almost every day.

"*Every time I see Yale at his home or at a coffee house, I give him all possible indication of my desire to be of service.*"

And less than two years later, my dear brother Daniel, our partner Elihu Yale, had altered beyond recognition. I penned sadly to Daniel:

September 1701. To my brother: "*Apropos of Mr. Yale, this man at first went abroad with a lackey, well-dressed and living like a gentleman. Now he has greatly modified his ways and lives in a secluded manner. I no longer go to see him at his house, where I went thirty times without once being able to get him to come to my house in the country. I found him timid, undecided, always on the defensive and in a word, of no great consequence, non e mi gran cosa.*"

■ RABBI NOSUN OF NEMIROV: Shaking—"*When the suffering of his sorrows came upon my master, Rabbi Nachman of Breslov, the pain was so great he said he could almost bite through wood with his teeth…*

Even when he was just conversing with people about worldly matters his body trembled greatly. His legs shook so badly that when he was seated at the table with other people, the whole table would shake on his account."

Our master, Rabbi Nachman never served as our prayer leader in Breslov. He never led the singing at his own Sabbath table. So great was his shaking, so heavenly his trembling.

Paul Gauguin, *The Mother of the Artist.*

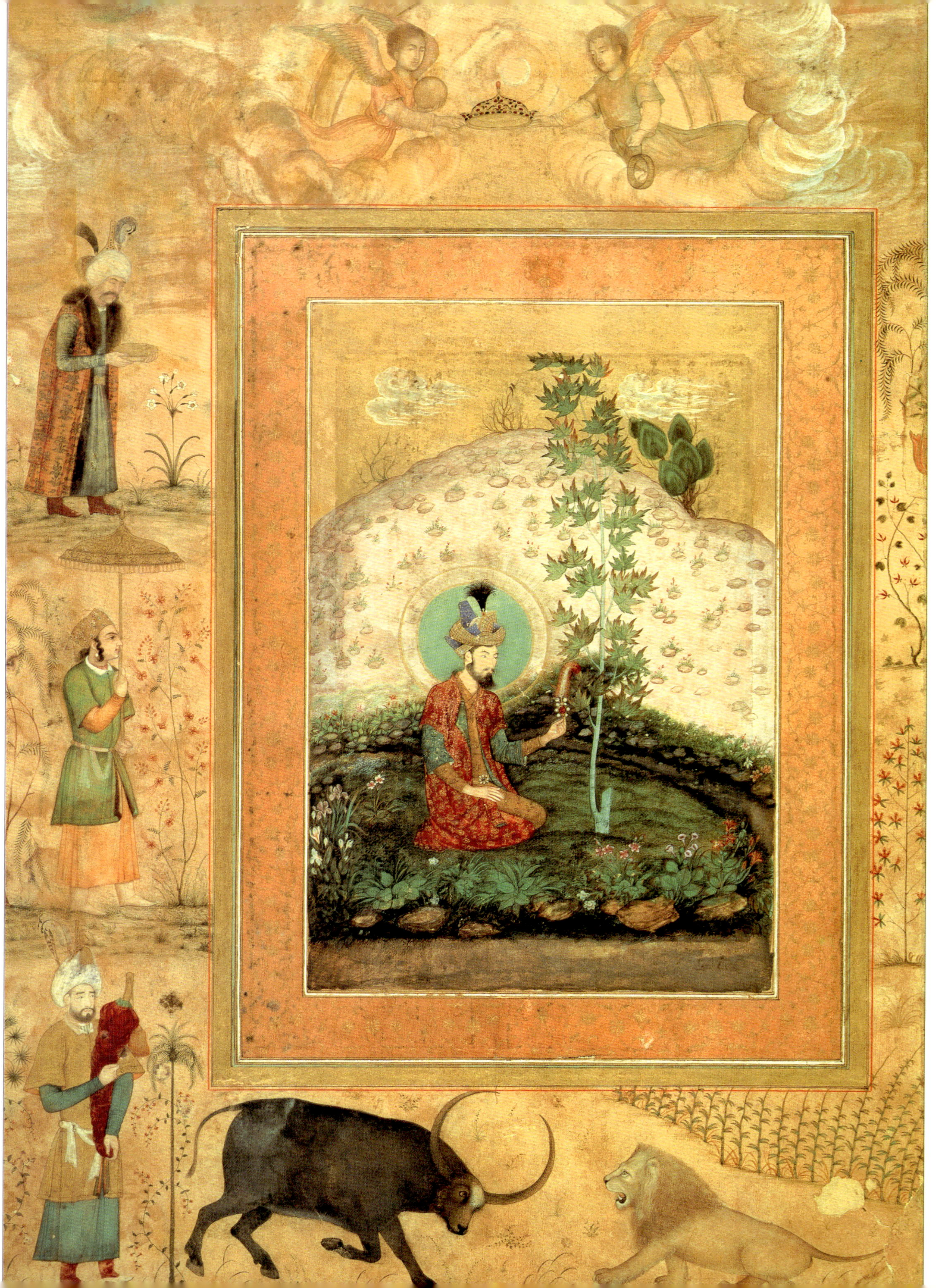

◆ EPHRAIM BEN JACOB KATZ, FISHER'S ANCESTOR: As a Rabbi's grandson—My grandfather Ephraim, a giant. "*And in those days giants walked the face of the earth.*" My grandfather Ephraim, a Rabbi in Jerusalem, a Dayan in Jerusalem. How many of us have the privilege of living in the city of Jerusalem: Ariel?

And my grandfather leaving the Holy City but only with the solace of the voice of Jeremiah echoing in his ear. *For I shall bring you from the lands of the North...and in my prayers. If I forget you, O Jerusalem, let my right hand fail*" and the ache of my arm, the trembling of my fingers, as I wrote in Ofen and in Prague and in Vilna. And Father, Father when will these works of yours see the light of day. And I replied to my dying son: Hezekiah: "*Or Hadash Mi Yerushalayim. A new light for Jerusalem. And the Lord giveth and the Lord taketh.*" My Hezekiah. And even myself, in place of my next born son Ayreh Leib. "Blessed be the name of G-d forever and ever."

■ HUMAYUN, SON OF BABUR: Father could never mention the word death— Father could never mention the word death as he walked around my bed. I, feverish, young and full of promise, set to inherit all of Hindustan and all the blessings of Timur. Yet I was dying. Father could not mention the word death. Take me, he prayed. Take an old man. Take one who has sinned. Do not take my son, Humayun. Judge me. Do with me what you will. Cast me off the knife's edge, a slender rope that leads to the greenest shores of paradise. May the *Peris* laugh at my song and be deaf to my praises of you!

But never the word death. The word life. A multitude of times poured from Father's lips. Breathe life onto my son's lips. Strength into his body. Warmth into his chest. Wisdom into his skull and brightness into his eyes. The All-Knowing One, never hearing the word death but only the word life over and over again, sent the contract of exchange through the angel Gavril. I to life and Father to the next life.

My life, my thoughts, my deeds, must forever be a testament to Father's memory. May all Hindustan be my witness.

And my brother smiled, and through my tears I could hear him say to me, "Haskel, you look like a greener."

"Of course, I didn't know what he meant. But he was right. I was a greener. And I've remained one. And if G-d forbid, something happens to me, I'll still be a greener."

Fisher laughed and put his arm around his father, "Here in New Haven, as a freshman, even as an immigrant, even as a Rabbi's grandson, I won't be a greener. I'll be an Old Blue."

Fisher's father stared blankly at him—no more understanding him than understanding his own brother, Nathan, eighteen years before.

And then, here he was, Raphael Fisher, four years later, a senior at Yale, standing at the back entrance of Woolsey Hall. Forty-five minutes after Joan Baez had finished her concert.

◆ ARYEH YEHUDA LEIB KATZ, FISHER'S ANCESTOR: A Rabbi's father...grandson —My father: both Abraham and Isaac. I pleaded with Father, "Do not pray for your own passage to the next world, Which of us can be Abraham, who of us can be Isaac, and Kal Va Homer, from minor to major, who can be both Abraham and Isaac. No man can bind himself." But Father would not listen. He was his grandfather. Then I pleaded further, "Who will print your words so that all of Israel shall read and understand?"

And my father—his name a blessing for me always—said, "You will be my scribe and my publisher and my light in Jerusalem."

Then I said, "But Father you are going to Jerusalem. You have agreed to take the post there, to return to the city of your grandfather." But Father would not move from the prayer circle he had drawn around my bed: Honi ha magel.

"Aryeh Leib, my son, you will be the blessed dew of my name. You will be the wind to scatter my words downward from the Heavenly City." "And will I be lain to rest alongside of you in Jerusalem, Father?" I pleaded.

If you remain in Jerusalem, the land of Moriah, yes, you shall rest. But if you leave, I bless you, your portion shall be Safed." And even after Father passed, I took his notes, his papers, his sayings, his hints, his questions, to Jerusalem.

His hand guided me and blessed be The Name who allowed me to bring to light my father's work: "*SHA'AR EPHRAIM.*" But having left Jerusalem and returned to Prague, I knew my lot would be to lie in rest in Safed. When the Dead shall be raised who shall rise first? Those in Safed. And then I will, please G-d, go and greet my blessed father, Ephraim, in the gates of Jerusalem, and my descendants ,all say Amen.

Payag, *Humayun Seated in a Landscape.*

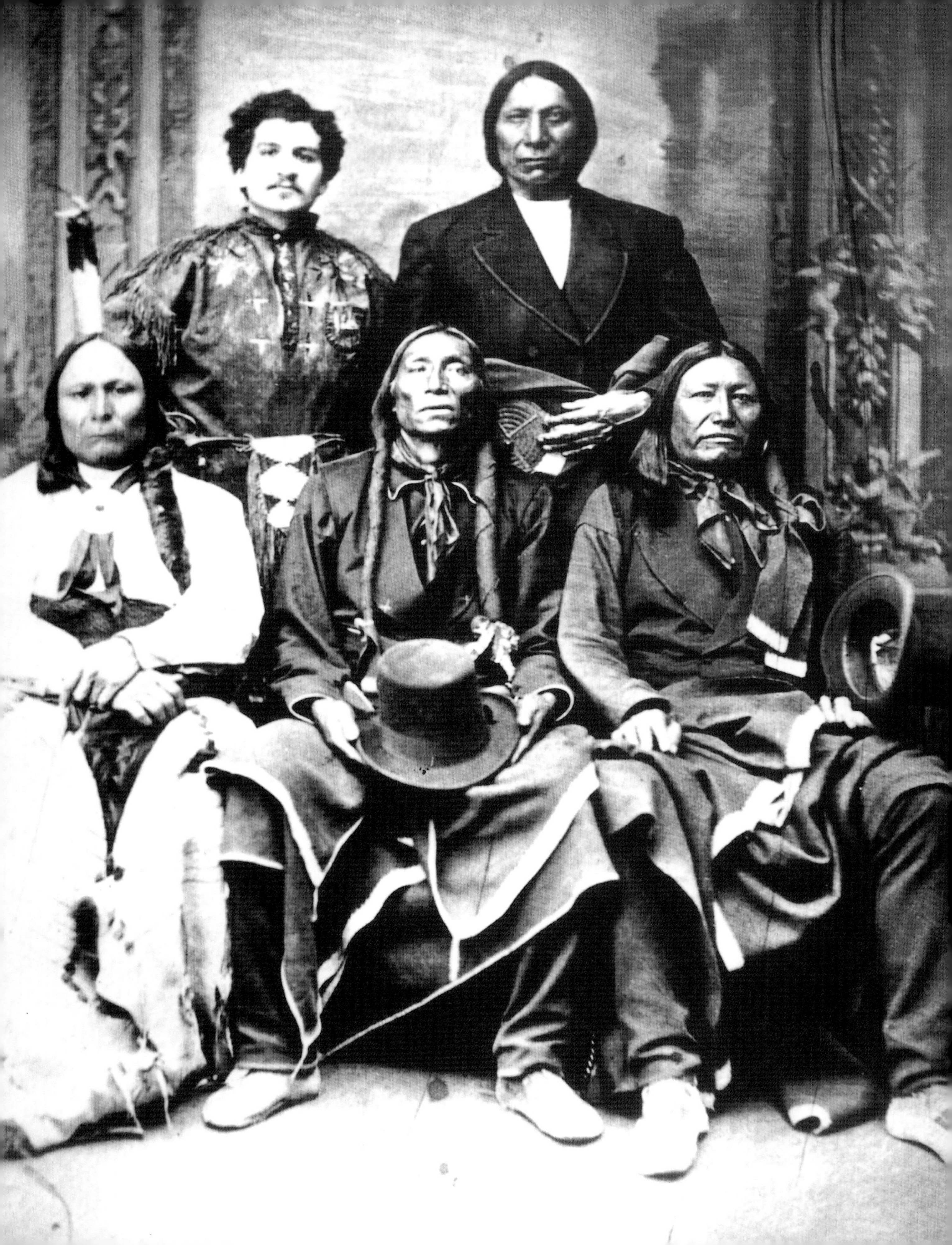

◆ JULIUS MEYER, DOSHA'S GREAT GRANDFATHER'S BROTHER: The image of—It was always the image. As seen by. Red Cloud. As a White man with a long black coat. Swift Bear holding Honest Abe's hat. Sitting Bull? He can only be dressed with an eagle feather in his Indian outfit.

For did not Sitting Bull defeat Custer? And Spotted Tail with his Indian moccasins peeping out from his severe banker's black, neither Sioux nor White.

Just what people would pay to see. In America, in France, in the Paris Exhibition of 1889 when I brought Standing Bear and a company of Omahas and Winnebagos to Paris. And what image of me did the Whites want? And the Indians? And who was I?

To Max? His youngest brother. To the people of Omaha, I was a magician with a China frock. Gold braid. Changing myself at will. My gold buttons reflecting in the eyes of those who saw me. And my image melded with Indians could sell out a hall from Omaha to Paris.

■ ABRAHAM ABULAFIA: Vision—Fisher is enraptured. He has been listening to her for years. She comes to him by night. Makes him complete. Brings him peace. Awakens him. Will not let him sleep. She comes in many guises. A vision. His Jerusalem: "Abraham called the place 'Yireh' as it is said: "And Abraham named that site Adonai-Yirch, whence the present saying, 'On the mount of the Lord there is vision' (Genesis 22:14). Shem called it 'Shalem' as it is said: 'And Melchizedck, King of Shalem' (Genesis 14:18). Said the Holy One, 'If I call it 'Yireh' as Abraham did, Shem, that righteous man, will complain. If I call it 'Shalem' as Shem did, Abraham, that righteous man, will complain. Therefore, I will use both names and call it Yirushalaym Yirah-Shalem. Genesis Rabbah 56:14."

Every fan had left and still she hadn't come out. There's another entrance just in front of Silliman College. Maybe she left through there, thought Fisher.

The image of Joan, the vision of Joan, had sold out the hall. Even the scalpers wouldn't sell their own tickets.

Fisher had come three hours early to the Woolsey Hall concert with his ticket, J-1. The tenth row wasn't good enough for him. He had to be in the front row.

Four years of listening to her. Amazing how he had remained enraptured, listening:

Oh Blue,
You Good Dog You

The impossibly high note held beyond human endurance. Resonating on a plane he felt he could see but couldn't touch. Over and over. Even after playing a hundred times.

■ MOZART: She...standing, enraptured, listening—"The voice of nature speaks as loud in me as in others, louder perhaps than in many a strong lout of a fellow. I simply cannot live as most young fellows do in these days. In the first place, I have too much religion; in the second place, I have too great a love of my neighbor and too high a feeling of honor to seduce an innocent girl; and, in the third place, I have too much horror and disgust, too much dread and fear of diseases and too much care for my health to fool about with whores...

But who is the object of my love? Do not be horrified again, I entreat you. Surely not one of the Webers? Yes, one of the Webers—but not Josefa, nor Sophie, but Constanze, the middle one. She is not ugly, but at the same time far from beautiful...

Her whole beauty consists in two little black eyes and a pretty figure. She has not wit but she has enough common sense to enable her to fulfill her duties as a wife and as a mother. It is a downright lie that she is inclined to be extravagant. On the contrary, she is accustomed to be shabbily dressed, for the little that her mother has been able to do for her children, she has done for the two others, but never for Constanze. True, she would like to be neatly and cleanly dressed, but not smartly...Moreover she understands housekeeping and has the kindest heart in the world. I love her and she loves me with all her heart. Tell me whether I could wish myself a better wife? And what should I tell Fathe? Better the introductory movement than the Allegro Andante."

■ CONSTANZE WEBER: Another entrance...just in front—He would hide, my Wolfgangerl, under the table and grab at my toes like a child of two—I would hear his footsteps at the hallway landing, but he would appear at another entrance, on the hallway, just in front of the kitchen.

Not that I was surprised to be ever surprised. Did I not keep his letter to me from Dresden inside my bodice: Wolfgangerl wrote me:

If I were to tell you all the things I do with your dear portrait, I think you would often laugh. For instance, when I take it out of its case, I say, "Good day, Stanzerl! Good day, little rascal, pussy-pussy, little turned up nose, little bagatelle. Schluck und Druck." And when I put it away again, I let it slip in very slowly, saying all the time, "Nu, nu nu." With the peculiar emphasis which this word so full of meaning demands, and then just at the last quickly, "Good night, little mouse, sleep well." Well I suppose I have been writing something very foolish (to the world at all events); but to us who love each other so dearly, it is not foolish at all."

Because he was such a foolish child, my Wolfgangerl was the wisest man in all the world.

Julius Meyer, Sitting Bull, Swift Bear, Spotted Tail, and Red Cloud.

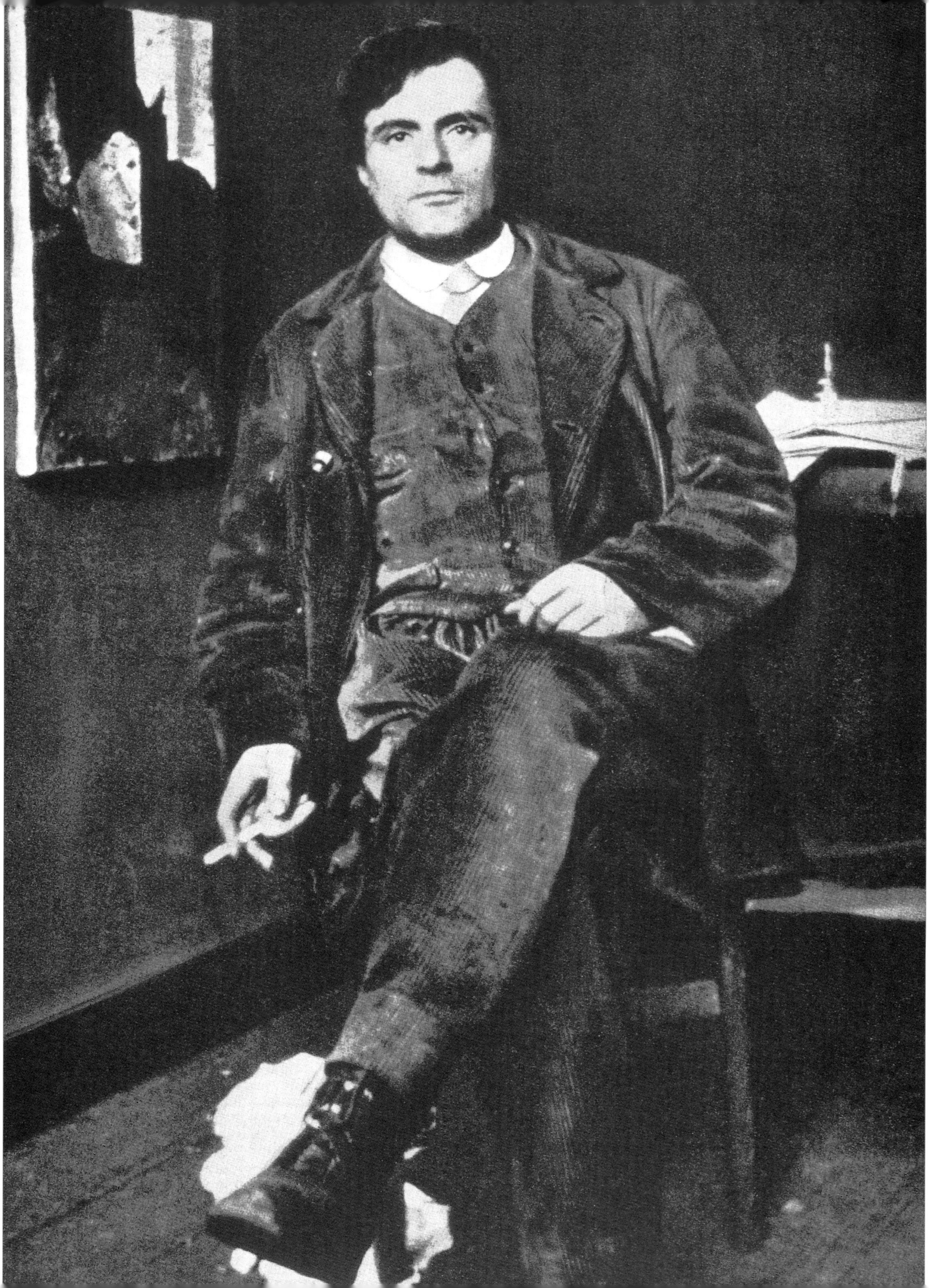

■ BEATRICE HASTINGS, MODIGLIANI'S GIRLFRIEND: All he had to do—Modigliani. "A complex character, a pig and a pearl. Met in 1914 at the crémerie. I sat opposite him. Hashish and Brandy. Not at all impressed. Didn't know who he was. He looked ugly, ferocious, greedy. Met again at the Café Rotunde. He was shaved and charming. Raised his cap with a pretty gesture, blushed to his eyes and asked me to come see his work. Went. Always a book in his pocket. Despised everyone but Picasso and Max Jacob. Loathed Cocteau."

Modigliani. All he had to do was stay with me. Forever.

■ QUEEN MARY at the Durbar in 1911: The Maharani of Patiala, Baktauar Kaur, walked ever so slowly toward me. In her hand, I could see what seemed to be a cup of the greenest water I had ever seen. An emerald brooch which glistened in the Indian sunlight, surrounded by diamonds. The Maharani, a wisp of a wisp, no more than eighteen she could have been, holding the gem brooch as my mother would hold an Easter egg before me, and bowing so low I thought the brooch would touch the ground and disappear into the arms of the earth again. I had never seen something so beautiful, and I spoke from my heart and proclaimed to the ladies of India:

"The jewel you have given me will ever be very precious in my eyes, and whenever I wear it, though thousands of miles of land and sea separate us, my thoughts will fly to the homes of India, and create again and again this happy meeting and recall the tender love your hearts have yielded me. Your jewel shall pass to future generations as an imperial heirloom, and shall always stand as a token of the first meeting of an English Queen with the ladies of India."

■ RABBI NOSUN OF BRESLOV: Golden Mountain—Rabbi Nachman looked at me, looked at all the Hasidim and paused. And with a smile—for here I knew that all the Hasidim knew that from here on in the story Nachman was utterly alone. And alone Nachman continued:

"He left the servant and went off himself to search for her. He searched for several years. Then he thought, "In places where men dwell one cannot find a golden mountain on which stands a castle of pearl [for he knew geography]. So I shall go into the desert and seek her there." He went tot the desert for many, many years. Then he saw a huge man, a giant, of a size that was not human, who was carrying a huge tree, of a size that one does not see where men live. The giant asked him, "Who are you?" He answered, "I am a human being." The giant was astonished and said, "I have been here in the desert for such a long time, and I have never yet seen a human being here." The chamberlain told him the story of what had happened and how he was searching for a golden mountain on which stood a castle of pearl.

The giant answered, "There can be no such thing. It cannot be. People have been telling you stupid tales."

Fisher didn't have to hear the song. All he had to do was hear the first note.

The song would play in his head even if he left his room and crossed the Silliman courtyard, leaving him with the most pleased expression on his face. Song after song, echoing in his head as Fisher finished a grilled cheese sandwich in George and Harry's—even while he discussed with Reilly Mrs. Wright's class on urban planning of Karakorum, the golden mountain Chinese capital.

It was all backdrop for the Princess' arrival. Although it had taken four years for her to come to Yale to perform at a concert, Fisher had always known she would.

There he was, waiting with his fable in hand. Thirty pages—a story of a princess in China, who could sing like a dove in an early southern Sung garden just south of Soochow. But her voice did not carry so that her parents and teachers thought she was mute.

■ MAHARAJA OF PATIALA: The Queen's arrival—In 1906, Rameshbhai the court astologer came before me in my private garden, just beyond the royal chambers. Lord Minto and his wife had just left that afternoon and Rameshbhai asked me, "What of your future do you wish to know?"

"How can I become lord of all India?" To my surprise, my astrologer answered, "You are Patiala—lord of the Punjab—and is not the Punjab first in all of Hindustan? But if you would be lord of all India, you must be crowned by a Queen of England."

I remember so clearly. How Lady Minto had peered at me never blinking, ever searching. I could feel her eyes on me even after she left. Then and there I resolved that should a queen ever arrive in Hindustan, I would take her hands and have them place the crown onto my head myself. It wasn't more than a week of years—in 1911—that Queen Mary, arrived at the Durbar in Delhi.

At first Bakhtaur Kaur, my wife, smiled when I said: "You will present this carved Moghul Emerald to her English Majesty, Queen Mary, and she will crown me ruler of India."

My Maharani ran her fingers across the folds of the emerald, caressing the lines of the carving as she did by the banks of the river palace where I would rest my head in her hands, night after night, when first she entered my palace.

"You would give her this wonder of wonders?" she said, after a long while. "How do you know that this gem gift will make you king? And if it doesn't, will you go to the land of the English and ask for it back?"

I held my Maharani's hand which held the Moghul Emerald from Akbar's time—and I whispered, "I have another yet more beautiful carved emerald, and the royal astrologer who is never wrong, has told me years ago I will be crowned king of India." My moon's delight—my Maharani laughed with a laugh that is only heard in the Punjab, and with a lightness of a *nilgai* leapt to her feet and said, "I will do this but remember to give me the other more beautiful dream of a gem. If you wish to remain king!"

■ LADY MINTO in her journal, Nov. 1906: Pleasing expression "*The Maharaja of Patiala is a boy of fifteen. He is six feet high and weighs fifteen stone. He has a pleasing expression and his brocade clothes and jewels are magnificent. In his tent Minto found a picture of his great-grandfather, under which was inscribed in golden lettering: Savior of the Patiala State.*"

Amedeo Modigliani.

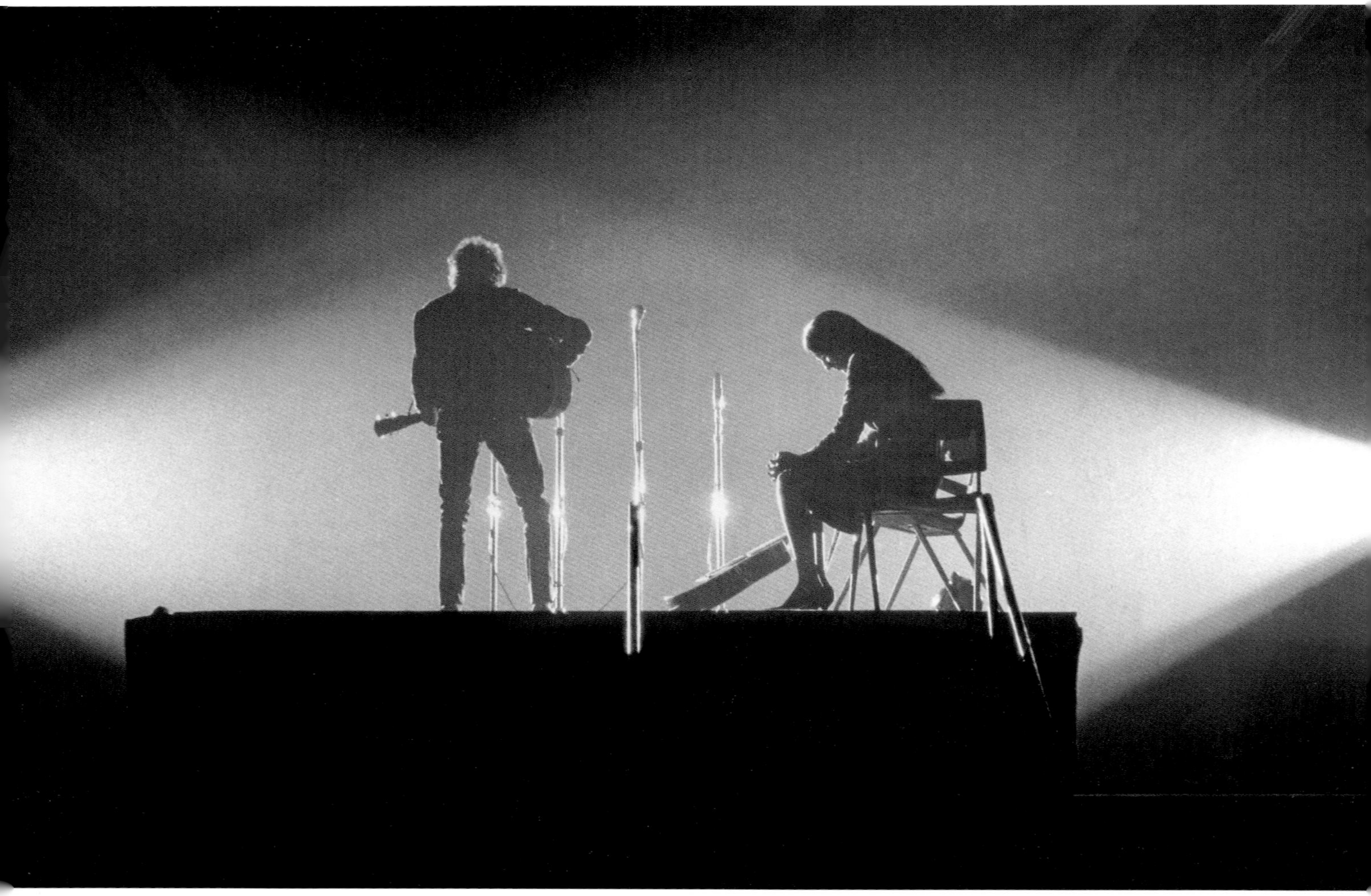

■ ABU MUHAMMED ALI IBN HAZM AL ANDALUS: Her lips moving, he began to sing—And why are her lips moving? Because she sees the troubadour. And why did he begin to sing? Because both the troubadour and the princess were parts of the same soul separated in the beginning of creation. And "*the soul is beautiful and passionately desires anything beautiful and inclines toward perfect images.*" The attraction between the troubadour and the princess is so great that were he in a garden in the farthest Maghreb of Andalus and she in an oasis in the Yemen, they would still draw closer and closer. She need not utter his name, merely move her lips, and he will fly to her. For is not the union of their souls a thousand times finer in its effects than that of bodies.

■ ELIHU YALE: Troubadour—
"*Gaily the troubadour*
Touched his guitar
As he was hastening
Home from the war

Singing from Palestine
Hither I come
Lady love, lady love
Welcome me home
She for the troubadour
Hopelessly wept.
Sadly she thought of him
Whilst others slept."

Odd these fifteen honored sons of Yale, standing in front of a small treasure house not much larger than my garden in Fort St. George and singing the same song twice weekly for more than a hundred years.

And not a damsel entering or leaving their crypt.

More Muslim than Christian. But weren't those troubadours that. Certainly no troubadour I, certainly not in the heat of Hindustan.

One day a troubadour, passing her parent's garden, saw her lips moving. He began to sing. She filled in melodic lines, each looking at the other's lips to complete each other's choruses.

The troubadour and the princess instantly knew every line of each other's songs.

Thirty pages long—a love note from Fisher, to Baez. And how to get the manuscript to her? Even if Fisher enclosed it in bouquets of flowers, he would be but one of a myriad of worshipers. Hadn't there been at least three thousand people overflowing the old town hall in Portland, Maine, in the dead of winter, just to catch a glimpse of her after her last concert the previous week? Baez, Mexican-Irish saint, beatified by throngs of her admirers.

■ ABISH RHEINHOLD, RAPHAEL FISHER MOTHER'S GRANDFATHER: sing—"To you belongs the day, and also to you the night," sings King David in Psalm 74:16. Yours and only yours. And did not Isaiah chant at night, "the song shall be for you as in the night when the festival is sanctified." And all songs from the heart directed to the One—do not all people hear them? A troubadour in the time of Rashi, my ancestor, sees the lips of a princess move and bursts into song. And do these songs not echo yet again in children, grandchildren, and later generation's ears? Will not Fisher's grandchildren's children sit at a seder and sing?

"*Yours G-d is the sovereignty. To you the song of praise is due. To you the song of praise is fitting.*" One song, one earth, forever.

■ ANDREAS CAPELLANUS, French writer for Countess Marie of Troyes: Her lips moving—And why are her lips moving and no words spoken? For he is a troubadour and he is singing, always singing. Songs of love. But first the troubadour "*should greet her in his usual way; this however should always be done and all lovers must realize that after the salutation, they should not immediately begin talking about love for it is only with their concubines that men begin in that way. On the contrary, after the man has greeted the woman, he ought to let a little time elapse so that she may if she wishes speak first.*"

But the princess is not speaking. She is mute. She is mute to all except the troubadour. If the princess begins the conversation," *her remark will give the troubadour plenty to talk about.*" But she is mute. "*There are men in the presence of ladies who so lose their power of speech that they forget the things they have carefully thought out and arranged in their minds; they cannot say anything coherent and it seems proper to reprove this foolishness, for it is not fitting that any man, unless he is bold and well-instructed, should enter into a conversation with ladies.*"

This troubadour will not stumble over his words, for he is always in song. His meter will save him as he chants: "*Oh if you should take service with love, blessed above all other will that man be whom you crown with your love.*" And so on and so forth for a thousand years in Troyes. And his song will fill Fisher's voice, echoing forever.

Bob Dylan and Joan Baez performing at Madison Square Garden.

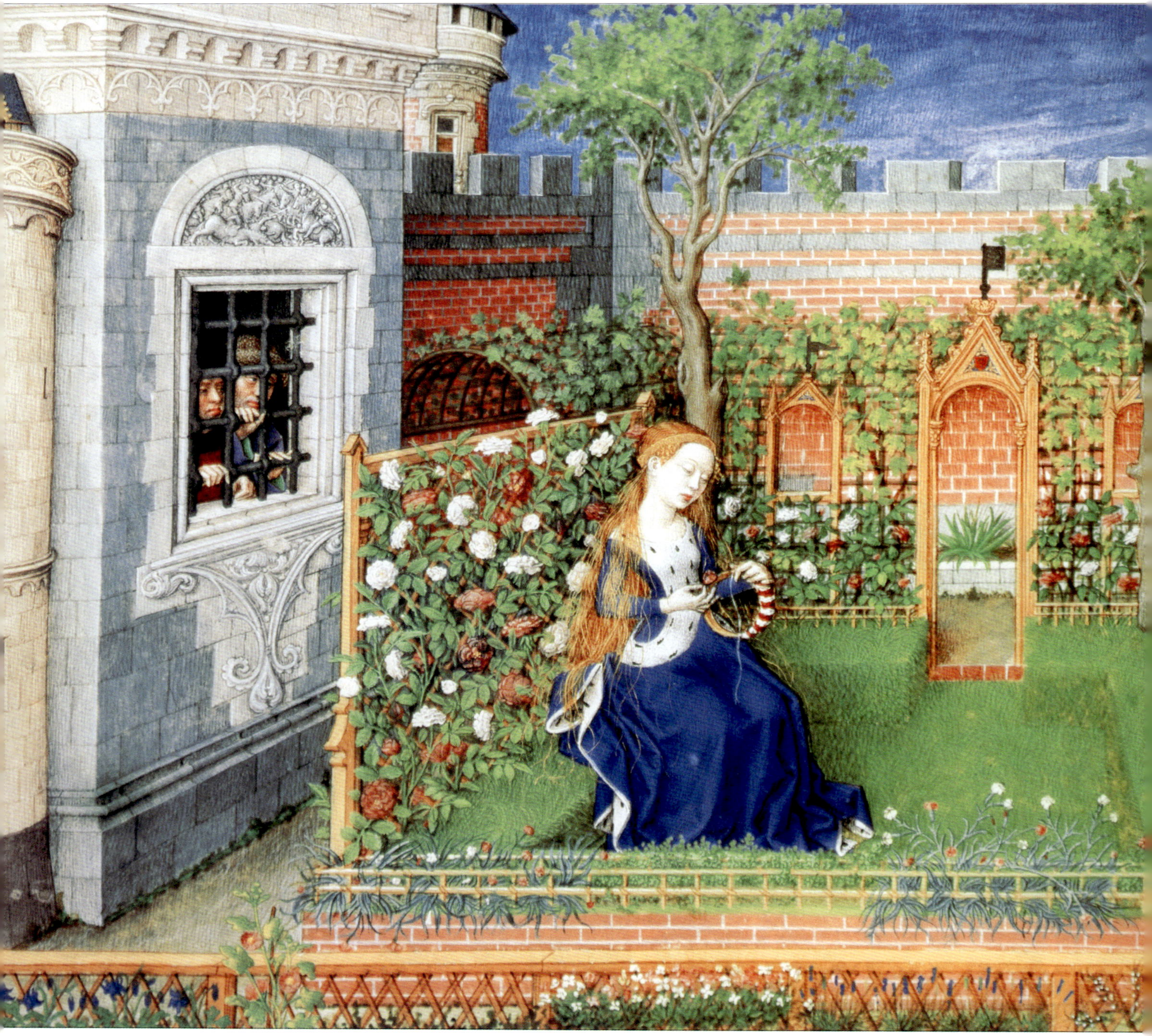

■ MODGLIANI: And it had started off so well. Hamilton had drawn—It isn't starting off so well at all. André Salmon, Picasso and I were seated at the Café Rotunde. It was August 1914. Just two months after I had met "La Belle Beatrice" Hastings. And Salmon was all aquiver. How did I meet her? Where did I meet her? Did I sketch her before I bedded her? But that question he barely stammered at me and stared at his shoes before he asked.

Beatrice was to join us but was an hour late as usual, half an hour to enrage me with jealousy and half an hour in fear that I had already left her. Salmon mumbled as he eyed each woman in the café. "You met her here, Amedeo! Did you speak to Beatrice first or did she speak to you?" "Oh," said Pablo, immediately, languidly pulling an artists chalk out of my pocket. "Momo does not speak. His hand simply draws the sketch of an invitation to his atelier." I interrupted, "Pablo, I suppose now you'll relate everything that followed these two honeymoon months. Are you also hiding in my broom closet?"

"I'm serious," André Salmon interrupted us both and said, "You two have it so easy. Momo, look at that woman at the table on our right, sketch her and I'll go over and your life will be my life at least for a night." And I did: the woman had her hands behind her head and she was stretching backward in her wicker chair. With an economy of line, I removed her hat, her dress, and drew her fait au naturel as I imagined her on Salmon's bed.

Salmon grabbed the sketch out of my hand before I finished. I guess he was afraid I would sign it, and before Pablo and I could believe it possible, André was at the woman's table, handing her my drawing, gesticulating wildly. Her eyes moved from the drawing to him, back and forth, just a hint of a smile, her hand still in that far-away-island staring arched position and André paying the bill resolutely and lifting her off her feet. His arm linked in hers but with her right hand clutching onto my drawing, it fluttered in the wind as they sailed up rue Casimir de la Vigne toward Andre's apartment off Rue Vaugirard.

At first we could not stop laughing, Pablo and I. We roared even after Beatrice joined us. She did not find it at all funny and took the woman's side. What kind of man would turn a woman into a "putain" and pay her in counterfeit art. On and on. Wait till I see André, Beatrice kept saying but the truth was we didn't see him for more than three months. When we did, once again, it was at the Café Rotunde. André walked to our table and sat down: a man who had come back from a voyage to a land no one ever had visited or heard of. He said with the gentlest of voices, "I don't wish to speak of it. Ever." Even Picasso did not press him.

It is not starting out well at all, in my opinion, for Monsieur Fisher. Or perhaps, just perhaps, it is staring out so well, so unbelievably well, that it cannot end well.

If she doesn't come soon, I might as well leave, thought Fisher, pacing back and forth in front of the stage door exit.

It had started off so well. Hamilton had drawn a cartoon badge with a line drawing of Baez, hair dragging down to the floor and a guitar resolutely hung over her shoulder. Across the badge in blue letters, BAEZ/SECURITY/YALE.

Fisher had simply walked in three hours and twenty-two minutes before the concert and sat down surreptitiously in house seat A1. And stared. And gazed. Frozen.

When she came in to tune up, she must have noticed him. She smiled directly at him, all teeth, with a glow that forced him to lower his gaze, only to discover that she had lowered hers.

■ ANDREAS CAPELLANUS: Started off so well— This love of Fisher for Baez has started off so well. For she is a treasure unobtainable. If Fisher "*preferred to save trouble by selecting a lover who has been trained rather than one he must go to the trouble of training, that deserves a good reprimand. For anyone ought to find that fruit from his own plantation tastes sweeter than what he gets from his neighbor's tree, and we value more what we have got with great labor than that which comes easily for 'without great labor, great things cannot be won…'*"

■ ANDRÉ SALMON (1881-1969), writer, art critic and friend of Modgliani: Started off so well—"*There is only one contemporary 'painter of women' from life (which rules out Van Dongen), the Italian Modigliani. Modigliani, whose origins were quite bourgeois, has been exhibiting between Fauves and the Cubists for more than ten years. But if I had to name a famous successor to Renoir, I'd say true to Cézanne's example, Modigliani would be hard to beat.*

Modigliani is not only a painter of nudes…A police inspector, or maybe an inspector for the Beaux Arts, once had Modigliani's contributions taken down in I don't remember which gallery. And yet what spiritually glows forth from so much beautiful, rich material, slimmed down by the controlled magnificence that the artist has striven hard to refine."

Years ago Modigliani once gifted me with a drawing. A drawing that launched me a romance that started off so well. To Momo undoubtedly it was of small account, and to Pablo even less—but to me, to me…

To start this way with Baez, for Fisher, will lead far beyond what his friend Hamilton or the woman or he himself can envision. Art always does.

■ SIR JOHN CHARDIN, ELIHU YALE'S PARTNER: Baez/security/Yale—Strange this university. These university students singing for G-d, for country and for Yale, and this young acolyte, a tidy Fisher, wearing a courtier's badge. Is Baez his G-d? And is his country his security? What are we to make of Elihu Yale, my client, my partner, my foundation in India, the confidant of my brother Daniel, the butt of a thousand jokes in Fort St. George and ten thousand rumors on Leadenhall Street in the East India Company's headquarters.

One had to be careful with Elihu Yale. In 1698, he purchased a bulse of diamonds, a horse and an elephant from me. I laughingly asked my brother Daniel, "Can Elihu Yale be three people?" Daniel replied, "I posed the question to the Governor himself and Elihu responded thusly. 'Indeed, I am three people, and of three faiths to boot. The good horse I paid you for, I ride to my garden house on Thursdays, like Galahad, to my good Mrs. Catherine Nicks to announce the sweet Catholic charms of Chrétien de Troyes. The elephant I reserve for my voyage to the garden house in Fort St. George when I visit my Oriental pearl, Hieronyma da Paiva, late of Portugal now of Hindustan, for she responds most lively to Eastern silk, luxury and pageantry.

The diamonds I overpaid you for, Frère Chardin, these I count in the Huguenot fashion, slowly, by moonlight, in my treasure house alone, preparing to meet my maker." And my good brother Daniel could not make out whether Elihu was jesting in claiming to be Jesuit, Jew and Huguenot at the same time. I dare say neither did Elihu himself know the answer to his life's riddle.

Hours of the Duke of Burgundy, *Emilia in her garden.*

תורה אור
והיה

נר מצוה | עין משפט

מסכת
כתובות
מן
תלמוד בבלי

עם פירוש רש"י ותוספות ורבינו אשר
ופסקי תוספות ורא"ש ופירוש
המשניות להרמב"ם ז"ל

ונלוו עליהם

חדושי מהרש"ל ומהרש"א ומהר"ם מלובלין ולמסכתות
יחידות תוספות שנ"ץ וחדושי רבינו יונה והלכות מרבינו
ישעיה הראשון וחדושים יקרים בישוב כל שאלות הגמרא
דסלקו בקשיא מהגאון בעל שושנים לדוד

ותשואות חן לה

הגהות מחוכמות מחכמי דור ודור אדירי התורה אשר כבר יצאו
לאור מלפנים אחת מהנה לא נעדרה והוספנו עליהן הגהות עתיקות
נעתקות ממכתב יד מרן הגאון בעל חתם סופר ז"ל
מקצת מאלה הגהות יחנו סביב הש"ס בגליון ולמקצתן שמנו מקום בסוף כל מסכת
והעולה על כלנה אשר ספחנו בסוף כל חלק וחלק את

התוספתא

ערוכה בכל ושמורה בהגהה מדויקת לזרות ולהבר גוסחאותיה

וזר זהב סביב לה

הגהות ותיקונים על פי כתב יד ישן בבית אוצר הספרים אשר לאדוננו הקיסר יר"ה ונקראו בשם

אור הגנוז

ישועה | חכמת | ודעת   אמונת | עתיך | חסן

זרעים | מועד | נשים
נזיקין | קדשים | טהרות

נדפס בהוצאות חברת המוציאים לאור | וויען | WIEN.
בדפוס האדונים זאמארסקי ודיטטמארש | | Druck von L. C. Zamarski & C. Dittmarsch.
בשנת תרכ"ב לפ"ק | Tom. IX. | Expedition des Talmud.

◆ Tuviah Gutman Gutwirth, Fisher's Grandfather: Motioned in the same direction with her eyes—During the war in 1944, I awoke in Cuba. Safe. Far from my Yeshiva in Tarnov, from my Bet Medrash in Riglitz and farther still from Jerusalem.

Instead of moving towards Jerusalem, I was moving ever so slowly away. I would awake and pray—toward the East, beyond the Europe of my birth, my boyhood, the Yeshiva of my blessed father-in-law, Abish Rheinhold—he was my blessing and he would tell me I was his memory.

He held his hand over my bride, Chaya, and me. My hand, white from having fasted all of my betrothed day and Chaya so close, so close to me under the Huppah. He blessed my wife and me, "You alone, for you will always be one, will be saved," he whispered. "And in your name, shall all nations be blessed, as were Sarah and Abraham." We held our hands together. Indeed, Reb Abish's words came true for us. We were saved. But what of the remnants of Israel?

Reb Abish had taught me from the Midrash: Before the binding of Isaac, Abraham awoke early and took Isaac, his son, his only son.

What did he tell Sarah? "I recognized our creator, the Holy One, blessed be He, when I was only three years old. Our son is now thirty-seven and never had an opportunity to study Torah outside our home. It is time to take him to a Yeshiva," Abraham was referring to the Bait Hamidrash of Shem, the son of Noah. Shem maintained a Yeshiva in which he taught the Torah that had been transmitted to the generations since Adam" (Zohar Hadash).

"You are right," Sarah agreed. Abraham instructed her, "Prepare provisions, because we intend to set out early on our trip tomorrow."

And Reb Abish, I implored in my prayers. I alone am saved. But where are the Yeshivot of my youth? Riglitz. Tarnov. Cracow. The Great Blue Domed Belzer Shul?

I prayed toward the East, but not a sound, not a whisper, no sense of motion, no feeling whatever came to me from that direction. The eyes of the Holy Shechinah were veiled and blinded.

I was without words.

She certainly must have noticed that he mouthed each line of every song.
Oh blue, you good dog you

At the very end of the concert, she stared straight at him, pointed her finger at the exit door at the far end of Woolsey, and motioned in the same direction with her eyes.

He was sure she'd done it. But no one had come out of that door for more than an hour. Suddenly he thought of his father: "You're a greener Raphael. You'll always be a greener here."

Even after getting tapped and even after the Ten Eyck prize for speaking, he was still a greener.

◆ Moses Gutwein, friend of Fisher's grandfather: Eyes—Tuviah Gutman Gutwirth could not speak. In the morning when I would walked to his house not far from the water on Calle Arroyo in Havana, he was sitting on a chair with Chaya.

I would say as softly as I could, "Reb Gutman, let's walk together to Shul for Shachris. He would mumble, "Where?" I would point toward the Calle Real just off Calle Arroyo and Reb Gutman's blessed wife would motion in the same direction with her eyes. With her blind eyes, she could see more than we. For during the war, only the blind could see, for they had always seen by faith alone. Reb Tuviah meekly asked, "Why? Why? They are dead. My sons, your sons, our sons, our Rebbeim, everything lost."

What could I say? Reb Gutman knew the entire Shas by heart. He was my Rabbi and I his Gabbai. So I said nothing. But the eyes of Chaya motioned us toward Calle Real, and we stumbled together, shipwrecked, toward the light.

■ Rabbi Joseph B. Soloveichik: Eyes—
*"If I forget you, O Jerusalem
Let my right hand fail."*

Clear. Even after one thousand years, If we forget Jerusalem, my right hand will fail. And my mother's hand, and my father's and my grandfather's and backward thousands of years. Thanks be to G-d, my mother's hand did not fail, and nor did her parents—all the way back to Abraham.

To all in the lands outside of Israel, I say: *"From the halachic point of view, the sanctity of the great ones of our people (Gedolei Yisroel) may well have increased when they stepped upon the ground of Eretz Yisroel. But from the personal, emotional angle, I am simply unable to accept the idea of diminished sanctity of these Gedolim I have abroad. Do you know why? Because in the spiritual sense, they were never abroad! The difference between Eretz Yisroel and outside of it was for them only a physical, geographical one but not a spiritual one. The spiritual Eretz Yisroel, as the Hasidim of R. Nachman of Breslov knew, always accompanied them."*

We are all travelers. Reb Gutman, his blessed all-seeing wife Chaya, their grandchild Fisher, Mr. Gutwein, we are all in motion toward Jerusalem, and the eyes of Jerusalem shine toward us. She is so, so far, a journey of a thousand years, and she is but a child's step away.

Ketubot: the Talmud.

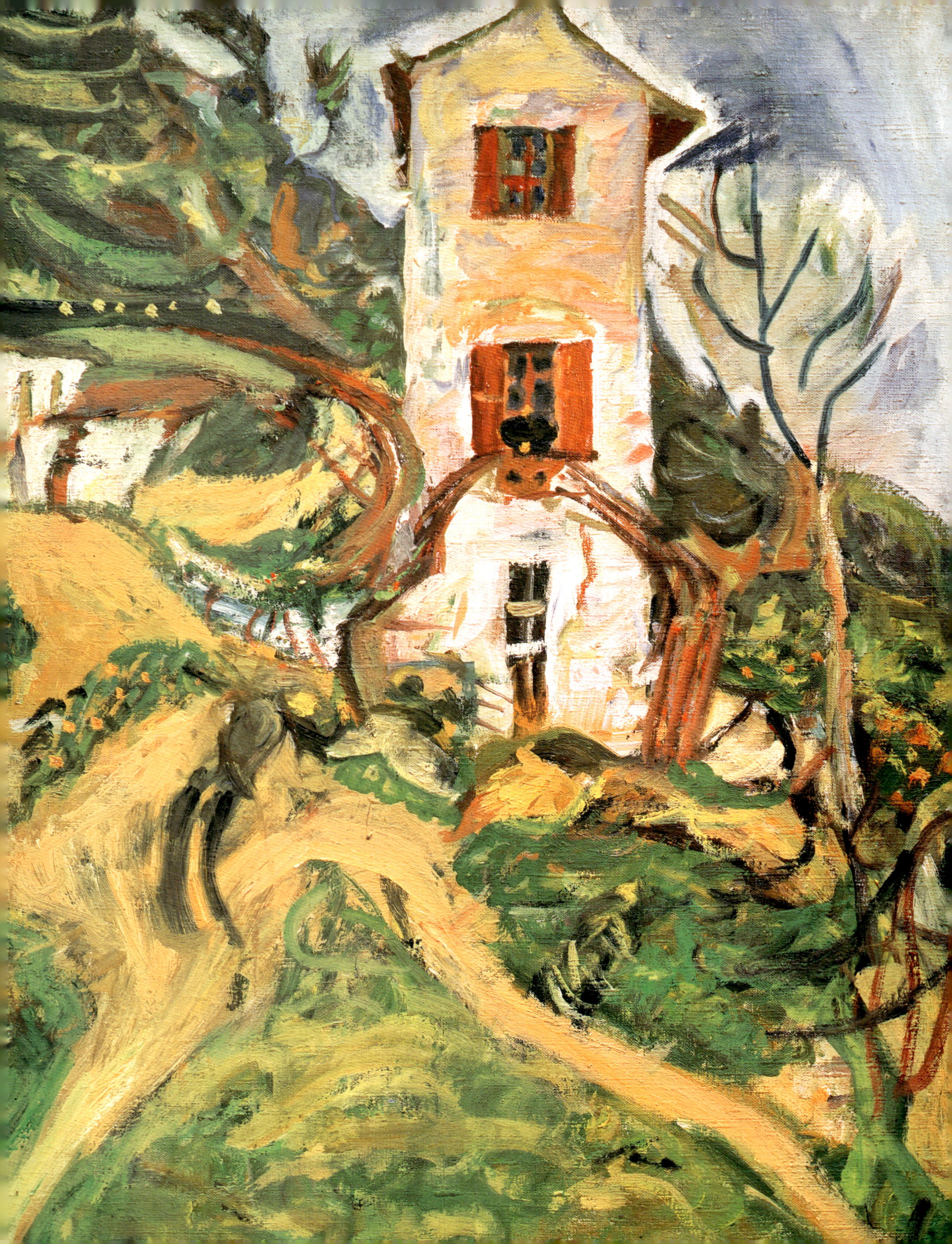

● SPIKE D'ARTHENAY: A proposal—Who is this young knight meant for? Is he not Tristan the sad looking for his princess?

This woman, who is she? Is she not Iseult the Fair? Are they part of a fate "*which they can never escape during the remainder of their lives, for they have drunk their destruction and death.*"

"*My Lords, if you would hear a high tale of love and death…*" Or is this princess Iseult of the white flag? So similar in form, even in name, to young Fisher's dream.

And should the princess be Iseult the Fair, what of their next three years "*harsh and hard*" and worse still when their love potion wears off after three years.

"*A combien fu determinez
Li lovedrins, li vin herbez
La mère Yseult, qui lebolli
A trois anz d'amisté le fist*

For how long was the love potion, the herb wine? Mother Iseult, who brewed it, made it to three years of love."

Not much of a choice. To marry Iseult of the white hand for "*her beauty and her name*" or to wed Iseult the fair—three years of love. And then…what…

The promise of all. Everything without end. Love conquering the teller of the tale himself. An endless ever-changing ending. What we all want and dream of when we are but half awake.

■ BEATRICE HASTINGS, MODIGLIANI'S GIRLFRIEND: Stared—And this young Fisher. What I would not do to meet him. With his bedroom eyes. How they would follow me as I criss-crossed the avenues of all the glittering boulevards of the world's cities.

Just like Modigliani. He fell in love with my eyelashes. My eyes, my neck, my right earlobe and on and on. Momo went plying down the rivers of my body, manning his gondola of love.

I, always two steps ahead of him. But leading him with my long flowing green veils, visible across the boulevards. Modigliani with his three Jewish jesters, all speaking a soupçon of Tatar—Soutine, Krémègne, and Indenbaum. "There she is," they would cry as I approached the café. So sweet they were, the three of them, the footmen of my prince, my Momo.

How sensible of them to leave us be when we needed to be alone. Art will always capture a princess's heart, for is it not through art that one becomes a princess?

Fisher fingered the rolled up story. He stared at the blank first page and turned to the second page.

A Proposal:
By Raphael Fisher
For You

Humming to himself, he started to read yet again about Soochow. About the lotus that could only open during the daylight if the princess were singing to it.

Suddenly he felt a touch on his shoulder. She was much tinier than he had imagined, her guitar in a ragged leather case with a deep viridian cloth strap, and while she walked, she used her guitar as a wand, waving at any oncoming traffic. He extended the manuscript roller to her. She smiled and accepted with one elegant sweep of her hand, and body.

She intently read, rarely looking up, devouring, each page.

In front of the Rialto bridge on High Street, she turned the last page and stopped.

■ AMEDEO MODIGLIANI: Princess—He will never, never, ever capture the princess. Though he is indeed playing the only card open to him—Art, which levels all people—princess or pauper, if only one is a prince of spirit.

He is so like Krémègne, that is how the princess must see him. An Eastern European Jew, Pinchas Krémègne, from the tiniest of villages in Lithuania. Krémègne and Soutine. Following me around. Up and down Boulevard Raspail.

Waiting on me, my two valets, footmen in waiting, eager to have a hand-me-down jacket or a discarded red scarf from my wardrobe.

Pinchas, Chaim Soutine, and Indenbaum, all gathered nightly after I ruled my Kingdom of Art by day. My evening companions until daybreak, when I returned to my English princess, Beatrice Hastings.

But the thought of Fisher and this princess together, impossible. Any more than Beatrice running off to Nice with Pinchas.

■ PINCHAS KRÉMÈGNE: The rolled up short story—Modigliani and I and Chaim Soutine. And Indenbaum. We offered Momo hot wine and canella. Modigliani drank and danced and laughed. His eyes drank in the colors of Le Passage Danzig. Momo's songs were half Ladino and half imagined magic. We all listened to his psalms of love and would have followed him to hell itself.

Hadn't we all three come from a Lithuanian winter? And Modigliani himself, the Prince of Parisian Palestine, knew our Jewish hearts and faces before we even introduced ourselves.

"We are all one," Momo shouted and we toasted Rembrandt—"Who must be a true Sephardi and by mother's Spinozan blood, I swear." Momo grandly exclaimed, "Look at Rembrandt's faces and his women and how the Jewish bride rolls up her ketubbah" and on and on.

But still Modigliani envisioned us all as visitors from a distant land, pilgrims to this Palace of Art . "Bring your winter coat when I paint you," Amadeo said to me though it was the summer of 1916. "That is how I see you!"

Chaim Soutine, *The White House*.

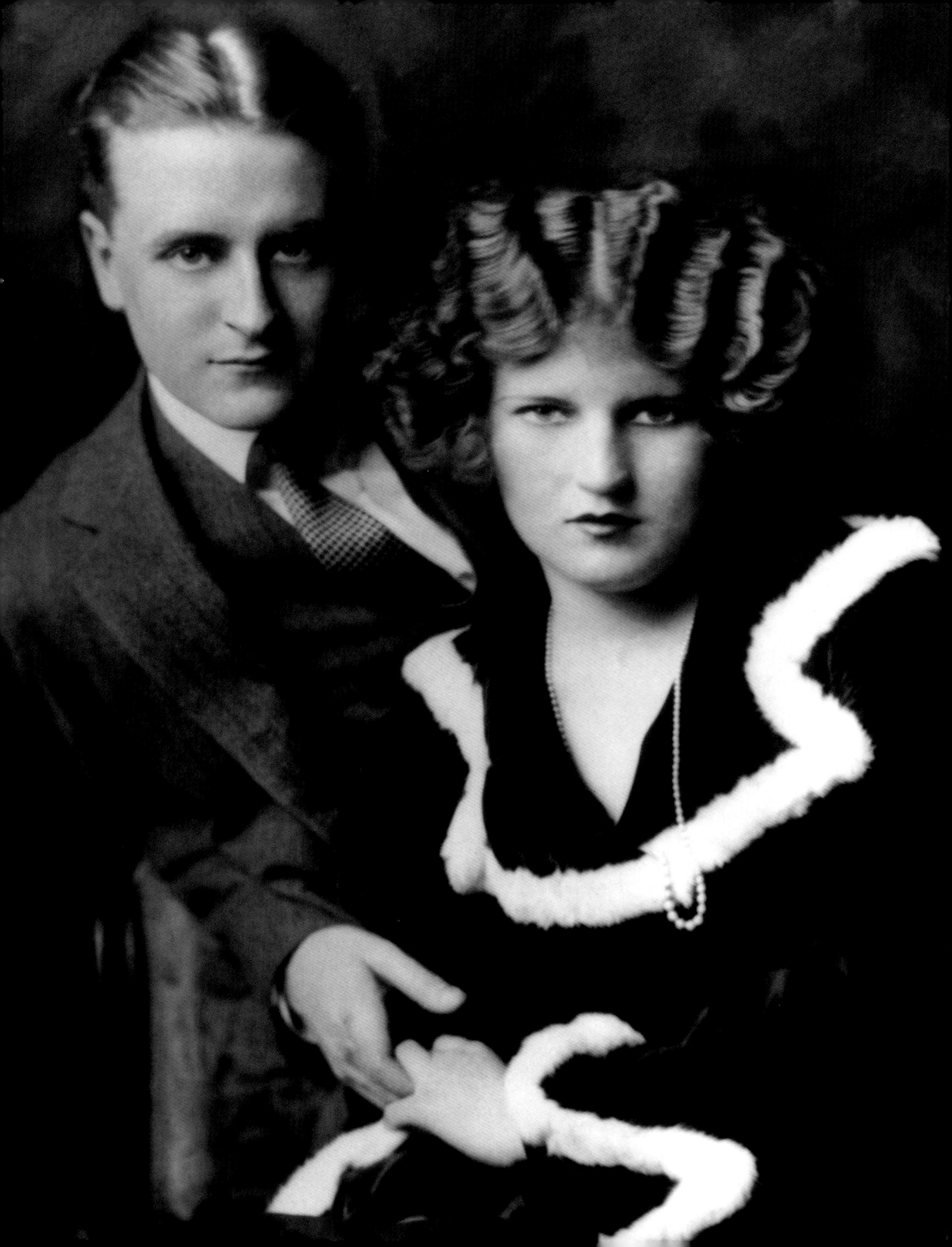

■ NORA JOYCE: Yes—"Ah," they would all ask me, "Are you Molly? And expect me to answer yes. And I would answer, "No. She was much fatter." And should I say yes to my Jim who never asked me to say yes to him? *Ulysses* was his life.

"How much will you give me for this?" I said to Arthur Power after Jim presented me with a copy of his *Ulysses*. *Ulysses*. Of course I was joking. Poor Jim, no jest to him.

"People say I have helped him to be a genius. What they'll be saying next is that if it hadn't been for that ignoramus of a woman what a man he would have been! But never you mind. I could tell them a thing or two about him after twenty years."

■ JOAN BAEZ: See me again—Bobby would be onstage. The overhead lights twinkling above his head. Klieg bouncing off his head like a halo. He'd snarl into the microphone:

"You can't...take fortune or fame. But neither of them is what they claim."

He'd look up at the tens of thousands in Skye,, in Waikiki, in Spokane, in Boston. An echo would roar back, "Fortune or fame!" By the time we'd get to the dressing room, he'd be drained. People in the hallway, outside the security area, a hundred guards couldn't keep them all restrained. Bobby seemed to have it all, fortune and fame. I'd hold his head in my hands and say, "Make a choice Bobby. Fortune or fame. Quit the road for a while and you'll keep your fame. For in America, only the mysterious, the reclusive and the dead are truly famous. Or keep performing day after day and watch your fortune grow. But forget everlasting fame."

As tired as he was, Bobby would say, "Tonto, are you telling me that you're not gonna see me again, that you're not gonna ride with me forever?" Of course, I'd laugh.

Inside I was weeping. For Bobby couldn't hear his own verse over the cries of his fans.

"Do you like it?" She looked up at him and breathlessy said "Yes."

To his amazement she opened the door of a battered 1958 blue Volkswagen and settled into the front seat. Taking the guitar from his hands, she put it on the passenger seat and simply gazed at him. Impossible for Fisher to invite himself along.

"Will you see me again?" he asked more as a prayer than a question.

For the longest of moments she stared at him from the wishing well of her car seat.

She handed the manuscript back to him through the open VW window, kissing the blank first page softly. Staring at her car pulling away from the High Street curb, he heard her answer.

"I will, yes."

■ GERALD MURPHY: Fisher—He asked young Fitzgerald. Young Fisher. First Fitzgerald writes. Then he gifts his precious prose as an engagement Golconda diamond—blue—white, of course. To Sara, to all, in his dreams, never mind that they've been bedded and wedded. A rival suitor. And then the questions. Words without end. Amen.

"His questions irritated Sara a good deal. Usually she would give him some ridiculous answer just to shut him up, but eventually the whole business became intolerable. In the middle of a dinner party one night, Sara had all she could take. 'Scott,' she said. 'you think if you just ask enough questions, you'll get to know what people are like, but you won't. You really don't know anything at all about people.' Scott practically turned green. He got up from the table and pointed his finger at her and said that nobody had ever dared say that to him, whereupon Sara asked if he would like her to repeat it and she did." Young Fisher. Writing. Asking. Plus ça change.

■ RICHARD WALLACE, a friend of James Joyce: Yes—Odd he was, Mr. James Joyce. In July '21, he visited us in Châtillon at our country house.

A glass of wine had put the Great Man to sleep on our sun porch early in the afternoon.

My wife, Lillian, was talking to a young painter. Suddenly I saw James stirring and as my wife repeated the word "yes" over and over again in different tones in her conversation, James retrieved a pencil from his pants pocket on which he wrote the word "yes" over and over again.

"By G-d, man," I said jocularly to Joyce. "What exactly are you doing?"

"*I have the opening and closing of Penelope. The last chapter in Ulysses.*" Joyce exclaimed triumphantly, standing up to his full height on the divan.

"And couldn't you remember the word yes without writing it down?" I said smilingly.

Joyce, without a smile, said, "Not if I wish people to remember my work for a thousand years."

■ BOB DYLAN: Prayer..."*But neither of them is what they claim*"—He quotes me, young Fisher. For she sings my song. He claims me as his Rabbi. He chants my words. He stands when I enter the concert hall. Repeats after me when I sing. Follows me across America and even abroad.

I'm no leader, follower, cantor or Rabbi. I am so tired, tired beyond what Fisher or any of the other Fishers can imagine.

Weary. Not from singing, not from writing, not from travelling but from all those expectations, all the demands, all the dreams that people write on little scraps of prayer paper and throw at me while I sing, leave on my doorstep, send via a friend's friend. I'm weary of not being their Rabbi. My only alternative to dying is to remain forever young.

F. Scott Fitzgerald with Zelda.

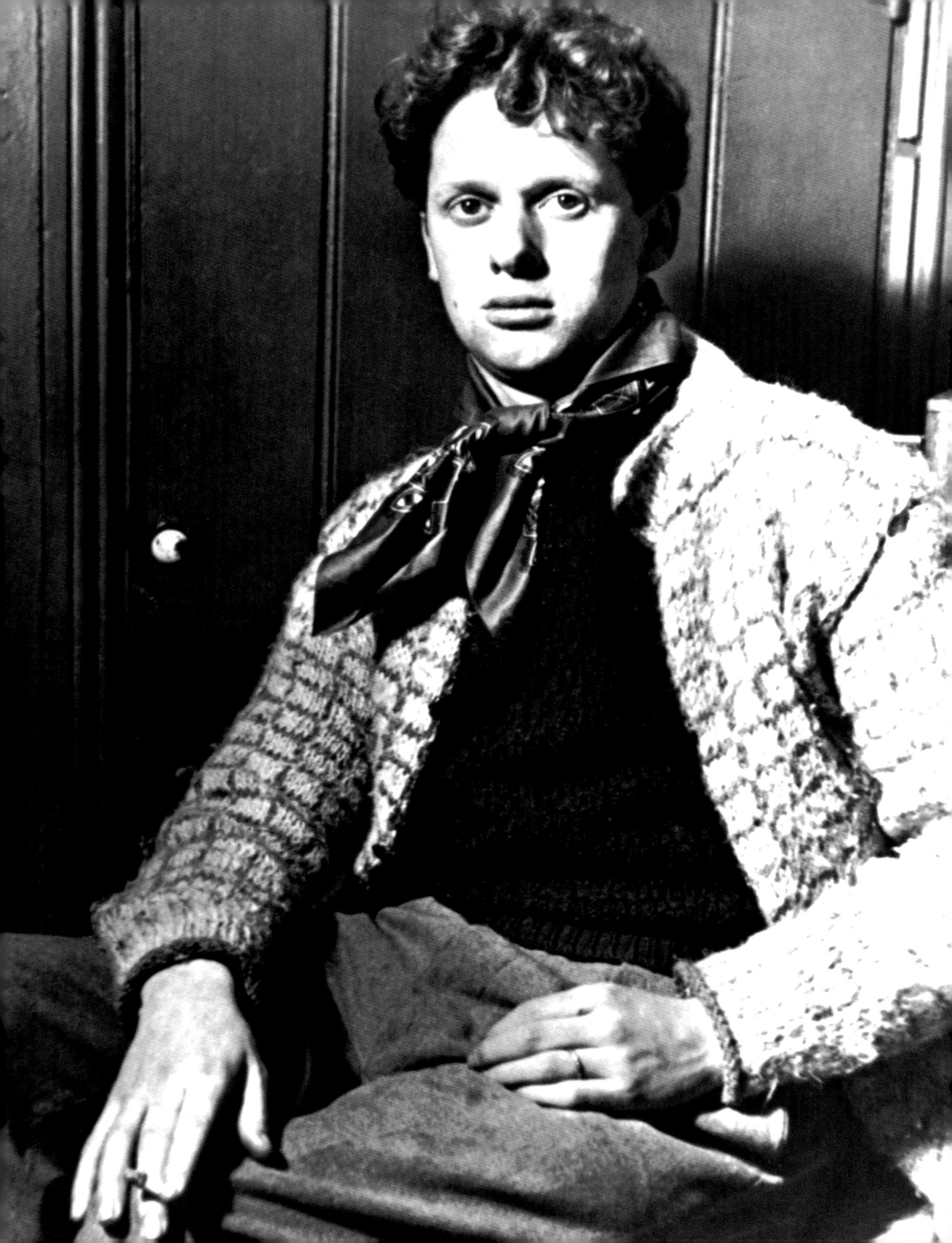

◆ Tuviah Gutman Gutwirth, Fisher's Grandfather: Calm down and listen—My grandson is sitting in an apartment quoting his "Rabbi" and Tal is telling him, "Calm down and listen."

Tal is dew from heaven. A Blessing to my grandson. My father Yekusiel Zalman always told me, "We are standing together in the middle of a long, long, tunnel. At one end is the light, the Holy Light, the Kabala. And Yekusiel Zalman can see it." But you, my son Gutman cannot see the Light. Thanks be to G-d that I am able to pass it along to you, and that is the Masoret, what I transmit. Then you will have received and it will be your duty to transmit. My grandson accepts that he has a Rabbi. He is willing to receive. G-d forbid, if a vessel is not open, no quantity of wine can fill it.

Tal is clear. "Calm down and listen," he is saying. Soon my grandson will be chanting Tal's teaching to another. The important thing is to listen with one's open eyes. As long as the tunnel may be, so great is the light that it may be seen at the end of it.

■ Dylan Thomas: Dying—
"*Time held me green and dying
And once below a time I lordly
Had the trees and leaves
Trail with daisies and barley
Down the rivers of the windfall light.*"

After so much death. Dying. Almost dead. As good as dead. The whole rotten war in October 1945. Cait and I, more dead than not dead. She massaging my fingers and blowing on my finger tips, breathing into the porch of my ear. "You must start to live again." And what is life but writing to me? I finished a line I wrote the year before the War.

"*Once below a time
When my pinned-around-the-spirit
Cut-to-measure flesh bit,
Summoning a child's voice from
A webfoot stone…I blasted in a wave.*"

My voice came back. A miracle. Lazarus rhyming. Time held me green and never dying, thanks to Caitlin and all the maidens in Christendom. Even a fisherman of Greenwich Village. My dying on his doorstep and he forever eulogizing me.

◆ Rachel Beller, Tal's girlfriend: Calm down and listen—Calm down and listen. He's been saying that for thirty years.

When we would walk in the park in Antwerp, how he would charm me. He could imitate the expression on everyone's face as they walked toward us. As soon as they passed, Abraham would mimic their speech, their very look. Sometimes he jumped on a park bench and folded his hands and rolled his eyes and started to bawl just like the crying infant in a carriage who had just passed.

Once a mother turned around and saw Abraham weeping, almost in unison with her own infant. The poor woman seemed more startled than angry and proceeded at a fast trot to escape the confines of the park and its crazed inhabitants. How we would laugh but, G-d forbid, if one subject came up—that Abraham should ask for my hand in marriage from my father, he would immediately pull me towards the nearest park bench, building stoop or just lean me against a parked limousine. "Calm down and listen!" he would shout.

I would put my hands on his face and say. "I'm calm! You calm down, Abraham." And he always would. But he would never listen.

Dylan Thomas.

CHAPTER 7

"Green with envy. Slip me the green. Time held me green and dying. Which is it to be, Tal? Fame or fortune? You can have one, to quote my Rabbi, but you can't have both, and none of them is what they claim," hissed Fisher to Tal. "Which is it to be now that we've moved back to my apartment?"

"Calm down and listen," said Tal to Fisher, staring at Fisher's writing table while absentmindedly stacking pencils and pens. "Calm down and listen," Tal placed the pens in a crossed position to create a three dimensional tic-tac-toe board, only to have the structure sway precariously in the gust of air that swept through Fisher's study from across the room. "Why don't you close at least one of these windows? It's freezing in here, Fisher."

◆ Bunam Fisher, Fisher's grandfather: Dying—Was I dying in Paris. In Montmorency, just outside of Paris. In Poland or just outside of Paris. And buried on the Mount of Olives in Palestine.

Dying. A score of children bearing my name. "*I shall multiply you as many as the number of sands on the shore and the stars in the sky.*"

My son Yehezkiel, the one who calls himself Emil, quoted me over and over again, things I said and even things I thought.

"*Honor your mother and your father that your days may be lengthened on earth.*"

I taught Yehezkiel. Why does this commandment alone bear a reward? The other commandments. Remember to keep the Sabbath holy, and indeed, all the other commandments are without rewards, because it is not natural. Children have to make the unnatural effort and not only are their days lengthened but our days also, even after we die. A person does not die until forgotten.

For as long as we are remembered, quoted, misquoted, thought of, as long as children are given our names, as long as charity is given in honor of us, as long as we are not, G-d forbid, forgotten, we live. We do not die.

◆ Emil Fisher, Fisher's father: Time held me green and dying——Dying. When I talked of my death, he couldn't accept it. Not really. Father, you'd be already… grandfather died young in Paris. But not you. You're vigorous. You don't smoke. You don't…you don't…

Of course, how could my wife talk to my son of death if she, master of silence, could not speak of death to me?

And he, trying to bring poems of that Englishman, Mr. Thomas. No, he's not English, he's Welsh. How am I to know what Welsh is? Polish, I know. French, I know. Not very well, but I know. Even Chinese or Indian, not the language, the people. And what is language but people?

The language of my parents—Yiddish. *Mama loshen*, I know, I think in, I dream in and for sure I cry in, but if your son will not cry, can a father cry? Certainly not in a hospital room. Not here in America. "If I didn't cry on the Maginot Line—*Gotse Helfen*," my mother would say. "Why should I cry in Mt. Sinai?"

Guldeneh Medineh, golden America, where all the streets are paved with rhyme, my son tells me. Of course he is looking for a father. Someone to clap for him whenever he writes a verse. I would have, if I could have.

But this old man, Tal. Is this how Raphael sees me? This Tal, what does he do? How does he support himself? I don't get it. What does he have that I didn't?

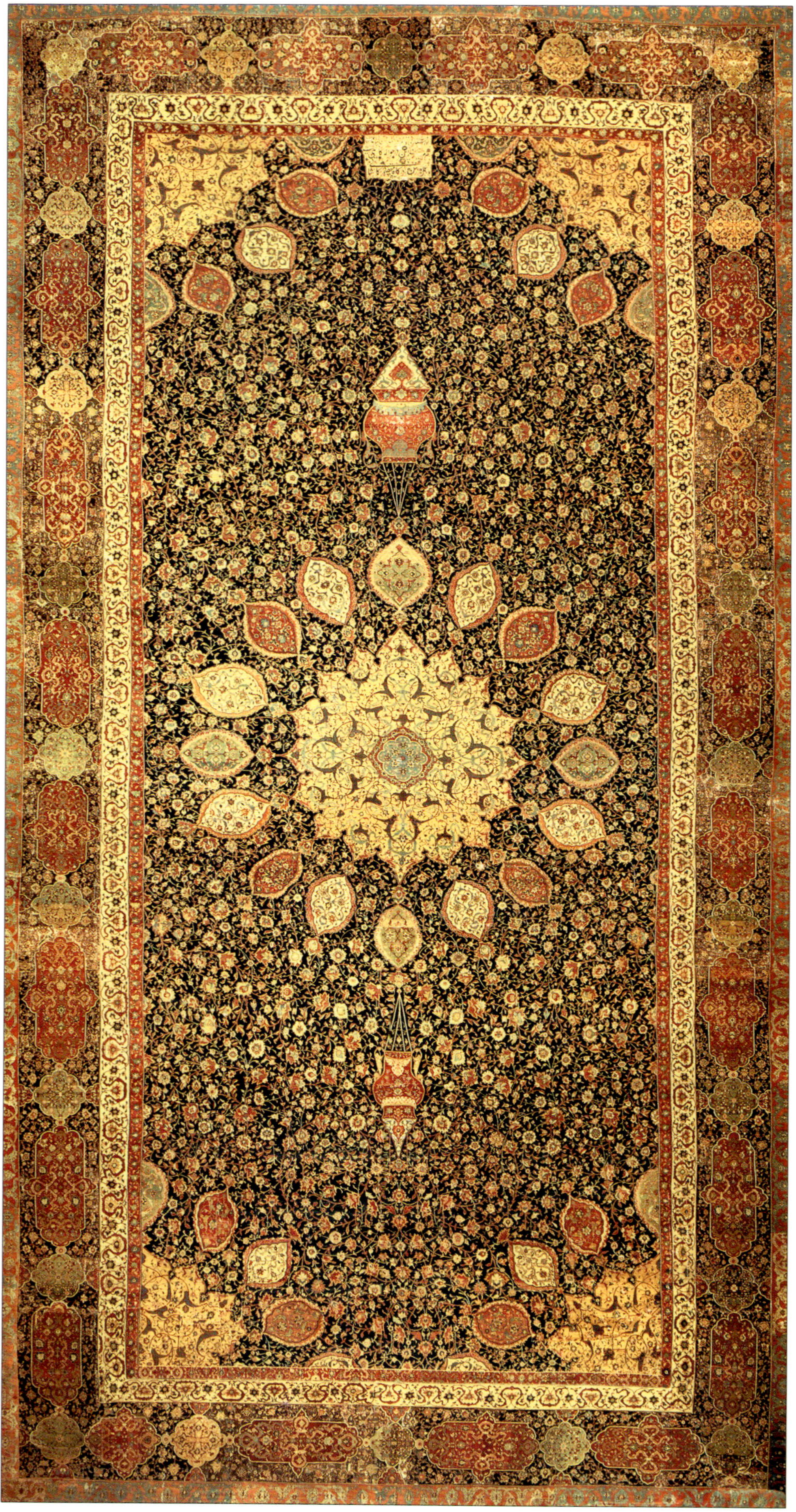

■ SHALOM ALKABETZ (circa 1505-1576), composer of "Lekhah Dodi": Three levels…invited and uninvited—We sat together, my student and my master, Moses Cordovero, and we looked at each other. We didn't speak. For my sister had left my house to go to her house across the garden to fetch some olives for Cordovero and me. How could we speak, when she was not with me?

Even more so, what could we say in her presence? Cordovero began as my student, and when I told him as he and my sister stood under the Safed star-filled Huppah:

"Now you will be my Rabbi, Moses, and so it has been."

What can we say of my sister and the holy olives she brings each day to sustain us?

There are three levels of the Paradise of the Torah. Peshat, Remez, and Drash. The simple meaning, the allusive meaning, the allegorical meaning. And then there is the secret of the secret, so simple that it eludes all of us without the Holy Bride of the Sabbath to rest our minds, and bring us the olive's sustenance of our soul.

Moses, my student, wrote Pardes Rimonim (the Paradise of Pomegranates) and I wrote "Lekhah Dodi". "Come My Beloved," to sing before the Holy Sabbath inviting the Bride of Israel. Blessed be the Lord, the one and the true, forever and ever, that pairs Rabbi and student into one song, a song so sweet that all the invited and uninvited stream from all places and times to glory in the beauty of Her Holiness.

■ EMILY POST: You invited yourself in—"One may never ask for an invitation for oneself anywhere! And one may not ask for an invitation to a luncheon or a dinner for a stranger. But an invitation for any general entertainment may be asked for a stranger, especially for a house guest.

Example:

"Dear Mrs. Worldly,
A young cousin of mine, David Blakely from Chicago, is staying with us.
May Pauline take him to your house on Friday the tenth? If it will be inconvenient for you to include him, please do not hesitate to say so frankly.
Very sincerely yours,
Caroline Robinson Town"

I quite like Mr. Abraham Tal. He presents Mr. Raphael Fisher with a green-lettered invitation to his apartment. Yet now Mr. Tal reverses himself by arriving at young Master Fisher's doorstep. If only these gentlemen could be consistent. If only they would apprise each other of their intentions, it would be so simple.

Answer:

"Dear Mrs. Town,
I shall be delighted to have Pauline bring Mr. Blakely on Friday the tenth.
Sincerely yours,
Edith Worldly"

The Ardabil Carpet.

"You invited yourself in, Tal. It's your vacation," said Fisher as he tried to stand one of his blue ballpoint pens directly in the center of Tal's jerry built, twelve pens, three levels, tic-tac-toe, structure. He jammed the pen into the center of the three level structure and then into a crevice in the table. The pen swayed back and forth, a barometric needle recording the Hudson Street weather, fulcrum to Fisher and Tal and even Dosha, not present but always present, along with their invited and uninvited guests.

"Why can't you leave what I do alone?" asked Tal, pointing to his elegant triple level structure, peeved that Fisher was damaging his antique table and might bring down his little edifice of pens. "You're ruining your writing table."

Fisher shrugged. "Listen Tal, speaking of writing, let's finish your lecture on what, how and where I should write. And as we say in twentieth century corporate America, let's firm up an agreement.

◆ TUVIAH GUTMAN GUTWIRTH, FISHER'S GRANDFATHER: "You invited yourself in, Tal. It's your vocation."—My grandson understands. And he speaks. But even he does not understand all that he says.

Some words are read one way and spoken another. Keri Ve-lo-Ketav—read although not written.

Tal's vocation is to invite himself in and my grandson knows this in his heart. But he has written it on his heart as Tal's pleasure, his vocation. Fisher is the writer and Tal his masoretic teacher. But Tal is also Fisher's teacher and Fisher the commentary on his teaching. If one inclines one's ear, one can hear the masoretic melody of Deuteronomy 28. As Tal and Fisher sing to each other.

"And it shall come to pass if thou shalt hearken diligently unto the voice of the Lord, thy G-d, to observe and to do all his commandments which I command thee this day, that the Lord will set the on high…and all these blessings shall come on thee and overtake thee."

Overtake Tal and Fisher though they run in all directions, sometimes away, sometimes toward the Heavenly Light.

"The Lord shall open unto thee his good treasure, the heaven to give the rain unto thy land in his season—"

What shall we say of a generation that moves forward and backward? Praise be to G-d that, in all times and in all places, every human can be the singer of G-d's word, one to another.

■ ANDRÉ GIDE: Jamming the pen into the center of Tal's jerry built…structure—"*All literature is architecture.*" All architecture is created in one person's dream. Every dream architect was a contractor.

Curious phrase these two Americans use. In any and all cases inferior, but is it inferior for it is a joint dream of the two of them.

Appropriate to the climate of their world, swaying in the breezes of their minds, swaying ever so slightly in the drying cement of the young man's writing table, an offering to his, and their, Muse, ever present, ever elusive.

Who needs the twenty thousand workers carving gemstones, planing marble, as though wood? Twenty years of labor and who needs the fabled jeweled building materials of the Taj?

No thank you, twelve pens will do just fine for these two playful people of the book. Father and son, lover and rival, emperor and prince, age and youth, charming Dosha. All of us in an ever growing pen house of their minds.

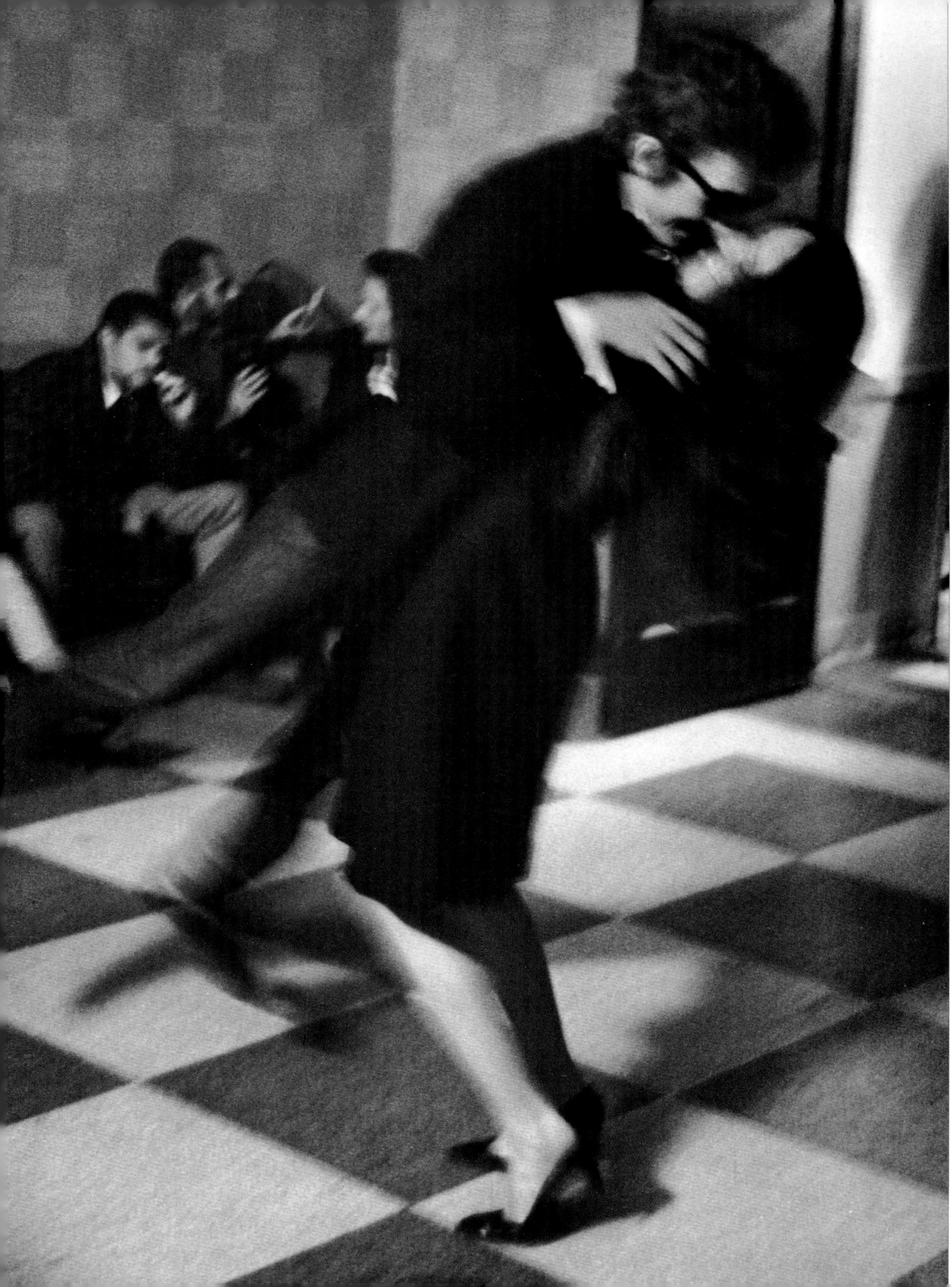

■ JAHANGHIR: Your family owns—My son Shah Jahan. *"His advent made the world joyous (Khurram)."* Light of my kingdom. The shadow of G-d on Earth, gifted me with treasures even from beyond Hindustan: Rubies and pearls from the North and East, diamonds from the flowing rivers of Hyderbad.

"Also a jeweled sash, a sword hilt made in my son Khurram's workshop…most of the jewels he had himself set and cut. He had brought great dexterity to bear on the design. Its value was fixed at Rupees 50,000. The designs were his own. No one else had up to this day thought of them. Undoubtedly it was a fine piece of workmanship."

Gifts to me from Prince Khurram. Then from me to my son, when he ascends to my throne as Shah Jahan. And from him to his son, or to another's son. Spilling downward through the rivers of time. The seed of Timur. Scattered. Does my family possess, or your family own, and what treasure does any family own? Forever?

■ MAHARAJA OF PATIALA: Paradise: My court jeweler, Muhammad Kassim, spoke to the European Imre Schwaiger, Cartier's agent in Delhi, who spoke to Jacques Cartier, the youngest of the Cartier brothers, who spoke to his elder brother, Pierre, who in turn could not answer before speaking to his eldest brother, Louis. The house of Cartier had told me that they would transform all my jewels, set in gold, into a new paradise, a platinum paradise, strong enough to last a lakh—a hundred thousand—of years. Beautiful enough to make me King of all Hindustan. Jewels befitting the King of the World.

Muhammad Kassim agreed but what would be the cost of all this remodeling, designing and setting? Months later the curious answer: My imperial jeweler should allow one gemstone from my sacred treasury to be sold and the revenues thereof would defray all costs of modernizing as well as net me a profit! I am not a merchant. I had Kassim reply; "The house of Cartier should choose the jewel and name the price they would charge." How was India to know what Paris desired? And they did. And clever the Cartiers were. They chose the Flowers of Paradise emeralds, six-sided, 141 Indian carats, gloriously carved. How they knew we had it in Patiala I'll never fathom. Cartier also named the price it would fetch in the European market. "An enormous price even after the five percent commission Cartier would charge for selling expenses," said Kassim to me. "Well then, multiply the price twofold, Kassim and tell them His Majesty accepts. Do it discreetly. Ever so discreetly. Let the family Cartier note in their cost books—for Europeans ever love their accounts—another of my fellow princes as the seller–Patiala, cares not a whit. But if my House's name is mentioned in their Holy account books, the self same "*30,000 sikhs who escorted me and our holy book–the Granth Sahib kept in a cavet placed in the silver howdah on the largest of eight elephants*" these self same warriors will march on Paris. All of Heaven's guardian angels will naught avail the House of Cartier. A Patiala who gifted a carved emerald to a British Queen does not intend to be the butt of Parisian wags.

"For reasons not altogether clear, you bring me this story about a 144 carat hexagonal moghul emerald carved by Shah Jahan that your family owns, and I am supposed to write it up, as you so elegantly put it.

"I'm dispatched to your diamondiferous brother at your family office, looking for you, and he too is looking for you, and then when I ask him for more details on the Green Mirror of Paradise, as you call it, he says 'Oh, yes, it's not his stone or your stone but Suleimani's." Fisher pronounced the name: SOO-LAY-MAH-NEE, with an exaggerated slowness.

"And is SOO-LAY-MAH-NEE the travel agent to whom I apply for my ticket to Agra to view the Taj personally, by moonlight?"

■ DARAH SHIKOH, SHAH JAHAN'S SON on his wedding day: Family—*"In the custom of Hindustan, on my marriage day, for good luck, His Majesty my Father, fastened around my head the Sehra (veil) which consists of strands of lustrous pearls with brilliant rubies and emeralds, and which His Majesty my Grandfather Jahanghir had fastened with his own blessed hand around His Majesty, my Father, Shah Jahan's head on the eve of his marriage…"*

My family's jewels, lovingly passed from father to son, and again on to me, lit the night with their lustre.

"The servants of the court at imperial command lit lamps in the garden below the private hall, and on the grounds beneath the Jharoka-I-darshan and brought boats on the Jumna and arrayed them with so many candles, torches and lamps that the stars of the heavens were jealous. Fireworks from the imperial establishment were lit and lighted up the earth like the heavens."

My brothers were jealous. Even I was jealous of myself, so beautiful was it all. And later by the lake in Kashmir, alone with my Sufi Chisti Master, I reflected upon his question: And where are the jewels your family owns? Your…family…owns. Then I realized who I am and I visualized my family for the first time. I beheld the truth in a green mirror of paradise: there is but One Owner.

■ GAUGUIN: The Green Mirror of Paradise—*"There are two things in the painter, the eye and the mind. Each of them should aid each other. It is necessary to work at their mutual development in the eyes by looking at nature, in the mind by the logic of organized sensations which provides the means of expression."*

I quite like this young Fisher. He understands the green emerald should be seen with one's mind, be understood with one's eye. What pleasure for Shah Jahan to feel the greenness of the stone. It must have been a green mirror of paradise for him—for Fisher, even for Suleimani—once the eye and the mind are merged—a painter, a collector, even a critic—we all can peer into a mirror of paradise.

■ LAWRENCE FERLINGHETTI: Family—*"I was looking at those great photographs of the Paris surrealists in the '20s and I thought it'd be a good thing to get one like that before the whole scene disappears in a cloud."*

And there the whole family was, and I mean the whole family: Richard Brautigan, Robert LaVigne, Shig Murai, Peter Orlovsky, David Melzer, Allen Ginsberg of course, right in the center, and I, opening my umbrella to give a soupçon of royalty to it all. Like every family photo, there's always one who just won't be in the picture. Too shy, too proud, too beyond it all, wants to watch but won't be included, maybe next time and of course more in the photo than anyone: Bob Dylan.

Pacing, smiling, standing inside of the City Lights bookstore, realizing that history was being made: Our family, all together, never again, but Bob content to have only his shadow fall across the negative.

■ BOB DYLAN: Diamondiferous brother—
*"Yes to dance beneath the diamond sky
With one hand waving free
Circled by the circus sands."*

Fisher's almost trained. Tal thinks he's calling the tune. So does Suleimani. So does Tal's diamondiferous brother—Big Jim. *"Who owns the town's only diamond mine."*

"They may own this emperor's emerald and they most certainly are '*little boys lost taking themselves so seriously.*' Dosha, '*radiant jewel, mystical wife*' owns them.

Joan Baez lifting and twirling Bob Dylan.

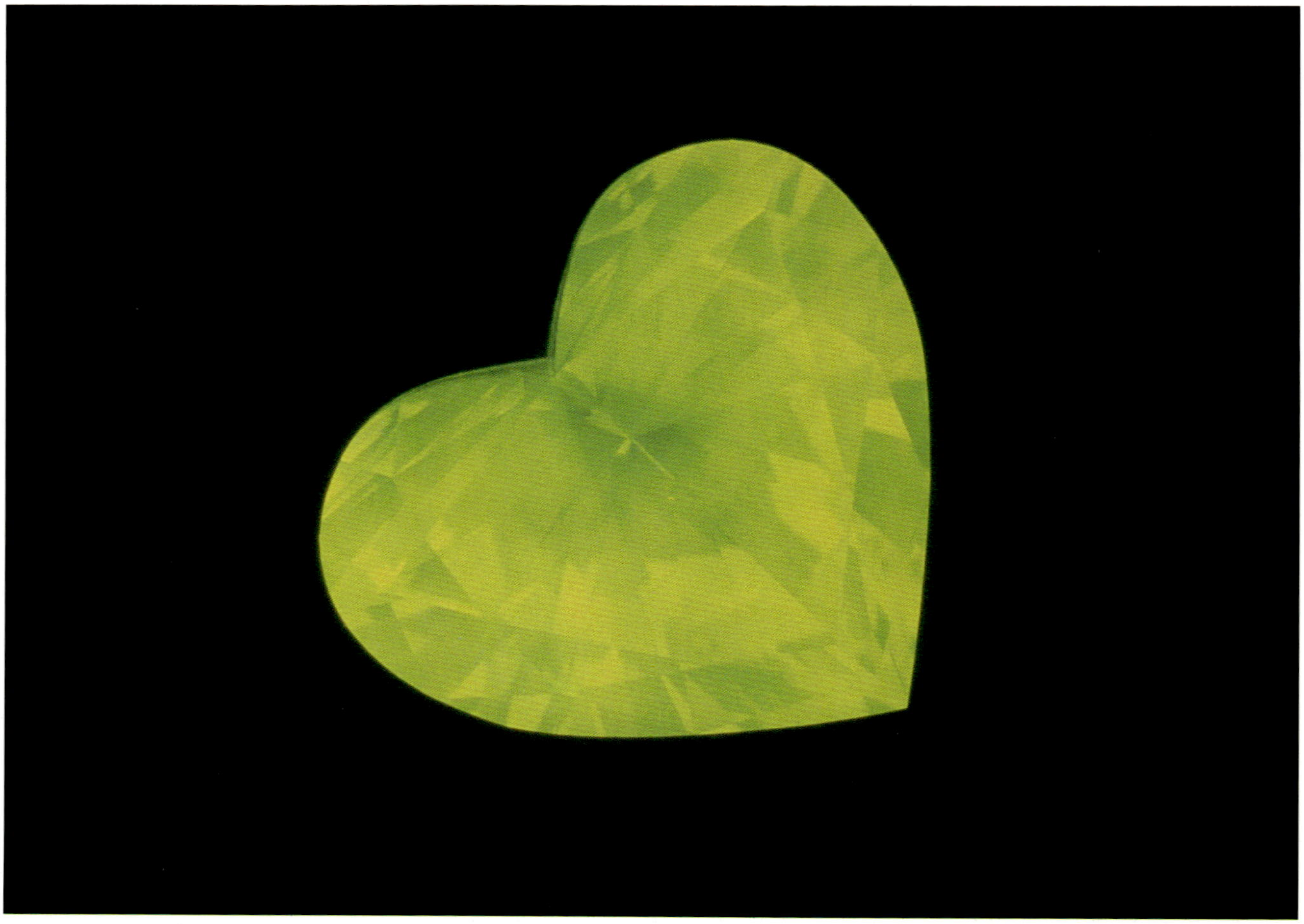

◆ HAHAM ZEVI, nephew of ARYEH LEIB KATZ, FISHER'S ancestor: Luminescent white gateway to Paradise—When I went East to Salonika to study with Elijah Covo, I was but sixteen years of age. Elijah blessed me when I arrived in his Yeshivah. "May your next thirty two years be as fruitful as your first." And when I objected to his counting, Haham Covo intoned: "*You shall love Hashem, your G-d, with all your heart, with all your soul and with all your resources. Let these matters that I command you today be upon your heart. Teach them thoroughly to your children and speak of them while you sit in your home, while you walk on the way when you retire and when you arise.*"

Then he put his hands, strong, steady hands on my head.'

Your mother's father taught you while you were awake and your father when you lay down. Thus your days have been doubled in blessing. Perhaps because I had come from so far away, from the West, from Moravia, I asked him, "And what of you Haham Elijah, are, you also twice your age?"

He closed his eyes and looked toward the East beyond the waters of Salonika, and he said, "I am looking at the East." That morning we were studying the Tractate Bava Basra. Rabbi Judah of India was fond of narrating tales. "*Once there was a great fish…*"

Even in Salonika we had heard of the Taj Mahal. the temple built in India. I asked, "Are you thinking of the Taj Mahal in Hindustan? Is that what you mean by looking at the East?" "No," said Haham Covo. "One cannot look at the temple of Hindustan. It is whiter than white. One averts one's eyes."

I am not looking so far. I am looking at the Eastern lights of Istanbul. My father Judah, may his light always illuminate me, journeyed there forty years ago. For in those days our holy congregation here in Salonika had to pay an annual tax. For five years we couldn't raise the enormous sums demanded. For those years the Turkish rulers allowed us to deliver clothing sewn by our people. But forty years ago, may the memory never leave me, the clothing did not find favor in the eyes of the Vizier to the Sultan. My father was put to death and the *Parnas* and *Gabbai* both tortured and imprisoned.

Haham Covo started to walk around me slowly, looking over my head and staring to the East to Istanbul, to Jerusalem, beyond to India and back on my other side and looking in the direction of Moravia, Prague, Ofen, all cities I had come from. He walked around me, time and time again. His lips moved but I could only make out a few of the sounds…"world" "crowns" "head." Years later, when I returned to Amsterdam, after Prague, after the Yeshiva in London, I could hear Haham Covo's benediction to me.

"In the world to come, there is neither eating nor drinking nor procreation nor business dealing nor jealousy nor hate nor competition. But righteous men sit with their crowns on their head and they enjoy the splendor of the divine Presence."

Then I understood that Moravia, Salonika, Belgrade, Venice, Prague, Altona, Hamburg, Amsterdam, London, Opatowa and Lemberg, all the Yeshivot I headed, were but luminescent white gateways to Paradise.

"Business Class, for I am in fact on a fact-finding mission. A free ticket made out to Raphael Fisher Esquire, as you so archaically put it. Or should I expect student fare accommodations as I will be teaching myself all kinds of valuable lessons—an autodidact of Moghul, Hindu and Sufi lore? How and why the Taj Mahal mausoleum stands elevated on a bed of marble flowers, a gateway to Paradise, a luminescent white gateway to Paradise."

"Is it to be business wages, Tal or student digs?" Fisher practically shouted, Tal winced, but didn't utter a sound.

■ PIERRE CARTIER: A fact finding mission—The young Fisher, just like young Jacques. Searching for the same prize and working at their elders bidding, half a century apart. C'est la bouquet vraiment.

Father said that Louis and I wished Jacques to go on a fact finding mission to India. Keep your eyes open and your pocket shut were our instructions to him.

Of course, Jacques knew that "keep your eyes open" were Louis' words. And why should he not "keep his pocket shut"?—Those Maharajas were worse than stall keepers in the marché aux puces.

With the earnestness of a school boy, Jacques left for the Darbar of 1911 in Delhi.

La Maison Cartier cares not a whit for whether Kapurthala or Nawanagar have a greater gun salute at the Darbar. Bring Fob Watches for all the potentates and, above all, bring back impressions of what they want, who they are, how they think.

What a success our student was in his opening semester: Brilliant grades: Hors concours. A platinum fob watch for Nawanagar; a blue enamel watch for the Maharaja of Kapurthala, a gold traveler's clock for the Rampur and of course…And of course, a gold fob watch for the Nizam of Hyderbad. But as for what intelligence Jacques brought back for us, all he could do is mumble over and over again: "Patiala, Patiala, Patiala is the key to it all!"

■ LOUIS CARTIER: An autodidact of Moghul and Sufi lore—Jacques was a brilliant student but I was an autodidact of Moghul, Hindu, and Sufi lore.

All one had to do is stare at the glorious miniatures—Akbar in battle, Jahanghir looking at his father's portrait, Shah Jahan floating on a flying howdah of gems called the peacock throne. Aurangzeb, his head in a Koran as he entered battle. "Patiala, Patiala, Patiala," Jacques would mumble. And I said simply, "Let Patiala bring his jewels to Paris to be remounted in white rivers of platinum. Les Freres Cartier will sit on the peacock throne and all the world from the Americas to the Ganges will prostrate themselves before us.

"Trés original," said Pierre to me, "but we can't afford it."

I chuckled and said, "Then we must figure out a plan for Patiala himself to pay the tariff."

■ BEBADAL KHAN GILANI: Paradise—And for the date of Mumtaz's death having vestiges of pardon, I wrote:

"May the Abode of Mumtaz Mahal be Paradise." "Ja-I-Mumtaz Mahal jannat bad."

This was the hemistich I received under the inspiration of the Inspirer of the unseen world."

■ KALIM, COURT POET OF SHAH JAHAN: Flowers—
The inlayer has set stone within stone,
As bold and precise as the dark spot within the tulip's heart.
Pictures become manifest from every stone;
Take a look at the garden in the mirror—
They have inlaid stone flowers in marble,
Which surpass reality in color if not in fragrance.
Nay not flowers, they are rather the fresh cheeks of Houris,
Or new drops engraved upon crystal.
Since the very first moment of creation,
Who till now has seen an edifice like this?

Heart-shaped diamond, 22.38 carats.

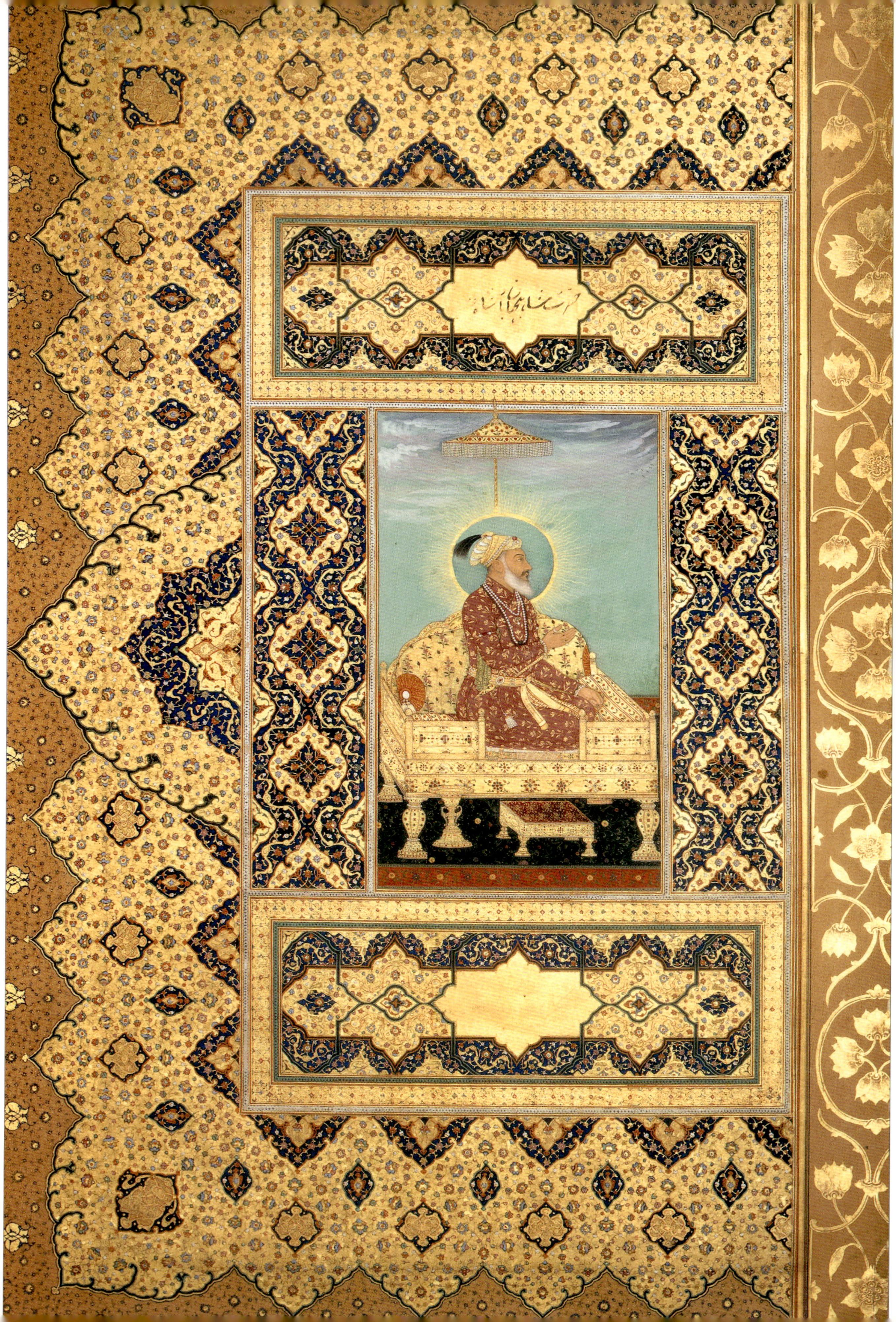

■ ABU SALIM, gem carver: Poppy—I could not stop shaking for a fortnight. "Not important. Not important." Suddenly I thought: I am a gem carver, not a painter. I went straight away to the Kharkana and there was the Hindu Payag.

I placed the mountain of green before him and told him what the Emperor had commanded me to do: Babur's lotus, Akbar's poppy of the mountains of Kashmir, and another flower to be chosen by me—all resting upon an acanthus base.

"What do I choose, Payag?" Payag was a painter. He was my friend. He knew my children. He ate in my house. But he was speechless: "I do not know the mind of the Emperor," he told me modestly. "I do not know even one word to tell you, Abu Salim." I was still shaking and I threw myself at his feet. "Payag, save me!"

Payag lifted me up and sat me on a divan opposite his painting space and within the briefest of intervals summoned his brother Balchand, who appeared, haggard, for he had been sleeping and was not well.

When Balchand heard our Emperor's words: "Not important, not important," he looked knowingly at his brother Payag. And suddenly burst out laughing. "Not important…not important. That means it is very important. More important than anything else. But how do we know the mind of Shah Jahan? Only an Emperor can understand an Emperor. We must ask how Babur and Akbar would portray Shah Jahan's emblem. It must be like them. It must be them. Yes, Shah Jahan must be like them. Be them."

"How do I do that? Draw it for me Balchand." I handed Payag's brush to Balchand. Balchand handed it back to Payag.

"Payag can sketch the crescent of the moon itself." Payag's hand started to move. Back and forth, back and forth. First he sketched the outline of the six-sided emerald. He inserted a lotus flower head and next to the lotus, the outline of a poppy. The same poppies we saw filling the mountain ravines of Kashmir and then a space and all rested on a bed of acanthus leaves.

Finally, after the three of us sat unmoving for hours, Payag, who had not lifted his head from his sketch, put down the outline of a third flower.

"But it's another lotus," I said and then caught myself and said, "No, it's another poppy." And realized what Payag had done. Back and forth, I moved my head between the field of flowers.

Yes, it was Babur's and Akbar's flowers: a combination of the two. I embraced Payag and his brother. Each night for four months, I came to the Kharkana just before dawn to show them the piece of emerald as I carved.

And when it was ready, just after the third Urs of the death of our Empress Mumtaz, I presented the emerald to Shah Jahan.

I never saw Shah Jahan again after that day. But my children's children will live on the lands the Emperor gave me as a prize. My Emperor recovered his spirit and next year voyaged to Kashmir after the fourth Urs.

I offered my daughter in marriage to Payag's son, even though he was a Hindu. Had Payag not saved my life? He refused and said laughingly, "It's not important."

"Or am I, perhaps, to pay you and your ever-obliging brother for all I'm learning about the mystic poppy, the lotus and the everlasting amaranth: the flowers carved on the Taj Mahal emerald. Amaranth that corresponds to the moonlit flowers that brighten the dreams of Shah Jahan and Mumtaz as they lie quietly in the Taj, the throne of G-d on the Day of Judgment."

"And now to the main event: the hullabaloo over the Taj Mahal emerald. A key to your past, Tal, Suleimani's past, and even my past. A key to a future treasure chest of riches. Yours, Suleimani's, and even mine, I am told."

Tal's silence was starting to unnerve Fisher as he roared to a finish. "A carved gemstone that will be explained totally by you. Tal, well?" Fisher stopped abruptly.

Finally, Tal was ready with a reply.

■ SHAH JAHAN: Lie quietly in the Taj—I and Mumtaz lie quietly in the Taj. For our seed is spread across Hindustan, flowering as the wind catches it, ever replanting in the earthly garden.

I am the illustrious heir of Jannat Makani—he whose place is in the heavenly garden—the Emperor Nur-Al-Din Muhammad Jahanghir; son of Arsh Asha—he whose nest is on the divine throne—the Emperor Jalal al-Din Muhammad Akbar; son of Jannat Ashyari (he who is nested in Heaven). The Emperor Nasir al-Din Muhammad Humayum; son of Firdaus Makani—he whose place is in paradise. The Emperor Zahir al-Din Muhammad Babur; son of Ustad Shaikh Shah; son of the martyr King Sultan Abu Said Shah; son of Sultan Muhammad Shah; son of Mirza Miran Shah; son of the Great Lord and Universal Conqueror, the pillar of the world and religion—Emperor Amir Timur Gurgan—the first Sahib-I-Qiran—Lord of the auspicious planetary conjunction.

Mumtaz and I, we lie quietly facing Mecca, as spring follows winter, as flower follows planted seed, as sun bursts forth day by day heated by the unending warmth of the wisdom of Timur.

■ MARCEL PROUST: Flowers—The moonlit flowers that brightened the dreams of Shah Jahan and Mumtaz as they lie quietly in the Taj. *"I never sleep except for a few minutes."* And in those few minutes, have I not written my Padshanama on the foolscap of my dreams?

"And it was perhaps also by the preposterous game they play with time that dreams had fascinated me. Had I not often seen them in one night, so far in the past that I could scarcely distinguish any longer the feelings I had at that time, come rushing down upon me, full tilt, blinding me with their brightness like giant airplanes instead of the pale stars I believed them to be, bringing me again all they had once held for me, giving me the emotion, the shock, the brilliance of their immediate proximity; and then when I awoke, retrace the distance they had so miraculously crossed at one bound and even make me believe, but mistakenly that they were one of the means of recapturing the past."

Shah Jahan has brought a bouquet of flowers to brighten the dreams of Mumtaz as he lies beside her in the Taj, both of them turned towards Mecca as they wait for the Judgment of G-d on the Day of Reckoning. They are facing me just as I am facing them, lying quietly in my bed, preparing to write my dream and dream of writing. *"For a long time I used to go to bed early."*

Shah Jahan.

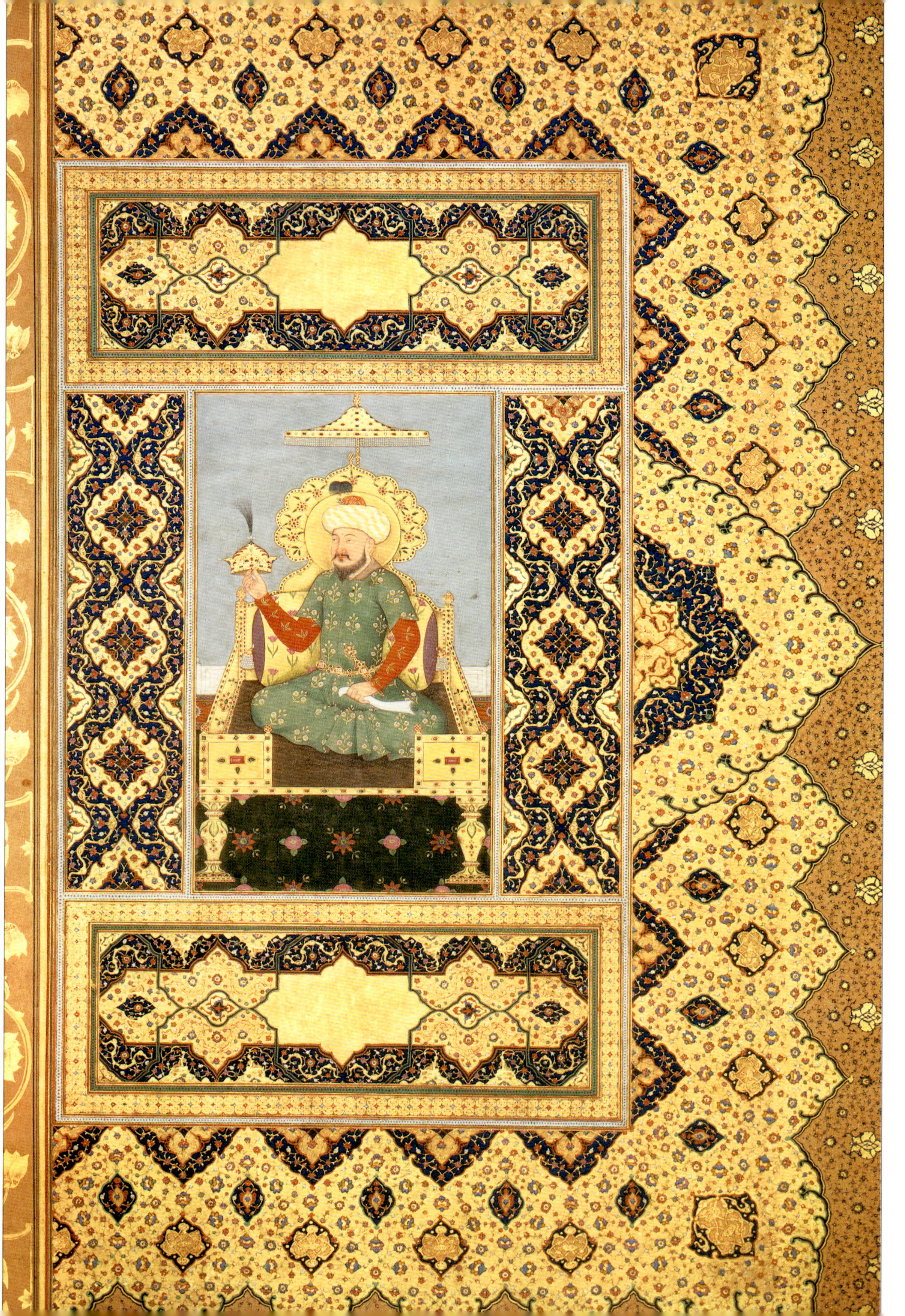

■ SHAH JAHAN: Not important—I spoke slowly and clearly, weighing each word to the Palace gem cutter, the wonder of the age: Abu Salim. It's not important how long it takes to cut this crystal. Was it important how long it took the emerald crystal to arrive here from the land of the Philippines? Was it important how long it took for the crystal to be mined by the *farangs* who rule in the land of Spain and whose boats sail across the waters to the Philippines.

Was it important how long this crystal has hidden in the ground before a *farang* stole it? No. We are here. And that is what is important. Now take this block of green and build me a green palace that my eyes can rest in. Bathe in. Swim in. Wander in. Be refreshed in.

And carve my House's voyage upon it. The Flower of Babur, my grandfather's grandfather. Like Dholpur—a garden of lotus buds. Ever-blossoming. And my grandfather's poppy, Akbar's flower. Did he not conquer the *Paradise Resembling Kashmir*. The same paradise I shall journey to in two months' time. The earthly paradise where I shall rest. Bathe in, swim in, wander in, be refreshed in. Yes, pluck a poppy that only grows in Kashmir as the fluttering flag of my grandfather Akbar. Choose a flower for me. Build the whole green palace upon a foundation of acanthus leaves. The same base I chose for the columns of all my palaces. Abu Salim, the carver, was shaking, so frightened was he. Finally he said: "Emperor—all seeing and all knowing—what shall be your flower?" Even I could not answer. I had not been able to sleep. Or eat. Nor to bathe. My hair had turned white. My trip to Paradise—Resembling Kashmir delayed. The third 'Urs (memorial saintly anniversary) of Mumtaz's death. The workmen bringing marble from the mountain passes of Amber had slowed to a trickle, new sources were needed, all was frozen, my heart, my will, everything in Hindustan. I could not open my mouth to speak more than two words.

"Not important...not important," over and over again. Until the carver Abul Salim retreated.

■ LAHORI, COURT HISTORIAN: Stone—"*[The two earlier histories by Tabataba, I and Qazwin's, as well as Salih's plagiarized version of the former, allude to Shah Jahan's despondency over the approach of the third death anniversary as one of the reasons for postponing his scheduled departure for Kashmir. In his officially sanctioned history, Lahori passes over the incident in silence, perhaps because he realized it could be construed in a negative way—seeing as how not departing was the fact that the passes to Kashmir were not yet clear of snow]*"

I wrote: [fol. 83A]: "*Among the events of these days was the cancellation, for the time being, of the journey to the promenade of Paradise–resembling Kashmir, and the postponement of that honored departure until the approach of some other chosen hour. Apart from the dictates of the Divine Decree and the will of the turner of men's hearts—which lie behind what are generally referred to as the cancellation of one's intentions and the annulment of one's design, the other obvious reason for the delay was that, after the second journey to the promised Paradise, namely the heart-pleasing Kashmir, had already been fixed and agreed upon, from the contents of the news reports of the official recorders (waqi'a–nawis) in these parts, it was disclosed that the roads and passes would not be clear from snow until the beginning of the month of Khurdad. Consequently, because of this news, the original plan was discarded.*"

Thus I wrote. But I did not write (for I was instructed not to write) that our Emperor His Highness the Shadow of G-d on Earth, who was unable to voyage to Paradise-resembling Kashmir had the hand of G-d design for him flowers of Kashmir on an emerald stone that he wore every day around his neck. I have not seen this green emerald, but if it be but a tenth part of what it is said to be, surely Kashmir itself has traveled to our glorious Emperor.

"The ownership of the stone is not important. I could tell you one thing right now, Fisher, as we talk, and it could be true right now. My brother could have sold the stone ten minutes before. The truth is not so simple. Nothing is so simple."

"You're pretty simple, Tal. You, omitting the name of the probable owner of the stone, Suleimani, whoever he is. You induced me to write up a proposal at my office, at my job, risking my reputation and that of my dear colleague, William Hamilton."

"The third probably," interjected Tal.

"No, just William Hamilton the First. If I had a dollar for each time, Tal, you used the word moghul—moghul mystery, moghul treasure, moghul secret, finest moghul gem—I'd be rich indeed."

■ PAYAG: The ownership of the stone—Shah Jahan summoned me. It was always in the middle of the night. Lahori was at his side. I suppose without his diarist-historian the Emperor's words would vanish in the wind.

On a string suspended, covered by the Emperor's hand, I was certain Shah Jahan's clenched fist hid Abu Salim's carved emerald, the one he had shown me in the unpolished state, a mountain of green light, just six months before.

Lahori bade me sit on a carpet spread on the garden grass not a distance greater than a Bukharan horse away from the Emperor.

Lahori spoke: "His highness wishes to have His Majesty's glory recorded forever, for more than one hundred generations of rule of the House of Timur. How would you do that, Payag?"

Does His Majesty wish to be portrayed sitting on the peacock throne holding in his hand the green miracle that Abu Salim is said to have cut? The emerald is said to be carved in the most beautiful fashion in all Hindustan—and His Majesty owns the stone.

The ownership of the stone is of no current central importance—that is what His Majesty told Lahori. He too suggested portraying His Majesty with the Green Mirror-of-Paradise Emerald.

No, Payag, what would you suggest?

Balchand had trained me well. Everything had to come from the Emperor. Even if the words emerged from Lahori's mouth.

Does the Emperor wish to be pictured as ever journeying toward the light, towards the Holy Place—I did not know whether I, a Hindu albeit a Brahmin could say the sacred name of Mecca—towards eternity? Walking ever onward, leading his people—and the future grandsons of grandsons onward?

Lahori looked at Shah Jahan whose head moved ever so slightly upward at the same instant my Emperor tightened his grip, yet more firmly around the gemstone hanging as a pendant from his neck—impossible though it could have been to see it clearly by torchlight in the middle of the night. A gesture was all Lahori needed, so long had they been together.

"The Emperor," Lahori said without hesitation, "Will not walk. He is to be portrayed on horseback. His Majesty will write your name on your painting if the portrait meets with his approval. And as far as your viewing the Green Mirror-of-Paradise Emerald, that will be quite unnecessary for Abul Hasan, for you or for anyone else." Immediately Lahori rose and with our Emperor, disappeared in the diwan-I-am.

I was afraid to smile—even in the dark. How could they possibly know that Abu Salim had brought the stone twenty times—to be viewed, discussed, planned, designed and yes, even blessed by me.

Timur (Tamerlane).

And the Thirty-two Counties of the Four Provinces of Ireland
Are thus divided: The Four Counties are in the Four Camps
Munster South in Reubens Gate, Connaut West in Josephs Gate
Ulster North in Dans Gate, Leinster East in Judahs Gate

For Albion in Eternity has Sixteen Gates among his Pillars
But the Four towards the West were Walled up & the Twelve
That front the Four other Points were turned Four Square
By Los for Jerusalems sake & called the Gates of Jerusalem
Because Twelve Sons of Jerusalem fled successive thro the Gates
But the Four Sons of Jerusalem who fled not but remain
Are Rintrah & Palamabron & Theotormon & Bromion
The Four that remain with Los to guard the Western Wall
And these Four remain to guard the Four Walls of Jerusalem
Whose foundations remain in the Thirty-two Counties of Ireland
And in Twelve Counties of Wales. & in the Forty Counties
Of England & in the Thirty-six Counties of Scotland
And the names of the Thirty-two Counties of Ireland are these
Under Judah & Issachar & Zebulun are Lowth Longford
Eastmeath Westmeath Dublin Kildare Kings County
Queens County Wicklow Catherloh Wexford Kilkenny
And those under Reuben & Simeon & Levi are these
Waterford Tipperary Cork Limerick Kerry Clare
And those under Ephraim Manasseh & Benjamin are these
Galway Roscommon Mayo Sligo Leitrim
And those under Dan Asher & Napthali are these
Donnegal Antrim Tyrone Fermanagh Armagh Londonderry
Down Monaghan Cavan. These are the Land of Erin

All these Center in London & in Golgonooza, from whence
They are Created continually East & West & North & South
And from them are Created all the Nations of the Earth
Europe & Asia & Africa & America, in fury Fourfold!

And Thirty-two the Nations: to dwell in Jerusalems Gates
O Come ye Nations Come ye People Come up to Jerusalem
Return Jerusalem, & dwell together as of old: Return
Return; O Albion let Jerusalem overspread all Nations
As in the times of old: O Albion awake! Reuben wanders
The Nations wait for Jerusalem, they look up for the Bride

France Spain Italy Germany Poland Russia Sweden Turkey
Arabia Palestine Persia Hindostan China Tartary Siberia
Egypt Lybia Ethiopia Guinea Caffraria Negroland Morocco
Congo Zaara Canada Greenland Carolina Mexico
Peru Patagonia Amazonia Brazil. Thirty-two Nations
And under these Thirty-two Classes of Islands in the Ocean
All the Nations Peoples & Tongues throughout all the Earth
And the Four Gates of Los surround the Universe Within and
Without; & whatever is visible in the Vegetable Earth, the same
Is visible in the Mundane Shell; reversd in mountain & vale
And a Son of Eden was set over each Daughter of Beulah to guard
In Albions Tomb the wondrous Creation: & the Four-fold Gate
Towards Beulah is to the South Fenelon, Guion, Teresa,
Whitefield & Hervey, guard that Gate; with all the gentle Souls
Who guide the great Wine-press of Love; Four precious Stones that
Gate

■ Nakahara Nantenbo (1839-1925), Japanese Buddhist monk, teacher of Deiryū Kutsu (1895-1954): Written—I was seventy-two years old in 1911 when Deiryū at the age of sixteen entered my temple. Each day we carried huge loads fire wood to the monastery.

Deiryū was athletic, but had pulmonary tuberculosis. The doctors predicted he would die within ten years. His parents had insisted on a military career for him—but relented when told this news by the doctors. When I was eighty, Deiryū painted my portrait. And I wrote in my own hand: His book, my writing; My Being, his hand.

Striking and pounding with the Nantenbo
I annihilate all false Zen;
This ugly old shavenpate arouses hate for
    a thousand ages
Extinguishing the transmission like a blind
    donkey.

And so we moved forward, I drawing my face in his style of drawing; his calligraphic writing indistinguishable from mine. Like Tal and Fisher, one moving closer to the other, day by day.

I remarked to a friend: *"Recently, copies of my writing are being sold. I think Deiryu is doing them."*

"What can I say?" Deiryū replied jokingly. *"Through Nantenbo Roshi's example, my calligraphy has become better. Do you think someone who can write better would dare to imitate inferior works?"* And I laughed in turn and said "That's true , Deiryū's writing may be better than mine, but people appreciate works by Nantenbo. Can we say the same about Deiryū?"

They are growing closer, Tal and Fisher, Fisher and Tal. It is becoming hard to distinguish the pen from the ink.

■ William Blake: Once this book gets written—
"Awake! Awake Jerusalem!…
For lo the night of death is past
And the eternal day
Appears upon our hills: Awake
Jerusalem and come away."

Tal is dew from heaven. Falling upon Fisher's pen and Fisher knows not how to begin. For Tal's heavenly flourish moves from right to left and Fisher has both forgotten and knows not how, yet. Yet.

"And of course, Tal, your repeating, your alluding to the fact that once this book gets written, not only would my star rise at Time Inc., traveling brightly over each American newsstand and subscriber's home, but also there would be 'a great deal' in it for me." Fisher paused and then crescendoed.

"What exactly do your brother, Suleimani, and you mean by 'a great deal' in it for me?"

"Suleimani has nothing to do with this," said Tal. "It's true that Suleimani brought the moghul jewel to my attention but he has relinquished control. As for my brother Tuviah, that is none of your concern. Our deal is between us—brother-partners. What do you want Fisher?"

"What do you want, Tal?" A simple question, thought Fisher.

■ John Linnel asked: Do you write Jerusalem from left to right in the manner of our countrymen, or right to left as the Seraphim do? And Blake replied sternly: This Jerusalem Book hismy feet one moonlit night and watched his hand move *"writing backward in a glutinous liquid in many instances in a highly ornamented and varied character."*

Tal is wakening Fisher and Fisher wakening his village and I could see Blake's hand moving, writing ever backwards but he could not see who moved his hand. For a book must be dreamed before it is written. Nor can Tal see what moves the hand. For it is Jerusalem that moves us all. If our right hand fails us, she has forgotten us.

■ Gauguin: Once this book gets written—Once Fisher's book gets written, it will not be written in a city nor will it be written with Tal by Fisher's side. Nor will it be written on paper, Heaven forbid, for paper will crumble and turn to ash. Fisher's book will not get on canvas, not even on a canvas of his midnight bride, Dosha, but rather his book will be written on his lovers lips in plain and bold script legible forever. As clear as my book: *Noa Noa*.

"As I left the quay at the moment of embarkation, I saw Tehura for the last time.

"She had wept through many nights. Now she sat worn out and sad, but calm, on a stone with her legs hanging down and her strong, lithe feet touching the soiled water.

"The flower she had put behind her ear in the morning had wilted upon her knee. Here and there were others like her, tired and silent, gloomy, watching without a thought. The thick smoke of the ship was bearing all of us—lovers of the day—far away, forever. From the bridge of the ship as we were moving farther and farther away, it seemed to us that with the telescope we could still read on their lips these ancient Maori verses."

■ René Descartes (1596-1650): Once this book gets written—Fisher's book is being written. Each day, each minute. In his apartment, as he walks to work.

Just as my books were written while I served Maurice of Nassau, Prince of Orange, fighting to keep Spain from reconquering Holland.

"The book of the world" written each day and edited, amended, corrected and abridged at night—this was the book I sought to write.

I had it all written, paginated, reasoned—*Le Monde*, my world—my book of the world, only to hear that my comrade Galileo's works of 1632 had been burned. *"I was so astounded that I quasi-resolved to burn all my papers or at least not to show them to anyone. I cannot imagine that an Italian and especially one well thought of by the Pope from what I have heard, could have been labeled a criminal for nothing other than wanting to establish the movement of the earth…I confess that if this is false, then all the principles of my philosophy are false also."*

Once Fisher's book gets written, it is not certain by any means whether his star will rise or fall. Tal's *Dubito, Ergo Sum*—I doubt, therefore I am—should well be his motto.

William Blake, *Jerusalem*.

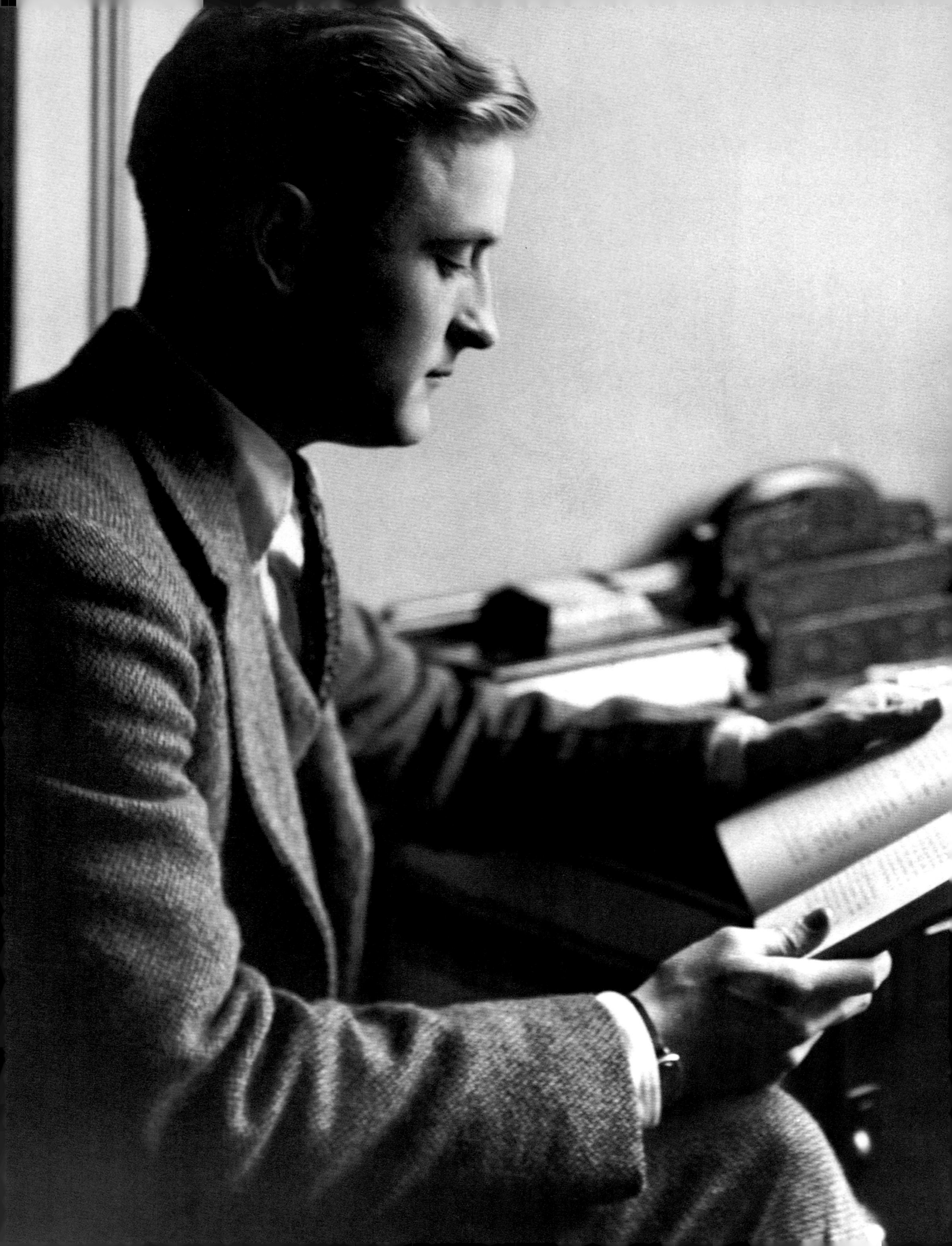

◆ RICKELE PADAWER, DOSHA'S GRANDMOTHER: Breath—Before Simha died, not in the hospital where they took him, but in our home in Brooklyn, when he held Jerusha's hand to mine and cupped his fingers over both of us—he looked at me but spoke to her, "What do you think the Rebbe was thinking when he walked us through the Yeshiva hall when you brought us there?"

Jerusha's eyes grew larger as he whispered, "Breath." That was what I was thinking. And neither Jerusha nor I answered. How could I? I suppose Jerusha expected what her mother used to joke about: Ask him the secret of life. I could not speak, for already I could see my bridegroom stepping beyond the canopy of this world. "Breath," Simha repeated. *"The world is sustained solely by the breath of schoolchildren. It ascends on high, is crowned with the upper crown, and is appointed to guard the world."*

■ SARAH CHOATE SEARS: What do you want? —I heard that Thomas Wittemore had gifted Mrs. Isabella Gardner with Matisse's glorious *The Terrace*. I invited her to my house. What did I care that Sargent always tried to play the J. Montgomery Sears fortune off against Isabella. They would never understand us— neither Mr. James nor Mr. Sargent. Isabella and I were friends.

As soon as Isabella entered my studio—I had invited her on the pretext of showing my latest work—I asked her what she wanted. She said nothing, moving her eye across two paintings by Picasso and a small water color of my own.

"Which do you want? You can take whatever you wish."

To her credit, Mrs. Gardner looked and looked and looked. And then said, "Why do young people always ask me what I want?"

I was quite nonplussed and before I could reply, she said, "I want you to tell me the truth."

I rested my arm on hers and said, "The truth, my dear Mrs. Gardner, is that Mr. John Singer Sargent and I have discovered the most extraordinary bohemian restaurant in town '*and we both request the pleasure of your company tomorrow evening.*'"

What do you want to do? Fisher's high school teacher had asked him years before. Mechanical Engineering? Tax? Lawyer? Graduate school in psychology? Apply to Grinnell? Winter in New Haven? What do you want, asked his father. You could have it all—more than your uncle, more than me. What do you want, asked his mother's eyes. And Dosha, at least she never asked but playfully whispered in his ear, walking down Perry Street. I know what you want Fisher, but he could still feel the question in her breath.

"I want you to tell me the truth, Tal. This isn't a game. It's a darn good job I've got. Not money wise, I couldn't care less about that right now, but it's a link in a chain. Just not the golden chain of your brother Tuviah's fantasy or the chain of justice of Shah Jahan."

■ ISABELLA STEWART GARDNER: Tell me the truth—"What do you want?" young Curtis would ask, his eyes never wavering from mine, brushing his long blonde hair behind his ear. A physician about to listen to my heartbeat beneath my chest. "What do you want?" he asked me over and over.

"I want you to tell me the truth," I said, throwing my body back as in my portrait by Anders Zorn, cupping my hands demurely together. "I want you to tell me the truth," I repeated.

And he said, *"Forty is the old age of youth…fifty is the youth of old age."*

It was touching, really. Young Curtis couldn't have been more than 35. All those young people always asking me the same question.

■ F. SCOTT FITZGERALD: What do you want?— "What do you want?" Zelda asked me in wartime Montgomery. And I would think, "You, Zelda," but would declaim:

"You as you are, not part of you, all of you. Part of a song, a remembered glory. Kisses, a lazy street—and night."

And I would spin the bottled question upon Zelda, "And, you, Zelda, what do you want." "Myself," she answered laughingly. "To be all of me. To be a flapper "*who bobbed her hair, put on her choicest pair of earrings and a great deal of audacity and rouge and went into battle…she flirted because it was fun to flirt and wore a one-piece bathing-suit because she had a good figure, she covered her face with paint and powder because she didn't need it…She was conscious that the things she did were the things she had always wanted to do.*"

Well then, we want the same thing. Let's get married. And we did but first we jousted, wrestled, bartered, raved, laughed, and cascaded down a white river of passion. *"Zelda was cagey about throwing in her lot with me before I was a moneymaker. And I cabled her from New York: while I fell sure of you[r] love everything is possible. I am in the land of ambition and success."*

And did I not compose the same telegraph each day and whisper it to my lady who deigned to receive my diurnal note penned with a feather, tongued to her, inside the porch of her delicate, oh so delicate ear?

And do I not still wait, like a child, for the messenger to return each day with an answer?

F. Scott Fitzgerald at his desk.

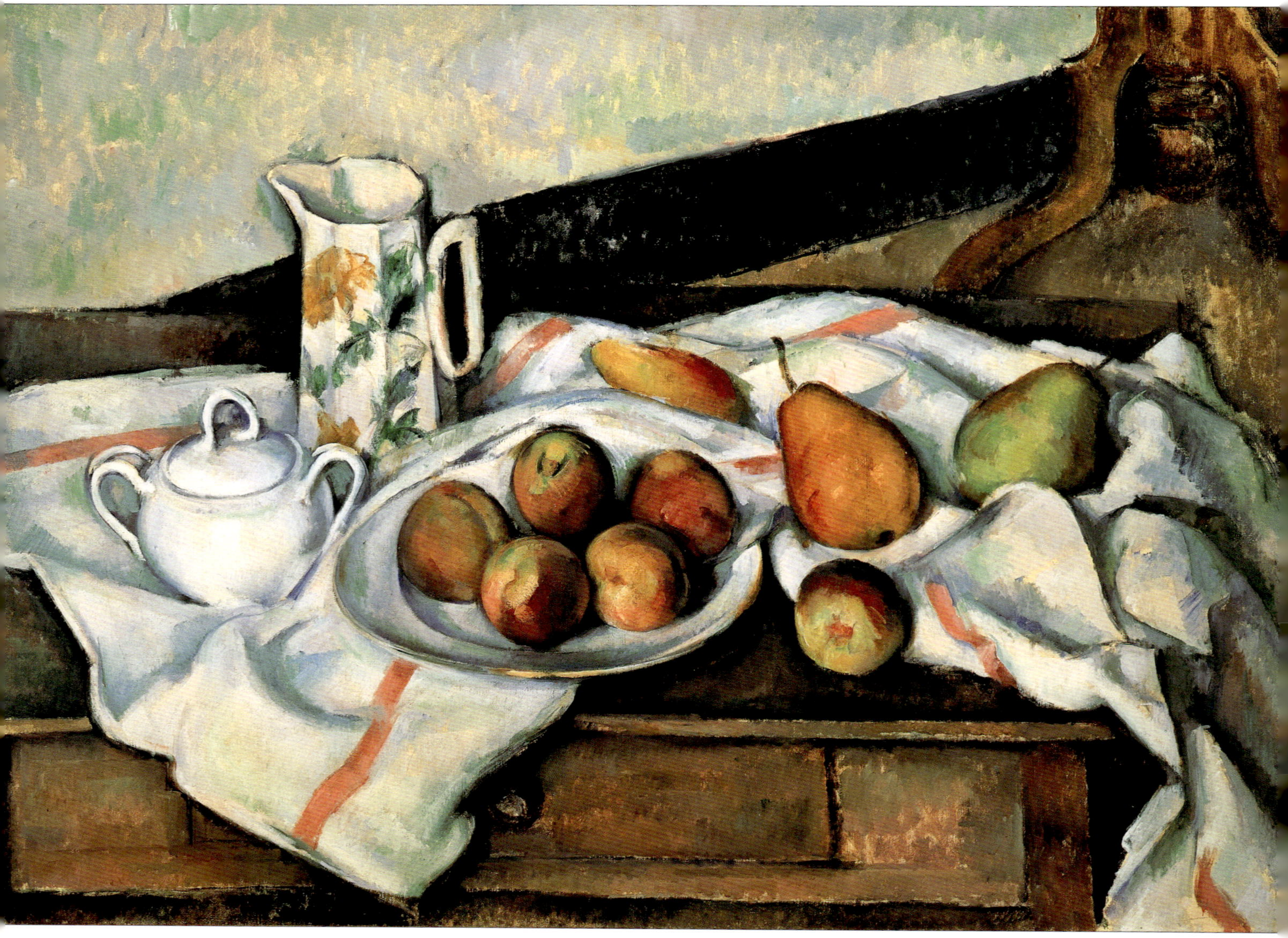

■ CÉZANNE: It's a chain of literary influence—It's a chain of literary influence but who is influencing whom? I, in Aix was premier in La Poésie and Émile Zola Premier in La Peinture. I wrote him from Aix, 3 May 1858.

"Are you well? I am very busy morbleu, very busy. This will explain the absence of the poem you asked me for. I am, you can be sure, most penitent not to be able to reply with a verve, a warmth, a spirit, equal to yours. I am studying for the matric…Ah if I had matric. If you had matric…but I am sunk, submerged, done for, petrified, extinguished, annihilated, that's what I shall be…"

Zola begged for poems. But my hand could not obey. "I see that after my brush, my pen can do nothing good and today I should attempt in vain:

To sing to you of some forest nymph
My voice is not sweet enough
And the beauties of the countryside
Whistle at those lines in my song
That are not humble enough.

I am going to stop at last, for I am doing nothing but heaping stupidity on absurdity."

Zola in Paris asking me for a poem. I, in Aix. How else could I reply!: *"As you say, there are some very beautiful views here. The difficulty is to reproduce them, this isn't exactly my line. I began to see nature rather late, though this does not prevent it being full of interest for me. I shake your hand ,Émile.*

Paul Cézanne."

Of course, merde, he was my literary chain of influence, but he was also my chain.

"Which chain?" asked Tal who was still riveted on the cross hatched pile of twelve pens pierced at the center by Fisher's addition.

"Which chain?" repeated Fisher.

"Yes, what's Shah Jahan's chain," persisted Tal.

"Tal, it's a chain of literary influence, my chance to write."

"But that's what I'm asking you to do, Fisher, to write about this emerald. Admit that when you came to my office and you saw the emerald, it was an amazing experience, even for you. You yourself said it was the deepest green you had ever seen in your life. You said it made you remember the stacks of peacock stick feathers in your father's warehouse when you were young. You said it was the green of the west of Connemara that you and Dosha had seen last summer. You were speechless."

■ MOZART: That's what?—That's what? Tal is saying. But Tal is merely echoing the world. Salzburg. Vienna. Paris. London. Even the New World. All the same. *"If a thing is not understood immediately no one has patience for it. And if it is only understood after great effort then it will not be given a chance."*

Young Fisher will do well as a writer of books. Those pens of his reveal disciplined understructure. And old Tal would put him in chains. *"The golden mean of truth in all things is no longer either known or appreciated. In order to win applause one must write stuff which is so inane that a coachman could sing it, or so unintelligible that it pleases precisely because no sensible man can understand it. This is not what I have been wanting to discuss with you; but I should like to write a book, a short introduction to music, illustrated by examples, but I need hardly add, not under my own name."*

Young Fisher had best not write music even under another's name. Odd lyrical taste he has.

■ ÉMILE ZOLA: A chain of literary influence—And am I not always on the ground in the courtyard of the Collège Bourbon pummeled by Gascoigne, Theriot and La Farge—even when I am standing in front of toute Paris at the Halle des Nations fêted by the entire Academie Française.

Cézanne smaller by far than La Farge and certainly not a match for Theriot or Gascoigne, routing the three of them. Saving me. Lifting me up. Dusting off my jacket. Making La Farge apologize. How could I repay him.

A basket of apples I sent him. And my emperor Paul replies, *"I wish to conquer Paris with an apple."*

It is with my apples and my blood that he has conquered. My literary influence. My books. My manuscript. I opened all of Paris to him. Walked him by the hand like a child from Aix to Montmartre. And what does he call me but his "chain" of literary influence. Why could Paul not have left off with his words: *"One does not put oneself in place of the past, one only adds a new link."*

■ JAHANGHIR, SHAH JAHAN'S FATHER: Chain—*"As a sign of divine grace and favor something happens around this time (23 April 1616) that is not a little strange. After defeating the Rana, my son Khurram presented a fine brilliant ruby to me in Ajmer. It was worth 60,000 rupees. It occurred to me that I should wear it on my arm. However, two rare and lustrous matched pearls worthy to sit with this ruby were necessary. Then when Muqurrah Khan obtained one superb pearl worth 8,000 rupees and offered it for Nawroz, it occurred to me that if a mate to this pearl could be found it would make a perfect armband. Khurram, who had been in my exalted father's service from childhood and had spent day and night with him, said, 'I have seen a pearl of this size and shape on an old headband.' A big old turban was brought and upon examination, it was found to contain a pearl of exactly the right size and shape. It didn't differ an iota in size. The jewelers were astonished that it matched in size, shape and lustre. You'd say they had been cast in the same mold. I had the pearls set on either side of the ruby and put it on my arm, lowering my head in gratitude upon the ground to render thanks to the Lord."*

Paul Cézanne, *Sugar Bowl, Kettle, and Plate with Fruit.*

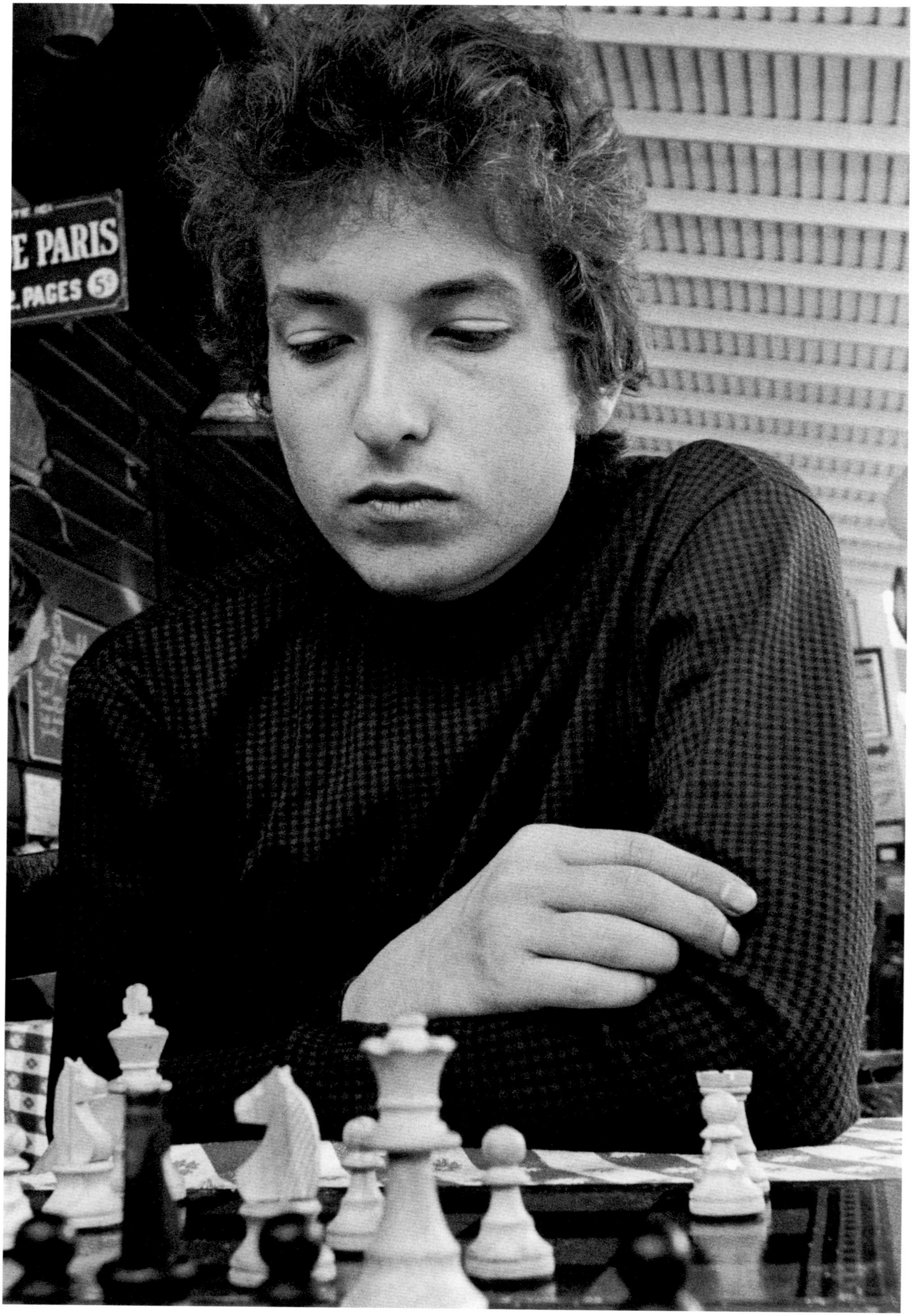
PARIS
PAGES

■ FRANTSEK LANGER (1888-1965), Czech playwright and brother of Jiri Langer: Speechless—"In 1913, my brother packed a small suitcase with a few essential clothes, some books and his phylacteries, and set out on a journey...It was only after a few weeks had gone by that a postcard arrived. It came from Eastern Galicia, from the town of Belz and it asked us not to worry for he was quite well and would be there for some time. This was Jiri's first journey to the Hasidim."

When Jiri returned, our Prague neighbors were speechless. Our family was stunned. Father was never to be the same. He "told me with a note of horror in his voice that Jiri had returned. I understood what had filled him with dread as soon as I saw my brother. He stood before me in a frayed black overcoat, clipped like a caftan, reaching from his chin to the ground. On his head he wore a broad round hat of black velvet, his whole face and chin were covered with a red beard and side whiskers in front of his ears hung in ringlets down to his shoulders...my brother had not come back from Belz to home and civilization, he had brought Belz with him...He used to cook various mashes at home on a spirit stove, but his staple diet was bread and onions, which could be smelled all over the house...The attitude of our family to Jiri seemed to us at the time to resemble the situation in Kafka's novel, Die Varwandlung—The Metamorphosis—in which an entire family finds its way of life completely upset when the son of the house is suddenly changed into an enormous insect and consequently has to be hidden from the rest of the world, while the family strives in vain to find some place for him in their affections."

My brother became Franz's Rabbi. He taught him Hebrew and regaled him with stories of Belz. Max Brod became my brother's Gabbai and welcomed him in Tel Aviv. I became my brother's editor and Franz wrote in his diary after reading Metamorphosis aloud to my brother's Gabbai Brod. "If one bolts the doors and windows against the world, one can from time to time create the semblance and almost the beginning of the reality of a beautiful life."

■ BOB DYLAN: Fisher pushing across the table—Fisher's pushing across the table. Tal's almost finished. Suleimani's dog tired. "But ain't him to blame. He's only a pawn in their game."

"I was speechless, Tal, because I heard pacing and walking and creeping around, Sam-Spade-like, in the next room. Now I understand it must have been the famous Suleimani, whom no man can speak of or see."

"It was Suleimani, Fisher, but that's not the point. Suleimani was there because he knew something of the emerald's origin."

"Oh, the handwritten, misspelled, one page account," Fisher didactically interjected, quoting Suleimani: "The Providence of the most famous emerald or coloured gemstone from the court of Shah Jahan," said Fisher, pushing across the table, a small single-spaced account of the emerald Tal had given him months before.

Tal looked perfunctorily at the note. Suleimani spelled "coloured" with a u because he'd grown up in India.

■ FRANZ KAFKA: Speechless—"When I was a child I opened my eyes after a brief afternoon nap, still not quite sure I was alive. I heard my mother (never 'mutter' in Prague German: it occurred to me that I did not always love my mother as she deserved and as I could, only because the German language prevented it, the Jewish mother is no mutter) up in the balcony asking in a natural tone of voice, 'What are you doing my dear? Goodness, isn't it hot?' From a garden a woman answered. 'Me, I'm having my tea on the lawn.' They spoke casually and not very distinctly, as though this woman had expected the question, my mother the answer."

My mother, what does she hear of me in the next room? My father, does he not hear me pacing and walking and creeping around in my room? And I am the famous Suleimani to Mother and Father, writer of misspelled one-page accounts.

"What is literature? Where does it come from? What use is it? What questionable things! Add to this questionableness the further questionableness of what you say and what you get is a monstrosity."

Fisher is me, the brother of Tal who is father to Tal himself. I am Gregor to Father and Suleimani is me in one room at three in the afternoon, pacing and walking and creeping, only to be me again at three in the morning, a writer, a fabulist, a teller of daytime tales of the office.

■ MAX BROD: Speechless—"He had pains, of course, throughout his whole body, but it seemed to him that they were gradually getting fainter and fainter and would finally go away altogether. The rotten apple in his back and the inflamed area around it, which were completely covered with fluffy dust, already hardly bothered him. He thought back on his family with deep emotion and love. His conviction that he would have to disappear was, if possible, even firmer than his sister's. He remained in this state of empty and peaceful reflections until the tower clock struck three in (the morning)."

When Franz finished reading this aloud to me, he stopped and put down the manuscript, stared straight at me and was totally speechless. Not a word. Not a sign. What could I say? That the story was profound. That he was a marvel. He simply froze before me.

I thought of his words: "Since the existence of the writer is truly dependent upon his desk and if he wants to keep madness at bay, he must never go far from his desk, he must hold onto it with his teeth."

Even if I could have wrestled him to the ground, pried his jaw open, I still would not have succeeded in removing one morsel of one word embedded in his throat.

■ JIRI LANGER (1894-1943), friend of Franz Kafka and author of Nine Gates to the Chasidic Mysteries: Speechless—Over and over Franz would ask me for a story from Belz—not the storyteller—for Franz could not believe my stories of the Rebbe or by the Rebbe. And speechless Franz would be as I told him stories I heard in Belz—stories from the Rebbe himself. But Franz always believed that the Rebbe was merly a story. As, indeed, I think I was but a story to him. A story that started in Prague and voyaged to a tiny town, Belz, in Poland. A school boy story begun in the Jewish quarter in Prague, edited in a Polish shtetl and written in my parents' house amongst my simmering potatoes and onions—edited by my brother and finally printed on Prague paper.

He is no story Franz, he is real and I will introduce you to him and Brod also. The Rebbe is in Marienbad. And what did Franz see? The Rebbe's silk caftan. His silver cane. The ten followers ever at his side. Franz saw Schlesinger—the rich Jew from Pressburg—who carried a bottle of spring water for the Rebbe. Franz saw the Gabbai. He saw the Rebbe's beard. A "long white beard, unusually long sidelocks...one eye is blind and blank," wrote Franz of the Belzer Rebbe. "His mouth is twisted awry which gives him a look at once ironic and friendly." Franz saw it all and through my eyes, for did I not teach both Franz and Max Brod Hebrew? But in Franz's heart, the Rebbe remained a story, a collection of words; they could not believe what they saw. If they had, they would have had to change their lives, and they could not. But on the deepest of levels, they were right. The Belzer was a story. So was Franz and so was Brod. And certainly what was I but a tale? We all are stories told forever by the Blessed One—Blessed be his name forever and ever.

Bob Dylan playing chess.

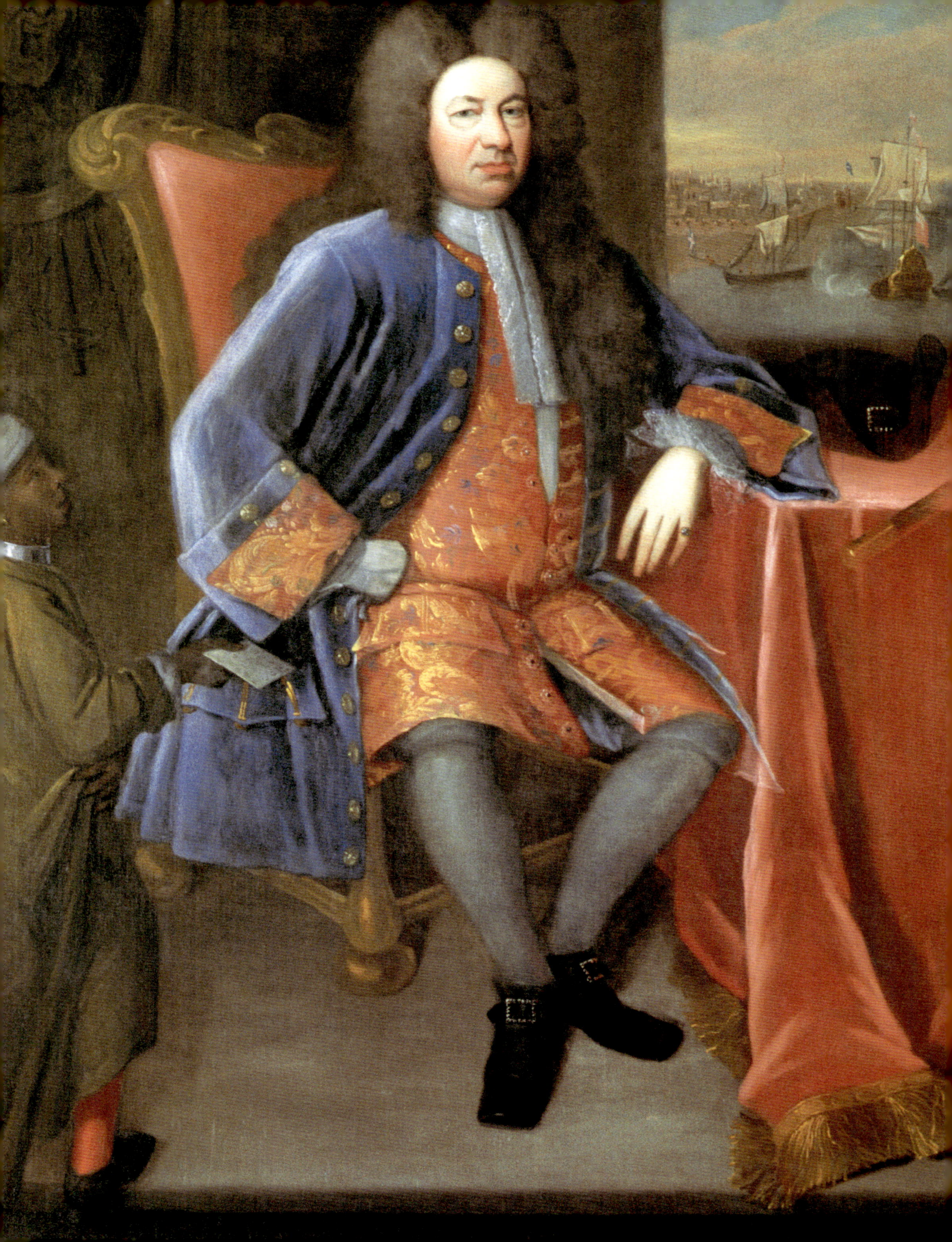

■ MRS. NICKS: The flowers in Kashmir—I told Master Yale to choose—upon my life and the life of my imprisoned husband—not that I believed for a moment that my Master Elihu could have him freed, for so grave were his sins and so many were Yale's enemies within the walls of Fort St. George, and even across the oceans in London in the boardrooms of the company of the East Indies, Elihu would have to choose either myself or the scourge of my life, the Portuguese woman, whom I would not dignify with the name Mrs. Paiva, for what did I or anyone know of her past or his past—Jacobo de Paiva, different he was from the other Portuguese or Armenians, even my John noted that, and my Master Yale, Governor of the Fort of six villages beyond, Master of the garden house that he called "our Kashmir" though was I in the "our," or was it he and she? I put it to my lord simply: Here is my open trunk. Either place my dresses of calico, all the diamond rosette necklaces you have given me, and the jeweled slippers you bartered for in the land of the Thais, or go to her room and put her precious Portuguese plate, her linen from her London Abendana family and send her packing. Even " "our Kashmir" is not vast enough for us three.

I could not hear the cooing of the Madrasi peacocks as they strutted across the lawn directly behind my lord Yale. Elihu often quoted his father, "a man's silence is heard far louder than his words," though I knew a shilling to a ha-penny that he'd made it up—as he fashioned so much to fit his own britches. And he said nothing. By the devil, who should appear from the garden house rear door but Herself, and she looked at my open trunk and at our Master Elihu and said, "Why is your trunk open? It's far too hot to pack or travel on a day like this." Master Yale, quite recovered and linking his arm in both mine and hers, said with all the sweetness of an eighteen year old, "Let us take the air amidst the flowers in Kashmir."

I gave him my arm as I always did and he took hers as he ever did. For who could defy Elihu when he was silent, and who could deny Master Yale when he spoke?

"It's not color I'm worried about. Nor even the quaint spelling and usage of the word provenance—the last refuge of art critics and scoundrels. It's the subtext. Your brother, Tal, is trying to set me up. Time Inc. isn't going to publish a movie script like book so that he can make a sale."

"This isn't about a sale, Fisher. It's a mystery. It's a research project. That's why I suggested it to you. And you yourself Fisher, found all the links to Paradise, to Agra, to the Taj Mahal, to the flowers in Kashmir, even to Elihu Yale. You should take yourself more seriously. And not be so strict with yourself. Even Dosha says that. Time should be thrilled with this opportunity to have you write it up."

■ HIRAM BINGHAM: Flowers in Kashmir. All the links:—Where are all the links that young Fisher found? Sitting on his desk among a pile of hand-copied documents from the Sterling Library. A catalog of the seventh sale of the most important collection of jewels…the catalog that eluded me as I excavated the mountain of Yale contracts, lawsuits, proclamations of the East India Company.

I knew it had to be jewelry as linkage. Was that not the solder that bound the Tiffany fortune into my betrothal to Alfreda Mitchell.

When I wrote my father-in-law, Alfred, in 1910 asking for $15,000 to purchase the lot on Prospect Hill, the lot that my wife had chosen mind you, I received a vengeful letter from Mother, as Alfreda always referred to Mrs. Annie Mitchell.

What happened to our wedding gifts, $10,000 each? Where was our trust distribution? Our allowance? I, a professor, was expected to make an accounting. As much as I could list, aid to my dying mother, a portrait painted of my father, investments, expenses to feed our five children. It all came back to the Tiffany fortune. Find the fortune and you find every link to every dream of Paradise Alfreda and I ever dared to dream.

What of Elihu Yale's dreams? His garden house, his wife, his Hieronyma de Paiva, even his Mrs. Nicks, they were all linked in a chain of diamonds. Fisher has found all the links. But in what order will he assemble them? That is the key. Does one place Mrs. Hynmers first and then Mrs. Nicks and then Hieronyma and then Cotton Mather and then the bequest? Or does it go back in quite a different order through a great sadness, a domestic revenge.

A thirst from a childhood spring once free flowing and then gone dry. Ordering is all, and having all links by no means assures that young Fisher will be able to make sense of it all.

Enoch Zeeman, *Governor Elihu Yale.*

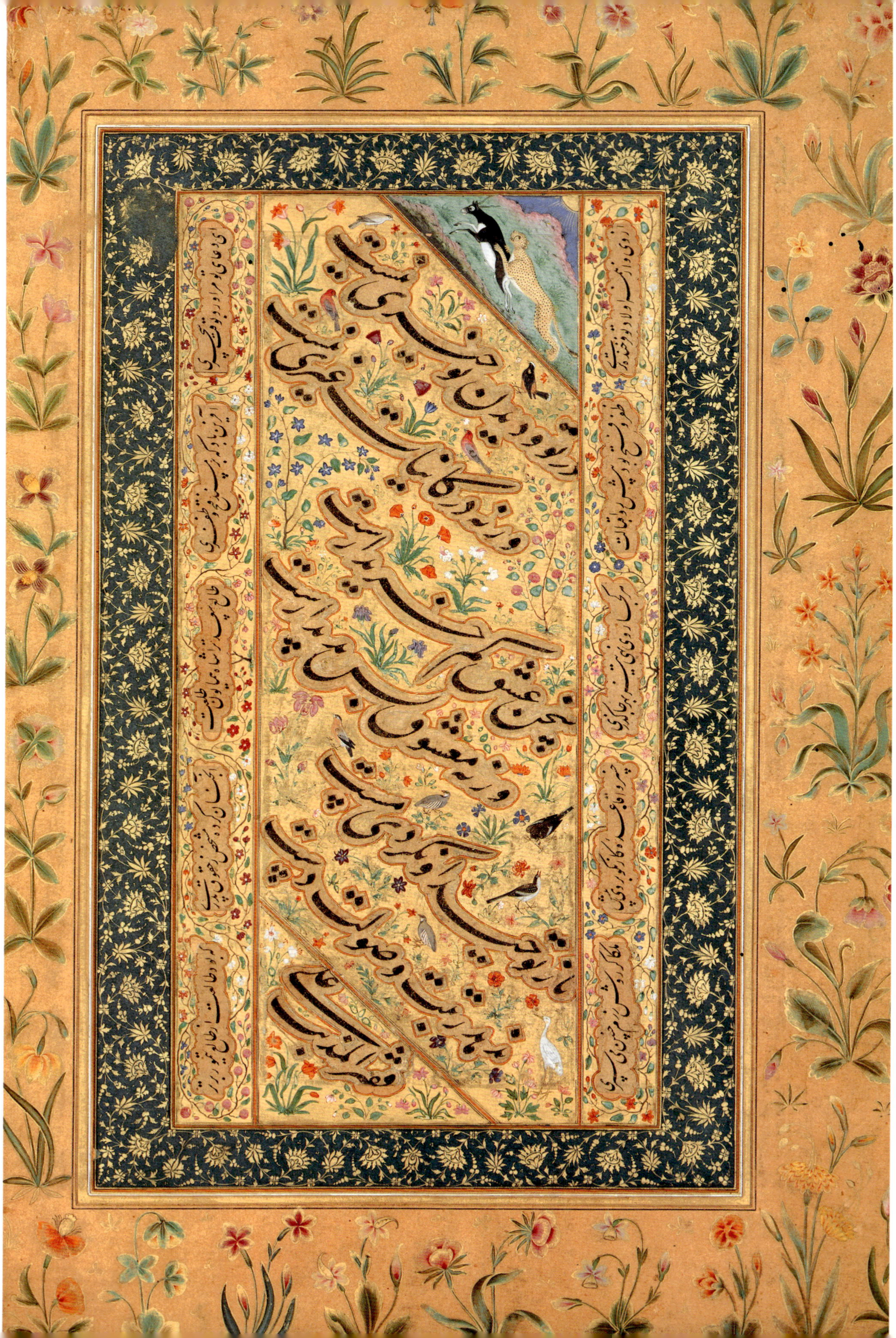

● SIMHA PADAWER, DOSHA'S GRANDFATHER: I've never even for a minute been to Yale—Here he is, Tal, the Rosh Yeshiva of Hudson Street. Two pupils, studying in Chavrusa, my granddaughter and Fisher. In America their Yale is our Pumpedita and their Harvard our Sura. When I studied Massechet Ketubot in Yeshivah in Slonim, we began: "*Rav Yosef said: Rav Yehudah said in the name of Shmuel: Why did the Rabbi say that a virgin is married on a Wednesday?*"

Avraham Weinberg looked at me, "And why does the Tractate Ketubot begin with Rav Yosef? He answered his own question: Rav Yosef was the head of the Yeshivah of Pumbedita in Babylon for two and a half years. He was called Sinai because of his prodigious knowledge of Torah, both oral and written. Abaye was his great student. When Rav Yosef became ill, his student Abaye helped him to recover all of his learning again.

What is a true marriage? When we forget, our true partner restores our memory. Here, who will be the head of the Hudson Street Yeshivah? My granddaughter or Fisher? For Tal has forgotten so much, but to his credit he is searching for his aide memoire. In America, can there not be two heads of each Yeshivah? When they wed, Dosha and Fisher will restore Tal. And he shall be a Sinai for them in the years to come.

■ RABBI NOSUN OF BRESLOV: Large and small—My master raised his hand slowly, to raise the spirits of the Hasidim around him, to raise mine, for we all felt close to exhaustion, lost, even more to raise himself—for my master felt the weight of all the story on himself, and he continued.

"But the chamberlain insisted, "It must exist somewhere." Then the giant said, "In my opinion, it is all nonsense, but since you insist, I shall help you. I am in charge of all beasts. For your sake, I shall summon them all here. They run all over the world, and perhaps one of them knows about your mountain and castle." So he summoned all the beasts, large and small, and questioned them. They all answered that they had not seen the mountain. He said, "You see, you have been told stupid tales. If you listen to me, you will turn back, because what you are seeking does not exist."

"If it's so worthy of writing up, why don't you bring it to them yourself?" snapped Fisher.

"Only a million reasons, large and small. The very last of which is I've never even for a minute been to Yale." Suddenly a weight fell from Tal's shoulders. He looked so small, so diminished, that Fisher said gently:

"Tal, I understand. And I think the gem is extraordinary. And I think what I've written is true. And wonderful. They pay me a salary at Time and I don't need your brother's money. I don't want to write a novel about the glistening paradaisical moghul stone. I want to write a novel about an auction of the Guggenheim Museum's art which never takes place, or perhaps will, but really I want to write a long novel about myself, and what I want is to get back right now, alone, without you, to Project Green."

■ MIR-'ALI OF HERAT, a 15th century Persian calligrapher: Worthy of writing—"*Whoever writes in the name of G-d the merciful and compassionate in fine lettering will enter Paradise.*"

Again and again I practiced. Mir-'Ali Tabrizi guiding my hand as I welcomed the bride among calligraphic styles, Nastaliq, into my dwelling. Over and over, two decades of spring and summer, winter and fall. "*Forty years of my life were spent in calligraphy. The tip of the tresses did not come easily into my hand. If one sits leisurely for a moment without practicing, calligraphy disappears from one's hand like the color of henna.*"

What is worthy of writing over and over and yet again other than "*the name of G-d the merciful, the compassionate G-d!*"

■ JAHANGHIR: Worthy of writing—If the style of writing is not worthy, then surely it is not worthy of being written.

My father Akbar's steadfast friend Khankhanan 'Abdul-Rahim gave him a copy of Yusuf and Zulaykha in Mir-'Ali's hand—beautifully bound and worth a thousand mohurs.

I would have paid a thousand thousands if my son Khurram had written the text himself. What would he have paid if his children had been like pages of Mir-'Ali's hand stitched together in a manuscript and not scattered and shredded, clawing at each other across the face of Hindustan?

■ F. SCOTT FITZGERALD: To Yale—To Yale. From Yale, for Yale. Over and over all I heard about at Princeton was Yale. In 1741, the New Lights battled with the established church leaders in Philadelphia town. Your inner experience counts for more than the accepted doctrines of the church. "*In a real dark night of the soul it is always three o'clock in the morning.*"

Six of the seven banished from the Presbyterian Philadelphia church were from Yale. But logical it was to form yet another college in New Jersey—for in '43 there was no college from the College of William and Mary in Williamsburg, Virginia, all the way to Yale in New Haven.

For God, for country, and for Princeton. "*It is in the thirties that we want friends. In the forties we know that they won't save us anymore than love did.*"

Young Jonathan Edwards went to Yale at twelve. Preached the great revival in Northampton. Came from Yale to serve as Princeton's first president. Died six weeks later from small pox. Princeton and Yale, twiddle dee and twiddle deedum.

Illuminated page of calligraphy, c. 1540.

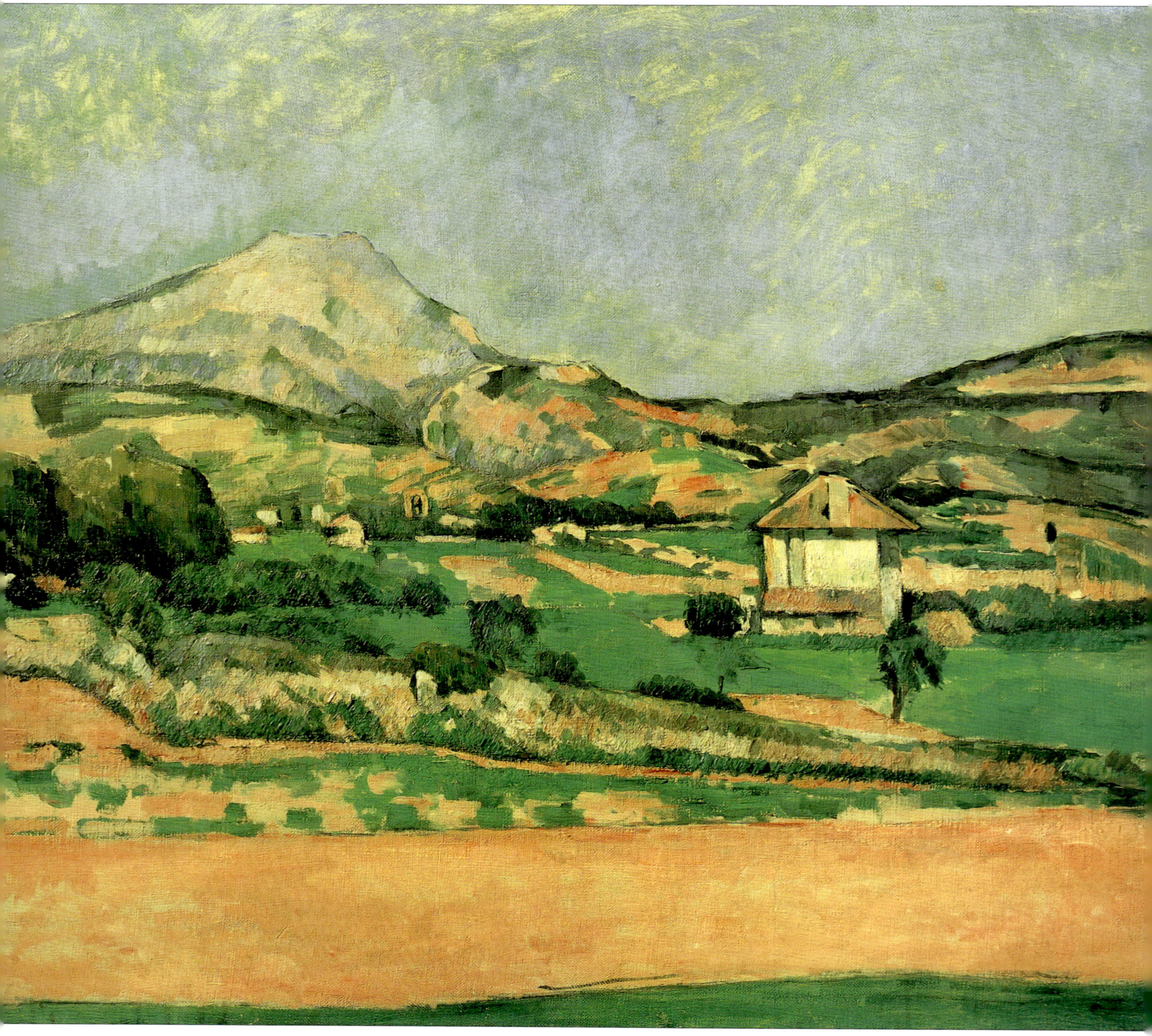

■ CÉZANNE: Green…green…he repeated the words over and over—Pissarro would circle around me in Auvers while I was painting and chant like a Zouave, "Green…green." He repeated the word over and over. Try as I might, it was near impossible to steady my hand.

So different from the Gilbert Salon in Aix—not a sliver of sound, not a whisper. I could hear my brush rub against the angel's wing as her chin touched my dozing poet. Over and over, green, green, green, until I exploded and shouted, "A fine dervish you are, and I a proper Christian from Áix."

"Speak to me, teach me, lecture me but don't circle about me, neither of us are Turks." Gentle Pissarro. He never angered, he simply fell silent. Only years later Zola commented to me: "Why do you mumble the word green, over and over again, while you paint?"

■ ÉMILE BERNARD, a conversation with Cézanne: See—Do you try "to see nature as no one has before you." I am a primitive of a new art.

Paul Cézanne, *Trees and Houses.*

CHAPTER 8

"Green," said Fisher to the secretary through the plate glass window. "Green, Project Green," he repeated the word over and over, as though the magic word would open the locked double entry to Tal's office.

"I'm sorry sir, Mr. Abraham Tal is not here today. His brother will be out to see you in a moment."

Fisher looked at his watch which was set, as usual, ten minutes fast. Almost 3:32. Why was Tal always late?

Suddenly, through the plate glass window, Fisher could see the same eyes as Tal's, dark, with deep set eyebrows, but more narrow. The man was immaculately dressed in a white shirt and jet black suit with a silk white handkerchief folded in his left breast pocket.

"Ah, Mr. Fisher, my brother's hasid. But where is the Rebbe?" said Tuviah Tal to Fisher through the grate in the glass window of the 47th Street gem merchant's office.

"Isn't Tal here?" asked Fisher, stooping over to get a better look at Tuviah's face through the waiting room window. "Tal said he wanted me to bring a copy of the report I've just finished and he would discuss it with me."

■ RABBI NOSUN OF BRESLOV: Brother—Rabbi Nachman looked at me sadly. For had he not always called me: My brother, my hasid. And I protested: My Master, you should write your own words down. "You will be my pen," Rabbi Nachman told me sharply: "These are your words. You, Nachman, must write them. "If they were mine, I would gladly write them. They come from a far higher place." Nachman said simply and with a sweetness of heaven. And I knew I must remember each of his words for I was a brother, a Hasid and a pen. My master continued.

"But the chamberlain insisted, "I know that it must exist."

Then the giant said, "I have a brother in the desert. He is in charge of all the birds. Perhaps they know, because they fly high in the air. Maybe they have seen the mountain and the castle. Go to him and tell him that I sent you." And the chamberlain went in search of him.

After many years, he met a huge man, a giant who was also carrying a huge tree and who also questioned him, as the first one had. And the chamberlain told him the whole story, and that the giant's brother had sent him. This giant, too, said that no such thing existed. But the chamberlain insisted that it must exist somewhere. Then the giant said, "I am in charge of all the birds, large and small. I shall summon them; perhaps they will know."

So he summoned all the birds, large and small, and questioned them. They all answered that they did not know of the mountain and the castle. He said, "You see, no such thing exists. If you listen to me, you will turn back because what you are seeking does not exist."

But the chamberlain persisted and said, "It certainly does exist, somewhere in the world."

The giant said, "Farther on in this same desert is my brother. He is in charge of the winds. Since they blow over the whole world, perhaps they will know."

And the chamberlain went on and searched for many years, and then he found another giant, who was also carrying a huge tree. The chamberlain told him the story of what had happened. And this giant also tried to discourage him, telling him that no such thing existed. But the chamberlain persisted. So the giant said, "For your sake, I shall summon all the winds and question them." So he summoned all the winds and asked them and not one of them knew about the mountain and the castle. The giant said to the chamberlain, "You see, you have been told stupid tales." Then the chamberlain began to weep and said, "I know that it does exist, somewhere in the world."

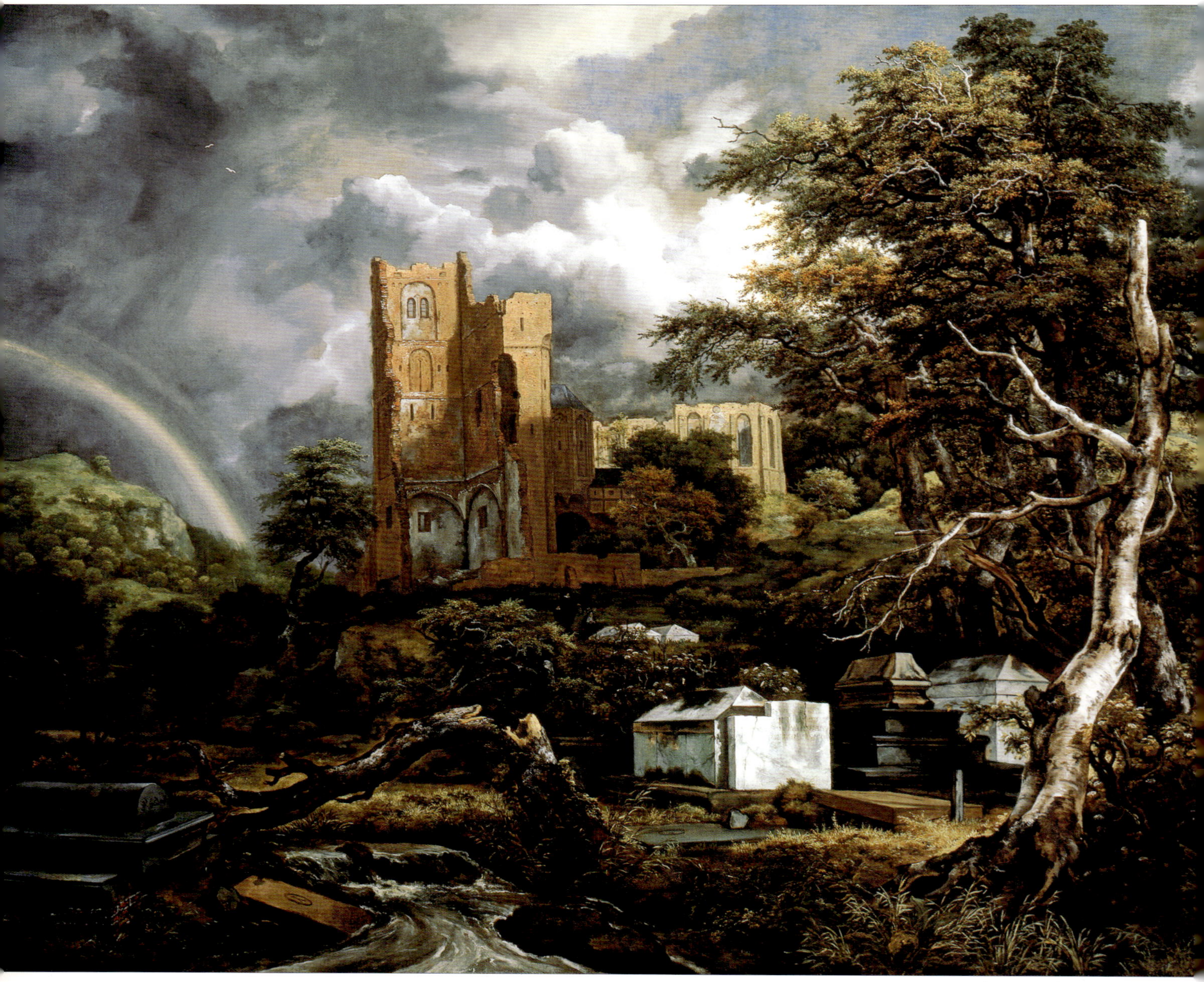

■ KAFKA: "Which room is Tal in?"—In the summer of 1916, I went out looking for a flat with my sister Ottla. *"Just for fun we asked in the little lane (the Alchemist's lane, the Golden lane). Yes there would be a little house to let in November. Ottla, who also seeks quiet though in her own way, fell in love with the idea of renting the house…*

It had many flaws stemming from its beginning. I do not have enough time to tell of its development. Today it suits me completely…I carry my supper up there, am usually there until midnight; then the departure and walk home, I take the path that cools my head. And life there: it is something special to have one's own house, to lock the door to the world not of the room, not of the flat, but of the house itself; to step out of the door of one's home straight into the snow of the quiet lane…"

That was my dream study. For my mind. And Tal's brother is also Tal's physician. Fisher is writing Tal's dream. Dr. Tal is making what appears to be a quite handsome living off of brother Tal's dream and Fisher's study. But which room is Tal in? Where is his body?

In my room of course, in the Schönbrun Palace. *"Two rooms, and an anteroom half of which was fitted out as the bathroom. Six hundred crowns annually. It was like a dream come true. I went there. Rooms high and beautiful, red and gold, almost like in Versailles. Four windows in a courtyard submerged in absolute quiet, a window on the garden. The garden! When you enter the gateway of the palace you can hardly believe your eyes. Through the high semi-circle of the second gate flanked by caryatids you can see standing on the beautifully divided curving stone steps of the large garden, a wide slope slowly and broadly climbing right up to a gloriette."*

"Well, Tal's here," said Tuviah, smiling. He buzzed Fisher in.

As soon as Fisher cleared the second double door, he spun around. "Which room is Tal in?"

Tuviah pointed at himself and said, "What your Rebbe has failed to make clear to you is that I'm Tal too." With an economic gesture, Tuviah stretched his hand out to Fisher. "Let's have a look at your dream study, Mr. Author."

Fisher froze. Exactly as he'd feared. Why didn't Tal ask to get his report at home? All Fisher had to do was walk across the hall and give it to him. If that weren't easy enough, they could have met downstairs in Tal's advice shop. "Where's Abraham? He said he'd be here."

"A lot of what Bram says and does don't match. Are you afraid if you show me what you've done, I won't pay you?"

"No. As a matter of fact, Mr. Tal's brother," said Fisher combatively. "I don't want to be paid. I'm already being paid by my employer, Time Incorporated."

"Well, then, you lose nothing by showing me." And before Fisher could protest, Tuviah was seated, absent-mindedly thumbing through the 112 page report, complete with photographs.

◆ RACHEL. TAL'S MOTHER: Well, Tal's here—When my son Abraham was here, he was not present. Not in any sense of the word. He would smile, he would nod, he would look but he rarely spoke in front of his father or brother.

But when he came home from school, early as he dared, he would race up to the kitchen on the second floor and stand on his toes and kiss me while I prepared dinner. "What happened while I was away?" he asked me as though he were an Abendana gone on a voyage to India to purchase gems.

If I left out a detail, where I had gone after the marketing, or if I stopped at the chocolate shop—and he would notice the sweet tray replenished, he would squeal: "But, Mother, you didn't mention that you went to the Lassères for chocolate truffles." And he would pout as though he had been betrayed. When Abraham was not with me, we were more together than ever.

■ VILNA GAON: I don't want to be paid—We were slaves unto Pharoah in Egypt. Unto. We made slaves of ourselves. So we read at the seder table each year. Twice outside the city of Jerusalem, twice outside the Holy Land of Israel. Once only in all the land of Israel.

And Fisher doesn't want to be paid. It is he who enslaves himself. But can he not free himself: twice a year in his native place—or better still through the miracle of the Holy Land—or best yet through the sanctity of Jerusalem itself.

■ JOHN DONNE: Author—*"All mankind is of one author and is one volume. When one man dies, one chapter is not torn out of the book, but translated into a better language; and every chapter must be translated—G-d employs several translators; some pieces are translated by age, some by sickness, some by war, some by justice; but G-d's hand is in every translation, and His hand shall bind up all our scattered leaves again for that library where every book shall be open to one another."*

Jan Isaaksz van Ruisdael, *The Jewish Cemetery.*

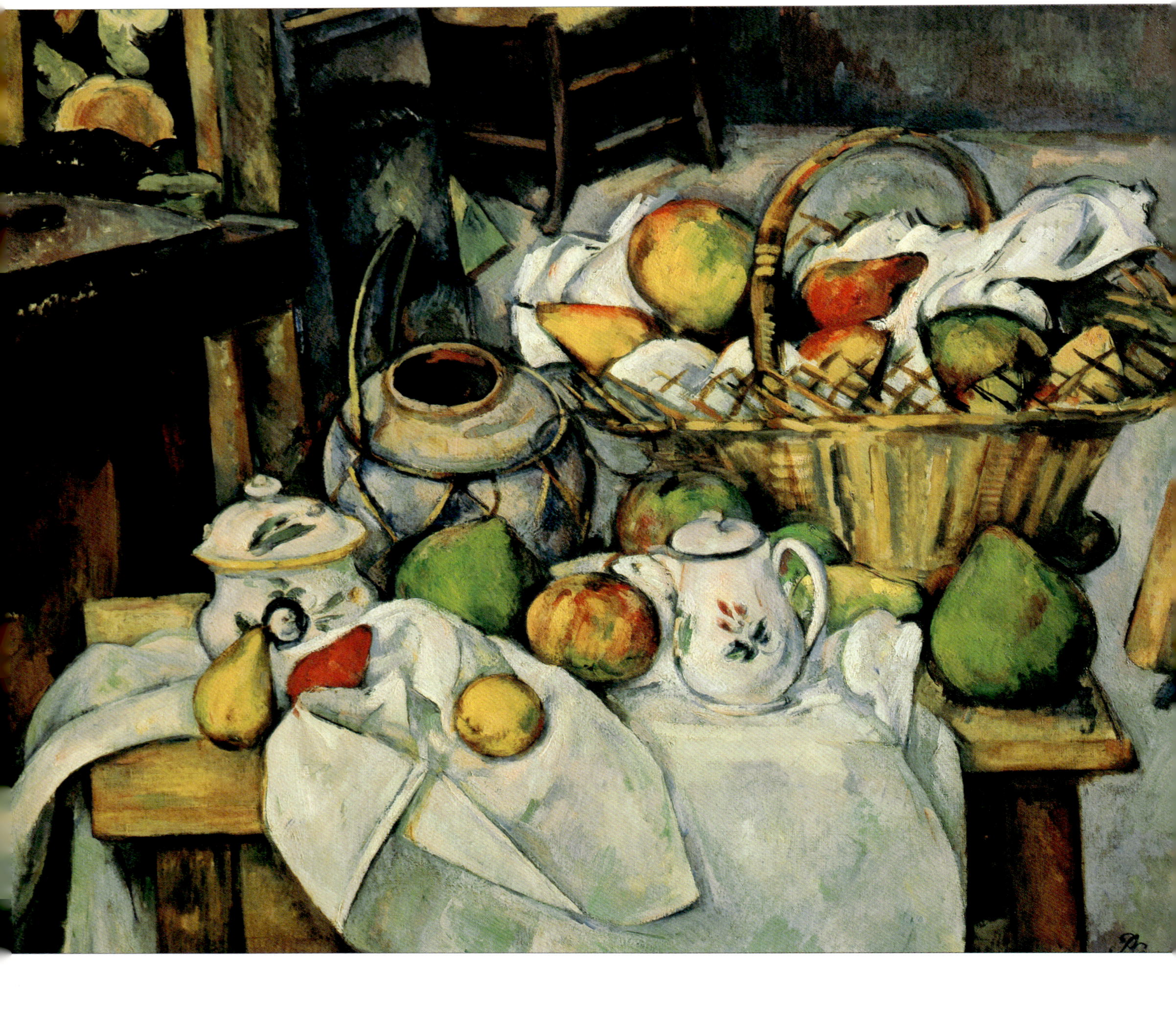

■ Cézanne: These dreams are not dreams they are object driven observations—To Émile Bernard, Aix, 23 October 1905:

"*Now the theme to develop is that whatever our temperament or form of strength face to face with nature may be, we must render the image of what we see, forgetting everything that existed before us. Which I believe must permit the artist to give his entire personality, whether great or small. Now being old, nearly seventy years, the sensations of colour, which give the light, are for me the reason for the abstraction which does not allow me to cover my canvas entirely nor to pursue the delimitation of the objects where their points of contact are fine and delicate; from which it results that my image or picture is incomplete…Nature, if consulted, gives us the means of attaining this end…*

Your old friend, Paul Cézanne,

A strong handshake and good courage. Optics which are developed in us by study teach us to see."

These apples of Zola, his gifts to me in our youth, these are not dreams, they are objects forever seen—night and day. The painted screen in the corner of my painting, this is no dream either, it too is a souvenir of Zola, when we decorated my home, Jas de Bouffan almost forty years previously.

Young Fisher—a poet manquée like myself—and these forever green flowers carved on a canvas precious beyond dreams—are they not poems fashioned in antique Hindustan.

Something neither Zola nor Tal's brother see—with their terror of the night—something veils their eyes of the glory of the day light; both fail to glimpse sun-drenched beauty.

Tuviah hummed to himself as he turned the pages, glancing from the color photographs to Fisher.

Fisher felt as if he were in his junior high school adviser's office who was thinking about how to tell him that he didn't have a wisp of a chance of getting into any of the fancy private high schools Fisher's parents hoped he'd be admitted to.

"I can't understand these dreams, Fisher. I'm only a diamond dealer. What do they mean?" said Tuviah Tal.

"These are not dreams, they're are object driven observations about the remarkable carved moghul your brother asked me to study."

"First of all, let me say the report submitted by the laboratory in Lucerne that tested the gem proves the emerald to have come from a Colombia mine," declared Fisher.

"Even a diamond dealer like myself can recognize the Colombia green shade of emerald," interrupted Tal.

■ Bereshit Rabbah: Look—"*G-d looked into the Torah and created the world.*"

◆ Shabbetai Suleimani, Suleimani's father: First of all…—Which of these Lucerne scientists were at the mine the moment when the gem was mined?

Which one was in the stifling heat of Muzo—the air so heavy one prayed for death to catch a reviving heavenly-breeze. The horrible toil, back breaking work, trapped in a pit, scratching for years on end, to find a crystal and not tell anyone of the miracle. For to reveal the miracle made one an instant mark for robbery at best, and most likely murder.

No, in the frigid air-conditioned laboratory—the fresh air of the Alps was not sufficient—these scientists are certain. They have proven the emerald to have come from a Colombian mine. But without having dug a gem, and certainly without having gone at least to Bogota and at best to Chivor or Muzo, having risked their money on a crystal, on a faceted stone, only then could we say that their judgment is anywhere near proving anything.

America is a land of laboratories, not a country that would believe a Marco Polo or a Tavernier, certainly not outside a movie theater.

■ F. Scott Fitzgerald: I can't understand these dreams—Alexander Woollcott and 'Chato' Elizaga being endlessly toasted. No one could match Gerald Murphy's Yale diction. Zelda languidly rising onto a table and singing out. "*I have been so touched by all these kind words. But what are words? Nobody has offered our departing heroes any gifts to take with them. I'll start off. And she stepped out of her black lace panties and threw them to Woollcott and Elizaga.*"

Was that a dream? And Hollywood not? Was that endless beach party real and Hollywood a dream? Was Sheilah Graham the dream? And Lily East End Sheil the reality? Or was Sheilah the dream brought into reality by me. I can't understand any of it.

Paul Cézanne, *Still Life with Fruit Basket*.

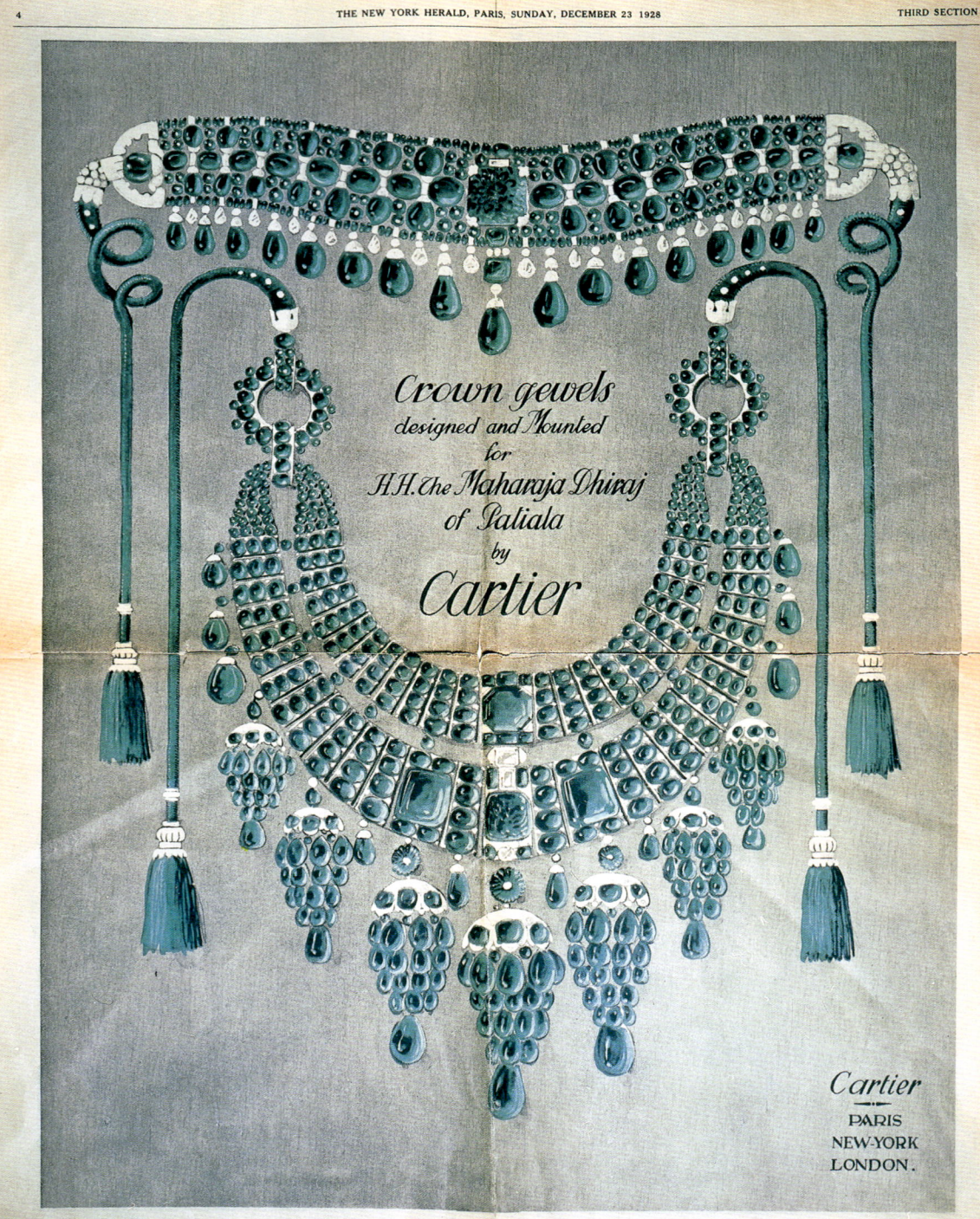

THE NEW YORK HERALD, PARIS, SUNDAY, DECEMBER 23 1928

*Crown Jewels
designed and Mounted
for
H.H. The Maharaja Dhiraj
of Patiala
by
Cartier*

Cartier
PARIS
NEW-YORK
LONDON.

■ LOUIS CARTIER: You know it from your brother—"How did I know Father would have told us to put the gloriously carved emerald up for sale—on a mere commission—and at a well nigh impossible price? Father is not here." Pierre would whine over and over again. His wife—the American—called the tune for him, and Pierre merely danced about, reciting her lines "One must quote a market price—or one is not a modern merchant," she would tell Pierre at breakfast, in turn quoting her American father, not that he would loan us a sou to get us through the Exposition.

"You know it from your brother, Pierre. That's how you know it." Grâce à Dieu for Jacques—India had opened his eyes.

When our agent Schwaiger Imre had picked the dazzling emerald from all the treasures of Patiala and said we would sell it for the royal family, and La Maison Cartier would use the proceeds to pay for the remodeling of all the Patiala gems into a silver snow-capped Kashmiri dream, I knew we had Patiala.

I asked Pierre to tell me the highest price we could get for the emerald and vain Pierre, he thought our only task was to achieve the highest world price for a gem we could. He named an astronomical sum.

I informed Imre to transmit the figure to Patiala. When Schwaiger asked what was the limit should the Maharaja raise our price, I answered grandly, "We will go as high as the Himalayas. What is the price of Paradise on earth?" Humorous, that Patiala, he doubled Pierre's boast.

But "Rome wasn't built in one day," Father always told us.

And if the Collier Bérénice wasn't sold, we still would have made Cartier *hors concours*.

And then we would decide what to do. In 1926 or '27 or later. We still weren't there. But I wasn't telling Pierre any of this.

■ JACQUES CARTIER: You know it from your brother—"You know it from your brother," Louis told Pierre, whenever Pierre questioned Louis.

Of course, Louis played the father. As Father had played his father to us. And as surely as I played the father to Pierre and Louis when I returned from the Delhi Durbar.

All Pierre could think of was selling diamonds to the Americans from the Parisian jewelers—Dreicer and the whole gang—at double the price.

Jewels from Sultan Abdul Hamid at treble the price they were auctioned off when that poor sot lost the throne—but kept his harem—G-d what a hell.

All Louis could think of was how to buy the jewels he saw in his night dreams after his days spent looking at his miniatures he kept in the library in the back of the ofice—

"Yes, but the inclusions! The record of crystallization pattern shows an interlocking stack of growth inclusions that perfectly matches an inclusion pattern on an emerald lost in a Spanish galleon sailing from Colombia in the early seventeenth century, 1607 to be precise."

Tuviah Tal read aloud from Fisher's report, as though the writer were not seated before him. "This emerald did not come from that shipwreck, but my surmise is that it came from the same level of the Colombian mine."

"Emeralds occur in a hexagonal crystal in the earth, and this crystal must have been originally thousands of carats to yield such a gem. A size and value that only Emperor Shah Jahan, the foremost lover of gems and jewelry in all history, who built the Taj Mahal in..."

"Don't tell me what I know, Fisher," said Tuviah Tal. "I may be only a diamond dealer, but I know who built the Taj as a monument to his wife."

"You know it from your brother Abraham, Mr. Tal," said Fisher, surprised at how annoyed he felt with his neighbor's officious sibling.

"Touché," said Tuviah. "You're probably right. Bram hasn't stopped talking about you or this treasure for six months."

"In any case," said Fisher, assuming a professional tone of voice and pointing to the photograph of the gem placed along side a line drawing of its carving design. "Shah Jahan commissioned a design on the gem that was both unprecedented and central to his view of himself."

the one we could only enter to discuss the absolute most secret plans for our future. Always buying, buying, buying.

He was crazed Louis, Pierre was right. Louis was trying to build a jeweled Louvre but alas he was no Napoleon, nor were we three together even half of a Napoleon.

Audacious it was, to put the Patiala stone at such a starry price alongside two other emeralds in the Bérénice Collier. And without a catch!

And when Pierre said, "Where's the catch, Louis?" Louis roared with laughter, "Oh the catch, there are two catches. One the piece will be on display on a mannequin's shoulders and the second catch, another Nabob, he'll be the eventual buyer."

I had been to the East. I thought I understood. In any case, what fun it would be to see it play out.

■ PIERRE CARTIER: "Don't tell me what I know," Louis kept saying over and over. "This will be our face to the world for the next fifty years." Father [Alfred Cartier] had died just before the Exposition des Arts Decoratifs was scheduled to open. 1925. My G-d, I lost one father and gained two, Imre Schwaiger, our man in Delhi, Louis and even Baby Jacques, whc said everything Louis said only, twice as slowly.

"I know. I know. But we have the Patiala hors d'oeuvres and we've been promised the rest within the year to remount."

"One year in the East is three years on the continent," said Louis glumly.

"Yes," said Jacques. "One year in the East, as I learned at the Delhi Durbar, is worth three on the continent."

Insufferable, he was—Jacques. A few months in India, and already he played Le Grand Mcghol. Probably planning to do us in Aurangzeb style.

"Well, we have the 141 carat hexagonal velvet paradisiacal carved emerald. Louis, when we show that, we can certainly make a display far superior to our neighboring jewelers," I ventured.

"We don't have any neighboring jewelers. We are the only jewelers in the Pavillior de L'Elégance," Louis quickly replied in an even tone.

"We stand next to your brother-in-law, Louis, and who will buy our jewelry there? At the price we have to get for the Bérénice Collier with its center 141, no one. No sooner did we follow your advice and tell Muhammad Kassim what we could sell the 141 carater for, he doubled the price and said he agreed...what are we, the Louvre for Patiala?"

And all Louis could say was, "Father would have told us this is our face to the world for the next fifty years."

Exhibition of Patiala Crown Jewels, Cartier, Paris, 1927.

ולכל שר אלירשי

ברביעי

בשבת ארבעה עשר יום לחדש אלול שנת חמשת אלפים וארבע מאות ושבעים וארבעה לבריאת
עולם למנין שאנו מנין כאן בפה סינגאליא מתא דיתבא על כיף ימא ועל נהרי ניפולא פינרא
ציסאנו מנחור היקר והנבון כמר אלישע יצו בן הבונה הזקן היקר כמר דוד חיים מקסטיל
לאוני זל אמר לה לבחורה הבתולה והצנועה מרת לא מבת בת היקר ויעלה כמר משה
מונטי פיורי מודיציא יצו הוי לי לאנתו כדת משה וישראל ואנא בסיעתא דשמיא אפלח ואוקיר
ואיזון ואפרנע ואכסה יתיכי כהלכת גוברין יהודאין דפלחין ומוקירין וזנין ומפרנסין
ומכסין לנשיהון בקושטא ויהיבנא ליכי מהר בתוליכי כסף זוזי מאתן דחזו ליכי ומזוניכי
וכסותיכי וסיפוקיכי ומיעל לותיכי כאורח כל ארעא וצביאת מרת ויולא כלתא בתולתא דא
מבתולתיה ותות ליה לכמר אלישע יצו חתן דנן הנל לאנתו ודא נדוניא דהנעלת ליה מבי אבוה
עשרין לטונין של כסף צרוף וצבי כמר אלישע יצו חתן דנן הנל והוסיף לה מדיליה וממונה
על חמשין ליטרין של כסף צרוף וצבי כמר אלישע יצו חתן דנן הנל והוסיף לה נדוניא ותוספאה
דבקין לטונין של כסף צרוף בשעתין זה ודא לית כתובתא דא נדוניא ותוספאה קבלית
עלי ועל ירתאי בתראי להתפרע מן כל שפר ארג נכסין דיקני דאית לי ונחות לי נחלת עפל
שמיא דקנית ודעתיד אנא למקני נכסין דאית להון אחריות ואגב דלית להון אחריות
כלהון יהון אחראין וערבאין עלי למפרע מירהון כתובתא דא נדוניא ותוספתא עד גמירא
ואפילו מן גלימא דעל כתפאי ולאחר חיי מן יומא דנן ולעלם וקבל עליו כמר אלישע
יצו חתן דנן הנל אחריות וחומר כתובתא דא כאחריות וחומר כל שטרי כתובות
דנהגין בבנות ישראל הבתולות הצנועות והכשורות הנעשין ככל
תקוני חכמינו זל דלא כאסמכתא ודלא כטופסי דשטרי וקנינא אן קהדי
די חתימי לתתא מהיקר כמר אלישע יצו בן המנוח הזקן היקר כמר דוד וחייב
מקסטיל לאומר זל חתן דנן הנל לזכות הצנועה והחשובה מרת ויולא כלת כמר
היקר ונגלה כמר משה מונטי פיורי מודיציא יצו הנל כלדיא בתולתא דלעיל אדא
אנדתיה על כל מיד דכתיב ומפרש לעיל במנא דכשר
למקניא ביה והכל שריר וקיים

■ LOUIS CARTIER: Unprecedented—At the Exposition des Arts Décoratifs in 1925 Pierre would arrive each day at twelve and at six. Like our mystery clocks, he would simply appear.

By my side, he would point at the Bérénice and move his eyes slowly from the emerald, pearl, and diamond tiara, down to the epaulette on the mannequin's shoulders. How sensual the mannequin's shoulders seemed in the reflection of the cascade of diamonds, highlighted by three glorious emeralds gently set at the neckline. How cunning and riveting to the eye: a spiral design flashing across the brooch of pearls, diamonds, and yet again emeralds tightly pinned to the mannequin's dress, chest high.

"Still here," Pierre would whisper. "Any interest in His Majesty's hexagonal Moghul 141 carat emerald." For never would the name of Patiala be spoken outside my hidden library in our office.

"Oh, Pierre, much interest, unprecedented interest, Tout le monde is coming, and tales are spreading back even to remote Hindustan."

"Yes, Louis. But interest, real interest, you know what I mean, Louis, genuine interest?"

"Oh, that. Real interest, as you would put it, Pierre. Interest to purchase, to take away, to disappear with, to decamp with, to walk off with now—Grâce à Le Bon Dieu—none of that kind of interest."

"Why unprecedented?" asked Tuviah.

"Unprecedented because the background was carved away by Shah Jahan's court gem cutter, leaving in the most perfect relief three flower heads, ten groups of three tight circles, and eleven single circles, a genealogical portrait."

"How do you know Shah Jahan, if he was such a maven on jewelry, didn't cut the stone himself?" asked Tuviah Tal.

"Carved, not cut. And in any case, a royal emperor, obsessed with power, flooded with responsibilities of ruling the richest empire in all the seventeenth-century world, could not have been the hand that carved a gem stone of this fragility."

Tuviah found himself increasingly impressed by Fisher.

"Please continue," he whispered.

"The central flower head is a rare Kashmiri poppy—-Meconopsis Aculeata—-symbol of Shah Jahan's grandfather, Akbar, who conquered Kashmir in 1586. The second flower head is the center of an opening lotus, symbol of Buddhist and Hindu India as well as a symbol used by the Timurid ancestors of Shah Jahan, but most especially the symbol of Babur who conceived of and caused to be built the first lotus garden in India, after he led the moghuls to first conquer the subcontinent. The third flower head, the one on the right, is a combination of the other two."

"Which is the right?" asked Tuviah Tal.

"What do you mean?" said Fisher.

"The right one from above or the right from below, as my brother Abraham would say." Suddenly Fisher understood that Tuviah Tal, like his brother, also understood. Now it was Fisher's turn to be impressed.

■ PIERRE CARTIER: A royal emperor: Twice a day, I would come to the Exposition—was I not a partner in the firm? It was all well and good to treat each day like a stroll through one's private garden. Oh, Louis was a master at that!

"Please do spare the time to view this marvel of nature– No, I cannot reveal from which princely collection we have acquired it," Louis would admonish the wealthy American couples who each day in endless numbers stood transfixed before La Maison Cartier's Manna–the epauletted mannequin.

I could see things were going nowhere. "Louis," I argued forcefully. "These rich Americans, they are not school children who should be punished and sent to bed early because they don't know Moghul history. They are Americans whose only sin is that they think Indian history begins with Louis and Clark, not with Louis and Pierre."

"Very sensitive. Why don't you lead the tour, Pierre?" And I did and said all the same words of incantation that I had to the Walsh-McLeans:

A royal Emperor…power…flooded with responsibility…ruling the richest empire in all the world.

Twice a day at twelve and six, I walked around our display. I would have sold the epaulette, by G-d I would have, but Louis and Jacques would gaze at each potential buyer I had with such a devastating glare that even I couldn't close the deal. If only Papa had been alive, he wouldn't have stood for it.

Montefiore Ketubah, Sinigalia, Italy, eighteenth century.

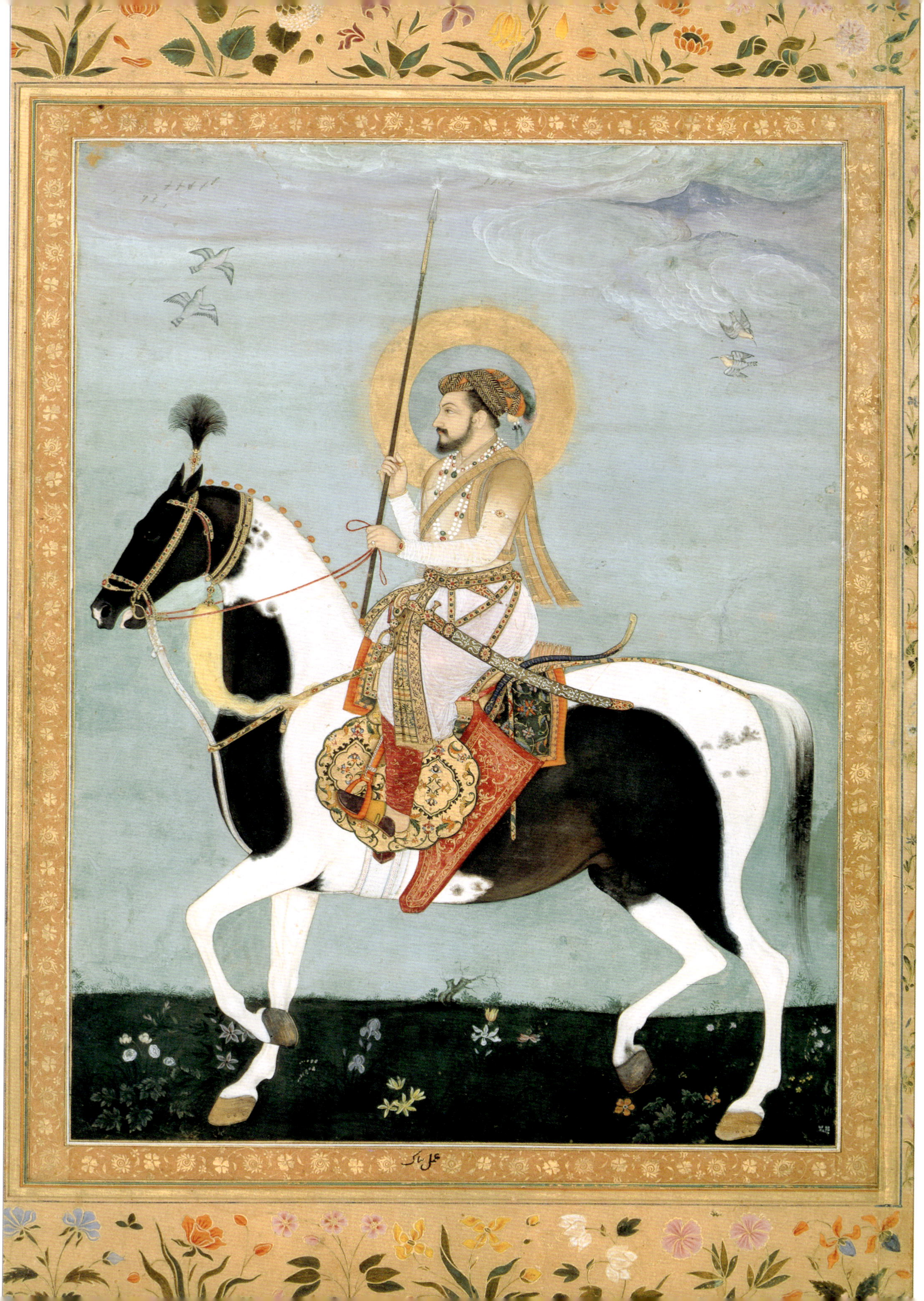
عمل

◆ HAHAM ZEVI, FISHER'S ANCESTOR: Genius skips a generation at best—And what does it mean to skip a generation?

And what does it mean for genius to skip a generation? Was I not with Elijah Covo in Salonika just before the dark days of Ofen? Did he not teach me that the word of Torah should not skip away from us for one week nor even one day, nor even one meal, for Torah too, G-d forbid, can go into exile.

Skip a generation. What did my blessed teacher, my grandfather Ephraim Ha-Kohen, pray for when the plague in Ofen hit my uncle? That the plague take my grandfather's life and pass over the brow of Aryeh Leib, his son.

Skipping a generation—what an idea! True my grandfather longed for the Rabbinical post in Jerusalem, the Jerusalem past of his grandfather. Not a day passed without Ephraim's father speaking of Jerusalem. Not a day when I was a student with my uncle Aryeh Leib that we didn't speak of Jerusalem. My uncle Aryeh Leib's son, Yedidiah, explained it most clearly, in the tongue of his father-in-law, the Sephardi Haham of Jerusalem.

Yedidiah asked if he took his bride to Europe, would they remain close to Jerusalem. The Haham asked his daughter to hand the pearl necklace he had just given her to Yedidiah. As she did Yedidiah's father-in-law said, "Are these pearls together?" Yedidiah said, "Yes." "And are there spaces between the pearls?" and Yedidiah said, "Yes."

The Haham gazed over the heads of his daughter and his son-in-law and said, "It depends on memory. On prayer. On love. The strength of the string. The skill of the knotting. And G-d forbid should the string break and the pearls scatter on the floor and roll into the Earth, all can be reassembled with the help of the Creator.

"We will all be connected, if you so wish."

"Shah Jahan is saying that he is a combination of his great great-grandfather Babur and his grandfather Akbar. By also including the ten triple circles, he is linking himself with Tamerlane (Timur), his tenth generation ancestor, the limping ravager of the East from Baghdad to Bukara, creator of the endlessly encircling gardens of Samarkand. Whom he is not linking himself with is his profligate father, Jahanghir, or his great grandfather Humayun, a weakling."

"Were they roommates of my brother in the Village?" cracked Tuviah, with a self-satisfied belly laugh.

"You know, you and blessed Abraham aren't that dissimilar," said Fisher. "In any case, genius skips a generation, at best.

"But to continue, Shah Jahan used the emerald as his symbol, wore it on a golden string when he sat on the peacock throne. He dominated and divided his family, buried his wife, built the Taj, and ruled the world."

"Only, according to your research, young man, to have his son Aurangzeb imprison him," interrupted Tuviah.

"But where did you get the gem from?" demanded Fisher. "Don't tell me Suleimani's family got it directly from the Maharani of Jodpur or Jaipur or any of the ruling families of India. Oh, no, the report Suleimani prepared for you wasn't worth the paper he wrote on." Fisher by now was fuming.

■ WILLIAM BLAKE A golden string—
*I give you the end of a golden String
Only wind it into a ball:
It will lead you in at Heaven's Gate
Built in Jerusalem's wall.*

What is the joy of Heaven but improvement in the things of spirit?

*England! Awake! Awake! Awake!
Jerusalem thy sister calls!
Why wilt thou sleep the sleep of death?
And close her from thy ancient walls.*

*Thy hills and valleys felt her feet,
Gently upon their busoms move:
Thy gates beheld sweet Zion's ways;
Then was a time of joy and love.*

*And now the time returns again
Our souls exult and London's Towers
Receive the Lamb of G-d to dwell
In England's green and pleasant bowers.*

A golden string containing Baghdad, Bukara Samarkand, London, Jodpur, Jaipur, and Jerusalem. All in all. Shah Jahan understands it all. *"The path to the house of enlightenment is through the path of excess."*

Payag, *Shah Jahan on horseback.*

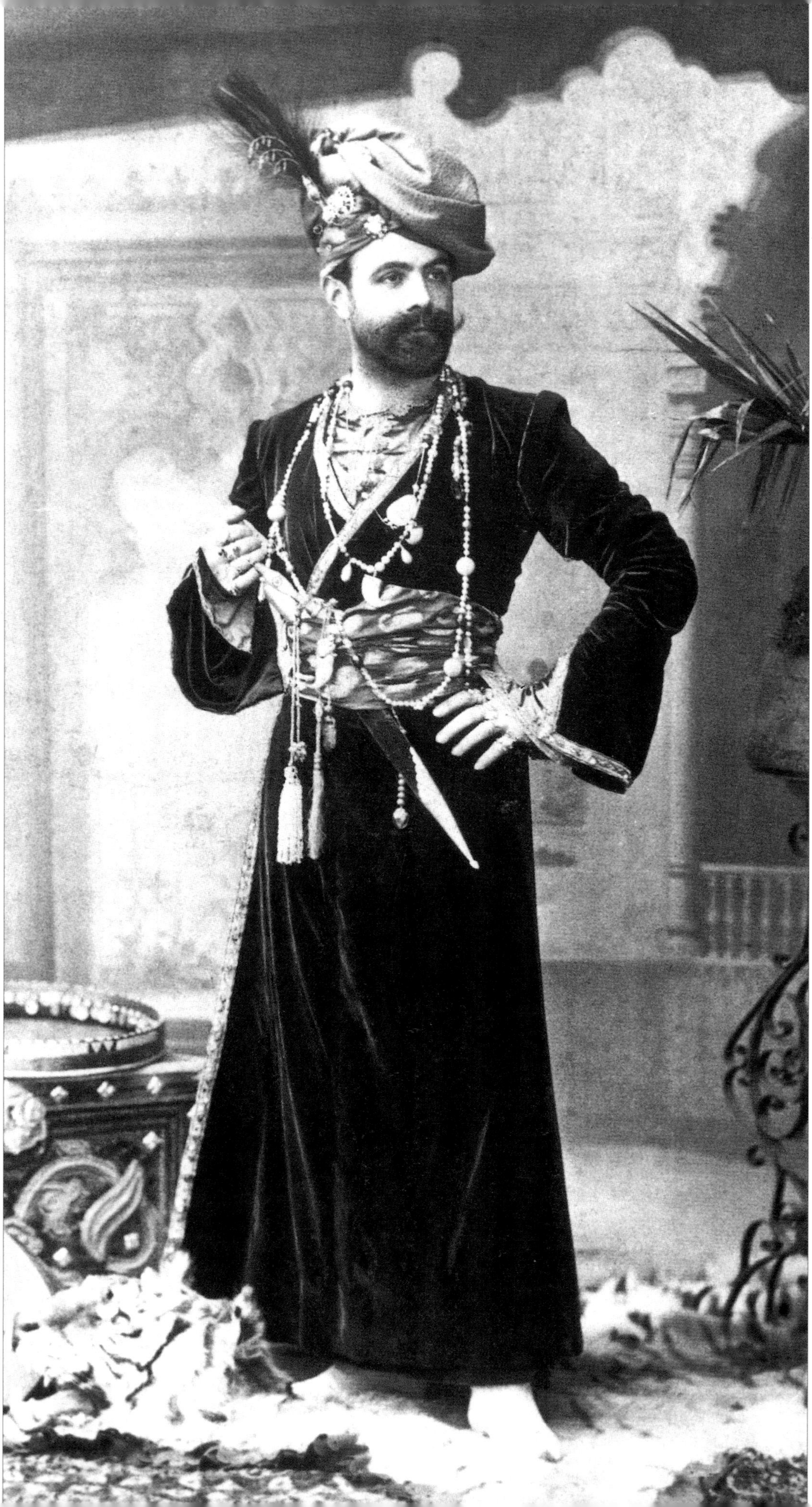

■ LOUIS CARTIER: Couturier Worth—I waited until Pierre came at six, on the minute as usual. Before he could mouth the words, "Any interest," I was ready for him.

My index finger was in front of my mouth and Jacques gesticulated with his eyes, pointed wildly to our right at the back of a tall, velvet-clad Indian potentate. Pierre could see the silhouette of the Indian figure with the epaulette around his shoulders.

In the case where the mannequin had worn the Bérénice tiara and the jeweled epaulette, now the tiara propped up against the side mirror and the vitrine.

"My G-d Louis, we've done it," said Pierre, practically dancing.

"How much did we make?" he whispered. "We can't close the deal. He's a slippery fellow. This Maharaja, more like a Frenchman he is, we're waiting for you to deal with him."

"Leave him to me Louis. I'll handle this one, Jacques" Pierre waved us away with the grace of a Ancien Regime nobleman. Jacques and I walked briskly by Pierre who immediately put his hand gently on the Maharaja's back.

"Permit me, Monsieur, to explain the royal history of the most magnificent emerald jewel in the world."

The figure did not turn toward Pierre.

"Sir," continued Pierre with contained gentleness. "Do me the favor of turning toward so that I might behold the beauty of La Maison Cartier's hexagonal 141 carat dream and at the same time have the honor of gazing upon your countenance." With the deftness of a Diaghilev dancer, the figure turned slowly, one hand on his sheathed scimitar, and gazed directly at Pierre.

Pierre whose back was to Jacques and myself was so startled he practically lept off the ground. At that moment, my father-in-law, Jean Philipe Worth, softly said, "Mon cher Pierre, comment allez-vous?"

And Pierre whirled around with not one trace of a smile and shouted, "Salaud prix, you're all crazy. Jean-Philipe, Jacques and especially you Louis."

Pierre charged out of the hall and didn't return for a week. And never until the end of the fair did he inquire of any further "interest" in the epaulette.

■ MOZART: Hissed—Tuviah is a snake to his brother. Once a serpent, ever a serpent.

Is a *vipere* less poisonous in Vienna than in its native land? Salieri, in the court, the conductor—*Kapellmeister*—no less, hissing at me to all who would hear, poisoning Hayden and even Da Ponte.

Also Venetian, not far from where Salieri was misbegotten. *"Da Ponte has to write per obbligo an entirely new libretto for Salieri [il Ricco d'un giorno] which will take him two months. He has promised after that to write a new libretto for me...If he is in league with Salieri, I shall get nothing out of him."*

Doesn't young Fisher know that a serpent's brother is a serpent? Let Fisher beware. Or first they will teach his knowledge, then his humors, and will they not after having poisoned his reputation turn their venom on his body itself?

"The Indian treasures accumulated by Akbar, Jahanghir and Shah Jahan were scattered in 1739 when Delhi was sacked. But this emerald miraculously survived, and I say miraculously because only one other gem—and I think this one is better and more delicately carved—has since surfaced." Fisher paused for a breath and then sailed onward.

"But in 1925, at the Exposition des Arts Décoratifs, Pierre Cartier, who had owned the Hope diamond (which was also a moghul jewel) set this emerald into a necklace—the Bérénice—that was a sensation in Paris. He exhibited the necklace in a hall next to the most fashionable dresses in all of Paris, those of the Couturier Charles Worth, dresses that sang of ostrich and rare Birds-of-Paradise feathers.

Holding up a photo of a stunning Worth 1920's flapper, outfitted and submerged under a marabou boa and ostrich feather aigrettes, Fisher smiled at Tuviah Tal.

"Drop the feather bit. We're in the gem business, Fisher, not selling feathers," hissed Tuviah Tal.

■ ALMA MAILMAN, JAMES AGEE'S WIFE: Drop the feather bit—Drop the feather, I told Jim. Or Luce will drop you. I could talk to Jim, I could play music with him. It was hard keeping up with him. Following as he paced, wandered. *"People's pain used to upset him. I remember Jim's dissolving into tears, crying over someone he didn't know—a bank teller, just a small person doing a job. He was thinking of him; thought of his whole life and the pain of it and the loss of it, I guess, and he just cried. He was a lovable, gentle, great guy. His lovableness, I think, was impossible for anyone to resist."*

Of course, Jim didn't drop the feather bit. He simply dropped me.

■ DA PONTE (1749-1838): Hissed—Look at him, Wolfgang hissed at me while we walked. Salieri, your fellow Venetian.

Should I plead that I was a Sephardi born? Better not, even a world away from España was too close to talk of one's Judaism. As much as I reassured Wolfgang that *Kapellmeister* Salieri was as necessary a patron as the Emperor—the court—all nobility—the way it had ever been—even the Garden of Eden had its serpent.

I would whisper to Wolfgang, sing to Wolfgang, declaim to Wolfgang the words of Figaro.

"My Lord Count, because you're a great aristocrat, you think yourself a genius!...Nobility, fortune, rank, influence, all that makes one so proud! What did you do to earn so many cdvantages? You just gave yourself trouble of being born and nothing more For the rest, you're a rather commonplace person. Whereas I, lost in the common herd, have had to use more thinking and scheming to get on than has been spent governing the whole of Spain for the past hundred years!"

But Wolfgang would not hear of the sangre d'azul of España, nor of the snake of Eden itself. All he would hear of was the hissing in his ears, all he could see was the serpentine form of Salieri.

Nadar, Jean-Phillipe Worth in Indian costume.

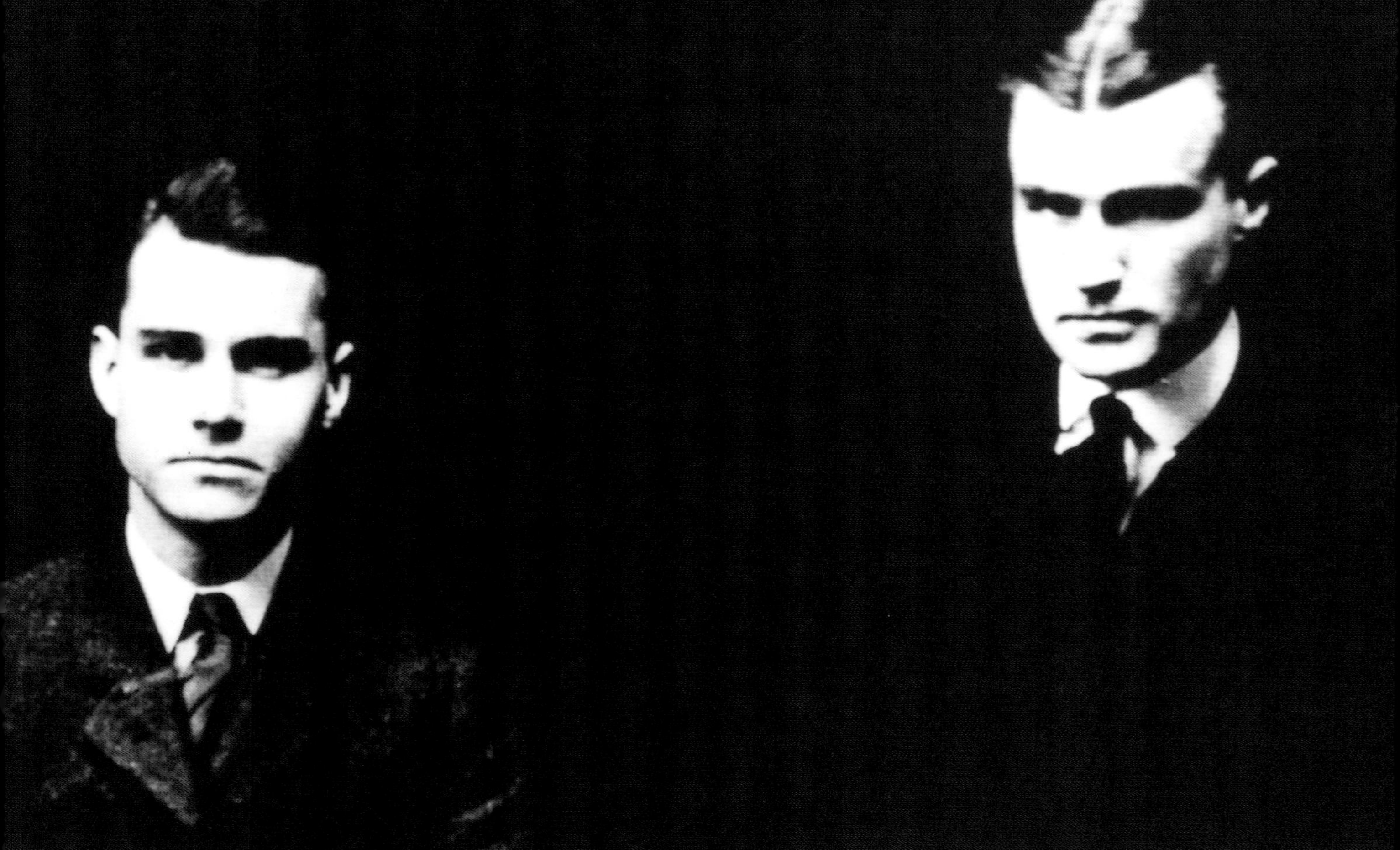

◆ EMIL FISHER, FISHER'S FATHER: My father was in Paris—In '25 my father was in Paris. On rue Faubourg Saint-Denis. Every day from Meletz, from Jeshev, from Tarnov, from Cracow. From all parts of Galicia, Shlichim knew they could get *Tzedaka*—never was anyone refused.

Years later, after the War, they wrote in the Yiddish paper about my father. His name itself was a blessing. One day a writer, a poor Yeshiva student traveling from Poland, came to my father's office. But he couldn't find rue Faubourg Saint-Denis—so he asked different people in the quartier. All the shops were closed and one person said, "The office you seek must be closed. Léon Blum has declared a work stoppage holiday."

Still, the Yeshiva boy went to our address, where else could he go?

There was my father, sitting on a chair in front of his locked office. "Reb Bunam, they told me all the shops in Paris were closed," the Yeshiva boy said.

"Oh, I am not in Paris, and perhaps someone might come to our office today seeking help."

One day I asked my father if he wasn't in Paris, was he still in Poland? Father answered with an ethereal smile, "Oh no, G-d forbid, I am on the road between Paris and Poland."

I knew Father was on Jacob's ladder, ascending.

■ MADANI PASHA, the brother of El T'hami's Muhammad: May consider himself a moghul—My younger brother may consider himself a moghul.

I would read his eyes as he looked at me and my ninety-six concubines. He considered himself the Pasha of Marrakesh.

But I could see the eyes of the French as they looked at me, looking at him, looking at him. *"They considered him to be a sword sheathed to be used and discarded."*

"My father was in Paris at the time, as a matter of fact," said Fisher in a faraway voice.

"As Pollock, the dealer in rough diamonds, would say," quoted Tuviah Tal slowly. "*Yeder Darshan darshan far siche*. Every preacher preaches for himself. In any case, will Time magazine publish this?"

"I don't know. But that's their business, not yours. In any case, they won't buy the gem. Luce may consider himself a moghul but at heart he's a missionary's son bent on power and not on Oriental splendor."

Tuviah Tal bent forward and pressed a buzzer. In walked Abraham Tal, smiling broadly.

"Didn't I tell you my pupil is extraordinary?" Tal said, looking more at Fisher than at his brother. "Here's your check, Fisher," he said with a flourish.

"I told you I don't want any of your money," said Fisher peevishly, peering down at the check.

"Then don't fill in the amount and don't cash it," said Tuviah Tal. "And while you're deciding what to do with our token of appreciation, leave my brother alone to decide what to do next. Thank you," said Tal dismissively.

Fisher, bewildered but charmed, got up to leave and out of the corner of his eye, caught Tal lunging to pick up his report. Project: Green.

■ EL T'HAMI: May consider himself a moghul—That *putain*. A certain charm she had. Violette le Duc, I believe, was her name in Marrakesh. Ahmad Ibn Yossuf had seen her in the train station with her friend, Annette La Cloche, who was carrying all four of their suitcases, although Annette was twice Violette's age and half her size.

Ahmed could read the past of a French woman by the way she walked, and invited both of them for dinner in the palace, with me if I so chose.

I looked through the grating at the second floor entrance before deciding how to spend my evening and perhaps how they would spend the rest of their lives.

Violette had a certain *je ne sais quoi*. I appeared at the end of the second course. Women love mystery, and the French above all adore suspense.

My translator, Hakim, conveyed my thanks in French to the both of them for deigning to dine with me. And my thousand questions in Arabic, all translated with alarming speed. "Do you like the wine, the bread, the cous-cous, the kidney beans, the weather?" All were met with amused, laughing hearty yesses.

Hakim excused himself during the après dinner cognac, and I remained silent. Mademoiselle La Cloche, who had eyed my emerald ring all evening, whispered in French to her companion, "This little *salaut-prix*, he may consider himself a moghul but he's just a barbarian *déclassé*."

I smiled throughout their cognacs. And then excused myself politely at midnight and looked the mademoiselle in the eye and said in perfectly accented French with a vocabulary I had learned with the aid of "*the long haired dictionary on my holidays at Cesar Ritz's in Paris. 'Because I am such a barbarian, it is only fitting a princess such as yourself should be gifted with this emerald, token of my obeisance.'*"

I went back to my harem, and had the ladies put on the first ship back to Paris to tell the tale.

Henry Luce and Briton Hadden.

BÉRÉNICE

DIADÈME ET COLLIER, DE CARTIER

■ RABBI VELVEL SOLOVEICHIK, in the name of his great-great-grandfather Reb Itzele Volozhiner: Green...Blue...White—"*The Talmud tells us that even the person himself who experiences a miraculous occurrence is unaware of it. A miraculous occurrence is always better observed from a distance (spatially or temporally) than from close proximity. Thus when the Prophets say that in the future G-d will show us wonders as in the days of the Exodus, this means that two salvations will appear to us as being of equal degree. But, as firsthand experience of the events, this view will be somewhat distorted. In order for the miracles of the future redemption to appear to be equal to those of the Exodus, they will have to be in fact of a much greater intensity.*"

The young man here is speaking of green and blue and the ground is white—rare for Jerusalem. Redemption has come for him.

For the green he speaks of, is it not Passover?

And the blue, is it not the land of Israel?

And the young man has returned—This year in Jerusalem—to be redeemed. And what can bring Redemption? Atonement, Yom Kippur, or marriage?

Here they are, all together, the man, the woman, and the color of Atonement: white.

■ PIERRE CARTIER: Miraculous—Louis smiled when I told him. "The Glaoui of Morocco, His Eminence El T'hami Muhammad Pasha of Marrakesh has purchased the epaulette."

I had showed El T'hami the photograph of the Bérénice piece with the emeralds: 141 carats and its shoulder companions, 153 and 86 carats. And what a price I achieved just for the necklace without Patiala's miraculous emerald.

"Now we can sell the remaining gems, pay Patiala, and show a profit on all of it, Louis." Louis continued to smile. He probably felt vindicated after putting La Maison Cartier in incredible jeopardy.

He also thought I was just lucky to have been in Paris when the Glaoui came by looking for something special for a very special friend, as he put it so coquettishly. His majesty didn't even have the necklace wrapped, he simply darted out of our office back to the top two floors of the Ritz he had taken to view the spring time chestnut arborial weather.

Even Jacques admitted to me later that it was foolhardy to build such an epaulette with a price higher than the Pyramids. I suppose Louis' smile was all the acknowledgment I could ever hope for. Father would have treated me differently, far differently.

Bérénice Emerald necklace.

◆ SIMHA PADAWER, DOSHA'S GRANDFATHER: Jerusalem...A miraculous blanket of snow—I would tell my Rickele, when we fled Slonim and were with the Partisans: "It's G-d's hand. A miracle."

In January '43 we were with Eric Stein on the Baranovici-Luninetz line, not far from Budi. The Germans everywhere looking for us and not with their own eyes only—also with the unflinching eyes of peasants. We were in eight feet of snow, everyday.

Every night a miracle. Our footsteps hidden by a miraculous blanket of snow. Manna from heaven. My granddaughter, my Jerusha, in Jerusalem not next year but now in Jerusalem.

"*And it came to pass at midnight.*"

How can redemption come at night? For Abraham? For Daniel, the man of G-d's delight? For me and Rickele, but not poor Eric?

But Thank G-d for my Jerusha.

CHAPTER 9

GREEN from blue. When you couldn't tell green from blue, as Tal always used to say to me," said Fisher wearily to Dosha, sitting down on a Jerusalem stone bench with his arm around her, more exhausted than chivalrous.

"Or was it blue from green," sleepily continued Fisher. "Or was it..." Fisher trailed off.

Dosha had been staring over Fisher's shoulder at the Jerusalem moon-full sky, which glistened on the windmill in the near distance. The walls of the Old City were under a rare carpet of white, a miraculous blanket of snow, the heaviest in twelve years in the Holy Land that bathed the entire heavenly cityscape in a diamondiferous haze.

Most High—make known that Yours are day and night
Appoint guards for your city all the day and night
Brighten the light of day and darkness of the night.

■ JORGE LOUIS BORGES: Staring—"*I suppose that the perception [of the two Borgeses] came originally from the mirror. Because when you stare into a mirror, well there you are, there you are yourself looking at it, and the image looking at you. As for two Borges, I have been made keenly aware of the fact that there are two, because when I think of myself, I think, let us say, of a rather secret, of a rather hesitant, groping man. Somehow that can hardly be reconciled to the fact that I seem to be giving lectures all the time and traveling all over the world. So I think of those two men as being different: the private man and the public man. Or if you prefer it, why not speak of the private man, the shy man, the man still wondering at things even as he did when he was a boy, and the man who publishes books, whose books are analyzed, who has symposiums and that kind of thing happening to him—why not think of those two as being different? I do.*"

■ LEONOR ACEVEDO BORGES, Jorge Borges' mother: Windmills—Dosha is staring over Fisher's shoulder at the glistening windmill in the distance. He will see the windmill through her eyes. Just as Georgie sees Geneva and London through mine.

At six, Georgie told Father he wanted to become a writer. His first jottings: "*Tiger. Lion. Papa Leopard.*" And Georgie's father reading to me in his library.

What is a writer? One who reads to his wife in his library. And not always aloud. Who is a writer? One who hears her father read to her mother in the library.

Georgie read aloud to me or was it I who read his words to him Father "*revealed the power of poetry to me. The fact that words are not only a means of communicating but also magic symbols and music. When I recite poetry in English now, my mother tells me I do so in his very voice.*"

I am reading Georgie's words to him in London "*Those who have insinuated that Ménard devoted his life to writing a contemporary Quixote besmirch his illustrious memory. Pierre Ménard did not want to compose the Quixote. Nor, surely, need one have to say that his goal was never a mechanical transcription of the original; he had no intention of copying it. His admirable ambition was to produce a number of pages which coincided—word for word and line for line with those of Miguel Cervantes...Every man should be capable of all ideas and I believe that in the future he shall be.*"

Do not all Argentines "*put Mother first*"? "*A characteristic of Argentine males is to hide behind the desire of the mother.*" I looked into Georgie's mirror and he spoke of the windmills that Menard and Jorge Louis Borges and Father and all, every reader saw.

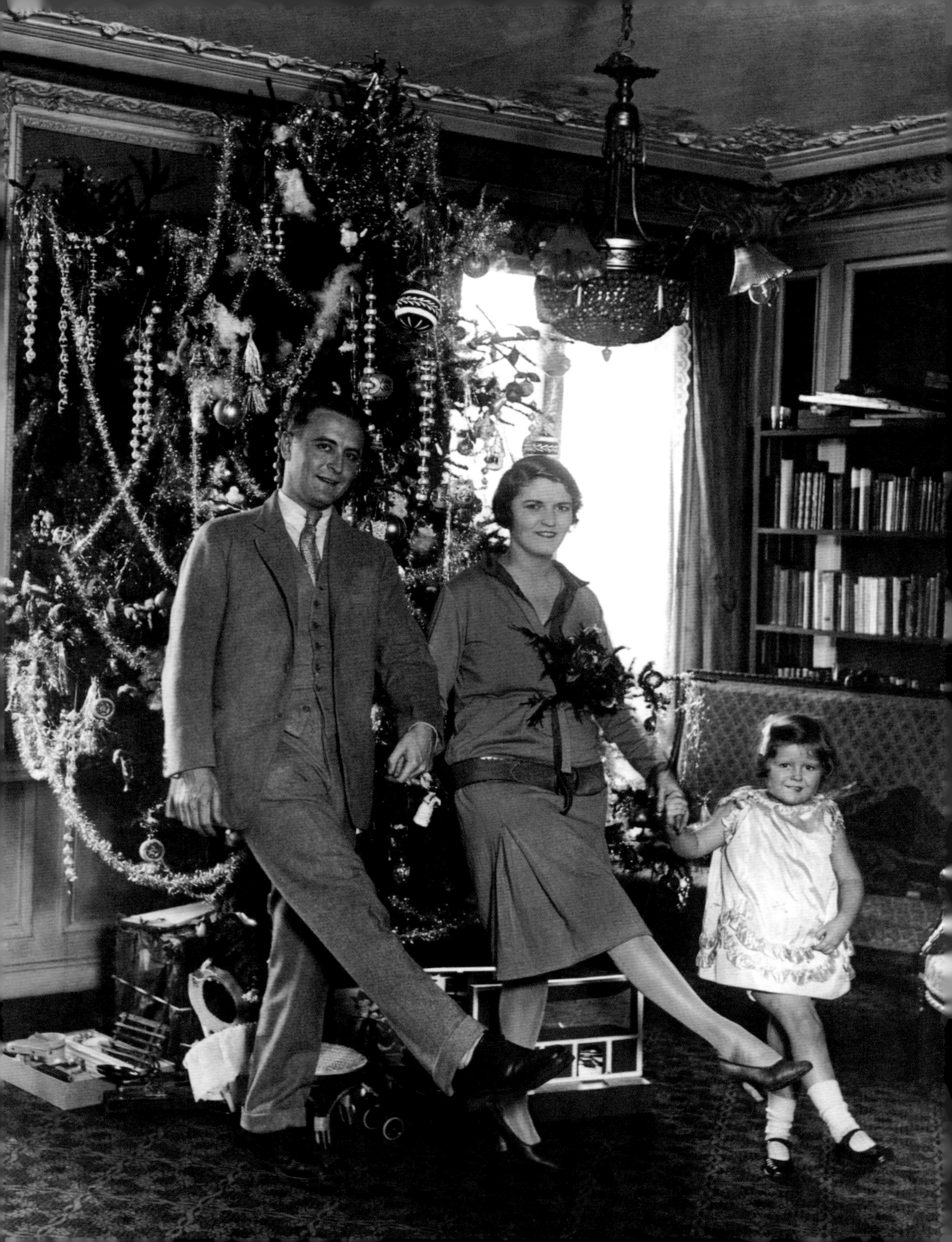

■ PAYAG: Daybreak—You will paint for his majesty Humayun, the glorious one, father of Akbar—whom destiny placed in your path. You will paint him as he was, a link in a chain of ten: Recall well that his majesty Shah-Jahan is the illustrious heir of Jahanghir son of Akbar, son of Humayun, son of Babur, son of Umar Shaikh Shah, son of the martyr King Sultan Abu Sa'id Shah, son of Muhammad Shah, son of Mirza Miran Shah, son of the Lord of the Auspicious Planetary Conjunction—Sahib-I—Qiran, Emperor Amir Timur.

I remembered how Akbar had spoken of Humayun's flight to Persia in the middle of the night.

His "army" of four, as he wandered and barely survived. And I knew what Balchand would advise: paint Humayun as he never was: with a ruby worth 150,000 lakhs—at peace in a garden, at daybreak with winged foreign angels crowning him with the first light of dawn.

How Abul Fazl smiled when I showed him my portrait of Humayun. The next day I was summoned to the court and promised that I would be forever the court painter of the Age—generation after generation Dara Shikoh and onward. I bowed as low as I could for fear that the Emperor's eyes might see the questioning expression in mine.

■ F. SCOTT FITZGERALD: Come to me dearest—I would look at Sara day after day. Directly into the Antibes light, hour after hour, dream after dream. To me dearest. But she would not move a bone in her blue-white body. "Sara, look at me." I would implore her. But she wouldn't. Or couldn't. Because of Gerald. Of Zelda, because of Honoria, of Baoth, of Patrick.

Never. Not ever, because of me. No, the beach at La Garope was not the venue, the lunches in Antibes not the improper occasion, the MacLeishes, Alexander Woollcott, and all the Hotel Du Cap not the proper people, inside the paradise of my head, come, come to me Sara Wiborg Murphy, and bring whomever you wish.

"Or was it black and blue, my love?" whispered Dosha into Fisher's ear. As exhausted as Fisher was, he leapt up from the bench.

"Don't do that! I can't move a bone in my body. We haven't slept in thirty-six hours." Fisher started to pace around Dosha, who had taken their knapsacks, tucked Fisher's neatly under her head and put the other under her feet. She lounged like a Turkish Courtesan.

"Come to me, dearest and we'll see if you can't move a bone in your body," Dosha sang.

Fisher laughed and walked toward her, resting his hand on her cheekbone. "Seriously, dear, Tal has a thing about daybreak. When you can't tell green from blue, you say the Shma—Hear Israel the Lord."

■ KORAN SURA 89 on the south gateway of the Taj Mahal: The Daybreak—
"In the name of G-d, the merciful, the compassionate
By the break of day!
By the nights twice twelve!
By the even and odd contrasted
And by the night when it passes away
Is there not in these an
Adjudication for those who understand
…O thou soul at peace
Return thou unto thy Lord, well-pleased
And well pleasing unto Him.
Enter thou around my servants
And enter thou my paradise."

■ ABRAHAM ABULAFIA: Or was it black and blue, my love?—Dosha is whispering into his ear. The bat kol is coming down from Heaven. Is he not bound and being prepared for…

And is his ear not Mount Moriah itself? And if Dosha spoke in a quiet voice, or G-d forbid shouted, it would be too great a voice for his ear. No, she must whisper or he will not hear. Or, if he hears, he will not understand. Or if he understands, he will not remember. Only a whisper will be remembered by Fisher. And his children's children.

She is whispering Tal's secrets. Of black and blue, and this Tal's pupils' pupil is singing back to her, of green and blue, and all the world is singing their song together:

Unhappy. Storm-tossed one, uncomforted
I will lay carbuncle as your building stones
And make your foundations of sapphires
I will make your battlements of rubies
Your gates of precious stones,
The whole encircling wall of gems.
And all your children shall be disciples of
*   the Lord,*
And great shall be the happiness of your
*   children.*
You shall be established through righteousness.
You shall be safe from oppression,
And shall have no fear; From ruin, and it shall not come near you.

F. Scott, Zelda, and Scottie Fitzgerald.

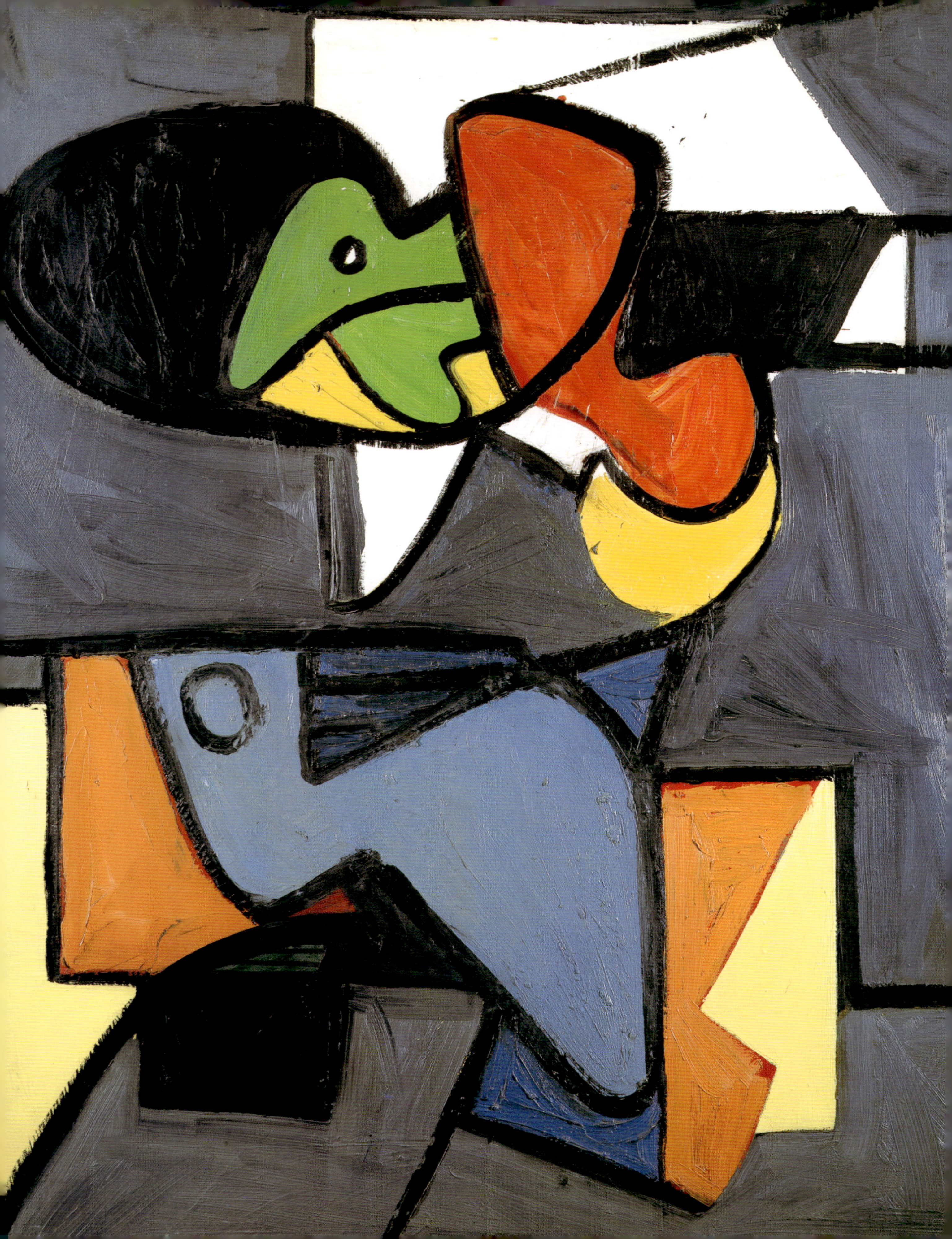

■ ARSHILE GORKY: A canvas…you're a Gypsy—And what is a canvas? Certainly not a square. Definitely *"a cone, a cylinder or a sphere"*—thus spake Cézanne. *"Cézanne is the greatest artist, shall I say, who ever lived."*

"Try to teach my girlfriend Siroon, my wild Armenian horse that—you're a Gypsy," she'd moan when I entered our apartment off Washington Square. She was from Van. For me *"it was like the sun had risen after a million years."*

She cleaned my brushes, she fed me from her own lips. She turned a Watertown summer into an Armenian spring but she wouldn't stay still for a moment. Asking questions about my name, my birth, my father.

With her I could never be an Armenian—and certainly never an American—and impossibility of impossibilities, never a Cézanne.

■ DA PONTE: Gypsy—How did I write the libretto of Don Giovanni—at a pace more furious even than Mozart managed? A girl. A Gypsy girl guided my hand, naturally.

"I sat down at my table and did not leave it for twelve hours continuous—a bottle of Tokay to my right, a box of Seville to my left, in the middle an ink well. A beautiful girl of sixteen—I should have preferred to love her (only as a daughter) but alas…! —was living in the house with her mother, my housekeeper, and would come to my room at the sound of the bell. To tell the truth, the bell rang rather frequently, especially at moments when I felt my inspiration waning. She would bring me now a little cake, now a cup of coffee, now nothing but her pretty face, a face always gay, always smiling, just the thing to inspire poetical emotion and witty thoughts. I worked twelve hours a day, every day, with a few interruptions for two months on end; and through all that time, she sat in an adjoining room, now with a book in hand, now with needle or embroidery, but ever ready to come to my aid at the first touch of the bell. Sometimes she would sit at my side without stirring, without opening her lips or batting an eyelash, gazing at me fixedly or blandly smiling, or now it would be a sign or a threat of tears. In a word, this girl was my Calliope for those three operas, as she was afterwards for all the verse I wrote during the next six years. At first I tolerated such visits very often; later I had to make them less frequent in order not to lose too much time in amorous nonsense, of which she was the perfect mistress. The first day, between the Tokay, the snuff, the coffee, the bell, and my young muse, I wrote the first two scenes of Don Giovanni, two more for the Arbore di Diana, and more than half of the first act of Tarar, a title I changed to Assur. I presented those scenes to the three composers the next morning. They could scarcely be made to believe that what they were reading with their own eyes was possible. In sixty-three days the first two operas were entirely finished and about two thirds of the last."

Arshile Gorky, Abstraction.

Dosha stood up suddenly. "Don't be ridiculous, Dreamboat. I know what the Shma is."

"But, well," stammered Fisher, "you're a Gypsy."

"But I've been grounded with you, you may recall, for more than two years and even a Gypsy knows…Thy G-d, the Lord is one. And speaking of that, what is it to be dreamboat? You told me in New York that a marriage license was simply a piece of paper not, 'a canvas,' as you so poetically put it. Nothing I could paint on. No, we had to come to the Holy Land. Whither thou goest, I go."

Not bad for a Gypsy, thought Fisher sardonically.

"Well, we're gone. We're here. We've walked," continued Dosha, staring straight at Fisher, whose eyes were downcast, as though being reprimanded by his mother for having gone out without his galoshes. Which he had.

■ SIROON MOUSIGIAN, a girlfriend of Arshile Gorky: You're a Gypsy—Arshile would shout, "I am from Van and you are from Van and we are from Van. And I am in love and you are in love and we are love itself."

It was like the sun had risen after a million years. Yet I needed love and security. Gorky did not know how to give that. Who was Gorky? He certainly was not Gorky—never a nephew of Maksim Gorky. Never the Russian author, even a child, even across the river of fire in Russia.

It could have been so simple. But he filled himself with so much coffee at the Gypsy Tavern that I could smell him half way up our walk-up. "You're a Gypsy," I shouted and he stormed into our apartment and kissed my toes, inhaled all of me, rolled across my body, told me tales that never were nor would be, pinched me hard if I didn't widen my gaze as he made a point. He wandered all over my body and followed me everywhere, even to my sister's home in Buffalo.

It could have been so simple. We could have turned a Watertown summer into a life together—an Armenian life. Arshile *was living in Armenia in Greenwich Village. If he hadn't told a lie so much he could have enjoyed being Armenian."*

■ CHESTER DALE, an American art collector, early twentieth century. Simply a piece of paper, not a canvas— Mary Cassatt's *Girl Arranging Her Hair*. Mary, staring at the girl. Louisine Havemeyer, looking at her friend Mary while Mary Cassat described her painting.

Of course, H.O.H., as Louisine called her husband, had to purchase the painting. Even Degas was overcome: *"What style,"* he exclaimed, when he saw the shimmering blues and white of the young woman's peignoir. My wife adored Mary Cassatt's work but said archly to me, "Isn't $8,500 quite a lot of money, Chester, for a canvas?"

"Oh, dear, money's simply a piece of paper not a canvas," I proclaimed, "And in any case, it was $4,600, the other canvas was $8,500."

■ F. SCOTT FITZGERALD TO SARA AND GERALD MURPHY: We're gone—We're gone. We're gone. Gerald gone from France, the Villa America: we're here. Hollywood. *"The bowl is broken but it was golden."*

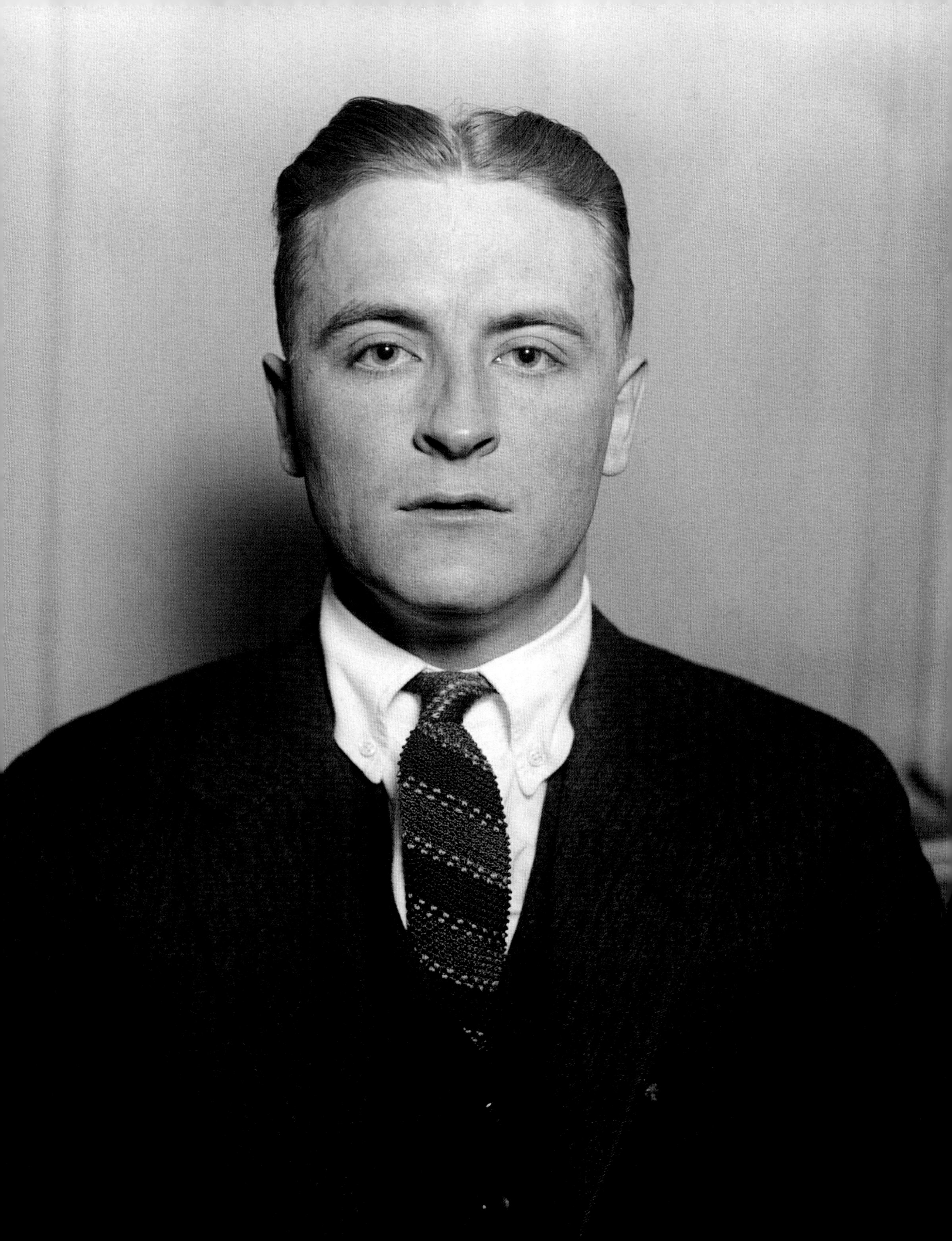

◆ TUVIAH GUTMAN GUTWIRTH, FISHER'S GRANDFATHER: We've come to—In Belz, and Belz existed in Marienbad as much as in Antwerp and will exist in Jerusalem, G-d willing, as much as in Poland—Blessed be the name of G-d, they used to tell about *Rabbi Samuel Shinyaver who came to Simha Bunam of Pshiske and introduced himself. Rabbi Bunam said: "If it is thy wish to be only a learned Jew, your coming was for naught; but if you wish to be a good Jew, it is well that you have come to me."*

Just as Simha Bunam had come to Shalom of Belz, my grandson has come to Jerusalem, come to the Western Wall.

May the Angelic teaching that Raphael taught him before he was born return to him now, and forever.

■ SHEILAH GRAHAM: Where art thou?—14th July 1937. When we met at Robert Benchley's, I asked Scott who he was. *"Five years have rolled away,"* said Scott looking down at his impossibly white shoes. *"And I can't decide who I am, if anyone."*

That is why I loved him. Lord Donegal knew exactly who he was. And what was worse, he would always remember who I had been—even if he made me his Lady.

But Scott, never was he so happy as while reading *Romeo and Juliet* aloud to me in bed—gently cuddled to my breast—brassiered, as always, mind you, so gargantuan my breasts seemed to my embarrassed self. And I disappearing into the bathroom only to find Scott hidden under the blankets.

"Romeo, Romeo where for art thou Romeo?" I would chirp, full-marks student I was, with a school girl's infatuation on the teacher.

It was ever so through the three years we rolled in the sheets of his prose. I once found a postcard he wrote to himself:

"Dear Scott—How are you? Have been meaning to come in and see you. I have [been] living at the Garden of Allah, yours, Scott Fitzgerald.

And one day too the postcard to her: *"Dear Zelda, I am deep in my novel, living in it, and it makes me happy."*

That very night Scott slept like the baby we never had, calling me darling. Calling me Zelda. Sara. Calling me Sheilah. But never my East End Jewish name, Lily Sheil, for I too was deep in my own novel, living in it, and it made me happy.

F. Scott Fitzgerald.

Who knew it would snow mightily in Jerusalem in the beginning of December?

Dosha bounded onto her marble divan and spoke.

"Raphael. Raphael. Where art thou? We've come to the Holy City. Our plane was delayed twelve hours. We arrived at nightfall. We walked all night through Jerusalem. You won't eat a thing. You're too fidgety to let me touch a bite of food. We've come to the Western Wall, which you call the Wailing Wall, which no one calls the Wailing Wall, not even Tal."

"He calls it the w-h-a-l-i-n-g Wall." Fisher, pursing his lips to underscore the pronunciation.

"Fisher, can't you be serious for a minute? At the Wall you disappear for two hours, and suddenly I find you lurking at the far end of the wall plaza. This is your trip. Your plan. Your scheme. Your dream. We're married."

■ RACHEL ZUCKER, American Poet: Snow—
    about this snow I'd say
little,
    less than necessary,
        it's so
readily available for metaphor or
    melting
which is not the same as transcendence or
    transformation, erosion—
we're not sure what it means…

■ PSALMS 137:5–6: Jerusalem—
*If I forget thee, O Jerusalem,
Let my right hand wither
Let my tongue cleave to the roof of
My mouth
If I cease to think of you
If I set not Jerusalem
Above my chief joy.*

■ THE KORAN: Jerusalem—
*Glory be to Him, who carried
His servant by night
From the Holy sanctuary (al-masjid alharan)
To the farther sanctuary (al-masjid al-aqsa)
Whose surroundings we have blessed,
that we might show him some
Of our signs,
He alone is the all-hearing, all-seeing.*

■ ABU BAKR MUHAMMAD BEN AHMAD AL WASITI: Jerusalem—Jerusalem and its merits—fada-'il al-quds.
    First, in the two directions of prayer,
    Second, of the two sanctuaries,
    Third, after the two places
    Of pilgrimage.

■ MELVILLE: Holy City—"*I am tormented with an everlasting itch for things remote. I love to sail forbidden seas and land on barbarous coasts.*"

Shall I never come to my own Holy City? A port where I might harbor forever?

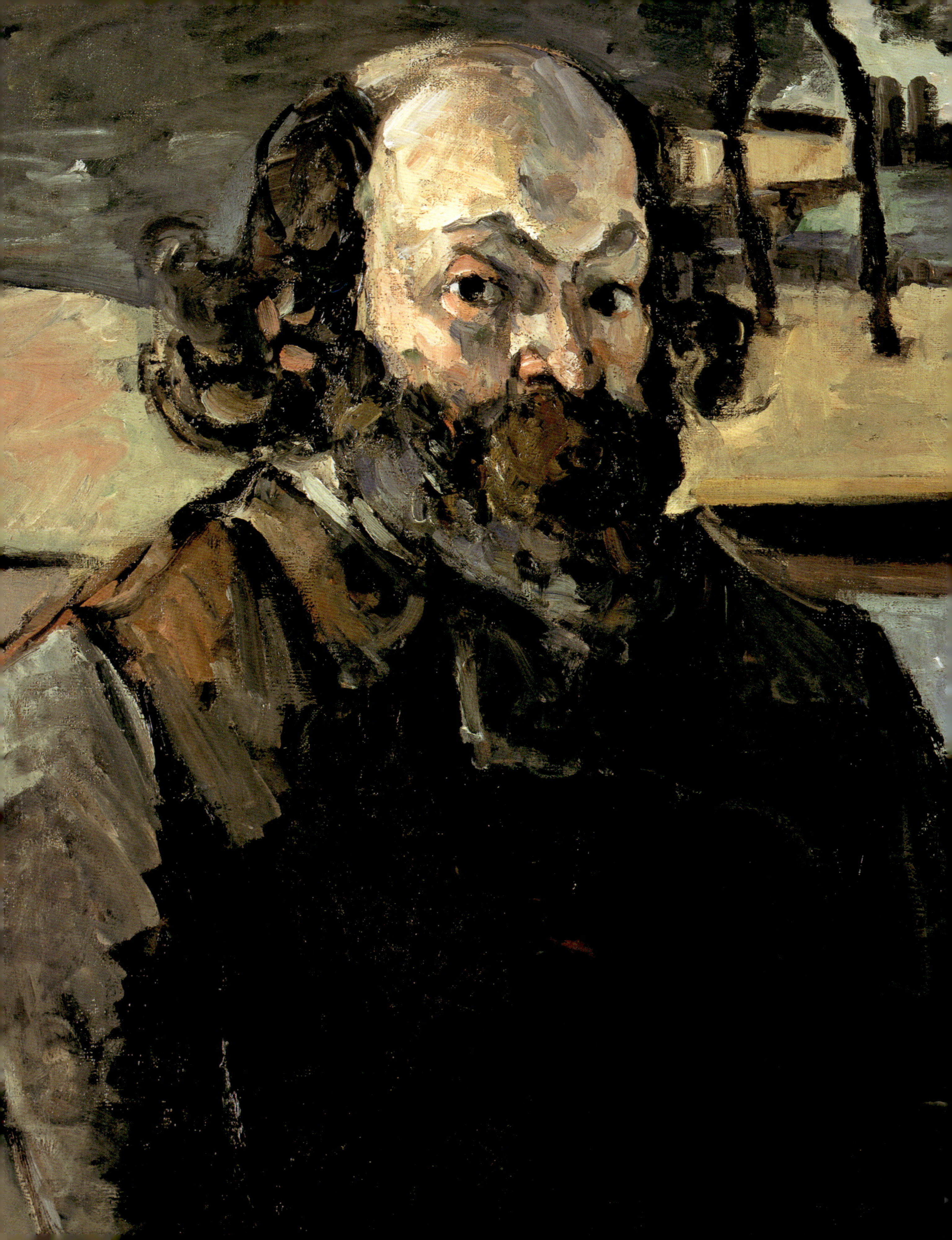

■ CÉZANNE: Married as much as your parents were married—Hortense would roar at me while I painted her: "Why can't we get married? Married, as much as your parents were married."

What did I care that she screamed, as long as she didn't move. Not a jot. I could barely catch her with my chalk. Before the torrent of words. What did I care about it all?

Father dared not change. And I couldn't change. And she wouldn't. They were two sides of a gold Napoleon—Monsieur Cézanne and my Madame Cézanne.

JAMES JOYCE: Married—Nora and I married? In London in '31, I wrote Miss Weaver "*In reading a book on the legal position of women, I find that under Scots law I am legally married, and my daughter-in-law tells me the same holds good in the United States. When I lived in Ireland, I always believed that marriage by habit and repute was recognized in the United Kingdom…If twenty-six years ago I did not want a clerk with a pen behind his ear or a priest in his nightshirt to interfere in my matrimonium I certainly do not want a score of journalists with pencils in their hands intruding where they are not wanted and as I am somewhat in the public eye, I wish I knew how to end the matter as quickly as possible.*"

Where's the hullabaloo? Why can't young Fisher and blushing Joshing Jerusha dally a quarter of a century until they wed?

◆ EMIL FISHER: Married, as much as your parents—My father knew I knew he wanted to marry me off but neither he nor my mother, Rickele, ever said a word. I was modern. Twenty-eight. In Paris. 1930. I told my father I was going to Antwerp to try to get a license to manufacture small light fixtures that shone under flat plastic holders "I will light all Paris," I told my father. He responded simply. "Rickele and I dream of a whiter light for you—one that will light the world. Would you agree to visit Gutman Gutwirth in Antwerp who has a wonderful daughter? She is…"

I interrupted my father, "Father, I will agree, but only this once, and never again. This is not Poland. I want to be married as much as your parents wanted to be married. But it is a new world."

I entered Reb Gutman's house, and all I saw was his daughter, radiant. She looked at me with eyes that smiled, I saw her lips moving as she sat next to me at the lunch table but I couldn't answer.

After Reb Gutman said the prayer over bread, his daughter waited for me to begin eating my soup. Only when my left hand touched the soup spoon did I start to hear and see clearly. "Marguerite," she laughed, and nodded, her hand, pointing to my hand and both she and her sister smiling followed me and began to eat. In Paris, it was different. There the woman started first. Something in the laugh, something at the table, the nine Gutwirth children, an equal match for my seven sisters and a brother, which lit even her mother's eyes. I knew then and there that I would be married, just as my parents were.

Married, thought Dosha, as much as your parents were married in Europe, with a wedding of hundreds dancing on the first floor of your mother's house. The Huppah in the street in front of the house. The honeymoon in Paris. And your parent's fifth floor walk-up apartment, which you never mentioned, but Tal did, to me. Why you keep the secrets you do, I don't understand, and why you tell me the things you do, I never will. Yet we are married with the same civil paper your parents were married with, and for that matter we're married, with the same paper my dear surrogate agnostic father, Richard né Reuben, and my atheist-Marxist-students-of-the-world-unite mother with her non-civil ceremony for seven years, her golden period, only to go Bougie and succumb to a civil ceremony certificate. So what if Mother's check bounced. They were married and we're most definitely married.

■ JAMES JESUS ANGLETON, head of counterintelligence: "Why you keep the secrets you do, I don't understand, and why you tell me things you do, I never will"—*In the C.I.A. I was known as the Gray Ghost, the Cadaver, the Fly, the Fisherman, Virginia Slim, the Orchid. Also as mother.*

I was ever a poet. But William Empson's ambiguity is at the center of the secret of poetry, and is not ambiguity the poetry of secrets? William told me as much when I invited him to Yale, "This year's friend might be next year's enemy, so that one limits even a friend's view of the real world to the short range. The enemy might be induced to act on false information and yet act in a way inimical to one's own interests, or reach a right conclusion from the wrong information…one might indeed become confused oneself. Further, there are ethical questions, profound ones in a democracy in which deception is considered wrong. And that which might be accepted as necessary in wartime would not be accepted in time of peace. But then, in a time of undeclared war, but war nonetheless, a cold war, a war of subversion, a war against terrorists what standards were to prevail?"

All the same, Fisher and Dosha—though that's not her name, why should she speak of her young lover's secrets?

What of her own?

He filled with Master Joyce's *silence, exile, cunning.*

But she too, and her very own name. In the Holy City, still keeping a secret. Just as I kept mine, and they gave me a statue not a mile from where Fisher and "Dosha" stand.

■ HORTENSE FIQUET: Married as much as your parents were—I muttered quietly under my breath. After Paul had asked me—after I had sat for an hour and a half, perhaps it was two, just "une petite blague", he so trying to please "mon chou chou"—what would you like?

"Like?" I mumbled. "I'd like to be married as much as your parents were married". And of course Paul started to scream: "Again! Again! The talk of marriage! We are married as much as my parents were married when I was born. When I was four. At five, I heard a snicker from Monsieur Le Temple on the rue Saint Jacques that my parents were now Monsieur and Madame and I asked Maman what Monsieur le Temple meant." And Paul kept screaming. I had heard it before…

"Father didn't marry until he was forty-six." And wasn't our young Paul worth a hundred notarial marriage contracts.

And on and on—all because my heart can't mutter an ache.

Paul Cézanne, *Self-Portrait.*

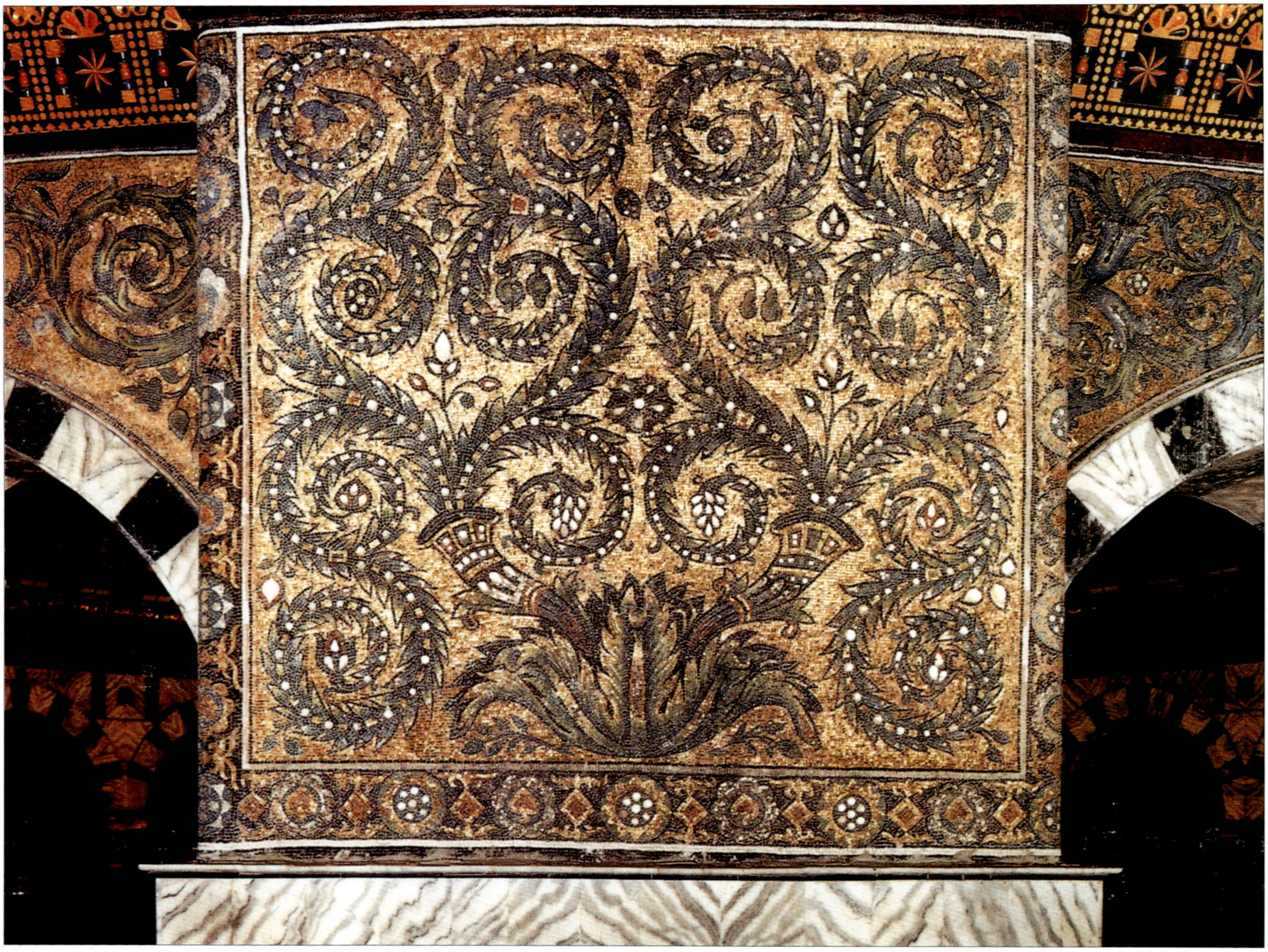

◆ TUVIAH GUTMAN GUTWIRTH, FISHER'S GRANDFATHER: We have to find a Rabbi—I sat in my chair in Havana. The War was drawing to a close. All the Yeshivot I had studied in—Riglitz, Tarnov, Cracow, Belz, even Belz, all were ashes. All my Rabbonin, where were they? If one Rabbi had survived, he was in Shanghai, perhaps in Cuba like me or in Lorenzo Marques where I had come from.

Mr. Gutwein came to my house, and he walked me to my library study and lifted the Talmud Berachot off the shelf. He said softly, "Where the Blessed Be He opens the page, we will read." He opened my tattered volume of Talmud, Berakhot to page 20a.

I couldn't open my mouth, but he read with the same voice when we had studied together in the Mahazikei Hadas each morning before the War:

"Rabbi Pape said to Abaye "What is the difference between us and the ancients? For them, miracles were done, and for us, no miracles are done. If it is on account of learning, in the years of Rav Judah they studied only Neziqin, and we study all six orders of the Mishnah, and when Rav Judah reached a certain passage, he was perplexed by it, while we cannot understand that same passage. But he could produce rain, and we cannot."

A voice within me rose to my throat. A voice of my teacher, my blessed father-in-law, Reb Abish Rheinhold, a voice of a boy of seven studying with his father in Riglitz. A voice that needed no text page. My eyes were rested on Reb Gutwein's and we both said aloud:

"Abaye replied to him, "The ancients gave their lives for the sanctification of G-d's name, but we do not do so.""

Reb Gutwein put his hand on mine. I don't know if he spoke, or I spoke, or a Bat Kol spoke for us but the words emerged "We must find a Rabbi."

"Married," said Dosha, "not with a 'a canvas' but with a New York City paper certificate."

"You don't need paper," said Fisher. "You need parchment. We have to find a Rabbi and I don't have the foggiest idea where to look. I explained all this to you. It's not so simple, especially with your Gypsy situation."

Fisher looked up pensively at the Jerusalem walls in the distance, the mosque of Omar covered entirely in snow.

Fisher continued to mumble, "Honey, where will I find a Rabbi?"

"Here I am." A figure dressed in a peculiar black suit beyond rumpledness moved towards them in a haze of tobacco smoke, although he didn't seem to be smoking and, in a lilting voice with a thick Viennese accent said, "Ready, villing, and able: a Rabbi."

■ CÉZANNE Certificate paper—Hortense never stopped. Even for an instant. Remarkable really. Never to have any other plan. Scheme. Hope. Desire.

Only marriage, the notarial certificate paper. Man and wife, just like Maman and Papa. I was offering far more than any diamond from rue des Petites Écuries, more than any pearl ring from rue Buffault in La belle Paris.

I was giving more than myself every day. Every month. Years of placing myself at her feet.

I was offering myself to her on a canvas. Caressing the planes of her cheeks with my brush, mixing my blood with hers, forever. But she would not accept me, or my offering, or my soul. She was a peasant. She would not budge.

■ TALMUD KIDDUSHIN 33: Rabbi—*An aged Rabbi who through no fault of his own forgets his learning shall be deemed as holy as the Ark.*

■ OLEG GRABAR, scholar of Islamic art: Mosque of Omar—"*The visual message of this initial program [of the Mosque of Omar] is quite clear to create on a gold background a seemingly continuous band of brilliantly lit green scrolls out of which sixteen colorful constructions culminate in the wings associated with royalty in the Iranian tradition surrounding a beautiful tiara, without apparent cultural identification and a variant of a lotus shape. The requirement that the mosaics in the lower drum be perceived as an unbroken entity is further demonstrated by the care taken to hide or, at the very least, to down play the separation between individual units of composition. Visible from everywhere but never seen all at once, the mosaics of the lower drum were intended to look the same from any vantage point, without a dominating movement or place, or in a single focus.*"

Fisher is seeing the Mosque of Omar covered entirely in snow, a white blanket on a green bed. Visible from everywhere, but never seen all at once, neither by Muslim nor Jew nor Christian.

Inside the buildings and outside. From the ground and, indeed, from above Jerusalem. An unbroken entity. Forever.

■ HORTENSE FIQUET: You don't need paper—"You don't need paper," Paul would roar at me. "You don't need marriage!" he would continue screaming. "You don't need a ring. Or a diamond or a pearl or a slice of a buttery gold ring. All you need is..." and suddenly he stopped badgering me and fell silent.

I looked at him and was silent though I wanted to scream myself, to shout, to talk, at the very least to whisper. I knew exactly what he would say for he said it each day for months, for years on end. He would pose my question and he would voice my answer, like the marionette at Le Petit theâtre that maman would take me to each Saturday.

Monsieur La Porte, holding all the marionette figures, making them bow, dance, kiss, collapse, die, jump up again.

Quite comical, Paul was and finally he whispered, all you need to do is be still...don't move. And of course, I hadn't moved, even a centimeter. Never in all the years of posing. And living. And listening to him. Never. I wouldn't budge. And my Paul knew it.

Mosaic column in the Dome of the Rock.

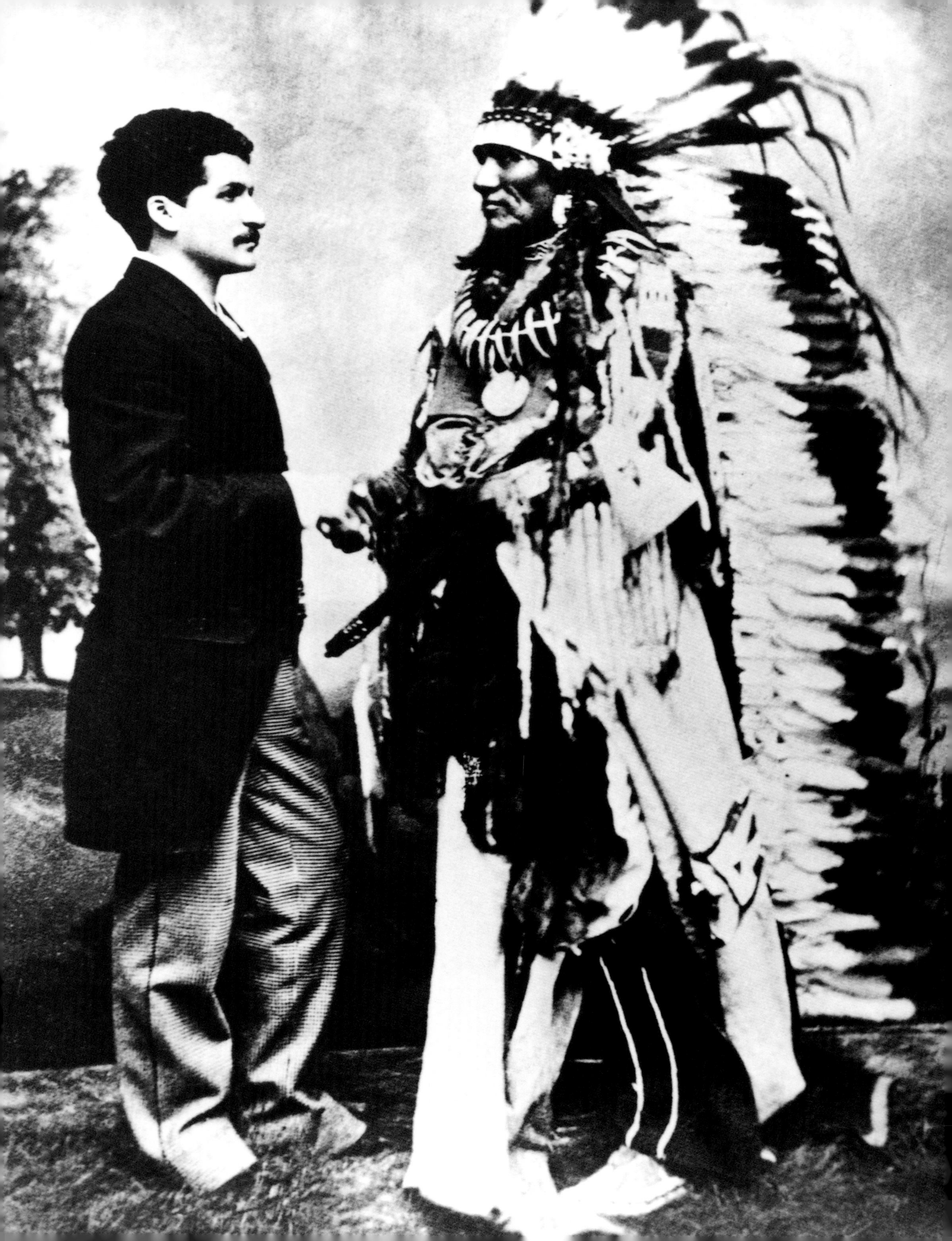

◆ ARYEH LEIB BEN JACOB HA KOHEN, FISHER'S ANCESTOR: Who are you?—My father, my friend, my blessed memory, would look at me and cup my face in his hands and whisper to me: Who are you?

Then he would answer his own question with a quotation from Proverbs 27:18.

Whoso keepeth the fig tree shall eat the fruit thereof; and he that waiteth on his Master shall be honored.

He would speak of the fig tree of his Jerusalem youth. How his father would place a fig shoot into the rocky ground behind their house in Jerusalem, how the figs would ripen.

I could not believe it—for where could I find a fig tree in Ofen? But Father would smile and in his eyes I could see him rising at dawn, for if he did not rise at dawn, birds would come and feast on the figs. Who was the master of these fig trees? Surely our Heavenly Father, *and he that waited on his Master shall be honored*, Father would whisper.

And gladly did I return to the Holy Land to taste the blessing of my father's figs.

■ JULIUS MEYER, DOSHA'S GREAT-GRANDFATHER'S BROTHER: Who are you?—"And who are you," Chief Standing Bear would ask me. "Are you me? A teacher of my brothers about shells from the coastal Indians, of Osage orangewood. Are you a *Teycha*, a friend, as we Caddos call our friends? Are you a burner of forests or a planter of trees? Are you an eater of dog at our festival time?"

I answered Chief Standing Bear, the greatest of all the Pawnee, beginning at the end For to all the Caddo tribes one begins at the end, since all on earth is a circle. "I do not eat dog for I am a child of Israel, and my tribe is a planter of trees. *If you study Torah, our holy book, you are joined to the Tree of Life. If you do not study Torah, you are joined to the Tree of Death.* And whosoever burns a forest, even a single tree, burns a part of my people's heart: our Torah. I am your Teycha, for did you not save my life, Chief Standing Bear. My people are traders as you are. As we both come from across the seas, perhaps in the beginning we were one tribe."

Chief Standing Bear reached behind him, and just as my friend Herman the Great, the magician, would delight the Pawnee by extracting gold coins from an empty top hat, so too Chief Standing Bear handed me an egg.

"Take this: Box-Ka-Re-Sha-Hash-Ta-Ka, Curly-headed White Chief who speaks with one tongue."

I took the egg and I took the name and I took the friendship and I took Chief Standing Bear to Paris in 1889.

Because we were so different, we were alike.

Fisher stared at the intruder. He asked, "Who are you? Have you been listening to our conversation? What are you, a peeping Tom? You know Mister, we're on our honeymoon."

The portly figure in black picked up a guitar case and wearily started to walk away. With genuine confusion and disappointment, he looked at Dosha and Fisher and muttered, "If you're on your honeymoon, why do you have to find a Rabbi?" He stared directly at Fisher.

Fisher had never seen such eyes before. He could not discern their true color by moonlight, but could feel their unwavering intensity. His arm tightened around Dosha.

■ MARCEL PROUST: Have you been listening to our conversations?—"Who are you?" asked the nineteen year old Marcel Plantevignes in 1908. Marcel visited my room each day to hear me read my work in progress:

Ask that young woman who teases me about…about…

I didn't complete my sentence. The younger Marcel, the one who was nineteen, replied astonished, "Have you been listening to our conversation?"

I didn't nod, but I simply continued reading from *Remembrance of Things Past*. For who was I, or he, or any of us but all the people who have conversed, conversed with our lips, with our hands, with our eyes. All our senses are but one.

Conversations heard or not heard. "What difference? Marcel told me of a pretentious lady asking Madame Leroi: "What are your views on love?" And Madame Leroi responding: "Love? I make it constantly but I never talk about it."

"*One no longer considers oneself to be more than the trustee, who can vanish at any moment, of intellectual secrets, which will vanish too, and one would like to check the inertia that proceeds from one's previous lethargy by obeying the beautiful commandment in St. John: 'Work while ye have light.'*"

"*Thus the empty spaces of my memory were covered by degrees with names which, in arranging, composed themselves in relation to one another, in linking themselves to one another by increasingly numerous connections, resembling those finished works of art in which there is not one touch that is isolated, in which every part in turn receives from the rest a justification which it confers on them in turn.*"

Marcel reading to Marcel of conversations eternal, spoken before the birth of one and after the death of the other.

■ ANNA L. WALTERS, PAWNEE: Change—"*Everything changes, and yet nothing changes but the holder of life. In the Great Mystery, it is unending. Grandma and Grandpa would say this is the way of the Great Mystery. It knows no time.*"

Julius Meyer with Chief Standing Bear.

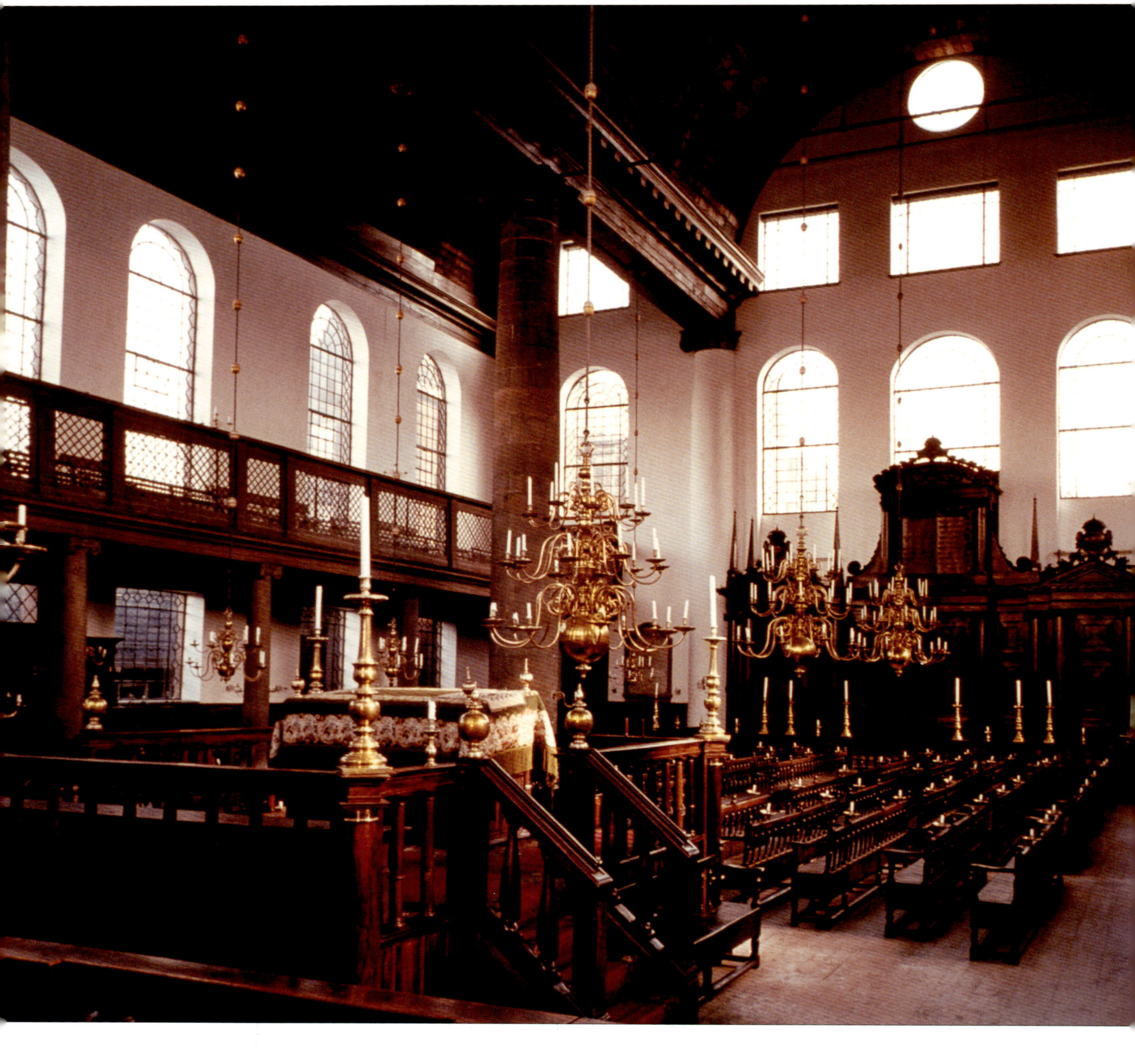

◆ RICKELE PADAWER, Dosha's grandmother How do we know this man is a Rabbi?—And how do we know the man with my Jerusha is a bridegroom, a *Hasson*? Because this young man is being told by his bride, his *Kallah*, my granddaughter, that they know they want to be married.

In Europe, it was the parents. And not even the parents. It was the *shadchen*, a matchmaker, who would come to a father and say, "Your Rivke, do I know someone for her." The father would then say, "I know you're thinking of Itzik. I don't need a matchmaker to tell me about a boy who lives five houses away from me. I'll ask my wife." Then the father would ask his wife and she would say, "What do we know of Itzik's family? They *daven* in a different synagogue." The father would say to the matchmaker, "What do we know of Itzik's family?" The matchmaker would answer, "That's why G-d created me a matchmaker, to answer. Do your shop customers tell you how to make the sides of their outsoles fit exactly to the welt of the shoe they're ordering? Do they talk of how tight you should make the heel grip?

"Enough already," the cobbler father would protest. "I leave it to you." The matchmaker exclaimed, "*Az a yid ken nit vern keyn shuster, troymter fun vern a professor* [when a Jew can't be a cobbler, he dreams of becoming a professor]." And the matchmaker did his job. Thank G-d, everything fit. But Europe was not only my home *Barnowicze* outside of Slonim. It was also Slonim. And not only Slonim but Pinsk. And Moscow, St. Petersberg. Even New York.

Not every marriage was a *shiddukh*. Even though for all the talk of love and the American so-called "Mr. Perfect" that I always heard of in Brooklyn, personally I'd rather trust in Reb. Weinstein's eyes and judgment. That *shadchen*, with G-d's help, missed nothing. Every groschen of his five percent of the dowry was worth it. *Got zitst oybn un port untn*, G-d sits on high and makes matches below. As for New York or anywhere, how do we know this guy is a Rabbi? It's a smart question. And the answer is simple. The Rabbi is my granddaughter. Didn't my Jerusha say, "We know we want to get married?"

She decided. Believe me, they're both the better for it. Not just because she's my granddaughter. They are young. They talk of love. They are in Jerusalem. *Nd'an kenen eltern gebn, ober nit keyn mazl* (parents can provide a dowry but not good luck). May the Lord bless them always.

■ LAURENCE STERNE: Do we know this?—Do we know this? My Uncle Toby knows that I know how we know that we know this. Alas, space does not permit me to share my knowledge, and time, ah, time, time is so sadly lacking for us to share the tale of our knowledge.

"We are looking for a Rabbi because we know we want to be married," said Dosha simply.

"Wait a minute, how do we know this guy is a Rabbi?" shouted Fisher.

"Well, honey, at five-thirty in the morning on a street in Jerusalem, facing the city walls, if it looks like a Rabbi and it talks like a Rabbi and it claims to be a Rabbi, it's good enough for me. And in any case, pet, where I come from, the wife's family makes all the arrangements," Dosha added brightly, without skipping a beat.

"Sir, we'd like to hire you as our Rabbi. What will the charges be? How much money dear Rabbi" said Dosha, smiling as sweetly as she could at Fisher and not at the guitar-toting, ever-moving, bobbing apparition in front of them.

"On the house, my dearest dearest friends," said the figure in black, before the words were even out of Dosha's mouth.

◆ SIMHA PADAWER, DOSHA'S GRANDFATHER: Rabbi—The *Tosefta* (Eduyos 3:4) tells us: "*The designation of a Rabbi is greater than that of Rav; the title of Rabban is greater than that of Rabbi; he who is known by his name alone is greater than Rabban.*"

For Rabbi comes from Rav, Biblical Hebrew for great. The title Rabbi does not occur in the Bible. And not in the early days of the Babylonian sages who were called Rav. For only in Eretz Israel could one get Semikhah, Rabbinical ordination.

Even later in Europe a Rabbi was originally an expounder of the law and earned his living elsewhere. In the Europe I knew, a Rabbi was a Rabbi. But my granddaughter Jerusha, though they call her Dosha, is she not the Rabbi?

Is she not the one who has decided that they want to be married? Is she not the one who has led them to Jerusalem? May the city be a blessing to them. My Jerusha, their Dosha. Said Dosa, first century Rabbi who saw the Second Temple and survived its destruction "*Morning sleep, midday wine, children's talk, and sitting in the assemblies of the ignorant, put a person out of the world.*"

My Jerusha, their Dosha, their Dosha's Fisher's Rabbi Dosha.

■ MARCEL PROUST: How do we know?—We know because we have seen. We have seen so long ago that we have forgotten. In the quietness of our rooms we begin to remember. We write. The words on the rolled-up pages bring back to us what we never have forgotten. How can I forget what I have known?

"I suddenly felt underneath me those twenty-three years, one going down from the other, deeper and deeper into invisibility and all that was still myself, lived by me, what I was seeing at a distance of twenty-three years, it was still myself twenty-three years away from me, and I felt almost fearful of not having the strength to stay for long at such a height of life already used, which I always had to keep under me, always tied to me, me with the feeling of my continuity into this immense depth, already of twenty-three years, a whole continuity, a lived and living thing, going down into darkness."

Even in the darkness we remember, we know.

■ RABBI NACHMAN: Money—My teacher, my Master Nachman lowered his eyes on mine. I always sat directly in front of his chair—listening, memorizing but in fact, each word was engraved on my heart. He continued.

Meanwhile, the giant saw that another wind had come. He was angry with it and said, "Why are you late? Did I not summon all the winds? Why didn't you come with them?" The wind answered, "I was delayed because I had to carry the daughter of a king to a golden mountain on which stands a castle of pearl."

The chamberlain was filled with joy. The giant asked the wind, "What precious things are in that place?"

The wind answered, "Everything there is precious."

Then the giant said to the chamberlain, "You have been searching for so long, and you have undergone many tribulations. Perhaps lack of money is troubling you. I shall give you a vessel when you put your hand into it, you will take out money." And he ordered the wind to take the chamberlain to the mountain of gold.

The Sephardi Synagogue of Amsterdam.

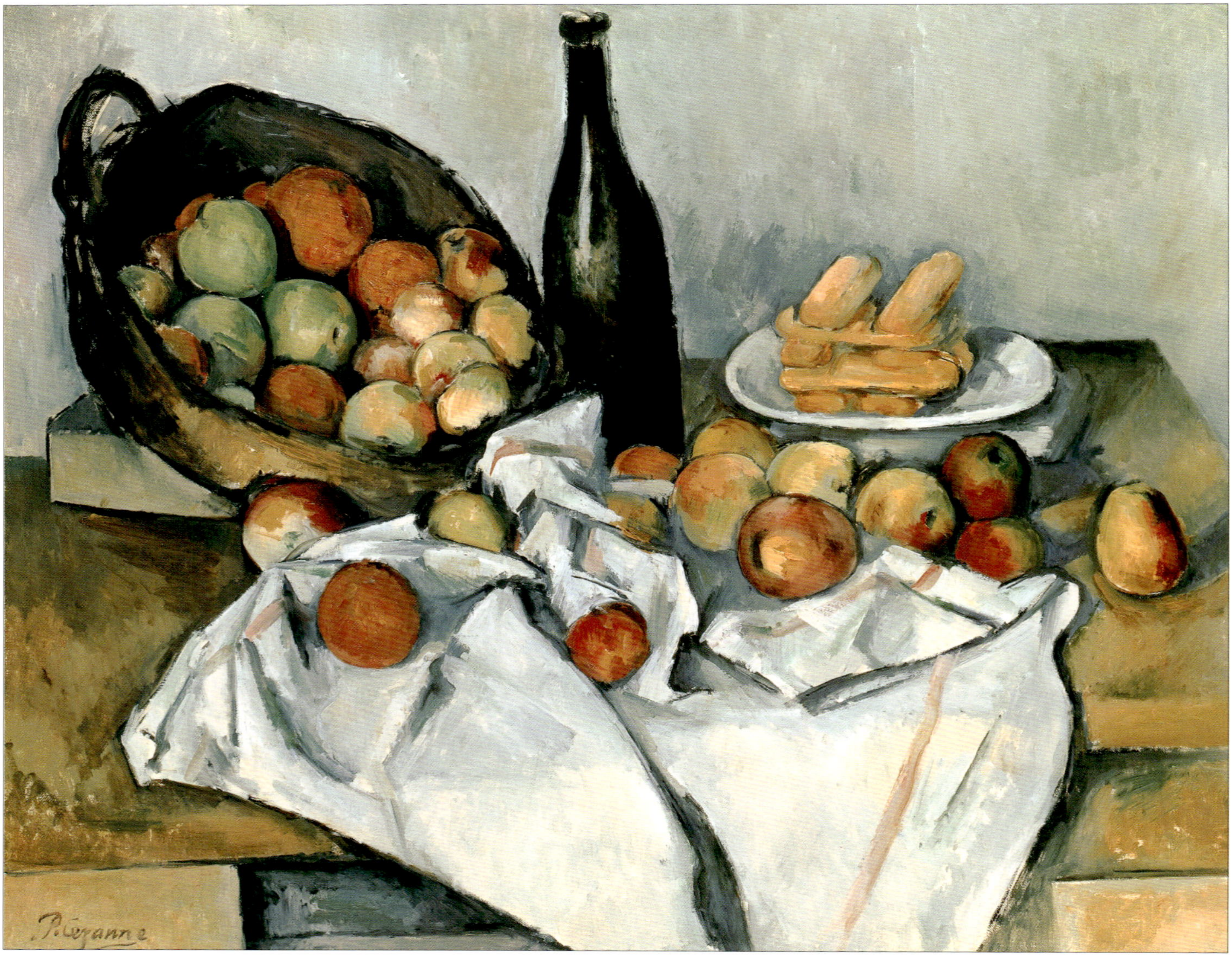
P. Cezanne

■ CÉZANNE: I think I saw—Vollard would ask me: "Do you paint what I see or do I paint what I think." I would answer: How do you wish me to answer, Ambrose?

"The truth, simply! The truth, Monsieur Paul." Of course I knew the truth was the truth that Vollard wished to tell all at my exhibition—enfin my solo exhibition in '95.

Therefore I said, "Monsieur Vollard, do me the favor of coming to my studio, and you will be my journaliste." He came and watched and returned. For a fortnight, even when it rained for three days straight, he didn't make a peep.

At the end of my private exhibition, I stared at him and said: "Now you have the answer." But Vollard was a donkey, and he, repeated, "Monsieur Paul, do you paint what you see or what you think?" "Neither."

I would not answer further. Certainly not for him. Or his audience, as he called La Publique. I simply waved my hat at the painting, as though it were the answer and Vollard retreated meekly from my studio and never again pestered me with school boy questions. Why should I tell him I painted what I think I saw.

■ CONSTANZE MOZART: The figure in front of her—He trembled before the apparition at the door. Why, why, Wolfgangerl, must it be an omen of doom? I pleaded with the father of our newborn—Franz Xavier Wolfgang. No, no, he wept throughout the night—The messenger asks me to write my own requiem. I held Wolfgangerl's hand on my breast, and indeed it stoked my body with a devilish flame.

I called to my precious one in my tears. Maybe the commission is proof of G-d's mercy. Did you not say to Abbé Joseph Bullinger before your saintly mother's death that "*You prayed to God for two things only—a happy death for her, and strength and courage for yourself—and G-d in His Goodness heard your prayer and gave you those two blessings in the richest measure.*"

But Wolfgangerl could not hear my voice weeping in the wilderness. And Fisher and this young woman. And the figure in front of her. Grey as night. It chills me. May all the saints of Jerusalem give her the strength to calm her beloved's fears. May theirs be a wedding of great jubilation filled with throngs of merrymakers. Not, heaven forbid, a solitary wintery funeral, a pauper's end, one witness, no cross to mark Wolfgangerl's passage. May the Archangel Himself protect this couple from my Wolfgangerl's dirge.

"What! This guy's no Rabbi," protested Fisher. "I think I saw him at the Wall before. Let's get out of here. This is too weird."

Dosha tightened her hand around Fisher's arm. Staring directly at the figure in front of her, she said, with absolute eveness, "Where would the ceremony take place, Rabbi?"

"HaKol Talui Be Mazal. Everything depends on luck." Suddenly Fisher felt faint. Tal's phrase, the phrase Tal repeated over and over again. Diurnal Dew.

And with the weakness of the day, not having eaten and all the walking. Fisher heard himself mumbling, "Don't we need witnesses?"

"Who's the Rabbi? Me or you?" came the cheerful response from the rumpled figure. "We can go into the Mishkenot Ra'ananim."

■ AMBROSE VOLLARD, Parisian art dealer: Staring…directly in front of him—"*No sooner was the cloth draped on the table with innate taste that Cézanne set out the peaches in such a way as to make the complementary colors vibrate, grays next to reds, yellows to blues, leaning, tilting, balancing the fruit at the angles he wanted, sometimes pushing a one-sou or two-sou piece under them. You could see from the care he took how much it delighted his eye.*"

Cézanne answered my question by letting me watch him paint, always standing…directly in front of him for hours. He neither painted what he saw nor what he thought. Cézanne painted what he dreamt. As soon as he set up his table in the morning, Les jeux étaient faits. Even Cézanne never understood that.

■ JEPTIMUS, A JERUSALEMITE (c. 340 C.E.): Jerusalem—At the Wall, I wrote this inscription one word at a time, at monthly intervals between each letter. Only by the light of a Jerusalem moon. Death by stoning if caught.

"*You shall see this and your heart shall rejoice, your limbs shall flourish like grass.*"

In the time of Julian there were plans to restore the Temple. Then Julian was assassinated and the further Christianization of Jerusalem continued.

■ MOZART: Faint at the figure in front of her—Constanze and I have two yearlings. Karl and Franz Xavier Wolfgang. We are blessed. We have little but we have everything. Suddenly he comes to the door. Tall. Impossibly thin. Wearing clothes the color of nightfall. A gray not of this world.

Constanze herself, my two blessings in her arms, answered the treble knock. I peered at the figure in front of her. He has left an unsigned note commissioning a Requiem—whose? Whose? I turn it over again and again in my mind. Who is this figure?

"*My head is confused. I can think only with difficulty, and cannot free my mind of the image of the unknown. I constantly see him before me; he pleads with me, presses me, and impatiently demands the work from me. I am continuing with it because the composing is less tiring than doing nothing. Besides, I have nothing more to fear. I can feel from my present state that the hour is striking. I am on the point of expiring. My end has come before I was able to profit by my talent. And yet life has been so beautiful; my career began under such fortunate auspices. But no one can change his fate. No one can count his days; one must resign oneself. What Providence determines will be done. I close now. Before me lies my swan song. I must not leave it incomplete.*"

I fear for Fisher. I tremble before the figure. Before him.

Paul Cézanne, *The Basket of Apples.*

183

שוש אשיש בי״י תגל נפשי באלדי כי הלבישני בגדי ישע מעיל צדקה יעטני

בסימנא טבא ובמזלא מעליא

למנצח על שושנים לבני קרח משכיל שיר ידידות

קול ששון · וקול שמחה
קול חתן · וקול כלה

בששי בשבת ארבעה עשר יום לחדש אב שנת חמשת אלפים וחמש מאות
וששים ואחת לבריאת העולם למנין שאנחנו מנין בו פה מודונא מתא
דיתבא על נהרי סיקייא ופאנארא ומי מעינות בא הבחור היקר והנכבד
כמר אברהם נחמן יצ״ו בן המנוח כמה״ר בנימין רפאל חזק זצ״ל ואמר לה
להדא בתולתא כבודה וצנועה מרת סטי״לא מבת בת כמהר שמשון חיים
פראנקיטי יצ״ו הוי לי לאנתו כדת משה וישראל ואנא בסייעתא דשמיא
אפלח ואוקיר ואיזון ואפרנס ואכסין ית נשייהון בקושטא וחזיבנא ליכי מהר
בתוליכי כסף זוזי מאתן דחזי ליכי ומזוני וכסותי וספוקיכי ומיעל לותיכי
כאורח כל ארעא וצביאת הבחורה מרת סטיל״א בתולתא דא והות ליה
לאנתו לכמר אברהם נחמן יצ״ו חתן דנן גדוניא דהנעלת ליה מבי אבוה
עשרין לטרין של כסף צרוף וצבי כמר אברהם נחמן יצ״ו חתן דנן ואוסיף לה
מממוניה עשרין לטרין של כסף צרוף נמצא סכום כתובתא דא בין נדוניא
ותוספא ארבעין לטרין של כסף צרוף בר ממאתן זוזי דחזו לה וכך אמר
לנא כמר אברהם נחמן יצ״ו חתן דנן אחריות וחומר כתובתא דא נדוניא
ותוספא קבלית עלי ועל ירתואי בתראי להתפרעא מן כל שפר ארג נפשי
וקנינין דאית לי תחות כל שמיא דקנאי ודעתיד אנא למקני נכסין דאית
להון אחריות ואגבן דלית להון אחריות דכולהון יהון אחראין וער באין
למפרע מנהון שטר כתובתא דא נדוניא ותוספא ואפילו מן גלימא דעל
כתפאי בחיי ובמותא מן יומא דנן ולעל״ם ואחריות וחומר כתובתא דא
נדוניא ותוספא קבל עליו כמר אברהם נחמן יצ״ו חתן דנן כאחריות וחומר
כל שטרי כתובות דנהיגין בבנות ישראל הבתולות הצנועות והכשרו״ת
העשויין ככל תיקוני חז״ל דלא באסמכתא ודלא כטופסי דשטרי וקנינא
אנן סהדי דחתימי לתתא מן כמר אברהם נחמן יצ״ו חתן דנן לזכות הבחורה
הכבודה מרת סטיל״א דא מברנ על כל מאי דכתיב ומפרש לעיל
במנא דכשר למקניא ביה והכל שריר · וברי״י · וקיים

שלמה יהודה בן כמהר״ר אריה סיניגאליא עד

יהי מקורך ברוך
ושמח מאשת נעוריך

● RABBI MOSES HAYYIM LUZZATTO, ANCESTOR OF SIMHA PADAWER: Fisher could feel himself being borne along— Fisher and his companion have spent a day and a night in Jerusalem. *"The entire day is also divided into four portions the morning and afternoon, and the two equal parts of the night. Each of these requires an appropriate transmission of G-dly illuminations in all of the universes for the true concept of the particular time of day.*

"Since morning is the time when G-d's sustenance is required for the day as a whole, it has a longer and more inclusive service of prayer (shacharit)."

Fisher is at the Western Wall at the end of his wanderings as I was from Padua, from Venice, from Amsterdam.

"In the afternoon, on the other hand, only the latter part of the day must be perfected and therefore a lesser effort is required."

And well for him, for weary he was as he wandered through Jerusalem's streets, his ears nodding Amen to what his eyes were saying.

"The evening service (Maariv) is longer than that of the afternoon. It also contains the Shema and its blessing, but since the substance of the morning service is still retained, the blessings are much shorter."

And has not the Holy One—blessed be He—provided a Rav for Fisher? All he need do is say Amen with all his heart. For those who are truly lost, one step alone brings one closer to redemption.

And now the latter part of the night: *"No universal service was ordained for the latter part of the night, since this would overburden the community. However, a midnight service (tikkun chatzot) does exist, designated for the especially devout, who rise and cry out to G-d, each according to his own understanding."*

Is not this man Fisher being led by his *Maggid* as I was by mine? Fisher can feel himself being borne along into the simplest and most elegant of structures.

Praise G-d, Jerusha guides him through his night. *"For I shall give you this land as an inheritance, Jerusha, forever."*

And Fisher felt himself being borne along into the simplest and most elegant of structures. A glorified dormitory complex, nineteenth century in style with crenellated parapets matching the facing Jerusalem walls.

"Right in here, my friends..." Fisher heard the Rabbi mumble. "They can be witnesses."

Suddenly two young Israelis stood with Dosha on a patio, directly looking onto a snow covered city in the distance. They were tapping their fingers as the Rabbi, who had taken his guitar out of his case, started humming a melody Fisher had heard somewhere before.

Suddenly, stopping singing but always strumming, the Rabbi asked the two bus boy-Israelis for a piece of paper "big as you have" snapping his fingers.

Fisher protested. "Paper? For what?"

The Rabbi answered: "The ketubbah."

■ JUDAH TOURO (1775-1854): The simplest and most elegant of structures— Personally, Sir Montifiore could have spared the crenellated roofs. The windmill was fine. I had wanted the simplest and most elegant of structures. For the poor, the simplest must needs be the most elegant. And for the wealthy too, for that matter.

How did I become wealthy? Simple. As I told Rabbi Isaac Lesser, *"I saved a fortune by strict economy, while others had spent one by their expenditures."*

How did these young Americans arrive in the Holy Land? Certainly not through their own resources. Probably through some childless bachelor like myself. Touching, really, though I would never permit myself to show my feelings to the world.

Ketubah, Modena, Italy, 1801.

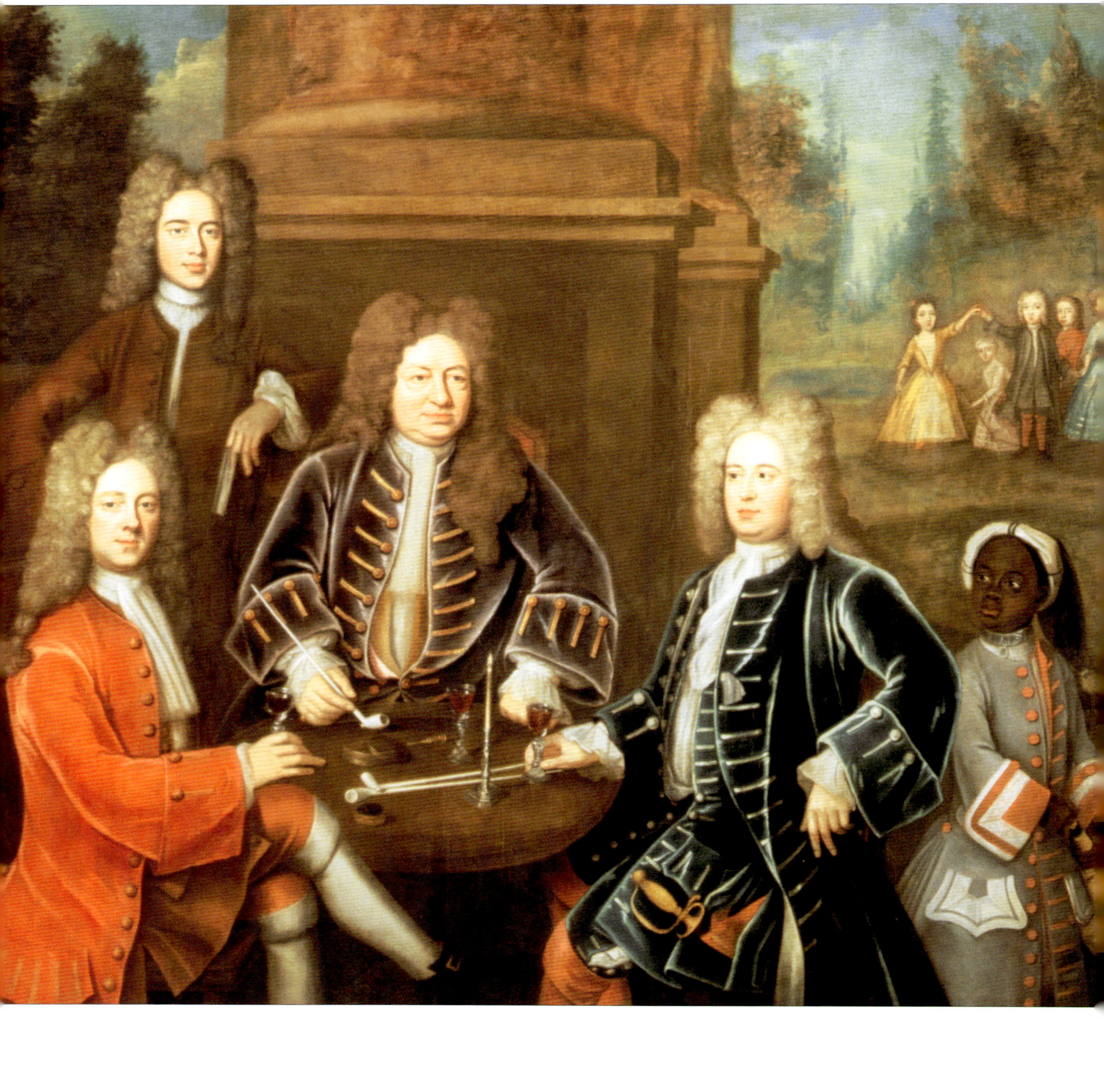

● Isaac. Tal, Abraham Tal's father: More from what he remembered in Tal's room—For weeks my son Abraham pestered me to bring him to Reb Amiel's house so he could ask if it were permissible to marry a woman with the same name as his mother, Rachel. Of course as soon as we were ushered into the Rabbi's study, Abraham could not bring himself to say Rachel's name, not even a complete sentence. All my son could do is look around Reb Amiel's room. I asked the question, and my Rabbi, without a trace of a smile, answered, "We shall find a way. The Talmud is a book of life…Perhaps a second name. Don't worry, my son."

Still Abraham said nothing. So I left them alone for more than an hour and sat outside the room. If they talked at all, I could not hear a word.

Abraham said nothing. Nothing at all, and nothing even to my wife, Rachel. Suddenly one day on 47th Street, after the War, Abraham said: "From Rabbi Amiel's room I learned everything."

How well I remember how he stacked his books on the chair behind him. *The Path of the Upright*, Moses Hayyim Luzzatto's *Mesillat Yesharim*, resting on top of *The Ways of Reason* (*Derech Tevunot*) and both balanced firmly on top of *Migdal Oz*, *The Tower of Strength*.

"The apple does not fall far from the tree," my Rachel would always say. "Of course this Fisher will learn more from what he remembers in Tal's room than from what he learned in his studies during his university years."

Fisher answered, more from what he remembered in Tal's room than anything he could call up from any course at Yale during all those years of auditing. "Paper? A marriage contract must be on parchment! Dosha, it must be on parchment!" exclaimed Fisher.

"Not in Jerusalem," said the Rabbi shyly. "Here it's paper."

Dosha brightened and said softly, "The Rabbi's right. The rules here are different."

"But we're not from here," protested Fisher.

The Rabbi interrupted while he was writing a long, long text to whisper to Dosha, "What's your name?"

"Jerusha bat Reuven." She said it before the name emerged from the Rabbi's lips.

■ Walter Camp, Yale Athletic Director: Yale—"It has been stated that the reason for Yale's triumphs lies in the fact that the institution is not situated in or near a large city. Probably the attraction offered by the social life, and the temptation of the pleasures of metropolitan life, are such as to take away some of the men who would otherwise prove acceptable candidates for athletic organizations."

■ Ralph Boas, a Dutch traveler who described Harvard College in 1680: Harvard—"Cambridge… is not a large village and the houses stand very much apart. The Harvard college building is the most conspicuous among them. We went to it, expecting to see something unusual, as it is the only college, or would-be Academy of the Protestants in all America, but we found ourselves mistaken. In approaching the house we neither heard nor saw anything mentionable; but going to the other side of the building we heard noise enough in an upper room to lead my comrade to say, 'I believe they are engaged in disputation.' We entered and went upstairs…we found there eight or ten young fellows sitting around, smoking tobacco with the smoke of which the room was so full, that you could hardly see; and the whole house smelt so strong of it that when I was going upstairs, I said, 'It must certainly be also a tavern.' We excused ourselves, that we could speak English only a little…However, we spoke as well as we could. We inquired how many professors there were, and they replied not one, that there was not enough money to support one. We asked how many students there were. They said at first thirty, and then they came down to twenty, I afterwards understood there are probably not ten."

Actually there were thirty, of whom about half, including Cotton Mather, were students."

■ Cotton Mather: Yale—"As I walk in the street, or sitt in the house, tho'I will not bee so pharisaical as to show it, yett I used frequently to lift up a Cry unto G-d, for some suitable Blessing to be vouchsafed."

Yale or Harvard?

May the name of Yale be blessed. Did I not promise Elihu Yale: "Sir though you have felicities in your family, which I pray G-d continue and multiply, yet certainly, if what is forming at New Haven might wear the name of Yale College, it would be better than a name of Sons and Daughters. And your munificence might easily obtain for you such a commemoration and perpetuation of your Valuable Name, which would indeed be much better than an Egyptian pyramid."

"When the servants of G-d meet at Yale commencement, I make no doubt that they will make it an opportunity in the most serious and mature manner to deliberate upon projections to serve the great interests of education, and so of religion, as well as whatever else may advance the kingdom of G-d, and not suffer an interview of your best men to evaporate such a senseless, useless, noisy impertinency, as it used to do with us at Cambridge."

This lad, Fisher, Praised be to G-d, more Yale than Harvard, has come to his Heavenly Jerusalem.

Elihu Yale and the second Duke of Devonshire, Lord James Cavendish, Mr. Turnstal, and a page.

hgeneratio

● MONTAGUE STANLEY NAPIER: Yours—Pierre Cartier was an impressive man. More Eton than Quai d'Orsay. Striped vest with morning coat over the whitest pants I had ever seen outside an Oxford wedding procession.

I had wandered into Cartier feeling quite lovely after an afternoon in Fouquets, with La Belle Suzanne. After returning to the Ritz, I thought I might do a spot of shopping. And there he was square in the doorway of the Cartier establishment, looking undecided whether to leave the shop or to stay. It must have been half after four. When my eyes met his, he smiled as though we had met after an absence of thirty years. "Cartier," he said loudly and whispered his first name, "Pierre," as an afterthought.

He grasped my hand and while I said, "Montague Stanley Napier," he turned into the Cartier shop.

More like an East End puller he was—Eton clothes notwithstanding. "Ah, Montagu," he mumbled. "India. Yes, India. Might I show you something lovely? To match your beloved's green eyes."

I jumped, for my wife's eyes were indeed a remarkable green. "Well," I countered, "make it quick for I've drinks at the Ritz at six."

Cartier placed me down at a schoolboy's desk in the corner of the shop and before my eyes was the loveliest, greenest brooch I'd ever seen. "Extraordinary," I said and meant it. "Where does it come from?" I expected a long-winded Cartier tale, like the one they supposedly spun for those young Americans about the Hopeless Diamond, as we called it at the Travelers Club. Henry Hope had been a member of our club for years. As had his son, whom we all called "Hopeless."

"Ah, this," said Cartier. "comes from your family's friend—a nameless Maharaja—richest in the world. Though I cannot breathe his name."

"How do you know everything about my family—right down to my wife's eye color?" I asked laughingly. And he said, "Why Montagu, I knew your brilliant relative Edwin Samuel Montagu who passed just two years ago, a great loss. I dare say, he would have recognized this gem—back to the peacock throne, in fact, its history weaves.

And I burst out laughing, to think he confused my first name with my last. Still, he had a point, for wasn't Samuel Montagu, Edwin's father, first Montagu Samuel.

I could see Cartier, who by now was swinging the emerald before my eyes—backward and forward—slowly, as though trying to hypnotize me.

It was uncanny. Not he but the gem. Greener than the library lawn at Eton, greener than anything. Flowers carved into the surface of the gem circling, almost growing, swaying in their green flower pot, back and forth, spiraling before my eyes. I was in over my head and I knew it. "What's the tariff?" I asked. He wrote it down on a piece of paper.

"For Montagu: Prix Special" and scrawled the cost figures so tiny as though the enormous sum would seem reasonable. I must have stared at the brooch containing the emerald for at least an hour. Finally I realized the shop would be closing and Suzanne was waiting for me back at the Ritz. I took my pen out and added a e onto Montagu and further added Stanley Napier. Then, with a flourish, said, "My solicitor Robert Wing Gray, as canny a Scot solicitor as you are a French jewel merchant, will be calling upon you next week to continue negotiations."

I arrived at the Ritz after six. Suzanne was furious. But when I told her my tale, she placed her arms around my shoulders and whispered in my ears, "Darling, cocktails are so tiresome. Let's spend the evening in." We did. And wasn't she in top form?

Robert W. Gray, wasn't he too in the finest form, more than a match for Cartier. And didn't the emerald brooch match Suzanne's eyes wondrously?

"And yours?"

Fisher could not speak but Dosha again anticipated the question, "Raphael ben Yehezkel Shraga."

How did Dosha know that so quickly? wondered Fisher, as he persisted in his question. "It should be parchment," he repeated. "We're not from here."

Writing in a cursive so minute it seemed like a flow of eddies from a mountain stream, the Rabbi said, "Oh but you are from here, Raphael ben Sheindel and so is Jerusha bat Suzanna. We're all from here. And we're all here and we all—we all are coming here."

Fisher looked at the small script in the center of the extra large sheet of paper.

● SIMHA PADAWER, DOSHA'S GRANDFATHER: How did Dosha know that so quickly—Either she knows or she doesn't know. What I and my Rickele heard under the Huppah from my Reb Weinberg was so simple:

The day of one's wedding is like Yom Kippur. On Yom Kippur we read of the High Priest in Jerusalem who performed the Temple service. The Temple has been destroyed. And Jerusalem too.

Every year on Yom Kippur we recall: "*Through performing the temple service on this day the High Priest will atone for you, cleanse you from all your sins, before Hashem you shall be cleansed.*"

"*The day itself is the atonement.*" My granddaughter has chosen Jerusalem. Did I not tell her, as a girl of seven what was said to her grandparents under the Huppah in Slonim? Her parents thought me half mad. They said: "What could a child understand?"

And is not my Jerusha, my Amen.

● THE GOLDSMITH ILLUMINATOR OF THE BOOK OF KELLS: It should be parchment—Surely, surely it should be parchment. For are they not, the angel Raphael himself and the maiden, in the Holy City of Jerusalem?

Parchment they shall have, and I too—to work my stylus on the parchment page, yellowing as I lay my gold upon it, hour after hour, day after day—My tears of longing running down my brow, melted in the fire, I feel for my Lord. We are all, all in a jewelers Jerusalem.

● YOCHANAN BEN ZAKKAI: Parchment—"*If all the heavens were parchment, all human beings scribes, and all the trees of the forest pens, it would be insufficient to write what I have learnt from my teachers; and yet I only took away from them as much as a dog laps from the ocean.*"

Chi Rho initial, *The Book of Kells: St. Matthew.*

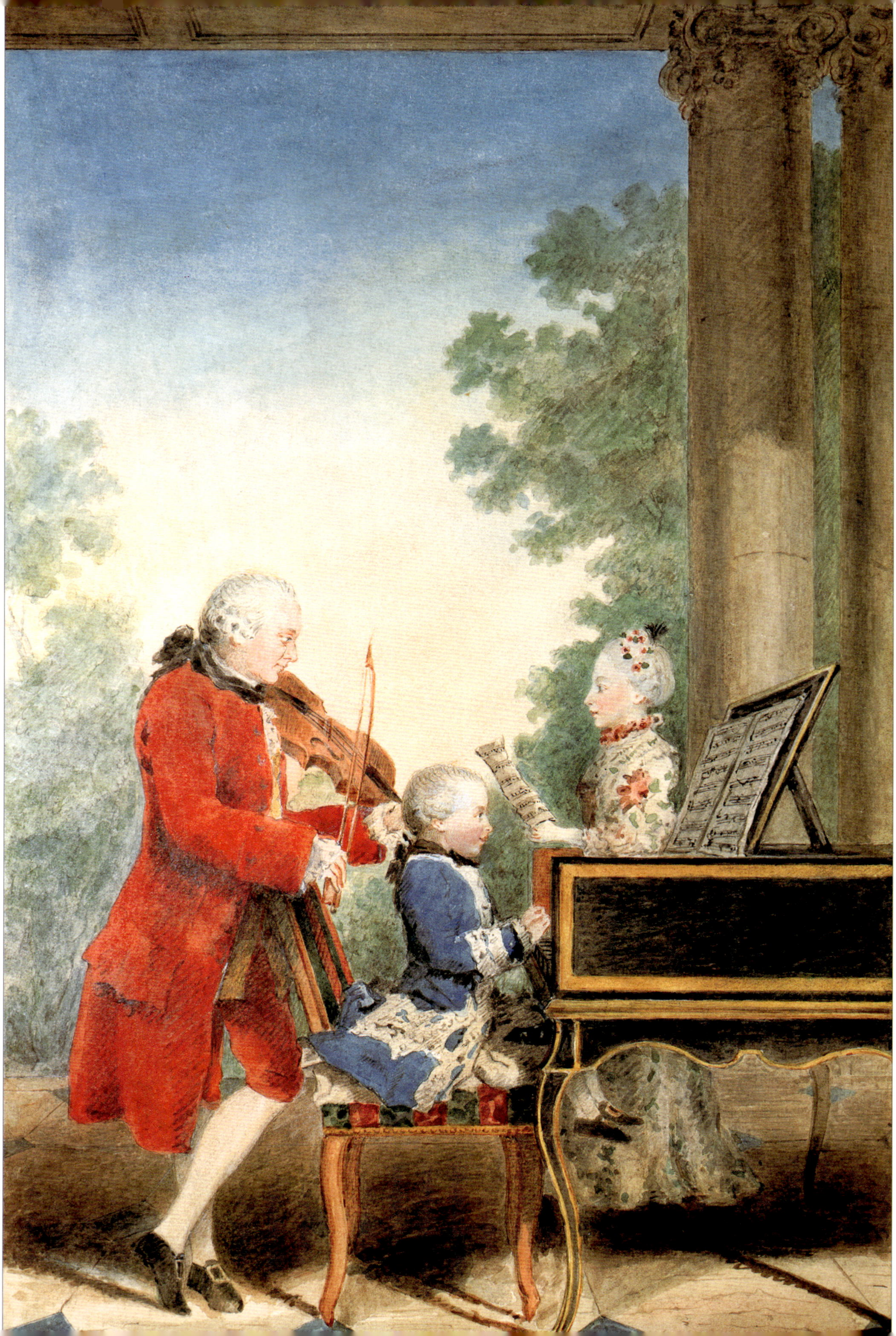

◆ RICKELE PADAWER, DOSHA'S GRANDMOTHER: "Oh, that's for the young couple to have illuminated"— Just when we were about to walk to the synagogue—my brother Yakov and my father and mother—my brother took me aside and showed me the ketubbah Reb Samuel Weinberg had written. It was the most beautiful script I had ever seen.

The letters danced on the pages. I could hear the Rebbe's voice singing between each word. Yakov, who had made the *shiddukh* for me with Simha, his *havrusa,* laughed when he saw me staring at the ketubbah.

"So, you see what I mean, isn't the Rebbe's writing as beautiful as his *niggunin*?" Though I understood what Yakov was saying, I couldn't open my mouth. One thing that puzzled me was the large border around the script. Wasn't parchment very expensive?

Yakov, who was almost as quick as my *hazzan*, Simha, saw me staring at the border and answered my unasked question: "I also asked the question, Why the huge, empty border? I don't know, maybe because Simha is a descendant of Moses Hayyim Luzzatto, it is a custom in their family."

Then as always, there he was when we wanted him, the Rebbe entered our house—for it was his custom to write the ketubbah and escort the *kallah* and her family to the synagogue before the wedding. Without hesitating, he answered, "Oh, that's for the young couple to have illuminated. I'm just a Sofer."

■ RABBI SAMUEL BEN ABRAHAM BEN ISAAC MATTATHIAS WEINBERG, Slonimer Rebbe: "Oh that's for the young couple to have illuminated. I'm just a Sofer."—I'm just a Sopher. Just a Sofer. I move my hand, and words are written. Does not the Heavenly Father move our hands.

Certainly what I write—the name of the bride Rickele bat Hillel and the name of the groom Simha ben Yitzhak, and the name of the place Slonim—these are given into my hand to write, letter by letter, crown by crown, space by space. I am just a sofer. Not a rabbi, not a *hazzan*, not even a *shammes*. And now standing before me is Simha Padawer and his kallah Rickele. I hold up the ketubbah that my hand has written. I see the sea of space around the letters.

I see the sea that Simha's ancestor Reb Moshe Hayyim crossed. From Padua to Venice, to Amsterdam, across the sea to Eretz Yisroel. I see my own grandson Noah in Tiberias, walking to Luzzato's grave, praying for all our Slonim Hassidim. For our *Hatonim*. All our *kallahs*, soon may their voices be heard in Jerusalem. Here we all are on the day of the wedding. All, my grandson, the Ramshal, even the grandchildren, may G-d be merciful of Rickele and Simha.

It is Yom Kippur and they have fasted and the day itself will act as atonement. And the wedding day of their grandchildren even if, G-d forbid, they do not fast, will act as an atonement. And I point with my hand trembling to the space of text at the ketubbah and words come pouring out of my heart: "That's for the young couple to have illuminated. I'm just a Sopher."

"What are the huge margins for?"

"Oh that's for the young couple to have illuminated. I'm just a Sofer, a scribe," replied the Rabbi instantly.

"I thought you were a Rabbi." Fisher heard himself ask, amazing at the purity of the singing, but not with the usual edge in his voice.

"Oh," smiled the Rabbi. "Today you can't just be a Rabbi." And as he tuned the guitar, the figure spoke. "In the highest of heaven there is a chamber that only music can unlock."

Dosha looked in Fisher's eyes and Fisher into hers. The Singer-Rabbi was swaying and chanting.

■ CÉZANNE: What are the huge margins for— To be filled in—later with music, Mozart, his parents, their children, everything.

A canvas ever being painted, even by the next generations, even those unborn.

◆ SIMHA PADAWER, DOSHA'S GRANDFATHER: "Oh, that's for the young couple to have illuminated I'm just a sofer."—I went to the Rebbe, Shmuel Weinberg, and asked for his blessing. Yakov, my schoolmate since I was four, was older than Rickele by two years.

All my life I had seen her and so often what you see all your life you don't see. It's right in front of your eyes and you don't see it. Reb. Shmuel put his hands on my forehead and said: "Simha ben Sheindel when you were three my *Heilege* grandfather Reb. Abraham blessed you. And the truth is, you should be blessing me for the Holy Ramshal, Rabbi Moshe Hayyim Luzzatto, his spirit is in your heart. Does not a grandfather's grandfather teach his grandson's grandson?

But in blessing, I will bless you. I could feel Reb. Weinberg's hands tremble as he blessed me.

May G-d make you like Ephraim and Menashe
May Hashem bless you and safe guard you
May Hashem illuminate His countenance
For you and be gracious to you
May Hashem turn his countenance to you and establish peace for you.

I understood each blessing: I was blessed for material support, for spiritual knowledge and, through G-d's mercy, blessed for beyond what I deserved.

Reb Abraham took my hands and put them around his. "This hand, Simha, is the hand that writes the ketubbah of each and every holy student I have in our Slonim Yeshivah. But I have heard that Sephardim illuminate their ketubbot. Do you have any illustrated ketubbot from your *heilige* Luzzatto family?

I held the Rebbe's hand and said: "All my life I wished a book, a bundle of papers, even a scrap of writing had been passed to me. But I have nothing from Moshe Hayyim Luzzatto or from any of my ancestors.

The Rebbe looked down at the ground. "I see. I see. I will ask Hashem what to do." The next month, a week before the wedding, the Rebbe himself came with our ketubbah. If someone had told me Gabriel himself wrote the text, so beautiful was the hand, I would have believed it. *Black fire on white fire*, glowing in the center of a huge sea of parchment.

I asked the Rebbe: "What are the huge spaces around the text for?" He smiled and said, "That's for the young couple to have illuminated. I'm just a Sofer."

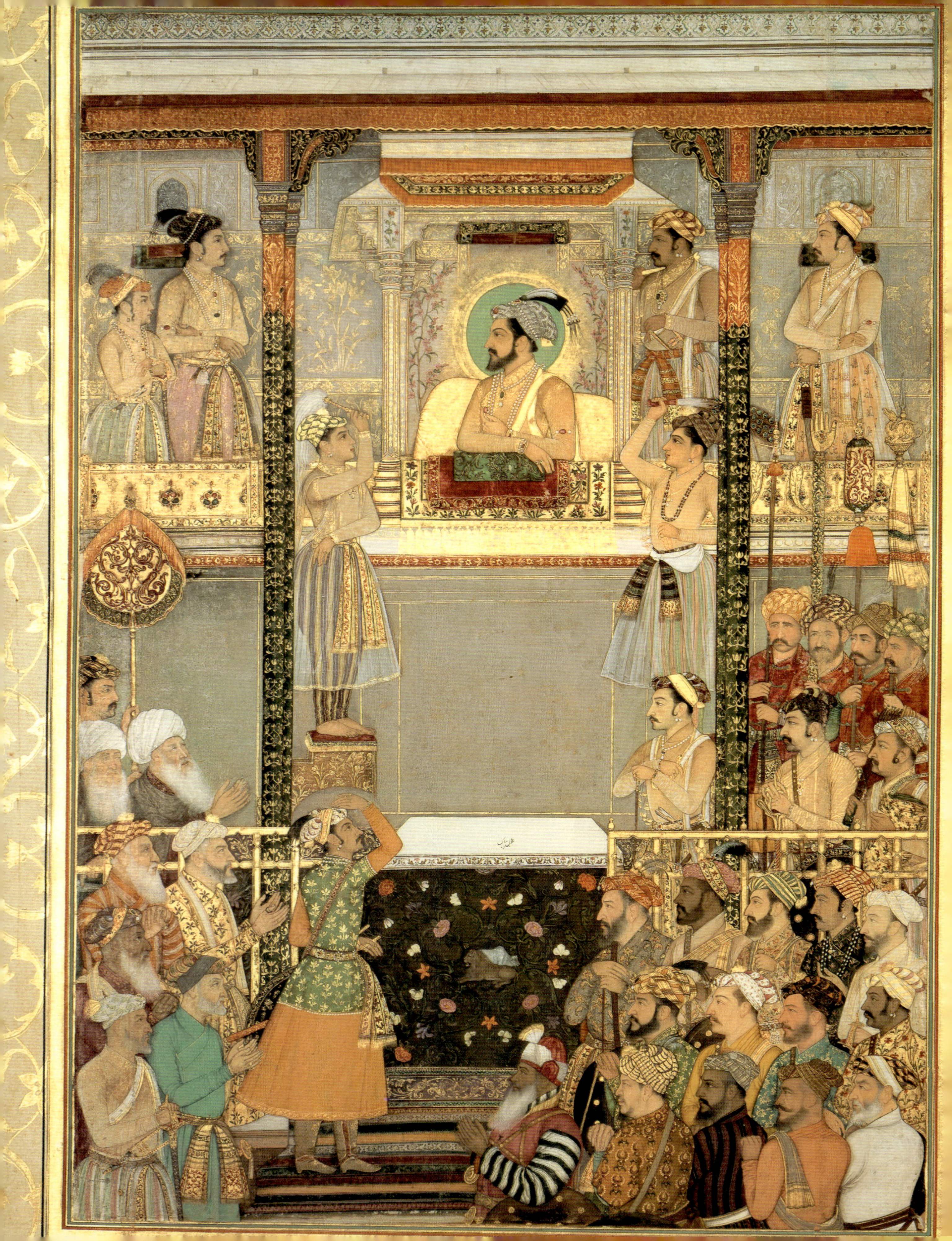

■ PAYAG: The sound of joy.—My brother burst into the atélier, waving a small miniature at me.

"What is this? What is this, Payag? Is this the sound of joy, the sound of gladness, the voice of the groom and the voice of the bride? Where is Prince Aurangzeb?"

"Look brother Balchand. You've still a keen eye. Look and then ask me," I replied cooly.

"Of course I can see him, you young fool," shrieked Balchand. "But what if Prince Aurangzeb sees where you have put him. With Asaf Khan the Wakil ready to receive his head with parted hands and Mir Bakhshi waiting to catch Prince Aurangzeb's turban after it falls from the Prince's severed head? You should have put Prince Aurangzeb directly next to the Emperor on the Prince's wedding day—his day of joy, even if he is a hater of Hindus."

"Balchand, do not call me a young fool, I have been painting for half a century for our Moghul Lords. For Akbar, for Jahanghir, and for Shah Jahan. I have done what the present Emperor wishes," I countered stubbornly.

Balchand whimpered, "We do not paint for the present, we paint for the future."

"For us, brother, there will be no future." I embraced my brother. We wept together—an old fool and a young fool—we wept for all of Hindustan.

"Hashem, our G-d, let there be soon heard in the cities of Judah and in the streets of Jerusalem the sound of joy and the sound of gladness, the voice of the groom and the voice of the bride, the sound of the groom's jubilance from their canopies and of youth's from their song-filled feasts. Blessed are you who gladdens the groom with the bride."

From a distance, both heard the Rabbi asking, "And the ring? Do you have the ring?"

Fisher couldn't move. He mouthed words but nothing came out. Dosha understood, reached into Fisher's pocket and slowly unwrapped Tal's ring—loaned to Fisher before they had left Greenwich Village. A glistening blue-roofed domed ring with gold now on fire from the rising Jerusalem sun.

◆ RACHEL BELLER, TAL'S GIRLFRIEND: Jerusalem—In the transport depot in Mechelin, after we were caught, my father held my hand tightly as we walked to the railroad siding. He was singing softly, so softly I could almost not make out the words—from when we sat on the floor in the Sephardishe Shul—for we always went there to pray on the ninth day of Av.

"Then Moses sang his never to be forgotten song,
    When I left Egypt,
    But lamentations did Jeremiah intone
    When I left Jerusalem."

And the wheel has come full circle. This Fisher, is he not my Tal? And is this Dosha not myself? And shall not finally their children's children be a blessing in our name?

Bhola, *Shah Jahan honoring Prince Awrangzeb at Agra before his wedding.*

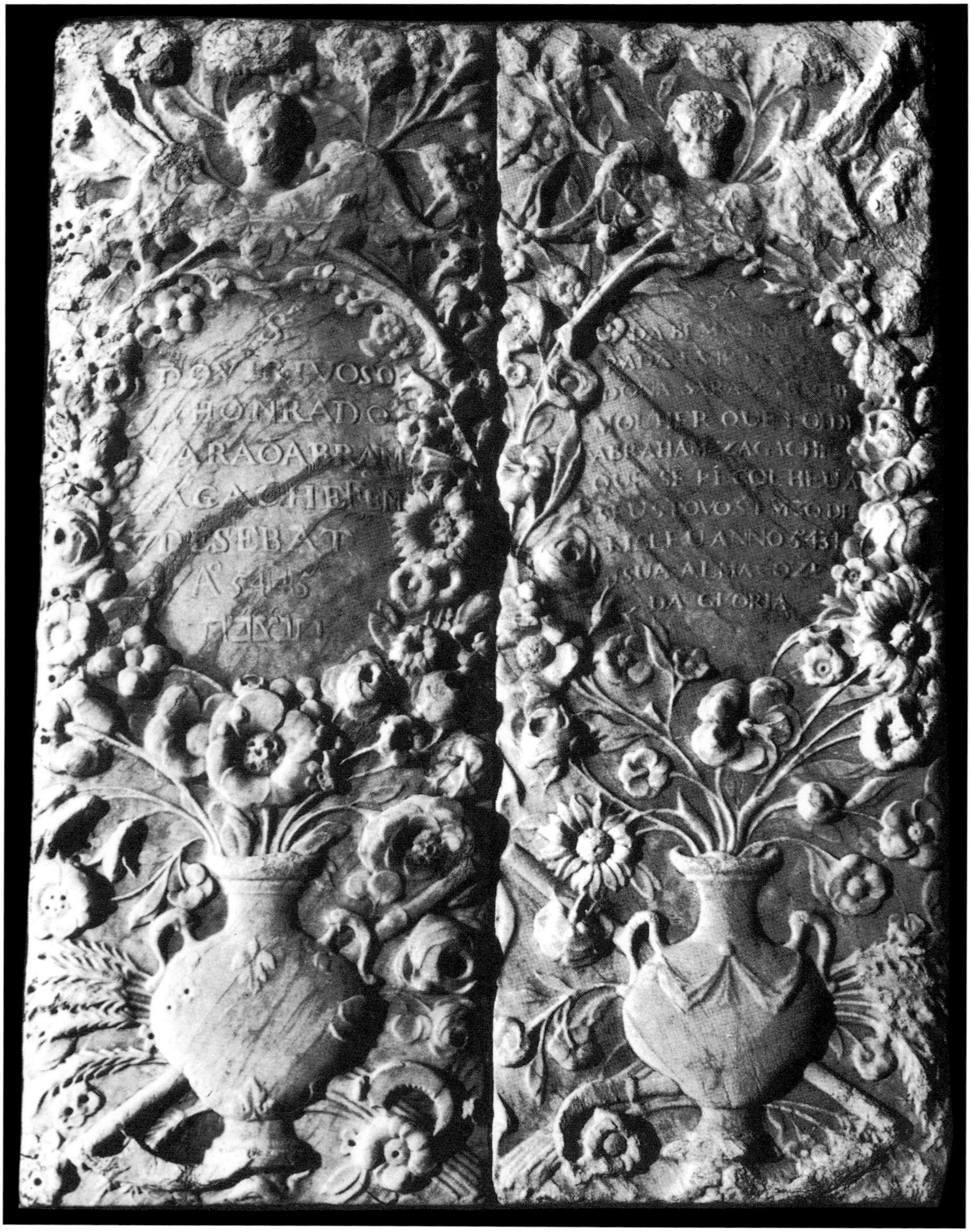
HONRADO
DESEBAT
DA GLORIA

- VAN GOGH: Finished—"*I am thinking about Gauguin a lot, and I am sure that in one way or another, whether it is he who comes here or I go to him, he and I will like practically the same subjects and I have no doubt that I could work at Pont-Aven, and on the other hand I am convinced that he would tremendously like the country down here.*"

Paul kept writing me: "Is my portrait—more an offering—finished."

Finished? What does it mean? Finished? To be finished? Patches of zinc white still not dry in this dry Arles climate.

And should I wait until my painting is finished to send it to Gauguin? Then it will be finished and I will be too.

"*I am pretty nearly reduced to madness...If it were not that I have almost a double nature, that of a monk and a painter, as it were, I should have been reduced, and long ago, completely and utterly, to the aforesaid condition.*"

Only Vermeer, with his yellows capable of charming G-d, could have the luxury of finishing.

- PAUL SACHS, December 1946: Finished—Wertheim's collection was on display in the spring of '46. I crossed the Yard with him, arm in arm. Maurice was especially jaunty—Fortieth reunion and all that—when just as we were about to leave through the wrought iron gate out of the yard, directly across from the Fogg. Maurice stopped and started to shiver as though in the dead of winter. I knew why but I didn't know how. He was a Jew, as I was, and an American. We both had gone to Harvard, but so much more than Harvard totally died for us during the War. Broken. Finished. Beyond repair. Beyond repair or conservation.

I put my hand on Maurice's shoulder to steady him and I said: "It's over, the winter. Spring is here, Maurice." I spoke of Europe, of France, of van Gogh, of the longing of the soul, of love, of new beginnings. Maurice did not nod in acquiescence, nor did he contradict.

To be on the safe side, for Maurice was Harvard but he was also a banker, I wrote him in December at the end of '46.

"*I have delayed writing to you after my return until I had an opportunity to present your grandiose idea to the colleagues to whom you authorized me to speak and I again assure you that nothing will be said to anyone else... And now I must say with the greatest pleasure and satisfaction that my colleagues saw eye to eye with you and with me and feel that in view of the homogeneous distinctions of your pictures they not only can but should be kept together in two rooms along the lines that we discussed.*"

Maurice, brief as ever, responded: "Yes, Paul, winter is finished."

"Where will we stay?" Fisher found himself asking, and in unison the two witnesses answered and with them a chanting voice, "Here," as an Amen, but best of all, it's on the house."

Suddenly Fisher and Dosha found themselves on the patio with a broken glass on the floor and the vision of the man in black departing from their marital chambers.

"By the way," the cherubic Rabbi face exclaimed as he left their room, "it wasn't daybreak that you can say the Shma from and it wasn't when you can't see green from blue, it was according to Rabbi Eliezer (Talmud Berakhot 9b) when you can't distinguish between blue and green."

- GAUGUIN: Finished—Finally, it arrived, finished. "À mon ami" Paul Gauguin scrawled across the top of the canvas with a mad flourish, and quite unnecessarily, "*Vincent*" on the bottom right. Who else could have finished with such great speed?

I had finished my self portrait with the haste of a bandit—my portrait. "The face of an outlaw, ill clad and powerful like Jean Valjean with an interior nobility and gentleness so the face is flushed, the eyes accented by the surrounding colors of a furnace fire. This to represent the volcanic flames that animate the soul of the artist...As for this Jean Valjean whom society has oppressed—cast out...is he not equally a symbol of the contemporary Impressionist painter? In endowing him with my features I offer you as well an image of myself. A portrait of all the wretched victims of society."

And all this panic of Vincent. Finish. Finish. Send your portrait. So we may all start again, in the yellow house, to create. To link our painting in a chain to oppose all our attackers.

They will burst the chain anyway, or crawl under it, as is their custom—And first your name, Vincent, will fade, and then mine, and then ourselves, and then perhaps even our portraits.

- MAURICE WERTHEIM: Finished—The Germany we knew was finished. The Jews were finished. America could be be finished. It was all in the air, the end of days when I arrived in Lucerne in 1934. Or, more precisely, my representative bid for me and acquired the self-portrait of van Gogh—a melange of emerald and viridian green and a yellow that haunted me throughout the war as a symbol of the fires that swept all of Europe.

After the War, I came to see van Gogh's invitation to Gauguin to create a home together as nothing so much as the displaced person wandering broken across Europe, searching for a home, a scrap of a meal or even a look that would show traces of human memory.

For a long time, Cecile would chide me for putting the self-portrait of van Gogh in the darkened room just off the library. "Maurice, darling, if you do not wish it to be seen, sell it, and if you wish it to be appreciated, bring it out into the light and let it breathe."

How could I tell her: It must sleep for a while, recovering, before it could again be a token of love.

And when had I first, and last felt, overpowering sunlight, far from the responsibilities of the minutes and hours, appointments that govern our weeks and years, than in my Harvard class of 1906.

As I walked about the Fogg with Paul Sachs in '46, he suddenly turned to me. "It is over Maurice, the winter of the war. Spring is here."

Paul waved his arms about, and suddenly I understood what should happen to van Gogh's gift to Gauguin—sold to Vollard for a song to be sung by Gauguin in Tahiti, washed ashore in Paul Cassirer's Berlin Gallery, acquired by the Neue Staatsgalerie Munich and disowned as "degenerate" by those more degenerate than even Gauguin could ever imagine.

"When I am finished and you, sweet Cecile, are finished, I should like van Gogh's valentine to hang in the Fogg at Harvard as an everlasting reminder of our Springtime love."

And, of course, Cecile listened.

Tombstone: Abraham Zagache and his wife, Sara.

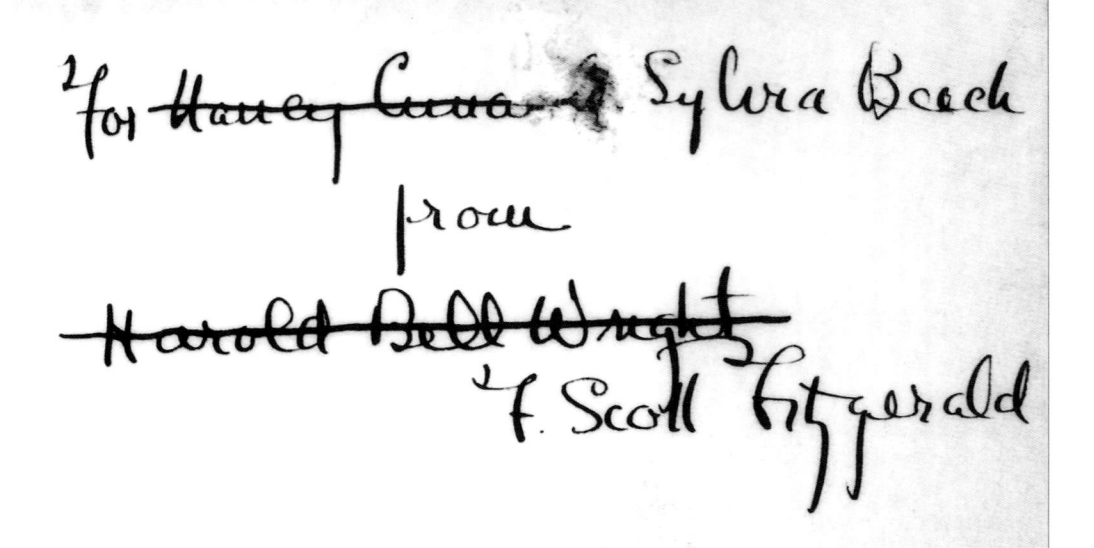

For ~~Harold Conrad~~ Sylvia Beach
from
~~Harold Bell Wright~~
F. Scott Fitzgerald

Paris, July 1928

18 Rue D'Odeon
Festival of St. James

◆ TUVIAH GUTMAN GUTWIRTH: Table—My great great grandchild under the table. Why is she there? Because she is the mystic spark of the All Creator. Brightness and illumination at once.

She is a daughter of Jerusalem. She is growing. Ever-growing. And she is reciting the order of the service.

■ EZEKIEL'S TABLE: 41:22
"The altar, three cubit high and two cubits in length, was of wood and so were its corners. Its length and its walls were also of wood; and He said to me, 'This is the table before the Lord.'" The Talmud explains: *"It begins by referring to it as an altar and concludes by calling it a table!? Both R. Yochanan and R. Elazar said, 'When the Temple stood, the altar made atonement for a person; now that the Temple no longer stands, a person's table makes atonement for him.'"*

Rachel will enlighten. She will awaken those around the Seder table from their slumber, she will sing and open their ears to song. She will cause this table to be an atonement for them all. Amen, and yet again Amen.

■ LAURENCE STERNE: Under the table—Of course Baby Rachel is under the table, as I was ever and always.

"If any free schooler upon due proof first hand shall be found altogether negligent or incapable of learning at the discretion of the Master he shall be returned to his friends to be brought up in some other honest trade & exercise of life."

Off to the streets of Halifax for me, or for her. Or has not her home been turned into a schoolroom?

And hide under the table, my schoolboy's table. What should I do, or she do, or any school do, child do but spoil paper with one's initials written over and over and yet over again draw one's friends: Christopher Welbery, John Turner, Nickibus Nukebus, Latin me that, and she a Hebrew? All the same in the end. Squeak out an acceptable answer from under a pile of papers, a sea of tables, an ocean of glares. Onward you are allowed to swim in the bosom of the classroom dreading to be exiled to the cold horror of the streets of a weaned world.

And what is Rachel doing under the table but singing her verdant song—and what am I doing but the self-same? *For to write a book is for all the world like humming a song—be but in tune with yourself.*

CHAPTER 10

"G R E E N" came the squeaky voice from under the seder table. "It's green, Abba," said Rachel in English to her father, Benjamin Tal.

"Yes, it's green but it's also *karpas*—the Passover vegetable," replied Rachel's father, glancing downward at the Seder table. Ariel, Benjamin's wife, had set the long oval table in the living room alongside the garden entrance, with a delicate beauty. Like her mother, Dosha's paintings, Benjamin thought, decorated around the edges and sober in the center. And only an hour before her American brother's family arrived from the hotel. Why did Ariel always leave everything for the last moment?

And how did baby Rachel, he still couldn't stop calling her that, know what he was holding up over her head while she was under the table?

◆ ISAAC TAL, ABRAHAM TAL'S FATHER: Table—My great, great grandchild under the table.

And why is she there? She is a tree growing from the ground up. She is small. And she will be very great. She is a seed, growing, sprouting, spreading, giving warmth, shade, and comfort to all around her.

And who is the *Shadchen* for all of this? For this child also comes from her mother's seed—and they from another's seed.

Her mother's mother Dosha and my son Abraham the blessed *Shadchen* of all this.

■ JAMES JOYCE: And how did baby Rachel know what he was holding up over her head?—*"Silence, exile and cunning."* Daedalus she is. Exiling herself under the table. Cunning too. Silent she be, for she is but the echo of her father's voice before he speaks. And how did baby Rachel know what He was holding up over her head.

Our Father. And fair Rebecca, ever darkened by the shadow of the table above her. *A dark coil of her slowly uncoils and falls.*

F. Scott Fitzgerald's drawing in Sylvia Beach's copy of *The Great Gatsby*.

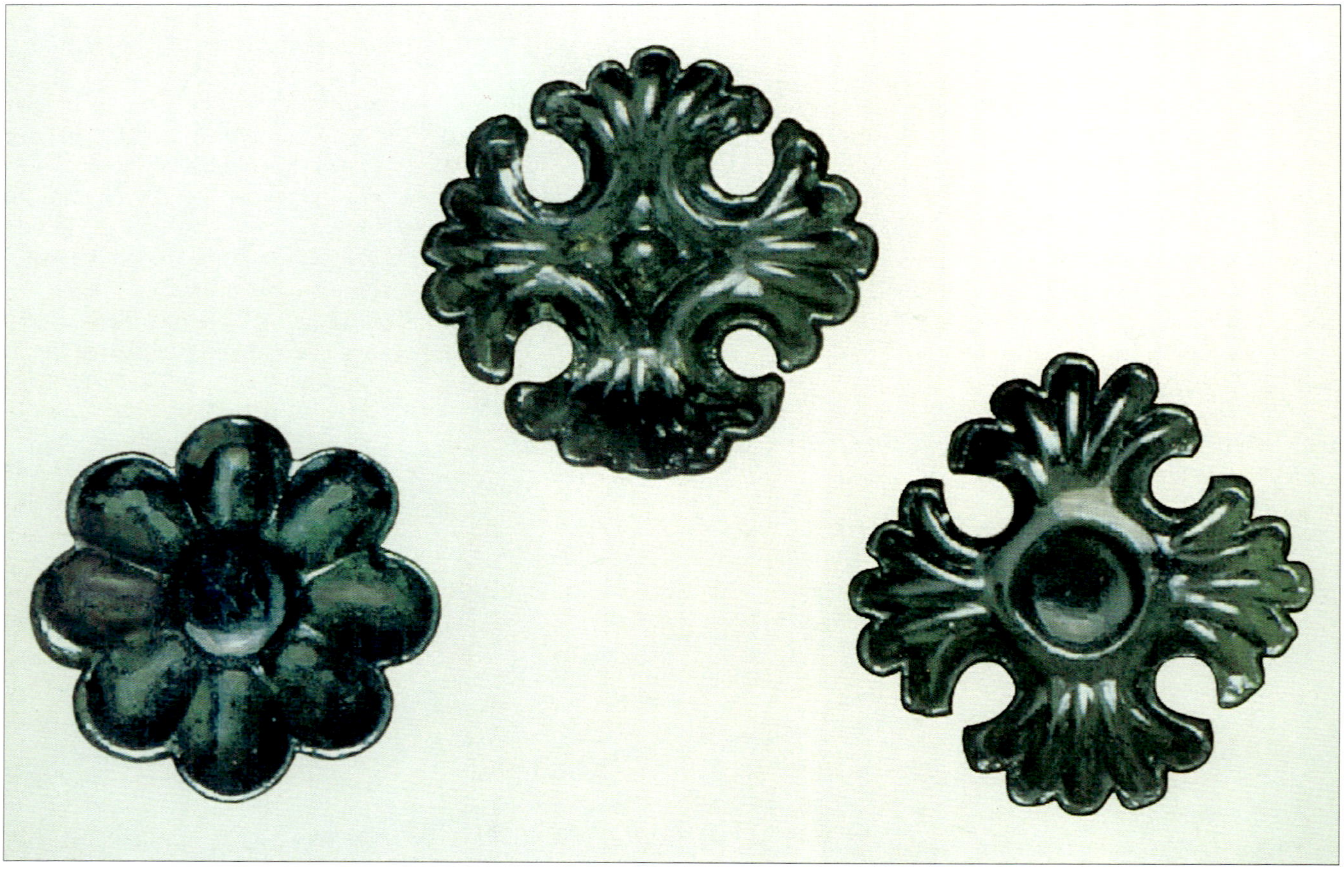

◆ SIMHA PADAWER, DOSHA'S GRANDFATHER: Rachel—My great-great-granddaughter: *"For out of Zion shall comeTorah."*

Her grandmother, Jerusha, danced under the table in my house in Brooklyn. I can remember my son-in-law looking everywhere for her. She must be in her room, she always hides under her bed. Dosha, where are you? He running around while I read the whole Seder in Hebrew. The first after the War. What did I care if Reuven couldn't understand a word. In America one prayed that one's prayers went straight down, to be picked and chewed at by grandchildren at least.

And here in Jerusalem, Rachel singing in Hebrew. Is not the Torah a song? And Rachel conceived in Tiberias on Benjamin and Ariel's honeymoon. And must be named after my Rickele.

So who should know how to sing better than this Tiberian bird fluttering from room to room. What does it mean: *"And they read in the book of the law of G-d distinctly. And they gave the sense, and caused them to understand the reading"* (Nehemiah 8:8).

Rachel is the reader. And sings in harmony with my wife Rickele, and speaks in their English language and she causes her parents, her cousins, and her offspring to understand. Blessed be G-d who causes the song of Tiberias to be sung forever and ever.

"Zeh Karpas, Abba, Avol be-emet low Kalkach yarok. It's Karpas, father, but not so green," chimed Rachel (although just seven years old) narrating and translating her words, brightly from Hebrew.

Rachel's three cousins—David, Jeremy and Daniel—burst into laughter. The lettuce from Degania did look a little ragged, Benjamin had to admit.

Out of the corner of his eye, he could see his wife standing by the garden window. His eyes were drawn to the arch of her long neck, sloping into her velvet dress, the one she had on when they had met in her Greenwich Village apartment after his American cousins had given him her address.

■ RACHEL ZUCKER, American poet: Narrating—
Whose place is it to say what happened?
　The snow is not a symbol
　　but literal.
　You happened
　　and happened to be here—
　where I am—
　　which changes and is always,
　from my point of view,
　　first person.
　I'm not the narrator or
　　speaker.

■ CRAZY HORSE: Out of the corner of his eye he could see his wife standing—Any white man could. And any Oglala too. Even a Bad Face. Not only one's own wife but another's wife. Could I not see No-Water's wife, Black Buffalo Woman in a crowd of a hundred at the Big Council in 1857.

Could I not see Black Buffalo Woman in No-water's tepee, after he left our raiding party with a toothache and rode back to our camp and married Black Buffalo Woman before sunset?

It was all Red Cloud's doing—he and his band of bad faces—never did the sun shine brightly for me again. But in the shadows I could see Black Buffalo Woman's long neck, could feel her lips part as I looked at her out of the corner of my eye. Another man's wife, but to be mine in the future. As sure as the light of the full moon rose to greet me each month.

■ RAHEL BLUWSTEIN (Israeli Poet): Rachel—
*For her blood runs in my blood
And her voice sings to me.
Rachel, who pastured the flocks of Laban
Rachel, the mother of the mother*

*And that is why the house is narrow for me,
And the city foreign,
For her veil used to flutter
In the desert wind.*

*And that is why I hold to my way
With such certainty,
For memories are preserved in my feet
Ever since, ever since.*

Carved flowerheads: Lotus, Poppy, and Amaranth, from The Taj Mahal Emerald.

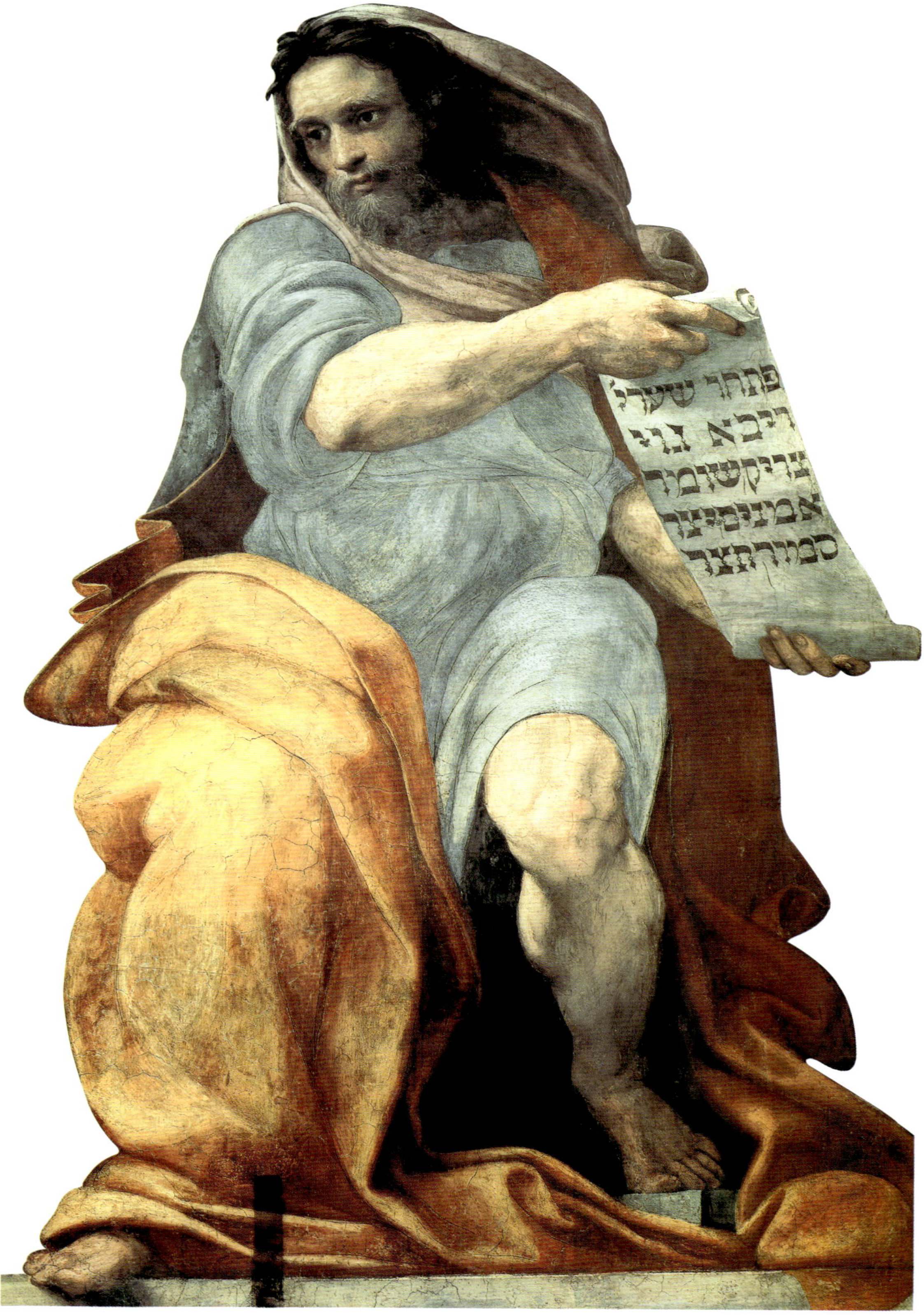
פתחו שערי
ויבא גוי
צדיקשומר
אמונים יצר
סמוך תצר

◆ MOSES HAYYIM LUZZATTO, DOSHA'S ANCESTOR: Beautiful—"*The Holy Zohar asks: Why does the Scripture tell us with so much detail that Isaac took Rebecca and she became his wife and he loved her. The last statement seems to be unnecessary, for naturally if she became his wife he loved her, as is the way of all men to love their wives. The explanation is that the attraction of the male to the female is derived from the left, as we read, 'Let his left hand be under my head (Song of Songs II, 6). The left being symbolic of night and darkness…Isaac had four spouses that mystically speaking combined in herself the virtues of four women. This is indicated in Scripture in the following manner: 'And he took Rebecca' alludes to one; 'and she became his wife' indicates a second; 'and he loved her' indicates a third: And Isaac was comforted for his mother…all was arranged by a divine dispensation to one and the same mystical purpose.*"

Could the *maggid* speak to me? Could he lead me to my beautiful, my celestial bride.

Not in Padua nor in Amsterdam only in the Holy land.

■ BLACK ELK: Great…Father…Great Spirit—"*The Hang-around-the-fort people said Crazy Horse was ready to tie up his horse's tail again and make war on the Wasichus*"—How could he do that when we had no guns and could not get any? It was a story the Wasichus told, and their tongues were forked when they told it. Our people believe they did what they did because Crazy Horse was a great man and they could not kill him in battle and he would not make himself into a Wasichu, as Spotted Tail and the others did. That summer, my father told me, the Wasichu wanted him to go to Washington with Red Cloud and Spotted Tail and others to see the Great Father there, but he would not go. He told him he did not need to go looking for his Great Father. Crazy Horse said: "*My father is with me, and there is no Great Father between me and the Great Spirit.*"

"Benjamin, you should meet her," said his cousin Jacob Tal. "Her parents were the reason your father, Isaac Tal, went to Israel.

"Is she beautiful?" Benjamin had asked Jacob. "As your Great-Uncle Abraham Tal would say, 'more beautiful than my lips could describe, more lovely than your eyes could imagine!'"

And of course, Benjamin had gone immediately, without phoning ahead. For had he not heard, in so many veiled references, of the enigmatic and mysterious Abraham Tal—almost a father to his father—almost a father to his Greenwich Village neighbors, the Fishers.

Ariel Fisher was coming down the stairs of her Hudson Street apartment. No less than seven years ago, he'd rushed to introduce himself, dropping his books in a fit of embarrassment. She laughed, helped him pick them up and put them in his backpack.

■ ISAAC LURIA: Your father, Isaac Tal, went to Israel.—Do not say your father, Isaac, went to Israel but say: Your father Isaac went to Israel. For only when your Patriarichal Father Isaac's Rebekah was brought by Abraham's servant to the Holy Land, did your Father, Isaac, truly arrive in Israel.

And more so, Father Isaac, alone among the patriarchs, must never leave the land: "*Isaac sowed in the land and reaped a hundred fold the same year.*"

And the seed? As the love begins so does it grow. "*Isaac went out walking in the field toward evening and, looking up, he saw camels approaching. Raising her eyes, Rebecca saw Isaac. She alighted from the camel and said to the servant, "Who is that man walking in the field toward us? And the servant said, That is my master: So she took her veil and covered herself. The servant told Isaac all the things that he had done…and Isaac took Rebecca as his wife. Isaac loved her.*"

Doubly loved Isaac: By his father Abraham: "Take your son, your favored one, Isaac. Whom you love."

And by the beautiful Rebecca. And his seed increased a hundred fold.

■ F. SCOTT FITZGERALD: You should meet her—"*Smiling faintly at him from not four feet away was the face of his dead wife, identical even to the expression. Across the four feet of moonlight the eyes he knew looked back at him. A curl blew a little on a familiar forehead, the smile lingered, changed a little according to the patter, the lips parted—the same. An awful fear went over him and he wanted to cry aloud.*"

She at the tips of my fingers. All I need is to summon her. But if there are no plot complications—no contrivances in *The Last Tycoon*. No silk scarf of d'Anjou to pledge my love. "No. I must not be the first Edna. No, Edna. It was nice of you to come. I've been stupid. Last night I had an idea that you were an exact double for someone I knew. It was dark and the light was in my eyes." No, not dead. My wife Minna fictively dead to me. Zelda breathing but comatose. Have Edna dead to me. Is she not Sara Murphy? To Kathleen, have her say simply: "You should meet her, my Zelda."

"*There she was—my face forms a smile against the light from inside. It was Minna's face—the skin with its peculiar radiance as if phosphurs had touched it, the mouth with its warm line that never counted costs and over the haunting jollity that had fascinated a generation.*" I could feel my fingers with my hand brushing the writing paper softly. I could feel Zelda's skin, see Sara's eyes, immobile on mine as I looked at Kathleen, I could feel Sheilah's form moving, slowly, ever so slowly under my body, my "*restless body which never spared itself in sport or danger, destined to give me one proud gallop to the end.*"

Raphael, *The Prophet Isaiah*, detail.

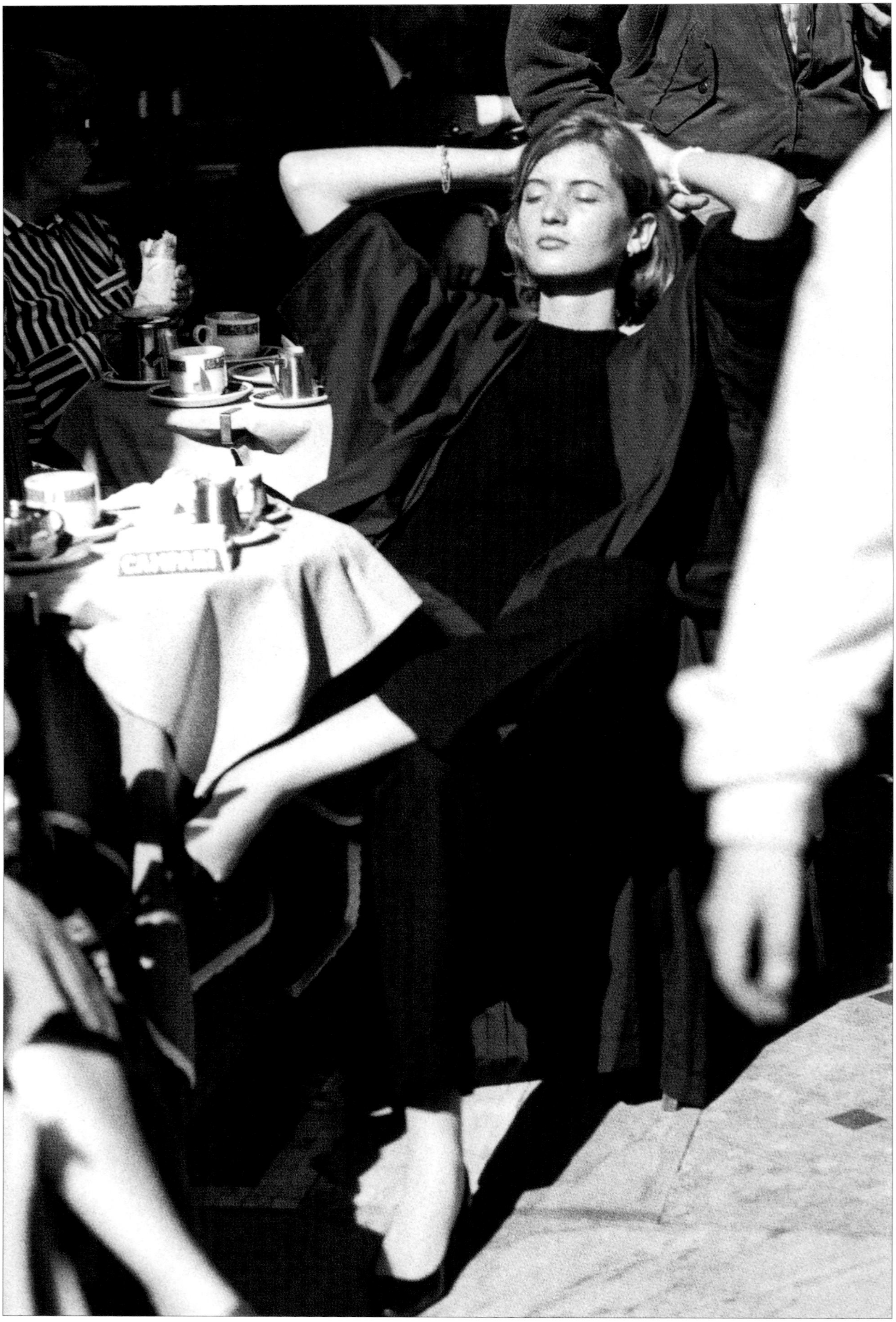

■ Rabbi Nachman of Breslov: All your books are in Hebrew—The ten characters in Fisher's tale parallel the ten sayings through which the world was created.

The mother and father of Tal, Tuviah Tal and Tal Himself, His nephew Isaac, Fisher, Dosha, Benjamin, Ariel, and the child to be born Rachel.

There are ten characters in my story of the Master of Prayer: The Master of Prayer and the warrior, the treasurer and the wise man, the bard and the faithful friend, the queen's daughter with her child, the king and the queen.

Does not the king tell us all? All your books are in Hebrew and therefore all your songs shall be sung generation upon generation.

Benjamin is rising to meet Ariel and she is raising him as he falls. Together they are already ascending toward Jerusalem to celebrate Passover. And Rachel is the Amen without which the first nine characters would–G-d forbid–wander forever.

■ André Breton: Ariel—"*She told me her name, the one she had chosen for herself: 'Nadja, because in Russian it's the beginning of the word hope: and because it's only the beginning.'*"

Ariel too has chosen her name for herself. In Hebrew it means the Lion of G-d: the Heavenly Jerusalem.

Young Benjamin has flung all his books at Ariel's feet. As I had, at the feet of Nadja, mine Greek to her, Benjamin's Hebrew to Ariel.

And what difference, for we all speak the language of the heart or else we are all mute.

"What an inventive way to pick up a woman!" she'd laughingly exclaimed. "And you're Israeli?"

"Oh, because of the accent," he'd answered.

"No, all your books are in Hebrew."

He blushed and she continued answering him with questions only, always questions. He kept asking her, asking her, and asking her, and finally she answered and here she was.

Their child Rachel bounced under the Seder table. As like her mother Ariel as two drops of water. Ariel's lips were moving, and suddenly it came to Benjamin that Ariel was mouthing the words for Rachel.

◆ Moses Hayyim Luzzatto: All your books are in Hebrew—"*When it will become clear to you that wherever you are, you are standing before the Divine Presence, you will arrive at the fear and dread of stumbling in action that would not be fitting before G-d's profound glory. That is what is indicated by the teaching (Avot 2:1), 'Know what is above you–a seeing eye, a hearing ear and that all of your actions are recorded in a book.' Since the Holy One (blessed be He) involves Himself in everything, and He sees and hears everything, you can be sure of the fact that all actions make an impression and are recorded in a book for merit or blame.*"

But our books are first written by ourselves, carried by ourselves, and the weight of our actions so often causes us to stumble. Praise be to G-d who has brought Ariel to Benjamin to help him gather up the books of his life–all praise be to Ariel to recognize the holiness of the language that he has written in and about himself, and is she not blessed to be able to speak simply and directly to him? The nations speak in many tongues–but all your books are in Hebrew.

Untitled photograph.

RVE OBSCVRE

CARRIERA SCVRA

■ ANDRÉ BRETON: "All the questions"—I awoke and she was next to me. I took her wrist, slender, a filament between the two pillows she always hid in between night after night in my apartment on rue Vaugirard–her wrist that seemed a directional marker. I took her wrist in my mouth and slid my tongue along her arm. Tonguing down the river of her arm and inhaling her breast with all my power. Out of the corner of my eye, I could see her erect nipple. An involuntary shudder acted as a wave crest, practically knocking me off the raft of our bed. But my lips held firm, gliding across her stomach, the insides of her arched legs. And the tiny streams between her toes, and all the while calling to her, whispering to her, Nadja, Nadja., and where was she? Certainly not here on rue Vaugirard. I left my apartment and stumbled down the stairs, still swimming inside her, along side of her, in search of her. "What are you?" I moaned, unaware of any of the passersby, repeating all the questions again, again, and yet again.

Suddenly on rue Royale, Nadja was before me in a green velour frock edged with pink pearls, singing to me under the arcade in the Palais Royale. We had taken refuge against a morning Parisian deluge:

"She uses a new image to make me understand how she lives: It's like the morning when she bathes and her body withdraws while she stares at the surface of the bath water. I am the thought on the bath in the room without mirrors. She had forgotten to tell me about the strange adventure which happened to her last night, toward eight o'clock, when supposing herself alone, she was singing and dancing as she walked beneath an arcade of the Palais Royale."

■ NADJA: Time—He would look at me when we were together on the street, or walking in the Bois du Boulogne, and most especially on boulevard de Montparnasse. He would gaze at me while I sipped a coffee in La Rotonde and a cassis afterward at Le Select. He looking at me, always, at my neck, my arms, my hands, undressing me with his eyes and what was I to say to his questions, repeated and insistent: I had but one answer for him: *"Time is a tease, time is a tease because everything has to happen in its own time."*

If he wishes to bed me now, amid the coffee cups and the cloth napkins, hoping all will avert their eyes, let him do it.

Or wait until I am in his arms yesterday. He has written his name all over my body and has sealed the envelope of my flesh with the words of his mouth.

It matters little which bed he or I are sleeping in, we are always and never together.

But time frightens him. In his bed, in mine, in our bed–on the street, in the parks of Paris, even in the coffee house of our dreams and especially when he chants my name, Nadja, again and again. I hold his head in my hands and write with my tongue on the walls of his eye: *"Nadja, because in Russian it's the beginning of the word hope, and because it's only the beginning."*

"My G-d, Ariel, you're telling our child what to answer."

Ariel raised her eyebrows in total astonishment and said, "My, my, you phrase all the questions, sweet Benjamin, so please don't worry about the answers. They'll come in due time, and if you're so worried about Baby Rachel cribbing from me, I'll turn around."

She pirouetted with the grace of a ballerina in a junior high school performance.

Gales of laughter again from the American cousins as Ariel gazed across the garden wall, at the Damascus gate wide open in the walls of Jerusalem.

■ CÉZANNE: And she pirouetted around with the grace of a young ballerina—Alone in the house with Felice. Shall I call her the maid? The housekeeper? A girl, a child? Maman, perhaps?

Alone, pretending to paint just outside the garden window, but peering in at her as she dusts the foyer cabinets. Reaching up, standing on a chair to clean the top of the hanging Gobelin chandelier. And as she pirouettes around the dining table with the grace of a young ballerina, she smiles directly at me.

"Can I help reach the highest cabinet, Félice?" I ask with my eyes.

And she walks out into the garden and looks at my canvas, blank for days. For how can I paint when I think only of her?

How can I paint her with Hortense returning in a fortnight, we, almost wed, if only Papa will finally bless us.

"Do you wish to paint me, Monsieur Paul?" she asks me gaily. And I cannot resist her voice, or her eyes, or her youth.

"Yes, but first I must arrange your outfit." I put my hands on her arms and place my index finger under the strap of her linen dress. "This will not do, this chemise, this cleaning outfit. I must have something regal for you to wear."

"Oh, Monsieur Paul, do not mock me," she squeals with delight. "What clothing do you suggest I model?"

"Le Bon Dieu's own finery. Nothing else would be grand enough." I pull her, not unwillingly, down to the stream in the corner of our property and slowly unfrock her and with the water falling on her glistening skin, I pile orange and yellow autumnal leaves all over her. "The dress of the gods," I murmur to her.

■ HORTENSE FIQUET, Cézanne's wife: All the questions—You stink of her. I am not a peasant for nothing. And I am not the fool you take me for.

If you think you will paint me as your grandmother and play the ladder game with that tartine Félice, you will paint me from memory. For you will never see me again, Paul.

Or Monsieur Paul, if you would like to be called that by me, as the so-called house maid Félice would call you. Ridiculous really. I your mistress, Paul, not even making love with you. And the house maid your mistress.

This is how it will be: I will be your wife or I will be your memory. And you may choose the mistress you wish. I held Paul in my arms and grabbed him by the ears and would not let him go, and slowly I lathered his eyes and his cheeks with my warmth.

I will be all the questions, mon petit, and I will be all the answers, and you will be my little cupid and paint oranges, pears and apples forever.

He wept and said he was sorry, and that how could Felice come between us. Never, never again. And I knew he meant it. And we would wed. But what an expensive victory.

清湘大滌子三十六峰意

■ Li Po: I believe you think I haven't put enough *Karpas* on the table—

*At dusk I came down from the mountain
That mountain moon as my companion,
And looked behind at tracks I'd taken
That were blue, blue below the skyline:
You took my arm, led me to your hut
Where small children drew hawthorn curtains
To green bamboo and a hidden path
With vines to brush the travellers
Clothes;*

*Coming down from
Ch'ang-an Mountain
By Hu-Szu Hermitage
He gave me rest for the night
And set out the wine.*

I believe you think I haven't put enough on the table, Tu Fu.

But I believe this child Rachel can see by the mountain moon's light that I have, and her mother, Ariel, also can see that I have put enough on the table.

*Did Chuang Chou dream
He was the butterfly
Or the butterfly
That it was Chuang Chou.*

*Down at the green gate
The melon gardener
Once used to be
Marquis of Tung-ling*

And what do I offer but a poem of green upon a paper tablet of memory to be sung together after a glass of wine?

Tu Fu, your back is to me. And to my family. To all who voyage beyond the gates: Nestorian Christians. Muslims. Jews and Zoroastrians. You think you know us for your back is to us. But we travel ever towards the same moon. They, you and I.

*And I rejoiced at a place to rest
And good wine, too, to pour out with you:
Ballads we sang, the wind in the pines
Till, our songs done, Milky Way had paled;
And I was drunk and you were merry
We had gaily forgotten the world!*

In any case, Tu Fu, it will not be I or you, mother or father, it will not be the Marquis or the melon gardener but the small children who will draw the hawthorn curtains to the green and hidden path.

"I believe you think I haven't put enough *Karpas* on the table," Ariel continued, still with her back to Benjamin and the family Seder table.

My G-d, thought Benjamin, even though her back's to me, she knows what I'm thinking. Of course, she's right. Before he could answer, the tiniest of fingers scooped up the green lettuce on the Seder plate just in front of Benjamin's seat.

Without turning around, Ariel shouted laughingly, "Rachel!" By this time Rachel was halfway across the room, lettuce in hand, sprinting across the dining room into the kitchen, through the entrance foyer they had completed last year with the geological study grant money from Belgium.

■ Emily Post: Rachel was halfway across the room…sprinting into the kitchen—This is quite extraordinary. "*At the end of dinner, when the last dish of chocolates has been passed and the hostess sees that no one is any longer eating, she looks across the table, and catching the eye of one of the ladies, slowly stands up and in the moment everyone is standing, the gentlemen offer their arms to their partners and conduct them back to the drawing room or library or wherever they are to sit during the rest of the evening.*"

Quite extraordinary, this Rachel halfway across the room…sprinting into the kitchen. Is she the hostess? How extraordinary. What manner of dinner parties will she host in the future?

■ Tu Fu: You think I haven't put enough on the table—I never turned my back on a Turk, a Jew, a Zoroastian or Nestorian, and certainly never on Li Po.

I was from Shao-ling and not from Ch'Ang-an. But you are right, Li-Po, that I did think you had not put enough on the table. For we are not preparing celebrations but an everlasting feast.

*A great dancer there was
The Lady Kung-lun
And her mime of the sword
Made the world marvel.
As she flashed, the nine suns
Fell to the archer
She flew, was a sky G-d
On saddled dragons
Her red lips and pearl sleeves
Are long since resting
But a dancer revives
Of late their fragrance*

They have danced for us. The mother and the daughter.

We have seen them dance, you and I, Li Po. Though their back be turned to us, or ours to them. We have sung to their dance:

*Those, many as the hills,
Who had watched breathlessly,
Thought sky and earth themselves
Moved to her rhythms*

And now Li Po—you and I, I know:

*An old man knows no more
Where he is going
On these wild hills, footsore,
He will not hurry!*

We know. We watch. We remember.

Shitao, Reminiscence of the thirty-six peaks.

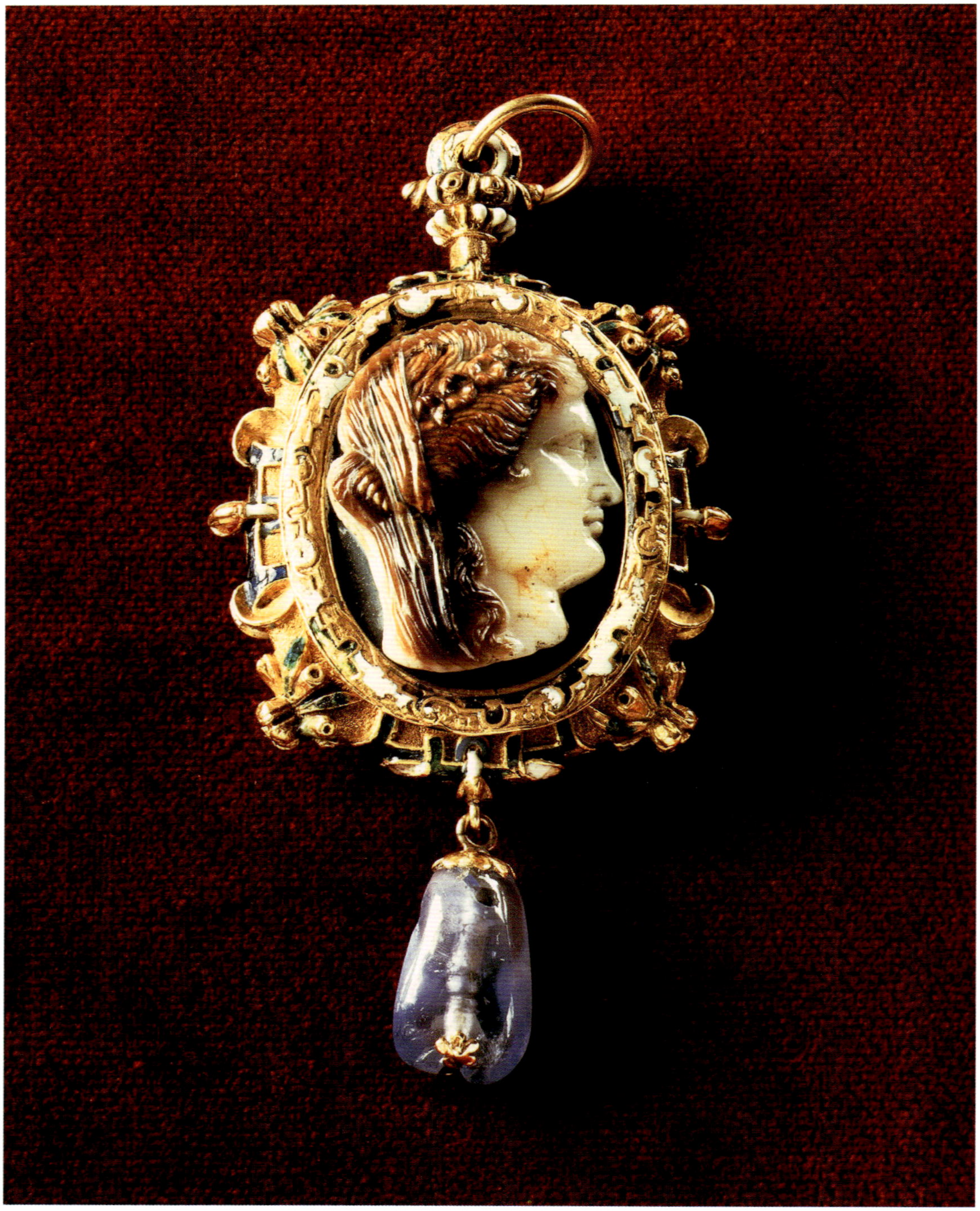

■ NINTH DUKE OF MARLBOROUGH: A merry chase—I was worried sick. With all the world giving Gladys a merry chase. That Prussian boy: Crown Prince William, certainly also the so-called Yank, Berenson, Monet maybe and who knows which Roman, a very merry chase indeed. And Gladys pretending all the while from her sixteenth birthday onward, on a birthday party on the sloping lawn at Blenheim, Consuela and I, and her mother, always her mother, Gladys stating she was the horse and I the fox. Clever she was. Always. And she went with the three Englishmen. To the land of the midnight sun, to the ends of the world, would I give chase to her. "*She sat reading on the beach for three hours with her legs buried in sand and then, as the afternoon melted into evening, she took up her pen.*

'*You devil! Why do you think I am out of temper? It looks as if thy conscience pricked thee…am I not the last of the Marlborough gems, Greek in temper with a more modern dash of Roman about certain parts.*'"

And then I knew the chase was over. I had won. Or had Gladys won? Or had Marlborough won? Devil take it, it was a merry chase.

■ MARCEL PROUST: A merry chase—It was I who gave Gladys merry chase: If one could term what I was able to do physically as a chase. But legs do not define a chase, the eyes and the mind define it.

From the day, lying on my bed, that I saw Gladys through my window, heavily veiled, stepping into an automobile, did I chase her.

And delicious it was that Gladys' mother informed me that she was ill and in bed and could not be wakened. "*A thin wall prevented me from seeing you, Gladys, and kept us apart. Alas it was a real wall and a symbolic one to extend endlessly in the plan of time. Very often I have thought of that evening…'When you were sleeping. And I denied the vision of you.'*"

Week after week, month after month, I could hear you pacing on the floor above me at the Hôtel des Réservoirs. I in a room hermetically sealed, lit by electricity—I might have had anywhere in the world rather than at Versailles, in the Hôtel des Réservoirs. I a floor below you, a world apart, chasing you in the day time dream of my life. Or was it you chasing me? Or was it a merry chase, each of each, like children dancing forever in a circle.

A merry chase—-first Ariel, then Daniel followed by Benjamin and David and Jeremy, leaving their astonished parents and the seated Abendana relatives wondering if this was some new American Jewish Passover custom, a kind of Native-American version of Find the Easter Egg in andante.

As soon as they entered the kitchen, the swinging door had swung from behind with Rachel again in the lead, racing at full throttle, leaving the large bowl with the green lettuce leaves on the table and tossing the Karpas directly into the bowl. Rachel sank into her chair, directly on her mother's right and smiled at the Abendana family with the sweetness of a teenager arriving home at two-thirty.

■ GLADYS DEACON, DUCHESS OF MARLBOROUGH: A merry chase—Of course it was a merry chase. And had there been no Marcel Proust, no Monet, no Ivor Guest, first cousin of Marlborough, no William, Crown Prince of Prussia— and that was the heart of a merry chase, to have him, HIM, propose, the Prince to me, had there been none of that, I only fourteen years old and looking at the October 1895 headline: DUKE OF MARLBOROUGH TO WED VANDERBILT HEIRESS, how could my merry chase come about? I wrote my mother:

"*I suppose you have read about the engagement of the Duke of Marlborough. O dear me if I was only a little older I might catch' him yet! But Hélas! I am too young though mature in the arts of a woman's witchcraft and what is the use of one without the other? And I will have to give up all chance to ever get Marlborough.*

But oh Miss Gladys don't you cry you sweetheart I'll come by and by. When he comes, he'll dress in blue, what a sign his love is true! You'll see what consolation there are in those simple lines!"

■ BLACK ELK: From behind—"*It was not long before we all knew what happened…because some of the people saw it happen, and I will tell you how it was. They told Crazy Horse they would not harm him if he would go to Soldier's Town and have a talk with the Wasichu chief there. But they lied. They did not take him to the wharf for a talk. They took him to the little prison with iron bars on the windows, for they had planned to get rid of him. And when he saw what they were doing, he turned around and took a knife out of his roll and started out against all those soldiers…Then Little Big Man, who had been his friend and was the one who told us boys that we were brave before my first fight, when we attacked the wagons on War Bonnet Creek, took hold of Crazy Horse from behind and tried to get the knife —and while they were struggling, a soldier ran a bayonet into Crazy Horse from one side at the back and he fell down and began to die. Then they picked him up and carried him into the soldier chief's office.*

That night I heard mourning somewhere, and then there was more and more mourning, until it was all over the camp. Crazy Horse was dead. He was brave and good and wise. He never wanted anything but to save his people, and he fought the Wasichu only when they came to kill us in our own country. He was only thirty years old. They could not kill him in battle. They had to lie to him and kill him that way."

Renaissance Frame, Hellenistic Cameo.

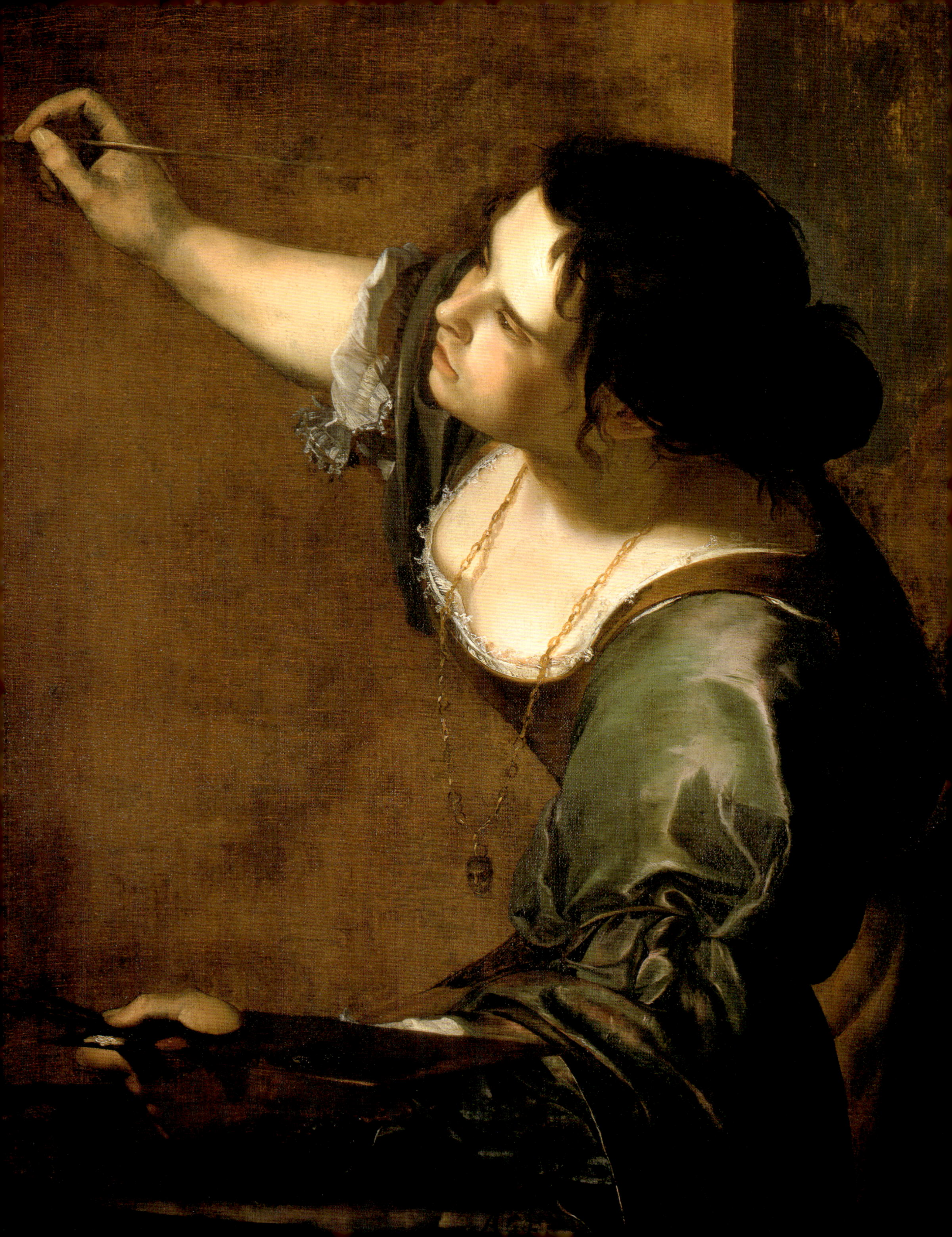

■ RABBI NACHMAN OF BRESLOV: Proceed—The night after the *shohet* brought me my wonderful chair, just before Rosh Hashanah 5569 (1808), I was given a dream:

A chair was brought to me, a chair surrounded by fire. All the world–all the men, women and children of the world—went to see the chair and circled around it. Upon their return, they immediately paired off and marriages were arranged between them. All the leaders of the world also went to see the chair.

"I asked, "How far away is the chair, and why were these matches made immediately?"

I was circling around them in order to get there when I heard that the Rosh Hashanah was coming. What should I do, proceed or remain there? I was torn. I felt: How can I stay here for Rosh Hashanah? But I thought, considering my physical weakness why should I go back?

So thus it was, I approached the chair and there I saw Rosh Hashanah, Rosh Hashanah itself, Yom Kippur, the true Yom Kippur and Succot, the real Succot.

I saw that the forms of all the creatures of the world were carved in the chair, everyone was there with his mate beside him. This was the reason that all the matches had been made, for everyone had seen and found his mate there."

I had been studying a verse from Daniel the previous few days, "*His throne was fiery flames.*"

The first letters of the Hebrew words *Korsyey Shevivim Di Nur* spell the word *Shadchen*, the matchmaker.

For it was by means of the chair that the matches were made. Furthermore, the word *Korsyey* is made up by the beginning letters of Rosh Hashanah, Yom Kippur.

"How shall I make my livelihood," I asked. They told me that I would be a matchmaker. The fire circled the chair because in truth, Rosh Hashanah is a great boon to the world."

And on Rosh Hashanah back in my home in Uman, I taught this, sitting in the chair given to me by the *shochet* of Teplik.

And what is happening here? What has happened always. And what will happen forever. First a voyage to the Holy City of Jerusalem–Ariel. And then a vision of Daniel: the fiery circle around the throne.

The true Rosh Hashanah, the true Yom Kippur, the true Succot and then speedily, in our day, the true Passover.

The family drifted back into the room and took their seats. Benjamin had no idea where he was, or how to proceed, or what to do—whether to laugh or to be sanctimonious, it was all so unexpected. He never knew what his wife or daughter would do. Was he so serious, so predictable, so scientific, that they had to be so frolicsome, so random? In any case, it was getting late and even though he knew that he wasn't leading the Seder but being led by Ariel and Rachel, he cleared his throat and sang.

■ ARTEMISIA GENTILESCHI, Roman painter (1590–1653): Benjamin had no idea where he was or how to proceed or what to do—If he does not know where he is, how can he proceed anywhere? And what can he do? Or I do?

In May of 1612, again and again, I was asked, questioned, bullied, beaten, railed at, sneered at, leered at, smirked at and patronized. Had I been violated by Agostino Tassi two years previous? My fingers in a vise, slowly being crushed, slowly crushing any of my dreams—the dreams of a nineteen year old—of art, of drawing, of painting as I had seen my brothers and father day after day do since I was a girl.

Did I know where I was or how to proceed or what to do? I screaming, "Yes! Yes!" He attacked. He and Tuzia trapped me like a dog in my bedroom, my father and brothers away in Florence.

And my fingers bleeding and I screaming, "Will I ever be able to use my hands again? Will they obey the command of my eyes?"

What a price to pay for revenge, more my father's hatred than my own, more my art than his.

Insane. Vile. The Devil's bargain itself. And for what? Agostino–exile–for five years. Or five hundred or five months. What did it matter? What was I but a skull kicked about the streets of Rome, picked up, fondled and dropped again, rolled by a whim into the alleys of Hell.

■ ORAZIO GENTILESCHI, Roman painter, father of Artemesia Gentileschi: Daughter—"*I find myself with a daughter and three sons, and this woman, it has pleased G-d, having been trained in the profession of painting, has in three years become so skilled that I can venture to say that today she has no peer; indeed, she has produced works which demonstrate a level of understanding that perhaps even the principal masters of the profession have not attained, as I will show your very Serene Highness at the proper time and place.*"

I showed these words on parchment to Artemisia, my daughter. In the sacristy of San Lorenzo in Lucina. We knelt, she and I, for hours.

Surely Cristina di Lorena, Dowager Grand Duchess in Florence, will heed these words. You will have a new life, Artemisia. You will have a new beginning. You will paint again. Artemisia held up her hand, fingers thrice the size they had been before her last deposition under pain of torture, and she said not a word but meekly looked at me through her distended fingers.

I led her back to our family studio and I took her right hand and slowly, slowly moved her hand, stirring the varnish. And then with her left hand in mine, I placed a spoon in a jar of ground amber and dipped the spoon, my fingers around her hand, pouring the varnish with its amber glowing onto a brush. Then with her hand safely in mine, I moved both of the interlocked hands, the brush in her hand, her hand in mine, backward and forward again and again across the canvas.

"You will paint again, Artemisia. You will wed. You will live again. We will be together."

Artemisia looked at me and said, "We will never be together again. We will be in exile."

It is a terrible thing to have a child who sees the truth and speaks it. May the archangel and all the celestial angels protect her, here and evermore. May my life be taken before she suffers one more day. Has any Lamb of G-d been so defiled?

Artemisia Gentileschi, *Self-Portrait as La Pittura*.

煙開蘭葉香風暖
岸夾桃花錦浪生
李青蓮鸚鵡洲句清湘老
人濟時亦拈出引興

◆ EMILE FISHER, FISHER'S FATHER: Remembered his father's words—I remembered my father's words and not only my father's words at a Seder but my father's words at all times.

How he would hold my hand and tell me when I said that I wasn't hungry, "The appetite will come with eating."

Father and I would go to Monsieur Droux, a feather customer. George Droux would push aside our ostrich feather samples and say, "Monsieur Emil, I have ostrich feathers up to here." Then he put his hand under his nose and pushed his head back while shouting, "I am choking on ostrich feathers."

My father offered, "Then give your customer this sample of ours for free. The appetite comes with eating, Monsieur George."

Maison Droux and Maison Judith Barbier did develop an appetite. But I remember best words, spoken by my father on any and all subjects. Words when I was afraid, words of comfort, words of encouragement when I was too afraid to ask, to talk, just the warmth of his heart, pouring out words more filling than any food.

Small wonder that I often make up words for Raphael and ascribe them to my father. I thought he would know they were not my father's but would understand why I needed to pretend that they were.

■ CÉZANNE: Has there ever been a greater miracle. The cone and the sphere and the cube and the line and the edge. Has there ever been a greater miracle? All from a cone, a sphere, and a cube.

■ LI PO: Raised his cup of wine and looking directly across the table—

"We both have drunk their birth,
The mountain flowers,
A toast, a toast, a toast,
Again another:
I am drunk, long to sleep;
Sir, go a little—
Bring your lute (if you like)
Early tomorrow!"

Tu Fu raised up his cup of wine and, looking directly across the table, understood my words. He bade a small child who was carrying his lute in a case to go back to the house.

Then he left. Softly treading on the path leading from the riverside hut we were sitting in. He walked on the pebbled path as though it were grass.

Not a whisper to disturb my sleep. I left the next morning before the house awoke. And never allowed myself another visit, so sweet it was.

Shitao, *Riverbank of Peach Blossoms.*

*"And I shall take you out as a people,
And I shall redeem you as a people,
And I shall take you to be mine."*

Benjamin leaned forward, and raised his cup of wine. He looked across the table at his wife, Ariel, remembering his father's words at a Seder table when he was ten years old. His father, very much a historian, first of Safed and then of Jerusalem:

"Has there ever been a greater miracle than the taking of Israel from Babylon, the taking out of the people of Israel from the midst of another nation? For Israel had become completely assimilated in the ways of Babylon."

■ PSALM 128: Wife—*"Your wife is as a fruitful vine within your home; your children as olive trees around your table. May the Lord bless you from Zion and may you see the good of Jerusalem all the days of your life. May you see the children of your own children, and peace upon Israel."*

◆ TUVIAH GUTMAN GUTWIRTH, FISHER'S GRANDFATHER: I shall take you out—Now they are a family singing together the words: "I shall take you out"—No family sings together. Always one starts and the rest continues. And who started? The child Rachel. And who delayed all this? The same child—my great great grandchild, Rachel. Is she not to be praised for leading her family in song, and is she not to be doubly praised for causing them to delay?

My father-in-law, Abish Rheinhold, would say at our Seders in Antwerp, quoting Rabbi Shmuel Sochatchor:

"We start eating the Karpas but make an interruption. Only after the Haggadah has been recited do we continue. First the children of Israel were told by Moses that they would be redeemed. But only after years of exile was the redemption accomplished.

For they were not ready for redemption. They lacked the genuine desire to come close to G-d, to be taken as G-d's own.

The Seder proceeds in stages, and by eating the Seder meal in stages we remember this pattern and stimulate a desire for physical and spiritual fulfillment."

The child Rachel knows when each is ready for each stage. She is the wise child who will teach for generations to come.

■ TU FU: Wine—
*"For Li Po, it's a hundred poems per gallon of wine,
Then sleep in the winehouses of Ch'ang-an markets.
Summonded by the Son of Heaven, he can't
    board the ship, calls himself your loyal
    subject immortal in wine."*

It was wine, always wine. Ever wine. We met in a wineshop near Lo Yang. The following year when he came to the hut that I had promised to build for us by the river in Sha Chiu in the east, if only he would grace it with his presence.

We gazed at each other across a table of wine cups. Li Po sang his verses softly, so as not to awaken the moon.

And he left. And is with me ever:

*"In these last outskirts of sky, cold
    winds rise. What are you thinking?
    Will geese ever arrive, now autumn
    Water's swamp rivers and lakes are there?
Art resents life's fulfillment, and goblins
    Dine on mountain travelers with glee:
    Why not send poems to that ill-used
    Ghost in the Mi-lo, and talk things over?"*

Benjamin is gazing at his wife across a table of wine cups. Even if they were separated for a thousand moons, the light in her eyes would be visible to him.

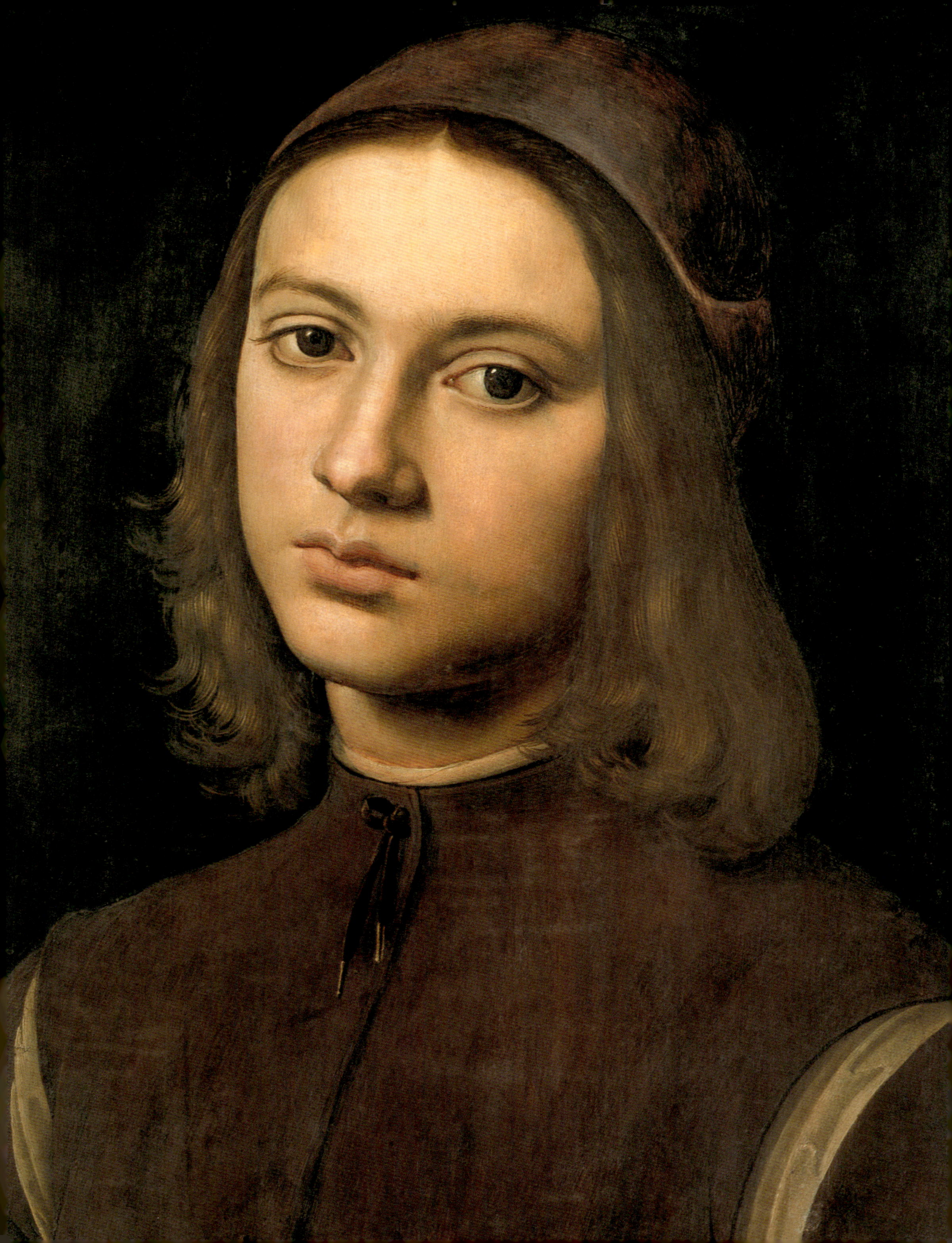

◆ ISAAC TAL, ABRAHAM TAL'S FATHER: Not even through a messenger, Abraham Tal—If it weren't so odd, it would be funny. If it weren't so funny, it would be so sad.

My son Abraham had everything. A quickness of mind, he could understand a problem from each and every angle.

A piece of diamond rough, he could draw on a scrap of paper, the stone, front, the top, the sides, and the bottom after looking at the diamond rough for not more than a minute. Once I put six pencils on my library desk, helter skelter, and asked Abraham and his brother, Tuviah, to stare at them for a minute.

Then I took my sons downstairs and asked each to copy what he remembered. When I returned an hour later, Abraham's rendition was perfect. He even remembered which color each pencil was and at which angle it had lain on my blotter. Tuviah's wasn't bad, but from the erasure marks on his scratch pad I knew that Tuviah had copied and adapted much of his work.

I marched the boys back to my library and showed them the originals. "Abraham, you've a perfect memory, a gift. Use it well. And Tuviah, all I can say is, stick with your brother's judgment." They did the opposite. Abraham, the advice giver, the *Etses Giber* as Pollak would call him. And Tuviah, who never would take advice from anyone.

Here are the three heroes: My messenger son Abraham and his two angelic clients, Raphael and Dosha-Jerusha. And their granddaughter Rachel. Is she named after my Rachel?

In each generation one is obliged to recall!

It's all too much, really.

■ RABBI NOSUN OF BRESLOV: get...out—*And my master, my teacher, moved his chair closer to us and though we were many, we were silent. He whispered:*

The storm wind came and carried him there and set the chamberlain down by the gate of a city. Soldiers stood there and did not let him enter. He put his hand in the vessel and took out money and bribed them, and he entered the city.

It was a beautiful city. And he went to a rich man and arranged to board with him, for he would have to spend time there; he would need to use wisdom and knowledge to rescue the king's daughter.

And how he got her out of there, he did not relate.

But in the end he succeeded.

And no one moved, and no one spoke. For did we not all know that the king's daughter would be taken out. And the tale—the first tale—all my Rebbe's—tales would be taken out—even the chair the Rebbe sat on, all, everything would be taken out. And where to, if not to Holy Jerusalem?

"And I shall take you out as a people," said Ariel, raising her cup of wine and quietly quoting from memory: "In each generation one is obliged to recall that one has gone out themselves from Egypt." Without lifting her gaze towards Benjamin, Ariel continued. "Hashem brought us out of Egypt not through an angel—Raphael, not through a seraph—Jerusha, not even through a messenger." She looked at Moshe Hayyim Abendana, Benjamin's cousin, and smiled, and repeated very deliberately, "Not even through a messenger, Abraham Tal, but by Himself, G-d, alone. In His glory."

Moshe Hayyim, agreed all the while, and chanting, "May you be blessed, Ariel."

Hearing her husband bless Ariel, Moshe's wife immediately winked at her.

Benjamin sensed that his Abendana cousins wanted to speak of their youth in Jerusalem—family gone, Seders past.

◆ RACHEL, TAL'S MOTHER: Not even through a messenger, Abraham Tal, but by Himself—Poor Abraham. Weeping in my arms and saying: "I will never marry my girlfriend. Never. It won't happen, she has nothing. Her father has nothing. Father will never accept her family. When would a Tal, let alone an Abendana, consent to wed their son to a Beller?"

Over and over, and he not yet eighteen. And I said to him: "Don't think for a moment, my son, that she has nothing. She has something. She has a good name."

He cried, "Yes, it's your name, Rachel." He crumpled at my feet, and I tried to reassure him, "It will work out, my son."

He looked up at me with the look of a five year old that he always had when he felt all was lost. "How, Mother, will it work out?" I answered with a voice that came from somewhere inside me, "It will come to pass after a long time. You will have your Rachel. Not through a messenger, Abraham Tal, but by Himself, G-d alone. In His glory."

■ RAPHAEL (1483-1520), Renaissance painter: In each generation one is obliged to recall—Perugino, my master, my guide. His hand on mine, guiding it in Perugia. I seventeen and he far older.: And telling me as we stood side by side before a canvas, "In each generation one is obliged to recall."

"Recall what?" I would ask, thinking he meant da Vinci. *Veramente mobile e celeste era Leonardo.* "This marvelously and divinely inspired Leonardo." Or did he mean the Soul of Art himself, Aretino's favorite, Michelangelo?

"I salute you with the greatest respect, for the world has many princes but only one Michelangelo," Pietro Aretino would bubble as Buonarotti would enter a room.

"No," said Perugino, looking at his canvas and not at me. "In every generation one is obliged to recall those who are obliged to recall." Then I looked at Perugino, my master.

I saw between him and his canvas, daVinci and Michelangelo and Giovanni di Paolo, the delicate mouth of the Madonna of Humility, through all these works Pietro gazed at his canvas.

And when I stood before the wall within the Stanza Segnatura Pope Julius' arm entwined in mine, "You will paint the history of all painting for me, for our church, for Rome, for ever."

And I placed the divine daVinci in the center, for was he not the pure Plato himself? And Aristotle too, and all of Athens but the simple key to it all, was my master Perugino recalling them all and I spoke to Pope Julius, "In each generation one is obliged to recall."

Julius held my hand tightly and said, "May G-d grant you the strength to fulfill these words."

Pietro Perugino, *Portrait of a Young Man.*

CAV. AMADEO WOLFGANGO MOZART ACCAD. FILARMON: DI BOLOG.
E DI VERONA

◆ Isaac Tal, Abraham Tal's father: His Abendana past. And why was my Rachel never anxious to speak of her Abendana past?

To talk of her father only occasionally, more in her silences than in her words. As though my sons Abraham and Tuviah could read her mind, or the mind of her father, whom they never met.

I would ask her to speak of the Abendanas, and she would say, "Whom should I speak of? Manuel Abendana, the Haham of Amsterdam? And should I speak of his father, Francisco Nunez Pereyra, and his cousin bride Justa whose children perished because Justa claimed that Francisco had not been received into the Covenant of Abraham and so Justa and Francisco separated until the rite was performed and Francisco changed his name to David? And shall these blameless children live? Ezekiel will provide, saith the Lord.

And should I speak of Isaac Sardo Abendana? Isaac supported his brother's scholarship in London and Amsterdam through his great wealth acquired in the Indies—only to perish and have his wife violate his deathbed wishes.

And what of the cousins of the Abendanas: the de Paivas. Abraham de Paiva, poet in Amsterdam, Jacob de Paiva, author of a Spanish arithmatic, and Jacques de Paiva, establisher of a Jewish cemetery in Madras, only to die in Golconda, leaving his jewel, Hierononyma Almonza de Paiva, floating like a cast-off bottle in the Hindustan ocean.

Such achievement and such suffering. Such wandering. If I began to speak of them, how shall I ever cease?

And so she refused to speak and what could I do but try to talk of their story when pressed by Abraham. Tuviah was never remotely interested in Hamburg, Amsterdam, Madras, London, or Castille. Strange how this Abendana is so anxious to speak of his Abendana past.

"And I will save you as Israel was saved in the land of Persia, referring to the Salvation of Purim," Benjamin continued.

But the word Purim was too great a temptation for Moses Hayyim—ever anxious to speak of his Abendana past: Spain, London, Persia, even India—more East than West, the Abendanas fancied themselves. He spoke up:

"Certainly Passover contains the salvation of Purim—the salvation of our entire people and the salvation of the entire universe. For the universe consists of the heavens, the earth and man. Man is the link between heaven and earth. Man's soul as part of heaven and his body part of earth and he himself a bridge between the two.

Passover isn't only like Purim but, as Yom Kippur is a day similar to Purim, Ke-Purim, so too are we all forgiven on this very holiday." Abendana paused and looked proudly around the table at each of his relatives.

◆ Tuviah Gutman Gutwirth, Fisher's grandfather: The word Purim was too great—Do not read the word Purim, but the world Purim. For the Maharal teaches us, in times to come the commandments of the Torah will be understood differently and observed differently from the way they are today. Shabbes will be observed with a heightened level of spirituality.

But the world of Purim, the holiday of Purim, will stand forever. Rabbi Eliezer says Yom Kippur, too, will not be nullified. And that is why this Jerusalem Abendana mentions Purim and is anxious to speak of his relatives at this Seder.

He is hoping, is he not, that their story will live forever, just like Ke-purim and Purim.

If a mother's longing is great enough, shall not her son or her granddaughter fulfill it?

May Jerusalem stir all their memories and may G-d be praised for having awakened these grandchildren from their parents' sleep.

■ Mozart to his father: Salvation—I wrote my father Leopold: Paris 31 July 1778. "My dear departed mother had to die. No doctor in the world could have saved her this time—for it was clearly the will of G-d, her time had come, and G-d wanted to take her to himself."

And what of me? My salvation? Not a witness at my grave site. Surely not Constanze, for she by custom was not permitted, a pauper's grave. Orphaned children without a father. Dear father, what of my salvation? Hyden granted me a century of fame: *Posterity will not see such a talent as his for this next hundred years.*

Beatified by others unborn, but my salvation lay in the movement of my fingers, moving along the pages of musical composition. My fingers caressing my children's cheeks, and of course, my Constanze my fingers on her—everywhere, at once and forever. Such pleasure!

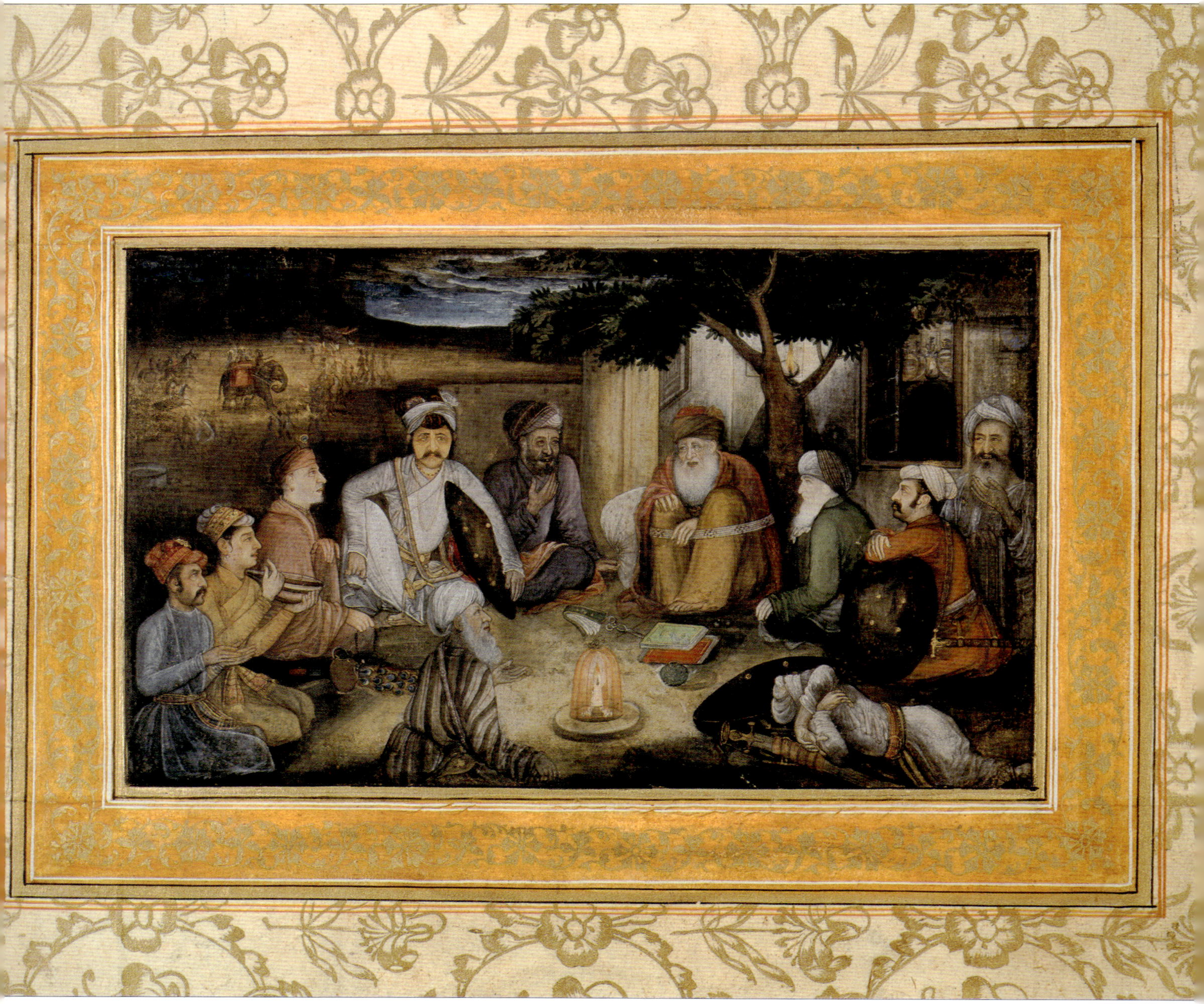

■ Rabbi Nahum Yanchiker, the Rosh Metivta of the Slobodka Musar Yeshiva: Words—On the day that the artillery of the Evil Ones—for I would not pronounce their defiling names in the Yeshiva halls—burst into the outskirts of Kovna in June 1941, I was asked by a student: "Rebbe, let our Master now teach us; do you not see that man is little lower than a wild beast? How can you, Rabbi Nahum Yanchiker, speak at this very moment about the dignity and nobility of man? The murderers slaughter Jewish babes without mercy...will you not realize that in but a few moments it will be shameful to be called a 'man'? Lift up your voice, therefore, and hurl this challenge against Heaven. Why are we punished so much and so exactingly?"

My students had been asking the same question for days—with their hearts, with their eyes, and now with their lips. I knew that now was the moment to speak.

"With the full weight of the authority granted to me as your Rabbi, I command you to leave me here. You must flee and save yourselves! Take heed of your bodies and your souls'. Do not place your lives in danger unnecessarily because of the lightning bolt that strikes from without. Do not think for one fleeting instant that you must sacrifice your lives for inner spiritual matters.

I beseech and adjure you to remember always those of your people who fell at the hands of the murderers. It is not for man to judge which one of them shall be a saint and which not. Everyone slaughtered by the wicked ones is to be judged a saint. My dear students always remember the Nehardea of Lithuania, the Yeshiva of Slobodka. And when the world returns again to stability and quiet, never become weary of teaching the glories, the wisdom, the Torah, and the Musar of Lithuania, the beautiful and ethical life which Jews lived here.

Do not become embittered by wailing and tears. Speak of these matters with calmness and serenity, as did our holy sages in the midrash," (Lamentations Rabbati) "And do as our holy Sages had done—pour forth your words and cast them into letters. This will be the greatest retribution which you can wreak upon the wicked ones. Despite the raging wrath of our foes the holy souls of your brothers and sisters will remain alive. These evil ones schemed to blot out their names from the face of the earth; but a man cannot destroy letters. For words have wings: they mount up to the heavenly heights and they endure for eternity.''

Cheered by her husband's eloquence Abigail put her hand on his head affectionately, like a schoolteacher's sign of approval.

"Thank you Moses Hayyim, words worthy of the Genius of Vilna," said Benjamin, smiling, a smile that only Ariel knew the nuances of.

"And I shall redeem you. Only when," he continued, looking across the table. Where was Rachel? Of course, she was under the table again.

"'And I shall redeem you.' The redemption is only complete when the Divine presence, the Shekinah, dwells over Israel. And this refers to the holiday miracle of the light of the menorah, and the verse '*I will redeem you*' continues with...' *an outstretched arm and great judgment*'—the overthrow of the Greek armies."

■ Cézanne: The miracle of the light—The miracle of the light is that the light itself comes from a solid, an apple that has weight, that does not roll off the table. A glass of liquid not reflecting to the eye but withdrawing into itself, sucking the light out of the atmosphere and congealing itself.

A tablecloth, crumpled on a table but able to hold on to itself, anchored by a bottle, myself in doubt. Although in truth am I not anchored by Hortense looming over me, steadying me?

The miracle of light is that it is seen, measured, observed, remembered, assimilated, understood, painted, frozen, transmitted. Chaos congealed. Solid, unchanging, aged yet not aging. Like myself, a miracle for a moment. I could feel it.

■ Payag: The holiday miracle of the light—A holiday, the wedding of Aurangzeb, was it not written in the Emperor Shah Jahan's history? Prince Aurangzeb and his bride, "*As they were crossing the field, the varieties of fireworks that lit up the night were beyond description. Towards the end of the night the Emperor Shah Jahan himself got into a royal ship and honored Shahnawaz Khan's [Aurangzeb's bride's father] house and in his presence the two were wed...congratulations and rejoicing rose from the earth to the highest celestial sphere, and singing and merriment engulfed time and space.*"

What a holiday. But read it holy day. And now the father Emperor cowers like a prisoner, across the river from his beloved Taj Mahal, staring at his sleeping Mumtaz. Aurangzeb rules. And the light has gone out in all Hindustan.

I weep for Balchand—but better for him that he doesn't see the darkness. Yet one light always remains. Even the Emperor knew this. I can see it in their painting. Across Hindustan, in the darkest night philosophers talk with officers, and one candle will ever light up the Hindustani night into a holy day.

◆ Rickele Padawer: Redeemed—Each Hanukkah my father would hold my hand after I had lit the Hanukkah menorah and looked at the Shamas candle I had lit, for only I was allowed to light the Shamas.

And my father would quote Hayyim ben'Atar: Let there be light—this is the wonderful Redemption that is to come. My father would place his hand upon my forehead and bless me with the words of the Yalqut Shim'oni. "*A generation is only redeemed by grace of the righteous women in it.*" From Hanukkah to Hanukkah, I felt the warmth of his hand on my forehead. And even after he died in '37, I felt the warmth of his hand upon my head—even in the frozen nights of the forests beyond Slonim during the partisan winters. I could feel my father's warmth, and I knew that I would be redeemed.

Payag, Officers and Philosophers.

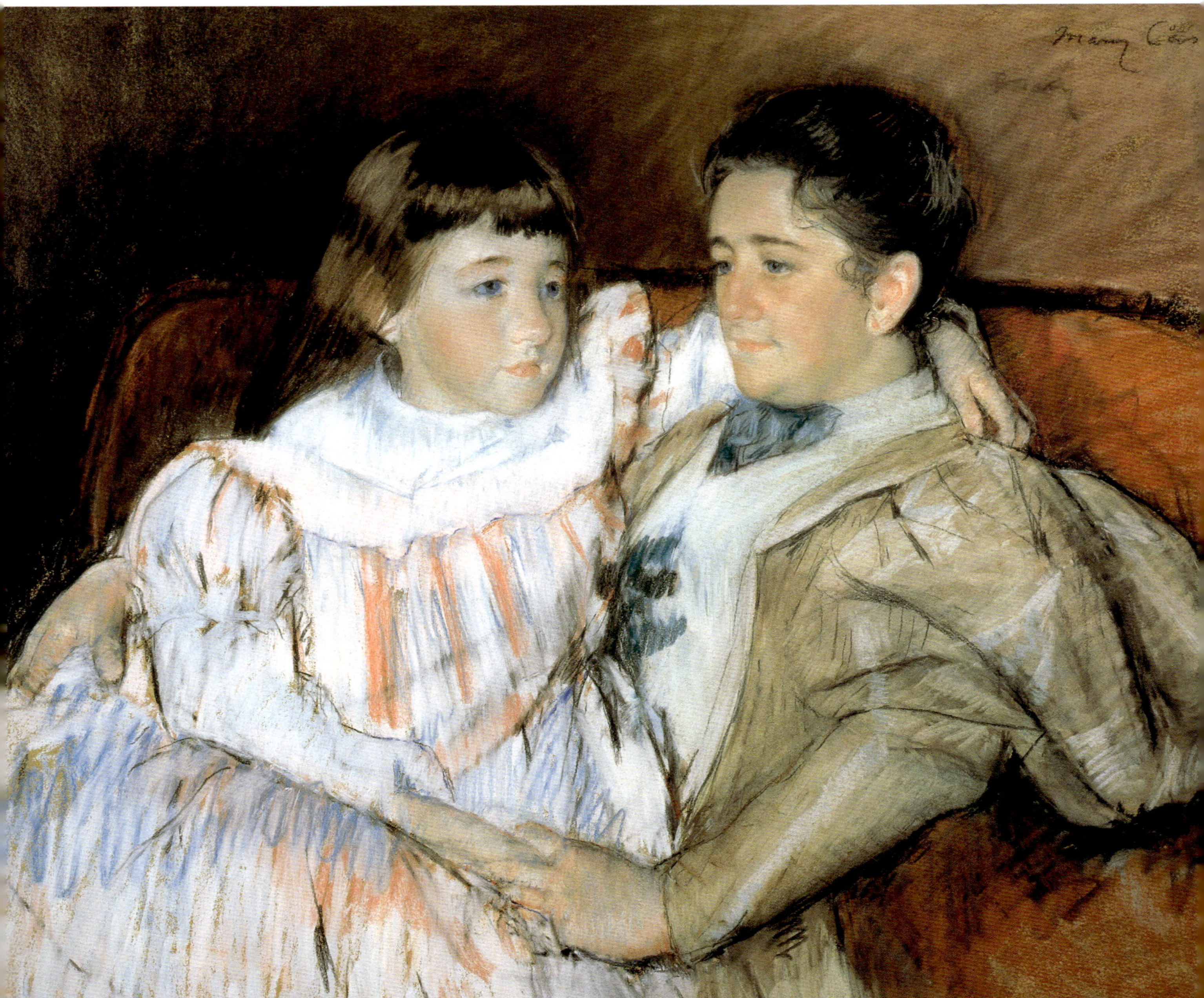

■ THOMAS JEFFERSON: And then I will take you to be mine—In the fullness of time, I would have voyaged up the Missouri to find my people: the Welsh speaking blue-eyed, blond, and red-haired Mandans.

I will take you to be mine, I grandly thought to say to these descendants of Prince Madoc who in 1170 sailed westward with ten ships, never to return to mother Wales.

I would have written the Mandan vocabularies and not theirs alone but others I had gathered through a lifetime of night time studies. I would have digested all of them, put them in collatoral columns, and joined them and myself through them to my ancestors.

"But the whole, as well digest as originals, were packed in a trunk of stationery and sent round by water with thirty other packages of my effects from Washington, and while ascending the James River, this package, on account of its weight & presumed precious contents, was singled out & stolen.

"The thief being disappointed on opening it, threw into the river all its contents of which he thought he could make no use. Among these were the whole of the vocabularies. Some leaves floated ashore & were found in the mud; but these were very few & so defaced by the mud & water that no general use can ever be made of them…Perhaps I may make another attempt to collect, altho' I am too old to expect to make much progress in it.

"…In truth, the ultimate point of rest and happiness is to let our settlement and theirs meet and blend together, to intermix, and became one people."

■ SHAH JAHAN: Each year we tell this story…for those of us outside this Holy City—I would stand beneath the archway in the Red Fort and stand and stand and stand all the day long. Often Jahanara would set my bed on the roof so that I could view Mumtaz's Taj Mahal by moonlight when my dream awakened me.

And I, Abu'l-muzaffar, shihab al-din Muhammad Sahib-I-Qiran-sani, Shah Jahan, Padshah ghai, son of Nor-al din Jahanghir Padshah, son of Akbar, son of Humayun, son of Babur Padshah, son of 'Umar Shaik Mirza, son of Abu Sa'id, son of Sultan Muhammad Mirza, son of Miran Shah, son of Amir Timur Sahib-I-Qiran, would speak of all my ancestors to my daughter Jahanara.

With my fingers on my Green Emerald of Paradise and my eyes on the Mahal of Mumtaz, Babur, Akbar, Jahanghir all would speak through my lips. In our eight year long captivity in Agra fort each year we tell this story for those of us outside this Holy City. And shall not this holy city and the Taj Mahal, even the Emerald Green of Paradise itself, forever be a witness to the Everlasting Glory of Timur.

And Ariel—without leaving the slightest pauses—from across the table, said, "And of course, what brings about this redemption is memory. Memory of where we, men, women, and children, have been. In Babylon, in Hellenistic Palestine, in Rome, and in modern-day Rome. What is the antithesis of memory but forgetfulness? What is the antidote of forgetfulness but study? And what is the music of study but repetition? And so each year we tell this story also for those of us outside this Holy City of Jerusalem who are, G-d-forbid, closer to forgetfulness, for those of us outside this blessed land." She smiled, looking at her family. "For those there is a repetition of our repetition of our Seder of remembrance—a second seder."

■ CHIEF LOGAN: Women and children—*"I appeal to any white man to say if ever he entered Logan's cabin hungry, and he gave him not meat; if ever he came cold and naked, and he clothed him not. During the course of the last long and bloody war [the French and Indian War, 1755-1763] Logan remained idle in his cabin, an advocate for peace. Such was my love for the Whites, that my country men pointed as they passed, and said 'Logan is the friend of white men.' I had even thought to have lived with you, but for the injuries of one man. Col. Cresap, the last spring, in cold blood, and unprovoked, murdered all the relations of Logan, not sparing even my women and children. There runs not a drop of my blood in the veins of any living creature. This called on me for revenge. I have sought it: I have killed many: I have fully glutted my vengeance. For my country, I rejoice at the beams of peace. But do not harbor a thought that mine is the joy of fear. Logan never felt fear. He will not turn on his heel to save his life. Who is there to mourn for Logan—not one."*

■ LOUISINE HAVEMEYER: Memory—Mary moved her pink pastel chalk across the paper as quickly as Electra skated across the lake near our winter home—faster even than the time it took for Electra to choose and put on a dress suitable for my portrait before we came to her mother Mary's home..

"What shall I wear, Mother?" Electra had asked me the week before. What was I to tell her? Anything pink and white or all white or all pink as Mary had instructed me but let her make the final choice Louisine, by all means, or she will never sit still even if I painted her with bolts of lightning.

How could Mary have known Electra's favorite frock, which she called her pink fairy dress, given to her by her grandmother, would be Electra's heart's choice?

But Mary knew my child better than I. She knew me better than I knew myself. And certainly far better than H. O. knew me.

"My, what a marvelous pink dream you have on," said Mary. "Like a queen do you look!"

"Oh no," Electra objected. "Mama is the queen."

"Oh no, Electra, momma is the Queen Mother. You are the queen," Mary said.

"Do you think you can pose without moving, Electra?" Mary asked her.

"Of course, a true queen never moves," said my child.

And so Mary sketched: Not Electra and me but rather our memory of women and children. Electra's memory of me. My memory of my child. Created by G-d, Mary, herself.

■ MARY CASSATT: Memory of…women and children—We would dine together and talk. She would listen and I would speak. We would walk into Duran-Ruel's art gallery and I would be on the verge of pointing out which of my paintings Mrs. H. O. Havemeyer, as Monsieur Durand-Ruel would unfailingly refer to her, Louisine would already have stretched out her long index finger, and languidly pointed it at the three figures and a landscape—"The Garden Lecture," as Durand-Ruel insisted it be called. The truth was after all those tea cups, walks, dreams exchanged, dresses ordered, girlish stories heard and reheard together the two of us didn't need words.

But how nervous Louisine always was. How very fidgety when I would do a pastel of her and her daughter Electra and gift it to her as a birthday present.

"But what should Electra wear?" she asked. "Pink," I said. "Pink." "But white is your favorite color, Mary," she interjected.

"Then white."

"But you said pink."

"Well, then, have Electra wear the pink one and it will become white in the future. But we will remember it as pink."

Louisine thought I was teasing. 'You told me my pictures will all find their way into American museums.' How will America remember Electra and me? America's memory of women and children will be of you and young Electra, but just as you are changing and she is changing, so too will my pastel change." And she thought I was teasing. But everything, Art included, changes.

Mary Cassatt, *Portrait of Mrs. Havemeyer and her daugter, Electra.*

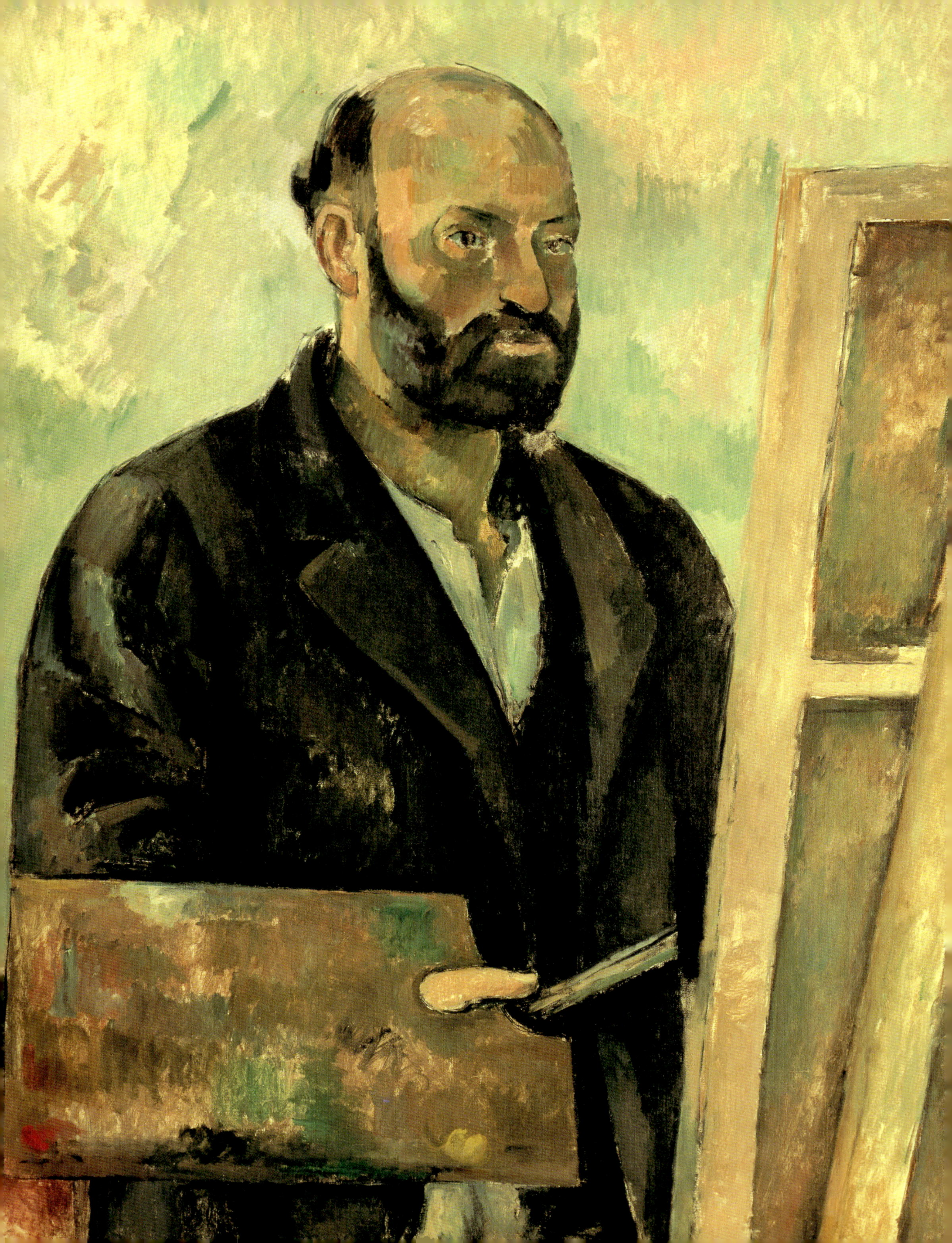

◆ TUVIAH GUTMAN GUTWIRTH, FISHER'S GRANDFATHER: Children—My son-in-law, Yehezkel Shraga, told me before he wed my daughter Sheindel, "Reb Gutwirth, I must tell you that I am not so religious. Considering this, may I still wed your daughter?" He paused a long time and waited for my response. And I paused a long, long time, for I was waiting for my answer. And each question that is asked in a generation often takes two or three generations to be truly answered.

Hashem Yisborah, G-d may He be blessed, put words in my mouth. "If one knows one is not religious, then there is hope one can become religious."

I put my hand on his shoulder and I said, "Your father, Yehezkel Shraga, was named after Simha Bunam of Pshiske, and who knows what children's children your children will have."
Simha Bunam said: "*We may learn three things from the child in serving the Lord. First, the child is always happy being alive. Second, the child is always active. Third, the child always cries for anything the child wishes for. In this fashion we should serve the Lord in a joyful mood; we should always be zealous to perform the Lord's commandments; we should tearfully implore the Lord to fulfill our aspirations.*"

■ IMMANUEL KANT: Children—Children ought to have their rights, but so should adults. "*Toby in Tristram Shandy, letting a fly which had long tormented him out of the window, addresses it: Go poor devil...this world is wide enough to hold both thee and me.*" And this, everybody should make his maxim. "*We must not harm each other; the world is wide enough for all of us.*"

■ TALMUD KIDDUSHIN: Green—"*The child shall keep the memory green of her parents, and whenever she speaks of them it shall be with words of loving veneration.*"

How does she know these things, thought Benjamin.

Suddenly he felt a patient little movement directly behind his pillow. In an instant he felt the pillow move and then saw a little hand remove the afikoman from behind him.

Without thinking, he reached down only to feel Rachel's forehead and then her tiny hand on his.

Once again he repeated, with the greatest patience "And what is the symbol of this remembrance?" As he listened to Rachel's voice, the daughter of a voice, *Bat Kol*, coming from under the table, and realized that in blessing his child he was truly blessed by her, children by parents, parents by children, and as a tear rolled down from his eyes, onto the lettuce leaf, he heard Rachel's tiny voice answer jubilantly.

"It's the Green!"

■ EMIL FISHER, FISHER'S FATHER: Blessing his child—I knew that Reb Gutman had heard reports from Paris of my father Bunam, who was a great Bal Zedakah, and must have assumed that I was of similar stock but I knew I must tell Reb Gutman that I was not so religious.

After he paused for the longest time, before responding to my confession that I was "not so religious," for me it seemed forever. Suddenly he spoke of children, of children serving G-d. I understood that in placing his hands on my shoulders, he was really putting them on my head, and not only on my head but that he realized he was blessing his daughter, Sheindel. He was a very wise man. He knew, in blessing his child, he was truly blessed by her.

And only now can I see what Reb Gutman could see long, long ago. My children's children jubilant, active, and speaking, so naturally, to the Almighty.

■ CRAZY HORSE: Green—The child has a tiny voice because her actions speak for her. She is their Chief. "*This world, the world we all live in is a shadow of the real world.*" It was from the real world I received my dream: In front of my eyes appeared a horseman, crazy-like, plainly dressed. Unpainted. The horseman floated above the ground: crazy-like.

And the secret was told to me: I was to be permitted but a few things. A single feather. A stone to wear behind my ear. I was never to take any plunder in battle. To put the dust of our sacred earth on my horse.

My own crazy horse: who could fly through bullets, with me unharmed, as long as one of my own people did not hold my arms behind me. Now I am dancing forever in the real world and I see all in the shadow world. I see the little children with tiny voices, leading jubilantly. never, never to be vanquished again.

The little lump of earth I sprinkled on my crazy horse before battle in the shadow land has taken to seed. And all people began to chant my name. His horse is crazy. "*One does not sell the Earth upon which the people walk.*"

Once again, in the geese laying moon by the slope toward Chankpe Opi Wakpala, the creek called Wounded Knee, my little lump of dust has turned green.

■ CÉZANNE: Green—Once in my life I permitted myself to paint myself painting. And what is a painter? All my life grâce à Dieu I permitted myself to paint my dreams of green.

■ F. SCOTT FITZGERALD: Head—"*Your books were in your desk. I guess and some unfinished Chaos in your head was dumped to nothing by the great janitress of destinies.*"

■ MARCEL PROUST: Patience—My last dictated sentence: *There is a Chinese patience in Vermeer's craft.*

Paul Cézanne, *Self-Portrait*.

NOTES

Guide to the Reader
First quote: James Joyce, *Finnegans Wake* (New York: Viking Press, 1976), p. 3. Copyright © 1939 by James Joyce; © renewed 1967 by Giorgio Joyce and Lucia Joyce. Used by permission of Viking Penguin, a division of Penguin Putnam, Inc.

Second quote: F. Scott Fitzgerald, *The Great Gatsby* (New York: Scribner, 1992), p. 152.

CHAPTER I

Page 1
Simha Padawer: Aubrey Rose, *Judaism and Ecology* (London: Cassell Publishers, 1992), p. 133. Quoting Norman Lamb's *Nature*.

Yiddishe Neshama: A warm Jewish soul. The soul and the Torah were likened to a candle. "The Lord said to Man: My candle is your possession and your candle is mine. If you preserve my candle, I shall preserve yours." (Pesichta Rabba).

Gauguin: Eckhard Hollmann, *Paul Gauguin: Images from the South Seas* (Munich: Prestel, 1995), p. 26, quoting Paul Gauguin, Jean Coize, ed., *Noa Noa* (Munich: Prestel, 1969), p. 8.

Dylan Thomas: Dylan Thomas, *The Poems of Dylan Thomas* (New York: New Directions, 1971), p. 195. "Fern Hill," copyright by Trustees for the copyrights of Dylan Thomas and New Directions Publishing Corporation; reprinted by permission of New Directions.

Menachem Mendel Schneerson: Chaim Dalfin, *Conversations with the Rebbe Menachem Mendel Schneerson* (Los Angeles: I.E.C., 1996), p. 205.

Laurence Sterne (1713-1768): Lodwich Hartley, *Lawrence Sterne* (North Carolina: North Carolina Press, 1968), p. 265. Laurence Sterne to Dr. John Eustace, a North Carolina physician who had sent him a curious walking stick.

The author of perhaps the most whimsical novel ever written. *The Life and Opinions of Tristram Shandy* (1760). "I begin with writing the first sentence," Sterne wrote. "And trusting to the Almighty G-d for the second." The book was an overnight sensation. "There is not a more perplexing affair in life to me, than to set about telling anyone who I am—for there is scarce anybody I cannot give a better account of than myself; And I have often wished I could do it in a single word—and have an end of it." "Through links to a great tradition of learned wit (Swift, Cervantes, and Rabelais) and through its artful, hilarious wandering through the mind of the characters and of the author, Sterne leads the reader, round and round, helter skelter, until one feels it is the reader merrily chasing Sterne, Tristram. Uncle Toby et al." See: Howard Anderson, ed., *Tristram Shandy* (New York: W. W. Norton, 1980), p. viii

F. Scott Fitzgerald: Edmund Wilson, ed. *The Crack-Up* (New York: New Directions, 1993), p., 140.

Rabbi Akiva Eger (1761-1837): A great Talmudist and Halachic authority. See: Benjamin Zucker, *Blue* (New York: Overlook Press, 2000), p. 240. Judah Leib ben Solomon Eger (1816-1888) studied with his grandfather Akiva whom he regarded as an exemplar of moral virtue. He also studied at the Yeshiva of Isaac Meir, the founder of the Gerer Hasidic Dynasty. Judah Leib Eger adopted many Hasidic ecstatic forms of prayer—marked by weeping and loud cries. His adherence to Hasidism met with strong family opposition.

Slonim: A city in Belorussia. See: Benjamin Zucker, *Blue* (New York: Overlook, 2000), p. 226.

Kotsker Rebbe: A Hasidic Rebbe, 1787-1859. Menachen Mendel of Kotsk, called the Master of Silence because of his many years living in seclusion. Said the Kotsker: "I have the power to revive the dead, but I'd rather revive the living." Emet Ve'emunah (truth and faith) p. 901 as quoted by Avraham Yakov Finkel, *The Great Hasidic Masters* (New Jersey: Jason Aronson Press, 1992), p. 137.

Proust: William C. Carter, *Marcel Proust* (New Haven: Yale University Press, 2000), p. 31.

Page 3
Elisabeth de Clermont-Tonnèrre: Ronald Hayman, *Proust: A Biography* (New York: HarperCollins, 1990), p. 262.

William Blake: "If the doors of perception were cleansed, everything would appear as it is, infinite." In 1804, William Blake, English poet, mystic, book engraver, and private printer, wrote: "Suddenly, on the day after visiting the Truchsessian Gallery of pictures, I was again enlightened with the light I enjoyed in my youth, and which has for exactly twenty years been closed for me as by a door and by window-shutters." Blake then began again to write his extraordinary illuminated books—among which *Jerusalem* is the longest and most complex. Morton D. Paley, ed.: William Blake, *Jerusalem* (New Jersey: Princeton University Press, 1991), p. 10.

Wallace Stevens:
John Richardson, *Parts of a World: Wallace Stevens Remembered*, (New York: Random House, 1983), p. 45. "Sweatered and moccasined" is from John Richardson, *Wallace Stevens: The Early Years, 1879-1923* (New York: Morrow, 1986), p. 171.

Heilige: Holy.

Mashgiach: The supervisor of the Yeshiva responsible for inculcating the ideals of *Mussar* (ethical teachings). "Among his duties were those of counseling students, disciplining them, giving a *shmues* (talk) aimed at the spiritual uplifting of the budding scholar. A good *mashgiach* was supposed to be sensitive to each student, and to know, often intuitively, how best to approach each individual: when to be stern and when to be kind, when to cajole and when to scold. The overall goal of the supervisor was to help in the development of the complete human being, aiding the young man in the successful integration of mind, body and soul…"

"One of the most famous supervisors was Rabbi Noteh Hirsch Finkel of the Slabodka Yeshiva (founded 1888). Rabbi Finkel lived as he preached, accepting no salary from the Yeshiva, existing on the meager income derived from a small store run by him and his wife. He was greatly respected and loved by his students, who affectionately referred to him as Der Alter fun Slabodka, the old one from Slabodka." William Helmreich, *The World of the Yeshiva* (New York: Macmillan, 1982), p.11.

Kafka: Franz Kafka was introduced to Hasidism by his friend Jiri Langer (1894-1943). Langer rejected his assimilated Prague family and journeyed to Belz, where he became a Hasid of Yisachar Dov, the Belzer Rebbe. In July 1915 Langer introduced Kafka to the Rebbe who was "summering" at Marienbad where he would greet his Hasidim from Western Europe. Kafka was awed, amused, and overcome by the encounter. On July 20, 1915, Kafka in his Diary addressed a direct plea to G-d: "Have mercy on me, I am sinful in every crevice of my being. Had talents, though, not wholly contemptible, some small abilities, but squandered them…am now close to the end, just at the moment when outwardly everything might turn out well for me. Do not consign me to perdition. I know that what we have here is self-love, absurd whether viewed from far or even from close at hand, but since I'm alive, I also have the self-love of the living and if the living escapes absurdity, so must its necessary manifestations. Poor dialectic." Ronald Hayman, *Kafka* (London: Phoenix, 1996), p. 210.

Page 5

William Blake: *Auguries of Innocence.* "God appears, and God is light…"

Isak Dinesen: Judith Thurman, *The Life of a Storyteller* (New York: Picador, 1995), pp. 13, 53, 55.

Dara Shikoh: Annemarie Schimmel, *Deciphering the Signs of God: A Phenomenological Approach to Islam* (New York: State University of New York Press, 1998), p. 226. Dara (1615-1659) was the eldest son of Shah Jahan, and was a philosopher and aesthete (see *Blue* p. 235). He was killed by his brother Aurangzeb (1618-1707), a religious fanatic. Aurangzeb seized the throne, and imprisoned their father. Aurangzeb's long reign was marked by intense antagonism to the Hindu majority of India. See *Blue*, p. 237.

Page 7

Simha Padawer: *Encyclopedia Judaica, Vol. XIV* (Jerusalem: Keter Publishing House, 1972), p. 1671-1674. Reb. Abraham ben Isaac Mattathias Weinberg (1804-1883) headed the world reknowned Slonim Yeshiva. Although the Belorussian Yeshiva had for generations been a *Misnagid* (opposed to Hasidism) bastion, Reb. Weinberg became a Hasid and the Yeshiva became a "hybrid" Hasidic-Misnagdic institution.

James Joyce: Richard Ellmann, *James Joyce* (Oxford: Oxford University Press, 1982), p. 440.

Gauguin: Belinda Thomson, ed, *Gauguin by Himself* (New York: Chartwell Books, 1993), p. 94.

J. P. Morgan: Andrew Sinclair, *Corsair: The Life of J. Pierpont Morgan* (Boston: Little Brown, 1981), p. 110.

Leopold Mozart: Maynard Solomon, *Mozart,* (New York: HarperCollins, 1995), p. 5.

F. Scott Fitzgerald: Edmund Wilson, ed., *The Crack-Up,* (New York: New Directions, 1945), pp. 154-156.

Zohar: The Zohar has been extraordinarily well described by Daniel Matt in *The Essential Kabbalah*: "The plot of the Zohar focuses ultimately on the Sephirot [The attributes of G-d]. By penetrating the literal surface of the Torah, the mystical commentators transform the Biblical narrative into a biography of G-d. The entire Torah is read as a divine name, expressing divine being. Even a seemingly insignificant verse can reveal the inner dynamics of the sephirot—how G-d feels, responds, and acts, how She and He relate intimately with each other in the world." Daniel C. Matt, *The Essential Kabbalah,* (New York: HarperCollins, 1995), p. 7. The Zohar is over 2,400 pages long—densely written—and only half of it is translated into English. Some ascribe its authorship to Rabbi Moses de Leon, a 13th century Spanish sage, others to Rabbi Shimon Bar Yohai, who lived a millenium earlier in Palestine. The Zohar writes:

> "So it is with a word of Torah,
> She reveals herself to no one but her lover
> Torah knows that he who is wise of heart
> Hovers about her gate everyday.
> What does she do?
> She reveals her face to him from
> The palace
> And beckons him with a hint."

Daniel Matt, Zohar, *The Book of Enlightenment* (New Jersey: Paulist Press, 1999), p. 124.

Page 9

John Malcolm Brinnin: John Malcolm Brinnin, *Dylan Thomas in America* (New York: Paragon House, 1989), p. XI-XII. John Malcolm Brinnin was the director of the Poetry Center at the Young Men and Young Women's Hebrew Associates (92nd Street Y). He invited Dylan to read in New York and elsewhere in America and Canada. Dylan died in St. Vincent's Hospital in Greenwich Village in 1953 after a long session of drinking at the White Horse Tavern.

Caitlin Thomas: Paul Ferris, *Caitlin: The Life of Caitlin Thomas* (London: Pimlico Books, 1993), p. 171. Caitlin Thomas (first the mistress of the painter Augustus John) was a writer, a dancer, and an extraordinary beauty. The tempestuous wife of Dylan Thomas and the mother of his three children, Llewelyn, Aeron, and Colm. Long after Thomas' death, she brooded and wrote about him.

David Slivka: He and his wife were close friends of Dylan Thomas.

Page 11

Paul Cézanne: Richard Kendall, ed., *Cézanne by Himself* (New Jersey: Chartwell Books, 1994), p. 19.

William Faulkner: David Minter, *William Faulkner: His Life and His Work* (Baltimore: The John's Hopkins Universtiy Press, 1980), pp. 95-96. on *The Sound and the Fury*.

Yehuda Halevi: 1075-1141. Hebrew philosopher and poet. Halevi longed to go to the Holy Land despite his great attachement to Spain (the land of his "fathers" and where his only daughter and son-in-law resided). Halevi was a doctor held in high esteem. In the last year of his life, he was able to undertake the dangerous voyage to the Holy Land, and was killed, as legend holds, at the very gates of Jerusalem, while kissing the ground of Zion.

"*My heart is in the East
And I am at the edge of the West*"

Quoted by Jessica Gribetz in her remarkable book, *Wise Words* (New York: William Morrow, 1997), p. 174.

Sarmad: Persian seventeenth century poet from a Kashani Rabbinical family. See *Blue* p. 231. Although he converted to Islam, he was called "the Jewish Sufi mystic." He was chosen by Shah Jahan to be the instructor of his son Dara Shikoh. Sarmad's lessons of tolerance shaped Dara Shikoh's ecumenical stance toward Hindus. Sarmad was beheaded by the fanatical Aurangzeb when he seized the moghul throne in Inida. Sarmad said: "Only when being has been left behind, canst thou the only source of Being find."

Page 13

Rabbi Nosun of Breslov: Chaim Kramer. *Through Fire: The Life of Rabbi Nosun of Breslov*, (Jerusalem: Breslov Research Institute, 1982), p. 116.

Rabbi Nosun of Breslov came from a wealthy, learned family, quite antithetical to Hasidism. In a dream, Rabbi Nosun saw a ladder that ascended to the Heavens. Each time Rabbi Nosun attempted to climb, he fell. Suddenly someone appeared at the top of the ladder and said: *Droppe Zikh un halt zikh* (Climb but hold yourself). A year later (1802), Rabbi Nachman went to Breslov, a few miles from Nemirov where he was living. When introduced to Rabbi Nosun, Rebbe Nachman said to him, "Now I am no longer alone. We've known each other for a long time, but we haven't seen each other for a while." Rabbi Nosun recognized the Rebbe's face. It was the face in his dream of the ladder. Rav Nosun recorded each story of the Rabbi and published his teachings. After Rabbi Nachman passed away, Nosun built many Breslov synagogues.

Theo van Gogh: Bernard Denvir, *Vincent: The Complete Self-Portrait* (New York: Courage Books, Running Press, 1994), p. 48.

Rabbi Nachman of Breslov: This tale, told throughout the novel, was taught to me by the remarkable Jonathan Omer-Man. I use his extraordinarily sensitive translation. I also thank Rachel Cowan and Nancy Flam for their wisdon and warm encouragement.

Payag: A brother of Balchand, a mogul court painter, he is believed to have been a Hindu, working as a miniature painter in the atélier of Akbar, Jahanghir, and Shah Jahan. Among the most evolved of Moghul painters. Payag grew from a rather journeyman artist under Akbar into one of the finest contributors to the Padshanama—the extraordinarily illustrated history of Shah Jahan.

"*Payag*," writes Milo Beach in his marvelous study *King of the World: The Padshanama*, "*does not present himself as humbly as his own brother Balchand [also a court painter of great note]. There is nothing reticent about Payag's paintings. More than any other artist, he flaunts his interest in European style…His portraits accentuate individual physiognomies—sometimes to such a degree that they seem statements about personality types, rather than individual likenesses.*" Milo Beach and Ebba Koch. *King of the World: The Padashanama* (London: Azimuth Editions Ltd., 1997), p. 217.

Page 15

Isaac Bashevis Singer: Dvorah Telushkin, *Master of Dreams: A Memoir of Isaac Bashevis Singer* (New York: William Morrow & Co., 1997), pp. 55, 230, 243.

Page 17

William Blake: "England! Awake, awake, awake" William Blake, *Jerusalem* (c. 1818-1820).

Ned McLean: Part of father's quote, "I don't need someone else to make me look foolish, I can do it quite well enough myself," is adapted from one of the author's remarkable friend and cousin Jesse Wolfgang's many wise sayings.

F. Scott Fitzgerald: Edmond Wilson, ed., *The Crack-Up*, p. 133.

Hexagonal Emerald Crystal: Nature expresses itself in straight lines. Emeralds crystallize in a six-sided form. Perfectly terminated crystals are exceedingly rare. Great skill is required to wrest the largest, purest, green gem from any given crystal. The most efficient cutting decision is to cut in an hexagonal shape mirroring the original crystal facing. It is a peculiarity of emerald (and sapphire and ruby) mining that the deeper one digs into the ground, the less pure the color of the gemstone and generally the smaller size of the crystal. The largest, purest green emeralds were found in the Columbian mines in South America (in the early days of the intensive exploitation of the mines in the 16th and 17th centuries) by the Spaniards who had forced the local Indian population to reveal the location of the Muzo and Chivor mines in Columbia. See: Benjamin Zucker, *Gems and Jewels: A Connoisseur's Guide* (London: Thames and Hudson, 1987) p. 54.

Bunam of Pshiske (1765-1827): A noted Hasidic Rebbe, Simha Bunam in his youth was a clerk in a timber concern, a graduate pharmacist, a player of chess, and a theater goer. He dressed in a non-Hasidic fashion. His teachings as a Rebbe stressed the importance of internal as well as external performance of mitzvot (commandments). See *Encyclopedia Judaica*, Volume XIV (New York: Macmillan, 1971), p. 157. Reb. Bunam once said, "*When I look at the world, it sometimes seems to me that every man is a tree in a wilderness, and that G-d has no one in His world but him, and that he has no one to turn to, save only G-d.*" Martin Buber. *Tales of the Hasidim* (New York: Schocken Books, 1991), p. 256.

Abraham Abulafia (1240-1291): Jewish Mystical thinker born in Saragossa, Spain, who interpreted the Bible by meditating all night, (dressed in clothing of white) on the true meaning of a single sentence of the Torah. Through word association and through *gematria* (numerical associations of words) Abulafia would arrive at the innermost secret of the sentence at dawn. His techniques of word association and use of dream imagery are considered to have been an inspiration of Sigmund Freud. See *Blue* p. 230.

Page 19

Evalyn Walsh McLean: "My friend came…one French compliment" from Judy Rudoe's wonderful study: *Cartier: 1900-1939*, (London: British Museum, 1997), p. 30. "You told me…fingers itch" from Hans Nadelhoffer, *Cartier: Jewelers Extraordinary* (New York: Abrams, 1984), p. 283.

Edward McLean: "That jewel is staring at me" from Hans Nadelhoffer, *Cartier: Jeweler's Extraordinary*, p. 284.

CHAPTER 2

Page 21

Kitab Khana: The artist's atélier.

Ein Eglaim: Perhaps the village of Ain el Feshkah at the Northwest end of the the Dead Sea. Rabbi Dr. S. Fisch, ed, *Soncino Books of the Bible, Ezekiel* (London: Soncino Press, 1960), p. 326..

Haim Vital: Ein Sof. The Hebrew name of God used by Kabalists meaning, "without end."

Rabbi Sol Fisch: *Ezekiel* (London: Soncino Press, 1960), p. 326.

Page 23
Simha Bunam of Pshiske: Martin Buber, *Tales of the Hasidim*, (New York: Schocken, 1991), p. 241.

Abulafia: Reuven Hammer, *The Jerusalem Anthology: A Literary Guide*, (Philadelphia: The Jewish Publication Society, 1995), p. 147.

Page 25
James Donoghue: from Jeffrey Meyers, *Scott Fitzgerald: A Biography*, (New York: Papermac, 1994), p. 334.

Sheilah Graham: *Scott Fitzgerald: A Biography*, p 334.

Dalai Lama: Mary Craig, *The Last Political Testament of the 13th Dalai Lama Kundun* (Washington, D.C.: Counterpoint Books, 1997), p. 1.

Page 27
Balchand: A Moghul court painter in the ateliers of Akbar, Jahanghir and Shah Jahan. A Hindu, the older brother of Payag. Much of what the author knows is owed directly to the warmth and knowledge—always given freely and enthusiastically—of Milo Beach. Director of the Sackler Museum, and writer of seminal texts on Moghul art, Milo Beach writes: "Whereas Payag was flamboyant in his composition, technique and depiction of physical appearances, Balchand is comparatively reticent…His figures also have character; he does not idealize. The figure of Karan Singh in "*Jahanghir Receives Prince Khurram On His Return From The Mewar Campaign*, for example, has a swarthy complexion, seemingly marked by smallpox scars—a detail absent from other portraits by other Indian Moghul miniature painters."

Rabbi Nachman of Breslov: *Advice of Rabbi Nachman* (Jerusalem: Breslov Research Institute, 1983), p. 107.

Bob Dylan: Bob Dylan, *Writings and Drawings* (New York: Knopf, 1973), p. 213. "Highway 61 Revisited." M. Witmark & Sons, copyright.

Moses Hayyim Luzzatto: Louis I. Newman, ed., *The Talmudic Anthology*, (New York: Behrman House, 1995), p. 216.

Page 29
Chusan boche: Young bridegroom.

Daitcher: German Jew.

Julius Meyer: Settled in Nebraska, joining his brother Max in 1866. He became a successful Indian trader. Meyer was given a Pawnee tribal name—Curly-headed-white-chief-who-speaks-with-one-tongue. He led a party of Indians to the Paris Exposition, 1889. See Harriet and Fred Rochlin, *Pioneer Jews* (Boston: Houghton Mifflin, 1984), p. 52 and *Encyclopedia Judaica*, Volume XII, p. 911.

Page 31
Oh but you will, you will, Gertrude: Pablo Picasso, after finishing a sturdy, rock-like portrait of Gertrude Stein, overcame her objections of "I don't look like that" with the answer, "Oh, but you will."

Mikhail Tal: Frank Brody, *Bobby Fischer: Profile of a Prodigy*, (New York, Dover Publications, 1989), p.79. Dmitry Plisetsky Sergey Voronkov, *Russian vs. Fischer*, (New York: Chess Books, 1994), p. 61.

Bjelica, Dimitrije: *Russian vs. Fischer*, p. 61.

Page 33
Cézanne: Richard Kendall, *Cézanne By Himself*, (New Jersey: Chartwell Books, 1994), p. 27.

Page 35
Tuviah Gutman Gutwirth: Benno Heinemann, *The Maggid of Dubno and his Parables*, (New York: Feldheim Publishers, 1978), p. 190.

The Vilna Gaon (1730-1797): Elijah (called Gaon or genius) of Vilna. He reputedly knew the Talmud by heart by the time he was nine. His glosses on the Talmud are a model of clarity. "*He toiled hard on emending Talmudic and midrashic texts. Subsequent discoveries of ancient manuscripts confirmed the soundness of his corrections, which appear in the Vilna editions of the Talmud (Haga'ot Hagra).*" Avraham Yaakov Finkel, *The Great Torah Commentators* (Northvale, N.J.: Jason Aronson Press, 1996), pp. 27, 29.
Wrote the Gaon of Vilna:
"*It is good to associate with the poor and humble people and to live among them. This way you will attain contentment and peace of mind. He who associates with the wealthy, although he may profit greatly, will never survive. He will continually run after more emptiness, as it is written, 'No man dies having even half of his desires fulfilled.'*" Also see Benjamin Zucker, *Blue*, p. 230.

Page 37
Tal's Father: Quotations are from Shemot Rabbah, I. Louis I. Newman, ed., *The Talmudic Anthology* (New York: Behrman House, 1995), p. 124.

Tal's Mother: Zohar III 93 a.See also Jerome R. Mintz, *Legends of Hasidim*, (Chicago: University of Chicago Press, 1968), p. 202.

Henry David Thoreau: Phillip Van Doren Stern, *The Annotated Walden* (New York: Clarkson Potter, 1970) pp. 24, 243.

T. S. Eliot: *The Family Reunion*, in T. S. Eliot, *The Complete Poems and Plays, 1909-1950* (New York: Harcourt-Brace, 1978), p. 227.

Page 39
Jacob Abulafia: Reuven Hammer, *The Jerusalem Anthology: A Literary Guide* (Philadelphia: The Jewish Publication Society, 1995), p. 186.

Page 41
Franz Kafka: Klaus Wagenbach, *Franz Kafka: Pictures of a Life* (New York: Random House, 1984) p. 162.

Milena Jesenska: Ernest Pollak was Milena Jesenska's husband. Frederick Karl, *Franz Kafka: Representative Man* (New York: Ticknor & Fields, 1991), p. 640.

Page 43
Vanse: A bug (Yiddish).

Page 45
Dylan Thomas: Paul Ferris, *The Life of Caitlin Thomas*, p. 96. Also: Dylan Thomas, *The Poems of Dylan Thomas* (New York: New Directions, 1971) p. 195. "Fern Hill" copyright by Trustees for the copyrights of Dylan Thomas and New Directions Publishing Corporation; reprinted by permission of New Directions.

Samuel Herman Reshevsky: 1911. Born in Poland, Reshevsky was a chess prodigy. At the age of 8, he defeated groups of adults. He became the American champion, defeating Reuben Fine and Isaac Kaufman. Reshevsky was an Orthodox Jew who did not play chess on the Sabbath or other Jewish holidays. *Encyclopedia Judaica*, Volume XIV, p. 82. An extraordinary careful player—Reshevsky sometimes lost "on the clock," running over his allotted game time. See also, Harold U. Ribalow and Meir Z. Ribalow, *The Great Jewish Chess Champions* (New York: Hippocreme Books, 1986), p. 81.

CHAPTER 3

Page 47
Sir Edward Coke: *The Case of Sutton's Hospital 10 Report*. P. 32.

Edward Thurlow: *Poynder Literary Extracts*, Vol. I, 1844.

J. B. Priestley: J. B. Priestley, *Man and Time* (New York: Doubleday, 1964), pp. 71-73.

Sir Henry Unton: The portrait of Sir Henry hanging in the National Gallery in London may be viewed as a philosophical key to the concept of time. J.B. Priestley notes: "The past, present, and future of the Elizabethan Courtier (seventeenth century) illustrate McTaggart's time series "A" in the form of one man's life from birth to death. In terms of this theory, past, present, and future are not "qualities" of Sir Henry, but relations that can be distinguished only by reference to some points outside of Time which therefore becomes meaningless. Also, every event must have a past, present and future; yet these factors cannot exist simultaneously. So, McTaggart concluded Time is only an appearance not a reality."

Page 49
Simha Padawer: *Rashi on Deuteronomy*. 17:11 citing Sifrei, Ronald Hoffmann and Shira Leibowitz Schmidt, *Old Wine, New Flasks* (New York: W. H. Freeman, 1997), p. 85.

Leon de Modena (1571-1648): Famous renaissance Rabbi in Venice who was a compulsive gambler. Born in Venice into a learned French Jewish family on his father's side and an Ashkenasic family on his mother's, de Modena was by turns a Rabbi; preacher; poet; a voice, music and Latin teacher; an essayist; a gambler; a proof reader and the writer of one of the earliest "modern" Jewish autobiographies. *"I have desired in the depths of my soul to set down in writing all the incidents that happened to me from my beginnings until the end of my life, so that I shall not die, but live. I thought that it would be of value to my sons, the fruit of my loins, and to their descendants, and to my students, who are called sons, just as it is a great pleasure to me to be able to know the lives of my ancestors, forebearers, teachers, and all other important and beloved people."* Mark R. Cohen, trans. and ed., *The Autobiography of a Seventeenth Century Rabbi: Leon Modena's Life of Judah* (Princeton, N.J.: Princeton University Press, 1988), p. 57.

Ambrois Vollard: Richard Kendall, ed., *Cézanne by Himself* (New York: Chartwell Books, 1988) p, 163.

Page 51
Rembrandt: H. Perry Chapman, *Rembrandt's Self-Portrait*: *A Study in Seventeenth Century Identity* (Princeton: Princeton University Press, 1990).

Rickele Padawer: Nachum Alpert, *The Destruction of Slonim Jewry* (New York: Holocaust Library), pp. 238-239.

Purim Spiel: A play staged on Purim by Yeshiva students, often ridiculing their rabbinical teachers.

Page 53
Dwight MacDonald: Dwight MacDonald, ed., *Remembering James Agee* (Athens, Georgia: University of Georgia, 1997), p. 167.

Robert Fitzgerald: A Harvard Professor of Literature and a translator of *The Odyssey*. He worked with Agee at Time Inc. in the 1930s.

Briton Hadden: Hadden, like Luce, prepared for Yale at Hotchkiss. Like Luce, Hadden "heeled" the news and was first in competition. Hadden was chairman, Luce merely managing editor. Both were tapped by Skull and Bones, but Hadden was tapped first. *"Luce and Hadden measured each other in a singular relationship that always contained more of rivalry and respect than friendship."* After graduating from Yale, they became partners in founding Time Inc. at age twenty-three. Hadden had a *"lighter touch"* than Luce, *"The reader was given a little story with a snappy title, beginning middle and end, sometimes complete with a bit of mystery or suspense."* Almost novelistic, rather than a news magazine. Virtually immediately, Time was an immense circulation success. On Feb. 26, 1929, just eight days past his thirty-first birthday, Hadden died from influenza. Henry Luce purchased enough of Hadden's shares to control Time Magazine. W. A. Swanberg, *Luce And His Empire* (New York: Scribner's, 1971), p. 32.

Gog and Magog: First mentioned in the vision of Ezekiel (38-39) of the end of days. "After the ingathering of Israel, Gog will come against Israel with many people from the furthest North…The Lord himself will go to war with Gog and punish him. These battles are said to be connected to the pangs of the Messiah and the great Day of Judgement. The war of Gog and Magog will be the final war. "During Islamic conquests, Christians believe Muslims to be the armies of Gog and Magog." *Encyclopedia Judaica*, Volume VII, pp. 691-692.

Page 55
Van Gogh: Cynthia Saltzman, *Portrait of Dr. Gachet: The Story of a Van Gogh Masterpiece,* (New York: Viking, 1998), p. 41.

Laurence Sterne: Arnold Wright and William Lutley Sclater, *Sterne's Eliza* (New York: Alfred Knopf, 1923), p. 52.

Simha Padawer: Søren Kirkegard, *Fear and Trembling* (New York: Penguin Classics, 1985), p. 45.

Apikoras: A person who has lost true faith. A Yiddish word derived from the Greek "Epicurean."

Page 57
Franz Kafka: Mary Hockaday, *Kafka, Love and Courage*: *The Life of Milena Jesenská* (Woodstock, N.Y.: Overlook Press, 1999), p. 47.

Milena Jesenská: Gabriel Josipovici, ed., Franz Kafka, *Collected Stories* (New York: Alfred A. Knopf, 1993), p. 128.

Page 59

Clarence Seward Darrow (1857-1938): A well-known Chicago criminal defense lawyer who argued in the Scopes trial: "I do not consider it an insult, but rather a compliment to be called an agnostic. I do not pretend to know where many ignorant men are sure—that is all that agnosticism means."

Milena Jesenská: Mary Hockaday, *Kafka, Love and Courage: The Life of Milena Jesenská*, pp. 51 and 57.

Shah Jahan: Annemarie Schimmel, *Mystical Dimensions of Islam* (Chapel Hill: University of North Carolina, 1975), p. 107.

Bat Kol: Literally in Hebrew: a small voice, a heavenly voice.

Yochanan ben Zakkai: Quote from Talmud, Chag 14b.

CHAPTER 4

Page 61

Van Gogh: Cynthia Saltzman, *Portrait of Dr. Gachet: The Story of a Van Gogh Masterpiece*, p. 21.

Assyrian Tablet: Sidney Homer, *A History of Interest Rates* (New Jersey: Rutgers University Press, 1977), p. 14.

Rabbi Akiva: *Encyclopedia Judaica*, Volume VII. p. 692.

Abdallah Ibn Salam: Abdallah Ibn Salam converted to Islam after Muhammad's arrival in Medina. *Encyclopedia Judaica*, Volume VI, pp. 884-885.

Gerald Murphy: Calvin Tomkins, *Living Well is The Best Revenge* (New York: Viking, 1992), p. 113.

Page 63

Archibald MacLeish: Archibald MacLeish, *Job: A Play in Verse* (Boston: Houghton Mifflin, 1958), pp. 2, 11.

Jahanghir: Wheeler M. Thackston, trans. and ed., annotated, *The Jahangirnama: Memoirs of Jahanghir, Emperor of India*. New York: Oxford University Press in association with the Freer Gallery of Art and the Arthur M. Sackler Gallery, Smithsonian Institution, Washington D.C., 1999), p. 146.

Page 65

F. Scott Fitzgerald: Matthew Bruccoli, ed., *The Notebooks of F. Scott Fitzgerald* (New York: Harcourt Brace Jovanovich, 1978), p. 45.

Cotton Mather: Ralph and Louise Boas, *Cotton Mather: Keeper of the Puritan Conscience* (New York: Harper & Brothers, 1928), p. 222.

Balchand: Ed. Milo Cleveland Beach and Ebba Koch, translator Wheeler Thackston, *King of the World: The Padshanama* (London: Azimuth, 1997), p. 28. Copyright, Her Majesty Queen Elizabeth II, Smithsonian, 1997.

Karan Singh, the "dark-skinned man in the yellow robe, was the eldest son of Rana Amar Singh. Sent to court as a mark of the Rana's capitulation to the imperial court he is shown being greeted 'with the usual ceremonials' by the imperial officials." *King of the World: The Padshanama*, p. 28.

Page 67

Sod Hatorah: Literally, in Hebrew: The secret of the Torah, the mystical secret of Torah.

Heder Boychik: Yiddish for school boy.

Mansur: Among the greatest seventeenth century mogul manuscript illuminators. His flower studies survive in the Leningrad library and in private collections. He was commissioned by the Emperor Jahanghir to draw flora and fauna in Kashmir.

Qarina: The "Shah-Jahani ideal of bilateral symmetry." The sense that there are mirror reflections and counter images of things sublime on earth and in paradise. See Ebba Koch's brilliant analysis in *King of the World: The Padshanama*.

Shah Jahan: Pratapaditya Pal, *Romance of the Taj Mahal* (New York: Times Books, 1989), p. 16.

Clint Murchison: An extraordinary Texas oil developer in the middle of the 20th century. Ferdinand Lundberg, *The Rich and the Super-Rich* (New York: Bantam, 1969), p 61.

Regine Schlegel: A woman whom Søren Kirkegaard fell in love with and was engaged to, but did not marry. *Encounters with Kierkegaard* (Princeton: Princeton University Press, 1996), pp. 34-35.

Page 69

Elihu Yale: Hiram Bingham, *Elihu Yale* (New York: Dodd Mead, 1939), p. 23.

Alfred Bingham: Alfred Bingham, *The Tiffany Fortune* (Chester, Mass.: Abeel and Leet, 1996), pp. 24, 263.

Tuviah Gutman Gutwith: Abraham Yaakov Finkel, *The Great Chasidic Masters* (New Jersey: Jason Aronson, 1992), p. 125.

Page 71

Mozart's mother: Maynard Solomon, *Mozart* (New York: HarperCollins, 1997), p. 177.

James Agee: Ross Spears and Jude Cassidy eds., with a narrative by Robert Coles, *Agee: His Life Remembered* (New York: Holt, Rinehart and Winston, 1985), p. 112.

Page 73

Leon de Modena: Mark A. Cohen, *The Autobiography of a Seventeenth-Century Venetian Rabbi* (Princeton, N.J.: Princeton University Press, 1988), pp. 105, 100.

James Joyce: James Joyce, *Finnegans Wake* (New York: Viking Press, 1976), pp. 26, 84. Copyright 1939 by James Joyce; renewed 1967 by Giorgio Joyce and Lucia Joyce.

Page 75

Archibald MacLeish: Mid-century American poet and playwright.

Rabbi Abba: Gustav Davidson, *A Dictionary of Angels* (New York: Free Press, 1967), p. 240.

Briton Hadden: W.A. Swanberg, *Luce and His Empire*, pp. 66-67

Clare Boothe Luce: Sylvia Jukes Morris, *Rage for Fame: The Ascent of Clare Boothe Luce* (New York: Random House, 1997), pp. 256-257.

The Vilna Gaon: Isser Zvi Herczeg, ed., *Vilna Gaon Haggadah* (New York: Messorah Art Scroll, 1993).

Page 77
Aryeh Yehuda Leib Katz: *Encyclopedia Judaica*, Volume III, pp. 667-734.

Golem: An artificial man-made person, a lump of clay like a human. A golem is created by a rabbi vouchsafed through great study and piety, with mystical powers.

Page 79
Mahlstick: A stick used to steady the hand of the painter.

Menachem Mendel: Abraham Yaakov Finkel, *The Great Hasidic Masters* (Northvale, N.J.: Jason Aronson, 1992), p. 102; I. Newman, *Hasidic Anthology*, p. 84.

Kay Glenn: James R. Phelan and Lewis Chester, *The Money: The Battle for Howard Hughes' Billions* (New York: Random House, 1997), pp. 125-126.

James Joyce: James Liddendale and Mary Nicholson, *Dear Miss Weaver* (New York: Viking Press, 1970), p. 191. Richard Ellmann, *James Joyce*, p. 352.

Page 81
Kalman Katz ben Zalman Gutwirth: Aryeh Judah Leib ben Ephraim HaKohen, 1658-1720: *Encyclopedia Judaica*, vol. 3, p. 667; Ephraim ben Jacob HaKohen, 1616-1678: *Encyclopedia Judaica*, vol. 6, pp. III, 667, 812.

Yihhus brief: A letter showing family genealogy.

Babur: Annette Susannah Beveridge, *Memoir of Babur* (1920), p. 483.

Hiram Bingham III: Hiram Bingham, *Elihu Yale: The American Nabob of Queen Square* (New York: Dodd Mead, 1939), p. 17.

Page 83
Henry Winters Luce: W.A. Swanberg, *Luce and his Empire* (New York: Scribner's, 1972), p. 17.

Elizabeth Middleton Root Luce: Henry Luce's mother. Before her marriage she was a YWCA worker among women factory workers.

Shachris: The morning prayers.

Thomas Pitt (1653-1726): Sir Cornelius Neal Dalton, *The Life of Thomas Pitt* (Cambridge: Cambridge University Press, 1915), pp. 236, 239. Pitt was a merchant involved in the diamond trade in India. Although arrested in 1674 by the British East India Company and fined for acting against the interests of the Company in 1693, he was eventually made Governor of Fort St. George, Madras. In 1701, Pitt acquired a great uncut diamond rough of 410 carats in the Kistna River alluvial deposits, called the Golconda mines (after the mountain fortress in which the "river" diamonds were traded). "Diamond Pitt," as Thomas Pitt came to be known, commissioned a Dutch Sephardi gem expert trading in Madras to make a model of the stone with a view toward cutting and polishing it. The stone was shipped to England and cut into a cushion shape brilliant weighing 140 metric carats. "Pitt was so fearful of the diamond being stolen from him that he never spent two nights running under one roof." Enlisting the aid of the founder of C. Hoare and Company (the oldest private deposit bank in England), Pitt finally succeeded in selling the diamond to the regent for Louis XIV and it has been known as the Regent diamond ever since. It is now on display at the Louvre in Paris. Arthur Balfour, *Famous Diamonds* (Carlsbad, California: California Gemological Institute of America, 2000), p. 68.

Page 85
Illui: a child genius.

Nogeh ba Davar: Touched by the matter (in Hebrew) not impartial.

Herman Melville: Jean-Jacques Mayoux, *Melville* (New York: Grove Press, 1960), p. 14; Herman Melville, *Moby Dick*, "The Child I Shared."

Gauguin: Michael Gibson, *Paul Gauguin* (New York: Editiones Poligrapha, 1990), p. 15.

Manna: Miraculous food that fell on Israelites in the desert, whatever they wanted it to taste like, it did.

Page 87
Proust: Alain de Botton quoted in Helen Sheehy and Leslie Stainton, *On Writers and Writing* (East Hartford, Conn.: Tide Mark Press, 1998).

Alma Mailman: Ross Spears and Jude Cassidy, eds., *Agee: His Life Remembered*, p. 118.

CHAPTER 5

Page 89
Nevil Maskelyne: Dava Sobel, *Longitude: The True Story of the Lone Genius Who Solved the Greatest Scientific Problem of his Time* (New York: Walker Books, 1995), pp. 166-167

William Empson: William Empson, *Seven Types of Ambiguity* (New York: New Directions, 1967), p. 193.

Alfred Dreyfus (1859-1935): A French officer wrongfully accused of passing secrets from the French military to Germany. The trial divided all levels of French society. After six years, Dreyfus was released from prison. Ernest Pawel, *The Labyrinth of Exile: A Life of Theodor Herzl* (New York: Farrar, Straus & Giroux, 1989), p. 229.

Emil Fisher: Reuven Alcalay, *Words of the Wise* (Jerusalem: Massada Press, 1973), pp. 322, 543.

Page 91
Rabbi Isaac Herzog: (1889-1959). Talmud Kiddushin.

"Herzog was nine when his father Rabbi Joel Herzog emigrated to Leeds, England, from Poland. He never attended a Yeshiva but achieved the highest standards in rabbinical scholarship, receiving semikhah (ordination) from Jacob David Wilkowsky (Ridbaz) of Safed. Herzog received a doctorate in literature from London University for his thesis *The Dyeing of Purple in Ancient Israel* (1919). Endowed with a brilliant analytical mind and a phenomenal memory...he was a linguist, jurist and at home in mathematics and natural sciences. The charm of his personality, which combined ascetic unworldliness with conversational wit and diplomatic talents, made a great impression."

Rabbi Herzog was my grandfather's (Yitzak Bunam Zucker, d.

1936 Paris) rabbi in Paris throughout the 1920s. In Paris, he made the *shidokh* (match) of my aunt Sarah Zucker and David Bezborodko (Z'L). He later became Chief Rabbi of Ireland and first Ashkenazi Chief Rabbi of Palestine in 1936. His son Chaim Herzog became president of Israel. Rabbi Herzog attempted to find a solution to the Arab-Jewish conflict over Palestine. In his lifetime, he was received by the Pope and many leading Jewish statesman.

Ephraim Zalman Margoliot: Rabbi Ephraim Zalman Margoliot quote from *Mateh Efrayim* as quoted by S.Y. Agnon, *Days of Awe* (New York: Schocken, 1965) p. 92.

Rabbi, author and businessman. It was said of him "*from the time of the minister Saul Wahl there had not been [such] Torah and wealth.*" His cousin was an ancestor of Abish Rheinhold, father-in-law of Tuviah Gutman Gutwirth (grandfather of Fisher). The Margolioth family traditionally traces its descendents from Rashi. See Encyclopedia Judaica, Volume XI, p. 963, and the Rheinhold family tree extraordinarily prepared by my wonderful friend David Hostyk

Laurence Sterne: *Wild Excursions*. p. 109.

Page 93
Sha'ar Ephriam: Talmud, Berachot, 1.5 b.

Shas: The Talmud.

Sabbetai Zevi: Sabbetai Zevi (1626-1676)), in 1666, claimed he was a messiah, splitting the Jewish world in two. From its beginings in Smyrna, Turkey, this largest messianic movement in Jewish history subsequent to the destruction of the Temple, spread as far as Western Europe. *Encyclopedia Judaica*, Volume XIV, 1220.

Posek: A judge on religious questions whose authority is accepted.

Gutman Gutwirth: *Jewish Encyclopedia*., vol. 3, p. 667.

Page 95
Arthur Power: O'Connor Cork, *Conversations with James Joyce* (London: Mercier, 1967), p. 185.

Marcel Proust: Ronald Hayman, *Proust: A Biography* (New York: HarperCollins, 1990), p. 475. *Proust*. A letter to Jacques Boulenger, p. 475.

Cézanne: In his painting, "In Hommage to Delacroix," Cézanne expresses his debt to previous schools of painting. "Like many of the impressionist painters, Cézanne retained a lifelong admiration for the works of Eugène Delacroix, who is seen in the sky between angels. Below are represented, from right to left, the painters Pissarro and Monet. Cézanne himself with a bag on his shoulder, the collector Victor Choquet, and another unidentified figure. According to the artist, the dog signifies envy, referring to the critics who continued to express their disdain for the art of a new generation. See Richard Kendrall, ed., *Cézanne by Himself* (Edison, N.J.: Chartwell Books), p. 59.

Page 97
Rebecca Neugin: "Memories of the Trail." *Journal of Cherokee Studies* 3:176. 1978. Rebecca Neugin as quoted in William L. Anderson, *Cherokee Removal* (Athens, Georgia: University of Georgia Press, 1991), pp. 35, 81, 176.

Rebecca Neugin's father: Anderson, *Cherokee Removal*, p. 81; *Journal of Cherokee Studies*, p. 3.

Father Spotted Tail: Ronald N. Saltz, "Rhetoric versus Reality: The Indian Policy of Andrew Jackson," in Anderson, *Cherokee Removal*, p. 35.

Page 99
Lee Krasner: Quoted in Deborah Solomon, *Jackson Pollock* (New York: Simon & Schuster, 1987), pp. 109, 111.

Tuviah Gutman Gutwirth: Isaiah 2: verses 2-4.

Wallace Stevens: Joan Richardson, *Wallace Stevens: The Early Years 1879-1923* (New York: William Morrow & Co, 1986). "The House Was Quiet and the World Was Calm" from Holly Stevens, ed, *The Palm at the End of the Mind* (New York: Alfred A. Knopf, 1971), p. 279.

Shlug Kapores: "*The custom in which the sins of a person are symbolically transferred to a fowl…often on the day before the Day of Atonement (Yom Kippur). The fowl is swung through the air and after the ceremony it is customary to donate it to the poor.*" Encyclopedia Judaica, Volume X, p. 756.

Page 101
Bava Metziah: Tractate in the Talmud that has to do with objects lost and found.

Luftmensh: Someone who has no visible means of income. "Makes money from air," in Yiddish.

Rabbi Naphtali Berlin (1849-1892): was the son-in-law of Reb Isaac Hayim Volozhiner. The Volozhin Yeshiva was the prototype of all Lithuanian Yeshivot. It emphasized learning, piety and rigorous self-improvement. From an article by Maidi Katz, "Secular Studies at the Volozhin Yeshiva" in Mikah D. Halpern and Chana Safrai, eds., *Jewish Legal Writing by Women* (Jerusalem: Urim Press, 1998), p. 290.

Page 103
Varmer Hend: In Yiddish, the term refers to the injunction to give charity while alive, with a "warm hand" as opposed to giving as a bequest.

William Blake: A poem from Stanza 2 of "The Crystal Cabinet" by William Blake. "Time will run…" from John Milton, "Hymn," Stanza 1, line 29. "From infancy…" from Peter Ackroyd, *William Blake: A Biography* (New York: Ballantine Books, 1995), p. 343.

Allen Ginsberg (1926-2000): Michael Schumacher, *Dharma Lion: A Biography Of Allen Ginsberg* (New York: St. Martin's Press, 1992), pp. 95-97.

Poet and essayist, Ginsberg was the hub of the ever-spinning wheel of Beat heroes and artists: Jack Kerouac, Bob Dylan, William Burroughs, Gregory Corso, Anne Waldman, Lawrence Ferlinghetti. Michael Schumacher wrote: "In 1948, shortly after Ginsberg's vision that "it was suddenly very clear to him that he and Blake shared the same consciousness though separated by centuries. Ginsberg had yet another mystical vision—in the Columbia bookstore. He was browsing in the poetry section, rereading a passage in Blake's "The Human Abstract," when he had the same shuddering sensation—a feeling that he had a few nights before. Looking around the bookstore, he was surprised to see that the people around him now had the faces of wild animals. The clerk, a man with a long face, had transmogrified into a giraffe. Looking at the man's face more closely, Allen sensed that he was a great tormented soul capable of the same elevated consciousness that he was experiencing in the store. Everybody in the bookstore knew these eternal truths, he felt, but they were so busy going about their daily lives that they did not dwell on their significance in the universe. Rather than face this cosmic consciousness, they hid their intelligence behind grotesque masks of self-deception. Perhaps this was for the best, he decided; if everyone faced this consciousness at the same moment, daily life should be terribly disrupted. People would be unable to accomplish even the most menial tasks. Passing along this consciousness was the duty of the poet. It was the supreme being—or New Vision."

It was at Ginsberg's concert in Woodstock that I was fortunate to meet Peter Mayer who encouraged my writing and agreed to publish *Blue*.

Zohar: Louis I. Newman, ed., *The Talmudic Anthology* (New York: Behrman House, Inc., 1945), p. 217.

Jahanghir: *Jahanghirnama* fol. 162A: translated by Wheeler Thackston; Milo Cleveland Beach and Ebba Koch, *King of the World; The Padshanama*, p. 96.

Page 105
Leonardo da Vinci: Michael J. Gelb, *How to Think Like Leonardo Da Vinci* (New York: Delacorte, 1998), p. 9.

"*From infancy, Leonardo would seem to have lived outdoors—he himself was later to write of the incident in which a kite swooped down upon his cradle, brushing its tail against his mouth.*" Da Vinci was very much self-taught. "*If you are alone, you belong entirely to yourself.*" At twenty, he entered the guild of Florentine artists, as a pupil of Verrochio. Da Vinci was the *uomo universale* with perfected interests in mathmatics, engineering, anatomy, architecture, music, drawing, painting and all forms of the arts. Da Vinci's anatomic renderings were based on extraordinarily few human dissections (though he perhaps viewed others). In addition, his view of the body was much limited by the medical knowledge of his times. "At the outset, it should be stated that Leonardo had no knowledge of the circulation of the blood and that his views of the function of the heart were in a continual state of flux." Charles D. O'Malley and J. B. de C .M. Saunders. *Leonardo da Vinci On The Human Body* (New York: Greenwich House, Crown, 1982), pp. 17, 18, 28.

Chief Joseph: Harold Lamar, *Encyclopedia of the West* (New Haven: Yale University Press, 1998), p. 200.

Leader of the Nez Perce Indians. *Young Joseph, or Hin-mah-too-yah-laht-ket (Thunder Rolling in the Mountains) as he was known, became chief after his father Chief Joseph died in 1871. He was always seeking to avoid war with the White Man. 'Rather than have war, I would give up my country…I would give up everything.' He agreed to lead his people out of the Wallowa Valley, along the Snake River, where the boundaries of Oregon, Washington and Idaho today meet.*

In 1877 the Nez Perce departed for the Lapwai Reservation. Bitterly attacked, stolen from and violated, the Nez Perce went to war. Chief Joseph tried to lead his band to safety into Canada, fighting his way "in a running campaign of over 1,000 mountain miles, conducted with a magnificent generalship that has been compared to Napolean's best. The war they fought, said General William Tecumseh Sherman, was "…one of the most extraordinary Indian wars of which there is any record. The Indians throughout displayed a courage and skill that elicited universal praise; they abstained from scalping, let captive women go free, did not commit indiscriminate murder of peaceful families."

Joseph led his tribe—men, women and children, sick, wounded, maimed and blind—through the Bitteroot Mountains, twice across the Rocky Mountains, through what is now Yellowstone National Park, across the Missouri River, to the Bear Paw Mountains, where on Eagle Creek, within thirty miles from the Canadian line, he finally surrendered on October 5th 1877," wrote Lieutenant Wood some years later. In his capacity as General O.O. Howard's aide, Lieutenant Wood recorded Joseph's oft-quoted surrender speech. See Alvin M. Josephy Jr., *American Heritage Book of Indians* (New York: Random House), p. 318.

Payag: Beach and Koch, *Padshanama*, p. 96.

Page 107
Hiram Bingham: Alfred M. Bingham, *The Tiffany Fortune* (Chester, Mass: Abeel & Leet, 1996), p. 351.

Monet: Monet to Evan Charteris. Judith Bumpus, *Impressionist Gardens* (New York: Phaidon, 1996), p. 13. Written three months before his death.

Proust: *Impressionist Gardens*, p.12. George D. Painter, *Marcel Proust* (New York: Random House, 1987), p. 94.

CHAPTER 6

Page 109
Nosun: Nathan

Sir John Chardin: Elihu Yale was a partner of Sir John Chardin, a Huguenot gem merchant, in England and Chardin's brother Daniel in Madras. In 1700 Sir John wrote his brother Daniel a 16 page letter describing the arrival of Elihu Yale to London. After 27 years of living in India, Yale found England "*a most chargeable troublesome place.*" Within a year, John Chardin wrote to his brother of Yale: "*I found him timid, undecided, always on the defensive and in a word, of no great consequences (non e mi gran cosa).*"

Elihu Yale spent the remainder of his years in England collecting art (over ten thousand works and objects) and dealing in diamonds, many of which he purchased with and from Governor Thomas Pitt of Madras, marrying off his daughters and finally assenting to Cotton Mather's request for a donation to the college at Saybrook, Connecticut. Mather grandiloquently prophesized that if the college could be moved to New Haven and be named Yale University—it would be for Elihu Yale a perpetuation of his "*valuable name, much better than an Egyptian pyramid.*" Yale gave the donation and Mather's prophecy proved to be true. Hiram Bingham, *Elihu Yale* (New York: Dodd, Mead, 1939), p. 184.

See also the extraordinary study by Edgar Samuel: "Gems from the Orient: The Acivities of Sir John Chardin (1643-1713) as a diamond importer and East India Merchant." (London: Proceedings of the Huguenot Society, xxvii (3) 2000), pp. 354-368. I would like to thank Edgar Samuel for his wide knowledge and ever-patient and warm encouragement in my study of this period.

Rabbi Nathan of Nemirov: Arthur Green, *Tormented Master* (Vermont: Jewish Lights Publishing, 1992), pp. 172, 180.

Rabbi Nachman of Breslov: *Tormented Master*, pp. 172-173.

Nabob: A person returning from India with a huge fortune. Originally a Muslim official, Nawab, acting as a deputy ruler in the Moghul Empire.

Place Fixe: French. Your own reserved regular table at a French restuarant.

Comme-il-faux: As it should be.

Gauguin: Marla Prather and Charles F. Stuckey, eds., *Gauguin: A Retrospective* (London:Park Lane, 1987), pp. 33, 34. Also see Paul Gauguin, *Avant et Apres* (Paris: Editions G. Cres et Cie, 1923).

Page 111

Ephraim: Genesis. The younger son of Joseph, based on the Hebrew word *Peri* "to be fruitful," brother of Menasseh. Jacob preferred Ephraim to Menasseh and crossed his hands, placing the right one on Ephraim, giving him the chief blessing. Rabbi Abba in the name of Rabbi Levi explains Jeremiah 31:19 to mean that Jacob blessed Ephraim thus: "You shall be the head of the tribes and the head of the academies; and the best and most prominent of my children shall be called after Thy name." The bones of the tribe Ephraim, fallen in the war the Philistines waged against them, were resuscitated according to the vision of the Dry Bones by Ezekiel." *Encyclopedia Judaica*, vol. 6, pp. 806-807.

Ariel: Another name for Jerusalem. The lion of G-d, or "mount of the world." *Encyclopedia Judaica*, vol. 3, p. 436.

Gavril: Jibril in Arabic of the "140 pair of wings" who dictated the Koran to Muhammad, Sura by Sura. To Muslims, Jibril is the spirit of truth. Gustav Davidson, *A Dictionary of Angels*. (New York: The Free Press, 1967), p. 117.

Peris : The word "fairies" is derived from the Arabic word *Peris*, for the inhabitants and companions of the righteous in Paradise. See *Paradise in Islamic Art*.

Honi: Honi HaMe'Agel in Hebrew, literally "Honi, who draws a circle."

"Once the people turned to Honi HaMe'Agel and asked him to pray for rain. He prayed but no rain fell. What did he do? He drew a circle and stood within it and cried out; 'Master of the universe, your children have turned to me because I am like a member of your household. I swear by Your Great Name that I will not move from here until you have mercy upon Your children.' A light rain began to fall. He said, 'It is not for this that I have asked, but for rain to fill cisterns, ditches and pools.' The rain began to come down forcefully. He said, 'It is not for this that I have asked, but for rain of favor, blessing and bounty.' The rain then fell in the normal way." Shulmanis Frieman. *Who's Who In The Talmud* (New Jersey: Jason Aronson, 1955), p. 121.

Page 113

Julius Meyer: Susanna Julia Meyer's (Dosha's mother) great-grandfather's brother. Born 1851. An Indian trader.

Max Meyer: Julius' brother, born 1831.

Sigmund Meyer: Max Meyer's son and Dosha's great grandfather. Born 1860. His daughter Susanna Meyer was born in 1908.

Amadeus Mozart: Peggy Woodford. *Mozart* (London: Ominbus Press, 1990), p. 93.

Constanze Weber: Robert L. Marshall. *Mozart Speaks*, p. 60.

Page 115

Beatrice Hastings: Carol Mann, *Modigliani* (London: Thames & Hudson, 1993), p. 106. Werner Schmalenbach, *Modigliani* (Munich: Prestel, 1991), p. 194.

Nilgai: A male antelope.

Lady Minto: K. Natwar-Singh. *The Magnificent Maharaja*, (New Delhi: HarperCollins, 1998), p. 41.

Maharaja of Patiala (1891-1938): Bhupindar Singh, ruler of the state of Patiala in the Punjab. "From his succession in 1910 to his death in 1938 the Maharaja Bhupindar Singh was Patiala, was perhaps the Sikh nation, and even for many in Europe was India." John Lord, as quoted in K. Natwar-Singh, *The Magnificent Maharaja*, p. 1. Patiala, as he was called, was the chancellor of the Chamber of Princes 1926-31, 1933-38, in India. He was at once a patriot, philanthropist, bigamist, father of Indian cricket, Cartier's greatest Indian customer, extraordinary gem collector (probable owner of the Taj Mahal emerald), and a friend of Motilal Nehru, Muhammad Ali Jinnah, Lloyd George, the Curzons and Minto.

The Coronation Durbar: In 1911 in Delhi, King George V, as Emperor of India journeyed with Queen Mary to greet and receive his Indian subjects. The Maharani of Patiala offered Queen Mary *"a large square emerald of historic interest engraved and set with diamonds. The Maharaja of Patiala made a sensational entrance to the camp of princes at the Coronation Durbar, leading a procession of 30,000 Sikhs all in flowing white garments, a group of eight elephants, the largest of which carried the Holy Book of the Sikhs."* The Magnificent Maharaja, p. 55.

Page 117

Abu Muhammad Ali: Andreas Capellanus, *The Art of Courtly Love*, ed. by John J. Parry, (New York: Columbia University Press, 1960), p. 9. From Parry's Introduction quoting the Dove's Neck Ring by Abu Muhammad Ali Ibn Hazm Al-Andalusi.

Andreas Capellanus: Andreas Capellanus, *The Art of Courtly Love*.

Abish Rheinhold: Rabbi Joseph Elias, ed., *The Haggadah* (Brooklyn: Mesorah Artscroll), p. 208.

Page 119

André Salmon: Werner Schmalenbach, *Modigliani*, p. 200. Ambrogio Ceroni, *Toute l'Oeuvre Peint de Modigliani*, p. 10f.

Page 121

Bet Hamidrash: School of learning.

Tuviah Gutman Gutwirth: Rabbi Moshe Weissman, *The Midrash Says* (Brooklyn: Benei Yakov, 1980), p. 195.

Gedolim: Great ones. Great scholars.

Joseph B. Soloveichik (1820-1892): Extraordinary Talmudist and teacher in Eastern Europe. He studied under his father, Isaac Ze'ev Soloveichik, and under Isaac, son of Hayyim of Volozhin. He became joint head of the Mussar Yeshiva in Volozhin along with Naphtali Zevi Judah Berlin. He subsequently became Rabbi of Slutsk. During the famine of 1866, he founded a society to aid the poor and personally collected donations from door to door. His son Hayyim, his grandson Moses, and his great grandsons each became Torah luminaries and maintained his vigorous, communally-responsible standards of Torah scholarship.

Joseph D. Soloveichik (1903-1993): His father was a rabbi in Europe and later professor of Talmud in Yeshiva University in New York. At the University of Berlin in 1930, Joseph was attracted to the neo-Kantian school. In 1931, he emigrated to the United States, becoming the rabbi of the Orthodox Jewish community in Boston. In 1941, he succeeded his father as professor of Talmud at Yeshiva University in New York. In keeping with family tradition, he wrote much but published little. See *The Lonely Man of Faith*, 1965. *The Rav Speaks*. Darryl Lyman. *Great Jewish Families* (Middle Village, N.Y.: Jonathan David Publishers, 1997), pp. 272-280.

Page 123
Spike D'Arthenay: First Quote: Denis de Rougement,. *Love in the Western World*. Second Quote: Bello, Hillaire, trans. *The Romance of Tristan and Iseult*. Final Quote: *Love in the Western World*. P. 28.

Pinchas Krémègne: June Rose, *Modigliani: The Pure Bohemian* (London: Constable, 1990), p. 132.

Beatrice Hastings: Rose, *Modigliani: The Pure Bohemian*, p. 133.

Page 125
Nora Joyce: Brenda Maddox, *Nora: The Real Life of Molly Bloom* (Boston: Houghton Mifflin, 1988), p. 198.

Richard Wallace: An American book illustrator. Wallace and his wife, Lillian, were great friends of the Joyces. Brenda Maddox, *Nora: The Real Life of Molly Bloom*, p. 177.

CHAPTER 7

Page 127
Mama Loshen: Language of mother, the Yiddish language.

Gotse Helfen: G-d will help.

Dylan Thomas: "Time held me green and dying…" Dylan Thomas, *The Poems of Dylan Thomas* (New York: New Directions, 1971). "Fern Hill" copyright by Trustees for the copyrights of Dylan Thomas and New Directions Publishing Corporation; reprinted by permission of New Directions.

Page 129
Tuviah Gutman Gutwirth: Low intonation. Deut. 28:15-68.

Masorah: The text of the Bible that is precisely transmitted. Some words in the Torah have different spellings or alternative meanings. Some are read one way in synagogue and written in another way; finally all the Bible is sung in synagogue according to masoretic note systems. Often the style of singing matches the text e.g. the low tones of Deuteronomy 28:15-68.

Emily Post: Emily Post, *Etiquette* (New York: Funk & Wagnalls, 1922), p. 117.

Solomon Alkabetz (1505-1576): Solomon Alkabetz, a Safed mystic composed the hymn "Lekhah Dodi" (Come My Beloved) sung each Sabbath eve to welcome the mystical bride of the Sabbath. See Benjamin Zucker, *Blue*, p. 227.

Page 131
Jahanghir: P. Pal, *Romance of the Taj Mahal* (New York: Times Books, 1985), p. 50.

Bob Dylan: "Tambourine Man." Copyright 1964, 1965 by Warner Bros., Inc.

Gauguin: Some of Cézanne's opinions by Émile Bernard. Richard Kendall, ed., *Cézanne by Himself*, p. 299.

Lawrence Ferlinghetti: In 1953, Ferlinghetti (with publisher/editor Peter Martin) founded City Lights bookstore. The store was a center for *"a substantial number of customers who would browse well into the late hours of the evening."* It published *Howl* by Allen Ginsberg and promoted *"little magazines like Circle Magazine…that didn't exist in the more-money-success-Time-magazine oriented New York scene."* Michael Schumacher, *Dharma Lion: A Biography of Allen Ginsberg*, pp. 183, 203.

Maharaja of Patiala: K. Natwar-Singh, *The Magnificent Maharaja* (New Delhi: HarperCollins, India, 1998), p. 55.

Carat: Comes from the weight of the Indian carob seed all of which have virtually the same weight.

Jharoka-I-Darshan: A balcony on the wall of the royal palace for the use of the Emperor. An alcove in the wall of the royal palace, known as Jharoka where the moghul Emperor made his most official appearance within the palace. Pratapaditya Pal, Janice Leoshko, Joesph M. Dye III and Stephen Markel. *Romance Of The Taj Mahal*, p. 80.

"*Before sunrise, from the time of Akbar until Shah Jahan, musicians played to wake the court and at the moment of sunrise, the Emperor presented himself in his Jharoka-I-Darshan, or balcony of appearance, high on the outside wall of the palace to reassure the people that all was well. Both Akbar and Jahanghir went back to bed for two hours after this early chore."* Bamber Gascoigne, *The Great Moghuls* (New York: Dorset Press, 1971), p. 184.

Page 131
Haham Zevi: Elijah Covo, died 1689. Judah Covo, died 1636.

Bebadol Khan Gilani: Wayne E. Begley and Z. A. Desai, *Taj Mahal: The Illumined Tomb* (Seattle: University of Washington Press, 1989), p. 16.

Howdah: A royal chair for royalty to be carried on.

Page 135
Marcel Proust: Marcel Proust in a letter to Jacques Boulenger: Quoted in: Bernard Strauss Holmes, *The Maladies of Marcel Proust* (New York: Meier Publishers, 1980), p. 69.

"And it was perhaps recapturing the past" from Marcel Proust, *Remembrance of Things Past* (New York: Random House, 1934), pp. 1024-1025.

"For along…bed early," from *Remembrance of Things Past*, p. 3.

Page 137
Farang: Foreigner.

Lahori: W. E. Begley and Z. A. Desai, *Taj Mahal: The Illumined Tomb*, p. 55.

Page 139
William Blake: Joseph Visconi, *Blake and the Idea of the Book*, pp. 50, 23. O. F. Theis, trans., *Noa Noa: The Tahitian Journal of Paul Gauguin* (San Francisco: Chronicle Books, 1994), p. 146.

René Descartes: Daniel Boorstin. *The Seekers* (New York: Random House, 1998), p. 142.

Nakahara Nantembo: Audrey Yoshiko Seo with Stephen Addiss: *The Art of Twentieth-Century Zen* (Boston: Shambhala, 1998), pp. 35-39.

Page 141
Rickele Padawer: Zohar II 225b, from Louis I. Newman, *The Talmudic Anthology* (New York: Behrman House, 1945).

Isabella Stewart Gardner: Douglass Shand-Tucci, *The Art of Scandal: The Life and Times of Isabella Stewart Gardner* (New York: HarperCollins, 1997), p. 76.

Sarah Choate Sears: Douglass Shand-Tucci, *The Art of Scandal: The Life and Times of Isabella Stewart Gardner*, p. 271.

Premier Poésie and Premier in La Peinture: First prize in poetry, first prize in painting.

F. Scott Fitzgerald: Arthur Mizener, *F. Scott Fitzgerald* (New York: Thames & Hudson, 1999).

Page 143
Cézanne: Richard Kendall, ed. *Cézanne by Himself*, p. 19. First excerpt from letter written 29 May 1858. Paul Cézanne in Aix to Emile Zola in Paris. Second excerpt from Kendall, p. 70. Cézanne L'Estaque/Provence to Emile Zola Paris. 19 December 1878.

Émile Zola: Marie Seillier, *Cézanne from A to Z*, p. 27.

Jahanghir: Jahangirnama, folio 132b-133 translated by Wheeler Thackston. Milo Cleveland Beach and Ebba Koch, eds., *King of the World* (Washington & London: Thames & Hudson, 1997), p. 92.

Mozart: Robert L. Marshall, *Mozart Speaks*, p. 184.

Page 145
Franz Kafka: Stanley Corngold, *The Necessity of Form*, (Ithaca: Cornell University, 1988), p. 61. Franz Kafka, *Dearest Father*.

Max Brod: Franz Kafka, *Metamorphosis*, pp. 53-54; Stanley Corngold, *The Necessity of Form*, p. 73.

Jiri Langer:Fredrick Karl , *Franz Kafka: Representative Man*, p. 404.

Frantsek Langer: Friedrick Karl, *Franz Kafka, Representative Man*, p. 344.

Bob Dylan: Only a pawn in their game, copyright 1963, 1964 by Warner Bros., Inc. © M. Witmark & Sons. Copyright reissued by Special Rider music.

Haham Zevi (1660-1718): Zevi Hirsh ben Jacob, known as the Haham Zevi ("learned Rabbi Zevi"), a Sephardic honorific although he was an Ashkenasi by birth. He studied in Sephardic Yeshivot in Salonica and Belgrade (1676-1679). His grandfather was Ephraim ben Jacob Katz (scion of the Gutwirth Family). See *Blue*, p. 227.

Page 147
Mrs. Nicks: When Catherine Barker Nicks came to Fort St. George, Madras, in the late 17th century she was unmarried. She "*set her cap*" for Elihu "*Yale but not successfully.*" Subsequently, she wed John Nicks, a merchant. In a trial of Elihu Yale by the East India Company, Yale was accused of being her "*secret partner*" and selling "*imported goods extraordinarily cheap to Mrs. Nicks and a native merchant.*" Several of the Nicks' children were named after members of the Yale family, Hiram Bingham writes in his seminal study of Yale. "*Scandal mongers whispered that there were more reasons for this than appeared on the surface; but there is no evidence of any real impropriety on the part of Mrs. Nicks, although it is said she sometimes stayed at Yale's house and that she had been in love with Elihu before he married Mrs. Hynmers. In fairness, it should be said that the governor frequently acted as G-dfather to babies born in the Fort. Mrs. Nicks was a shrewd, smart woman engaged in private trade and was probably often a partner of the governor's in transactions which however legal did not sell well in public gossip.*"

One of Yale's successors, Governor Higginson, thought differently. "*Mrs. Nicks lived with Mr. Yale at his Garden House, (where she and Mrs. Paiva, a Jew, with their children have and do frequent to the scandal of Christianity among the heathens.*" Hiram Bingham, *Elihu Yale*, pp. 39, 253, 298.

See also Elizabeth Lee Saxe's dissertation. *Fortune's Tangled Web: Trading Networks of English Entrepreneurs in Eastern India* (1657-1717). Yale University (Doctor of Philosophy), May 1979.

Page 149
Chavrusa: In pairs. The Talmud in the world of the Yeshiva was traditionally studied by a pair of students—one questioning, the other answering with both reading in unison.

Sura: "Sura, a town in southern Babylonia, Sura was not an important Jewish community until Rav moved there and established the Sura Yeshiva (c. 220 C.E.). He was called Rav because he was "*the teacher of the entire Diaspora*" (Talmud Beitzah, 9A, Rashi). Rav said: "*The future world is not like this world. In the future world, there is no eating nor drinking nor propagation nor business nor jealousy not hatred nor competition, but the righteous sit with their crowns on their heads feasting on the brightness of the Divine Presence.*" Dr. I. Epstein, editor, *Talmud Berakhot* (London: Soncino Press, 1990), p. 17a.

Pumpedita: An important study center of the Babylonian Talmud from the 259 C.E. onwards. Rav Yehuda founded the Academy of Pumpedita. Rav Yehuda "*used to don special clothes for prayer and prepare himself for prayer. He composed blessings for the New Moon and blossoming trees. He prayed only every thirty days. And in the intervening period, he occupied himself with Torah study.* Shulamis Frieman, *Who's Who in the Talmud* (Northvale, N.J.: Jason Aronson, 1995), p. 358.

Simha Padawer: *The Talmud*, Steinsaltz edition, Volume VII. Tractate Ketubot Part I. (New York: Random House, 1991), p. 8.

Mir-'Ali of Herat: A late fifteenth century calligrapher. Stuart Cary Welch, Annemarie Schimmel, Marie Swietochowski, Wheeler N.

Thackston, *The Emperor's Album* (New York: Metropolitan Museum of Art, 1987), p. 31.

An extraordinary Muslim calligrapher, Mir-'Ali of Tabriz in c. 1400 applied the rules of measuring the letters with dots and circles to the hanging style. With him began the style called Nastaliq. Nastaliq, called by its admirers "the bride among calligraphic styles," proved an ideal vehicle for poetry. *The Emperor's Album.*

Jahanghir: Stuart Cary Welch et al, *Emperor's Album*, p. 34.

F. Scott Fitzgerald: Edmund Wilson, *The Crack-Up* (New York: New Directions, 1945). Don Oberderfer. *Princeton University: The First 250 Years* (Princeton, N.J.: Princeton University Press, 1965), pp. 10, 12.

CHAPTER 8

Page 151
Cézanne: Henri Callemand, *Visions of a Great Painter*, p. 4.

Émile Bernard: Richard Kendall, ed., *Cézanne by Himself*, p. 289.

Zouave: A member of the light infantry in the French army, originally from North Africa.

Dr. Gachet: Dr. Paul Ferdinand Gachet (1828-1909) was an ardent collector of impressionistic painting in Auvers, France, and a "father figure" and doctor to Pissarro, Cézanne, and especially to van Gogh. Gachet offered to van Gogh, when he insisted on leaving the asylum at St. Rémy, that "*Vincent should lodge in a nearby inn so that he should be able to visit the doctor's home whenever he wished.*" Van Gogh ate many meals at Gachet's home and wrote his sister Wilhelmina that Gachet was "*a true friend...something like another brother.*" Gachet's stupendous collection of Impressionists was eventually donated by his son Paul to the Louvre and is presently on display in Gare d'Orsay in Paris. David Sweetman, *Van Gogh* (New York: Crown, 1990), pp. 326, 365.

Page 153
Franz Kafka: Harold Salfellner, *Franz Kafka and Prague* (Prague: Vitalis, 1996), pp. 93- 95.

Vilna Gaon: Yisrael Isser Zvi Herczeg, ed., *Vilna Gaon Haggadah* (New York: Messorah Publications, 1993), p. 17.

John Donne: This quotation from John Donne was found in Jonathan Rosen's remarkable book examining the parallel universes of the Talmud and the Web, *The Talmud and the Internet: A Journey Between Two Worlds* (New York: Farrar, Straus & Giroux, 2000), p. 5.

Page 155
Cézanne: Richard Kendall, ed., *Cézanne by Himself*, pp. 241-242.

Page 157
Bérénice: An extraordinary tiara, created by Cartier especially for the 1925 Exposition des Arts Décoratifs in Paris. Also Coma Bérénices—exquisite hair like Bérénice (a Latin phrase).

Named for Bérénice, a Roman queen of legendary beauty. This name "*invented by the Gazette du Bon Ton in 1925 has since applied to both the necklace (epaulette containing the Taj Mahal emerald) and the diadem.*"

Judy Rudoe, *Cartier 1900-1939* (New York: Harry N. Abrams, 1997), p. 316.

Page 161
William Blake: Morton D. Paley, *Jerusalem* (Princeton, N.J.: Princeton University Press, 1991), pp. 258-259.

Page 163
Alma Mailman: "After their marriage in 1938, they lived in New Jersey where Agee wrote *Let Us Now Praise Famous Men,* and then in New York until their separation in 1941." Ross Spears and Jude Cassidy, eds., Narrative by Robert Coles, *Agee: His Life Remembered* (New York: Holt, Rinehart & Winston, 1985), p. 112.

Mozart: Robert L. Marshall, *Mozart Speaks* (New York: Schirmer Books, 1991), p. 353.

Lorenzo Da Ponte: Eighteenth century Italian librettist, worked with Mozart on *Figaro, Don Giovanni,* and *Cosí Fan Tutte*. Peggy Woodford, *Mozart* (London: Ominibus Press, 1990), p. 110.

Page 165
Shlichim: Literally "to send" in Hebrew. Emissaries who are sent to raise money for charity. "*The almighty has many agents*" (Numbers, Rabbah). Individuals sent by a Hasidic Rebbe to found a synagogue or perform some religious mission. "People sent on pious missions will meet no evil" (Talmud Pessahim). Rabbi Shlomo Carlebach acted as a "traveling musical Sheliach" of the Lubavitcher Rebbe from 1951-1954.

El T'hami: See Gavin Maxwell, *Lords of the Atlas: The Rise and Fall of the House of Glaoua, 1893-1956,* (New York: E. P. Dutton & Co., 1966), p. 153

"*Madani and his brother T'hami El Glaoui, sons of a Moraccan Cadi by an Ethiopian concubine rose to power in "the almost medieval state of Morocco at the end of the nineteenth century.*" T'hami ruled until 1956 from his castle in the High Atlas mountains, as well as in Marrakesh. T'hami, the Glaoui of Morocco, lived life as a potentate out of the Arabian nights. Drawn to Paris and all things French, he purchased the epaulette necklace, without the Taj Mahal emerald, perhaps because of the emerald's "asking price" from Cartier in 1928.

CHAPTER 9

Page 167
Rabbi Velvel Soloveichik: *The Haggadah of the Roshei Yeshiva: Book Two.* Adapted by Rabbi Blinder from the Hebrew compiled by Rabbi Asher Bergman in association with Rabbi Shalom Meir Wallach (Brooklyn: Mesorah Publications, 1999), p. 260.

Simha Padawer: Nachum Alpert, *The Destruction of the Slonim Jews* (New York: Holocaust Library, 1989), p. 304.

Leonor Acevedo Borges: First quote: James Woodall, *Borges: A Life* (New York: Basic Books/HarperCollins, 1996), p. 210. Second quote, "revealed...very voice": Edited with forward by Carlos Continez, *Simply a Man of Letters* (Maine: University of Maine at Orono Press, 1982), p. 177. Third quote, "Those who...shall be": Jorge Louis Borges, *Pierre Menard, Author of the Quixote, Collected Fictions,* trans. by Andrew Hurley (New York: Viking Press, 1998), pp. 91, 95.

Fourth quote, "put mother...the mother" from Woodall, *Borges: A Life*, p. 11.

Gemara: The commentary on the Mishnah. The Mishnah and the Gemara together are called the Talmud.

Page 169
Abraham Abulafia: Reuven Hammer, *The Jerusalem Anthology*. Isaiah 34:11-14. pp. 60-61.

Koran Sura: Wayne E. Begley and Z. A. Desai, *The Taj Mahal: The Illumined Tomb*.

Page 171
Arshile Gorky: "cone, cylinder..." from Matthew Spender, *From a High Place: A Life of Arshile Gorky* (New York: Knopf, 1999), p. 80. "Cézanne...has lived" Spender, p. 70.

Siroon Mousigian: Matthew Spender, pp. 79, 81.

Chester Dale: Thomas E. Norton, *100 Years of Collecting in America: The Story of Sotheby Parke Bernet* (New York: Harry N. Abrams, 1984), p. 13.

Lorenzo Da Ponte: Peggy Woodford, *Mozart*, pp. 118-119.

F. Scott Fitzgerald: Honoria Murphy Donnellly with Richard N. Billings, *Sara and Gerald: Villa America and After* (New York: Times Books, 1982), p. 105.

Page 173
Tuviah Gutman Gutwirth: Louis I. Newman, *The Hasidic Anthology*, p. 458.

Koran: Sura 17:1.

Abu Bakr Muhammad ben Ahmad al wasiti: I. Hasson Jerusalem 1973. *Fada'il al-Bayt al Muqaddas* by Abu Bakr Muhammad ben Ahmad al-Wasiti, p. 483. From Chapter 5, "The Spiritual Meaning of Jerusalem" in *City of the Great King*. Nitza Rosovsky, ed., (Cambridge, Harvard University Press, 1996), p. 94.

Sheilah Graham: Arthur Mizener, *Fitzgerald*, p. 101.

Page 175
James Jesus Angleton: Robin W. Winks, *Cloak and Gown* (New Haven: Yale University Press, 1996), pp. 332, 343.

Page 177
Tuviah Gutman Gutwirth: Jacob Neusner, *There We Sat Down: Talmudic Judaism in the Making*, (New York: Abingdon Press, 1972), p. 83.

Talmud Kiddushin: Lewis I. Newman, *The Talmudic Anthology* (New York: Behrman House, 1983), p. 406.

Oleg Grabar: Oleg Grabar, *The Shape of the Holy* (Princeton, N.J.: Princeton University Press, 1996), p. 84.

Page 179
Marcel Proust: Edmund White, *Marcel Proust* (New York: Penguin Books, 1999), p. 102. Marcel Proust, C.K. Scott Moncrieff and Terence Kilmartin, trans. *Remembrance of Things Past; Guermantes Way* (New York: Random House, 1981), p. 558.

Aryeh Leib ben Jacob Ha-Kohen: Yehuda Feliks, *Nature and Man in the Bible* (London: Soncino Press, 1981), p.242.

Julius Meyer: Zohar I, 152 b. M. L. Marks, *Jews Among the Indians* (Chicago: Benison Books, 1992), p. 53. Howard R. Lamar, ed., *The New Encyclopedia of the American West* (New Haven: Yale University Press, 1998), p. 149.

Anna L. Walters: Lee Francis, *Native Time* (New York: St. Martin's Press, 1996), p. 235.

Page 181
Hasson: Bridegroom in Hebrew and Yiddish.

Daven: "To pray" in Yiddish. "*All are equal in prayer before the Lord,*" Exodus Rabah.

Simha Padawer: Avot (3:10).

Marcel Proust: Ronald Hayman, *Proust*, p. 315. Cahier 51, p. 53.

Rabbi Dosa ben Harkinas: A second century Rabbi in Palestine. Rabbi Dosa lived a very long life. His maxim: "Morning sleep, midday wine, put a person out of the world" Avot 3:10.

Page 183
Ambrose Vollard: Henri Lallemand, *Cézanne: Visions of a Great Painter* (New York: Todtri Press, 1994), p. 88.

Page 185
Judah Touro (1775–1854): American philanthropist born in Newport, Rhode Island, raised in New York and Jamaica, British West Indies (1782). He went in 1801 to New Orleans where he made a great fortune as a merchant and real estate owner. "*He left $60,000 in his will to be used to help the poor in Eretz Israel with the funds to be managed by Sir Moses Montifiore. His gifts to non-Jewish institutions in New Orleans, Boston, and Newport totaled $153,000. No American Jew has given so much to so many agencies and causes; nor has any non-Jew done so much in such varied ways.*"

Encyclopedia Judaica, vol. 15, (New York: Macmillan, 1971), p. 1289.

Moses Hayyim Luzzatto (1707-1746): Mystical Rabbi, born in Padua, Italy. His *Path of the Upright* (Mesillat Yesharim) is considered to be one of the great ethical guides in Judaism. Rabbi Moses Hayyim Luzzato said: "We note at all periods and at all times, between all lovers and friends—between a man and his wife, between a father and his son, in fine, between all those who are bound with a love which is truly strong—that the lover will not say, "I have not been commanded further. What I have been told to do is enough for me." He will rather attempt, by analyzing the commands, to arrive at the intention of the commander and to do what he judges will give him pleasure. The same holds true for one who strongly loves his Creator; for he, too, is one of the class of lovers." Moses Hayyim Luzzatto, *The Path of the Just* (Jerusalem: Feldheim Press, 1996), p. 219. See Benjamin Zucker, *Blue*, p. 226.

The Book of Kells: An Irish manuscript with interlocking patterns, written in the ninth century. Bernard Meehan, *The Book of Kells*, pp. 9, 78.

One of the finest illuminated manuscripts, containing the Gospels and filled with Byzantine, Celtic (and even Coptic-style) decorative patterns. The manuscript was illuminated c. 800 by many different hands in Ireland, beginning at the monastery at Iona and then completed at Kells. The book has been at Trinity College, Dublin, since the seventeenth century where it can be viewed, with a page of the manuscript turned each day.

Page 187
Cotton Mather: Ralph and Louise Boas, *Cotton Mather, Keeper of the Puritan Conscience* (New York: Harper and Brothers, 1928), pp. 37, 63, 222.

Page 189
Simha Padawer: Leviticus 16:30.

Goldsmith Illuminator: Françoise Henry, *The Book of Kells,* (New York: Knopf, 1993).

Yochanan ben Zakkai: As quoted in Jonathan Rosen. *The Talmud and the Internet: A Journey Between Worlds* (New York: Farrar, Straus & Giroux, 2000), p. 34.

Page 191
Simha Padawer: "Black fire on white fire." From the Zohar. An oft-used description of the Torah.

Shidduch: The mutual promise between a man and woman to contract a marriage at some future time and the formulation of the terms on which it shall take place. In Yiddish vernacular to make a "shidduch" is to arrange a match. A matchmaker (Shadchan) has been an integral part of traditional Jewry for millennia. "*A woman asked Rabbi Yossi ben Halafta: How many days did it take the Lord to create the world? He answered: Six. And since then, what has he been doing? The reply came: Arranging marriages.*" *Genesis Rabbah*.

Niggunin: Songs (in Hebrew).

Minhag: Custom or usage from the Hebrew "to lead." These are customs in areas of Jewish law and practice. A local custom of praying for example, Minhag Romani is binding on Jews who pray in Romania. Some customs, demonological for example, connection with circumcision (the night of vigil before the circumcision) or the Ashkenasic custom of a person whose parents are alive leaving synagogue when the souls of the dead are mentioned, are maintained as law.

Heilige: Holy in Yiddish and German.

Shammes: A person who does odd jobs in the synagogue; sexton.

Hatonim: Bridegrooms.

Ramshal: Initials for Rabbi Moses Hayyim Luzzatto.

Montague Stanley Napier: The purchaser of the Taj Mahal emerald in a clip brooch mounted by Cartier in 1927. The gem colored hexagonal 141 carat emerald had been a spectacular highlight of the Cartiers in the 1925 Parisian Exposition des Art Décoratifs, where it was displayed as a shoulder ornament and diadem. The ornament itself, without the emeralds, was sold to the Glaoui of Marrakesh, leaving Cartier to offer the emerald in a redesigned jewelry piece. See Judy Rudoe, *Cartier 1900-1939*, p. 317.

Samuel Weinberg: Died 1916. Grandson of Abraham ben Isaac Weinberg, founder of the court of the Slonim Hasidim, and a great influence on "one of the oldest and most honored Lithuanian Yeshivot. Samuel's Hasidic court was known through the world for its special melodies. His brother, Noah, founded a branch of Slonim Hasidism in Tiberias in the late nineteenth century." *Encyclopedia Judaica,* vol. 14, p. 1673.

Tiberias: A city on the western shore of Lake Galilee. Founded by Herod in 14 C.E., named after Roman Emperor Tiberius. After the destruction of Jerusalem, the city became the capital of Jews in the country until the Arab conquest of the seventh century. The "Jerusalem Talmud" was composed largely in Tiberias. In the seventh century it was the center of the Masoretes who standardized the spelling and vocalization of the Torah. Maimonides is buried in Tiberias. It is one of the four holy cities of the Land of Israel. *Encyclopedia Judaica,* vol. 15, pp. 1130-1132.

Page 195
Van Gogh: Vojtech Jirat-Wasiutyaski, H. Travers Newton, Eugene Farrell and Richard Newman, *Vincent Van Gogh's Self-Portrait Dedicated to Paul Gauguin* (Cambridge: Harvard University Museum, 1984).

Paul Gauguin: Debora Silverman, *Van Gogh and Gauguin* (New York: Farrar, Straus & Giroux), p. 32.

Maurice Wertheim: James Cuno, *Harvard's Art Museums: 100 Years of Collecting* (New York: Harry N. Abrams, 1996), p. 32.

CHAPTER 10

Page 197
Laurence Sterne: Arthur Cash, *Laurence Sterne, The Early and Middle Years* (London: Methuen & Co., 1975), pp. 34-35. Also, Lawrence Sterne, *Tristram Shandy,* Book IV, Chapter XXV, p. 221.

James Joyce: *Giacomo Joyce* (New York, Viking Press, 1968).

Shadchen: Matchmaker.

Page 199
Bad Face: A Native American tribe, a subset of Oglala Sioux.

Crazy Horse: Larry McMurtry, *Crazy Horse* (New York: Viking Books, 1999), pp. 51, 68-69.

Israeli Poet: Jessica Gribetz, *Wise Words* (New York: William Morrow and Company, 1997), pp. 233-234.

Rachel: Rahel Bluwstein (1890-1931) was a poet who emigrated to Eretz Israel in 1909. She abandoned her native Russian language and learned Hebrew. In 1913, she went to Toulouse to study agriculture to prepare herself to "*work the land.*" Unable because of the War to return to Eretz Israel, she went to Russia, where she taught Jewish refugee children. Because she had contracted tuberculosis in Europe, when she returned to the kibbutz in Degania she spent the rest of her life in hospitals and sanatoriums. Rachel was "*the first poet to write in a conversational style. Her poems are characterized by a clear, uncomplicated lyrical line and a musicality, then rare in Hebrew poetry.*" *Encyclopedia Judaica*, vol. 13, p. 1515.

Rachel Zucker: American poet. "A Kind of Catastrophe" (Iowa City: *The Iowa Review*, Volume XXVIIII, 1999), p. 78.

Page 201

Isaac Luria: Nahum M. Sarna, ed. *The JPS Torah Commentary* (Philadelphia: Jewish Publication Society, 1989), p. 185. See Genesis 22:2, p. 51. Sarna, *JTS Bible*. Also, Harry Sperling and Maurice Simon, trans. *The Zohar, Volume II* (London: The Soncino Press, 1949), pp. 31-32.

F. Scott Fitzgerald: Edmund Wilson, ed., *The Crack-Up: Fitzgerald*, p. 152. F. Scott Fitzgerald, Mathew J. Bruccoli, ed., *The Love of the Last Tycoon*, p. 26.

Page 203

Moses Hayyim Luzzatto: Yaakov Feldman, trans., *The Path of the Just*, (New Jersey: Jason Aronson, 1996), p.216.

André Breton: André Breton. *Nadja* (New York: Grove Press, 1960), p.66.

Wasichu: A term used to designate the White Man but making no reference to his skin color.

Black Elk: *Black Elk Speaks,* as told through John G. Neihardt (Flaming Rainbow), introduction by Vine Deloria, Jr.

Page 205

André Breton: André Breton. *Nadja*, p. 101.

Nadja: Breton, Ibid., pp. 66 and 102.

Page 207

Li Po: Arthur Cooper, trans. and ed., *Li Po and Tu Fu* (New York: Penguin Books, 1970), p. 15.

Eighth-century T'ang Dynasty poet. His poems are much influenced by Ch'an (Zen) Bhuddism and Taoism. He and his friend Tu Fu are considered the finest classical Chinese poets. Ezra Pound's translation of Li Po's poems entered them in the Western poetry canon. Arthur Cooper, trans. and ed., *Li Po and Tu Fu* (New York: Penguin Books, 1970), p. 1.

Tu Fu: Li Po and Tu Fu. Tu Fu's poem: "Ballad on seeing a pupil of the Lady Kung-sun dance the sword mime."

Tu Fu (712-770 CE). T'ang Dynasty poet. David Hinton has called him "*the first complete poetic sensibility in Chinese literature.*" Tu Fu said "*a poet's ideas are noble and simple.*" David Hinton, translator. *The Selected Poems of Tu Fu* (New York: New Directions, 1989), p. 105.

Page 209

Ninth Duke of Marlborough: Hugo Vicker, *Gladys, Duchess of Marlborough* (New York: Holt, Rinehart & Winston, 1979), p. 130.

Gladys Deacon: Vicker, *Gladys, Duchess of Marlborough*, p. 41.

Black Elk: *Black Elk Speaks*, p. 143.

Page 211

Shochet: Ritual slaughterer, who ensures that the meat is slaughtered according to Talmudic law.

Page 213

Tuviah Gutman Gutwirth: Rabbi Eliyahu Touger, Trans. *The Hasidic Haggadah* (New York: Moznaim Publishing Corporation, 1988), p. 31.

Rabbi Nachman of Breslov: From a personal communication to the author from the remarkable craftsman, Catriel Sugarman (Fine Judaica in Rare Woods. Jerusalem. October 1985.)

Li Po: Poem: "Drinking with a Gentleman of Leisure in the Mountains," David Hinton, trans., *Selected Poems of Li Po*. Arthur Cooper, Trans. "At Sky's End Thinking of Li Po," *Li Po and Tu Fu* (Penguin Classics, 1973), p. 110.

Tu Fu: Poem: "Song of the Eight Immortals in Wine." David Hinton. Selected Poems of Li Po (New York: New Directions, 1996), p. XIX.

Page 215

Raphael: Vasari, *Lives of the Artists.*

Page 217

Center text: Deuteronomy 4:34. Rabbi Davin Cohen, *Haggadah Simhas Yabetz,* (Brooklyn, New York: Messorah Publications, 1993), p. 15. Also: Yisrael Isser Zvi Herczeg, *The Vilna Gaon Haggaddah* (Brooklyn, New York: Messorah Publications, 1997), pp. 55-56.

Tuviah Gutman Gutwirth: Rabbi Noson Scherman, *Yom Kippur* (New York: Mesorah Publications, Ltd., 1989), p. 35.

Mozart: Robert L. Marshall, *Mozart Speaks*. (New York: Schirmer Books/Macmillan, 1991), pp. 176-177.

Page 219

Payag: Milo Cleveland Beach and Ebba Koch, *The Padshanama: King of the World,* p. 108.

Rabbi Nahum: Pesha Marcus, the Lithuanian Yiddish writer records the last Mussar lecture in Slobodka—as described by Joseph Gutferstein: *The Indestructible Dignity of Man* in *Judaism Magazine* (New York: American Jewish Congress, 1970), p. 262.

Page 221

Chief Logan (1725-80): "*Chief of the Mingo—those Iroquois who had located the Ohio country…*" "*In the Yellow Creek massacre of April 1774, some of his family were killed by whites. He refused to be reconciled after the Indians were defeated at Point Pleasant. On this occasion, he expressed his feelings so movingly to a Virginia emissary, his words gained wide currency in colonial newspapers and were incorporated by Thomas Jefferson into his book* Notes on Virginia 1781." Howard R. Lamar, ed., *The New Encyclopedia of the West*, p. 648.

Page 223

Bal Zedakah: A person who gives a great amount of charity.

Cézanne: Henri Lallemand, *Cézanne: Visions of a Great Painter*, p. 91. "The only self-portrait in which Cézanne depicted himself as an artist. The back of the palette, tilted up so that it appears parallel to the picture frame, blocks off any immediate access to the sitter, whose eyes are focused on the easel in front of him. The dark beard framing his features is echoed by the brown overcoat, leaving his white shirt visible, for Cézanne the artist had to remain in the background, while the pleasure must stay in the work."

Crazy Horse: Dee Brown, *Bury My Heart at Wounded Knee* (New York: Henry Holt & Co, 1970), pp. 289, 441. Larry McMurty, *Crazy Horse* (New York: Viking Penguin, 1999), p. 33.

Immanuel Kant: Arthur H. Cash and John M. Stedmond, eds., *The Winged Skull* (Ohio: Kent State University Press, 1971), p. 205. Quoting Kant, *Gesammelte Schriften IX* (Berlin und Leipzig, 1923), p. 469.

F. Scott Fitzgerald: Mizener, *F. Scott Fitzgerald* (New York: Thames & Hudson, 1999), p. 108.

ACKNOWLEDGMENTS

Many, many thanks to Peter Mayer who elegantly and patiently encouraged me to follow *Blue* with *Green*.

All at The Overlook Press helped create this book. It has been a great pleasure to work with Tracy Carns, David Chestnut, Caroline Trefler, Hermann Lademann, Steven Cipriano, Bruce Mason, Steven Cooper, George Davidson and Janet Hotson Baker. Miracles are not believed to occur twice but they did for me with Bernie Schleifer.

Each variation of the manuscript was expertly and enthusiastically edited by Tasha Blaine and skillfully molded by George Blecher and by Rachel Zucker. Alison Jasonides' wonderful eye and spirit shaped the art work. Mary Flower graciously gathered the rights.

Keys to the glorious Moghul Garden of Art—and indeed many other forms of art—were gifted to me by Jan Mitchell, Alastair B. Martin, Martin Norton, Nicolas Norton, Jonathan Norton, Francis Norton, Diana and Peter Scarisbrick, Ralph Esmerian, Ralph Pinder Wilson, Dr. Assadullah Souren Melikian-Chirvani, Robert Skelton, Michael Spink, David Khalili, Richard Camber, Susan Stronge, Elizabeth Moynihan, Daniel Walker, Martin I. Harman, Stuart Cary Welch and Gary Vikan.

Barbara and I went to India on a most wonderful trip organized by Milo Beach, seeing India through his enthusiastic eye and having discussions with Terence McInerney, who suggested Payag and Balchand as characters, Sir Howard Hodgkin, Ebba Koch, Benno Koch, and Dr. Gursharan Sidhu. have been the core of the mogul part of *Green*. A museum trip years ago with Amy and Robert Poster, whose encouragement and friendship have been extraordinary, began these musings. My remarkable friend Jesse Wolfgang started the whole endeavor.

Sustained conversations about writing with good friends over the years and often over coffee have been a fabulous delight for me: John Flattau, David Birnbaum, Derek J. Content, Al and Harry Kleinhaus, Jim Traub, Lee Grove, Josh Goren, Milton Ginsberg, Ricki Borger, Alfred Moldovan, Daniel Friedenberg, Bill Gross, Tom Powers, David Jaffe, Isaac M. Heschel, Bill and Libby Reilly, Willliam Hamilton and Eden Collingsworth Hamilton.

My friends at the Golden Notebook (Woodstock, NY) and the Gotham Book Mart are just terrific.

My inspiration for *Green*, like *Blue*, flows from the teachings of Elie Wiesel and Jay Margolis.

My family has been so supportive and has considered my eccentricities entertaining during the writing of *Green*. Above all, Barbara's marvelous smile, laughter and love have made writing this book a joy.

My warmest thanks to everyone.

ART SOURCES

Frontispiece (Opposite Title Page)
The Taj Mahal Emerald, 141 carats. Courtesy Michael Freeman.

Opposite Guide to Reader
Paul Cézanne (1839-1906), *Green Apples*, ca. 1873. Musée d'Orsay, Paris. Credit: Erich Lessing/Art Resource, NY.

Page viii
Paul Gauguin (1848-1903), *Noa Noa Album: Landscape*, 1893. Watercolor. Louvre Museum, Paris. Photo: Gerard Blot. Credit: Reunion des Musées Nationaux/Art Resource, NY.

Page 2
Paul Cézanne (1839-1906), *Camille Pissarro on his way to paint*. Black chalk drawing. Louvre Museum, Paris. Credit: Scala/Art Resource, NY.

Page 4
Govardhan, *Akbar with Lion and Heifer*. Leaf from an album made for Emperor Shah Jahan., ca. 1630. Ink, opaque watercolor and gold on paper. Credit: The Metropolitan Museum of Art, Purchase, Rogers Fund and The Kevorkian Foundation Gift, 1955. Photograph ©1980 The Metropolitan Museum of Art.

Page 6
Photograph of F. Scott Fitzgerald writing at his desk. Credit: Bettmann/CORBIS.

Page 8
Photograph of Dylan Thomas, 1946. Credit: Hulton-Deutsch Collection/CORBIS.

Page 10
Photograph of the Taj Mahal, Agra, India. Credit: Scala/Art Resource, NY.

Page 12
Vincent van Gogh (1853-1890), Self-Portrait, 1889. Oil on canvas. Collection of Mr. and Mrs. John Hay Whitney, Photograph © 2001 Board of Trustees, National Gallery of Art, Washington, D.C.

Page 14
Anonymous artist, *Portrait of Wolfgang Amadeus Mozart as a child*. Mozart House, Salzburg, Austria. Credit: Scala/Art Resource, NY.

Page 16
Page of the Talmud: Ketubot. Gutman Gutwirth's study copy.

Page 18
Photograph of the American socialite Evalyn Walsh McLean wearing the 44.5 carat Hope Diamond on a diamond chain which Cartier Paris sold to her around 1912. Credit: Bettmann/CORBIS.

Page 20
Nanha, *Prince Khurram (Shah Jahan) with his son Dara Shikoh*. Leaf from an album made for the Emperor Shah Jahan. Credit: The Metropolitan Museum of Art, Purchase, Rogers Fund and the Kevorkian Foundation Gift, 1955. Photograph © 1980 The Metropolitan Museum of Art.

Page 22
Paul Cézanne (1839-1906), *The Card Players*. Musée d'Orsay, Paris. Credit: Reunion des Musées Nationaux/Art Resource, NY.

Page 24
Gordon Bryant, *Portraits of F. Scott Fitzgerald and Zelda Fitzgerald*, ca. 1921. Credit: Arlyn Bruccoli Collection.

Page 26
Daniel Kramer, photograph of Bob Dylan playing the harmonica. © Daniel Kramer.

Page 28
Photograph of Julius Meyer's Indian Wigwam, Omaha, Nebraska. Credit: Nebraska State Historical Society, Julius Meyer Collection.

Page 30
Rembrandt van Rijn (1606-1669) *Rembrandt and, Saskia in the Parable of the Prodigal Son*, ca. 1635-39. Gemaeldegalerie, Staatliche Kunstsammlungen, Dresden, Germany. Credit: Erich Lessing/Art Resource, NY.

Page 32
Johannes Vermeer (1632-1675), *The Art of Painting*, detail. Kunsthistoriches Museum, Vienna. Credit: Erich Lessing/Art Resource, NY.

Page 34
Photograph of Briton Hadden, ca. 1923. Credit: TimePix.

Page 36
Eightteenth century Prague Haggadah. Private Collection (ZFC/RCZ). Photograph courtesy Jewish Theological Seminary, Suzanne Kaufman.

Page 38
John Tenniel (1820-1914), "The Mad Tea Party." Proof for *The Nursery Alice* by Lewis Carroll. AAH 590. The Pierpont Morgan Library, New York. Credit: The Pierpont Morgan Library/Art Resource, NY.

Page 40
Photograph of Franz Kafka as a young man in front of a toy horse. Credit: Klaus Wagenbach.

Page 42
Daguerrotype of Emily Dickinson. Credit: Amherst College Archives and Special Collections.

Page 44
Augustus John (1878-1961), *Portrait of Caitlin Thomas*. Credit: Glynn Vivian Art Gallery, Swansea, Wales. © Courtesy of the Estate of Augustus John/The Bridgeman Art Library International Ltd., London/New York.

Page 46
Anonymous artist, *The Life and Death of Sir Henry Unton*, detail. Courtesy of the National Portrait Gallery, London.

Page 48
Paul Cézanne (1839-1906), *Portrait of M. Ambrose Vollard, the art dealer* (1865-1939), 1899. Musée du Petit Palais, Paris. Credit: Erich Lessing/Art Resource, NY.

Page 50
Rembrandt van Rijn (1606-1669), *Portrait of Nicolas Ruts*. Copyright The Frick Collection, New York.

Page 52
Photograph of James Agee, ca. 1940-50. Credit: Bettmann/CORBIS.

Page 54
Emerald shoulder clip brooch made by Cartier, owned by Marjorie Merriweather Post, L. 19.5 cm. Large carved emerald 3.2 x 3 cm. Credit: The Hillwood Museum and Gardens, Washington, DC. Photograph by Edward Owen.

Page 56
Delhi Coronation Durbar, 1903.

Page 58
Portrait of Shah Jahan on horseback with his son Dara Shikoh from *The Minto Album*, seventeenth century. Credit: The Victoria & Albert Museum, London/Art Resource, NY.

Page 60
Necklace made for Cartier London to the order of Lady Granard, 1932. Emerald is 143 carats. Credit: Art of Cartier Collection, © Cartier. Photograph by N. Welsh.

Page 62
Payag, *Man Singh of Amber*, ca. 1615. Reproduced by kind permission of the Trustees of the Chester Beatty Library, Dublin.

Page 64
Balchand, *Jahanghir receives Prince Khurram*. From the Padshanama. The royal Collection, Windsor. © 2001, Her Royal Majestly Queen Elizabeth II.

Page 66
Roman Vishniac, *Searching for truth in the Talmud*, Lublin, Poland, 1938. Gelatin silver print. © Mara Vishniac Kohn, courtesy of the International Center of Photography.

Page 68
Fort St. George (Vestiges of old Madras) at the time of Elihu Yale, 1680.

Page 70
Paul Cézanne (1839-1906), *Madame Cézanne* (Hortense Fiquet, 1850-1922) in the Conservatory, ca. 1890. Credit: The Metropolitan Museum of Art, New York. Bequest of Stephen C. Clark, 1960 Photograph © 1980 The Metropolitan Museum of Art.

Page 72
Photograph of Nora and James Joyce on their wedding day. Credit: State University of New York at Buffalo, Poetry/Rare Books Collection.

Page 74
Ark of the Torah, eighteenth century, Sephardi Synagogue, Amsterdam.

Page 76
Roman Vishniac, *Jewish Street*, Slonim, Poland, 1937. Gelatin silver print. © Mara Vishniac Kohn, courtesy of the International Center of Photography.

Page 78
Johannes Vermeer, *The Art of Painting*. Kunsthistoriches Museum, Vienna. Credit: Erich Lessing/Art Resource, NY.

Page 80
Photograph of the Maharajah of Patiala, © Cartier Archives. Courtesy of Cartier

Page 82
Seventeenth century Italian octahedral diamond ring (side view). Photograph by Peter Schaaf, private collection (ZFC/RCZ). Courtesy Walters Art Gallery.

Page 84
Paul Gauguin (1848-1903), *Self-Portrait*, 1889. Chester Dale Collection. Photograph © 2001 Board of Trustees, National Gallery of Art, Washington, D.C.

Page 86
Paul Cézanne (1839-1906), *The Artist's Father*, 1866. Collection of Mr. and Mrs. Paul Mellon. Photograph © 2001 Board of Trustees, National Gallery of Art, Washington, D.C.

Page 88
Photograph of Marcel Proust, playing on a tennis racket, with Jeanne Pouquet 1892. Credit: Snark/Art Resource, NY.

Page 90
Raphael (1483-1520), Detail of Raphael's self-portrait in *The School of Athens*. Stanza della Segnatura, Vatican Palace, Vatican. Credit: Erich Lessing/Art Resource, NY.

Page 92
Roman Vishniac, *Altar of the Lask Synagogue*, Lodz, Poland, ca. 1938. Gelatin silver print. © Mara Vishniac Kohn, courtesy the International Center of Photography.

Page 94
Paul Cézanne (1839-1906), *Apotheosis of Delacroix*. Musée d'Orsay, Paris. Credit: Giraudon/Art Resource, NY.

Page 96
Edward S. Curtis (1868-1952), *A Comanche Mother*, 1927, from

The North American Indian (1907-1930), vol. 19, pl. 685. Credit: The Pierpont Morgan Library, New York/Art Resource, NY.

Page 98
Rudy Burckhardt, *Jackson Pollock pretending to paint for the photographer*. Credit: Estate of Rudy Burckhardt.

Page 100
Rembrandt van Rijn (1606-1669), *Abraham and Isaac* (B. 34), 1645. Etching. Credit: The Pierpont Morgan Library, New York/Art Resource, NY.

Page 102
William Blake (1757-1827), Etching from *Jerusalem*. Paul Mellon Collection, Yale Center for British Art, courtesy of The Bridgeman Art Library International Ltd., London/New York.

Page 104
Payag, *Jahangir Presents Prince Khurram with a turban ornament* Credit: The Royal Collection © 2001, Her Majesty Queen Elizabeth II.

Page 106
Leonardo da Vinci (1452-1519), *Study of a Woman's Hands (Probably Ginevra de' Benci)*, ca. 1474. Photographer EZM. Credit: The Royal Collection © 2001, Her Majesty Queen Elizabeth II.

Page 108
Paul Gauguin (1848-1903), *The Mother of the Artist (Aline Marie Chazal)*, 1890. Credit: Staatsgalerie, Stuttgart.

Page 110
Payag, *Humayun Seated in a Landscape* (S1986.400,), ca. 1645. Courtesy of the Arthur M. Sackler Gallery, Smithsonian Institution, Washington D.C.

Page 112
Photograph of Julius Meyer, Sitting Bull , Swift Bear, Spotted Tail and Red Cloud. Credit: Nebraska Historical Society, Julius Meyer Collection.

Page 114
Photograph of Amedeo Modigliani. Credit: The Modigliani Committee, Legal Archives of Amedeo Modigliani, Livorno and Paris.

Page 116
Daniel Kramer, "Crossed Lights,"photograph of Bob Dylan and Joan Baez performing at Madison Square Garden, 1965. © Daniel Kramer.

Page 118
Hours of the Duke of Burgundy, *Emilia in her garden*. Oesterreichische Nationalbibliothek, Vienna. Credit: The Bridgeman Art Library International Ltd., London/New York.

Page 120
The Talmud: Ketubot.

Page 122
Chaim Soutine, The White House. Musée de l'Orangerie, Paris. Credit: Scala/Art Resource, NY/ ARS/NY.

Page 124
Photograph of F. Scott Fitgerald with Zelda. Credit: Underwood & Underwood/CORBIS.

Page 126
Photograph of Dylan Thomas, ca. 1925-35. Credit: Hulton-Deutsch Collection/CORBIS.

Page 128
The Ardabil Carpet. 1539-40. Credit: The Victoria & Albert Museum, London/Art Resource, NY.

Page 130
Daniel Kramer, Photograph of Joan Baez lifting and twirling Bob Dylan. © Daniel Kramer.

Page 132
A chameleon diamond, 22 carats, under fluorescence. Photograph Gemological Institute of America and Tino Hammid.

Page 134
Shah Jahan from the *Padshanama*. Photographer EZM. Credit: The Royal Collection © 2001, Her Majesty Queen Elizabeth II.

Page 136
Timur (Tamerlane) from the *Padshanama*. Credit: The Royal Collection © 2001, Her Majesty Queen Elizabeth II.

Page 138
William Blake, Etching from *Jerusalem*. The Paul Mellon Collection, Yale Center for British Art. Credit: The Bridgeman Art Library International Ltd., London/New York.

Page 140
F. Scott Fitzgerald at his desk, c. 1925. Credit: Minnesota Historical Society/CORBIS.

Page 142
Paul Cézanne (1839-1906), *Sugar Bowl, Kettle and Plate with Fruit*. Hermitage, St. Petersburg. Credit: Scala/Art Resource, NY.

Page 144
Daniel Kramer, Photograph of Bob Dylan playing chess. © Daniel Kramer.

Page 146
Enoch Zeeman *Governor Elihu Yale*. Credit: Yale University Art Gallery, New Haven, Ct. Gift of Dudley Long North, M.P., in 1789.

Page 148
Illuminated page of calligraphy, c. 1540. From an album of 37 leaves, assembled for Emperor Shah Jahan. Colors and gilt on paper. Credit: The Metropolitan Museum of Art, Purchase, Rogers Fund, and the Kevorkian Foundation Gift, 1955. Photograph ©1980 The Metropolitan Museum of Art.

Page 150
Paul Cézanne (1839-1906), *Trees and Houses*. Pushkin Museum, Moscow. Credit: Scala/Art Resource, NY.

Page 152
Jan Isaaksz van Ruisdael (1628/9-1682), *The Jewish Cemetery*, ca. 1655-60. Gift of Julius H. Haass in memory of his brother Dr. Ernest W. Haass. Photograph © 1996 The Detroit Institute of Arts.

Page 154
Paul Cézanne (1839-1906), *Still Life with Fruit Basket*, 1888-90. Musée d'Orsay, Paris. Credit: Erich Lessing/Art Resource, NY.

Page 156
Drawing of a necklace and a head ornament for an advertisement for the exhibition at Cartier Paris in 1928, of the jewels created by Cartier for Bhupindar Singh of Patiala. Credit: Cartier Archives, © Cartier.

Page 158
Montefiore Ketubah. Credit: Private Collection (ZFC/RCZ).

Page 160
Payag, *Shah Jahan on horseback*. From an album of 37 leaves, assembled for Emperor Shah Jahan. Color and gilt on paper. Credit: The Metropolitan Museum of Art, Purchase, Rogers Fund, and The Kevorkian Foundation Gift, 1955. Photograph © 1980 The Metropolitan Museum of Art.

Page 182
Nadar, Jean-Phillipe Worth in Indian costume.

Page 164
Photograph of Henry Luce and Briton Hadden when they both worked at the Yale Daily News. Credit: TimePix.

Page 166
Bérénice Emerald necklace, from the Gazette du Bon Ton. Paris Exhibition of 1925. Courtesy of Leonard Fox Gallery, New York.

Page 168
Scott, Zelda and Scottie Fitzgerald doing the kick step in front of their Christmas tree. Undated photo. Credit: Bettmann/CORBIS.

Page 170
Arshile Gorky (1904/05- 1948), *Abstraction*, ca. 1936. Credit: Art Resource, NY/Artists Rights Society, NY.

Page 172
F. Scott Fitzgerald. Credit: Bettmann/CORBIS.

Page 174
Paul Cézanne (1839-1906), *Self-Portrait*. Musée d'Orsay, Paris. Credit: Reunion Musées Nationaux/Art Resource, NY.

Page 176
Mosaic in the Dome of the Rock, Jerusalem. Credit: Art Resource/NY

Page 178
Photograph of Julius Meyer with Chief Standing Bear. Credit: The Jacob Rader Marcus Center of the American Jewish Archives.

Page 180
Synagogue hall, eighteenth century, Sephardi Synagogue of Amsterdam.

Page 182
Paul Cézanne (1839-1906), *The Basket of Apples*, ca. 1895. Oil on canvas, 65 cm. x 80 cm. Helen Birch Bartlett Memorial Collection. Photograph courtesy of the Art Institute of Chicago.

Page 184
Ketubah from Modena, Italy. Credit: Private Collection (ZFC/RCZ).

Page 186
Elihu Yale and the Second Duke of Devonshire, Lord James Cavendish, Mr. Turnstal and a page. Credit: Yale Center for British Art.

Page 188
The Book of Kells: St. Matthew, *Chi Rho* initial, ca. 800 CE. Ms. A16, f.34r. Trinity College, Dublin. Credit: Art Resource, NY.

Page 190
Luis Carrogis Carmontelle, *Leopold Mozart playing music with Wolfgang and Nannerl*, 1763. Musée Conde, Chantilly. Credit: Erich Lessing/Art Resource, NY.

Page 192
Bhola, *Shah Jahan honoring Prince Awrangzeb at Agra before his wedding*. Exhibition catalogue no. 43. (Photographed for gold). Photographer EZM. Credit: The Royal Collection © 2001, Her Majesty Queen Elizabeth II.

Page 194
Zagasche Tombstone (De Paiva family), seventeenth century, Ouderkerk, Amsterdam.

Page 196
F. Scott Fitzgerald's drawing in Sylvia Beach's copy of *The Great Gatsby*, commemorating her dinner party for James Joyce. Credit: Department of Rare Books and Special Collections, Princeton University Library, Princeton, NJ.

Page 198
Flower-head patterns carved onto the Taj Mahal Emerald. A lotus, a meconopsis, and an amaranth. Photograph courtesy Peter Schaaf.

Page 200
Raphael (1483-1520), *The Prophet Isaiah*, detail. S. Agostino, Rome. Credit: Scala/Art Resource, NY.

Page 202
John Flattau, *Untitled*. Credit: John Flattau.

Page 204
John Flattau, *Rue Obscure*. Credit: John Flattau.

Page 206
Tao-chi (Shitao, 1642-1707), Hanging scroll: *Qingxiang Dadizi's Reminiscence of The Thirty-six Peaks of Mount Huang*. Ink on paper. Credit: The Metropolitan Museum of Art, Gift of Douglas Dillon, 1976. Photograph © 1980 The Metropolitan Museum of Art.

Page 208
Twentieth century cameo pendant consisting of a Roman cameo in a Renaissance frame. Gift of the Ninth Duke of Marlborough to his American wife, Gladys. Photograph by Peter Schaaf. Credit: Walters Art Gallery, Baltimore, MD (Private Collection, ZFC/RCZ).

Page 210
Artemisia Gentileschi (1593-1652/3), *Self-Portrait as La Pittura* Photographer: A. C. Cooper. Credit: The Royal Collection © 2001, Her Majesty Queen Elizabeth II.

Page 212
Tao-chi (Shitao, 1642-1707), Album of twelve paintings: Wilderness Colors. Leaf c: Riverbank of Peach Blossoms. Ink and colors on paper. Credit: The Metropolitan Museum of Art, The Sackler Fund, 1972. Photograph © 1984 The Metropolitan Museum of Art.

Page 214
Pietro Perugino (1448-1523), *Portrait of a Young Man*, 1495. Uffizi, Florence. Credit: Scala/Art Resource, NY.

Page 216
Portrait of Mozart. Civico Museo Bibliografico, Bologna. Credit: Scala/Art Resource, NY.

Page 218
Payag, *Officers and Philosophers seated around a candle at night*, ca. 1630. Credit: San Diego Museum of Art (Edwin Binney 3rd Collection).

Page 220
Mary Cassatt (1844-1926), *Portrait of Mrs. Havemeyer and her Daughter, Electra*, 1895 Credit: © Shelburne Museum, Shelburne, Vermont.

Page 222
Paul Cézanne (1839-1906), *Self-Portrait with Palette*. Collection E. G. Buehrle, Zurich. Credit: Erich Lessing/Art Resource, NY.